THE STONE OF THE EKLEKTOS

THE STONE OF THE EKLEKTOS

CREATURES OF DARKNESS: BOOK ONE

BRITNEY JACKSON

Noctem
Publishing

CONTENTS

Published by Noctem Publishing
Second Edition, May 2016

www.britneyjackson.com

SUMMARY

Rose Foster is just your typical, bisexual, smart-mouthed, socially awkward genius from a family full of felons. Okay, fine, so maybe there's nothing typical about her. But she'd at least maintained a semblance of normalcy in her life until the night a stranger gave her a red stone and disappeared without a trace.

Rose suddenly finds herself hunted by monsters that she never believed existed. A vampire, named Theron, is particularly interested in killing her. Her only hope of survival is to work with Kallias, a cynical, ancient Greek vampire with the ability to read and control minds. As a vampire, he hardly seems trustworthy, but he has his own reasons for wanting Theron dead, which works in her favor.

With the help of Kallias, Rose finds unlikely allies among an unusual group of vampires. The only problem is… these vampires seem to be hiding an important detail about what she is. In her quest to defeat Theron and the vampires who follow him, Rose must face the possibility that she might, in fact, be an even darker monster than the ones trying to kill her…

SUMMARY

In the first installment of the *Creatures of Darkness* series, find out how our perpetually sarcastic, bisexual protagonist found herself in the world of vampires in the first place.

ABOUT THE SERIES

The *Creatures of Darkness Series* is a queer fantasy series, centered around Rose Foster—the perpetually sarcastic, bisexual protagonist—and an unlikely group of vampires who try to save the world.

There's also a bit of queer romance going on in the midst of the chaos—especially once seductive, Viking warrior, Kara Unnarsdóttir, comes into the picture in *The Tomb of Blood*.

Follow Rose and her companions as they fight to stop a nefarious plan that was set into motion thousands of years ago, and as Rose unravels the mystery of what she really is.

The fourth and final book of the series, *The Reign of Darkness*, is available now!

CREATURES OF DARKNESS

SERIES

Book One: *THE STONE OF THE EKLEKTOS*

Book Two: *THE TOMB OF BLOOD*

Book Three: *THE ASSASSINS OF LIGHT*

Book Four: *THE REIGN OF DARKNESS*

Find out more at:
britneyjackson.com

DEDICATION

*This book is dedicated to anyone who's in a period of darkness right now —
whether that be depression or grief or something entirely different.*

*I want you to know that you're not alone, even when it feels like you are, that
someone understands, even when it seems like no one does, and that someone
cares, even when it feels like no one does.*

You're stronger than you know.

Keep fighting.

"The scariest monsters are the ones that lurk within our souls."

— often attributed to Edgar Allan Poe

PROLOGUE

471 BC in Ancient Greece...

Kallias should've known something was wrong the moment he saw the flickering candlelight in his bedroom window. By this hour of the night, his wife, Phoebe, had usually left for the Temple of Artemis.

His footsteps echoed through the empty halls of his home. Firelight, cast by the torches, flickered along the mud-brick walls.

His bedroom shone like a beacon at the end of the hall, candles illuminating every corner of the room. When he reached the room, he leaned in the doorway, watching his wife with a frown.

She was beautiful.

As always.

Phoebe sat in a wooden chair in front of the small, stone table. Her sheer, white chiton clung to her curves, and her sleek, black hair fell to the base of her spine in a tightly woven, elegant braid.

She wrote quickly, her quill scratching against the papyrus scrolls.

Kallias crossed the room and peered curiously over her shoulder.

But at his approach, Phoebe screamed and jumped to her feet, knocking the scrolls into the floor. She spun to confront him, but when

1

she realized it was just Kallias, she laughed and placed a hand over her racing heart.

Kallias raised his eyebrow at her reaction. "I seem to be having that effect on people today."

Phoebe waved a hand at his towering height. "Honey, you *always* have that effect on people," she teased. "You're not exactly small and meek."

He knelt to pick up her scrolls. "Sure, but I've never made *you* scream before." As he returned to his feet, a playful smile tugged at the corners of his lips, and he added, "Well, not in terror, at least."

Phoebe rolled her eyes. "Don't be crass," she whispered, as if there were someone there who might hear them. "And give me those."

Kallias glanced down at the scrolls. "What were you writing?"

"Nothing," she said, snatching them with a swiftness that surprised him. She rolled up the scrolls and returned them to the table.

He scowled. "Is something wrong?"

"No, I just..." she sighed. "I'm a little on edge tonight." She shrugged. "I was just writing a journal of sorts. I prefer to keep it private."

"Even from me?" Kallias said. With a bit of insecurity, he ran his hand through his long, brown hair. "But I'm your husband."

"Are wives not allowed privacy," Phoebe asked, "even from their husbands?"

His father would say no.

But Kallias wasn't his father.

"If you wish it," Kallias said softly.

Phoebe's brows furrowed. "What's gotten into you tonight? You seem...unsettled."

Kallias looked away and sighed, "I spoke with my father, and he got under my skin a bit. That's all."

Phoebe nodded. "Have a seat. We can talk about it."

Kallias's dark gaze shifted toward her. "You're not going to the temple tonight?"

Unease flickered across her face. "Not tonight."

Kallias lowered himself into the chair that Phoebe had been using.

When she folded herself affectionately into his lap, a smile quirked at one side of his lips. "I can't say I'm disappointed. I've missed you."

A hint of guilt seemed to flash in her large, brown eyes, but it disappeared as quickly as it came. "Tell me what happened."

Kallias sighed, "Is it wrong that I sometimes wish I was an illegitimate child?"

Phoebe trailed a finger along the soft fabric of his chiton. "That depends," she murmured. "Could you forgive your mother, if she were promiscuous?"

Kallias scowled. "My mother would never..."

Phoebe lifted an eyebrow. "That's not what I asked."

Kallias's brows furrowed. It was odd that she'd ask that—so soon after his father had made some...suspicious accusations of his own. She couldn't have known what they'd discussed, could she? "Chloe came to the temple while I was teaching," he admitted. "I think my father's mistreating her again."

Phoebe nodded sadly. "He means to control her. As she gets older, it'll only get worse."

"I went to talk to him," Kallias said.

"She's only your sister, darling," Phoebe said. "Legally, there isn't much you can do."

Kallias touched the braid that hung over Phoebe's shoulder, feeling the sleek hair beneath his fingertips. "So, I should just look the other way?"

"What else can you do?" Phoebe said, shrugging. "You can't save everyone, Kallias."

She'd said that before, and Kallias hadn't listened then, either.

"You're awfully cynical for such a young woman," Kallias told her.

A slight prick of pain pinched Phoebe's brows. "Well...I have my reasons."

"And what are those?" Kallias said. Her dark braid fell between her soft breasts, and he began to loosen the braid.

Phoebe swallowed uneasily. "Perhaps I'll find the courage to tell you one day."

Kallias frowned at that remark, but before he could ask about it, an ear-piercing scream echoed through the street.

Kallias glanced toward the window, but he saw only darkness outside. He gently pushed Phoebe off of him and went to check the window. The Mediterranean breeze caressed his skin, as he ducked his head through the window to listen to the sounds outside.

But he heard nothing.

He sighed and decided he'd have to go outside to check.

Phoebe was more than aware of what had caused that scream, however, and she panicked at the thought of Kallias coming into contact with the source. She ran to him and grasped his hand. "Kallias, you can't."

He turned to her. "I have to check. Someone just screamed."

"No, you don't," she argued. "Let someone else check."

"And what if there is no one else? What if no one else heard it? What if whoever *did* hear it decides to ignore it, like you want me to do?" He started toward the door. "Someone could need my help."

She clutched his chiton. "Stop. *Please!* Don't go out there."

Kallias hesitated. He pinned her with a suspicious look. "What is it, Phoebe? Do you know something?"

"Of course not," she lied. "What could I possibly know?"

His gaze darted toward her trembling hands. "Baby, you're shaking," he said worriedly. "What's the matter?"

"Just don't go, okay?" Phoebe pleaded. "I'm afraid for *you*."

Kallias laughed. "Don't worry about me. I'll be fine."

"No," she said, chasing after him, "you won't!"

"Stay inside," Kallias told her, but she didn't listen. He heard her quick footsteps behind him, even as he stepped out into the street.

"Please, Kallias," his wife pleaded. "Let *me* check!"

"Don't be ridiculous," he scoffed.

"Then, we can both stay inside," Phoebe offered. "Just come back in. Please."

"You're making no sense, Phoebe," Kallias said irritably. "If you know what's going on, just tell me."

"I don't know anything," Phoebe insisted. She chased him through the street. "I just…need you to come back inside."

The street looked as dark and desolate as it did when he'd made his way home. He couldn't think of a reason for anyone to be outside at this hour, much less scream out like that. "I don't understand why you're acting like this."

"That doesn't matter," Phoebe said dismissively. "Just…please, listen to me. Before something terrible happens!"

He spun to face her. The moonlight illuminated her face, her ghostly pale skin, and her wide, frightened eyes. "Enough with the games, Phoebe. Tell me why you're acting like this."

She pursed her lips. "It's not a game."

"Go inside," Kallias said, too frustrated to argue with her anymore. "I'll return soon enough."

He turned and began walking in the direction he'd heard the scream.

But Phoebe didn't do as he asked. Instead, Kallias heard her quick footsteps behind him as she practically jogged to keep up with his long strides. "He doesn't listen to me, Kallias," she cried out. "I don't know if I can convince him to spare you!"

He froze. "Who?"

But Phoebe wasn't looking at him anymore. Her dark brown eyes shifted past him—and widened. "Oh, gods, no," she whispered.

Kallias followed her gaze.

Outside a small home, he glimpsed silhouettes of a man and woman, cloaked in shadows. He inched closer, determined to understand what he was seeing.

The man had a woman pinned against the outer-wall of the small home.

At first, Kallias assumed the man was kissing the woman's neck, but as he moved closer, the stream of blood pouring from the woman's neck glistened in the moonlight.

His confusion morphed into horror.

The man in the maroon chiton held his lips to the pale woman's neck. With her drab peplos lifted around her hips, the woman leaned limply against the wall with her eyes closed. Blood flowed from her neck, down to the bottom of her peplos, staining the fabric and her bluish-white skin. Even her brown hair was matted with blood.

Snapping out of his shock, Kallias rushed to the woman's aide, pulling the monster away from her, but as he did, the woman collapsed on the ground in a crumpled heap.

The creature laughed.

It was a dark, sadistic laugh—one that sent chills down Kallias's spine. He turned to face whatever kind of monster this was.

Only his blood-soaked lips and teeth distinguished him from a human. The rest of him didn't look much different from Kallias.

He leaned lazily against the wall, like a man drunk on too much wine. Blood spilled from the corners of his mouth—blood that he didn't bother wiping away. His long, dark brown hair was woven in a braid down his back, and his eyes were dark and hungry.

Kallias had never found himself attracted to other men, but he thought, if he were, that he'd find this terrifying monster attractive.

What kind of monster looked like *that*?

Kallias turned his attention toward the woman. He knelt next to her curled up body to take a closer look. He shook her, but her skin felt as cold as ice.

"She's dead," the monster laughed, as if this were amusing to him.

Kallias stood and faced the creature. "What are you?"

The monster stepped forward—and staggered, as if the blood had intoxicated him somehow. He smiled, his razor-sharp fangs wet with the dead woman's blood.

He grasped Kallias's chiton and slammed him into the wall. Then, he leaned in close—close enough for Kallias to smell the metallic scent of blood on his breath.

"You've heard stories of my kind, haven't you?" the creature said. He licked his fangs for emphasis. "Undead monsters that feed on the blood of humans?"

Kallias shook his head in disbelief. "Impossible."

"You think so?" The creature shot a pointed look at the woman on the ground. "Who do you suppose killed her, then?"

Kallias tried to pull himself free, but he was no match. This creature was stronger than anything Kallias had ever encountered.

"Theron," Phoebe said. She stepped forward, clasping her hands together in an attempt to stop them from trembling. "Please, let him go."

Kallias glanced at his wife, stunned that she'd called the monster by name.

"And why would I do that?" Theron sneered.

Not a shred of shock passed over Phoebe's face. She wasn't shocked by the creature's strength, the blood that coated his face, the razor-sharp fangs in his mouth, or even the fact that he'd just killed a woman.

As Kallias glanced back and forth between Phoebe and the murderer, he realized...they knew each other. Phoebe had already known what they'd encounter out here. That's why she'd begged him to stay inside.

"He's my husband, Theron," she said, though there was already resignation in her tone. "Please. Let him go."

"Phoebe," Theron said in a cruel, patronizing tone, "you know better than to make demands of *me*."

And as soon as those words left his mouth, Theron jerked Kallias forward and slammed him against the wall with enough force to knock him out. As Kallias quickly lost consciousness, he thought, for a moment, he'd heard his wife cry.

PHOEBE SLIPPED QUIETLY INTO THE EMPTY, WINDOWLESS ROOM. LIGHT danced across the wall, keeping time with the flickering fire that burned in the stone furnace.

She gasped when she saw her husband.

It was even worse than she'd feared.

So much worse.

Kallias hung from the wall, his wrists shackled above him. He still wore his chiton, but it was torn to the waist and stained red. The once smooth, golden skin of his chest was covered in dried blood.

His long, brown hair hung around his shoulders, matted with blood. Countless burns and gashes marred his torso.

She barely recognized him in this state.

Phoebe ran to him and fell to her knees. "What has he done to you?" she whispered.

Kallias opened his eyes. "Phoebe?"

His voice came out as nothing more than a croak.

Tears streamed down her cheeks. "Yes," she whispered. "I'm here."

"Get," he gasped out, "away from me."

Phoebe froze. "Away?" she breathed. "Why?"

"I don't want," Kallias sucked in a ragged breath, "to look at you."

A prick of tears burned her eyes. She'd never known Kallias to be cruel. He'd always been so kind to her—so trusting.

"I begged him to let you go, but he doesn't listen to me," she tried to explain. "I never meant for this to happen, Kallias."

His tired, brown eyes seared her with accusation. "I trusted you."

"He told you?" she said softly.

"He didn't have to," Kallias scoffed. "I'm not an idiot." His voice grew stronger the longer he spoke. "Or perhaps I am. I should've realized it before now. You were never even *at* the temple, were you?"

She didn't dare meet his shaming gaze. "No, but," she sighed, "I tried to end things with him so many times, but he wouldn't let me. He has this sort of...*control* over me—some sort of power I can't resist."

"Convenient excuse," Kallias snarled.

She flinched at his tone. "You don't understand."

"I understand perfectly, Phoebe," Kallias said hoarsely. "The worst part is I defended you—when my father was right the entire time."

Phoebe kept her gaze on the blood-stained floor. "You can see he's not human. Is it so hard to believe he has inhuman power, too?"

"You just had to prove him right, didn't you?" Kallias muttered, as if he were somehow more bothered by his father being right than by the gashes and burns on his skin.

Phoebe forced herself to meet his gaze. Gone was the amusement and humor that usually lightened his brown eyes. His eyes looked lifeless now—the eyes of someone who'd endured too much. She could almost *see* the despair in those cold eyes. "I'm sorry."

"Why are you even here?" Kallias said. "What do you want from me?" He scoffed in disgust. "Forgiveness?"

Phoebe leaned back on her knees, ignoring the blood that stained her peplos. "Ideally," she said warily, "yes. I want you to understand that I never meant to hurt you—and that I…"

"No," Kallias interrupted.

The pain spread slowly through Phoebe's chest, as if her nerve endings were as stunned as she was. "What?"

"Your *lover* has tortured me," Kallias said, a surprising amount of venom in his voice, considering how weak he was. "You're not getting anything from me, Phoebe. No understanding, no forgiveness. Now, *leave* me to die in peace."

The pain and guilt took Phoebe's breath. "How can you be so cruel?" she gasped. "This isn't you. You're not like this. You never have been."

"Well, I have news for you, Phoebe," Kallias said. "Pain changes people. There's nothing left of *me*." He let his head fall back against the wall, too tired to hold it up any longer. "You have no idea what that monster has done to me. You have no idea the kind of pain he's inflicted on me. Hell, you don't even seem to understand the kind of pain *you* caused me. I'm tired. I'm wounded. And I'm dying. And it's *your* fault."

"I couldn't stop," Phoebe said. "You don't know what it's like. I don't even feel like I'm in control of my own *mind* when I'm around him!"

Kallias closed his eyes, pain radiating throughout his body. "Do you love him?"

Phoebe hesitated at that. "I—I don't know," she stammered. "I think I hate him sometimes, but when he bites me, I—"

"Never mind," he said with a grimace.

"You don't understand," she said—for what was probably the twentieth time. "It's such a euphoric feeling. It confuses me."

He frowned at her. "Drinking too much wine can make you feel good for a little while. That doesn't make it *love*."

"And maybe it's not!" Phoebe said. "Perhaps it's just an addiction— or some kind of mind-control."

"Anything to make it not your fault, right?" Kallias said.

Phoebe looked down at the floor, guilt twisting at her face. "I only know that I've never been able to escape him—not since I was fourteen."

"All this time we've been together, and you were with him all along," Kallias scoffed. He didn't have enough life left in him to even *feel* the proper amount of betrayal. "Phoebe, just leave."

"It was so hard to sneak in here," Phoebe tried to explain. "I don't know if I'll be able to do it again."

His eyes narrowed. "Good."

"At least tell me you don't hate me," Phoebe pleaded.

If he'd had any more energy, he might've rolled his eyes at her. "I don't. I should, but...*somehow*, I don't."

"Really?" Phoebe said, breathless with relief. "Oh, Kallias..." She rose up on her knees, as if she meant to kiss him, but he turned his head away from her.

She hesitated. "Kallias?"

"I said I don't hate you," Kallias snarled. "That doesn't mean I want to kiss you."

Phoebe fell back on her feet. "But...why not?"

With an incredulous glare, Kallias snarled, "Because you disgust me —sleeping with that...blood-sucking monster."

The pain that tore at Phoebe's face was almost enough to make him regret his words—but not quite. Her eyes filled with tears, and she jumped to her feet, fleeing as quickly as she could.

Unfortunately, before she could escape, the door flung open and Theron snatched her up by her arm, jerking her against him.

"Did you really think you could sneak in here without me knowing? Sensitive hearing, remember?" Theron said, pointing to his ears. He threw her against the wall with enough force to make her cry out in pain. "Since you wanted to be in here so badly, I don't see any reason to let you leave."

Too terrified to defy him, Phoebe just sobbed, "I'm sorry!"

Theron's cold, black eyes held no sympathy.

Kallias, on the other hand, cast a worried glance at her.

Theron noticed—and laughed. "She did this to you, and you still care about her?"

Kallias looked down at the floor. "*You* did this to me," he said quietly.

Theron shrugged. "I suppose I did. I'm quite proud of my work, too."

With no emotion whatsoever, Kallias watched Theron approach. His throat burned. He could barely breathe. His entire body ached, burned, and stung. His stomach clenched in the most agonizing hunger he'd ever felt. There were no words or emotions that could express his misery, so his body seemed to choose stoicism, instead.

Theron grasped his face roughly and lifted it, staring into the deadness of Kallias's eyes. "I've never seen a human last this long. Most are either insane or dead, by this point. But here you are, still alive."

"Why won't you just kill me?" Kallias said tiredly.

Theron laughed, "Most humans plead for their lives, not their deaths."

"Most humans aren't *tortured*," Kallias said.

Theron smiled. "Perhaps you should try begging."

Kallias forced himself to make eye contact with the monster. His eyes full of hatred, Kallias assured Theron, "I will *never* beg you for anything."

Theron's smug smile didn't falter. "In that case," he said with a smile that looked almost...*delighted*, "perhaps it's time for more torture."

"No!" Phoebe gasped. She rushed to her husband's side, attempting to put herself between them. "Leave him alone!"

Theron's sick, sadistic smile might've turned Kallias's stomach, even if he *weren't* already so sick. His own blood was splattered across Theron's pale chiton in such copious amounts that Kallias wondered how he hadn't bled to death already.

But that was just wishful thinking.

"What have I done," Kallias said, his voice still weakened by the pain, "that upset you so much that you find such delight in torturing me?"

Theron waved a hand dismissively. "Oh, it's not about *you*," he scoffed. "It's just a hobby of mine."

"I don't believe you," Kallias said.

Phoebe must've realized what he was doing—because she shook her head worriedly. "Kallias, don't push him. You'll make it worse."

But Kallias *wanted* to make it worse. He was tired and ready for death, and the only way to make death come quicker was to manipulate Theron into giving him what he wanted.

Theron lifted a dark eyebrow. "You think I care enough to have some grudge against a *human*?" he laughed.

"From what I hear, she was with you first," Kallias said weakly, "and yet, she still married me. It seems you weren't good enough for her."

"Kallias, please," Phoebe whispered, "he will hurt you even worse."

But Kallias ignored her.

Rage flashed in Theron's dark eyes, but he kept his voice even somehow. "You know nothing, human," he sneered. "I could ensnare almost any woman I wanted with one look. I was more than enough for your insignificant human wife."

Kallias frowned at that. One look? Was it possible that Phoebe *hadn't* lied about his control over her?

"And yet," Kallias said slowly, "she still married me."

A growl that was unnervingly animalistic resounded from Theron's throat. The taunting had succeeded in causing Theron to lose his temper.

In the few days since Kallias had met him, he'd realized the monster was easy to manipulate in that way—always just a few words away from a temper tantrum.

One that would bring the sweet release of death just a bit closer.

Kallias was *so* tired, so ready for the pain to end.

With a speed that Kallias couldn't follow, Theron pulled out a dagger and thrust it into Kallias's stomach. As Kallias yelled out in agony, Theron pulled it free and plunged it into him again. He twisted the blade, determined to do as much damage as possible.

Kallias's head fell forward, and warm blood spilled over his skin. He welcomed the waves of dizziness that cascaded over him, as he lost more and more blood.

Phoebe had been right about the pain. Theron had ensured its severity, but Kallias was grateful for it, still, because it meant it would all be over soon. He'd rather feel agony now than endure Theron's endless torture for another day.

Phoebe screamed out, but Kallias couldn't hear her. His ears rung, and his head spun violently, so violently that he thought—or hoped, really—that he might pass out soon.

Kallias thought he heard Phoebe pleading with the monster, but the ringing in his ears only grew louder, drowning out the noise around him.

After several moments of hearing only the pounding of his own pulse and the ringing of his ears, Kallias felt Theron grab his face roughly and force him to meet his gaze.

"Are you listening to me, human?" Theron growled.

No, Kallias thought, but he was in too much pain to speak.

"These last few days," Theron said with a strange, almost manic laugh, "those were just me having a bit of fun." His smile faded. "But there *is* information I need from you before you die, and now, you've gone and messed it all up."

"How is it his fault that *you* hurt him?" Phoebe cried, as if she actually thought the monster might respond to reason.

Kallias almost admired her hope. *He* had none left.

His vision blackened at the edges, and he felt a coolness spread slowly through his body.

"I need answers, and now, he'll die before I can get them," Theron continued. His voice seemed to move, as if he were pacing, but Kallias could no longer see him clearly.

Phoebe said something, but the sound was garbled.

Theron bared his fangs and sank them into his own wrist. He returned to Kallias and pressed his bleeding wrist against Kallias's mouth. "Drink."

Kallias tried to turn away, but Theron held him firmly by his hair.

"I said *drink*," Theron growled again.

Kallias clamped his jaw shut.

"We don't have time for this, human. You're dying," Theron said, as if Kallias were simply playing a game.

"I'd rather die," Kallias tried to explain, "than become like you."

Theron glared at Phoebe. "What is his problem *now*?"

"He's afraid it'll turn him," Phoebe said. Her voice sounded hoarse from all the screaming and crying she'd done. She looked at Kallias, desperate to help him avoid more pain. "Theron feeds me his blood often, and I'm still human. It won't change you, I promise."

Theron rolled his eyes. "You humans are so stupid. Your heart is still beating," he snarled at Kallias. "Only the dead can become what I am. My blood will heal you. That's all."

Kallias didn't trust the word of a monster. He didn't trust his wife, either, for that matter.

Besides, even if the blood *would* just heal him, he didn't *want* to heal. He wanted to die.

But of course, Theron wouldn't give him that.

He pushed Kallias's head against the wall and pried his mouth open. Then, Theron held his wrist over Kallias's open mouth and let the blood pour into it.

Kallias tried to pull away, but Theron held him firmly. Only after Kallias finally swallowed some of the blood did Theron pull his wrist away. He left Kallias there, as he waited for the blood to take effect.

A strange disorientation washed over Kallias's mind, and he wondered if the blood had intoxicated him somehow. His pain dulled, and there was some kind of...*pleasant* sensation, as well.

He watched in horror, as his wounds began to heal.

Eventually, Phoebe's broken voice found its way through his disoriented haze.

"You should've let him die," she sighed.

With a laugh, Theron said, "You've begged me to spare him all week, and now, you want me to kill him?"

"What I want," Phoebe said, sniffling as she held back tears, "is to have never met you, but I can't have that. So, yes, I'd rather him be dead than endure what you've done to him."

Theron scoffed, as if she were simply a child who couldn't take no for an answer. "We both know you can never keep up this...insolence of yours long. You'll get over it eventually."

At that, Phoebe only sobbed—as if she knew he was right, as if she knew there was no free will, no escape.

Theron walked over to Kallias and kicked him in the side.

Kallias groaned, as pain spread through his ribs.

"You should be able to talk now," Theron said. "Speak, human."

"You could've just asked," Kallias muttered.

"Tell me where to find the Stone of the Eklektos," Theron said.

"What?" Phoebe breathed.

Kallias frowned. "I don't know what you mean."

"Don't play games with me, human," Theron said with a growl. "Where is the Stone?"

"What stone?" Kallias said with an incredulous stare.

"The Stone of the Eklektos," Theron said again, "prophesied to hold the power to either save or destroy the world."

Those words pricked a memory, but it'd been so long that Kallias had nearly forgotten it entirely.

Phoebe climbed to her feet. "*That's* what this was about?" she said, anger rising in her voice. "You're still fixated on that Stone?"

Theron turned his glare toward her. "Take care how you speak to me, Phoebe."

Phoebe took a step back, clearly intimidated by the threat. "Why didn't you tell me?" she breathed. "If I'd known that was what you were after, maybe I could've prevented all of this."

The priest with the strange, emotionless eyes, Kallias remembered. The one from Aphrodite's temple. Theron was referring to that odd, red stone the priest had given him.

"Why would you want that?" Kallias said. He hadn't even wanted it —nor had he thought about it in years.

"The power," Theron scoffed. "Obviously, I want the power."

"There's no power. It's just a rock," Kallias muttered. "The priest was clearly out of his mind—or playing some strange trick." His frown deepened. "How did you even know about it?"

But then, he remembered. Phoebe had been with him that day.

The guilt he saw in her dark brown eyes confirmed his suspicion. "I didn't know he'd become obsessed with it."

Kallias mentally rolled his eyes, too tired to do so physically. "I haven't seen it in years."

"You were told it was powerful, and I'm supposed to believe you just…threw it away?" Theron snarled.

Kallias scowled at him. "It was just a stone—an ugly, red stone. Stones don't have power. That's impossible."

"Until you met me, you thought that undead creatures who feed on blood were impossible, didn't you?" Theron countered.

Kallias couldn't deny that, but he still didn't see a connection. "It doesn't change the fact that I haven't seen it in years."

Theron knelt in front of him and waved a blood-soaked knife. "I'm sure a bit more torture would help you remember."

"No!" Phoebe cried. "Please, Theron. Just listen to me."

He ignored her. "What will it be?" he asked Kallias. "The truth or more pain?"

"I've told you the truth already," Kallias said tiredly.

Theron shrugged. "Pain, it is, then."

"No," Phoebe said. She grasped his arm to get his attention. "You don't need to hurt him. Just listen to *me*."

With a slight flick of his arm, the monster managed to throw her across the room somehow. Kallias had never seen anything like it.

She crumpled into the floor, sobbing, and Theron turned his attention back toward Kallias.

But Kallias was looking at Phoebe now.

Theron stepped forward with his blade.

"Please," Phoebe cried out, her voice broken with pained sobs, "he's telling the truth. He doesn't know where it is."

Theron glared at her. "Don't lie for him."

"I'm not," Phoebe said, tears streaming down her cheeks. "I've been trying to tell you, but you won't listen to me. He doesn't *know*."

But he *still* wasn't listening to her. Instead, he seemed suddenly intrigued by the concern in Kallias's eyes. With a slight smile, he turned and walked toward Phoebe.

She cowered against the wall, terrified of what he might do to her.

But he grasped her arm and jerked her to her feet. Phoebe tried to pull her arm free, but his tight grasp bruised her.

With just the hand on her arm, he spun her around so that her back pressed against his front. He moved his face to her neck and inhaled her scent.

Phoebe shivered. "Theron, what are you doing?"

"I'm hungry. I need blood," he growled, the words vibrating against her neck. "You know I can't be around this much blood without feeding."

Her wide, brown eyes shifted toward Kallias. "Not here."

Theron swept her waves of soft, black hair aside, baring her neck. As she tried to pull away, he wrapped his arm around her waist to hold her still. He moved his lips to her ear and growled, "I'll feed anywhere I want."

"Please, Theron," Phoebe whispered. "We can do this in your room."

Theron smiled. She couldn't see him, but she knew that he was smiling because she felt his lips curve against her ear. "I'm hungry now. I don't want to wait. What's wrong, Phoebe? You've never denied me before."

Phoebe closed her eyes in shame. He was mocking her. He knew exactly why she didn't want him to feed, and he apparently found it amusing. She glanced at Kallias and sighed, "Because I don't want you to feed from me in front of my husband."

"He knows about us now," Theron said. "Why hide it?"

Like always, Phoebe's blood responded to Theron's hunger, and her reluctance began to fade. She shivered when his lips pressed against her neck. "I'm not hiding anything. I just don't like it."

"But of course you like it," Theron whispered. "You couldn't possibly like anything more. Now, stop fighting it, and let me feed."

Phoebe's blood called to him, and she didn't have the strength to resist it. "Fine."

Kallias turned his face away, nausea twisting at his stomach. He tried his best to block out what was happening, but when he heard Phoebe whimper, he glanced at her, afraid she was hurt.

What he found, instead, was that Phoebe seemed to *enjoy* what the monster did to her. With her head leaned against Theron's shoulder and her eyes closed tightly, Phoebe appeared to be feeling some sort of plea-sure. Repulsed by what he'd just seen, Kallias returned his gaze to the floor, wishing he'd never looked at all.

After a few moments, he heard Theron's voice again. "All right, human. Would you tell me where to find the Stone of the Eklektos, if your wife's life depended on it?"

Kallias looked up. Theron still held Phoebe, but he'd stopped feeding from her. Blood stained his lips, and a stream of blood trickled down Phoebe's neck, as well, staining her light blue peplos. Horror had replaced the pleasure that had been apparent in Phoebe's expression moments ago.

"Don't hurt her," Kallias said, unable to stop himself. "Please."

Theron laughed. "Do you see that?" he whispered in Phoebe's ear. "He still cares about you. Doesn't that make you feel terrible?"

Her eyes glistened with tears. "Yes," she said hoarsely. "It does."

He licked the blood from his lips. He looked at Kallias, victory in his dark brown eyes. "If you want her to live, tell me where to find the Stone."

"And if I don't know?" Kallias asked worriedly.

Theron shrugged. "Then, she dies."

Kallias cast a distraught look at Phoebe. She met his gaze, and he was surprised to see...not fear, but *regret*.

"I told you, Theron," Phoebe sighed. "He doesn't know."

"Then, I'll kill you," Theron told her.

Kallias pulled at the chains holding him to the wall, but it did no good. If he hadn't been able to loosen the chains when he'd had all of his strength, he certainly couldn't do it now, when he was injured and weak. "Let her go."

"Only if you tell me where it is," Theron said again.

"You're *still* not listening to me!" Phoebe said. Though tears still wet her cheeks, anger tinged her voice now. "He can't help me. He doesn't know where it is. *He* hasn't seen it in years."

"You said he had it," Theron snarled.

"I said that years ago!" Phoebe scoffed. "He doesn't have it anymore."

Theron twisted her arm painfully and snarled, "Then, who has it now?"

When Phoebe cried out in pain, Kallias pulled again at the chains, ignoring the way his body protested the movement. "Let her go!"

"I knew I couldn't resist you!" Phoebe cried, unable to stand the pain in her arm. "I realized I'd made a mistake by mentioning it to you, and so I took it and gave it to someone who *could* resist you."

"You did what?" Theron growled.

"It was the only way to correct the mistake I'd made," Phoebe said, despair in her voice now. "I had to make sure neither of us could find it. Kallias never even noticed I took it."

"Phoebe," Theron growled, "you'll tell me where it is, or I *will* kill you."

Phoebe's despair grew more visible with each passing moment. "I didn't trust myself with you. I made sure I'd never know where it was, as well. I can't help you, Theron. It's gone."

Theron growled—the sound frightening and inhuman. He twisted her arm further, causing her to scream out in pain. "Well, you're just absolutely worthless, aren't you?" he sneered in her ear. "I'll enjoy killing you."

Phoebe sobbed, but she knew it was useless to fight him. He was infinitely stronger than her—than any human, really.

Kallias's heart raced. He jerked pointlessly at the chains, using more strength than he'd thought he had left. And when he couldn't free himself, he dropped his pride and did what he'd promised he'd never do. He begged.

"Please, don't kill her. I'll do whatever you want."

Theron smiled maliciously. "I think I'll especially enjoy the look on *your* face as you watch your wife die."

The next few minutes were the worst minutes of Kallias's life. He could do nothing to stop Theron from killing Phoebe. He fought against the chains harder than anyone in his state should've ever been able to do, but it didn't help. He begged Theron to release her, but Theron ignored his pleas.

Kallias watched in horror as the color drained from his wife's face. Her body weakened and slumped against Theron. But Theron continued feeding until he'd drained her completely. When he finally released her, her pale, lifeless body fell to the ground with a *thud*.

Kallias stared at her, praying that she would move.

Theron smiled and wiped the blood from his face with the back of his hand. "She's dead, human. No use in staring at her now."

Kallias barely heard Theron.

In fact, as the minutes and hours passed, he was only vaguely aware that Theron had returned to torturing him. His mind seemed to distance itself from everything around him.

He continued to stare at his wife's body. She lay facedown on the floor with her arms sprawled on either side of her. A stream of crimson blood coated her bluish skin and her peplos.

Watching her die was more painful than anything Kallias had ever experienced. As a matter of fact, he felt so much pain over her death that he didn't even notice the physical pain, as Theron sliced at his skin.

Theron eventually lost interest in torturing Kallias. It ceased to bring him satisfaction once it stopped affecting Kallias. With a disappointed sigh, Theron plunged the dagger into Kallias's heart.

When the darkness began to overtake him, Kallias felt relief. His suffering was finally over.

He welcomed the cold embrace of death.

But when Theron heard his heart stop, he found himself even more disappointed. Killing Phoebe had brought him no satisfaction. Torturing Kallias had brought him no satisfaction. And killing Kallias had brought him no satisfaction either.

He still didn't have the Stone of the Eklektos, and instead, he had given Kallias what *he* wanted, which was death.

Kallias had said he'd rather die than become what Theron was.

Theron smiled, as he realized one last way he could torture Kallias. He used his fangs to pierce his wrist and then knelt in front of Kallias's lifeless body. He let his blood pour into Kallias's mouth.

And then he waited for the change to begin...

1

THE OLD, STONE BOX

2,485 years later…

*E*arly for class, as usual, Rose Foster waited in the empty college classroom for her classmates and art history professor to arrive.

In her boredom, she let her gaze wander, and a painting on the wall caught her eye. It was a painting of two women—one woman lying on the floor, her eyes closed and her head tilted back, and the other woman lying on top of her, her mouth against the woman's throat. Red paint colored the first woman's neck and the second's mouth.

A vampire.

Rose imagined her art history professor would interpret it as a demonization of women—or a religious critique of some kind.

But Rose found the image strangely…erotic.

The vampire didn't look like a monster. She looked beautiful.

And the victim looked less like a victim and more like a…lover.

But maybe that was just Rose's own queerness influencing her interpretation of the art.

In the silence of the room, the buzzing of the fluorescent lights and the clicking of the color-wheel clock on the wall were much too loud.

Deciding she had time to waste, Rose pulled her worn, black backpack into her lap and unzipped it. She reached in and pulled out the old, stone box she'd brought back from Greece. She opened it gently, not sure how much the ancient relic could handle.

Her long, red hair fell around her shoulders, as she leaned forward to peer inside the box.

A strange, blood-red stone lay inside.

Rose hesitantly reached toward the stone, and when her fingertip brushed it, it glowed red at her touch.

She jerked her hand back.

"Family heirloom?"

Startled, Rose jumped and slammed the box shut. Her wide, blue eyes shifted toward the guy in the chair next to her. His sleek, black hair brushed his brows, as he leaned over his bag, pulling out books for class.

"It's...nothing," she said with a nervous laugh.

He watched, as she hastily shoved the box back into her backpack. His thick, black eyebrows arched curiously, and his lips twitched, as he glanced between the box and her. "You all right, Rose?"

"Yeah, I just..." She shook her head at her own paranoia. She'd been on edge since her trip to Greece. "Sorry, Liang. I'm acting weird today, aren't I?"

His dark eyes studied her. "I would say yes, but you always act weird." He shoved his bag under his chair. "No offense."

She laughed. "None taken."

"So," Liang said, glancing at her closed bag, "what was it?"

"Nothing," she said—a little too quickly. "Just something I'm studying."

His laughter caught her off-guard. "Is there anything you *don't* study?" he teased. "I mean, it's just some ugly, old necklace."

"It's an ancient relic," she said defensively.

"Right," Liang said, grinning. "Rose, what do you do for *fun*?"

"Rose doesn't understand the meaning of the word *fun*," said a familiar voice.

Rose glanced toward the doorway, narrowing her eyes at her best friend. Audrey stuck out her tongue, and then, she crossed the room and took the seat next to Rose.

"That's not true," Rose told both of them. "I *read* for fun."

Audrey snorted. She propped her legs—which were clad in tight jeans that were permanently stained with neon pink paint-splatter—on the table, and her thin lips tilted into a grin. "Nerd activities don't count."

Rose lifted her eyebrows in disbelief. "What are you? Five?" she scoffed. "Never mind. Don't answer that. Of course you're five."

"*Twenty*-five, next month, actually," Audrey said, plucking playfully at the sleeve of Rose's T-shirt. "I expect a birthday party, by the way— with dancing, alcohol, and socialization."

Rose shuddered at the thought. "All three of those activities are way too dangerous for *me*, Audrey. You'd be better off asking one of those daredevil boyfriends of yours."

Audrey waved a hand at that. "No boyfriend would ever remember my birthday, Rose. Only you remember stuff like that." She offered Rose a teasing grin. "You're like the perfect back-up boyfriend—just without the sex and stuff."

"Oh, good," Rose said dryly. "That's my life's aspiration, you know. Being a back-up boyfriend for a straight girl."

Audrey tilted her head back and laughed loudly.

"Speaking of my usually-accurate memory," Rose said, pointing at Audrey's shirt. "That's not yours, is it?"

Audrey glanced down at the pale yellow, Beatles shirt. "Damn. You don't miss a thing, do you?"

It really wasn't hard to guess. The shirt was at least three sizes too big for Audrey's pencil-thin figure.

Not to mention the fact that Audrey listened almost exclusively to heavy metal, and the Beatles were, you know, not that.

"I lost my shirt at some point last night," Audrey said with a shrug, "so I stole one of his."

Rose stared blankly at her. "You lost a whole shirt? The shirt you were *wearing*?"

Audrey placed a hand on Rose's shoulder. "Rose, has anyone ever explained to you how sex works?"

Rose rolled her eyes at her friend's teasing. "Do I know him?"

"I doubt it," Audrey said. "He's this hot guy from my pottery class."

"Will there be a second date?" Rose asked curiously.

"Probably not," Audrey muttered. "He was a bit self-obsessed."

Rose squinted at that. "That sounds like an unpleasant date."

"Not at all," Audrey said with a smile. "He was a good kisser."

As it grew closer to the class's starting time, students filled the room. Their voices blended into unintelligible noise, but Rose thought she heard Liang talking to another student about someone who'd gone missing the night before.

"Audrey, sometimes, I think you'd forgive murder, if the guy could kiss," Rose muttered.

"Nah," Audrey said. She placed a neon-paint-stained bag in her lap and unzipped it. "For *murder*, I think he'd need to be good at a little more than kissing."

Rose shook her head. "So, what else did you do last night?"

Audrey smiled. "You want details?"

"No," Rose said quickly, "not the kind you mean, anyway." She blushed. "I just meant: what did you actually *do* on the date? I don't think kissing and sex count as a date."

"Like you would know," Audrey scoffed, as she continued to rummage through her messenger bag. "It's been two years since *you* went on a date."

"Wow," Rose said sarcastically. "What ever would I do without you to constantly remind me of my nonexistent love life?"

"You'd brood in our apartment with your books," Audrey said, "like you do now." She triumphantly retrieved a crushed bag of barbecue chips from the bottom of her bag. "And you'd forever hold the record for World's Oldest Virgin."

"I don't think that's a real record," Rose muttered, "and I don't *brood.*"

"And you'd forever be a smartass," Audrey added.

Rose shrugged. "That's not going to change anyway."

Audrey ripped open the crushed bag of barbecue chips, completely ignoring the '*No Food or Drinks*' sign on the wall beside her. "To answer your question, though," she said, tossing a handful of crushed chips into her mouth, "we ate at this nice spaghetti restaurant, and then, we went to a concert."

"You mean an Italian restaurant," Rose said with a frown.

Audrey ignored the correction. "By the way, if you *want* to go on a date, I could set you up with someone. I made a list of guys that I think you'd like."

"You made a *list*?" Rose repeated.

"It's only two pages," Audrey said with a mouthful of chips.

Rose blinked. "Two pages?" She grimaced as she remembered the last guy Audrey had tried to set her up with. "Umm, no, thanks."

"Ah, come on," Audrey whined. "I left the ex-convicts off this time!"

"I'm just not interested in dating anyone," Rose told her.

"Well, I made a list of women, too, but I can't promise they're all gay," Audrey said. "We could ask them, though!"

All Rose could think to say to that was, "Wow."

At her reluctance, Audrey said, "Do you want me to ask them *for* you?"

"No," Rose said, her eyes wide. "Please, don't."

"I don't mind," Audrey assured her.

Rose didn't doubt that. "It's *really* not necessary."

"Do you *want* to become a lonely, old cat lady?" Audrey scolded.

Rose shrugged. "Well, considering our current apartment doesn't allow pets, the ability to *have* cats sounds like a step up to me."

Audrey rolled her eyes. "There's just no hope for you, is there?"

"I'm focusing on my studies right now," Rose said dismissively.

Audrey snorted at that. "Rose, you have a perfect GPA, and you're *literally* a genius," she laughed. She turned the chip bag upside down, letting the crumbs fall into her mouth, like some weird potato-waterfall. "You could ace your classes with your eyes closed."

"Well, let's hope so," Rose muttered. "I forgot my reading glasses at home."

Audrey laughed, and apparently, her potato-waterfall didn't like that

—because she choked. After she recovered from her short coughing fit, Audrey fell serious. She leaned toward Rose and whispered, "Not everyone is like Ethan, you know."

Rose froze at the mention of her ex-boyfriend. She closed her eyes, counting the seconds, as she waited for the sick feeling in her stomach to pass. "I know that. It has nothing to do with Ethan."

"If you say so," Audrey said with a worried frown. "So, how was your trip to Greece?"

Excitement lightened Rose's bright blue eyes. "It was interesting."

Audrey held her hand up and gave Rose a bored look. "Interesting by Rose-standards or interesting by Audrey-standards?"

Rose frowned. "What's the difference?"

Audrey fished out a candy bar from the bottom of her bag. "Interesting by *my* standards includes meeting a bunch of sexy men. Interesting by your standards usually involves looking at old, boring things and learning about dead people."

"Mine, obviously," Rose said. "It was a study trip."

"Ugh," Audrey groaned. "All those sexy accents, and you *studied*."

Rose frowned. "Do you even know what a Greek accent sounds like?"

Audrey shrugged. "It's an accent. Who cares how it sounds?"

Rose rolled her eyes. "You know, if you devoted half as much attention to your classes as you do to guys, you wouldn't be failing so many classes."

"Yes, *mother*," Audrey said, flashing a sarcastic smile. "If I only had to take art classes, I wouldn't be failing *any* classes. I care about art. I don't care about all this other stuff. Oh, that reminds me: I need your Psychology notes."

Rose pulled a thin, black notebook out of her backpack and set it in front of Audrey. As Audrey busied herself in copying them, Rose leaned closer so she could speak quietly. "Something *did* happen on the trip, though."

Audrey glanced at Rose. "What kind of something?"

Before Rose could speak, the art professor hobbled into the room and dropped an armful of books down on her desk. She glared at the noisy students, as if she weren't fifteen minutes late for her own class. Rose cast a wary look at the irritated professor and pulled her books out of her backpack.

"I'll tell you after class," she whispered.

Audrey pouted. "Dang it. Now, I'm curious."

The art history professor spent most of the class lecturing on the use of nudity in art throughout history—from the Ancient Greek kouros to contemporary art and performance art. Rose listened closely and tried to take detailed notes, but Audrey was more concerned with making silly comments about the examples.

"Look at *this* one," Audrey whispered, pointing at a picture in the book.

"Shhh," Rose hissed.

Audrey shrugged and returned to flipping through the examples in the textbook. A few minutes later, however, as the professor discussed a Renaissance painting, Audrey leaned over and whispered in Rose's ear, "Is it just me, or is Dr. Grandma a little too excited about these naked men?"

Rose scowled at her immature friend. "Pay attention."

The professor continued chattering excitedly about the paintings of that time period, and Audrey listened quietly for maybe fifteen minutes, at *most*, before she leaned in again. "Do you know who I would like to paint naked?" Audrey whispered. She pointed at a blonde man at the table in front of them and said, "Him."

Rose rolled her eyes and then blushed, as the guy Audrey pointed at turned to look at them. Audrey just smiled and waved.

He seemed amused. "Were you talking about me?"

Rose's blush deepened. "She was talking about the penguin," she blurted out, and then, she pointed at a strange penguin statue on the windowsill.

Audrey clamped her hand over her mouth to muffle her laughter.

The blonde man stared at Rose for several moments, as if he were trying to figure out whether she was joking or not. Finally, he just laughed and turned to face the professor again.

Audrey, on the other hand, continued to stare at Rose with raised eyebrows, her lips twitching as she tried not to laugh.

As soon as the class ended, Audrey fled the classroom and fell against the brick wall, finally allowing herself to burst into hysterical laughter.

Rose slung her backpack over her shoulder, grabbed her coffee thermos from the table, and joined Audrey outside. She sighed as Audrey continued to laugh.

The Florida sun felt too hot and bright on her skin for the autumn morning.

"It's not that funny," Rose muttered.

Audrey snorted. "Penguin? Really, Rose?"

Rose sighed. "What was I supposed to say?"

"Anything but *that*," Audrey laughed.

Rose pursed her lips. "Well, it's *your* fault. You're the one who embarrassed us," she grumbled. "You know I can't lie when I'm embarrassed."

"I know you can't lie *at all*," Audrey said with a grin. "And what I said wasn't embarrassing. What *you* said was embarrassing."

Rose rolled her eyes. "Can we just…forget this happened?"

Audrey continued to smile at Rose. "Deal," she said, offering her hand for a handshake, "as long as you buy me lunch."

"I was already planning on it," Rose laughed.

"Well, aren't you a gentleman?" Audrey teased.

Rose rolled her eyes. "I need to tell you about my trip anyway."

Audrey nodded. "I guess I'll see you at lunch, then."

Audrey bit into her second cheeseburger. "Aren't you going to eat?"

Rose continued picking at her salad. "I *am* eating."

Audrey set her half-eaten cheeseburger on the plate next to her side of French fries and slice of chocolate cake. Rose was convinced that her slender friend could win national eating contests if she tried.

"You know, a wise woman once told me that if God wanted us to eat grass, we'd have been born cattle," Audrey said in the most sage-like voice she could muster.

Rose laughed. "And who was this wise woman?"

Audrey tossed some French fries into her mouth. "My grandmother, of course."

"Your grandmother also tried to feed me an entire chocolate pie once because she said chocolate was the cure for a bad day," Rose reminded her.

Audrey frowned. "Chocolate *is* the cure for a bad day."

Rose smiled. "Yeah, well, it's easy for you to say. You eat whatever you want and never gain a pound. I don't have that problem."

"Oh, shut up," Audrey scoffed. She swallowed her food and pointed a finger at Rose. "You've been barely eating and making those little, insecure remarks since Ethan, and I'm finding it harder and harder to believe that asshole isn't to blame for it all."

Rose didn't meet her gaze. "Why are we talking about him again?"

"Because I'm your closest friend, and I always tell you the truth," Audrey said, "and the truth is: you did not walk away from that asshole unscathed. You *say* it's nothing compared to what you went through as a child, but that doesn't mean it's not still trauma."

Rose chewed a mouthful of tomato and lettuce, before mumbling, "It's a good salad, actually."

Audrey shook her head. "Besides, I'd *love* to have your curves. I mean, just look at your boobs."

Rose nearly choked on her salad. Even though she wore a T-shirt that definitely covered everything, she still threw her arm over her chest, when an elderly couple turned to glare at them. "Audrey."

"What?" Audrey said with a mouthful of burger.

Rose leaned over the table and whispered, "I don't know if everyone in this restaurant is enjoying your boob lecture."

Audrey shrugged and grabbed another fry.

Rose eyed Audrey curiously. Even though Audrey was acting like her usual fun-loving, obnoxious self, something still felt…off.

Every now and then, Rose would glimpse a brief flicker of fear in those amber of hers, but then, Audrey would launch into another silly lecture or playful remark—and Rose would never have time to ask about it.

So, while Audrey silently chewed a mouthful of fries, Rose asked her, "Are you all right?"

Audrey looked up, her eyes wide. "Yeah! Fine," she said—a little too quickly. "I'm just waiting to hear about this study trip of yours."

She said *'study trip,'* as if she'd never heard those words in the same sentence before.

Rose set down her fork and pushed aside her half-eaten salad. The noisy chatter, the clanging of forks against plates, and the scuffing chairs resounded loudly enough throughout the busy restaurant that Rose doubted anyone would overhear them.

She leaned forward, resting her arms on the dark, wooden table. "There was nothing unusual about the trip, really—until the last day."

"What happened on the last day?" Audrey asked.

"We were touring a temple in Athens, when this strange man pulled me aside," Rose explained. "I'd never seen him before in my life, but he acted as if he knew me."

Audrey picked up another fry. "Define *'strange man.'*"

"Pale and emotionless," Rose told her, "like some kind of ghost."

Audrey's brows furrowed. "So, what did Creepy-Guy say?"

"He said he'd been waiting for me, and then, he gave me this box that he said *belonged* to me—whatever *that* means," Rose said. She blew out a slow sigh. "I wanted to tell him he had the wrong person—that I'd never seen the box before—but he disappeared before I could."

Audrey looked up, alarm widening her golden-brown eyes. "What do you mean *'disappeared?'*"

Rose shrugged. "I looked down at the box for maybe a second, and when I looked back up, he was gone."

Audrey's fair skin paled. "That...sounds familiar."

Rose frowned worriedly. "What do you mean?"

Audrey shook her head, as if shaking herself out of a haze. "Nothing," she said—a bit too quickly. "Just tell me what was in the box."

Rose hesitated. She was more sure than ever that something was bothering Audrey, but she didn't want to push her when she looked so uncomfortable. "Some scrolls and a necklace of some kind."

Audrey squinted. "A necklace?"

Rose sipped her coffee. "Well, more like a large stone, attached to a chain."

"Stone?" Audrey repeated. "What kind? Like a diamond?"

"No," Rose said, shaking her head. "It's dark red—but not a ruby, either."

"Garnet?" Audrey guessed.

"I don't think so," Rose said. "It's old and asymmetrical—with a lot of sharp edges. I've never seen anything like it."

"Weird," Audrey said.

Rose nodded. "And sometimes, Audrey, I swear it glows."

"*Very* weird," Audrey amended. Her frown deepened. "Creepy-Guy —what did *he* look like?"

"Pale blonde hair. So pale it was almost white," Rose said, "and pale blue eyes, too." She squinted, as she tried to think of a way to explain it. "And sort of...perfect? Like so perfect that it feels wrong, you know?"

Audrey leaned forward. "So, you *did* meet a sexy, foreign guy!"

"That's what you got out of all of that?" Rose said with a frown.

Audrey focused her attention on the chocolate cake in front of her. "And he gave you a gift, too! I hope you got his number. When a hot guy gives you jewelry, you're supposed to get his number."

Rose stared blankly at her. "That's not even—"

"Oh, right! Speaking for myself, of course," Audrey added, before Rose could finish her sentence. "I am totally supportive of you getting women's numbers, too."

Rose just sighed. "It wasn't jewelry, Audrey," she tried to explain. "It was an ancient artifact, and last I checked, giving ancient artifacts to people didn't mean you wanted to date them."

"It could, if he's weird like you," Audrey suggested.

Rose frowned. "When have I ever given anyone an ancient artifact?"

"No, what *you* do is worse," Audrey told her. "You just blush from afar and then ruin your chances with them as soon as you meet them by opening that sassy mouth of yours."

Rose flashed a sarcastic smile. "Thanks, Audrey."

"You're welcome," Audrey said. "So, what did the scrolls say?"

"I'm still working on that," Rose admitted. "From what I can tell, they're written in Ancient Greek. I've been trying to translate them for days."

Audrey frowned. "But aren't you like an expert in Greek?"

"Expert? Hardly," Rose scoffed. "I'm fluent—technically—in *Modern* Greek. But Ancient Greek? Not so much."

"Ancient?" Audrey repeated. "How old *are* those scrolls?"

"It's hard to say," Rose said, picking at her salad. "It seems unlikely that they're as old as they seem. Surely, they would've fallen apart by now." She shrugged. "It could be a forgery."

"And if it's not?" Audrey said, her eyes wide. "They'd be…what? Hundreds of years old?"

Rose lifted her eyebrows at the guess. "Try thousands."

"No way," Audrey said, her fork still in hand. "Is there anyone who could help you make sense of it?"

"Possibly," Rose said. She sighed. "Honestly, I should've taken it to a museum as soon as he gave it to me. If it *is* ancient, that's where it belongs—in a museum, not in the hands of a college student. At the very least, I should've shown it to Dr. Parker."

"So, why didn't you?" Audrey asked.

Rose swallowed uneasily. "Before he disappeared, he gave this warning. I know it's silly to even take it seriously, but it just…unsettled me, for some reason."

But Audrey didn't act like *she* thought it was silly. "What was it?"

"He told me not to tell anyone," Rose said. "He said to guard it with my life and that people would die if it landed in the wrong hands."

A flicker of fear flashed across Audrey's face. "The wrong hands?"

"He said the stone is—and I quote—*the key to the destruction or the salvation of humanity.*" Rose let out a small, nervous laugh. "And I know that sounds totally insane, and yet, I can't shake the feeling that I should listen to the warning."

Audrey lifted her eyebrows. "You told *me.*"

Rose laughed, "Well, I trust you to not kill a bunch of people, Audrey."

"You never know," Audrey said with a grin. "I could be a secret serial killer."

Rose shook her head. "You're too forgetful. You'd get caught within the first week."

"Well, that's what I have you for," Audrey teased. "You'd be in charge of all the brain stuff."

Rose wanted to ask what *'brain stuff'* even meant, but instead, she said, "Wait, when did *I* become a serial killer?"

"When I asked for your help," Audrey said easily. "You know you'd do anything for your best friend."

Rose rolled her eyes, but she couldn't help but laugh.

Audrey smiled. "So, if you can't translate it, what will you do?"

"I can translate some of it," Rose assured her, "but at some point, I'll need help. I might ask Dr. Parker."

"Well, of course *she'll* help you," Audrey laughed. "She loves you."

Rose smiled shyly at that. She'd always had a lot of admiration for her ancient history professor, and her ancient history professor seemed to appreciate Rose's passion for the subject, as well.

"Do you think the scrolls have something to do with the stone?" Audrey asked curiously.

Rose shrugged. "I assume so, but I haven't figured out what yet." Growing more exhausted by the moment, she drank a bit more of her coffee. "At first, I thought it was meant to be some sort of journal, but now, I'm thinking it must be fiction."

"What makes you think that?" Audrey asked.

"Well," Rose said hesitantly, "if what I've translated so far is correct, then…the scrolls are about a vampire."

Audrey froze, alarm flickering in her golden-brown eyes. "Vampire?"

Rose frowned at Audrey's reaction. "It seems that way," she said, "but like I said, I haven't translated much yet. There are a lot of words in the scrolls that are unfamiliar to me."

"Vampire?" Audrey said again, like a scratched CD, stuck on that one word.

Rose nodded slowly. "The person who wrote the scrolls had a lover who drank her blood," she explained. Again, the painting of the two women flashed through her mind. "He didn't age, and she only saw him at night." She set down her coffee. "His name was Theron."

Audrey stared at the table, her narrow shoulders rigid. "Theron," she mumbled under her breath. "That sounds familiar, too."

With a worried frown, Rose said, "Are you all right, Audrey?"

Audrey looked at her, but she didn't answer. "Did they even have stories about vampires back then?"

"Sure," Rose said, surprising Audrey. "Almost every culture throughout history has had myths of *some* kind of vampire-like creature. The term *'vampire'* wasn't used until the 1700s, but the myths predate the term. Ancient Hebrew cultures had their stories of Lilith, and Ancient Babylon and Assyria had similar myths about Lilitu. Jewish folklore also had stories about Estries, which were female vampires who preyed on men. The Ancient Greeks and Romans had myths about blood-drinking creatures, including the Lamia, the Empusae, and the striges. Eventually, the Greeks used the term *vrykolakas* to describe undead creatures—and some people equate that with the modern-day vampire myth. And then, of course, you have the well-known Slavic vampire mythology. And really, that doesn't even scratch the surface. Until a recent point in history, almost every culture believed in some kind of vampire myth."

Audrey scowled. "You're like a human textbook."

"You asked," Rose muttered.

Audrey's hands fidgeted on the table. "So, if all of those cultures had stories about vampires, why don't *we* believe in them?"

"Because we know more now," Rose said. "Our culture is guided by science, by concrete evidence, and there's none of that for vampires."

"How can you be so sure?" Audrey asked.

Rose shrugged. "Logically, it doesn't make sense. Everyone dies. You can't defy death. No one drinks blood, and no one bursts into flames because of a few UV rays, not even pale, freckled redheads like me."

"I seem to remember someone saying—can't remember *who* but… someone—that all fiction originates from fact," Audrey said.

"That would be your literature professor from two years ago," Rose reminded her. "We took that class together, remember?"

"Why would I remember that?" Audrey said with a frown.

Rose suppressed a laugh. "It was an enjoyable class."

"There's no such thing," Audrey said dismissively.

"Well, he wasn't saying that all stories are true," Rose told her friend. "He was simply saying that there is a *bit* of truth in every story."

"What's the difference?" Audrey said.

"The story of Dracula, for instance," Rose offered. "It's likely based on the true story of Vlad the Impaler. Vlad Dracula *did* exist, but he was human. He was definitely bloodthirsty in the figurative sense of the word, and some say he put the blood of his victims in a goblet and dipped his bread in it." She shrugged. "Clearly, there were bits of truth in his story, but that doesn't mean he was a vampire."

Audrey didn't seem convinced. "But what if the vampire part *is* true?"

"Vampires aren't real," Rose insisted.

Audrey stared at her plate, picking nervously at her cake. "Well," she said uneasily, "let's hope not."

Rose's stomach twisted with worry. She leaned forward, resting her hand on top of Audrey's, hoping to soothe the fear she saw in her best friend's face. "Please, talk to me. Something's clearly bothering you."

Audrey squeezed Rose's hand, and when she looked up, Rose was stunned to see that Audrey's golden eyes glistened with unshed tears. "Can we get out of here?" she asked, suddenly. "I need air, and...we need to talk."

Rose nodded. "Go on. I'll meet you out there after I pay the bill."

AFTER ROSE LEFT THE RESTAURANT, SHE FOUND AUDREY SITTING ON THE bench outside. She hunched forward with her face in her hands, her narrow shoulders lifting and falling with each shallow breath.

Rose set her backpack on the sidewalk and sat down next to Audrey.

"I had one of my dreams," Audrey said into her hands.

Rose pressed a comforting hand against Audrey's shoulder. "The bad kind?"

Audrey lifted her head to look at Rose, and she nodded.

Audrey's dreams had a tendency of coming true. She'd discovered this *condition* of hers, as she often called it, when she was a child. For weeks, she had a recurring, vivid nightmare about her parents dying in a car crash, but she was only five years old, and no one would listen.

The doctors blamed her vivid and disturbing dreams on a worse-than-average case of night terrors. Unfortunately, the doctors were wrong. Even though Audrey had begged them not to leave that night, her parents left her with a babysitter while they attended a wedding.

On their way home, a tractor-trailer slammed into their small car. Her parents died exactly as they had in Audrey's dream.

Afterward, Audrey was diagnosed with post-traumatic stress disorder—much like Rose had been at a similar age—and her nightmares were blamed on that, instead.

After kids at school began to call her crazy, she'd stopped talking about the dreams altogether. The only person who'd ever believed her was Rose—which was strange, since Rose wasn't the type to believe in anything she hadn't seen with her own eyes.

But Rose had seen the pain in Audrey's eyes, and she'd responded to it with nothing but acceptance.

"Are you ready to talk about it?" Rose said softly.

"Oh, Rose, it was horrible," Audrey cried.

Rose moved closer to Audrey and slipped an arm around her. Audrey rested her head on Rose shoulder and began to sob.

How long had Audrey been holding this back?

And why?

Rose held Audrey while she cried, her tears soaking into Rose's thin, black hoodie. "It's going to be fine," Rose said in the most comforting tone she could. "Whatever is going to happen—we'll get through it."

"No, *we* won't," Audrey sobbed. "That's the problem."

Rose's brows furrowed. "What do you mean?"

Audrey pulled away, tears flowing down her face, smearing the thick, black eyeliner beneath her eyes. "Rose, in my dream, you died."

Rose nearly fell off the bench, when Audrey latched onto her and started sobbing again. Rose's hand absently rubbed Audrey's back, and her mind whirled with the gravity of what Audrey had just said.

"Maybe it was just a dream," Rose heard herself say.

Audrey jerked back, glaring at Rose through the tears. "I know the difference, Rose! You know I do. Do you think I'd be this upset over a normal dream?"

"But it *could* be," Rose said—in one, final desperate attempt.

"Don't do that," Audrey said, her eyes narrowed. "Don't be like everyone else who doubted me. You've always believed me!"

Guilt twisted in Rose's stomach. "You're right. I'm sorry," she sighed. "It's just hard to accept when someone tells you you're going to die."

"How do you think it feels for *me*?" Audrey said, her voice cracking. "I can't lose you! Who would I have without you?"

"Your grandparents," Rose said, trying to be helpful.

Apparently, she wasn't.

"You know what I mean, Rose," Audrey said irritably.

"Audrey," Rose said with a nervous laugh, "out of the two of us, you're not the one who has problems making friends. You'd find someone to replace me *easily*—someone less awkward, less sarcastic..."

She was honestly trying to be encouraging, but based on the glare Audrey gave her, she'd clearly failed.

"Rose, the only thing I want to hear you say right now," Audrey said, tears shining in her eyes, "is that you'll stop it from happening."

"Is that even possible?" Rose said.

They'd tried before and failed.

"You believe me, don't you?" Audrey said. "You're already a step ahead of anyone else I've tried to warn."

"Okay," Rose said, nodding. "I guess...first, I'll need to know how it will happen."

Audrey shifted uneasily, as if she'd hoped Rose wouldn't ask that. "Promise me that you'll believe me, no matter how crazy it sounds."

"I promise," Rose said. She'd believed in the precognitive dreams, hadn't she? What could be more unbelievable than that?

With absolutely no build-up, Audrey blurted, "A man bit you and drank all of your blood."

Rose blinked. "Uh, what?"

"He bit you and drank all of your blood," Audrey repeated slowly.

Rose laughed in disbelief. "*Who* bit me?"

"The murderer," Audrey said.

"You're joking," Rose assumed.

There was no other explanation.

Audrey glared at her. "No, I'm not joking! Rose, you promised."

"I know, and I do believe you," Rose assured her, "but...my blood?"

It had to be some sort of prank. What other explanation was there?

"You have to take this seriously," Audrey told her.

"I know. I'm trying. I just," Rose said, "don't understand." With a sigh, she said, "Just start from the beginning."

"It was night, and you were outside," Audrey explained. "You were walking down an alley. You were nervous—I think something must've set you on edge beforehand." She frowned thoughtfully. "Then, just as you were about to step out of the alley and onto a main road, this attractive guy attacked you."

Rose lifted her eyebrows. "I'm sorry. Did you just say *attractive*?"

Audrey shrugged. "It feels weird to call him hot, considering he killed you."

"But it *doesn't* feel weird to call him attractive?" Rose asked.

"It's just a fact, Rose. Don't take it personally," Audrey muttered.

"I'm not," Rose said with a bemused frown. "I'm just—" She shook her head in defeat. "Never mind."

"He was tall—sort of. Compared to you and me, anyway," Audrey told her. "He had dark hair and dark eyes. Very sexy."

"Audrey," Rose said, eyebrows high, "can we focus, please?"

Audrey rolled her eyes. "I changed my mind about his sexiness after he killed you, okay?"

"I appreciate that," Rose muttered.

"No problem," Audrey said. "Where was I? Oh, right, his appearance. His complexion was dark—or maybe just tanned? It was too dark to tell, really. He was kind of seductive—in this weird, unsettling way."

Rose's frown deepened. "The murderer was...seductive?"

"In a weird, unsettling way," Audrey repeated, as if that changed the fact that she was calling a murderer seductive.

"Let me get this straight," Rose said. "You're telling me you had a dream that a tall, dark, and handsome *vampire* killed me?"

Audrey's eyes narrowed. "You promised."

"I'm not saying I don't believe you," Rose assured her. "I just...don't believe in vampires. There must be some other explanation."

"Like what?" Audrey said.

Rose shrugged. "Have you read any horror novels lately? Could they have influenced the vision or something?"

"No," Audrey assured her. "What I saw was real."

Rose nodded slowly. "There has to be an explanation."

"And what if there's not?" Audrey challenged. "You said yourself that most cultures believed in them. Is it really so hard to think they might exist?"

"Yes," Rose said. "If they did exist, there'd be evidence."

"Don't you believe in God?" Audrey said.

Like most people from their small town, Rose was raised Christian. Well, 'raised' wasn't exactly the right word.

She wasn't really *raised* at all.

"Sure," Rose said.

"You have no proof *He* exists," Audrey pointed out.

Rose nodded. "Well, no, but...people kind of *feel* God—when they pray or worship. Right? That's why they believe," she suggested. "No one has felt or seen vampires."

"Or maybe they have," Audrey argued. "Maybe the stories are true."

Rose leaned back tiredly. The combination of stress, jet lag, and now the news that she'd die soon was beginning to get to her. "There must be another explanation," she said—for the third time.

Was she trying to convince Audrey or herself?

"Before my dream, I would've laughed at the mere idea that vampires might be real, but Rose, I *know* what I saw. He bit you and drank your blood. My dreams are always right," Audrey said. She sighed and added, "Besides, don't you think it's kind of weird that those scrolls described a vampire, and now, I've dreamed that you'll be killed by one?"

"Of course I think it's weird," Rose agreed, "but that doesn't mean I can just reverse my worldview in a matter of minutes. I don't believe in the supernatural. I never have."

Audrey tried a different approach. "Fine. Then, let's just say it wasn't a vampire at all. Let's think of him as an insane human who *thought* he was a vampire. Either way, I saw him bite you. I saw you die."

Rose nodded. "Okay. I believe you. Of *course* I believe you."

Audrey breathed a small sigh of relief. "So, how do we stop it from happening?"

"Your guess is as good as mine," Rose muttered.

KALLIAS SWIRLED THE WHISKEY IN THE SHORT, SQUARED GLASS, AS HE listened to the voices around him. The thunderous, bass-heavy music easily drowned the other sounds, but Kallias's inhuman hearing allowed him to discern each voice, despite the music.

A beautiful, blonde woman slid onto the barstool beside him, but he ignored her lustful gaze and continued to stare at the glass.

Unfortunately, the woman didn't take the hint.

Most vampires enjoyed this aspect of who they were.

Kallias did not.

The woman set a pink purse on the bar, intentionally brushing her hand against Kallias's arm. A thick, Southern drawl colored her words, as she said, "Can I buy you a drink, sugar?"

Kallias set his drink on the bar and glanced at her. Curly, blonde tendrils framed the woman's slender face. Her short, red dress barely covered the tops of her thighs, much less her perfectly-tanned legs.

Her dress barely even covered her breasts at all, and her ruby-red lipstick drew attention to her curved, full lips.

Kallias figured that most sane men—the ones who liked women, anyway—would've forgotten their quests, in favor of such a woman, but he didn't consider himself a sane man.

Not anymore.

Instead, he scowled at his full glass of whiskey. "I already have one."

If she'd noticed his irritation, she gave no indication of it. "In that case, maybe I can help you with something else."

Kallias studied the woman curiously. He decided that, though she did little for *him*, she was certainly attractive enough to capture Theron's attention—even if she *was* wearing such an excessive amount of perfume that it was borderline nauseating.

He returned his glass to the bar and turned toward her. "Well, I suppose there is one thing you might be able to help me with."

Excitement flickered in her hazel eyes. "Anything, darling."

"I'm looking for someone," Kallias told her. "Have you seen anyone new lately? He would've been tall with brown hair and a dark complexion. And to you, he would've seemed very attractive."

The woman's hazel eyes roamed Kallias's body, noticing the long, brown hair that brushed his black, leather jacket, his golden skin, and his tall, muscular body. She offered him a charming smile.

"I've seen *one* person that fits that description," she said.

Kallias gave her a peeved look. "Not me."

The woman scowled, clearly stunned by his rudeness, but she recovered quickly. She propped her elbow on the bar and leaned her cheek against her hand. "You'll have to give me more details, then, honey."

Kallias sighed, "He would've introduced himself as Theron."

The woman traced a manicured fingernail along the tattooed flames that crept up his neck and then along the zipper of his black, leather jacket. "No, I haven't seen anyone who calls himself Theron. Sorry."

Kallias frowned, as the woman trailed her hands past his unzipped leather jacket to the thin black T-shirt he wore underneath the jacket.

The woman began to trace the muscles of his abdomen, before trailing her hand down to his thigh, allowing the rough texture of his jeans to scrape across her hand.

"Maybe I could help you in a more...*physical* way," she offered.

Kallias grasped her wrist a moment. He removed her hand from him, ignoring her gasp of surprise. "I'm not in need of that kind of help," he said coldly, and he picked up his glass and sipped the whiskey.

Apparently offended by his cold refusal, the woman glared at him and hopped off the barstool, snatching her pink purse from the bar.

"Asshole."

Kallias shrugged carelessly—and continued drinking his whiskey.

It wasn't her fault. Humans couldn't help themselves around vampires, but Kallias was in no mood to deal with it today.

"Not your type?"

Kallias glanced at the bartender, who leaned against the bar, directly across from him. The bartender crossed his arms, his muscles bulging from the short-sleeved, flannel shirt. His stout frame, buzz-cut hairstyle, and botched tattoos gave him a rough, intimidating appearance, but Kallias supposed that in comparison to his own tall, muscular form, the bartender probably looked docile.

"I'm not sure I have a type," Kallias said.

When the bartender noticed Kallias's empty glass, he reached down and grabbed a bottle of whiskey. He held it up questionably, and when Kallias nodded, he refilled the glass. "You probably made a good choice, anyway," he muttered. "She leaves with another man every night. She'd probably give you an STD or something."

Kallias raised an eyebrow. Apparently, he wasn't the only rude person in this bar tonight. He wondered what this guy's excuse was. "You must be a hit with the ladies," he said sarcastically.

The man laughed, and the smile softened his brown eyes. He leaned lazily on the bar. "Yeah, asshole is their *nice* name for me."

Kallias's gaze roamed the dark bar, even though he already knew Theron wasn't there. He knew Theron had been there recently because Theron's scent still lingered, but he was long gone now.

His gaze returned to the bartender, whose uneven tan looked more like a suntan than a natural complexion. "You're from here, I assume?"

"Yep," the bartender said. "Born and raised Floridian. How about you? You don't sound like you're from around here. Your accent is...different."

"I travel," Kallias said. "I live in New York at the moment."

"Ah," the man said, as if that somehow explained the Greek accent.

"My name is Kallias," he said, attempting to be polite for once.

"Kallias?" the man repeated. "I'm Jack. It's nice to meet you."

"Yeah," Kallias replied insincerely.

Jack looked down at the cherry-wood surface of the bar, and his brows furrowed. "That man you described," he said. "Why are you looking for him?"

Kallias glanced curiously at the bartender. "He's an old friend." It took all of his restraint to resist sneering the word *friend*. "Why? Have you seen him?"

"Maybe," Jack sighed. "There was a man named Theron who came in last night. A bit odd—the ladies were all over him." A worried frown twisted at his face. "One of my waitresses went home with him, and she didn't show up for her shift tonight."

"Of course she didn't," Kallias said, finishing his drink. "Do you know where he might be staying? Or any other information about him?"

Jack blew out a sigh, as he debated whether to tell Kallias the next part or not. "*He* was asking about someone, too."

Kallias set down his glass. "Who?"

"Rose Foster," Jack sighed. "He seemed keen on finding her."

"Did anyone tell him where this Rose Foster might be?" Kallias asked.

Jack shook his head. "No, none of them knew her. She isn't really the type to frequent a place like this." He offered a wry smile. "I think she prefers libraries."

Kallias raised his eyebrows. "Then *you* know her."

Jack's brown eyes seemed startled for a moment, but then, he nodded. "Your, uh, *friend* seemed dangerous, and Rose is a nice, young woman. I'm not sure how she managed to get noticed by someone like him, but I wouldn't have wanted to be responsible if he hurt her."

"Good call," Kallias assured him. "Now, tell *me* where to find her."

"No offense, but you look dangerous as well," Jack said.

"I *am* dangerous," Kallias agreed. "But if you don't want this Rose Foster to wind up as dead as the girl Theron took home with him last night—which she is, by the way; *dead*, I mean—then, you need to tell me where to find her."

Jack paled. "Well, you don't break it easy to someone, do you?" he complained. He sighed and answered, "Rose works with my little sister at a café about two blocks behind the University. Rose is one of the servers. She'll be working tonight."

Kallias nodded and stood. "What's the name of the café?"

"Eleanor's," Jack said.

Kallias stood and pulled his wallet from the back pocket of his jeans.

"Should I call the police about the waitress?" Jack asked.

Kallias shrugged and handed Jack a wad of cash. He wasn't sure how much he owed, but he figured that would cover it. "It'd be kind of pointless, wouldn't it? There's nothing they can do for her now."

"What is that man?" Jack called out, as Kallias headed toward the exit. "Some kind of a criminal or something?"

"Worse," Kallias said, as he left in search of Rose Foster. "Much worse."

2

HUNTED

*I*t was nearing closing time, when Kallias reached the restaurant, and a crisp coolness had settled in the night air. Nestled in a strip mall of shops and stores that were already closed for the night, the small café emitted a soft, golden glow across the deserted street.

Kallias pulled open the glass door and stepped inside the small café. The scent of grease overwhelmed his senses, but the faint, warm scent of coffee soothed those same, hypersensitive senses.

Photos of Florida beaches and college jerseys lined the log-cabin-style walls. Barely large enough for its six booths, four tables, desert counter, kitchen, and hostess podium, the empty café felt small and crowded.

A tanned, brunette woman, who looked strikingly similar to the bartender, stood behind the hostess podium, scrolling through her phone. A peek inside her thoughts confirmed for Kallias that she was indeed Jack's sister.

The vampiric allure affected her immediately, and she gasped when she saw him behind the counter. She scanned his features, her brown eyes widening.

She slipped her phone into the pocket of her small, white apron. She wore the apron over a short, black skirt and a white, button-down shirt, its top three buttons left undone.

The black name-tag attached to the left side of her shirt revealed that her name was Ashley. The hostess licked her lips and straightened her clothes nervously.

"Hello, sir. Can I get you a seat?" she asked.

Kallias glanced around the empty restaurant and then returned his attention to the hostess. "Perhaps," he said—and began to listen to her thoughts.

Unfortunately, instead of hearing information about the servers on the forefront of the young woman's mind, he heard her thoughts about him. It wasn't unusual for a human—just a little inconvenient.

He sifted through her thoughts, searching for something useful—something beneath the haze of desire.

As the hostess glanced around the restaurant, considering where to seat him, her thoughts shifted to the waiters and waitresses serving each table, and he found the information he needed.

With his telepathy, Kallias took control of her mind. "I need you to seat me at one of Rose Foster's tables."

The hostess's brown eyes glazed over, as his mind-control took effect. "Of course," she said in an emotionless tone. "Follow me, sir."

The short, young woman led him to a booth in the back corner of the restaurant. Kallias thanked her, as he slid into the red leather seat and stretched his legs out in front of him. The hostess placed a laminated menu in front of him and turned to leave.

Kallias grasped the woman's wrist to stop her before she could walk away. Her eyes widened in panic, but he quickly took control of her mind again. "Forget what I asked you to do," he commanded.

The woman's brown eyes glazed over again. "Okay."

Kallias offered her a polite smile and released her wrist. Oblivious to what had just happened, she smiled sheepishly at him.

She returned to the podium, her black heels clicking against the tile floor. He scanned the room again from this side of the restaurant, and he froze, when his gaze met a pair of curious, azure-blue eyes.

The woman sat on a barstool, behind the counter, long, red hair cascading around her shoulders. An anxious flush reddened her fair skin, and she chewed on a pen, stressing over some kind of document that was spread out over the counter.

Kallias felt his lips lift slightly, as he met her curious stare with his own.

The woman sighed. It wasn't an annoyed sigh—more like a wistful one, as if she'd been so engrossed in the document in front of her that she could barely tear her attention from it.

She slipped her pen behind her ear and hopped off the barstool.

Unlike the stylish hostess, the woman dressed as comfortably as possible, opting for loose-fitting dress pants rather than a short skirt, and a pair of worn, black Converse, rather than heels. Even her white, button-down shirt hung loosely from her curves.

There wasn't anything special about her, really—nothing to explain why Theron was so interested in her.

That being said, her eyes *were* a stunningly bright shade of blue, and her long, red hair swayed around her shoulders, like fire.

He looked away. He didn't have time to waste on a human. He was here to find Theron, and that was all.

Besides, even if he were interested in a human, he wouldn't chance it with his hunger so out of control, at the moment.

"What can I get you to drink?" the woman asked.

Kallias glanced at the menu—the one he hadn't bothered to look at yet. "Do you have any type of alcohol here?"

Rose struggled to remember the question, as she considered the eerily perfect man in front of her. She felt that same twinge of unease while looking at him that she'd felt while looking at the man in Greece. It felt as if she were looking at an optical illusion—as if her brain were trying to warn her that something wasn't quite right.

His long, brown hair brushed the collar of his black, leather jacket, and the black T-shirt underneath the jacket clung to his muscles. His light, brown eyes seemed almost...*hypnotizing* each time they met hers, and his golden skin was luminous beneath the soft glow of the café's lighting.

Brightly colored flames crept up his neck, only partially hidden by his jacket, and his facial structure seemed strangely symmetrical, reminding her of the Greek statues she'd studied.

Even with his long legs hidden underneath the table, she could tell he was tall—and muscular, too. That alone made him intimidating, but it was more than that.

Rose could *feel* in her gut that he was dangerous.

Rose frowned, as she realized that he was watching her with an amused smirk, as if he knew, somehow, what she was thinking. She pulled a notepad from her apron. "This is a café, not a bar."

Kallias raised an eyebrow at the woman's snarky tone. He rarely encountered anyone bold enough to speak like that to him. Most humans were either too intimidated by him or were too affected by his allure. He wasn't sure whether he found her unusual reaction amusing or annoying. "A cola will be fine, I suppose."

Rose scowled and began patting her apron and the pockets of her dress pants, as she searched for her pen. She remembered having it just a moment ago.

The man suddenly stood, and she took a startled step back, as he dwarfed her. That half-smirk still tugged at his lips, as he reached toward her and pulled the pen from behind her ear.

He held out the pen.

She blushed and snatched it from him.

Kallias returned to his seat, chuckling at her reaction. He glanced at the name-tag on her shirt, reading the four, white letters. "Your name is Rose?"

"No. It's Cleopatra," Rose said, as she wrote in the notepad. "I just wear a name-tag with 'Rose' on it for no apparent reason."

A smile tugged at the corners of his lips. "Does sarcasm usually earn you big tips, *Cleopatra*?"

"Massive," Rose said sarcastically.

Kallias laughed, entertained by her snarky remarks. When he noticed the dark circles beneath her bright blue eyes, he wondered if there were a reason she hadn't slept—one related to Theron's sudden interest in her, perhaps. "Have you seen any scary men lately, Rose?"

Rose glanced at him, her brows lifting in disbelief. "You mean besides *you*?"

With a smirk, he said, "You think I'm scary?"

Rose closed the notepad and scoffed, "You don't scare *me*."

Kallias chuckled. "Yes, I meant besides me."

Rose frowned suspiciously at the stranger. "What kind of question is that anyway? No, I haven't, not that it's any of your business."

Kallias frowned, when the woman turned on her heel and headed toward the kitchen. Why would Theron be interested in *this* woman?

She wasn't his type.

Theron preferred compliant, docile types like Phoebe, the type of human he could manipulate. As a matter of fact, Kallias was sure that Theron would've lost his temper and killed her if she'd spoken to him like that even *once*, and since this women was still alive, Kallias figured it was safe to assume that Theron hadn't met the woman yet.

Which once again begged the question: Why would Theron be hunting this woman that he'd never even met?

Rose opened the door of the kitchen and frowned, as she noticed one of her closest friends, Owen, sitting in a chair behind the counter, spreading icing on a cake with a spatula.

Since Owen was also a server, he wore a similar outfit to hers, although his dress pants and button-down fit closer to his lean body than her own uniform. He wore his short, ashy-blonde hair spiked with gel.

His hazel eyes were narrowed on the cake, and he bit his lip in concentration, as if he were conducting an experiment, rather than putting icing on a cake.

Of course, Owen did major in biology, so that might not have been too far from the truth.

Rose tucked her notepad into the pocket of her apron and walked over to the counter to take a closer look at the cake. "What are you doing?"

"I have no customers," Owen explained. "So, I'm baking a cake."

"Oh," Rose said, nodding. "I didn't realize you knew how to cook."

He placed a slice of the cake on a small, round plate. "I don't."

Rose laughed, "Oh."

Owen dug his fork into the slice of vanilla cake with white frosting and held out the bite of cake to Rose. "Here, try a bite, and tell me what you think."

Rose grimaced at the cake that looked just a *bit* too mushy. "I can't. You know I'm on a diet."

"You're *always* on a diet," Owen complained. "Don't worry. With any luck, you'll get food poisoning and won't keep it down anyway."

"Nice advertisement," Rose said. "You should put that on a billboard."

Owen stood and held the fork closer to her mouth. "One bite."

"Fine," Rose said, but when she opened her mouth, Owen shoved the rest of the cake in her face, smushing it against her mouth and nose.

She glared at him, as he doubled over in laughter. She wiped the cake off of her face—as much as she could, anyway, with the back of her hand. And she licked the gooey mixture from her lips.

Owen licked the cake from his fingers, as well. "Are you angry?"

"Not at all," Rose said sarcastically. She grimaced at the strange taste of the cake.

Owen went to the sink to wash his hands. "How did it taste?"

Rose tried to think of something nice to say. "The icing was all right."

Owen laughed. "Probably because Betty Crocker made the icing," he said, pointing at the container of store-bought icing on the counter.

Rose grabbed a white washcloth from a cabinet and took it to the sink. She held it beneath the hot water. "Did you even put it in the oven?"

"I did," Owen said, frowning, "for a few minutes."

Rose glanced back at him. "I think it takes more than a few minutes."

Owen braced his hands on the counter behind him. "Probably."

Rose wiped her face with the rag, cleaning the cake from her face as well as she could with no mirror. She dipped the washcloth under the warm water again. "Thank you, Owen. I've *always* wanted icing in my nose."

"You're welcome," Owen said. He froze by the kitchen door. His eyes widened, as he peered through the window that opened into the restaurant. "Holy shit! Is that your customer?"

"Yeah," Rose said, her voice muffled by the cloth, "unfortunately."

Owen spun toward her. "What's wrong with you? He's hot."

"You have a boyfriend," Rose reminded him.

"That doesn't mean I'm blind," Owen said. "Oh! Now, I get why you're so afraid to date! Someone must've told you that sex makes you blind." He grinned. "It doesn't. I promise."

Rose tossed the washrag in the sink and turned toward him. She crossed her arms, as she leaned against the sink. "Hilarious," she muttered. "Why are all my friends so concerned with my love life lately?"

"Because you don't have one," Owen answered.

"So?" Rose said.

"And because you apparently can't see how hot that guy is," Owen added.

Rose lifted her eyebrows. "How would Jared feel about his boyfriend calling another man hot?"

Owen shrugged. "He'd want to see for himself."

Rose rolled her eyes. "Well, *I* don't think he's attractive."

"Uh-huh," Owen said skeptically. "Then why are you blushing?"

"I'm not," Rose muttered. She turned toward the sink and turned on the water again. She washed her hands so that she could fix the strange man's drink. "He's probably a criminal. He looks dangerous, and he has a tattoo."

"*You* have a tattoo," Owen reminded her.

Rose scrubbed her hands irritably. "Well…yeah, but mine's smaller."

Owen started laughing. "Okay, now you're just grasping at straws."

"There's something…off about all of this," Rose said honestly. "He asked me a weird question."

"A weird question?" Owen said. "Oh, no! Let's call the police!"

Rose dried her hands with a white towel. "Jerk."

Owen just laughed and returned to his failed experiment of a cake. He slid onto the stool and watched Rose fix the customer's drink.

Eleanor emerged from her office, resting a wrinkled hand on the door. "Does anyone know Mike's number?"

Rose turned to look at her boss. Eleanor wore her gray and black hair in a tight bun, and her purple dress clung to her wide hips.

"Sorry," Rose said dryly, "I don't talk to people enough to know it." With an apologetic smile, she said, "Why do you need it?"

Eleanor sighed. "I need someone to work the weekend. I was going to ask him."

"I can come in, if you need someone," Rose offered.

"Honey, you've worked every off-day for the last two weeks," Eleanor said, "not including the days you were on that trip—but that wasn't exactly a vacation either, was it?"

Rose shrugged. "I don't need an off-day."

Eleanor pursed her lips skeptically. "When was the last time you slept?"

"I have coffee to keep me going," Rose said.

"No offense, but I don't think coffee's doing the job, hun," Eleanor laughed. Her brown eyes scanned Rose's face, lingering on the dark circles beneath her eyes. "You need to get some sleep."

Owen jotted down a number in his notepad and ripped out the page. He handed it to Eleanor. She glanced at the number and thanked him. Then, she returned to her office.

Owen scowled at Rose. "What kind of person willingly gives up their off-days every week? Don't you have anything better to do?"

"No," Rose said. "Not at all, actually."

"So, let Audrey drag you to a party, for once," he suggested.

"Um, no," Rose said, horrified. "Besides, Audrey's going to see her grandparents this weekend. And I've run out of books to read."

Owen snorted. "I'm sure you'll find more. But if you want, you could stay at my apartment this weekend. It's been forever since our last sleep-over. We could marathon *The Lord of the Rings* movies and then go to a bookstore."

Rose's eyes lit up with excitement. "Now, that *is* an appealing offer."

He laughed. "I figured you'd think so."

"I don't know," she said worriedly. "What about Jared? Are you sure he'd be okay with it? He doesn't seem to like me very much."

He sighed. "No, no, it's not that. Jared doesn't *dislike* you. That's just how he *is*. He treats everyone like that."

Rose raised an eyebrow. "The most he's ever said to me is, 'Hello, Rose.'"

Owen shrugged. "He's a man of few words." He cocked his head to the side and grinned. "Except in the bedroom. He's a little more talkative there."

"Owen," Rose said, "there are things I *don't* need to know."

He laughed loudly. "Sorry. I'll be more considerate of your virgin ears."

She rolled her eyes. "They'll be grateful." She glanced down at the glass in her hand and sighed, "Crap, I'm a terrible waitress, aren't I? I better get this drink out to the guy. Did I get all the cake off of my face?"

A smile tugged at the corners of his lips. "Yeah, you're good."

Rose nodded and pushed the door open with her shoulder, making her way to the strange man's booth. She set the glass of cola on his table and tried to ignore the way he watched her.

Why *did* he watch her like that? Dodging eye-contact with him felt like an impossible task.

Rose pulled out her notepad and clicked her pen. "Are you ready to order your food?"

Kallias glanced back at the menu. "What do you recommend?"

Rose shrugged. "I eat salad."

He watched her expectantly. "And is...the salad good?"

"It tastes like salad," Rose muttered.

Kallias lifted an eyebrow. The woman ran from small talk faster than anyone he'd ever met. "Right."

"Rose, be nice to the man," Eleanor scolded, joining Rose by the table. "How will you get a husband, talking to men like that?"

"Why would I want a *husband*?" Rose muttered.

Eleanor ignored her, apparently used to her snark. Instead, she gazed curiously at Kallias. "Oh my, you are an attractive one, aren't you?"

Kallias snorted at the older woman's bluntness.

Eleanor tapped a wrinkled finger against the menu. "A big, tall man like you would probably like the Breakfast Platter. It has plenty of bacon," she whispered, as if she were sharing a secret with him.

"It's 10:30 at night. Why would he want breakfast?" Rose asked.

"It has bacon," Eleanor answered, as if that explained it all.

Rose laughed and shook her head at Eleanor. The older woman patted Rose's back affectionately and turned to leave.

When Rose turned back toward her customer, she realized he was watching her with that strange smirk again. "What?"

Kallias stood, causing her to, once again, take a startled step back.

He took another step toward her, their bodies nearly touching.

The soft scents of honey and vanilla clung to Rose's hair and skin, filling his senses, as he moved closer.

Rose squinted, watching him curiously, as she wondered what he intended to do.

Kallias lifted his hand and ran a thumb over her full, pink lips, surprised to find that her lips felt as soft as they looked.

Rose froze, clearly stunned by his actions. He raised an eyebrow and pulled his hand back to show her the icing on his thumb.

He wiped the icing on a napkin. "There was something on your lips."

Her cheeks flushed a dark pink. "I'm going to kill Owen."

He collapsed back into his seat. "The Breakfast Platter sounds fine."

"Fine," she said, jotting that down in the notepad. "I'll be back with it soon."

She turned on her heel and marched back into the kitchen, flinging the metal door open so fast that it continued to swing back and forth for several moments. She ripped the slip out of the notepad and handed it to the cook at the other end of the kitchen.

She turned and saw Owen still peering through the window, and she marched over to him, glaring murderously at her friend.

"Damn, he really is the hottest man I've ever seen," Owen muttered. "Looks sort of familiar, too. Not sure how, though."

"I'm going to kill you," Rose warned, "slowly and painfully."

He spun around and held up his hands in a gesture of surrender.

"Relax," he laughed. "It was a little white lie. There's no need to resort to murder."

"Oh, I think lying is a severe offense," Rose argued. "You *purposely* let me go out there with icing on my lips."

"Oh, come on. You should be grateful," he said. "A hot guy touched your lips. Because of me! I think that makes me the best friend ever."

Rose backed him into a corner. "I think it makes you a liar."

Owen leaned against the wall. "Any normal woman would *thank* me. Do you even *like* men, Rose?" he laughed. "I can't say I haven't wondered. It's not like we haven't all *seen* the way you look at women."

Rose froze, momentarily forgetting her irritation. "Way?" she sputtered. "There's no...*way!*"

"Sure there isn't," Owen teased.

"And who is *we*?" Rose said.

Owen just laughed.

She rolled her eyes. "Yes, I like *some* women," she admitted, "but I also like some men. Just not *that* man." She jabbed her finger in the direction of the dining room. She was too flustered by his teasing to complain any more about the cake incident. So, she turned and headed toward the counter, as she waited for the food to cook.

She perched herself on top of one of the stools.

Owen sat beside her and smiled. "But I think you do," he whispered. He poked her arm playfully. "I think you're being overly judgmental of him because you don't *want* to like him."

She rolled her eyes. "What would *you* know?"

"I know *you*," he said, "and I know sexual tension when I see it." He leaned closer to her again, as if he were going to tell her a secret. "And Rose?"

"What?" she snapped, louder than she'd intended.

"You're *tense*," he teased.

"I am not," Rose grumbled. "He's not even my type."

"Uh-huh," Owen said skeptically. "And who is your type, Rose? Ethan?"

Every bit of humor faded from her face. "No. Not Ethan."

Owen's hazel eyes softened with regret. "Sorry, I shouldn't have..."

"It's fine," Rose assured him. "I just hate that everyone keeps mentioning him. It was two years ago. Break-ups happen. It's not the end of the world."

He grimaced. "Break-ups may not be, but what he did to you…"

"I don't want to talk about it," Rose interrupted.

"Of course not," Owen said sympathetically. "I'm sorry."

She hopped off of the stool. She headed toward the back of the kitchen, where the cook was preparing her customer's food. She felt someone come up behind her. "It's fine, Owen."

"No, it's not," he sighed. "I feel terrible for mentioning him."

"Don't," she said tiredly. "I'm fine. I'm not a fragile, little girl."

He slung one arm around her shoulders. "I know."

Eleanor chose that moment to walk out of her office. She stopped in the doorway and stared at them, placing a hand on her hip. "You two would make such a cute couple."

Rose snorted at that.

"Thanks, Eleanor, but we're just friends," Owen said.

"I'm not his type," Rose said, earning a scowl from Owen.

Eleanor just frowned at them. "If you say so," she said in a puzzled tone. "Anyway, you two should go on break. We'll be closing in about fifteen minutes or so, and I want you to eat something before you go home."

"I have a customer," Rose reminded Eleanor.

"*One* customer," Eleanor said. "I've run this restaurant for longer than you've been alive, young lady. I can handle one customer."

"You want me to go on break, too?" Owen asked.

Eleanor scowled at him. "Yes! *Please!* The last thing I need is you getting bored again and trying to bake another cake—if you can even *call* that a cake."

He laughed and went to his locker to grab his phone.

The cook who worked that night was Eleanor's nephew, a broad-shouldered man with short, black hair. He handed a large plate of food to Rose.

Rose smiled. "Thanks, Tyler."

"Eat something," Eleanor told Rose. Then, apparently not satisfied with Rose's lack of response, she looked at Owen. "Make sure she eats something, and I mean something *worth* eating, not that rabbit food she usually eats."

Rose suppressed a laugh. What was it about older women in this region and their hatred of salads?

"Yes, ma'am," Owen said.

"Like he could make *me* do anything," Rose scoffed.

KALLIAS LEANED FORWARD, SUDDENLY, SURE HE'D SEEN SOMETHING OUTSIDE. He listened in the stillness of the almost-closed restaurant to the heart-beats—six separate people, he counted—but he heard nothing outside, just the rustle of leaves in the wind.

Still, he watched the window, wondering what he'd seen.

"Uh…are you okay?" Rose said, following his gaze.

Kallias glanced up at the waitress. "I thought I saw something," he said, curiously watching her reaction.

Rose glanced at the window. "Was it a window? Because that's a window."

He sighed and flashed a sarcastic smile. "I'm aware."

Rose set the plate of food in front of him, the glass clanging against the table. "I'm going on break. My boss is supposed to check on you, but…" She shrugged awkwardly. "If you need anything, you can let me know—if you want."

He blinked, so surprised by her sudden politeness that he nearly let her walk away without saying anything. But then, he grasped her wrist, forcing her to stop. He must've grasped her wrist harder than he'd meant to because she gasped. He loosened his grip a little, still holding her wrist. Their gazes met, and quietly, he said, "Thank you."

Rose glanced down at her wrist, frustrated by the way his touch raised chills along her skin, affecting her more than it should have. She tried to pull her hand from his grasp, and Kallias, not wanting to hurt her, immediately let go. Awkwardly, she muttered, "It's my job."

More than a little curious about this strange human, he watched her walk away.

She slid into a booth by the window.

Kallias raised an eyebrow in surprise, as he noticed her glance out the window, just as he had earlier. As he noticed the spike in her pulse, he realized…maybe she *did* know something.

ROSE FOUND HERSELF STARING OUTSIDE INTO THE SHADOWS OF TREES YET again. She couldn't shake the feeling that someone was out there, watching her, but there was no one—just as there had been no one there the last several times she'd checked. She reminded herself that she wouldn't be so paranoid, if it weren't for Audrey's dream.

As she considered Audrey's dream again, she found her attention drifting back toward the man sitting on the other side of the restaurant. She had the distinct feeling that he was watching her right now, but she didn't want to turn and look—for fear of meeting his gaze.

There was something dangerous about him. She felt it in her gut.

On top of that, she hadn't missed the fact that he resembled the killer from Audrey's dream a little too closely for comfort. His dark hair and eyes, his golden skin, height, and attractiveness all fit the strange description Audrey had given her.

Especially after he'd asked such a strange question earlier, Rose had begun to wonder if he might be her murderer.

She jumped as a crash beside her jolted her from her thoughts. She glanced up and sighed in relief, as she realized it was just Owen. A plate with a small cheeseburger set in front of her, the likely cause of the crash.

Owen slid into the seat opposite her. "Are you okay? You seem jumpy."

Rose nodded, casting another glance at the window beside her. "Yeah, sorry. I've been like this for days. I think it's the lack of sleep."

He seemed worried. "Why haven't you been sleeping?"

"I've been busy," she said nervously, "studying."

His eyes narrowed just slightly, as if he didn't quite believe her. "You really do need to learn to relax every now and then, Rose."

"Now, you're starting to sound like Audrey," she complained.

"Good," Owen said, as he picked up his burger and bit into it. He shot her a half-grin-half-glare and said, "*I'm not his type*. You think you're *so* clever."

With a cute smile, Rose said, "I am clever."

He rolled his eyes at her, laughing.

"You should tell her," she suggested.

Owen scowled at her. "She's Christian."

"And what am I? A chicken?" Rose asked.

"You're different," Owen said, "and queer yourself. That makes a difference."

"Believe it or not, Jesus taught love, not hate," she said.

"I guess," he said, "but not everyone sees things the way you do."

"I'm only suggesting you give her a chance," Rose said. "Eleanor cares about you. I can't imagine her not accepting you. I think you should give everyone a chance—because people surprise you, when you let them."

He fell serious. "I wish I had your faith in people, Rose, but I don't. All I see is a dark world full of hate with maybe a *couple* of decent human beings."

"I get that," Rose admitted. "I guess I just...want to find good in everyone."

"I know you do," he said with a smile. "I'll think about it."

"Fair enough," Rose said.

He scowled at her and pointed at her food. "Eat your cheeseburger. *Now*," he said, clearly trying to sound intimidating.

Rose laughed at the failed attempt. She picked up the cheeseburger and took a bite. Glaring playfully, she said, "Happy now?"

Before Owen could respond, both of them froze and glanced up at Rose's scary customer, who'd suddenly appeared beside their table. His light brown eyes studied Rose with a scrutiny that made her squirm. She wondered how he'd moved so quietly.

"Do you need something?" she said.

He looked up suddenly, staring out the window. His eyes narrowed, as he watched something in the trees outside. Rose frowned curiously and followed his gaze, but she saw nothing. "I'm leaving now," he said, drawing her attention back to him. She noticed that he still wasn't looking at her. He was watching something outside. "I've already paid my bill. I need to give you a tip."

Rose's frown deepened. "*Ohhh*-kay," she said slowly.

Even Owen turned and glanced curiously at the window.

Without looking at her, Kallias shoved a crumpled dollar bill into her hand. Then, he spun on his heel and hurried to the door, as if he were trying to catch up with someone. As he walked away, Rose glanced at her hand and gaped at the crumpled one-hundred-dollar bill. She scrambled to her feet and chased after him, grasping his leather jacket before he could leave.

He sighed and turned back toward her, giving her an annoyed glare.

She clearly had no useful information about Theron, and he didn't have the time to waste on her right now.

"What is this?" Rose said, holding up the ridiculously large tip.

"It's money," Kallias said with a shrug. "That *is* what people usually give as tips, right?"

Rose couldn't tell if he was being serious or sarcastic. She hoped for sarcasm. "Your meal was barely ten dollars. This isn't ten or twenty percent. This is *one thousand* percent. No one tips this much. *No one.*"

He sighed tiredly, like someone dealing with a difficult child. "So, what do you want? Do you want me to order more food? I *could* do that, but I'm not hungry anymore." His gaze drifted down to the pulsing artery in her neck, and under his breath, he muttered, "Not for human food anyway."

"Huh?" Rose said, not catching that last part. She shook her head. "No, I don't want you to order more food. I want you to take this money back."

"You've got to be the most difficult human I've ever met," Kallias complained.

Rose frowned at the way he said that. "I...*guess* humans are difficult —compared to inanimate objects."

Kallias closed the space between them with one single step, and Rose stumbled backward, swallowing nervously. "You're complaining because I gave you too *much* money?"

His closeness confused her. One moment, her mind was forming coherent arguments, and the next moment, the scent of leather and after-shave scattered those thoughts, leaving her standing there dumbly, trying to remember why she was angry.

"I didn't even give you good service," she said in a quiet voice.

His lips twitched, almost unnoticeably. "I enjoyed it well enough."

She took another step back—so she could think clearly. "I don't understand why you'd give me so much money," she said, trusting him less and less by the moment. "I hope you're not expecting…*something* for this," she muttered, "because that's disgusting."

He raised his eyebrows, and an incredulous smirk tugged at his lips. "You think *I* would need to pay someone for sex?"

Rose scoffed in disgust. "Wow, you are arrogant."

"And you're stubborn and frustrating," Kallias countered.

"No one *gives* someone this much money," Rose said. She'd grown up poor. She was *still* poor. She barely trusted people with a surplus of money in their banks, much less people with it in their pockets. "How did you expect me to react?"

He stepped forward and leaned closer to her. His eyes darkened slightly, and the corners of his lips twitched upward. "I expect you to thank me and come back to my hotel room."

Rose blinked in shock. "What?"

He laughed. "That was a joke. I figured you would know that, considering how well-versed you seem to be in the art of sarcasm."

She stared at him, still confused. "Right."

"Goodbye, *Cleopatra*," Kallias called, as he turned and left.

Rose just stood there for several moments, clutching the ridiculous tip.

"Who is Cleopatra?" Ashley asked.

Rose glanced at her and blushed—as she realized that both Owen and Ashley had witnessed that entire conversation. "Long story."

She turned and stalked grumpily to her booth, sliding in across from Owen and tossing the wrinkled dollar bill on the table.

"That was interesting," Owen said, grinning at her.

"Shut up," she grumbled.

"I don't think I've ever seen anyone get you so worked up," he teased.

"Shut up," she said again.

Owen picked up the one-hundred-dollar bill and turned it over in his hand, smoothing the wrinkles with his thumb. "It's a pretty impressive tip."

"It's probably drug money," Rose said bitterly.

He snorted. "This guy doesn't stand a chance with you, does he?"

"Nope," she said easily, glaring at a random spot on the wall.

"Maybe now, you can pay your phone bill this month," he said.

"I've paid it the last several months," Rose grumbled.

She took the money and stuffed it in her pocket, still unsure of whether she should chase the guy down and insist he take it back.

Again.

Rose felt a chill run down her spine, and her stomach turned with dread. She straightened and glanced out the window, watching the trees, as she searched for the source of the bad feeling.

"Okay, Rose," Owen sighed, "it's time for you to tell me what's wrong."

Rose shook her head and tried to ignore the feeling. "It's nothing."

"Liar," he said. "Now, let's try that again."

She sighed. "Do you ever get the feeling someone is watching you?"

"Yeah," Owen said, "when someone is watching me."

Rose sighed. "Yeah, well, I feel like I'm being watched right now. I've been getting this horrible feeling all night, and it's got me on edge."

Owen glanced around at the empty restaurant. Everyone was in the kitchen, except for Rose, the hostess, and him. He looked out the window, but he saw nothing but darkness. "Do you think it could be the lack of sleep?"

She considered telling him the truth—that no, she didn't think it was the lack of sleep, that she thought someone was actually watching her—

but Audrey had never told Owen about her precognitive dreams, and it wasn't Rose's secret to share. Not sure of any other way to explain it, she just nodded. "Yeah, it's probably nothing. I just need some sleep."

Owen seemed unsure. "*Is* there someone who could be watching you?"

Noticing that concerned, protective scowl twist at his face, she shook her head quickly. "You know what? It's probably just those scrolls making me paranoid."

Owen picked up a French fry. "Scrolls?"

"Yeah. Long story. Basically, when I was in Greece, someone gave me a necklace," she said tiredly, "and some ancient scrolls about a vampire."

A necklace was a vague enough description, she thought.

Owen froze mid-fry. "Vampire?"

Rose frowned at his reaction—and the fry hanging out of his mouth. "So it seems. They describe a woman and a vampire named Theron."

"Theron?" He seemed pale, all of the sudden. "That was the name? You're sure?"

"Yes," she said slowly. "Owen, what's wrong with you?"

Owen stuffed the rest of the fry in his mouth and shrugged. "Nothing. I'm just interested. Who knew ancient people had stories about vampires?"

Rose watched her friend suspiciously. "Lots of people, actually."

"Well, there's your problem there. Ancient vampire stories would make anyone uneasy," Owen said, as he finished off his last few fries. "You should lay off the horror for a few nights and watch a chick flick or something."

"Chick flick?" Rose repeated bewilderedly.

"Romance, Rose. Romance," he chuckled.

"Actually, the horror novels I read usually do have *some* romance," she said. "They just *also* have blood and guts everywhere to make it interesting."

He snorted, "That's an endorsement for horror, if I've ever heard one."

Ashley walked over to their table. "Hey, I just locked the door," she said, as she untied her apron. "We're closed."

Rose glanced out the window again, a little uneasy about walking home soon. She blinked, as she saw something in the shadows.

"I could walk you home," Owen offered, "if you want."

Rose continued to stare out the window. Whatever she'd seen was gone now. "You live on the other side of town," she argued. "I'll be fine."

"I can be pretty intimidating when I want to be," Owen bragged. "Besides, Jared's meeting me after work, and fighting is pretty much his job."

She frowned. "What does he do? I don't think you've ever told me."

Owen seemed uncomfortable, all of the sudden. "Uh, a few things," he muttered, "but during the day, he teaches martial arts at the gym."

Rose nodded. "I'll be fine," she assured him. "I don't need bodyguards."

He scowled at that, as if he didn't quite agree. "If you say so."

It was nearly an hour later when Rose and Owen left the café—which was now dark and empty—to make their way home. Rose nearly jumped, when she saw a dark, human-shaped silhouette, leaning against the streetlight, but as they neared him, she recognized his features.

The man was shorter than Owen—but taller than her, still—and his brown skin glistened in the light, as if coated with sweat. His thick, curly, black hair hung around his face in a wild mess. He wore a tank top and shorts, his muscles visible beneath them.

As soon as Owen neared the man, he closed the space between them.

Rose hung back to give them privacy as they kissed.

"You smell terrible, by the way," Owen teased, pushing Jared away.

"Love you, too," Jared muttered. "I just left the gym."

"Hi, Jared," Rose said, as she joined them under the streetlight.

Jared offered her a polite smile. "Hello, Rose."

Owen scowled at her again, his brows knitted with worry. "Are you *sure* you don't want us to walk you home? We don't mind."

"We don't?" Jared asked bluntly.

Owen glared at him. "No, we don't. Rose is feeling uneasy because she's been translating scrolls about *vampires*. I figured our presence would help."

Jared's entire countenance changed. "Vampires?"

She frowned at his reaction. "I'll be fine," she told Owen.

Jared glanced around, his brown eyes narrowing at the empty dark street. He glanced at Rose. "Are you *sure*? Because I don't think you should take any chances."

Well, *that* was a quick change in attitude, Rose thought.

"I'm sure," Rose said with a frown.

Owen and Jared exchanged a strange look.

Just as she started to ask them to explain what was going on, Owen turned toward her and pulled her into a bear hug that took her breath. With her face crushed against his chest, Rose felt less like her friend was telling her goodbye for the night and more like he was telling her goodbye for *good*.

"You'll text me as soon as you get home, right?" Owen asked.

Rose pushed back on his chest, extracting herself from his arms so that she could breathe. She stared at him, her brows furrowing. "Yeah, of course."

Jared glanced around the street suspiciously. "We need to go, Owen."

Owen glared at him. "I'm coming." He stepped closer to Jared and leaned in close, whispering something too quietly for Rose to hear.

"Well, what do you want *me* to do? Force her?" Jared snarled back.

Rose pursed her lips. "Guys, is there something I should know?"

They both turned toward her. Owen looked startled, but Jared just looked irritated. Jared grabbed Owen's arm. "Goodnight, Rose," Jared said, and he dragged a reluctant Owen in the direction of their apartment.

Rose stood there for a while, under the streetlight. She frowned after them, puzzled by their behavior. Deciding their lover's quarrel was none of her business—even if it *did* seem to have...*something* to do with her— she turned to head home.

But as she started off in the direction of her apartment, she couldn't shake the feeling that she was being followed.

WHEN ROSE TURNED THE CORNER ONTO A DARK ALLEY, SOMEONE GRABBED her. Her back collided with a tall, muscular form behind her, and an arm wrapped around her chest and shoulders, effectively restraining her. She opened her mouth to scream, but a large, rough hand covered her mouth to muffle the sound.

She fought and kicked, but her strength didn't compare to the person who held her. His grip tightened, as he tried to force her to stay still.

"Damn it, woman. I don't want to hurt you!" he hissed. "Stop fighting!"

Rose froze, as she recognized that voice. Even though he'd spoken quietly, she still recognized that slight accent, that melodic tone.

Since he'd rendered her unable to voice her anger, she settled for biting his palm, instead.

To her surprise, he didn't remove his hand from her mouth. As a matter of fact, he didn't even flinch. He just laughed. "That's cute," he growled in her ear, "but *my* bite is a lot harder."

She realized that the only way to get him to loosen his grasp was to temporarily stop fighting. So, she relaxed, letting her body fall limply against him.

Kallias shoved her against the wall of the alley and pinned her hands above her head with just one of his. He leaned against her to hold her still.

Now that she could see him, Rose pinned him with the most murderous glare he'd ever seen. He raised an eyebrow, amused by her courage. He could smell the adrenaline pumping through her bloodstream, but she hid her fear well.

With his hand still pressed against her lips, Kallias leaned closer. His face was only inches from hers, and he spoke in a dangerously low tone. "I'll take my hand off of your mouth now, but only if you *don't* scream."

Rose's bright blue eyes darkened angrily. She looked as defiant as ever.

Kallias sighed tiredly, already sure this wouldn't end well. "Do *not* scream," he said again, before he removed his hand from her mouth.

"I knew it was you," Rose snarled.

His brows furrowed. "You knew *what* was me?"

"Let me go, or I swear you'll regret it," she warned.

Kallias laughed, "I will? What are you going to do to me?"

Rose narrowed her eyes at his patronizing tone. "I'm not afraid of you."

"You should be," Kallias said simply.

"Well, I'm not," she said, as she tried to pull her hands free. Her wrists twisted in his grasp, and she whimpered at the pressure of his rough hands.

His gaze darted toward her hands. "Stop. You'll bruise your wrists."

"Why do you care?" Rose said, and she jerked at her wrists again.

"I told you. I don't want to hurt you," he sighed. "I just want to talk."

"Yeah, that makes sense," she snarled. "You attacked me just to talk."

"*Attack* is a bit of an exaggeration, don't you think?" Kallias grumbled.

"If you wanted to talk," she grunted, as she fought against him, "why didn't you just talk to me in the restaurant?"

"Because I needed to talk to you *alone*," he said. His gaze darted toward her wrists. "Stop fighting."

Her eyes narrowed. "Let go of me."

"If I knew you wouldn't run, I would," Kallias said, trying his best to hold her still without harming her. "But considering your track record of *insanity*, I'm almost positive that letting you go would be a bad idea."

"*I'm* insane?" she said. "You're the one attacking women in alleys!"

His eyes widened. "Would you shut the hell up?"

"No," she snarled. "Now, let me go, you creepy drug dealer."

He laughed in surprise. "That's your brilliant conclusion? I'm a *drug dealer*?"

"That's just the nicest accusation I could think of," she said. She winced, as she continued to pull at her hands. "You might be a kidnapper. Or a murderer. Drug dealers are nicer than both of those, don't you think?"

Kallias struggled to process her logic. Was she insinuating that accusing him of a being a drug dealer was a compliment? "I'm not a kidnapper."

She raised an eyebrow. "Murderer, then?"

He didn't answer that. "What I *am* is a dangerous and impatient person, who happens to be trying to *help* you," he growled, "and you're making that very difficult." His brows furrowed, as she whimpered in pain. He suddenly grabbed her face and forced her to meet his gaze. He forced his way into her mind with his telepathic abilities and commanded, "Be still, and stop fighting me."

Rose felt a strange wave of dizziness fall over her mind, but at that same moment, she realized the guy had loosened his grip. She took advantage of the wider range of motion and stomped on his foot.

A sharp pain shot through Rose's head, and Kallias released her with a grunted curse. But she ignored the pain and fled as fast as she could, stumbling as she ran.

"What the hell?" Kallias said under his breath. No one had ever resisted his telepathic control before. No one. He narrowed his eyes at the woman fleeing from him—and yelled, "Fine! If you want to die, go ahead! Just remember: I tried to warn you!"

She froze. She turned back toward him, surprised to find he hadn't moved. She'd halfway expected him to come and snatch her up again, but he didn't. He just stood there, glaring at her.

"Warn me about *what?*" Rose asked.

Holding his hands out on either side of him, he stepped toward her, like someone afraid of spooking a wild animal. "You're in danger."

Rose snatched the first thing she could from her pocket and held it out toward him. "If you grab me again, I swear I'll use this."

He glanced down at her hand and laughed, "You'll *see* me to death?"

Rose grimaced, as she realized she'd threatened him with her reading glasses, of all things. "I'll stab you with them," she improvised, "in the eye."

He snorted at that. "I'd love to see you try."

She glared at him. "What do you want?"

Kallias sighed. "Someone is looking for you, Rose Foster."

Rose frowned. "How do you know my last name? I never mentioned it."

"That doesn't matter," Kallias said dismissively. "You were being watched by someone while you were at the café. Did you notice?"

"No," she muttered, but then, she shrugged. "Maybe. I don't know."

"Which is it?" he asked irritably.

"Who was watching me?" Rose countered.

Kallias shrugged, as if the question were irrelevant. "No one important. It's the one who *sent* him to watch you that you should worry about."

When he took a step toward her, she took another step backward. "Who sent him?"

"A very dangerous person," Kallias answered. He continued to approach her. "And when he finds you, Rose, he will kill you."

She glanced behind her, preparing to run. She wanted to believe him, honestly. His warning did match Audrey's dream, after all. And yet, every bone in her body told her *not* to trust him. She could *feel* that he was dangerous. She could see it, even.

On top of that, he also fit the description of the killer in Audrey's dream. "Who is he? Because *you* seem pretty dangerous to me."

"I am," he said. "But luckily for you, I have no interest in killing you."

"Yeah, lucky me," Rose scoffed. "So, who *does* have an interest in killing me?"

"Someone just as dangerous as I am—but a lot more insane," he answered.

Rose narrowed her eyes. "And how would you know?"

"That's none of your business." He took another step toward her. "All you need to know is that if you want to survive, you'll need my help."

Rose didn't buy it. "I'll scream, if you come one step closer."

He froze, frustration flashing in his light brown eyes. "I'm trying to help, but I only have so much patience. If you walk away, your death is on your own hands."

"I think I'll take my chances," Rose said.

"Fine. Go. Die," Kallias growled. "I don't give a shit."

Rose watched him warily for a moment. Then, she turned and ran.

Kallias raked a hand through his hair, as he watched her flee. "Stupid human," he said bitterly. "You deserve to die." He stood there for a few moments, trying to talk himself into going back to his hotel room and forgetting about her. She hadn't wanted his help, and that was fine with him. He didn't care about some stubborn human.

Yet, his thoughts kept drifting back to that moment after he'd used telepathic control on her—the way she'd just ignored it. He'd never seen anyone resist his telepathy like that. He wondered if *that* had something to do with why Theron was looking for her.

She certainly smelled unusual for a human.

Too sweet. Too powerful.

Kallias was just about to turn around and go back to his hotel room, when he noticed Theron's scent.

And immediately after he noticed it, he heard a woman scream.

Kallias rolled his eyes. "Damn it."

A VAMPIRE

*A*n involuntary scream escaped Rose's mouth, as someone
stepped out of the shadows and grabbed her.

Again.

This time, however, the person didn't seem to be trying *not* to hurt
her. His hands gripped her arms roughly, and his fingernails dug deeply
into her skin. Up until that point, Rose would've assumed that no one
could break a person's arms just by grabbing them, but she began to
doubt that, as intense pain splintered through her arms, reaching down
into her bones. She cried out, but he made no move to cover her mouth.

He didn't seem to care whether or not anyone heard her.

Instead of grabbing her from behind as the other man had, this man
grabbed her from the front, giving her a clear view of him. Though darkness cloaked the rest of the alley from her, the streetlight behind her cast
enough light onto his face for her to make out his appearance.

Her eyes widened, as she took note of his tawny skin, his dark,
brown eyes that looked cold and cruel, his short, brown hair that was
combed neatly, his strong jaw, his height, and that strange symmetry of
his features. Her stomach turned with dread as she realized: *this* was the
man from Audrey's dream.

Ironically, he didn't look much like a killer. The man from the restaurant—he'd *looked* dangerous. He probably even made an effort to look dangerous.

But this man was different.

The man who gripped her now wore neat, black slacks and a gray sweater. He looked more like someone who worked in an office somewhere than a murderer.

But she knew, now—with the way he gripped her, with the way his black eyes scrutinized her with cold curiosity—that *this* man was evil.

His smile alone could've told her that.

That *smile* sent chills down her spine.

Rose fought against him. "Let me go."

His fingernails dug deeper into her skin, and she felt the bruises begin to form along her arms.

But it was no use. He held her easily, no matter how hard she fought.

Disappointment flickered in the man's dark brown eyes. She, apparently, wasn't what he'd expected. "You don't *look* like much of a threat, do you?" he said, the Greek accent clear in his voice. "You smell amazing, but your appearance is lacking."

"Oh, thanks," Rose muttered. She struggled still, unwilling to give up, even though she was only hurting herself worse. "Let me go."

With a cruel smile, he said, "You'll only make this more painful, if you fight."

Twisting in his grasp, Rose gasped, "What do you want with me?"

"I should be asking *you* that question," he said.

She froze. She cast a brief, puzzled glance at him, but then, she pulled back and kicked him in the leg as hard as she could.

He made a low, terrifying sound in his throat—one that sounded more animal than human—and then, Rose cried out in agony, as he twisted her arm behind her, until she could no longer stand. She fought back tears, as he held her in that painful position.

"If you were smart, human, you'd stop fighting and save yourself some pain," he growled in her ear. "Because I can make this *very* painful."

Practically kneeling on the pavement, she gasped out, "Human?"

"Well, that's what you are, isn't it?" the man said.

"No, I'm a fish," Rose said sarcastically. "Don't you see the fins?"

The man squeezed her arm tighter. "I don't like your attitude."

Her entire body trembled under the force he applied to her arm, and she was sure it'd break at any moment. "Well, *I* don't like being attacked."

He jerked back on her hair, and his breath fell against her ear, as he snarled, "Your fragile, human bones will snap if you keep fighting." His breath smelled of copper.

Or...*blood*?

Impossible.

"I have to admit," he laughed cruelly, "for a human, you have a lot of fight in you."

"Why do you keep saying that?" Rose scoffed. "You're a human, too, idiot!"

He suddenly released her arm, sending her sprawling face-first onto the pavement, but before she could scramble away, he grabbed her and dragged her back to her feet. He pulled her against him, and that metallic scent fell against her face again. "Do *not* insult me," he snarled, "and no, I'm not human. But you already know that, don't you?"

Rose hesitated, caught off-guard. "What?"

"You were looking for me," he told her. "Well, here I am."

"You obviously have the wrong person," Rose assured him. "I don't make a habit of looking for creepy men who attack women in dark alleys."

He offered her a derisive smile. "You didn't ask anyone about me?"

"I don't even know who you are!" Rose snarled.

"Theron," the man said. "My name is Theron."

Rose went totally still. She looked up at him, her eyes wide.

No.

It couldn't be the same Theron from the scrolls. She refused to believe it. The scrolls were likely hundreds of years old—if not *more*.

The Theron from the scrolls, if he ever existed, would be long dead by now.

Wouldn't he?

Vampires didn't exist.

Theron's smile grew when he saw the flash of recognition in her bright blue eyes. "Ah. You recognize me now, don't you?" He leaned closer, and she cringed away from him. "You have something I want, human. Tell me where it is."

Her brows furrowed. "I don't know what you mean."

Theron dipped his head and pressed his face against her neck. He either didn't notice or didn't care, when she cringed away. "Why do you smell so powerful?"

"What are you *doing*?" Rose said, shoving against him. She kicked him again, but that only caused him to growl and grip her harder. Her voice grew more strained by the moment. "Let me go, you sick *creep*!"

"No," Theron said. His voice vibrated against her throat, and her stomach turned. "I'm hungry, and your scent is *very* appetizing."

Rose didn't even have time to process that strange remark—because she suddenly felt two, razor-sharp teeth press against her neck.

Her eyes widened in horror.

Before his fangs could pierce her skin, however, Theron stopped. His mouth remained against her skin for a moment—as if that moment had been frozen in time—but then, he straightened and looked up.

"I know that scent," Theron said under his breath. He peered into the shadows near the end of the alley. "Kallias," he sneered. "What a pleasant surprise!"

Rose turned—as much as she could in Theron's grasp, anyway—to glance further into the alley, into the shadows, where this *Kallias* must've stood. She watched as a tall form stepped forward.

"This is what you have to do to get women now?" Kallias taunted.

Even before she saw him, Rose recognized the man's voice. It was the same deep, slightly accented voice that had growled into her ear only a few minutes before.

The man from the restaurant—his name was Kallias, she realized.

It was a strange name. *A Greek name*, she thought.

She watched him warily, as he moved out of the shadows and into the dimly lit part of the alley. She didn't know whether to feel relieved by his presence or afraid of it.

It all depended on whether he'd come to help *her* or Theron.

A malicious smile curled at Theron's lips. "I don't recall having to resort to *anything* in order to obtain Phoebe."

Kallias said nothing, but Rose noticed his jaw tighten.

"Oh, I'm sorry. Was that a sensitive topic?" Theron said.

Rose stared incredulously at the two men. She wasn't sure why they were choosing now to do this—whatever *this* was. If Kallias planned to help her somehow, she'd be grateful, of course, but she wished he'd hurry—preferably *before* Theron shattered her arm.

She liked her arm.

And if he planned to kill her, well, that would just irritate her more.

She froze, as she noticed his light brown eyes shift toward her. His lips lifted into an amused smirk, almost as if he *knew* she was chewing him out in her mind. He took a step closer, still watching her.

"Release the woman so that you and I can talk," Kallias told Theron.

Theron glanced down at her. "Why would I need to release her?"

"She shouldn't hear our discussion," Kallias answered.

Theron shrugged. "Why not? It's not like she can repeat it—when she's dead."

"Yeah, the *dead* part doesn't sound too appealing to me," Rose said.

Theron twisted her arm again. "Shut up, human."

Rose whimpered involuntarily, her muscles buckling under the pain. Out of the corner of her eye, she saw Kallias glance at her, and if she didn't know any better, she would've thought that was concern she'd seen in his light brown eyes.

"My name," she said, gasping at the pain, "is Rose."

Kallias turned to Theron. "What do you want with her?"

"Why does it matter to you?" Theron asked. "Are *you* interested in her?"

"No," Kallias said. "I just find it strange that you would be."

"Wow. Thanks a lot," Rose muttered under her breath.

His lips twitched as he suppressed a laugh, and he gestured toward her, as if she'd just illustrated his point. "We both know this type of woman isn't *your* type."

"Ah, I guess that'd mean she isn't yours either," Theron said with a cruel smile. "I seem to recall us having similar taste in women."

"We don't," Kallias assured him. He took a slow, measured step toward them. "Answer the question. Why were you hunting her?"

"Hunting?" Rose repeated incredulously. "I'm not a deer."

"No," Theron agreed, and he leaned closer. "You're much tastier."

Rose kicked him again, irritating him enough that he, *at least*, moved his face away from her. "Get away from me."

Theron's lip curled. "Do you want free, little girl?"

Rose frowned. She was almost positive it was some sort of trick, but she nodded, anyway.

Rose realized she'd answered too soon, though, when Theron threw her against the wall with so much force that she felt her feet leave the ground. Pain shot through her skull, when the side of her head hit the wall.

Her mind swirled with dizziness from the impact, and she vaguely noticed a warm liquid pouring down the side of her face and sliding down her neck. She touched the thick, sticky liquid and pulled back her hand. Her own blood coated her fingers.

She groaned, as her body ached and her eyesight blurred.

Theron snatched her up, clutching the front of her white button-down shirt that was now stained with large drops of blood. Her eyes fluttered closed, even as she fought to stay conscious.

She felt his fangs dig into her neck.

Theron suddenly dropped her, and Rose collapsed onto the ground.

With a surprised gasp, Theron looked down.

Through her disoriented daze, Rose vaguely noticed the tip of a blade sticking through Theron's stomach, the blood stain steadily growing on his grey sweater.

Just as Theron realized what happened, the blade twisted, causing him to cry out in pain and fall to his knees. She watched as Kallias, standing behind Theron, removed the blood-coated dagger from Theron's back.

Kallias watched Theron writhe in pain. He raised his eyebrows and flashed a bitter smile. "It hurts, doesn't it?"

"I should've killed you when I had the chance," Theron growled.

"I seem to remember you did," Kallias reminded him.

"I should have left you dead," Theron amended.

"I can't disagree with that," Kallias said bitterly. He kicked Theron across the alley, causing the vampire to land in a crumpled, whining, heap.

Kallias turned back toward the human, scowling as she continued to lie there on the pavement. Her bright blue eyes were open, but they looked so blank. He grabbed her hand and jerked her to her feet. "What are you waiting for?" he snarled. "Run!"

But she didn't respond. Instead, her eyes fluttered closed, and she swayed unsteadily on her feet. He sighed as he realized what was happening. He barely had time to loop his arm around her back before she fell limply in his arms.

He stared blankly at the unconscious, bleeding woman. "Shit."

The scent of fresh blood filled his senses, and he felt the warm liquid coating his palm, as it streamed down from her head. His breath came in harsh pants as he fought against his hunger.

Involuntarily, he lifted her in his arms, moving his face closer to her neck. There was more power in her blood than anyone he'd ever encountered before, and his body craved it.

Her blood would sate him, perhaps even make him more powerful.

Theron wouldn't stand a chance against him, if he had *her* blood.

He pressed his mouth to her neck. As he listened to her blood course through her arteries and smelled the unusual scent of her blood, he almost bit her. His fangs dug into her skin.

But then, she murmured something unintelligible and shifted in his arms, as if falling into a comfortable sleep, and he suddenly realized what he was doing.

He dropped her, horrified by what he'd almost done. He stared at the dark crimson blood that coated his hand, unable to tear his gaze from the one substance that drew out his true nature.

He *still* wanted to taste it.

Theron laughed. "How long has it been since you fed?"

Kallias finally managed to tear his gaze away from the blood on his hand, and he narrowed his gaze on Theron.

No longer lying on the ground, Theron sat, leaned up against the opposite wall of the alley, and he watched Kallias with an amused expression, even as his stomach continued to bleed, darkening his gray sweater.

Kallias returned his attention to the blood, unable to look away for long. "It's none of your business."

Theron shifted, wincing as pain tore through his body. He clutched the stomach wound. "You nearly bit her just now," he said with a weak smile. "A twenty-five-hundred-year-old vampire should have more control over his hunger than that—unless he's starved, of course." He smiled. "So, tell me, Kallias. How long has it been? Days? Weeks?" He laughed. "Tell me it hasn't been months."

Kallias stared hungrily at the blood, his mouth watering.

"Feed from her," Theron suggested. "She's unconscious. She'll never know."

Kallias squeezed his eyes shut, breathing in short, harsh gasps. "No."

"Why not?" Theron said. "It's what we are. It's what we do."

"It's what *you* do," Kallias snarled. He opened his eyes to glare at Theron. He walked over to where Theron sat against the wall. "Now, I'll ask you one more time. Why were you hunting this human? What are you up to?"

Theron shrugged. "You can smell her blood," he said. He glanced down at the blood drying on Kallias's hand. "As a matter of fact, it's driving you mad with hunger at this very moment. I can see the hunger in your eyes."

Kallias clenched his jaw in frustration. He couldn't argue with Theron's observation. The scent of the woman's blood intoxicated his senses, and it was all he could do to keep his focus on Theron. "What's your point?"

"She smells incredible," Theron said. "Why *wouldn't* I want her blood?"

Kallias pinned him with a suspicious look. "Why *does* she smell like that? Why does she smell more powerful than any human should?"

"I don't know," Theron admitted, "*yet*. I'd like to find out, though."

Kallias frowned. He saw in Theron's mind that he was being honest about that part, at least. "Fine, but I still don't believe her blood is the reason you were hunting her. No vampire would go to the trouble of hunting a human just because her blood *might* make him more powerful for a few nights."

"I would," Theron said, smiling. "I *enjoy* the hunt."

Kallias tried to sift through the vampire's thoughts to find the answer to his question, but between the scent of blood distracting Kallias and the pain distracting Theron, his telepathic abilities were practically useless. "I'm not leaving without answers. You're up to something. I feel it."

Theron frowned for a moment, clearly confused, but then, recognition lightened his dark brown eyes. He began to laugh. "You're still bound to me? It's been twenty-five hundred years, and you haven't broken the bond?"

Kallias gripped his dagger tightly. "Just answer the question."

Theron pulled his hand off of his stomach to see if the wound was healing yet. He smiled, when he noticed Kallias's eyes darken with hunger. "I'll answer your question, if you answer mine."

Kallias forced his gaze away from the blood. "What's your question?"

"Why do you care?" Theron asked. "Have you finally decided to get your revenge?" He laughed. "No, I doubt that. It's been twenty-five hundred years. You could've found me long before now if you'd wanted. So, what is it? Did you decide you wanted to befriend me?" He laughed again, when he noticed the disgust on Kallias's face. "I didn't think so. Just, *please*, tell me it doesn't have anything to do with the woman. You've already died because of a woman once. I'd hate to see it happen again."

Kallias clenched his jaw. "I don't care what happens to the human."

"Then, feed from her," Theron demanded. "Kill her."

Kallias glanced back at the woman, who lay unconscious on the ground, blood sticking to her skin and matting her long, red hair. "Why would I do that?"

"To prove you don't care, of course," Theron answered.

Kallias turned back toward him. "I don't need to *prove* anything."

"If you say so," Theron said in a patronizing tone. He winced when his hand brushed the wound in his stomach. He looked up at Kallias.

"You're also starved, which means you can barely even concentrate right now—much less win a fight."

"I think I beat you easily enough," Kallias scoffed.

"It also means you're weaker than usual," Theron continued, as if he hadn't said anything, "and *that* means that I'm stronger than you. The only thing keeping you alive right now is the fact that I'm injured, and in case you haven't noticed, my injury is healing as we speak."

Kallias shrugged. "Let it heal. I'll just stab you again."

"Are you sure about that?" Theron asked.

Kallias heard the whistle of movement only a moment before the approaching vampire would've reached him. He spun around and shoved his dagger into the vampire's stomach.

Kallias kicked him to the ground just in time to catch the blade that a second vampire swung near his neck. He grasped the vampire's wrist, knocked the knife out of his grasp, and flipped the vampire over him.

By this point, the first vampire was on his feet again with the other vampire's knife in his hand. As he tried to stab Kallias again, Kallias sliced his own dagger swiftly through the vampire's neck, decapitating him in one swing.

As the headless corpse of the vampire fell to the pavement, Kallias noticed the second vampire approaching him from the side. He waited until the vampire reached him, and then, he shoved his hand into the vampire's chest and ripped out his heart.

Blood seemed suspended in air, as Kallias killed the vampires with a speed a human couldn't have seen.

Kallias froze, as he suddenly felt a cold, sharp blade against his own throat.

"I should kill you now," Theron growled into Kallias's ear, digging the blade into his skin. "But I enjoy watching you suffer."

And in the blink of an eye, Theron had disappeared down the alley, leaving Kallias in the blood-covered alley with the dead vampires.

"Freeze!" a man yelled, as he stepped into the alley with his gun drawn.

Kallias rolled his eyes. He turned toward the human man, sighing as he noticed the police uniform. He watched as the police officer registered the sight before him. The officer's grey eyes widened with alarm when he saw the blood that coated the pavement and the headless corpse lying near his feet.

His voice trembled. "Drop whatever you have in your hand."

Kallias opened his hand. "You mean this? It's just a heart."

The officer glanced at the crushed organ lying in Kallias's open palm and the dark, sticky blood that coated his arm from elbow to fingertips. And he gulped audibly. "What the hell? Drop that!"

"What? Are you afraid I'll use a heart as a weapon?" Kallias scoffed.

The man looked ghostly pale. "How did you kill these people?"

"Well, first, they're *not* people," Kallias said, as he dropped the heart. He wiped his bloodied hands on his black jeans and frowned at the unconscious woman lying a few feet in front of him. "Well, okay, *she* is a person, but she's also not dead. And as for how I killed *them*," he paused, as he held up his hands, "With my hands, of course."

"If they're not people, what are they?" the man asked nervously.

He screamed and fell back, when Kallias suddenly appeared in front of him. Scrambling to his feet, the man stared at Kallias, his grey eyes wide with horror.

"They're the monsters that lurk in the darkness, waiting to prey on unsuspecting humans," Kallias answered.

The gun shook in the man's hand. "How did you move so fast?"

"Because I'm just like them," Kallias answered. "A monster."

The man tried to pull the trigger, but Kallias moved too quickly, ripping the gun out of his hand and tossing it aside. He reached for another weapon, but Kallias caught his wrist before he could get his hand around anything.

"If I wanted to kill you, those weapons wouldn't save you," Kallias said.

The man's heart raced—so fast that Kallias worried he might have a heart attack. Kallias sighed and stepped closer, still holding the man's wrist.

He met the man's gaze and took control of his mind. "Whatever you thought you saw or heard on this alley wasn't here. You checked, but you found nothing out of the ordinary. As a matter of fact, you're certain there will be no need to check this part of town for the rest of the night. Do you understand?"

The man's pulse immediately slowed, returning to its usual pace. His grey eyes glazed over, as Kallias's telepathic control took effect. "Yes," he said.

Kallias nodded and let go of the officer's hand. He knelt and picked up the gun from the ground. He held it out toward the man, nodding at the man to take it. "Go on. You can have it back now."

The man took the gun and returned it to its place on his belt. Then, without another word, he turned and left the alley, rubbing his eyes and mumbling to himself about needing sleep, as he walked back to his car.

Kallias turned back toward the darker end of the alley, sighing at the dismembered bodies of the vampires who attacked him. "If you were going to send your friends to their deaths, Theron, you could have at least cleaned up the mess," he muttered.

He closed his eyes and listened closely to the sounds around him. After the officer left, a silence settled in the air. Only two heartbeats echoed in his ears now—his own and *hers*. He glanced at the young woman who still lay unconscious on the ground. Sticky blood coated her forehead, but she seemed to have stopped bleeding for the moment.

Her red hair fanned around her head, matted with blood. Drops of blood stained her wrinkled, white, button-down shirt. Her skin looked softer and fairer than before, and her soft, pink lips were parted. Although less strong than it'd been a few minutes ago, the scent of her blood still enticed his senses, along with the blood from the two dead vampires, as well, and Kallias felt his throat burn with hunger.

Kallias ignored his hunger and returned to the task at hand. He tossed the headless body over his shoulder and carried it to the dumpster. He threw it in on top of the trash and grabbed the head that had already rolled away, tossing it inside, as well.

He grabbed the other corpse and the crushed heart and threw them inside, too. Then, he pulled a bottle of lighter fluid from his pocket and poured it over them. He lit a match and tossed it inside.

Flames consumed the trash—and the inhuman corpses, as well.

Kallias started to leave, but then, he glanced back at the woman and sighed. "What the hell is wrong with me?" he said—and returned to her.

He knelt in front of the unconscious woman. "I should leave you here," he grumbled.

With a defeated sigh, Kallias scooped the woman's long, soft body into his arms. He cradled her against his chest and carried her to his car. After a few steps, she groaned in pain and shifted in his arms.

Her eyes fluttered open slowly, and she squinted, as if suffering from a severe headache. As her azure-blue eyes met his gaze, she murmured, "You."

———

Rose woke in a panic. Her head pounded in time with her racing heartbeat, and she had the worst headache of her life.

Bright light flooded her eyes as she opened them, and she winced, as pain shot through her skull.

She blinked slowly, as her eyes adjusted to the light, and she frowned at the empty, white walls around her. Another spike of panic buzzed through her, as she realized that she had no idea where she was.

Rose attempted to sit up in her bed, only noticing the IV needle in her wrist when it tugged at her.

Only then did Rose realize that she was in the hospital, and she couldn't remember why.

She grimaced at the dry, soreness of her throat. She spotted a tall, blue glass of iced water on the rolling tray near the door. She tried to crawl out of the bed.

But as soon as her bare feet touched the cold, tile floor, a wave of dizziness rushed over her, and she fell face-first into the floor. She managed to pull her IV loose in the process, and the machine began to beep angrily at her. She groaned as the incessant noise worsened her headache.

A middle-aged woman in pale pink scrubs rushed into the room—with Audrey trailing behind her. "What on earth are you doing out of bed, Miss Foster?" she cried. She helped Rose back into bed, ignoring

Rose's protests. "You could've hurt yourself. And look! You've pulled your IV loose."

"Sorry," Rose slurred. "I was just so thirsty." Her brows furrowed, as she noticed how strange and lethargic her own voice sounded. "What happened? Why am I in the hospital? Why does my head hurt so badly? Why does my voice sound weird?"

The nurse raised her eyebrow, as she reconnected the IV. "One question at a time, honey," she laughed. "Your head hurts because you have a head injury. Your voice sounds funny because of the medicine the doctor gave you. And concerning what happened, well... we were hoping you could tell *us*."

"Stop plugging me up," Rose said drowsily. "I'm thirsty."

"Well, sweetie, *that* is why you have this button," the nurse scolded. She pointed to the call button on the side of the bed. She walked over to the tray and grabbed the blue glass. "That way, *I* can bring what you need, and *you* don't have to hurt yourself."

With shaky hands, Rose took the glass of iced water from the nurse. She sipped, still a little mopey about not being able to get it herself. "Thanks."

"How are you feeling?" she heard Audrey ask.

Rose looked up, squinting at Audrey's blurred, slender form next to her bed. She tried to concentrate on the question, but her mind felt too foggy.

Shooting a worried glance at the nurse, Audrey said, "Are you sure she's all right?"

"The doctor thinks she'll be fine," the nurse said. "She just needs—"

"I'm fine," Rose said, suddenly. "Is that what you asked?"

Audrey turned to her. "Do you remember what happened?"

Rose tried to shake her head, but the movement rattled her head. "No," she said, clutching her glass. "What happened?"

"I don't know. The hospital just called and said someone had dropped you off at the hospital," Audrey explained. "You were unconscious, and you needed stitches. Are you sure you don't remember? You're pretty bruised up, Rose."

"Give her time," the nurse scolded. "She just woke up."

Rose felt a pang of guilt as she noticed Audrey's clothes. Dressed in a lacy pink camisole and short pink shorts, covered in penguins with top hats, Audrey had clearly been in bed when she got the call. "You didn't have to come."

Audrey waved dismissively. "I didn't come for *you*," she teased. She held up a frozen coffee drink so that Rose could see it. "The hospital has Starbucks."

Rose laughed and returned to drinking her iced water.

"You listed Miss Audrey Stevens as your emergency contact," the nurse said. "They tried to find your parents' contact information, but it wasn't listed."

"You should have checked the cemetery," Rose blurted.

"Huh?" the nurse said, taken aback.

"That's her contact information," she said calmly. "My mom's dead."

The nurse stared at Rose, her eyes wide. "Oh! I'm..."

"I don't have a clue who my dad is," Rose said, "but he's probably dead, too, considering the kind of men my mom used to interact with."

The nurse was stammering, "Oh, bless your heart, I—"

"My brother's still alive," Rose said, "but you'd have to call the prison to get in touch with him because he's an idiot and a criminal—but mostly just an idiot."

The nurse just blinked. "I'm sorry."

"She's pretty talkative on this medicine, isn't she?" Audrey said with an amused smile. "Let's keep her on it until I get some good blackmail material."

Rose blinked, as if just realizing what she'd said. "Why did I tell you that? I never tell people that. Did I make things awkward?"

"A little bit, yeah," Audrey said.

Rose sighed.

"It's perfectly fine, Miss Foster," the nurse assured her. "Right now, just focus on getting some sleep. The medicine will make you drowsy. That's what you need most right now: rest."

"Yeah. Drowsy," Rose said, her eyelids suddenly heavy.

"We'd like to know what happened when you're ready to talk," the nurse said. "I can even call the police for you so that you can file a report."

"Why would I need police?" Rose asked.

The nurse frowned. "Well, I just assumed this wasn't self-inflicted or anything. I mean, I don't see how it could be. You had a deep gash in your head that needed stitches. You're covered in bruises. And you have a concussion."

Rose just shrugged. "I don't remember anything."

The nurse nodded. "That happens sometimes. Just, when you *do* remember something, let me know. My name is Harriet. Call, if you need me."

"Thanks," Rose mumbled, as she watched the nurse leave.

The bed dipped as Audrey crawled onto the bed. She lay beside Rose and crossed her legs, her thin body easily fitting in the small space.

She leaned toward Rose and whispered in her ear, "Did you really not remember anything, or did you just not want to talk in front of her?" She pulled back, frowning curiously. "It wasn't the vampire, was it?"

To her surprise, Rose laughed, "You still think a vampire's after me?"

Audrey scowled. "Rose, *someone* attacked you last night."

Rose blinked, waves of drowsiness drowning out her thoughts. *Had someone attacked her?* She couldn't remember. She touched the bandaged cut on her head. "Why?"

"I don't know," Audrey sighed. She glared at Rose and slapped her hand away from the bandage. "Stop touching it! You'll mess up your stitches."

"I'm so sleepy," Rose announced.

Audrey snatched the television remote from Rose's nightstand and started flipping through the channels. "Sleep. I'll be right here, stealing your blanket and cable TV. Maybe you'll remember something when you wake up."

"Oww," Rose complained.

Audrey looked up from the romance novel in her hand. "Oh, good, you're awake. Owen called while you were asleep. He's pissed at you, by the way. And now, I am, too. Is it true that you refused his offer to walk you home?"

Rose winced at the quickness of Audrey's words. It was like watching headlights buzz by on the interstate. Speaking of lights, why were the lights at the hospital so harsh? Did the hospital workers *enjoy* having pain stab through their skull, like it was doing to Rose now? "Uh, yeah? Maybe? I think I remember that."

"I *told* you about my dream!" Audrey snapped. "How could you tell him no when you *knew* that someone would attack you?"

Rose cringed, her headache worsening with each loud shriek of Audrey's voice. She rolled onto her back, giving Audrey a frustrated look. "You know, people with concussions *love* being yelled at."

Audrey continued to glare at her. "If you had let him walk you home—"

"If I had, *he* would've been attacked, too," Rose interrupted.

"See, that's the problem with you," Audrey said. "Twelve times out of ten, if it comes down to you or someone else, you'll sacrifice yourself every time."

"You know twelve times out of ten is impossible, right?" Rose said.

Audrey rolled her eyes. "I was exaggerating for effect."

Rose closed her eyes. "Hyperbole," she said drowsily.

"This really isn't the time for a vocabulary lesson, Rose," Audrey complained. She shook her head and sighed, "I don't want to lose you!"

Rose opened her eyes again, stunned by the fear in Audrey's amber eyes. With great effort, she managed to pull herself into a sitting position and lean her head on Audrey's shoulder. "You won't," she promised.

Audrey didn't have any siblings. She didn't even have parents anymore. She and Rose really only had each other.

"Do you remember anything yet?" Audrey said.

Rose frowned, as she tried to recall the events of the night before. Her mind felt heavy, and her memories blurred together like one, long trail of disjointed pictures that made no sense—flickering images of cold, dark eyes, a sadistic smile, a man in the shadows, blood, so much *blood*...

"I'm working on it."

"Do you know if it was the man from my dream?" Audrey asked.

Rose squinted. That seemed to prick at a memory. "If it were him, I'd be dead, wouldn't I?" she said, but even as she said it, her stomach sunk with dread.

"I thought so, too, but..." Audrey trailed off.

"But what?" Rose asked. She pulled back to look at Audrey. Noticing Audrey's sweaty palms, she realized, "You had another dream."

Audrey's worried, golden-brown gaze darted toward the closed door of Rose's hospital room, and then, she nodded. "It was different this time. The same person attacked and killed you, but it didn't happen in an alley. You were inside," she explained. "If the dream had been exactly the same, I would've just assumed that last night had nothing to do with it, but since it changed..."

"Why does Theron want to kill me so badly?" Rose wondered.

Audrey spun toward Rose. "Theron? You said Theron!"

Rose frowned. "Hmm. That *is* weird."

"You remember his name," Audrey said. "What else do you remember?"

Rose shook her head, her thoughts rattling. "I don't know. I don't remember anything."

"Except his name," Audrey corrected. "That's something!"

"That can't be right," Rose mumbled. "Theron is the name of the vampire in those scrolls. That's too much of a coincidence."

"Unless they're both the same person," Audrey reminded her.

"Vampires aren't real," Rose insisted.

Audrey scowled. "*Something* attacked you last night, Rose."

Rose shrugged. "That doesn't prove that vampires exist. It only proves that crappy people exist, which isn't much of a surprise to me, by the way."

"Crappy people with the name Theron," Audrey added.

"It *is* a weird coincidence," Rose admitted. "But it doesn't mean the person who attacked me is some kind of mythological creature. Besides, if a vampire *had* attacked me, wouldn't I have bite marks on my neck or something?"

"I guess," Audrey said. "Are you *sure* you don't remember anything else?"

Rose replayed the hazy, partially forgotten events of the previous night in her mind, recalling the walk to work, the scrolls, the customer who asked her that creepy question…

Her eyes widened. "The man from the restaurant!" she blurted. "I think he might've saved me."

"The man from the restaurant?" Audrey repeated.

"Kallias," Rose whispered in shock. "That arrogant jerk saved my life."

Audrey blinked. "Well, that's a strange thing to call your hero."

Rose turned to Audrey. "Who brought me here last night?"

Audrey shrugged. "They just said a man found you in an alley."

Rose frowned at that. "And they didn't ask for his name?"

"I guess that is weird," Audrey admitted. "Does it matter who it was?"

"It could," Rose said quickly, lost in thought. "I wonder why he saved me. He said he didn't care whether I lived or died."

"He said *what*?" Audrey sputtered.

"We have to go," Rose announced, as she threw her legs over the bed.

"Whoa! Slow down!" Audrey shrieked, as she jumped off the bed and rushed to the other side. She shoved Rose back into bed before Rose made another disastrous attempt to stand. "They haven't even discharged you yet!"

"I have to figure this out," Rose complained.

"You have a concussion, Rose. You need rest," Audrey scolded.

"A *mild* concussion," Rose said, though she wasn't actually sure. She fumbled with the IV in her wrist. "And a few stitches. I'm not dying. *Yet.* I might if I don't figure this out, though."

"Fifteen is *not* a few," Audrey argued.

"Seriously, I just need some Tylenol," Rose said stubbornly.

"I'm pretty sure you're on something stronger than Tylenol right now," Audrey said. She glared at Rose. "Would you leave your IV alone? You're going to hurt yourself! I swear I'll puke if you start bleeding everywhere!"

Rose ignored her. "I have to figure this out."

"Okay, look! Just be still, dang it!" Audrey said frantically, throwing up her hands. "At least let me see if I can get them to discharge you first."

"Yes, ma'am," Rose said, offering her friend a sarcastic salute.

Audrey raked a hand through her frizzy mess of brown hair. She sighed loudly at Rose, "Okay. Just stay here. Don't touch anything."

"I ASSURED THEM THAT I'D TAKE YOU DOWN IN THE WHEELCHAIR!" AUDREY complained, as she abandoned the wheelchair in the hallway and ran after Rose.

Rose shoved open the door to the stairway and started down the five flights of stairs. "Well, why would you do that?" she asked. "Wheelchairs and stairs are a bad combination. I'd end up injured even worse."

Audrey rolled her eyes. "Obviously, we would've used the elevator… like *normal* people," she said, breathless as she rushed after Rose. "Dang it. Are we really going to walk down five flights of stairs?"

"You know how I feel about elevators. They're tiny," Rose said. It was a bit more serious than that, but she purposely kept her voice light. "You're welcome to ride the elevator if you want."

"And leave a concussed, crazy woman to walk down five flights of stairs by herself?" Audrey scoffed, as she took two steps at a time to catch up with Rose. "Ugh, I'm going to be sick. I shouldn't have eaten those six donuts."

Rose tapped on the beige '*Level 2*' sign with her fingertip, as they passed the door and continued down another set of stairs. "Relax. We're almost there."

"Where are you in such a hurry to get to?" Audrey said, nearly tripping over her own feet. "Owen's already told Eleanor what happened, and she gave you the next few nights off. And your classes are over for the day."

"I need to figure this out," Rose repeated.

"Figure *what* out?" Audrey asked breathlessly.

Rose pushed open the door beside the *'Ground Floor'* sign and stepped out into the hall. "Several things, but first, I want to know who brought me here."

"I told you," Audrey sighed. "The nurse said she doesn't know."

"*Someone* must know," Rose insisted, as they neared the Emergency Room floor. "They said he brought me in through the ER, right?"

Audrey cast a wistful look at the snack machines, as they passed them. "Yeah, but what are you going to do? Break into the office? Watch the cameras?"

"That's illegal," Rose muttered, as if she'd do it otherwise.

As they entered the empty waiting room. Rose glanced around, looking for someone to ask. Audrey crossed her arms and sighed, ready to sink down on one of the sofas and watch some television if Rose didn't hurry. She glanced around the room, looking for a comfortable place to sit. She froze as she saw a familiar, brown-haired woman behind the desk. "Hey, that's Meg. Rose! We can ask Meg!"

Rose glanced at Audrey. "I'm not sure I know a Meg."

"I went to high school with her," Audrey explained. "Come on."

Rose followed Audrey to the desk, where a pretty, curvy woman in a brown suit and a crisp, blue button-down shirt sat, typing something into her computer. She held a black, corded phone to her face with her shoulder, and soft, brown tendrils of hair fell around her face, as she typed.

When she noticed Audrey, she smiled and mouthed what appeared to be an enthusiastic hello. She then frowned curiously at Rose, her green eyes lingering on the blood that stained Rose's shirt and the bandage on her head. After a few moments, she finished the call and returned the phone to its receiver.

"Audrey! It's so good to see you!" she exclaimed. "How have you been?"

"Good," Audrey assured her. "And you?"

"Well, I'm taking a few classes at the University," Meg told her.

"That's great!" Audrey said. She scratched her head, tangling her already messy hair. "I was wondering if you'd answer a question for my friend."

Meg nodded. "Of course." She glanced at Rose, glancing once again at the bandage on Rose's forehead. "Shouldn't you be in a wheelchair?"

"Nope," Rose said, offering no further explanation.

Audrey leaned against the desk. "Rose wanted to know if you knew—"

"How much my bill will be," Rose interrupted.

Audrey frowned at her. "But I thought you wanted..."

Rose cut her off again. "Can you tell me that?" she asked Meg.

Meg nodded and began typing. "Possibly. I should at least be able to tell you how much the ER portion will be. What's your name?"

"Rose Melanie Foster," Rose answered.

Meg smiled kindly at Rose, although her gaze remained on the computer. "I'm glad you're feeling better, by the way. I was worried when he brought you in last night. You were unconscious, and there was just so much...*blood*."

Rose raised an eyebrow. "You were here last night?"

She continued typing. "Yeah."

"Then, you saw the person who brought me in," Rose stated.

Meg grinned. "Pardon the lack of professionalism, but he was *hot*."

Audrey raised her eyebrows. "Really?" she asked excitedly. "How hot?"

Rose rolled her eyes at them. "Did he give you his name?"

Meg frowned. "Honestly, I don't remember him mentioning a name, but I'm sure we asked." She hesitated. "That *is* strange, actually. I don't remember asking."

"Is it on the report or anything?" Audrey asked.

Meg scanned at the screen, as she pulled up the report. "No," she said. Her frown deepened. "That's weird. It doesn't mention him at all."

"Okay," Audrey said, drawing out the word in confusion.

"Describe him to me," Rose suggested.

"Tall. *Very* tall. Sexy. Long hair. Black clothes. Tattoos," Meg listed.

Rose grimaced. "Yeah. That sounds like the guy from the restaurant."

"Arrogant-Jerk-Hero?" Audrey asked. "You didn't tell me he was sexy."

"Attractiveness is subjective," Rose muttered. "It would've been a completely useless observation."

Audrey sighed, "Why are you so boring?"

"Okay, this is really weird," Meg announced, that frown twisting deeper at her brows. "Most of the report is blank. It says your bill's already been paid, but the details are missing."

"Huh," Audrey said. She glanced at Rose and asked, "Do you think Tall-Sexy-Arrogant-Heroic-Jerk-Guy might've paid your bill?"

Rose raised an eyebrow at the ever-lengthening name. "Why would he do that? I mean, he did give me a *huge* tip. So, it's possible he has the money, but—"

"Call me crazy, but this guy isn't really sounding like a jerk," Audrey said.

"You're only saying that because she called him sexy," Rose scoffed.

"Am I losing my mind?" Meg asked suddenly.

"I'm not sure we're qualified to answer that," Rose said.

Meg shook her head in confusion. "This has my signature, but I don't remember this at all."

"Well, that's creepy," Audrey said.

"This is my handwriting," Meg said. "Why don't I remember?"

Rose frowned, not sure what to think. "Did you hit your head, too?"

Meg scowled at Rose. "No."

"We should get you home," Audrey said, pulling Rose by the arm.

"Thanks, Meg! It was nice to meet you!" Rose called, as Audrey dragged her through the door and outside into the hot afternoon sun.

As soon as they were outside, Audrey turned back toward Rose. "Why do you think I didn't see the man who saved you in my dream?"

"I have no idea," Rose admitted.

Audrey frowned thoughtfully. "Did he seem to know your attacker?"

Rose considered that for a moment, recalling the night again. "Well, I don't think they were friends, but yes, they did seem to know each other. I think they might've, umm, *known* the same girl? In the biblical sense, I mean."

Audrey raised her eyebrows. "And how exactly do you know this?"

"The way they were talking," Rose answered.

"Wait! Does that mean you remember *everything*?" Audrey asked.

"It's all starting to come back to me," Rose confirmed. "We need to go."

Audrey frowned at the urgency in Rose's voice. "Why?"

"Because I have *a lot* of questions I need answered," Rose said.

4

SWORDS AND FANGS

*A*udrey placed a hand on her hip. "Rose Melanie Foster, I *know* you heard that doctor tell you to rest."

Rose suppressed a smile. Audrey would never believe it if Rose told her, but every now and then, she sounded *just* like her grandmother.

Rose glanced up from her books and scrolls to find Audrey standing in the doorway of the empty classroom. "Relax. I'm not going to rip open my stitches by *reading*," she scoffed.

She straightened her reading glasses on her nose and returned her attention to the book in front of her.

Audrey stepped into the room, depositing a half-empty box of donuts on the table. "You should be in bed, eating chicken soup."

"I have a concussion, Audrey, not the flu," Rose scoffed.

Audrey hesitated near the door. Something about the maps and artwork on the walls of this classroom felt so familiar to her. She looked around, noticing the familiar arrangement of desks, as well, and the wooden podium at the front of the classroom.

"Have I been here before?"

"I doubt it," Rose said, without looking up. Her long, red hair—still wet from the shower she'd just taken—fell forward, leaving damp spots on her blue, button-down shirt. "As far as I know, they only use it for the upper-level history classes."

Audrey frowned. "But it looks so familiar."

Rose shrugged. "Have you come here with *me* before?" She jotted something down and turned to the next page.

"I don't think so," Audrey said.

Dismissing the strange feeling as just that—a *feeling*—Audrey dragged a chair over to the table with Rose. She sat down and opened the box of donuts. "I brought donuts," she announced, as she plucked her favorite one from the box. "I already ate half of them, though."

Rose laughed. "I'm fine. I'm on a diet, remember?"

"But they're jelly donuts," Audrey said.

Rose looked up at Audrey, her brows furrowing. "So?"

Audrey bit into it. "So, they're technically fruit, right?"

Rose blinked slowly. "I...don't think it works that way."

Audrey took another bite of the donut, not even bothering to wipe away the glob of red jelly that dropped onto her thin, pink hoodie.

"You can go on home, if you need to," Rose said distractedly. "I know you still need to pack for the weekend."

Audrey scowled at her. "Look, I get that you have that head issue right now—"

"Concussion," Rose provided.

"But," Audrey continued, "surely, you haven't forgotten that someone attacked you *last night*! You're not walking home again tonight."

"I could've driven myself here, if you'd let me," Rose muttered.

Audrey rolled her eyes. "The doctor hasn't okayed you to drive yet."

"I feel fine," Rose said. She flipped open another oversized book and began thumbing through it, as well.

"Why can't you do this at home?" Audrey asked.

"There's no room in our apartment for all of these books," Rose said.

Audrey glanced at the pile of books and decided Rose had a point about that. "There's no room *anywhere* for this many books. If you ask me, it shouldn't even be legal for someone to check out this many."

Rose looked up, horrified. "Well, I *didn't* ask you," she muttered, "and I definitely won't *now*."

Audrey stuck out her tongue, like a child—a silly, jelly-covered child. "I guess I *could* come back later to pick you up. I was planning a midnight run for ice cream anyway."

Rose laughed at her friend's junk-food obsession. "Only if you're sure it won't be an inconvenience," she said. "I really don't mind walking."

"You're *not* walking!" Audrey snapped. "You are not to leave this classroom until I get back, okay?"

Rose glanced at Audrey, her brows high. "Yes, ma'am."

Audrey sighed and slid back her chair. She grabbed the box of donuts and cast one last glance at Rose. "Promise me you'll be careful."

Rose flashed a cute smile. "Now, if I did that, how would I carry out my brilliant plan of hunting down Dracula and asking him to *drink my blood*?" she said, adopting a cheesy, fake accent for the last part.

Audrey rolled her eyes. "Not funny."

KALLIAS SIGHED, AS HE FOUND HIMSELF STANDING IN THE ALLEY NEAR THE café for the second time in one night. He knew Rose Foster wasn't there tonight. He would've recognized her scent if she was.

Still, he hated that he kept finding himself back there. He had no interest in running into *her* again, but it was the last place he'd seen Theron. It was the only starting place he had.

Just as he was about to leave, he noticed movement in the shadows.

Near a wooden fence that separated the residential neighborhood from the main street, someone waited.

Kallias closed his eyes and inhaled, discerning the many scents in this part of town. There was food from the café, car exhaust from the street, trash from the alleyways, and beyond all of that, a vampire.

He opened his eyes and watched the moving figure. He kept to the shadows as he inched toward the vampire, careful not to let his boots thud too heavily against the pavement.

He'd nearly reached the fence when his phone vibrated.

As hypersensitive to sound as any vampire, the one near the fence straightened at the sound, and she glanced at him with wide, brown eyes —before leaping over the fence and disappearing into the night.

With a frustrated growl, Kallias shoved his hand into his pocket. He pulled out the phone and answered it without even checking the caller ID.

"Erik, you have the worst timing," Kallias complained.

"Aww, I miss you, too," Erik quipped on the other side of the line.

Kallias sighed, "Shouldn't you be busy right now?"

The sound of a car buzzing past and the quiet giggle of a woman filled the line. "I am. Kind of," Erik said distractedly. "Have you killed Theron yet?"

"I'd be on my way home if I had," Kallias said. "Guess where I am?"

"*Not* on your way home?" Erik guessed.

In the background, Kallias heard a woman telling Erik goodbye and then the thud of the front door closing. Kallias rolled his eyes.

"I told you I'd help if you needed me," Erik said, after she left.

"What would be the point?" Kallias said. "If you'd come with me, you'd just be doing the same thing here you're doing there."

"What?" Erik asked.

"Sleeping around," Kallias said, "and being no help whatsoever."

"That's not fair," Erik whined. "I've helped before."

Kallias rolled his eyes—even though Erik couldn't see it.

"I have a talent," Erik told him. "Not everyone can mix work and pleasure." He let out a quick, playful laugh. "*You* sure as hell can't. I mean, how long *has* it been since you had sex?"

Kallias noticed movement in the trees. "Too long."

"So, what happened last night?" Erik asked. "I thought you had a lead."

"I did," Kallias said. He stepped back into the shadows so that whoever it was he'd seen between the trees wouldn't see him. He lowered his voice. "I did find Theron last night, actually. I even managed to injure him."

Erik was quiet for a moment. "So, why didn't you kill him?"

"He had other vampires helping him. They attacked me," Kallias said.

"What vampire in their right mind would want to help *Theron*?" Erik asked.

"A vampire who doesn't want to die, I assume," Kallias said. With a scoff, he added, "Of course, that didn't work out very well for them because they still died—just at my hands, instead of his. I'm not sure they fully appreciated the mercy of that."

"Why didn't you go after Theron afterward?" Erik asked curiously. "If he was injured, he would've been an easier target."

Kallias sighed, "I had to deal with a...distraction."

Erik laughed. "Distraction, huh? Was she hot?"

Kallias rolled his eyes. "Why do you assume the distraction was a she?"

"Am I wrong?" Erik asked expectantly.

"It wasn't like that," Kallias muttered. "I had to take her to the hospital."

"Damn, Kallias. You can't be that rough with humans," Erik said.

"Funny," Kallias said sarcastically. "Theron attacked her. She was unconscious and bleeding. I couldn't just leave her there."

"But you didn't answer my question," Erik complained. "Was she hot?"

"She's the most annoying human I've ever met," Kallias answered.

Erik laughed, "I knew it. You're attracted to her."

"I'm speaking English, right? Because that's *not* what I said," Kallias said.

"Is she blonde?" Erik asked, ignoring Kallias's objection. "Brunette?"

Kallias just rolled his eyes. "Neither."

"She's a redhead, then?" Erik continued. "Not *my* type, but..."

"Erik," Kallias interrupted. "I don't have time for this."

"Of course," Erik said. "I should let you get back to *not* killing Theron."

Kallias scowled. "Fuck you."

"No, thanks," Erik said.

"Bye."

Kallias hung up on his friend and slid the phone in his pocket. His eyes narrowed, when the woman emerged from the trees and started walking toward him.

"Is someone there?" the woman called.

Kallias stepped out of the shadows, and the tall, slender woman froze in shock. The flickering streetlight behind her cast an orange glow on her chin-length, brown hair. Her short, khaki skirt revealed long, tanned legs, and her green, sleeveless shirt seemed to draw his attention toward her hazel eyes.

Those large, hazel eyes dilated, as they lingered on him.

Like most humans, she was affected by the allure.

Unlike Rose Foster, Kallias thought.

He hadn't thought much about it the night before—because he'd been more concerned with how she'd resisted his telepathic control. But it came to mind now, and he wondered if the problems were related.

It was possible she just didn't experience attraction to men at all. He'd yet to see her around a female vampire, after all.

But sexual orientation only affected so much. It wouldn't have affected her response to his telepathic control.

No, that was something he'd *never* seen before.

"Wow," the human said, though Kallias suspected she hadn't meant to say it out loud. She stepped forward, joining him in the dark alley. "Why were you hiding back here?"

"I was hiding for your benefit, not mine," Kallias muttered. "I'm not in the best mood tonight."

"Oh," she said. "Maybe I could help?"

"I doubt it," Kallias said. He stepped toward her, causing her to stumble backward. "*Although*...I do have a question for you."

Her hazel eyes darted toward the fence. "Uh...okay."

He leaned in close. "Who told you to hide in those trees?"

She paled. "I—I just... I was supposed to watch for someone."

"Who?" Kallias asked. "Rose Foster?"

The woman gave a nervous nod. "He said there'd be someone else here. Was it you?"

"No," Kallias told her. "The other person ran. You should, too."

The woman offered him a smile. "Why would I do that?"

Kallias grasped her wrist and jerked her forward, until her body collided with his. With his hands tight around her arms, he leaned down and sniffed her neck. "Because I smell his scent in your blood," he growled. "You're bound to him."

Her heart raced. She pulled back, her eyes wide and frightened.

He took control of her mind. "Tell me who you are, why you're here, and anything you know about Theron."

The emotion faded from her hazel eyes. "My name is Lori."

"Yes, keep going," Kallias said impatiently.

"I met someone last night," she admitted. "He had blood all over him. He bit me. I was dying, and he forced me to drink his blood, said it would heal me. It did."

"Yes, what then?" Kallias prompted.

"It felt...*good*," the woman admitted.

Kallias rolled his eyes. "Skip ahead."

"He said I could feel what I felt last night *every* night," the human said, "as long as I did as he said. He told me to watch the café during the day and report back to him if I saw Rose Foster. He said another vampire would meet me here later."

Kallias nodded. The vampire by the fence had been the one he'd sent to meet her, then. "Is that all?"

"I know who you are," the woman said, blinking, as if she'd only just realized it. "You're Kallias." She pulled a dagger out of her small, green purse and held it up to show him. "I'm supposed to stab you."

Kallias glanced down at the dagger in her hand. "Yeah, you won't be doing that," he said, as he pulled the dagger from her grasp. He released her arm and stepped back.

He brushed past her, as he turned to leave.

The woman stumbled backward, rubbing her head as she regained control of her mind. "What did you do to me?" she mumbled. Her eyes widened. "Hey! Wait! You can't leave!"

"I assure you: I can," Kallias muttered.

The woman chased after him, nearly falling in her heels. When she caught up with him, she grasped the corner of his leather jacket and pulled him back toward her.

Kallias could've kept walking. No human was strong enough to pull *him* to a stop. But he didn't want to hurt the human, so he stopped and turned back toward her.

"I have to do what he told me to do," the woman tried to explain.

He shrugged. "That's *your* problem, sweetheart, not mine."

She stared at him, her eyes wide. "You're like him, aren't you?"

His eyes narrowed. "I am *nothing* like Theron."

She reached up toward his mouth, but he grasped her wrist before she could touch him. She pursed her lips. "Fangs," she said breathlessly. "Do you have fangs?"

Kallias released her wrist. He stepped toward her and growled with his fangs bared, causing her to fall backward. "Does *that* answer your question?"

The woman stared up at him, visibly trembling. She nodded and stuttered, "Y-y-yes." Somehow, she managed to pull herself to her feet, even as she continued to tremble in terror. "Would *you* do it? Would you bite me?"

"You humans are so stupid," Kallias snarled. "Do you want to *die*?"

The woman paled. "Umm, n-no?"

"See, that's how this ends," Kallias said. "You were lucky last night that Theron found a use for you, or you'd already be dead. But I can assure you that if you return to him, he'll eventually kill you." He felt no sympathy for the human, but he continued his warning anyway, "Maybe he'll grow tired of you. Maybe you'll get too old for him. Or more than likely, you'll just piss him off, and he'll end your life without a second thought. Theron doesn't care about you. He doesn't value your life. He's a monster, just like me, and you can *always* expect him to do what monsters do."

Her eyes were wide. "What?"

"They kill," he told her.

"Are you going to kill me?" she asked.

"I should," he said tiredly, "but I have a better idea."

The woman frowned. "What?"

"You drank his blood, which means you're bound to him," Kallias said. He leaned in close. "So, you're going to lead me to Theron."

She shook her head quickly. "I don't know where he is."

"No, but your body does," Kallias said. "Use your blood bond."

The woman swallowed. "I don't even know what that means."

Kallias grasped her chin and forced her to meet his gaze. He then took control of her mind. "Use the blood bond to lead me to Theron."

"Yes," the woman replied. "Follow me."

ROSE JUMPED, AS A CREAK OF THE DOOR INTERRUPTED THE SILENCE OF THE empty classroom. Her reading glasses fell crooked on her nose, as she glanced at the door. She sighed in relief when she saw a familiar, middle-aged woman in the doorway.

A few strands of ashy-blonde hair hung around the woman's narrow face, falling from the loose bun that held the rest of her long, blonde hair. She carried a pile of textbooks in her arms.

"Rose!" the woman said with a smile. "I should've known I'd find you here."

"Hi, Dr. Parker," Rose said, smiling back at her professor.

Rose straightened her glasses and returned her gaze to the computer screen in front of her, browsing articles from the school's database.

Dr. Parker crossed the room and dropped an armful of books on the desk with a loud crash. She leaned forward and sighed, as she rubbed her sore arms. "We missed you in class today."

Barely missing a beat in her typing, Rose pointed at the bandage on her head. "The hospital held me hostage."

Dr. Parker frowned at her nonchalant tone. "What happened?"

"Ah, nothing," Rose muttered. "Some psycho attacked me."

"What?" Dr. Parker sputtered. "Someone attacked you? Are you okay?"

Rose looked up from the computer screen. "Yeah, I'm fine."

Dr. Parker shook her head and laughed, "You're so strange sometimes."

"So I'm told," Rose agreed. "Did I miss anything important in class?"

Dr. Parker leaned her arms on the desk and waved her hand dismissively. "Nah. Don't worry. You're already months ahead of everyone else, anyway."

Rose nodded—and frowned at the demonology article in front of her.

The professor walked around the desk, raising an eyebrow at the article on the computer screen. "What are you working on?"

Rose turned to Dr. Parker. Should she tell her or not? Rose wasn't sure. "How much do you know about vampire mythology?"

Her interest officially piqued, the professor grabbed a chair and pulled it over to the desk, the metal legs scraping loudly across the floor. She sank into the chair and leaned forward, resting her elbows on the desk. "Not much," she admitted. "Are we talking modern mythology or medieval mythology?"

"Both," Rose answered, "and…earlier."

Dr. Parker frowned. "What do you mean by *earlier*?"

Rose pulled off her reading glasses so she could rub her temples tiredly. "Ancient Greece, for example," she told her. "How much do you know about the ancient versions of the vampire myth?"

The professor nodded, her brows furrowing as she considered the question. "I doubt I know any more than you do," she admitted. "I know Jewish folklore ascribed vampire-like qualities to the infamous Lilith. I also know that Ancient Greek mythology suggested that the demigoddesses Lamia and Empusa fed on the blood of humans."

Rose knew that, too, of course, but these scrolls weren't about goddesses. They were about a man—a cruel, monstrous man.

"They were said to be beautiful and seductive," Dr. Parker continued, "and if you're interested in later lore, I believe later Greeks believed in some sort of blood-drinking creatures."

Rose nodded, lost in thought.

Dr. Parker shrugged. "Besides that, I'm afraid my knowledge on the topic is limited."

"Beautiful and seductive," Rose mumbled.

"Can I ask again?" Dr. Parker said. "What *exactly* are you working on?"

Rose snapped out of her daze and glanced back at her teacher. She smiled shyly, as she met Dr. Parker's curious gaze. "It's a long story," she said slowly, "but the short version is that I'm trying to translate a set of scrolls. They're written in Greek, but dialect seems...ancient. And they describe a vampire-like creature."

The professor blinked at that. "Interesting."

"Yeah," Rose agreed. "The word *vampire* is never used, of course, but it didn't exist at the time. But the scrolls do refer to him as a monster, a blood-drinker, and a creature of darkness. So...vampire, right?"

"May I ask *how* you came to possess these scrolls?" Dr. Parker said.

"That part is even weirder," Rose said with a wince. "Someone gave them to me."

The professor raised an eyebrow. "Someone *gave* you ancient scrolls that could be worth an undetermined amount of money?"

"Like I said," Rose repeated, "it's weird."

"Did you know the person who gave them to you?" Dr. Parker asked.

Rose shook her head. "It was a total stranger."

Dr. Parker stared blankly at her. "That is *beyond* weird," she said, her eyes wide. "Do you have the scrolls with you?"

"Not at the moment," Rose said honestly.

Dr. Parker nodded. "My guess is that they're a forgery."

Rose nodded. She'd considered the same.

"Preserving ancient documents is no easy task," Dr. Parker told her. "If they were as old as they seem, I doubt they'd be legible—or that there'd be much left of them at all. If I could see them, maybe I could tell."

"I could bring them tomorrow, maybe," Rose offered.

The professor smiled. "You do that, then, and we'll go over them together. Maybe I can help you translate them, as well." She gave Rose's shoulder an affectionate pat. "The husband and kiddoes are waiting for me, so I need to get home. Try not to get attacked by a psycho again, okay?"

Rose laughed at that. "I'll try."

Dr. Parker headed toward the door. "Lock up for me, okay?"

"Of course," Rose said, returning her attention to the article.

She'd nearly given up on finding anything useful, when her phone rang.

Rose pulled the phone from her pocket and answered it. "Don't worry. I'm not walking. I was just about to call you," she laughed.

"Rose! You answered! Thank God!" Audrey squealed in her ear.

Rose winced and pulled the phone away from her ear. "Why wouldn't I answer? When have I *not* answered?"

"Are you okay?" Audrey asked. She sounded as if she were almost in tears.

Rose frowned at her friend's panicky tone. "I'm fine. What's wrong?"

"You need to leave! Now! Get out of that room!" Audrey cried.

"Okay," Rose said. She held the phone with her shoulder and began to shut down the computer. "But…I thought you told me *not* to leave the room."

"Yeah, well, I was wrong! Leave now!" Audrey shrieked.

"Okay," Rose said, her confusion growing. She pulled off her glasses and slipped them into her pocket. "I'm turning off the computer now. What's going on?"

"There's no time for this, Rose," Audrey said breathlessly.

Rose hesitated. "No time for what? What's wrong?"

"I remembered where I've seen that room before," Audrey told her.

"Oh," Rose said. She rolled her eyes, as the computer informed her that it'd be installing updates. "Where, then?"

Audrey's voice cracked with panic. "In my dream, Rose! That's where he'll kill you!"

Rose didn't have time to respond—because at that moment, her gaze darted toward the door, and she saw him.

Dressed in brown dress pants and a green sweater with a small, almost-unnoticeable, red stain on the collar, Theron stood, staring at her.

Was that blood?

Saying nothing to Audrey, Rose pressed the end button and dropped her hand to her side. She stared warily at the man who would kill her.

With that same, sickening smile he'd had the night before, Theron announced, "Found you."

Rose stood slowly and grasped the closest thing to her: a ballpoint pen. "If you come any closer, I'll scream."

Theron seemed to take that as a challenge. He approached her, slowly and predatorily, his dark eyes wild and manic. "Go ahead. Scream."

"That's not the response I was hoping for," Rose complained.

Theron chuckled, "No one will hear you. I made sure of that."

Rose frowned, her stomach twisting with worry. She glanced again at that red stain on his collar and then at the red stain that darkened his mouth. "Why are you here?"

"We were interrupted last night," Theron said, as he carefully avoided the desks. "I figured the least I could do was finish the job."

"Oh," Rose said with a nod. "Well, I appreciate the thought, but believe it or not, I'm actually okay with that job never being finished."

Theron rounded the computer desk. "I'm not."

Rose took another step backward, gasping, as her back hit the wall.

Theron shoved the computer chair aside and cornered her against the wall. His eyes darkened with hunger, as he neared her.

With no possibility of escape, Rose pressed her back against the wall, desperate to keep space between them. Her best option was to keep him talking. "Why do you want to kill me, anyway?"

Theron stepped closer, ignoring the way she cringed away from him. He raised a hand and touched her neck, feeling her rapid pulse beneath his finger. He leaned in and sniffed her neck, inhaling her enticing scent. "You smell delicious."

Anger and disgust boiled inside of her, and she barely resisted the urge to shove him or punch him—actions she knew would only succeed in hurting *her*. "That's all?" she said incredulously. "I smell good, so you decided to *kill* me?"

His hands skimmed her shirt, and she recoiled. "Essentially."

"In that case, maybe I should've skipped that shower," Rose muttered. He tried to touch her again, and she shoved his hands away. "Get your hands off of me, you—"

"Or what?" Theron interrupted. "What will you do, if I don't?"

Rose didn't have an answer. She only knew panic and revulsion were swirling inside of her, and she'd die before she let him touch her in a way she didn't want. "Something."

Theron gave her a condescending smile, as if he saw her as no more than an ant with a battle cry. "The truth is I didn't come here to kill you. I came for something *far* more valuable than you—something I was told *you* possess."

"Oh," Rose said, "so you're *not* going to kill me?"

"Of course I'm going to kill you," Theron said, rolling his eyes. "It's just not *why* I'm here."

"Right," Rose muttered.

He leaned closer to her and hissed, "Killing you is just a bonus."

Rose forced a smile. "Flattering."

Theron licked his bloodstained lips. "I need to taste you."

Rose frowned at that—and at the way he stared so hungrily at her neck. "Taste me? What are you going to do? Barbecue me?"

Theron scowled, as if *she* were the one talking nonsense. "No."

"Wait. Valuable?" Rose remembered. "Who told you *I* have anything valuable?" She scoffed, "I'm a college student. If I can afford coffee and Ramen noodles, I'm doing well for the week."

"I've had people watching you. I *know* what you have," Theron said.

"Stalking is illegal, you know," Rose said, "but then, so is murder, so..."

Theron traced a finger over the pulsing artery in her neck.

"Stop," Rose snarled, "touching me."

"No," Theron said, clearly unconcerned. "I had people watching you because *you* were looking for me. I wanted to know why. And when I realized what you had, I had to come."

"I don't have anything," Rose said. She tried to keep the tremor of panic from her voice, as she shoved his hand away. "And I was *not* looking for you! I don't even know you."

"Does the name Calista Petrakis ring any bells?" Theron asked.

"No," Rose said slowly. "Should it?"

"Short. Brunette. *Much* prettier than you," Theron taunted.

Rose rolled her eyes. "Trying to destroy my self-esteem before you kill me is a little excessive, don't you think?"

"She worked in a library you visited while you were in Greece," Theron continued. "You asked if she'd ever heard of any Greek stories or myths about a vampire with the name *Theron*."

Rose froze. She *did* remember. She just hadn't known her name. "What does that have to do with you?"

Theron gave her that condescending smirk of his. He gestured toward himself and said, "Theron." Then he flashed his fangs at her and said, "Vampire."

Rose's eyes widened at the sight of those sharp, inhuman teeth. "No. Those are fake. They have to be. They're…costume teeth. Right?"

Theron suddenly grasped her wrist and leaned forward. Before she even realized what was happening, one of his fangs sank so deeply into her finger that it hit bone.

When she cried out in pain, Theron pulled back. "Did it *feel* fake?"

Icy shock washed over her, as she watched the thin stream of blood slide down her finger. She glanced up at him, watching in horror, as he licked the blood from his razor-sharp fang—where his canine tooth should've been.

The realization left her disoriented. She felt as if everything she'd ever known about the world was wrong.

Her horror and disgust only increased as Theron placed her finger in his mouth and sucked the blood from it. She tried to snatch her hand away from him, but no amount of force could remove her hand from his grasp.

A strange wave of pleasure cascaded through her body, eating at Rose's awareness—disorienting her like some sort of hypnotism.

Thankfully, it didn't last long. It faded the moment he relaxed his grip and allowed her to pull free.

But he immediately fixed his ravenous gaze on her neck. "You taste," he breathed, "so powerful."

"What?" Rose mumbled.

He moved his mouth to her neck. "I need more."

Panicking, Rose ducked beneath his arm and tried to escape. She didn't even make it one step before he'd wrapped both arms around her and jerked her back against him.

He pushed her against the wall and ripped the collar of her shirt with enough force to send a button or two flying. Rose shoved his hands away, but he seemed unfazed by her fighting.

She realized she needed to stop fighting long enough to *think*.

As his fangs brushed her neck, she gasped out, "What do you want? The valuable item—what is it?"

Theron pulled back to glare at her. "You know."

"Oh, sure," Rose said sarcastically. "I'm just asking for no reason."

Theron growled. "Didn't I tell you that I don't like your attitude?"

"Didn't I tell *you* I don't like being murdered?" Rose countered. She gave him a sarcastic shrug. "I guess I'm just weird that way."

"It doesn't matter what I want," Theron told her. "You won't survive long enough to see me take it."

"What if I gave it to you?" Rose said. "Would you let me live?"

Theron's dark gaze roamed her body, and the cold lust in his eyes nauseated Rose. "No," he said with a cold laugh. "Now that I've tasted your blood, I couldn't possibly spare you. You taste too good to waste."

Her heart raced, and Rose knew when she saw the smile that curled at his lips that he *knew*. He knew he'd scared her. He knew he'd won. Still, she tried her best to hide it. "It was stupid of you to tell me that."

Rage flashed in Theron's dark brown eyes. "You're calling me stupid?"

"No," Rose said, ignoring his increasing fury, "I'm calling what you *did* stupid." She held his gaze boldly. "It's really simple. You see, if you hadn't told me you'd kill me either way, you could've used that as leverage—to make me give you the item you want so badly."

Rose held back a cry, when he grasped her face hard enough to bruise her. She could put on a brave face in the face of a monster, but hiding her body's natural response to pain was a bit harder.

His fingernails dug into her skin. "Do you know what I think is stupid?" Theron snarled. He leaned in close, blood on his breath. "Insulting the person who means to kill you. I can make your death *very* painful. Is that what you want?"

Rose desperately tried to pry his fingers from her skin. It felt as if he might crush her jaw with just his hand. The pain brought tears to her eyes, tears she *tried* to hold in.

Having proven his point, he released her with an arrogant smirk.

She touched her bruised jaw. "It wasn't so much an insult as it was advice."

Again, he moved closer, ignoring the way she cringed away. "Now that I've tasted your blood, my body knows your scent. I'll be able to track your scent anywhere—to places you frequent, to people you're close to." She gasped as he wrapped his hand around her throat. He snarled in her ear, "Maybe I'll kill everyone you care about—the girl you live with, that boy who works with you. If you want to save them, you can hand over the item. How's *that* for leverage?"

The panic coursed through her with even more strength than before. "Let me go," she pleaded.

Theron smiled and removed his hand. "I'm listening."

She coughed, struggling to pull breath back into her lungs. "I still don't know what you want."

"Fine," Theron said. His gaze narrowed on her neck, and he licked his lips. "I'll find it myself."

But before he could lower his head toward her neck, Rose gripped the pen in her hand and shoved it into his eye.

He screamed and stumbled backward, blood spewing from his eye, and Rose seized her one chance to escape. She bolted toward the door, knocking over desks and chairs in her clumsy rush.

She scrambled to a stop, as she found him in the doorway already, blocking her escape. Blood coated his face, still gushing from his eye, but he stood in front of her as if she'd only scratched him.

She could see—from the paleness of his skin and the way he gasped for breath—that the injury caused him pain, but apparently, it took more than that to slow him down.

"You'll pay for that," he growled.

His voice sounded more like that of a beast than a person. He caught her in his grasp, twisting her wrists painfully, and he shoved her against the wall. She fought with every bit of strength inside her, but she couldn't stop him from pressing his fangs against her neck.

Suddenly, Rose felt his body ripped away from hers, and she heard a series of crashes throughout the room as desks and chairs scattered across the floor.

She glanced across the room, her brows furrowing at the sight of Theron crumpled against the opposite wall.

"Not *you* again," said a lightly accented voice beside her.

Rose spun toward him, her relief shifting to annoyance, as she realized who stood beside her. "Oh, sure, get irritated at me," she said sarcastically, "because I totally asked to be stalked and murdered by that psycho."

Kallias stood just inside the room. He tilted his head to the side, his long, brown hair brushing the collar of his black, leather jacket, and the annoyance and impatience was evident in his narrowed, brown eyes.

Behind him, Rose saw Theron returning to his feet. When he charged at Kallias, she warned, "He's behind you!"

Kallias spun on his heels and stepped aside just before Theron would've reached him. He caught Theron by the shoulder and tossed him across the room again. Rose frowned, puzzled by how easily he'd just thrown a grown man.

Kallias grimaced at the blood oozing from Theron's eye. "What the hell happened to you?"

Theron turned his murderous glare back toward Rose.

Kallias glanced at her, raising an eyebrow. "Impressive."

Rose blinked in surprise. "Did you just compliment me?"

"Don't read too much into it," Kallias said. "I still find you frustrating."

Rose smiled. "And I still think you're a jerk."

She pointed behind him, when she saw Theron on his feet again, but before she could *voice* a warning, Kallias had already spun around and grabbed Theron. Her confusion grew, when he threw Theron across the room again, as if he were simply tossing a tiny doll.

Theron groaned in pain and crawled unsteadily to his feet. When he finally managed to stand, he glared murderously at Kallias. "Why do you keep *interrupting*?" he growled. "You shouldn't even be here."

"You shouldn't have sent your girlfriend to me, then," Kallias said.

Theron frowned for a moment and then shot a glare toward the door.

"I appreciate the gesture, but she's not really my type," Kallias continued to taunt. He pulled out the dagger and held it up for Theron to see. "The dagger was a nice gift, though."

"It wasn't meant to be a gift," Theron snarled. "It was meant to be *painful*."

"I'm aware," Kallias assured him. He smiled. "By the way, she seemed awfully interested in me, considering what you wanted was for her to stab me. Are you sure you're pleasing your women well enough?"

His taunts succeeded in enraging Theron, which had been his intent, of course, and Theron immediately charged at Kallias.

As Theron neared him, Kallias stepped to the side again, causing Theron to slam into the brick wall at a supernatural speed.

Kallias approached him, but he stopped just out of reach. "You're *so* easy to manipulate," he laughed. "All I have to do to turn you into a mindless idiot is piss you off. One, little taunt, and you charge into walls, like a bull."

The sound Theron made, at that moment, was the *least* human sound Rose had ever heard. It was a beastly snarl—the kind of sound that sends chills down your spine.

At a speed no human could follow, he raced across the room and shoved Kallias into the wall behind them.

Rose blinked. She'd missed it. She'd been looking right at them, but she'd missed the movement. How was that possible?

When she heard the crash, she turned to look at them.

How had they gotten there?

Theron held Kallias against the wall, and for a moment, Kallias seemed unable to escape his grasp. But then, he swept his leg under Theron's feet, knocking him flat on his back.

He stepped away from the wall, and his eyes narrowed, when they landed on Rose. "Why are you still standing there like an idiot?" he snarled. "Run!"

"Oh, right. Of course it's idiocy," Rose scoffed. "It couldn't possibly be that I just refuse to leave you here."

Kallias frowned at that. "You think I need *your* help?"

115

Rose scowled. "That's not—"

But before she could finish her sentence, Rose saw the flash of a blade behind Kallias. "Watch out!" she shouted.

Kallias turned slightly, just in time to catch Theron's wrist before the blade reached his neck. He twisted Theron's wrist, and Theron fell to his knees, groaning in pain.

Kallias twisted Theron's wrist to its breaking point. "Drop the weapon."

Desperate for relief from the pain, Theron opened his hand, allowing the weapon to fall. The metal blade clanged against the tile.

Theron glared at Kallias, snarling a string of Greek curse words under his breath, as his wrist ached. Kallias released his wrist, and Theron scrambled several steps backward to put space between them.

Glancing from Theron to Kallias—to make sure neither of them were paying attention—Rose used her foot to drag the dagger behind her. She quickly knelt and picked up the weapon. She hid it behind her back, watching the men warily.

Kallias's gaze darted toward her, but he gave no other indication of noticing what she'd done. The moment he looked away, Theron attacked him, but Kallias caught him and shoved him back.

Theron growled and attempted to punch him, but Kallias blocked the blow with his forearm. This provoked an onslaught of attacks from Theron, all of which Kallias skillfully blocked.

Rose managed to make out a few punches and kicks, but as their speed increased, the fighting soon became a blur. She watched the blur of movement in stunned confusion, trying to make sense of what she was seeing.

She blinked several times. "What the heck?"

The fighting ended with a thunderous crash, as Theron landed against the farthest wall with enough force to shake the room.

Rose stared at Theron in shock, as he slumped against the wall and wiped the blood from his face with the back of his hand. His eye had stopped bleeding and appeared to be healing.

"I told you to run," Kallias said, his voice much too close.

Rose gasped and spun around, stunned to find him right behind her.

He seemed mostly unscathed from the fight—with the exception of the blood that trickled from his bottom lip. "How did you…" she trailed off in confusion, as she glanced back and forth between the man standing next to her and the injured vampire across the room.

"Do you have a death wish or something?" Kallias snarled.

"According to my therapist, yes," Rose muttered. She shook away the confusion, deciding to blame what she'd just seen on the concussion. "I won't leave you with him. He's dangerous."

With no warning whatsoever, Kallias shoved her into the wall. She gasped, and her bright, blue eyes darted toward her left hand, which held the dagger. He'd been careful to pin it safely beside her head, proving that he *had* noticed her take it.

His face was so close enough that she could smell the mint on his breath, and his eerily-attractive face suddenly looked terrifyingly furious.

Kallias smelled the adrenaline in her blood, and the scent only intensified his predatory hunger. He could feel every inch of her soft body pressed up against his, as he held her against the wall.

It took an unbelievable amount of self-control to resist the urge to sink his fangs into her neck.

He sounded breathless, as he growled, "In case you haven't noticed, I am dangerous, as well. So, when I tell you to run, you run."

"Fine," Rose snarled. She might've been depressed and a little self-destructive—okay, a *lot* self-destructive—but even *she* had limits.

"Good," Kallias said, and he pushed himself away from her.

Rose truly had every intention on running, but before she reached the door, she saw Theron grab Kallias from behind and press a long, sharp blade against Kallias's throat.

Was that a *sword*?

It was just a short sword, but still…

"Where the hell did you have *that* hidden?" Kallias asked.

As always, Rose's concern overrode her reason. "Don't hurt him!"

Theron glanced at her, a sinister smile curling at his lips. He pressed the blade closer to Kallias's neck and said, "I think you have an admirer."

Rose rolled her eyes. "I am not, nor will I ever be, his *admirer*."

Kallias stared blankly at her. "What do I have to do to get you to run?"

"You do realize he has a knife on your throat, right?" Rose said.

"It's a sword, smartass," Kallias informed her. "Knives are *much* shorter."

"Oh, congratulations, you know more about weapons than I do. Shucks, I was *so* hoping to win that award," Rose said sarcastically.

It did sound like a cool award, though, now that she thought about it.

Frustrated that neither of them were paying attention to him, even though he was the one with a sword, Theron glared at them. "Do you want me to leave the room so you can just have sex and get it over with?"

"Eww," Rose said.

Kallias raised his eyebrows in disbelief. "Eww?"

"Hello? Remember me? The one who's going to *kill* you?" Theron said. He pressed the sword into Kallias's skin until it drew a thin line of blood.

Rose gasped, when she saw the blood. "No! Leave him alone!"

"I don't need your help. I need you to run," Kallias reminded her.

"I wouldn't listen to him, if I were you," Theron warned. "If you take one step toward that door, I'll decapitate him without a second thought."

"I won't," Rose assured him. "Just don't hurt him."

"Good," Theron said. He leaned in and sneered in Kallias's ear, "I find it interesting that a human would risk her life for someone she doesn't know."

"Not interesting," Kallias said, glaring at her. "*Foolish*."

Rose shot an annoyed glare at Kallias, before returning her gaze to Theron. "He risked his life for me. Why does it surprise you that I'd do the same?"

Theron offered her a taunting smile. "If you only knew."

"If I only knew *what*?" Rose said irritably.

"I think, if you knew what Kallias really was, you'd *want* me to kill him," Theron said. To Kallias, he sneered, "What do you think? Should I tell her?"

"I don't give a shit what you tell her," Kallias snarled. "Either kill me, or get the damn sword off of my throat. I'm sick of your psychotic games."

"I don't care what he is or what he's done," Rose said, earning a surprised look from *both* of them. "It's not my place to decide if he deserves to live or die."

Kallias frowned, both shocked and confused by her answer.

With a sigh of disappointment, Theron tapped the blade against Kallias's throat—the way a normal person might tap a pen on their notebook when they're thinking. "*Should* I let him go, though? He's interfered a few too many times. I think I should just kill him, after all."

"I said I won't run," Rose reminded him. "Don't hurt him."

Kallias's gaze darted toward her left arm, just as she tightened her grip around the dagger's handle. Since he had no other option, he used his telepathic abilities.

"*Keep the dagger hidden,*" Rose suddenly heard his deep, accented voice say, the sound resonating deep inside her head.

She froze, startled and confused. She glanced his way. "Did you just say something?"

Theron frowned. "What are you talking about? No one said anything."

Rose glanced back and forth at them, noting the bewildered look on Theron's face and the glare Kallias shot her way. "But I heard him," she mumbled.

"She did hit her head pretty hard last night," Kallias commented.

She scowled at that. "I'm not hallucinating! I know what you—"

"Shut up!" Kallias said, suddenly.

They both frowned at him. "What's going on?" Theron asked Kallias.

Rose opened her mouth to demand an answer, but when her gaze dropped toward the floor, she stopped. Theron stood behind Kallias with his legs positioned a comfortable distance apart. At least a foot separated his brown loafers, and Kallias's large, black boots filled that space.

She watched as Kallias carefully inched his left foot toward Theron's foot, seeming to feel for the distance between them. Rose returned her gaze to his face, and she froze as she found his warm, brown eyes studying her.

Rose mouthed the word *left* to Kallias, and she noticed his lips tug upward in response. With a speed she could barely see, he quickly shifted his foot to the left and hooked it behind Theron's ankle.

He simultaneously grasped Theron's arm with his hand to prevent the blade from slicing through his neck.

In a swift, fluid motion that looked like a blur to Rose, Kallias swept Theron off his feet and took the sword. As Theron fell backward, Kallias flipped the sword and pointed it at the vampire.

Theron swallowed and began to back away from him, but Kallias pursued him slowly.

"Retreat is cowardly," Kallias said.

Theron eyed the sword warily. "I'm a vampire. We're not exactly known for being virtuous." As his back collided with the wall, he began to slowly circle the room back toward Kallias, rather than allowing himself to be cornered. Kallias mimicked the action, stepping sideways to keep Theron in his line of sight. Theron smiled and added, "Frankly, Kallias, I think you place too much importance on the foolish virtue. Courage has always been your downfall."

The way the two men circled the room reminded Rose of the way predators might circle their prey in the wild.

She frowned at the natural way in which Kallias held the sword, almost as if he'd been formally trained to wield it.

"How so?" Kallias asked.

"Well, it was courage that landed you in my hands," Theron said. "If you had just ignored that scream like any other human would've, you could have gone on living your boring, human life, blissfully ignorant of Phoebe's nightly activities, but you couldn't do that, could you?" He laughed. "And now, here you are, repeating history. Mark my words, Kallias. Courage will be the death of you. *Again*."

"You're a disgrace to your kind. You always have been," Kallias said.

"Do you know what I think is a disgrace?" Theron said, as he stepped over an overturned desk. Without waiting for an answer, he continued, "A vampire desperately clinging to his last shred of humanity thousands of years after that humanity died. You haven't heard of any vampires like that, have you, Kallias?"

Kallias's jaw tightened, and he glanced back at the human, frustrated that she still hadn't run. "Why are you hunting the woman, Theron?"

"Why do you keep asking? Why do you even care?" Theron countered. "If I want her, I'll have her. You can't stop me. I'm stronger than you are."

Kallias smiled. "Stronger, maybe, but your combat skills are laughable."

"I don't need combat skills to kill you," Theron said.

"You know, I actually have no idea who you were before you were turned," Kallias said suddenly. A taunting smirk curved at his lips. "But I guess you must've been pretty lowborn to have not been trained in combat."

Theron froze. "Lowborn?" His lip curled in disgust, and his eyes narrowed. "You know nothing! I was a Macedonian prince when I was human!"

"Ah, that explains it," Kallias said. "Pampered and spoiled."

"As if *you* have room to talk," Theron scoffed. "I know who your father was. You weren't lowborn either. Of course, I also know how much of a disappointment you were to him. You weren't good at pleasing *anyone*, were you?"

Kallias ignored Theron's attempt to provoke him. "Macedonia, huh?" he said with a mocking smile. "That explains a lot, actually. You know, I heard the Macedonians were incestuous. Is that why you're so insane, Theron? Were Mommy and Daddy really brother and sister?"

A guttural growl resounded from Theron's throat. He raced toward Kallias so rapidly that his movement blurred, but just as Theron reached him, Kallias twisted and shoved the sword into Theron's stomach. A strangled sound escaped his lips, as the sword impaled him. Kallias jerked the sword out of his stomach, and Theron fell to his knees. He clutched at the gaping wound, blood pouring through his fingers, soaking into his sweater.

"You should really work on that anger," Kallias said.

With another growl, Theron sank his fangs into Kallias's leg, ripping the jeans and jerking out a chunk of flesh and muscle.

The bite caused enough pain to knock Kallias off of his feet. He fell to the floor, cursing under his breath.

Theron spit out a mouthful of bloodied clothing and flesh on the floor, and then his feral eyes shifted toward Rose, darkening with hunger.

"Oh my goodness," Rose whispered in shock. "Kallias! Are you okay?"

Kallias glanced at Theron, and he panicked, as he realized Theron's attention was on Rose. "Run! Now!" he shouted, but it was too late.

Rose never even saw him move. One moment, she'd seen Theron kneeling in a pool of his own blood in the middle of the room, and the next moment, she felt his hands grasp her arms and shove her against the wall. His heavy, blood-soaked body practically fell onto her, and his two, abnormally sharp teeth sank into her neck.

Rose cried out as the fangs tore roughly through her skin, and acting mostly on instinct, she shoved the dagger into his left side.

Theron pulled away from her neck and glared at the dagger stuck in his hip.

In shock, Rose stared at the blackish burgundy blood that coated his face and flowed down his chin and neck, realizing...it was *her* blood.

Theron's own blood drenched his sweater, still flowing from the sword wound. His eyes were dark and manic, and he looked more feral and terrifying than she'd ever seen him before.

Theron jerked the dagger from his side and tossed it aside.

"You stabbed me," Theron said, as if he couldn't believe it.

"Well, you *bit* me!" Rose said defensively. She covered her neck with her hand, and her eyes widened, as she felt the warm blood.

"And I'm going to do it again," Theron growled.

He froze, as a sharp blade suddenly slid in front of his neck.

Rose leaned back in shock, blinking at the blood-coated blade and then at Kallias who stood behind Theron, leaning heavily on his unin-jured leg. He wrapped one arm around Theron, restraining him, as he pressed the sword to Theron's throat. Rose frowned, as she realized that

that Kallias's eyes seemed darker now, dilated too much for the fluorescent lighting of the room.

"Please, Rose," Kallias said, shocking her, "I need you to leave."

Rose wanted to argue. She wanted to tell him that she couldn't just leave him, that it'd be wrong, but there was something about the weak desperation in his voice—she couldn't argue with it.

She nodded and ran from the classroom.

Rose froze, as she found a beautiful, brunette woman standing in front of the hall door, blocking the only way out of the building.

Rose frowned at the woman. "Who are you, and why are you standing in front of the door?"

The woman stared at her. "You have red hair."

Rose blinked and then nodded slowly. "Congratulations. You're not colorblind. Now, can we go?" she asked, pointing at the door.

The woman continued, "You have blue eyes, fair skin…"

Rose stared blankly at the woman. "Correct," she muttered. "Seriously, now that we've established that you have great eyesight, can you please move?"

"You're Rose Foster," the woman said.

Rose raised an eyebrow. "Okay. Now, I'm impressed."

"You're the one he wants," the woman stated.

The woman slid her hand into her green purse and pulled out a handgun. With shaky hands, she pointed the gun at Rose and curled her finger around the trigger.

5

DEATH AND BAD GUYS

*K*allias slammed Theron into the wall. He pressed his forearm to Theron's chest to hold him still and pressed the blade against his throat.

"I could overpower you," Theron said.

"And I could let this blade slide through your neck the moment I see even one muscle twitch," Kallias countered. "So, I'd suggest you hold *very* still, and answer my questions. Unless, of course, you'd prefer death?"

"Fine," Theron said between clenched teeth.

"I want to know," Kallias said, "why you're hunting the woman."

"You seem awfully concerned with that question," Theron remarked.

"Well, your refusal to answer it makes me suspicious," Kallias said.

"It's a matter of pride," Theron said. "I can't let a *human* escape me."

Kallias shook his head. "You're lying. There's more to it than that."

"Is there?" Theron taunted. "And how would you know?"

"I'm asking the questions, not you," Kallias said. Growing impatient, he took control of Theron's mind and commanded, "Tell me the truth."

A blankness came into Theron's dark eyes, as the telepathic control took effect. "She has something I want."

"And that something *is*?" Kallias prompted.

Theron opened his mouth to answer. "The Sto—"

A distant voice captured Kallias's attention. It was the woman Theron had sent to stab Kallias—the woman he'd *also* sent to watch Rose during the day.

Without waiting for Theron to finish his answer, Kallias rushed out of the room to stop the human before she did something stupid.

Kallias found Rose and the woman in the hallway. He snatched the gun from the woman's hand before she could pull the trigger.

He emptied it of bullets before he returned it. With a murderous glare, he said, "Did you not understand what I told you earlier?"

The woman looked terrified. "I just… I just wanted to—"

"To kill someone?" he interrupted.

While Kallias handled the strange, gun-toting lady, Rose found herself face-to-face with Theron yet again.

She gaped at the blood that soaked his sweater, wondering how he was even able to stand, much less move so fast she couldn't even *see* the movement.

Before she could react, he grasped her shirt and jerked her forward. She held back a cry when his fangs tore into her neck.

The pain was as intense as it was the first time, but she preferred the pain over the strange, disorienting sensation that came afterward.

Before the pain could subside, she kneed him in the groin.

Theron released her with a curse. He staggered, nearly falling to his knees, and he snarled every Greek insult she'd ever heard—and a few she hadn't.

Rose cupped her fingers over the bite wound, but the bleeding had already slowed. How was that possible?

She lifted her eyebrows, when Theron let out another pained groan. "Well," she said, her tone surprisingly optimistic, "it's nice to know *that* still works on…whatever you are."

She heard a laugh, and she looked up to find Kallias watching her, amusement glittering in his light brown eyes.

She glanced down at the gun-lady, who lay motionless at his feet. "What did you do to her?" she said worriedly.

"Don't worry about it," Kallias told her. He opened the door the woman had been guarding and gestured impatiently. "She's fine. Just go."

Rose cast another concerned glance at the woman—and only breathed a sigh of relief after she saw the rise and fall of her chest. She still wanted to know what he'd done to the woman, but at least he hadn't killed her.

"Now," Kallias snapped. His amusement was gone now.

She narrowed her eyes at his tone—but left anyway.

KALLIAS APPROACHED THERON FROM BEHIND.

Theron stiffened. He tried to climb back to his feet, but before he could, Kallias shoved a dagger into his back.

Theron collapsed again, growling at the pain. Kallias jerked the blade upward, slicing through his torso, as well—an action that would've killed a human.

Unfortunately, Theron hadn't been human in a *very* long time.

Theron fell back, choking on his own blood. Thick, crimson blood flowed from his body, pooling on the white, tile floor beneath him.

"You'd think you'd see that coming every now and then," Kallias muttered.

Theron tried to speak but couldn't—blood still gurgling in his throat.

Kallias quickly returned to the unconscious human. He picked her up, cradling her small body in his arms. He shouldered the door open and hurried down the hall. The hall opened into a foyer before he reached the exit, and he froze in the doorway, as he caught sight of Rose, kneeling in the floor of the small room.

"Damn it. Can you not follow a simple..." Kallias trailed off, when he noticed the middle-aged, blonde human lying in the floor, next to her. He watched, as Rose pressed trembling fingers to the woman's wrist to check her nonexistent pulse.

He noticed the quiver of Rose's lips.

"Shit," Kallias breathed. "You knew her."

Rose didn't hear him. She didn't even notice him standing there—when she started to cry.

Kallias stepped back into the hall and lay the unconscious human across a side table, sweeping aside a vase of fake flowers as he did so.

He leaned over the woman and focused his attention on breaking into her mind. "Wake up."

Her hazel eyes fluttered open. The woman gasped the moment she saw him, and she began to flail.

Kallias grasped her wrists to hold her still, and her heart raced even faster. "Calm down," he demanded. "I'm not going to hurt you."

"Please," the human sobbed, "let me go back to Theron."

This woman was even worse off than Phoebe had been. At least Phoebe had been *somewhat* aware of what Theron's blood was doing to her.

"I should," Kallias said with a cynical glare, "but then, he'd drain every drop of blood from your body in order to heal himself." His eyes narrowed. "It's not that I care about *you*. I just don't want him to heal too quickly. So, you should count yourself lucky."

"Then, just let me go," the woman pleaded.

"Look at me," Kallias said, and his voice echoed deep in the woman's head. The emotion dulled from her eyes. As soon as he had control of her mind again, he commanded, "Forget what happened here. Forget you met Theron, and forget he bit you. Forget about Rose Foster. And most importantly, forget you ever knew about the existence of vampires. Leave, and find somewhere safe to stay for a few weeks—somewhere out of town. Do you understand?"

The thin, brunette woman stared blankly at him, as if she were in a trance. "Yes," she confirmed.

"Good," Kallias said. He stepped away from the human. "Now, run."

The woman scrambled from the table and fled from the building as quickly as her feet would take her.

Rose looked up, frowning as she watched the previously unconscious woman flee the building, as if she were being chased. Thinking that perhaps she *was* being chased, Rose peered into the hallway.

She blinked, as she found Kallias there, watching her.

"Call 911," Rose gasped out. She wiped angrily at the tears beneath her eyes. "Please!"

"Why would I do that?" Kallias asked.

She stared in disbelief. "I dropped my phone back there. Please, you have to call!"

Kallias pushed away from the doorway. "It's too late for that."

"We have to help her," Rose pleaded. "She's— She's—"

"Dead," Kallias finished. "*Dead* is the word you're looking for."

Rose glared at him. "Don't say that! You don't know that!"

"I do, actually," Kallias corrected. "And so do you. She's not breathing. Her heart isn't beating. Her skin's cold, ashen… Her eyes are—"

"Yeah, I know what a dead body looks like," Rose muttered.

Kallias couldn't shut out her thoughts fast enough. An image flashed through his mind—through *her* mind, but he saw it as a clear as she did: a long-dead corpse lying in the middle of a dirty living room floor.

He turned away, taking deep breaths as he tried to disconnect his own mind from hers. "Then, you know she's dead," he said slowly, "and there's nothing you can do for her."

Rose looked at the woman, her eyes blank. "I have to do something."

"Like what?" he snarled, suddenly. He took a step toward her, his eyes narrowed. "What do you want? To wait until she feels stiff? Until her corpse stinks? By then, you'll be as dead as she is!"

Rose just stared, stunned by his cruel tone. "What's wrong with you?"

"Me?" he said, stepping toward her. "What's wrong with *you*? I'm trying to save your life! *Again*, might I add. But you insist on making it difficult!"

"I never asked for your help," she said quietly.

Kallias stiffened as he heard movement somewhere behind him. He turned and glanced down the hallway—and then, he turned back to Rose, who continued to shake her lifeless teacher in desperation. "Damn it, I am *not* watching you die."

Rose gasped as he grabbed her arm and jerked her to her feet. With her emotions still reeling, she snapped at him, "Let me go!"

He dragged her toward the door by the arm. "You'll thank me later."

She continued to fight, though it didn't seem to bother him. "No, I won't," she said, kicking. "I'll hate you! I *do* hate you!"

He pulled her roughly along the breezeway. "That's fine with me."

She struggled more. "Let...me...*go!*"

Kallias ignored her. He dragged her by the arm—with her fighting the whole way. By the time they reached the next building, he'd lost his patience. He shoved her into the grey, stone wall of the college building, and she gasped at the sudden impact.

"Do you *want* to die?" Kallias said, pinning her wrists to the stone. He leaned in close, his eyes dark with a mixture of anger and hunger. "If you do, just tell me so I can stop wasting my time. I'll even kill you myself. Just say the word."

Rose swallowed at the threat. Those terrifyingly furious eyes seared her. Before she could respond, she heard the history building's doors swing open, and she glanced down the breezeway—in the direction they'd just come.

She gasped, as she saw Theron leaning wearily against the wall, drenched in blood and ripped open from stomach to chest.

Theron eyed her with a crazed, feral hunger, his fangs flashing in the moonlight.

"How is he even walking?" Rose muttered.

"*Skata*," Kallias cursed. He glared at her. "We're running. Now."

Rose didn't argue this time. Reality had finally caught up with her shock and grief, and though her emotions still whirled within her, she let him take her hand, and together, they ran.

They ran across the dark campus, toward the main street, and then, they kept running, street after street, through the city.

Rose's lungs ached and burned, reminding her of one of the *many* reasons she preferred the library to a jogging track.

She couldn't even see in front of her anymore. Everything blurred around her, as if they were moving too fast for her brain to process the images. Since she couldn't see, she had no choice but to let Kallias pull her in whichever direction he chose.

She wondered, as they ran, how he always seemed to know when to turn. It was almost as if his eyesight processed the images quicker than hers did.

They'd just turned onto a well-lit street, when Rose's shoestrings got caught beneath her shoe.

She fell flat on her face, her lips smashing painfully against the pavement. She pressed down on her hands, pushing herself up.

Kallias knelt beside her and helped her to her knees. He pushed her messy, auburn waves out of her face. "Are you okay?"

Rose wiped the blood from her lips with the back of her hand.

Kallias paled, as the sight of her blood and the scent of it hit him, all at once. He cursed and jumped to his feet, distancing himself from her as quickly as possible. He took deep breaths, fighting to regain control of the burning hunger inside of him.

Rose looked up at him, confusion creasing her brows.

"Do you have to bleed every time you're around me?" Kallias snapped.

Rose blinked in shock. "Oh, I'm sorry," she scoffed. "Next time, I'll just tell my blood not to come out—since I have *so* much control over that."

Kallias looked away, unable to bear the sight of the blood.

Rose eyed him suspiciously. "Why does my bleeding bother you anyway?"

Kallias walked away, putting as much distance between them as possible. Even several feet away from her, the scent of her blood still enticed his senses—more sweet and powerful than any human blood should be.

He faced away from her, staring into the dark alley they'd just run through. He feared he'd lose control, if he saw her blood again. "Theron can smell fresh blood from miles away. With you bleeding, protecting you will be even harder than it was before."

"Oh." Rose seemed to accept that answer. She climbed clumsily to her feet, wincing, as her hands, knees, and lips burned from the fall. She scowled at Kallias's back. "Why are you standing all the way over there?"

"I'm watching for Theron," Kallias said, irritated that she was asking questions—questions she *shouldn't* ask. He spun around and narrowed his eyes at her. "Why were you out alone again, anyway?"

"Not that it's any of your business," she muttered irritably, "but I was studying."

"Studying?" he repeated. He gave her an incredulous scowl. "Who *studies* after being released from the hospital? After an attack on her *life*?" He shook his head in disbelief. "And that still doesn't explain why you were alone at night."

"My mistake! I thought it was the twenty-first century," Rose said. She placed her hand on her chest, pretending to be appalled. "How *dare* I leave my home without a male escort? Next thing you know, I'll start thinking for myself."

Kallias rolled his eyes. "How did I get myself into this?"

Rose winced, as her palms burned from the bite of the pavement. She spread her hands in front of her to look at them, but the cold, night air only seemed to make the raw, peeled skin hurt worse.

As they stood there quietly, Rose found herself fighting back tears again. "I can't believe I left her there," she said, mostly to herself.

"It's all you could do," Kallias muttered, "if you wanted to survive the night."

"She's my teacher," Rose said, pleading pain in her voice.

Kallias spun on his heels to face her, noticing with relief that her lip had stopped bleeding. "Correction: She *was* your teacher. Now, she's dead."

Rose glared at him. "How can you be so heartless?"

Kallias felt his hunger ignite again when Rose's cheeks flushed pink with anger, and he quickly looked away, choosing to focus, instead, on a closed thrift shop. "I'm not heartless," he said under his breath. Truthfully, he often wished he were heartless. It would've saved him a lot of frustration and suffering. "I'm just realistic. People die. The sooner you accept that, the better."

"She was a good person," Rose tried to explain.

"And good people die," Kallias said. He turned to look at her, his gaze dark and intense. "This isn't one of your fairy tales where the bad guys die and the good guys live happily ever after. This is real life. And in real life, it's the good guys that die and the bad guys that are immortal."

A soft, disbelieving breath escaped her lips. "*My* fairy tales?" she repeated. Her words sounded quiet and measured, as if there were *so* many emotions brimming just beneath the surface. "What makes you think I *ever* believed in fairy tales?"

It happened again.

His breath caught, as her thoughts flooded his mind. He blinked and looked away, stunned by the horrifying memories. "You're right. I shouldn't have assumed..." he trailed off. "I'm an asshole. I'm sorry."

She raised an eyebrow at the sudden shift in behavior. She nearly laughed at how uncomfortable he looked. "You don't apologize much, do you?"

His lips lifted into a small smile. "No, I don't."

Rose watched, as he returned to scanning the street for any sign of Theron—or anyone who might've been helping him. "So...she's dead," Rose admitted to herself, her voice catching. "We still need to call the police."

Kallias shook his head. "You underestimate Theron's speed. By the time human police reach the college, Theron will have already disposed of the body."

"Disposed?" she repeated. "What do you mean by that?"

Kallias turned to her. "I *mean*...if I were you, I wouldn't expect an open casket funeral," he said bluntly, "that is, if she ever has one at all."

Rose stared at him in disbelief. "Are you always like this?"

"Yes," he said easily.

She crossed her arms and nodded bitterly. For a while, she just glared, as he continued to watch for Theron. "Do you know what I can't seem to make sense of?" she asked.

Kallias looked at her curiously, wordlessly urging her to continue.

"If you're so cold and heartless, why would you save my life?" she asked. "If you *really* don't care for others, why would you care whether I lived or died?"

He sighed, "I'm not cold. I'm just...callous."

"Why?" Rose asked curiously. "What made you so callous?"

He watched her for a moment, as if he couldn't decide how to answer the question. Then, in just four long strides, he closed the distance between them.

Rose let her arms fall to her sides, as he moved so close that their bodies nearly touched. She gasped, as his large, rough hand closed around hers.

He stared at Rose's hand for a while. Her skin felt so soft against his.

Then, finding what he was looking for, Kallias traced his finger over a rough spot on her finger—a spot calloused from writing. He looked at her. "When something endures injury, stress, or wear for too long, it hardens itself for its own protection. It's natural."

Rose glanced down at his hand and swallowed. His feverish touch caused her skin to tingle and burn, and she blushed as she saw chill bumps rising on her skin. Almost as soon as she noticed it, he let go of her hand. She watched as he stepped back awkwardly, putting an appropriate distance between them.

Her chest tightened with sympathy, as she wondered what had happened to him to make him harden his heart. She might've asked, if she thought he'd answer. "*Or,*" she said softly, biting her lip, "it can heal."

"Some wounds never heal," Kallias said, unable to meet her gaze. He shoved his hands in his pockets. "Come on. We have to keep moving."

Rose frowned at his urgency. "Why?"

"Because if Theron tasted your blood, he can track you by scent, and the longer you remain in one spot, the easier that will be," he said. He pointed at the pavement near her feet. "And that blood on the ground won't help matters."

Rose frowned at the dry spot of pavement. "What blood?"

"It's there," Kallias said impatiently. "Let's go."

"Fine," Rose sighed. "Just let me tie my shoes first—so I don't fall again."

He nodded and waited, as she knelt to tie the shoestrings of her old, black Converse.

He cast a quick glance at her and froze, his eyes widening. He suddenly realized that with everything going on, he hadn't really looked at her—because if he had, he would've *definitely* noticed *that*.

Her long, red hair fell forward, partially shielding her face. Dirt and rocks clung to her jeans, which were torn at the knees from the fall. And, *well*, her shirt was torn, too.

It hung open, revealing nearly every inch of her large, shapely breasts.

When Rose finished tying her shoes, she stood and frowned—as she found Kallias watching her with an amused smirk. "Why are you smiling like that?" she said warily.

Kallias didn't answer. He just shrugged off his jacket and held it out.

Rose scowled at the proffered jacket. "What are you doing?"

"What does it look like I'm doing?" Kallias asked.

Her frown deepened. "You don't really strike me as the chivalrous type."

His smile widened. "I'm not."

She gestured at the jacket dangling between them. "Then, what is this?"

His eyes drifted downward again, and his lips twitched, as if it were taking all of his strength not to laugh. "Your shirt is torn, and you can see...*a lot*."

Rose's eyes widened, and she quickly looked down at her shirt. Her cheeks burned with embarrassment, as she noticed that the first several buttons of her shirt had been ripped off, leaving only a pale blue, cotton bra to shield her breasts from the night.

"And you know, your breasts are just so," Kallias could barely hold back his laughter, as she glared at him, *"distracting."*

Surprisingly, Rose's face managed to turn a darker shade of red than before. Unable to look at him, she fumbled nervously with her shirt, trying and failing to pull it closed. "That stupid psycho ripped my shirt."

Kallias pulled his jacket back toward him and teased, "I mean, if you don't mind me staring, then I certainly don't mind..."

Rose snatched the jacket from his hand. "Pig!"

Kallias had never seen anyone shove their arms into a leather jacket with such...*fervor*. He couldn't help but laugh harder.

Rose zipped the jacket all the way up to her neck, covering the exposed breasts—*and* everything else. The black, leather jacket hung nearly to her knees, and the sleeves hung well past her hands.

With one last glare, Rose turned and marched off in the direction they'd been running before she fell.

Kallias shoved his hands in the pockets of his jeans and caught up with her in two easy strides. "Hey, I could've just kept my mouth shut and kept looking."

Rose rolled her eyes. "Now, you're just digging yourself into a hole," she muttered. "You should've stopped while you were ahead."

Kallias laughed, "Yeah, I probably should've stopped at *'distracting.'*"

She surprised herself by laughing along with him. "Probably."

Kallias watched her laugh, surprised by how attracted he was to that cute smile of hers and the way her face flushed when she was embarrassed or angry. He looked away, falling silent, as they wandered the streets.

After a few minutes, Rose realized that they were circling the town. She looked up at him curiously. "I have a question."

"You seem to have a lot of them," Kallias muttered.

Rose pursed her lips at that comment. Then, she started speaking rapidly, "Anyway, I know it might sound like a bad question, but I promise I don't mean it in a bad way. And I also know it's none of my business, but I'm a really curious person. And I ask a lot of questions, and it irritates everyone, I know, but—"

"Are you ever going to ask this terrible question of yours," Kallias interrupted, "or are you just going to keep rambling about why you shouldn't?"

Rose exhaled slowly. "Are you Greek?"

Kallias suddenly froze and burst into laughter. He laughed so hard that he nearly doubled over. *"That* was your question?"

She turned toward him, scowling at his sudden fit of laughter that seemed just a little too melodramatic, in her opinion. "What's so funny about that?"

"Well," he said, still laughing, "with all of that build-up, I was afraid you were going to ask my penis size or something."

Her jaw dropped. "What? No. No! I would never ask about your... I don't want to know your..." She gestured blindly toward his crotch. "I'm not interested in your—your... I'm not interested!"

Kallias watched her with raised eyebrows, as she continued her loud, mortified stammering without ever managing to finish a sentence. He glanced at a man and woman on the street, who'd turned to watch Rose's strange outburst.

Rose followed his gaze—and blushed, her cheeks practically crimson. "Why does this always happen to me?" she grumbled.

"*This* has happened before?" Kallias snorted.

She spun back toward him. "The point is: I couldn't care less about how big or small your..." she trailed off. Giving up on what was clearly an impossible sentence for her, she marched off in the direction they'd been walking.

Kallias followed, easily catching up with her. He leaned toward her with a playful grin. "I'm offended that you'd even think *small* is an option."

Rose rolled her eyes.

"Yes, I'm Greek," Kallias said. "How did you know?"

She shrugged, temporarily forgetting her embarrassment. "Well, I didn't know. I just suspected. I noticed you have an accent, although it doesn't sound *Greek* exactly, and I noticed that you seem to have some Greek features. But that doesn't mean much because we're all from somewhere originally, right? And then, I noticed that you have an unusual name—a *Greek* name, specifically. Of course, your parents could've just liked Greek named—"

"You've been thinking about me an awful lot," Kallias interrupted.

Rose scowled at him. "Oh, don't flatter yourself. It took *maybe* a total of three minutes for me to make all those connections."

"But I was still on your mind," Kallias teased.

She threw her hands up. "Well, yeah," she said, as if it were obvious. "A strange guy showed up at my work, asked me a weird question, and then attacked me. Then, I realized that the same rude jerk who'd attacked me and said he didn't care whether I lived or died *actually* saved my life and even went to the trouble of dropping me off at the hospital. So, yeah, obviously, you were on my mind!"

Kallias sighed, "I thought we'd established I did *not* attack you."

"You established that. I didn't," Rose clarified. "You forcefully grabbed me. The definition of the word 'attack' is an act of aggression that—"

"Do you always define words in the middle of an argument?" he asked.

"I, uh… Well, yeah, sometimes," Rose admitted. "What's wrong with that?"

Kallias shrugged. "I didn't attack you."

"Fine," Rose countered. "Then, what would *you* call it?"

"Restraining," Kallias replied. "Restraining is defensive, not offensive."

Rose glared at him. "I didn't need to be restrained."

Kallias raised his eyebrow. "Speak for yourself," he muttered. "I don't think there's a person alive who has the patience to deal with you."

"Funny," Rose said. "I was thinking the same thing about you."

Kallias chuckled. He wasn't *fully* endeared to her snark yet, but he couldn't deny that it was amusing. "So, what else made you think I was Greek?"

"Well, if you hadn't interrupted me, you'd know I was almost finished," Rose sassed. She shrugged. "You spoke in Greek. After that, I kind of figured."

Kallias frowned. "When did I speak in Greek?"

"You said the Greek equivalent of the S. H. word," Rose reminded him.

"S. H. word? You mean *shit*?" Kallias laughed. "Do you always refer to curse words with vague letter references the way a five-year-old *child* would?"

"Do you always *say* the words?" Rose countered.

He laughed. "I do, actually," he answered. "You see, my father used to tell me that respectable, high-class men should avoid vulgarity, but I never much cared for his political, self-righteous bullshit, so…" He completed the sentence with a sarcastic bow to no one in particular.

"There were a lot of adjectives in that sentence," she said playfully.

"A lot of adjectives come to mind when I think of him," he muttered.

Her smile faded. She stared at him, surprised that he'd actually revealed something about himself, even if it was only his dislike for his father. "Where is your father now?"

"Dead," Kallias answered with no emotion whatsoever.

"Oh, no," Rose said, sympathetic pain burning in her eyes. "I'm sorry."

"Don't be. The world was better off without him," Kallias said. No emotion—not even anger—showed in his expression. "I only wish I'd been the one who had the privilege of shoving the sword through his heart."

Rose froze. "Your father was murdered? With a sword?"

Kallias grimaced, mentally cursing himself for saying too much. He wasn't accustomed to making such ridiculous mistakes. "It was a metaphor."

"Oh," Rose laughed, "of course." But her smile faltered again, when she thought about what he'd said. "You didn't really mean that you wish you could've killed him, though, right? Because even if you didn't like him, that's a little—"

Kallias turned to look at her. He sighed, and she thought he looked sad, all of the sudden. "Rose, I'm *not* a good guy. I thought I made that clear already."

Rose watched him with a frown. "Yeah, I guess you did."

"Come on. We have to keep moving," Kallias reminded her.

Rose followed, as he continued to lead her down random streets. She struggled to keep up with his brisk pace.

Rose fiddled with the sleeves of the leather jacket, as she walked. "Where did you get this jacket?" she said, finally breaking the silence. "Giants-R-Us?"

Kallias laughed. "It's custom-made."

She sighed, "It was Theron who murdered her, right?"

He didn't even seem surprised by the sudden change of subject. "Yes."

"And he killed her because of me," Rose said quietly.

Kallias glanced at her. "It's not your fault," he assured her.

"Isn't it, though?" Rose asked, her voice cracking. "He wanted to kill *me*. He wouldn't have even encountered her, if he hadn't been looking for me."

Kallias came to a stop, suddenly, and he turned toward her so abruptly that she collided with him. He grasped her shoulders to steady her, vaguely noticing the way her cheeks flushed at his closeness. "You cannot do that," he said, enunciating each word. His dark gaze softened. "Believe me, Rose. No one can shoulder that kind of guilt. Theron killed her. *He* is to blame. Not you. Not anyone else."

Rose tried to argue, "But—"

"You didn't choose for him to come after you," Kallias interrupted, "now did you?"

Rose shook her head. "I don't even know why he wants to kill me."

"Then, like I said," Kallias said, "it's not your fault."

"There was blood on her neck," she added.

Kallias watched her warily. "Yes."

"But Theron can't be a…" Rose trailed off. "Tell me it's not true."

"But it *is* true," Kallias said. "Theron is a vampire."

She shook her head in denial. "It's impossible. Vampires don't exist."

Kallias sighed, "If I thought you really believed that, I'd let you continue to believe it. It doesn't help anyone's cause for humans to know about vampires. But there's no point in denying it when I know you already *know*. You saw his kill. You saw the blood on her neck. You *felt* his fangs when he bit you. You know what he is, whether you want to believe it or not."

"I don't believe in the supernatural," Rose insisted.

"Well," Kallias said bitterly, "considering you're being hunted by a vampire—maybe even more than one—you might want to start."

"Why do you keep calling it that?" Rose asked. "I'm a human being. You're talking about me like I'm an animal or something."

"To a vampire, you might as well be," Kallias said, shrugging. "You're just food to vampires, similar to how animals are just food to you."

"Now, that's not fair," Rose muttered. "I love animals."

"And some vampires like humans," he said. "But they also eat them."

She sighed. "Have you ever heard of something called tact?"

Kallias shrugged. "If you're looking for sensitivity, you should look elsewhere. You won't get it from me."

"Because you're a jerk?" Rose asked with raised eyebrows.

"Sure," Kallias said, smiling, "but I'm an honest jerk. Usually."

"Usually?" Rose repeated.

"Come on," Kallias said, and he continued to walk.

"So, how do *you* know about vampires?" Rose asked.

"I just do," Kallias said dismissively.

Rose gave an exasperated sigh. "It irritates me that you refuse to answer my questions."

"It irritates *me* that you ask so many," Kallias countered.

She wasn't surprised. "How do you expect me to trust you if you won't answer my questions?"

"I don't," he told her. "I'd actually advise you *not* to trust me. I'd advise you not to trust anyone, for that matter. I sure as hell don't."

"Surely there's someone you trust," Rose said skeptically.

Kallias looked at her. "Only a fool trusts someone willingly, and I am no fool," he said with a bitter edge to his voice. "When you trust someone, you might as well have given them a knife and said, 'If you want to slice open my heart, go ahead.' You deserve to have your heart broken if you're that stupid."

"You must have *loads* of friends with that attitude," Rose said sarcastically.

"I have very few," Kallias confirmed, "and I prefer it that way."

"So, you expect me to do what you tell me to do, but you don't want me to trust you," Rose said. "Don't you think those expectations clash a little?"

"I *expect* you to be smart. I expect you to do what you need to do to survive," he corrected, "and right now, I am your only chance of survival."

"Yeah, well, I don't like being told what to do," she said stubbornly.

Kallias chuckled at that. "I've noticed."

Silence fell between them, as they wandered the city. Kallias turned on one street after another, as if he were trying to keep moving but not trying to *go* anywhere.

Kallias watched every shadow and every corner, looking for Theron or anyone that might be doing Theron's bidding, but the streets grew quiet and deserted, as restaurants and stores closed for the night. Now, only the soft sound of her footsteps and the harsher sound of his own echoed through the streets.

After a while, he asked, "So, how do you know Greek?"

Rose glanced at him. In his black jeans and black button-down shirt, he blended into the shadows of the alley. She had to squint just to see his face. "I study Ancient History. I had to choose between Latin or Greek. I chose Greek."

Kallias nodded. "And are you fluent?"

Rose shrugged. "Technically, yes. I aced all six classes."

His eyebrows lifted. "They teach profanity in academic classes?"

She laughed, "Ah, you know. Someone always asks."

They'd reached the busiest street of the city, by this point, but aside from a man sitting on the hood of his car, talking on a cell phone, the street was empty.

Dark stores and restaurants lined the street, but only the hotels and gas stations near the highway seemed to be lit at this hour.

Kallias figured he would've noticed Theron's scent by now, if Theron had been following them.

He turned to her. "Where do you live?"

Rose pinned him with a suspicious scowl. "That's none of your business."

He sighed, "Do you want to get home safely or not?"

"Oh, but I can't trust you, remember?" Rose reminded him. She flashed a sassy smile. "It'd be unwise to tell someone I can't trust where I live."

He gave her an exasperated look. "What could I *possibly* do?"

"Well, you could kill me or rob me," she suggested.

Kallias laughed. "No offense, sweetheart, but I'm fairly certain I have more money than you do. I have no reason to rob you," he pointed out. "And believe me, if I wanted to kill you, you'd be dead already."

"For all I know," Rose said, "you could be some sort of predator, planning to sneak into my apartment and watch me shower or something."

"Predator. Interesting word-choice," he muttered—too quietly for her to hear. He smiled. "Don't flatter yourself. I have better things to do."

As tall as he was, he couldn't hide in her little bitty apartment, anyway.

"Fine," Rose said. She crossed her arms. "But what makes you think I *need* you to walk me home?"

Kallias frowned. "Do you suffer from memory loss or something? Have you already forgotten that I've had to save your life? Twice?"

"Have *you* forgotten I helped?" Rose countered. "Theron was going to kill you. I might not have cool weapons like you. Or...height. Or muscles. Or anything useful, really. But I still helped!"

Kallias snorted at that. "He was bluffing."

"I do need something sharper than a pen, don't I?" Rose mumbled to herself. "Paper clips? No. Staples? Staples are good."

Kallias ignored that. "He would've never killed me."

"Oh?" Rose said skeptically. "And why not?"

Kallias stepped closer. The gentle scents of honey and vanilla filled his senses, along with the scent of her uniquely powerful blood. He couldn't help but let his gaze drift toward her neck, and his mouth watered as he watched and listened to the pulse of her artery.

Rose lifted her head to meet his gaze, and her blue eyes dilated.

"Theron is sadistic in the worst of ways," he informed her. He struggled to focus on their conversation, rather than on her soft, full lips. "Humans fight harder to survive than any other creature. They fear death and love life. So, Theron takes great joy in taking that life. But I'm different. I have no love for life anymore. So, he doesn't get that joy from taking my life."

Rose looked away, blushing at how his closeness had affected her. She laughed nervously, "You say that like he's killed you before."

He shifted uncomfortably. "I guess that *was* a strange way to say it."

She stared at him for a moment. Sadness softened those bright blue eyes of hers. "Kallias, you're not saying that you," she hesitated, breaching the topic carefully, "want to die, are you?"

If she were being honest…Rose knew that feeling all too well. She'd been there before, and she couldn't bear to leave anyone else in that darkness.

But Kallias just grinned and changed the subject, "I guess you did help a *little*," he teased, "but you still wouldn't survive Theron. Not by yourself."

"You don't know that," Rose challenged. "I bet I could fight just like you if I knew how. If I set my mind to do it, I could learn. No one can stop me once I've decided to learn something."

Kallias chuckled. "I don't doubt that."

Rose blinked in shock. "That sounded…*positive*," she said slowly, as if he'd just sprouted horns or something. "Was that a compliment?"

Arrogance pulled at his smile. "I'm sure that if you weren't such a weak and incompetent human, you'd be a formidable foe for Theron."

"Well, the compliment-part didn't last long," Rose muttered.

He laughed, "You disagree?"

"Well," Rose said, frowning, "the incompetent part was a little—"

Her sentence ended abruptly, as Kallias shoved her into the wall. He pinned her wrists on either side of her head and leaned against her.

His breath fell against her face, and his gaze lingered on her lips, as if he were thinking of kissing her. Eventually, however, his light brown gaze returned to her eyes, and smug grin spread across his face.

"Overpower me, then," he challenged, "if you think you're strong enough."

Rose started to point out that she'd never called herself '*strong*,' but there was something about the curve of his lips that made her think that this challenge of his was some sort of…*game.*

Was this flirting?

Now, that was one language Rose *wasn't* fluent in.

Rose glanced at the large, rough hands that pinned hers to the wall. She jerked them in multiple direction, but no matter which way she tried, they didn't budge in his grasp. She returned her attention to him, when she heard him chuckle at her fourth failed attempt.

"This proves nothing," she muttered.

With another soft laugh, Kallias released her and stepped back, instantly missing the feel of her soft form against his own. He caught her elbow when she nearly fell, but apparently, that only made matters worse—because she stubbornly jerked it away from him.

"Nothing," Rose reminded him. "It proves nothing."

He laughed. "It proves you need to tell me where you live."

Rose rolled her eyes, but her defeat was obvious. "Just so you know, I dislike you," she grumbled.

He smiled. "The dislike is mutual, sweetheart."

"Yeah? Well," Rose countered, "I kind of hate you."

"Hate is a passionate emotion," he said with a smirk.

Rose set off in the direction of her apartment—*without* telling him where she was headed. "So?"

He fell into step beside her. He leaned in close, until her shoulder brushed against his chest, and his lips curved into that arrogant smile he wore so often. "Passionate women are good in bed," he whispered.

The warmth of his breath on her ear made her shiver, but when she'd recovered from that temporary lapse in judgement, she shot a glare his way. "I— You have some nerve to— You have no business considering how I would— You'll *never* know how I am in—"

Kallias raised his eyebrow at the sheer number of unfinished sentences. "Do you always become incapable of finishing a sentence when a sexual topic's brought up?"

She blushed. "Maybe," she mumbled. When she heard him chuckle, her blue eyes narrowed. "I can't help it that I'm not a pervert like you."

He snorted. "You think *I'm* a pervert? In that case, I'd *love* to hear what you'd call Erik. He makes me look like a blushing schoolboy."

Rose frowned worriedly. "Who is Erik?"

"A friend," Kallias answered. "My closest friend, actually."

She placed her hand over her chest and gasped, "*You* have friends?!"

He rolled his eyes at her teasing. "I told you I have a few."

His defense only encouraged her. "And what do you do when you're hanging out with your friends?" she said with a cute smile. "Brood in your pessimism and black clothes?"

He scowled. "What does the color of my clothes have to do with anything?"

Rose laughed. "Come on," she said, finally giving in. "My apartment's this way."

Kallias shoved his hands into the pockets of his black jeans and followed her toward the darker end of the street—where the alleys led into residential neighborhoods. "Okay, I'll give you the pessimism," he said, as he fell into step beside her. "But I'm not the *brooding* sort. I'm more of the *killing things* sort."

"Killing...*what* things?" Rose said with a frown. "What do you do for a living, anyway? Are you a hitman?"

"Why do you keep assuming I'm a criminal?" he asked.

She held out a hand, as if it were obvious. "You just said that you like to kill things," she reminded him. "You also said you weren't a good guy, and apparently, you're walking around with one-hundred dollar bills in your pocket."

Kallias frowned. "Is that unusual?"

"It is to *me*," Rose scoffed. She glanced at him. "You're also secretive, and you fight like someone who's been professionally trained."

Kallias nodded. He had to admit: aside from her strange issue with putting certain dollar bills in pockets, the rest of her reasons *were* pretty rational. "I hunt and kill vampires," he said, giving her the closest thing to the truth that he could—without revealing his own secret.

"You hunt *vampires*?" she repeated.

Kallias shrugged. "I found Theron well enough, didn't I? I stopped him from killing you," he reminded her, "and if I hadn't needed to help you, I would've killed him."

Rose's frown deepened. "I mean, I guess, if he really is a vampire..."

"Rose," Kallias said with raised brows. "He bit you. You *felt* his fangs rip into your neck." He sighed, "Deep down, you know what he is. You're just afraid to admit it."

Her hand strayed toward her neck at the memory of Theron's bite, but she didn't feel any cuts or torn skin. "Where did it—"

"It's already healed," he said—before she could finish asking that question. "The body of a vampire is designed to heal from almost anything. Healing and regenerative enzymes run through the vampire's entire body—through the bloodstream and even the saliva. That's what makes...*them* immortal." He'd almost said *us*. "It's what allows them to heal so quickly, and it's what keeps them from aging. Their bodies don't deteriorate the way a human's does—because those enzymes are constantly healing them. But they serve another purpose, too. When Theron bit you, his saliva healed the bite wound."

Rose blinked. "So, when a vampire kills a human, there's no proof?"

"Nothing as definitive as a bite wound, anyway," Kallias said with a shrug. "It'd be clear the human died of blood loss, but there wouldn't be any wounds to explain how the human lost so much blood."

"So, vampires leave no trace?" Rose said. "Besides the dead body, I mean."

Kallias nodded. "But most vampires dispose of the bodies, anyway, so..."

"So, humans never know what's really out there," Rose finished for him.

"Exactly," he agreed. "After years of being hunted by humans, vampires retreated to the shadows—and they learned to cover their tracks."

Rose's frown turned suspicious. "Then, how do *you* know about vampires?"

"I already answered that question," Kallias said.

"No, I already *asked* it," she corrected, "but you didn't answer. You evaded the question and thought I wouldn't notice."

Kallias narrowed his eyes at her.

"All right," Rose said. "You don't want to answer that one? Fine. We'll try a simpler question. How do you know *Theron*?"

"I just do," Kallias muttered.

"Evading a question is a sign of guilt," Rose informed him.

Kallias ignored her, frustrated that he'd somehow wound up stuck with a human who asked way too many questions.

But Rose refused to give up, practically jogging to keep up with him. "It has something to do with the woman Theron mentioned, doesn't it? Phoebe?"

Kallias froze—and grabbed her elbow to stop her from running into him. "*That* is none of your business," he snarled.

Rose stared at him, torn between her irritation at his reaction and her curiosity over why the name would provoke so much emotion. Irritation won. "Well, I honestly don't understand what this woman could've seen in either of you," she muttered. "Theron is obviously psychotic and evil, and you are just… Well, a woman would have to be insane to want to be with you."

"Insane, huh?" Kallias said. His gaze, dark with anger and hunger, swept over her. "Well, I suppose that means *you* want me, then."

Her eyes narrowed, and she jerked her arm away from him. "Never."

Kallias watched, his brows high, as Rose, in her frustration, set off in the wrong direction. She took several large steps before realizing it. Then, without missing a beat, she spun on her heels and started off in the other direction, as if nothing had ever happened.

He chuckled and followed her.

They traveled in silence for the rest of the walk. They'd passed so many residential streets, and she hadn't turned onto any of them.

Now, the lights and noise grew sparse.

Kallias found that listening to Rose's thoughts was almost as amusing as listening to her talk. It'd been forever since he'd made that comment, and she was still coming up with sassy comebacks in her mind. She'd even caught him laughing at her several times.

When she heard him laugh for the *fifth* time, she turned and asked, "What's so funny? Are my boobs showing again?" She looked down at her chest.

He snorted, "No. Believe it or not, I can't see through leather."

Rose suddenly came to a stop near a cracked, unevenly lined parking lot, which set in the middle of four, identical, brick buildings.

Kallias squinted at the apartment sign, but there was too much graffiti to make out the name.

She turned to him, even as they remained in the middle of the street. "This is it."

He raised an eyebrow. "You live in the street?"

Rose crossed her arms. "No, but I can handle it from here."

"I rarely do anything nice for anyone," Kallias informed her. "At least let me walk you to your door—just this once."

The request was strange enough to break through Rose's stubborn, little walls. With a slight stutter, she said, "F—fine."

He followed her across the cracked parking lot, weaving through the maze of old, used cars. When they reached the third apartment building, Rose trudged up a set of creaky, metal stairs.

Kallias wondered once or twice if the stairs would even hold their weight. When he saw how close the apartment doors were to each other, his frown deepened. These apartments made the ones in the residential neighborhoods look like mansions.

And those hadn't been large either.

Rose hesitated in front of a red door with the number seven on it, and she started fishing through her pockets for the key.

"Seven?" Kallias said with a frown.

"Forty-seven," Rose said distractedly. "The four's been missing since before we moved in, but our address is forty-seven."

Kallias leaned against the rail. Was she married? "We?"

"My roommate, Audrey," Rose said. "You haven't met her yet."

Kallias nodded. So, *that's* why she wasn't affected by the allure. She liked women. He'd wondered before, but he'd clearly dismissed the idea too quickly. It all made sense now.

"Well, is your girlfriend home?" Kallias asked.

She glanced back at him, her eyes wide and confused. "Roommate."

"Right," Kallias said. Clearly, she didn't want to talk about it. So, he changed the subject. "This is the bad part of town, isn't it?"

Rose squinted at him, but then, she returned her attention to her empty pockets, searching for something that obviously wasn't there. "Uh," she mumbled, "it's not too bad. It's a college town. Even the *'bad'* parts of town aren't that bad."

Rose had grown up in a neighborhood with a much higher crime rate than *this* one.

Kallias raised an eyebrow, as she continued to search her pockets. "Do you need help?"

"No," she sighed. "I just...misplaced my key." She shook her head in frustration. "I don't lose keys. That's Audrey's job."

Kallias thought that sounded like a strange relationship, but he kept that thought to himself.

Rose gave up on finding her key and knocked on the door. The lock clicked as Audrey unlocked it, and then, the door swung open to reveal Audrey in the doorway.

Her frizzy, brown hair looked as wild and messy as ever, and there was a smudge of blue paint on her cheek. The same blue paint had apparently left splatters of blue on her shorts and on the lacy, white camisole she wore. Like everything else Audrey owned, that camisole would never be its original color again.

"Rose Melanie Foster," Audrey shrieked. "I'm going to skin you alive!"

Kallias winced at the loudness of her voice. Couldn't Rose have picked a lover who didn't shriek like a damn pterodactyl?

"I don't think you have the tools to do that," Rose said dryly.

"You hung up on me!" Audrey said. "I called you back *three* times, and you never answered! I thought you were dead! I was going to call the police! See?" Audrey held up her phone to show Rose that she'd already pressed 9-1-1.

"You're right," Rose said with obvious sarcasm. "It was inconsiderate of me. Next time I'll tell the murderer to wait, while I answer the phone and tell you I'm still alive. Of course, then, he'll kill me, which means that I'll have lied to you, so..."

Audrey's eyes widened. "Murderer? Then...the dream came true?"

"You know," Rose said with far too much levity for Audrey's taste, "I think you should consider going into meteorology, instead of art. Then, the news might actually get the weather report right."

"Oh, Rose!" Audrey cried.

Without warning, she threw herself at Rose, latching both arms around her neck. The force of the hug sent them backward and would've probably sent them over the railing, if Kallias hadn't been there to catch them.

Rose tried to shoot an apologetic look over her shoulder, but Audrey held her too tightly. She patted Audrey's back. "I'm all right, Audrey," Rose told her best friend, "I promise."

"I'm so glad you're alive," Audrey said, pulling back, "but how?"

Rose pointed her thumb behind her. "The, uh, arrogant jerk?"

Audrey blinked, and then, her gaze shifted in the direction of Rose's thumb. Her eyes widened when she saw Kallias for the first time.

"Oh, my, my," Audrey breathed. "Can I get attacked next?"

Kallias frowned. He didn't know how to break the news to Rose, but it seemed her girlfriend or wife or whatever was a little...*into men*.

Then again, perhaps she was into both.

Rose closed her eyes, clearly mortified. "Audrey."

Audrey blinked innocently at her. "What?"

Rose turned to Kallias and spread out her arms. "As you can see, I'm safe. You can go now."

Audrey slapped Rose's arm. "Rose! Don't be rude! Invite him inside!"

Rose gave her an incredulous look. "You can't be serious."

She blinked, as she realized that Audrey was staring at Kallias with a strange, dazed look—much like Owen and Eleanor had.

"He saved your life, and he's hot," Audrey hissed. "It's the least we can do."

Kallias didn't exactly want to cause problems in their relationship, so he tried to decline. "Actually, I need to find Theron before sunrise."

Audrey beamed. "Dude! Is that an accent? Say something else!"

Rose sighed heavily. "He's busy, Audrey," she said, ignoring her friend's fascination with his voice. "He doesn't want to come in."

Kallias scowled. Rose was awfully eager to get rid of him. He cast a quick glance behind the women, into the tiny apartment, and he realized that a look at the place Rose lived might help him figure out what Theron wanted with her. "On second thought, maybe..."

"No," Rose said worriedly. "No second thoughts."

"Rose can make you a cup of coffee. She's good at that," Audrey offered. "She's terrible at cooking, though, so I wouldn't ask for food, if I were you. Unless you *like* the taste of burnt food?" She shrugged her mostly bare shoulders. "I can't cook either, but that's irrelevant."

"I'm *not* making him coffee," Rose grumbled.

Audrey patted her shoulder. "Sure, you will. He saved your life, and we both know that deep down, underneath a thick layer of sarcasm and stubbornness, you're like the nicest person ever." She glanced past Rose, smiled at the tall, blindingly attractive man that leaned against the metal rail, and said, "Would you like to come inside?"

Flashing a wry smile at Rose, he said, "A cup of coffee does sound nice."

Rose glared at him. "You said you have things to do tonight."

He seemed amused. "I changed my mind. Those things can wait."

"Yay!" Audrey sang. She smiled at the man who, unbeknownst to them, happened to be a vampire and said, "What are you waiting for? Come inside!"

Kallias offered a smug smirk to Rose, as he brushed past her and stepped into her apartment. Rose's eyes narrowed, and she glared murderously at the back of his head, as she followed him inside.

Kallias circled the small apartment, as Audrey and Rose both headed toward the kitchen area. The tiny, one-room apartment basically consisted of just a bathroom and closet along the right wall and a kitchen area along the left wall. The center of the room was filled with a desk, several bookshelves, and one queen-sized bed.

Despite the fact that the apartment was nearly spotless, Kallias could barely move because of its small, cramped size.

"You both live here?" Kallias asked in disbelief.

"No, we live outside," Rose said sarcastically, as she grabbed a pot.

Audrey hopped on top of the counter and crossed her legs. "Yep! We've lived here for four years. We moved in here during our first semester of college."

Kallias frowned at the one bed in the center of the room—a possible confirmation of his suspicions. "Where do you sleep?"

"In the bathtub," Rose muttered. "The bed is just decoration."

Kallias snorted at her continuous sarcastic remarks. "Both of you?"

"It's a big bathtub," Rose said.

Audrey rolled her eyes. "Actually, it's a tiny bathtub like everything else in this apartment, but we don't sleep in it either," she said with a laugh. "We sleep in the bed."

Clearly, she was more open about things than Rose. "Oh," he said slowly, "so you two are—"

Audrey caught on before he could finish. "Oh! No! No, no."

"It's not any of his business, anyway," Rose grumbled.

Audrey smiled and shook her head. "I'm straight," she assured him, "and Rose is...well..." She cast a playful look at Rose and shrugged. "Well, she's single, anyway."

Rose glanced up at her. "Really, Audrey?"

Audrey gave her an innocent look. "You *are* single!"

So, Rose *was* into men—and women, too, from the sounds of it.

So, why the hell wasn't she affected by the allure?

Kallias was back at square one.

He made a slow circle around the apartment, searching for some clue as to what would make this woman catch Theron's interest.

He noticed textbooks and notebooks on the black desk against the back wall—but nothing out of the ordinary. A worn, black backpack set beside the bed, leaning against a nightstand that matched the bed-frame. He absently scanned the bookshelves for anything peculiar, but he found only a large collection of fiction novels and history books.

A few pieces of artwork, depicting sunsets and oceans, decorated the wall. He stared for a while at a painting of a sunset, unable to remember how the last one he'd seen looked.

"Audrey painted that," Rose said from beside him. "She's an art major."

Kallias glanced down at her, suddenly aware of her closeness. "Oh."

Rose held out a cup of dark liquid. "Coffee?"

The scent of coffee and hazelnut soothed his senses, dulling the scent of her powerful blood. Kallias blinked at the proffered coffee mug, surprised that she'd actually made him coffee. He'd mostly been joking. "Thank you," he murmured.

Rose's entire stance seemed to soften at his tone. She smiled a little, when he lifted the cup to his lips. "You're not afraid I poisoned it?"

Kallias chuckled. "You underestimate me, sweetheart. It'd take a lot more than poison to kill *me*," he said with a playful grin. He sipped the hot liquid, and his eyebrows lifted—because it was actually really good.

"Well?" Rose asked. She held her own cup in her hand, still full.

"It's good," he admitted. "Maybe you *are* competent at something."

"Maybe?" she repeated in disbelief.

Audrey still sat on the counter, watching their banter with amusement. "Rose, you didn't do him justice in your description! Sexy is an understatement!"

Kallias raised his eyebrow at Rose. "You called me sexy?"

"No!" she scoffed. She glared at Audrey. "I did not call him sexy, and you know it! Your hospital friend called him sexy. Not me!"

Audrey held her hands up in surrender. "I plead the fifth."

"So, you *don't* think I'm sexy?" Kallias asked in an amused tone.

Rose blushed. "I— Well, what kind of question is that?"

Kallias shrugged and sipped his coffee. "I thought it was a simple one."

"Uh," Audrey said, much too excited, "are you wearing his jacket?"

Rose glanced down at the oversized leather jacket. "It's a long story."

Deciding his chances of finding anything significant in this tiny apartment were slim to none, Kallias set his cup on the counter. "I should go."

"No, wait!" Rose called, as he headed toward the door. She set her coffee cup on the nightstand and rushed after him, determined to stop him before he disappeared again. "I need to talk to you."

Kallias paused in the doorway and looked down at her. "Alone?"

Rose blushed and glanced at Audrey who was watching them with some sick kind of satisfaction. "Yeah," she said, "but we're just going to talk."

One corner of his lips curved into a smile. "Of course."

"Bye, Mr. Tall-Hunky-Scary-Guy!" Audrey called out.

Rose closed the door, shutting them outside. With a nervous laugh, "I'd say she's not always like this, but that would be a lie."

Kallias chuckled and leaned against the railing. "You wanted to talk?"

Rose blushed and looked down at her feet, as if her shoes were the most interesting things in the world. "I just wanted to thank you for saving me."

He raised an eyebrow. "Oh, you're actually grateful for something?"

She looked up, glaring at him. "You know what? I take it back!"

"It's too late now," Kallias teased. "You've already said it."

Rose crossed her arms. "I *really* don't like you," she said matter-of-factly.

"Your friend doesn't seem convinced of that," Kallias teased. He glanced back at the door, still hearing the peculiar, brunette woman's thoughts.

"Audrey's a hopeless romantic. She probably thinks I've found my knight-in-shining-armor, and you're obviously nothing of the sort," Rose scoffed.

Kallias grinned. "I agree. My armor's pretty shitty, and I never had the etiquette to be a knight," he joked. He watched, as she laughed softly at him, amazed by how much her smile brightened her already luminous azure eyes.

She sighed, "So, uh…do you think Theron will come after me again?"

"Probably," Kallias said honestly. "You seem to have piqued his interest somehow."

"Which is weird because I'm not a very interesting person," she laughed.

"You seem *very* interesting to me," Kallias said before he could stop himself. He winced, when she blinked at him. He hadn't really meant it that way—or had he? He cleared his throat and added, "And by interesting, I mean annoying."

Rose nodded, as if that made more sense. "Kallias, why did you save me?"

He just stared at her for a moment. "I don't like to watch people die."

She smiled. "Maybe you're not as terrible as you think you are."

Kallias looked away. "You wouldn't say that if you knew my secrets."

Rose frowned curiously at that, wishing he'd go on, wishing he'd divulge those secrets to her. She wasn't sure why she even cared, but then, she supposed it was just her insatiable curiosity.

Nothing more than that.

She *hoped* it was nothing more than that, anyway.

As a tense silence spread between them, Rose found herself wishing she could forget the whole night—not because she wanted to forget about what had happened to *her*, but because she wanted to forget what had happened to her teacher. She was sure the image of Dr. Parker's lifeless body would haunt her nightmares, just as the memory of her mother already did.

"Why didn't you save her," she said, her voice breaking, "instead of me?"

A slight prick of emotion irritated his calloused heart. "It was too late," he said, fighting to stay in control of his emotions. "She was already dead when I got there. There was nothing I could do."

Rose glanced down at her hands, her fingers trembling. "She had kids, a husband, people who will miss her. If anyone had to die, it should've been me."

"Don't say that," Kallias said, stunned by her statement.

Rose shrugged, spiraling quickly, as she often did. "Why not? It's not like *I* would've been missed." She said it as if it were a simple fact that held no meaning. "For whatever reason, Theron wants to kill me. If he'd just killed *me*, then Dr. Parker might still—"

"Stop," Kallias said, and without thinking, he pressed a finger to her lips to stop her. Both of them froze, both surprised that he'd reacted like that. Their gazes met, and almost involuntarily, his finger traced the curve of her soft mouth.

For a moment, Rose thought he might kiss her, and for some reason— a reason she couldn't possibly understand—she *wanted* him to kiss her. This man had frustrated on several occasions, and yet, her mind betrayed her, longing for something she'd told herself she no longer cared for.

It wasn't that she hadn't thought she was capable of desire anymore. It was just that…she'd been sort of scared of it.

For quite some time now.

Luckily for the part of her that was still afraid, he didn't kiss her.

Instead, Kallias pulled away, scowling at his hand, as if confused by its action. He cleared his throat and turned to leave, but she grabbed his arm to stop him.

When he turned toward her, she blurted out, "Your jacket."

She shrugged off the jacket and handed it to him. He took it from her and pulled it on, leaving it to hang open over his black shirt.

With a sheepish smile, Rose crossed her arms to hide her torn shirt and the blue bra that was getting a lot more fresh air than it needed.

"Thanks," she mumbled.

Kallias nodded. "Stay home tomorrow night," he told her. "Don't leave for any reason."

"Okay, first of all," Rose said with lifted eyebrows, "I don't know what kind of lifestyle *you* live, but some of us actually have to work and go to class." She pointed a finger threateningly at him. "And second, don't tell me what to do."

His lips twitched. She clearly thought she was intimidating, but at this exact moment, she was mostly just cute. "What good will your job and classes do if Theron kills you?"

Rose pursed her lips. "I can't just stay home forever."

Kallias sighed. "I didn't tell you to stay home forever. I told you to stay home tomorrow. I need time to deal with Theron. That's all."

"Fine," Rose muttered. "I'll...think about it."

He watched her, suddenly reluctant to leave. "Goodbye, Rose Foster."

As he turned to leave, Rose stopped him again. "I—" she stammered. She bit her lip nervously and muttered, "Just... Thanks again."

Kallias nodded. "Stay safe tomorrow night."

"Should I expect to see you again?" Rose asked curiously.

"No," Kallias said, and then, he turned and walked away.

6

QUESTIONS

*A*s soon as Rose opened the door, Audrey fell out onto the ground.

She'd been listening at the door.

Typical Audrey behavior.

With an exaggerated sigh, Rose offered her hand, and Audrey took it; pulling herself back to her feet. Audrey straightened her clothes and followed Rose inside, grinning as if she'd just found her favorite paint-brush on sale.

Rose grabbed her coffee. "Stop looking at me like that."

"You like him," Audrey said in a sing-songy voice.

Rose crawled into bed with her coffee cup and leaned wearily against the headboard. "I don't know where you and Owen are getting these ideas, but you couldn't be more wrong. I don't like him."

Audrey smiled. "Owen thinks you like him, too?"

Rose scowled at Audrey's triumphant smile. "That is *not* confirmation."

Audrey tilted her head to the side and squinted. "Your boobs are showing."

Rose grimaced at her torn shirt and set her coffee cup on the nightstand. She hopped out of bed to change clothes. "Why do you think I was wearing his jacket?" she grumbled.

She rummaged through the dresser for a pair of pajamas.

She pulled out a pair of red and black flannel pajamas and headed to the bathroom to change and brush her teeth. She unbuttoned what was left of her shirt and tossed it into the small garbage can beside the sink.

When she stepped out of her blue jeans, she heard a loud gasp.

Audrey stood in the doorway of the bathroom, a glass of sweet tea in her hand and her eyes wide with shock. "Rose! Look at your arms!"

Rose frowned and glanced at the mirror above the sink, blinking at her reflection. New, reddish purple bruises marred her arms, joining the older bruises from the night before.

She traced the deep, red marks on her forearms where Theron's fingernails had dug into her skin.

She found it strange to see the evidence of the attack on her skin, when the evidence of the bite had already left her neck.

"Maybe you should go to the hospital," Audrey suggested, "just in case."

Rose tossed her jeans in the laundry hamper. "I'm fine, Audrey."

Audrey frowned worriedly. "You already had a concussion, and now—"

"And now, I have a few more bruises," Rose said, shrugging. She grabbed the pajama pants from the counter. "I'll be fine. Besides, it'd be stupid to waste time in the hospital, while this...*killer* is out there, looking for me."

She still couldn't bring herself to say vampire.

"I guess you're right," Audrey admitted. She leaned against the door.

Rose stepped into the flannel pants. "Did you finish packing?"

"Not so fast, missy," Audrey scolded, wagging her finger in a way that earned a giggle from Rose. "We're talking about you and Mr. Tall-Hunky-Scary-Guy *first*. Did you get his number?"

Rose rolled her eyes and grabbed the pajama shirt from the counter. "His name is Kallias, and no, I didn't get his number. *Why* would I do that?"

"To call him," Audrey said, "and ask him on a date, obviously."

Rose slipped her arms into the flannel shirt. "I already told you: I *don't* like him," she insisted, despite Audrey's unfazed smile. "Why would I want to go on a date with him?"

"Because you're wrong," Audrey said. "You're obviously hot for him."

"I am not 'hot' for him—whatever *that* means," Rose scoffed.

"Oh?" Audrey said. She raised an eyebrow in disbelief. "Then, what *do* you feel for him? Because you obviously feel something."

"Yes. Hate," Rose said, as she buttoned her shirt.

"Uh-huh," Audrey said. She leaned lazily against the door.

Rose grabbed her toothbrush from the counter. "I'm serious," she said, as she squeezed toothpaste onto the toothbrush. "He's a jerk. I don't like him."

"Well, when will you see him again?" Audrey asked.

"I won't," Rose said with a mouthful of toothpaste.

Audrey straightened. "What? Why not?"

Rose shrugged nonchalantly, as she continued to brush her teeth. She leaned over the sink and spit out the toothpaste so she could speak clearly. "Tell me the truth," she said, glancing at her friend. "What do you think of him?"

"I think he's the sexiest man I've ever seen," Audrey answered.

Rose pursed her lips. "I was being serious."

"So was I," Audrey responded easily.

Rose turned and leaned against the bathroom counter. What was it about this guy that made Audrey and Owen both act like hungry wolves around fresh meat? He was attractive, sure. Even Rose could see that, but their reactions seemed…extreme.

Well, Owen's had.

This was all kind of typical for Audrey, actually.

"I'm not looking for your expert opinion on his attractiveness," Rose said. She sighed, "I want to know if you think he seems dangerous."

Audrey sobered at the serious question. "I mean, yeah, there is something off-putting about him, but that probably has more to do with the fact that he's a hundred feet tall and muscular." She shrugged. "Besides, an *animal* is dangerous when it needs to be, but that doesn't mean it'll ever harm you."

Rose nodded, considering that. "I don't know. I just get this feeling that there's something off—something I need to know."

"He saved your life twice, Rose," Audrey reminded her.

"I know, I know," Rose said with a guilty sigh. "But you didn't see the way he fought."

"Being able to fight doesn't make him evil either," Audrey argued.

"He's also secretive," Rose added. "He refused to answer my questions."

Audrey shrugged. "In his defense, you *do* ask a lot of questions."

Rose pursed her lips. "He's hiding something—something *bad*. I can feel it."

"Okay," Audrey said slowly, as if she were plotting something. She walked into the bathroom, standing in front of Rose. She crossed her arms. "How did he react when you told him about your dead mother and your brother in prison?"

Rose frowned. "Why would I tell him that? I just met him."

"Exactly," Audrey said. "Rose, you open your heart to so many people, and you trust so easily. And yet, when your mother died, you told everyone that you were going to visit her—not *bury* her. And each month, when you visit your brother at the prison, you tell everyone that you're just going to an *appointment*."

Rose bit her lip. "Technically, it is an appointment."

"You have your own dark secrets, Rose," Audrey reminded her.

"I just don't need people judging me or feeling sorry for me," Rose said.

Audrey leaned against the counter, beside Rose, and crossed her arms. "Don't you think he's probably keeping his secrets for the same reason?"

"But I wouldn't judge him," Rose argued. "I'm not that kind of person."

"He doesn't know that. He just met you," Audrey reminded her.

"Okay, I see your point," Rose said with another guilty sigh, "and I may have been a little...uncharacteristically judgmental toward him already."

"See?" Audrey said, smiling. "Maybe he's actually a good guy."

Rose stepped away from the counter. She left the bathroom, heading to the bookshelf to look for a book. She trailed her finger across a few worn book spines. "Well, he seemed pretty determined to convince me otherwise."

Audrey followed her. "That's a good sign. The ones you really have to watch out for are the ones who try to convince you they're good."

"Right. I forgot that I have my very own *bad-boy* expert," Rose said dryly. She tugged a tattered horror novel from the top shelf.

"Oh, you mock now, but when you see that I'm right..." Audrey said, pointing her finger playfully. She scowled at the novel in Rose's hand—one of the many books on that bookshelf that Rose had already read a hundred times. "How many times are you going to read the same books?"

Rose crawled into bed, pulling the quilts over her and wiggling her toes to get comfortable. She flipped open the familiar book and smiled at Audrey. "You can never read a book too many times. Each time is like a new experience."

Audrey rolled her eyes. "You know what else is like a new experience?" Without waiting for an answer, she provided, "An *actual* new experience."

"Ha. Ha. You're hilarious," Rose said sarcastically.

"I know I am," Audrey said. She hopped on the other side of the bed and snatched the novel from Rose's hand. "So, what *exactly* happened tonight?"

Rose pouted. "I need my book."

Audrey patted Rose on top of the head, as if she were a puppy. "You'll be okay. I have faith in you. Now, tell me what happened."

Rose sighed and shifted in the bed, leaning against the headboard. She then proceeded to describe the events of the night, exactly as they happened—even the parts that were difficult to relive.

Audrey listened until Rose finished.

"Eww! You stabbed him in the eye?" Audrey groaned in disgust.

Rose stared blankly at her. "Is that all you heard?"

"Why would you do something so disgusting?" Audrey whined.

"I'm sorry. Next time, I'll choose a less disgusting way to defend myself against a psychotic murderer," Rose said, "because your weak stomach is far more pertinent in my mind than the threat of my impending death."

"Hey, my weak stomach takes offense to that sarcastic tone," Audrey complained. Then, she suddenly fell serious. "But your teacher—is she really..."

Rose's smile faded, and her gaze immediately fell to her lap. "Unfortunately," she sighed. She squeezed her eyes shut, trying not to let herself cry again. "I kept hoping I'd feel a pulse, but..."

"Rose, I'm really sorry," Audrey said. "I know how much you liked her."

"What am I supposed to do, Audrey? She has a family," Rose said, her voice cracking. "Kallias said I shouldn't call the police. He said it would do more harm than good, and I can't be responsible for more people getting killed..."

"Then, it sounds to me like you should listen to him," Audrey advised.

Rose looked at her. "But is that right?"

"If it keeps innocent people from dying," Audrey offered, "how could it be wrong?"

"It's against the law," Rose reminded her.

Audrey rolled her eyes. "You know, for a woman from a family full of felons, you sure do have a strong respect for the law," she scoffed, earning a scowl from Rose. "Okay, think of it this way. Worst case scenario is that Theron is still there with the body, and in that case, if the police were to arrive, he'd kill them." She spread her hands as she spoke, as if she were speaking in a grand hall, rather than on the corner of a thrift-store mattress. "Best case scenario is that Theron has already disposed of the body, like Tall-Hunky-Scary-Guy said, and then disappeared. And in that case, the police would think you were insane."

"Yes," Rose said flatly. "Thank you for explaining that to me."

Audrey laughed. "Shut up."

Rose suppressed a smile, as the sadness began to seep in yet again. She could never push it away for long. "Surely, they'd realize I was right when they see she's missing."

"Or," Audrey pointed out, "they'll think you had something to do with it."

Rose leaned forward and rested her face in her hands. "Yeah, I guess it would look suspicious."

"No one wants to believe in things that scare them," Audrey said. "Take it from the girl who dreams about people dying before it happens. People would rather assume you're insane than consider the possibility that you might be right. If I've learned anything from it all, it's that some things are best left quiet. If you tell them about vampires, you'll end up in a mental ward before the end of the night."

"Or just referred to a new psychiatrist," Rose muttered. She lifted her head. "You know, maybe that's where I should be. Maybe I *am* losing my mind."

Audrey glared at Rose, as that remark had been directed at her. "Are you kidding me? You're not losing your mind, Rose. You saw the vampire. I saw him, too, remember? In my dream."

"Oh, that's reassuring," Rose said sarcastically. "My friend who sees the future saw the vampire in a dream." She shook her head and muttered, "What if *you're* a figment of my imagination, too?"

"Okay, now, you *are* losing it," Audrey said, rolling her eyes. "You think you've just been *imagining* my existence for four years? If you are, your imagination sucks—because I could use some improvement. Imagine me with boobs, please. And money. And a hot boyfriend."

Rose's brows furrowed. "*Those* are your three choices?"

"See? I'm shallow," Audrey pointed out. "I need improvement."

"Maybe I'd be safer in a mental ward," Rose offered.

"I doubt it," Audrey said. "He nearly killed you at the university."

"You're right," Rose acknowledged, finally. "This really isn't the best time to get locked in a padded room. I have an important exam in the morning."

Audrey blinked. "Your priorities are *so* messed up."

"Speaking of priorities," Rose said, "give me back my book."

AS DAWN CREPT CLOSER, A QUIETNESS SETTLED OVER THE CITY, MARKING that short stretch of time between the night owls finally stumbling *into* bed and the early risers stumbling *out* of bed.

It was during that time that vampires could usually take their victims with less fear of being seen—that dark hour when no human should ever stray into the streets.

With all the shops already closed, the only sound echoing through the street was the low, dull thud of his boots, as Kallias searched for Theron.

Rose's scent clung to his jacket, still, even though she'd worn it for only a short time, and each time the warm breeze swayed the corners of his jacket, her scent seemed to envelop him.

He clenched his jaw as his hunger surged.

Kallias froze, as the scent of fresh blood filled his senses. Without making the conscious decision to do so, he followed the scent.

He moved with the supernatural speed of a vampire, traveling in a fluid blur of movement, rather than the step-by-step pace of a human.

The scent led him to a dark parking garage.

Kallias stopped just past the parking garage's entrance, and he kept to the shadows, as he watched what appeared to be a woman and a man in a tight embrace, leaning against a lone car on the first level.

With his nocturnal eyesight, he could discern the two figures in the darkness. A man leaned limply against the side of the car, as a tall, slim woman clung to him. She wrapped her legs and arms around him, as she mercilessly drained him of blood.

Kallias cleared his throat.

The woman pulled back, suddenly. Her dark eyes shifted directly toward him, and her bloodstained lips curled into a smile.

Her straight, black hair brushed her chin, not quite reaching her neck, and a short, black dress hugged her tall, slim figure.

She was as beautiful as any other vampire, her perfect features marred only by the blood that coated her face.

Kallias approached her, and her smile deepened.

With that old, Spanish accent of hers, she cooed, "Kallias of Athens."

He came to a stop several feet away. "Sofia Pérez," he replied curtly.

The human—still conscious, despite the blood loss—glanced back and forth from the blood-coated vampire to Kallias. Yet, his eyes remained blank, as if he still weren't aware of his surroundings.

Perhaps she'd taken too much already.

Blood stained the collar of the man's tan button-down shirt, seeping slowly from a wound in his neck that was already beginning to heal.

"It's been a long time," the woman said.

"Fortunately for you," Kallias told her.

She stiffened at his tone, as if his hostility surprised her. She glanced at the human. "I wasn't going to kill him, if that's what you thought."

"Huh," Kallias scoffed. "You cut it awfully close, don't you think?"

Sofia offered a guilty smile—that only angered Kallias more. "So, I may have taken a little too much," she said with a shrug of her bare, slender shoulders. "I have an insatiable appetite sometimes, and it's just...*so* hard to stop once I've started. I'm sure you understand."

"Not really," Kallias said. "I have something called self-control."

Her smiled faded. "Where is your empath? He was *far* more charming."

"By charming, I assume you mean gullible and ready to sleep with just about anyone," Kallias said.

"Anyone?" Sofia said. She stepped closer to him and trailed a manicured fingernail along the zipper of his jacket. "Different country, different language, different century, but you're still the same rude, mysterious vampire, permanently in a bad mood." She smiled. "But I suppose mysteriousness *does* have a certain appeal."

Kallias grasped her wrist to stop her. "Refrain from touching me," he muttered, his eyes narrowed with suspicion. "What are you doing here, Sofia?"

"Am I not supposed to be here?" Sofia said, feigning concern. "Is this *your* territory?"

"I don't have territory," Kallias said. "I know how to behave like a human, rather than an animal."

Sofia gave a soft, derisive laugh. "But you're an animal, nonetheless."

Growing impatient, Kallias said, "Are you working with Theron?"

Sofia tapped her finger against her chin. "Theron? Never heard of him."

"You're lying," Kallias stated.

"Am I?" Sofia murmured.

Kallias leaned closer. "He's twenty-six hundred years old. You've at least heard of him," he told her, "and I think *he's* the reason you're here. Why else would you be?" He lowered his voice to a growl. "As a matter of fact, I think you're the one I saw by the fence earlier tonight. Tell me. Does the name Rose Foster ring a bell?"

"Why?" Sofia whispered. "Does she taste good?"

The human began to stir. "What... I don't understand..." the man stammered. His eyes widened as he realized that it was *his* blood that coated Sofia's face. "You... You bit me! Why—why would you do that?"

Sofia grimaced at the terrified human. "Well, shit."

As the human pulled desperately at the handle of his car door, Kallias reached out and grasped his forearm. He jerked the human around to face him, and the human gulped audibly.

The man tried to pull his arm free from Kallias's grasp, but he couldn't. "Please, man, I don't know what you are, but I—I have parents and," he stammered, "a girlfriend... I should've been home hours ago. Please!"

Kallias took control of the human's mind. "Calm down."

The human stilled, his eyes suddenly blank.

Kallias pulled his dagger from its sheath and sliced the man's arm open. He tensed as the scent of *more* fresh blood filled his senses, intensifying his already ravenous hunger. As blood flowed down the man's arm, Kallias continued to use his telepathic control. "You need to go to the hospital, and tell them you've cut yourself. Tell them that it was an accident. Tell them you think you've lost too much blood."

"Hospital," he said in an eerie tone. "Yes."

"For what happened," Kallias continued. "Forget seeing us."

"Of course," the human responded.

"Good," Kallias said, releasing the man's arm. "Now, go."

The human turned and left, walking out of the parking garage without question or afterthought.

Sofia turned to Kallias, her eyes wide. "The rumors are true!" she gasped. "You *are* a telepath! I heard stories, but I never believed them. I've never met a telepath before. Oh, Theron will be so—"

Her sentence ended in a sharp cry as Kallias shoved her against the car, his hand closing around her throat. "So you *do* know Theron."

Sofia pulled at his hand, but his fingers didn't budge. "Let go of me."

"Tell me where he is," Kallias demanded.

"Damn you and your ancient," Sofia wheezed, "strength."

Losing patience, he used his telepathic control on her. "Where is he?"

Sofia fell still. "He's already taken shelter for the day. He told no one where he'd be," she answered honestly.

Kallias sighed in frustration. "Fine," he growled. "Forget about this. Forget I'm a telepath. I'd like to keep Theron in the dark about that for a bit longer."

"Yes," she said, her large, brown eyes blank.

Kallias released her. He turned to leave, ignoring the sound of her breathless gasps. "For your sake, Sofia, I hope that you're not killing humans again. Because if you are, you will die."

THE MIDMORNING SUN BURNED ROSE'S SKIN, AS SHE HEADED TO HER FIRST class of the day. She crossed the lawn that stretched between the history building and the linguistics building, and she slowed her steps, when she neared the place where Theron had attacked her one night earlier— the same place he'd also killed Dr. Parker.

Her stomach lurched, as the image of her teacher's corpse flashed through her mind again. She considered running back to her car. She didn't want to step foot in that building again.

She didn't know if she *could*.

Even worse, her next class *was* Dr. Parker's class.

Rose had nearly decided to leave when she noticed a familiar form in the breezeway. A guy dressed in a college hoodie and faded jeans leaned against a pillar, his brownish blonde hair stuck up in short, gelled spikes.

It was Owen.

She took slow, deep breaths to calm herself.

She couldn't run now. Not without worrying Owen.

Rose stopped in front of him. Adjusting her backpack on her shoulder, she frowned at him. "I thought you had Organic Chemistry right now."

Owen shrugged. "I wanted to catch you before your first class."

Rose looked horrified. "You skipped class for me? Now, I feel evil!"

Owen laughed, "Well, if it makes you feel any better, I skipped class last week to take Piper to the vet, and she's probably the *least* evil dog on the planet."

"That's true," she agreed. "She doesn't even bark at the mailman."

He nodded. "She loves the mailman."

Rose sighed, "Audrey said you were angry at me."

"Audrey exaggerates," Owen said. He touched Rose's stitches warily. "I really wish you would've just let us walk you home, though."

She shrugged. "It wasn't that big of a deal. I'm fine, as you can see."

"Not a big deal?" Owen repeated. "Rose, someone tried to *kill* you!"

Rose frowned. "How did you know about *that*? I never told—"

"Audrey told me," Owen interrupted.

"Right. Of course," she said, shaking her head at herself. She'd always trusted people easily. So, why was she suddenly suspicious of her own friends?

"Speaking of Audrey," he said, slipping his hands into his pockets, "is she still planning on visiting her grandparents this weekend?"

"She better be," Rose muttered.

"I don't think you should be alone right now," Owen said worriedly.

She shrugged. "I'll be fine. Audrey's been planning this visit for months."

"Yeah, I know," he said. He shifted uneasily. "Which…is why I think you should stay with us this weekend. You can't just stay alone while someone is out there trying to kill you. You'll be safe with us." He avoided her gaze. "Jared—he, uhh, has experience with this kind of thing."

"Umm," Rose said, frowning, "what kind of thing?"

Owen suddenly looked uncomfortable. "Did you ever wonder how Jared and I met?"

"I assumed high school," Rose said. They'd been together since before she'd met either of them.

He shook his head. "We didn't go to the same school—at least not at first." He sighed. "Do you remember how I told you that I switched schools during my senior year?"

She nodded. "You said the people at your old school treated you badly."

He winced. "And they did. That was the truth," he said hesitantly, "but, actually, I switched schools because I moved in with Jared's family. After my parents died."

"Your parents," Rose breathed. "Owen, you never told me."

"I know. I should have," Owen said. He glanced around to make sure no one was listening. "Especially you, especially after your mom died. You, of all people, would understand. But then, you would've had questions about how it happened, and I would've had to tell you they were murdered, which is hard to—"

"Murdered?" Rose repeated, a little too loudly. She winced at her mistake, grateful no one had chosen that moment to walk by. "By whom?"

Owen looked a little greenish. "It doesn't really matter."

She decided not to press. "I'm so sorry, Owen."

He offered her a weak smile. "Thanks."

She frowned. "So, then, was Jared your foster brother or something?"

"No," he said with a small laugh. "It was nothing like that. I met Jared the night my parents died. It was his family who saved me from the...*people* who murdered my parents."

Her frown deepened. "How?"

"It's a long story," he said. He seemed a bit nervous, which was unusual for Owen. "The point is...they know a lot about this kind of thing." Before Rose could ask what sort of thing he meant, he added, "Rose, I told you all of this because I want you to understand that Jared knows how to protect you."

"Okay," Rose said, drawing out the word in confusion. "I have a few questions—and by a few, I mean a billion or more."

"I know," Owen sighed, "but I can't. I don't want to talk about it—no more than we already have, anyway. I know it sounds confusing, but you just have to trust me. You'll be safe with us."

Rose wanted to tell him that he didn't understand, that it wasn't a typical murderer who'd tried to kill her, that no matter what kind of murderer Jared's family had *somehow* taken down, it didn't even compare to Theron. But she couldn't say any of that. "I can't. I'm sorry. I have plans. A date! I have a date!"

Owen raised an eyebrow in amusement. "Really? With whom?"

Rose grinned. "Oh, you know. Just a certain tall, dark, and handsome...*bookshelf.*"

He stared blankly at her. "You have a date with your books?"

"Yep," Rose confirmed. "I need to brush up on my knowledge of creepy, psychotic murderers, and I have just the horror novel collection to do so."

Owen rolled his eyes. "I worry about your sanity sometimes."

Rose's eyes shifted toward the history building, her gaze immediately freezing on the wall Kallias had shoved her against the night before. She glanced at the doorway, and the image of Theron, cut open and bloody—still standing somehow, despite that gruesome injury—flashed through her mind.

She jumped, as she felt Owen grab her shoulder, and she shoved him away unintentionally.

"It's just me, Rose," Owen said, his hazel eyes wide with concern.

Rose stared at him, embarrassed by her own panic. "Owen, I'm so sorry. I didn't mean to..." she trailed off. "I guess I kind of...forgot where I was."

"I know," he said. "I said your name, and you didn't even hear me."

She glanced down at her feet, her cheeks flushing. "I'm sorry. I—"

"Rose, I get it," Owen said. His hazel eyes were soft and sympathetic. "After what happened to you, anyone would feel a little traumatized. It's normal."

She sighed, "I better get to class before I'm late."

He nodded, his brows still creased with worry. "Reconsider. Please."

"I'll be fine," Rose assured him. She looked toward the building, as the door opened and students filed out from their classes. A brief glimpse of the foyer, where Dr. Parker had been killed, took her breath.

"What if he doesn't stop until you're dead?" Owen asked, suddenly.

She glanced at him, her anxiety and suspicion rising in tandem. "Is there something you're not saying, Owen?"

He looked away. "No. Nothing."

Rose continued to frown. "I have to go now."

"I'll see you later," he said—without looking at her.

She watched as he walked away, more than a little confused about how he'd acted the last few days. It just wasn't like Owen to look so nervous. He'd always taken everything in stride.

Finally, Rose sighed and continued her walk to class. When she reached the door, she hesitated with her hand on the door handle, as she tried to muster up the courage to go inside.

"Rose! Wait!"

Audrey ran through the breezeway, toward Rose, like a bull charging at the color red.

Rose inched a little closer to the door, afraid that her friend wouldn't be able to stop in time.

But Audrey did stop, and she leaned froward, her hands on her knees, as she tried to catch her breath.

"Why didn't anyone tell me that today is Stop-Rose-On-Her-Way-To-Class Day?" Rose asked. "I would've bought banners and party hats."

"You were gone when I woke up this morning," Audrey panted.

"I had to leave early to drive to the prison," Rose reminded her.

"Oh!" Audrey exclaimed. "Today's the day you visit your brother!"

"Yeah. Same day every month," Rose said, adjusting her backpack.

Audrey straightened and ran her hand through her disheveled brown hair. "Of course. My brain's just been all over the place today."

Being 'all over the place' was sort of Audrey's m.o., but there was clearly more to it today.

"What happened?" Rose asked.

"My grandparents are here," Audrey said breathlessly. "They

picked me up because they didn't want me to attempt such a long drive in my car, which is probably a good idea because I'm sure it'd break down before I reached the Georgia state-line. They're actually parked right over there." Audrey pointed to a small, silver car parked beside the 'No Parking' sign. Apparently, the disregard for signs was hereditary.

"Slow down, Audrey," Rose said worriedly. "What's wrong?"

Audrey exhaled shakily, and then, she began to speak again—slowly, this time, "I had another dream last night, and Rose, it was the worst one yet."

Rose pushed her hair out of her face. "What do you mean by that?"

Audrey grimaced, her hazel eyes wide with horror. "It... I—I can't..." she stammered, unable to finish. "Look, I think you should come to my grandparents' house with me. Just get out of town."

"No," Rose said with a regretful sigh, "I can't do that. You know I can't do that."

"Oh, come on!" Audrey said, her voice strained with desperation. "My grandparents *love* you, which is saying something because they hate everyone else I've ever brought home."

Rose laughed, "Probably because the others were boyfriends."

"You're right," Audrey said, seemingly calmed by that thought. "They hate everyone I date."

"I don't blame them," Rose commented.

Audrey grinned. "Maybe I should just marry *you*, then," she teased.

Rose smiled and shook her head. "Then, they'd hate me, too."

"Nah," Audrey said, waving her hand. "Seriously, though, Rose, I think you need to get out of town. In my dream...you were in our apartment when he killed you."

Rose froze. "Are you sure?"

Audrey suddenly looked sick. "I could see the apartment, the bed..."

"But Kallias said that I should stay home," Rose said worriedly.

"I know," Audrey said with hopeless shrug. "Maybe he was wrong."

"Or maybe he was lying," Rose said with a bitter edge in her voice.

"He saved your life two nights in a row," Audrey reminded her. "Why would he do all of that just to let you die now?"

"I don't know, but it's what you saw, right?" Rose sighed. "Do you what night it will happen?"

"No," Audrey said. "I never know that. Just come with me, okay?"

"No," Rose said firmly. "Absolutely not."

Audrey wrung her hands anxiously. "Rose, please!"

Rose moved closer so she could whisper, "What if Theron follows me? He'd kill you. He might even kill your grandparents. I would never let that happen to you, Audrey."

Audrey sighed in defeat. "Fine. Then, I'll tell them I can't go."

"No, you won't," Rose said stubbornly. "They've already driven all the way here to pick you up. You're not sending them home without you. You're going."

"I'm not leaving you here to die!" Audrey argued.

"It may not even happen this weekend," Rose reminded her.

Audrey ran her fingers through her tangled mess of hair. "But at some point, it *will* happen. Unless you do something to stop it."

"Then, that's what I'll do," Rose said.

Audrey scowled at her. "What will you do?"

"Research," Rose said.

Audrey rolled her eyes. "Research? Really, Rose?"

Rose shrugged. "There has to be something helpful out there. In the past, when I've read about vampires, I've done so with the assumption that the stories were fiction. Now, I know the truth—that the fiction is fact, that *any* story might be true. So, I'll read them again," she told her. "I just have to find a way to stop a vampire."

"And if there isn't a way?" Audrey asked worriedly.

"I will find a way," Rose assured her, "I promise."

Audrey's shoulders fell slightly, and then, she leapt forward and threw her arms around Rose's neck. "Please, please, don't die," she whispered, hugging Rose tightly. "Promise me you won't die."

"I promise," Rose said. "Now, go. Your grandparents are waiting."

Audrey pulled back. "You can't die this weekend anyway," she said with a half-smile that *barely* hid her panic. "We have to look for wedding dresses on Monday."

Rose smiled at Audrey's teasing. "I wouldn't wear a dress, even if I were getting married. Well, maybe for Wonder Woman." Her lips pulled to the side thoughtfully. "Nah. Not even for her."

Audrey laughed, "Fine, I'll wear the dress. You can wear the tux."

"Bye, Audrey."

Rose didn't let the smile slip from her face, until Audrey turned to job back to her grandparents' car. She hated lying to her friends, pretending that she believed everything would be fine when she knew it wouldn't, but she couldn't put them in danger.

Struck by a sudden sense of dread, Rose yelled out, "I love you!"

Audrey spun around and grinned playfully. "Now you're *really* making us sound gay," she teased. But then, her smile faded, and she said, "I love you, too."

Rose nodded and opened the door of the building. She nearly screamed, as she ran into someone, sending their books scattering across the tile floor.

She blinked at the small, mousy woman in front of her.

"Riley," Rose acknowledged, blushing. "I'm so sorry."

She knelt and began gathering up Riley's books.

"N-n-no, it's my f-fault," Riley stuttered, her hands fiddling with the corners of her purple plaid skirt. "I s-shouldn't have been in front of the door."

Rose stood and placed the books in Riley's arms. "No, it's mine," she argued. Her gaze shifted toward the corner of the room, where she'd found Dr. Parker's body the night before, and her stomach turned at the memory. She exhaled shakily. "I'm not thinking clearly today."

Riley fiddled nervously with her long, black hair that was bound together in braided pigtails. "It's okay. Really. It's g-good to s-see you today."

Rose smiled. "It's good to see you, too."

Riley adjusted the crooked, black glasses that framed her green eyes. Her cheeks flushed a bright pink. "I'm sorry. I can't s-seem to stop s-stuttering."

"I told you before," Rose said. "You don't need to apologize for that. If other people have a problem with it, that's *their* problem."

Riley smiled and ducked her head shyly. "So, um, are you r-ready for that exam we have in Dr. Parker's class today?"

Rose's smile faded at the mention of her teacher's name. "Sure."

Riley laughed softly. "Then, why do you look so pale?"

Rose sucked in a shaky breath. "Maybe I *am* a little nervous," she lied.

"Why?" Riley asked. "You've probably *never* made lower than an A."

Rose frowned. "Not that I can remember, no."

Riley giggled, "Then, you shouldn't be nervous. You'll do fine."

Rose forced herself to smile, despite the anxiety. "Thanks."

She scanned the room for any sign of the murder. Some small part of her probably hoped—against all reason—that her teacher would show up for class, still alive, somehow.

But the more rational part of her had come to class today for another reason. She needed to know what had happened after they left.

Surprisingly, the room looked exactly as it always had. Rose saw no sign of blood or struggle in the foyer. She stared at the white floor—determined to see at least one blood stain—but the floor was spotless.

Riley placed a hand on Rose's arm. "Are you okay?"

Rose jumped at the touch, her heart racing inside her chest.

"I'm sorry," Riley stammered. "I d-didn't mean to s-scare you."

Rose raked her hand through her long, wavy red hair. "It's okay. I'm fine," she assured Riley. "I just kind of spaced out for a minute."

"Oh, I do that, too, when my sugar gets low," Riley told her. "Have you eaten today? I have some peanut butter crackers in my bag, if you want some."

Rose laughed. "I am *not* taking your crackers. You might need them."

Riley blushed. "I have plenty."

"I'm fine. I promise," Rose said. "I just had a rough night."

Rose cast one last glance at the floor, and her breath caught in her throat, as the image of her dead teacher flashed through her mind yet again. She squeezed her eyes shut, waiting for the memory to subside. She'd been through this before, after her mother's death.

Rose hated not being in control of her own mind.

"You're not hallucinating, are you?" Riley asked worriedly. She blushed. "S-sorry, I...noticed your stitches. And my brother played football. He had concussions all of the time, and he used to have these weird hallucinations."

Rose laughed softly. "Are you sure that wasn't the drugs?"

Riley gave a small smile. "It may have been."

"Yeah," Rose agreed. "Come on. Let's get to class before we're late."

They shuffled through the crowded hallway, as they made their way toward the classroom that Dr. Parker usually used. Rose worried about what she'd find when she reached the classroom.

But when she reached the classroom, she stopped in the doorway—and found that, like the foyer, the classroom looked as it always had.

All of the desks and chairs set upright in even rows.

The floor looked spotless, any sign of blood wiped clean.

Even the wall looked perfect—despite the fact that she remembered it caving in when Kallias had thrown Theron against it.

"Are you gay?" Riley asked suddenly.

Rose turned toward her. "W-what?" she sputtered.

Riley's face reddened. She stared at her feet. "S-sorry. I-I just heard the l-last part of what you and Audrey were s-saying, and it was a l-little confusing."

"It's just a joke she likes to make with me sometimes," Rose laughed. "Audrey's as straight as it gets."

"And you?" Riley asked quietly, fiddling with her skirt again.

A classmate chose that moment to squeeze between them on his way to his seat.

Rose glanced curiously at Riley after he passed. "Uh, why do you ask?"

"No reason," Riley said quickly. She'd apparently changed her mind about the question. "Just forget I asked. It's embarrassing. I need to sit down."

Rose stood there, dumbly, as Riley found a seat on the other side of the classroom. "That was weird," she said under her breath.

Rose took a seat near the back of the classroom. As she waited for the rest of the students to arrive, she once again found herself scanning the room for anything out of place.

It seemed impossible that every trace of what happened could've been wiped clean. It made her feel as if she'd imagined the entire night.

When silence fell over the classroom, Rose snapped out of her thoughts. She glanced back at the door that had opened and realized the reason for their silence.

A tall, middle-aged man stepped through the door and walked slowly toward the front of the classroom. He wore a perfect suit, as always—the kind that clearly hadn't come from a thrift store—and though his face looked young, his hair was totally grey.

Rose knew him well, as did any history major. He was the Dean of the History Department.

He leaned on the teacher's podium and folded his hands on the wooden surface. His body language seemed far more relaxed than Rose had expected.

"Good morning. My name is Dr. Davidson, as I am sure you're all aware."

"Is something wrong?" asked someone in the front row.

"Nothing that I know of," Dr. Davidson told them. "I just came to announce that Dr. Parker isn't here today, so all of her classes have been cancelled." As the class sighed in relief, he laughed, "I can see you're all devastated."

The rest of the class laughed at the sarcastic remark, but Rose didn't.

Rose stared at the head of the department, studying his expression and his body language, looking for any sign that he knew what had happened to her teacher.

"Have a nice day," the Dean said, as he turned to leave.

Rose grabbed her books and jumped out of her seat, rushing after him as he left. "Dr. Davidson!" she called, following him into the hallway.

The professor turned around, smiling kindly when he recognized her. "Oh, hello, Miss Foster. How was your trip to Greece last week?"

She smiled nervously in return and tightened her grip on her books, as people filed out behind her. "Great," she said quickly. "I wanted to ask you, um... Do you know why Dr. Parker is out today? I mean, is she okay?"

Dr. Davidson laughed. "I knew you'd be the only one to actually be *disappointed* that classes are cancelled." He shrugged. "But no, I have no idea. She just didn't show today." His smile didn't waver. "I'm sure she has a good reason, though. She never misses."

"You didn't think that maybe you should call the police?" Rose asked.

Dr. Davidson frowned. He focused his attention on his tie, straightening it. "Calling the police because a teacher took a sick day is a bit extreme, don't you think?"

"But you haven't heard from her, have you?" she argued.

He shrugged, still messing with his tie, as if he were bored with the conversation. "I tried her cell phone, but if she's at the hospital, her phone's off, anyway," he said. "Look, I'm sure she would be flattered to know that she has a student so concerned for her, but you really should relax, Miss Foster."

"Have you tried calling her husband yet?" Rose continued.

He narrowed his eyes. "Is there a reason you're so worried," he said, a strange note in his tone, "Miss Foster?"

Rose pursed her lips, realizing she had to stop talking before she got herself into trouble. "No, I just... I've never known of her to miss before."

Dr. Davidson nodded and placed his hand on her shoulder. "I'm sure she's fine. One of her kids probably got sick, and work was the last thing on her mind. It's still early in the day. I'm sure we'll hear from her soon."

A strange, uneasy feeling traveled through her, as she glanced at his hand on her shoulder. Though his expression and his tone gave no indication of deception, something felt...off.

Disingenuous.

But then, she remembered that she'd felt suspicious of Owen, as well, and she realized that she was just being paranoid.

She distrusted everyone right now.

"Yeah," Rose said, unable to meet his gaze. "Thanks."

She shook off his hand with a quickness that she *hoped* wasn't rude, and she hurried toward the door.

Rose didn't stop walking until she was halfway across the lawn, and she only stopped then because someone called her name.

She turned around to find Owen and Jared sitting on a bench, shaded by a tall tree.

"I thought you had class," Owen said.

Rose walked toward them. Owen and Jared sat next to each other with a bag of fast food sitting between them. "They cancelled it," she explained.

"Awesome," Owen said. "You're welcome to hang out with us."

"No, thanks," Rose said with a nervous smile. "I wouldn't want to interrupt your breakfast date."

Jared held out the fast food bag, wordlessly offering her a biscuit.

She shook her head. "I'm not hungry. But thanks, Jared."

He shrugged and dropped the paper bag on the bench between them.

"Well, what will you do with all your free time?" Owen asked playfully.

Rose shrugged. "I figured I'd just go to the—"

"Library?" Owen finished for her.

She laughed. "You know me well."

"You really should reconsider staying with us," Jared said, suddenly. His deep voice caught her off-guard. He'd said so little around her that she barely recognized it, still. "I highly doubt *you* even own a gun."

Rose glanced at him. His dark eyes studied her suspiciously, and something about that set her on edge. "Who says a gun would protect me?"

Jared shrugged. "Guns kill humans."

Owen elbowed him. "Shut up," he hissed.

She frowned at Jared, once again feeling a sense of apprehensiveness twisting at her gut. Something about his use of the word *'human'* bothered her.

"I have to go," Rose said nervously. "I'll see you guys later."

OWEN WATCHED, AS ROSE LEFT, CROSSING THE CAMPUS, TOWARD THE library.

When he was sure that Rose was too far away to hear them, he twisted toward Jared. "What the hell is wrong with you?"

"I don't trust her," Jared stated.

"She's my closest friend. I'd trust her with my life," Owen told him.

Jared barely even spared him a glance. "She was attacked by a vampire."

Owen looked around to make sure no one was listening. "You don't know that."

"Yes, I do," Jared said.

Owen shook his head in frustration. "Either way, I don't see how that would make you not trust her. She didn't ask for it to happen."

"But she survived," Jared said. "Would you like to explain to me how?"

"I don't know," Owen admitted. "Maybe she just got lucky."

"I doubt it," Jared muttered.

Owen narrowed his eyes at that. "But as you can *see*, she's still human."

"For now," Jared said.

7

NOT AN ORDINARY HUMAN

*R*ose made it halfway through the mountainous pile of books before she passed out.

Her small apartment looked as if it'd been hit by a rockslide of books. Both fiction and nonfiction books scattered the floor, and notebooks filled Rose's bed and the nightstand beside it.

Lying on her stomach after tiring of sitting up, Rose slept with her face mashed against an open book—the one she'd been reading before she'd passed out.

Aside from the steady tick of the clock on the wall, the only sound that filled the room was the sound of her slow and steady breathing.

After Rose left the library, she'd spent the entire night mulling over every vampire myth she'd come across, trying to find some pattern to separate fact from fiction.

But she'd only come away with more questions.

Earlier in the night, she'd jumped at every sound outside her door, afraid that each one might've been Theron, but as dawn drew closer, the sleep deprivation overtook her anxiety.

And eventually, she'd fallen asleep.

She awoke, suddenly, as three short knocks sounded at her door.

Rose scrambled out of bed and stared in horror at the door. She kept as quiet as possible, still hoping that she'd only dreamed the knock.

But the three knocks came again.

Rose quietly crept toward the kitchen area and pulled open a drawer. She took a kitchen knife and returned her attention to the door.

She knew it wasn't Audrey. Audrey had a key.

Audrey *never* knocked, and Rose knew of no one else who would come to her apartment at such a late hour of the night.

She held out hope that it was Kallias checking in with her or that it was Owen and Jared, but hope wasn't a strong enough reason to abandon caution.

She stayed as far away from the door as possible, determined to show no signs that she was home.

The thought of calling the cops briefly crossed her mind, but what she could tell them that *wouldn't* make her sound insane?

Besides, there was also the small matter of her phone being lost.

The knocking stopped.

Silence stretched on for several moments.

Rose wanted to peek behind the curtains and see if the person had given up, but she couldn't risk him seeing her. So, she inched toward her bed, instead.

Before she reached the bed, however, a loud crash resounded through the apartment.

The door fell open.

Literally.

It just...fell.

The old, orange streetlight outside outlined the silhouette in her doorway. She didn't even need to compare the figure to the one from her memories—because he spoke, then.

And she recognized that sneering voice of his.

"I tried to be polite, but you wouldn't answer the door," Theron said.

"Yes, that's code for *I-don't-want-you-to-come-inside*," Rose informed him.

"You're being rude," Theron scolded.

The lamplight finally illuminated his features, allowing her to actually see him for the first time since he'd kicked down her door.

He leaned against the doorframe, dressed in a white button-down shirt and black slacks. His short, brown hair fell around his forehead. His injuries from the night before were gone.

He was fine.

In just one night, he'd completely...*healed*.

"My mistake," Rose scoffed. "I forgot the proper etiquette for murderers who kick down your door. Remind me. Am I supposed to curtsy or shoot you?"

Theron smiled. "You can shoot me, if you want. It won't kill me."

"I'd test that theory if I had a gun," Rose said. "How are you even *alive*?"

"It takes a lot to kill a vampire," Theron said.

"You were practically gutted. It takes more than *that*?" she asked.

Theron rolled his eyes. "You'll be dead in a matter of minutes, and you're wasting your last words on pointless questions?"

Rose shrugged. "I like learning."

"I like killing," Theron told her.

She frowned as he stepped into the room. "I didn't invite you inside."

Theron approached her slowly. "I know. Like I said, you're rude."

Well, at least that answered Rose's question about *that* myth.

Rose stepped backward, keeping as much distance between them as possible. She kept the knife hidden behind her back, and she glanced at the door behind Theron, hoping she could reach it before he killed her.

"Well, this sucks," she remarked.

"Literally," Theron said, flashing his fangs.

Her pulse spiked at the sight of those sharp, inhuman teeth. "I'm sure you're the first vampire to make *that* joke," she muttered.

He narrowed those cold, dark eyes of his, and he took slow, measured steps toward her, backing her toward the wall. "I don't often kill the humans that appeal to me. Not immediately, anyway. I usually like to keep them around—for feeding and other...*recreation*."

Rose didn't bother to hide her disgust.

"But *you*," Theron said. "Well, I think you're one human I'll like better *dead*."

Rose swallowed uneasily, when she realized he had her cornered. "Dude, I want no part in your necrophilia."

Theron snatched her off the ground by her throat. "I'm so sick of your little *jokes*. I should just snap your neck and be done with you."

Rose's lungs screamed for air, and blotches of red and purple colored her skin.

Theron tossed her onto the bed. "But that would be a *much* too easy death for you."

Disoriented and gasping for breath, Rose rolled onto her stomach and crawled toward the edge of the bed. Her muscles didn't move as quickly as they should have, and she'd barely made it to her feet before Theron grabbed her again.

His arms circled her waist, and he jerked her back to the bed.

Rose cringed when she felt his breath on her ear.

"This will be much worse if you fight," he warned.

That only made her fight harder. "Let go of me!" she gasped.

Theron tossed her back onto the bed. "I don't think so."

Out of the corner of her eye, Rose saw the knife she'd dropped when Theron attacked her. Only a few feet from her, it set between the two pillows, the blade gleaming against the headboard.

With her methods of survival quickly dwindling, Rose lunged for it, but before she reached it, the knife was…gone.

She looked up at Theron, who stood over her, and saw the knife in his hand. She blinked, stunned by how quickly he'd moved.

"Humans are such slow creatures," Theron said, and he tossed the knife aside.

Metal clanged, as the blade hit the floor and slid toward the kitchen area.

Rose made another attempt to run, but Theron easily shoved her down. This time, to her horror, he climbed on top of her to hold her still.

The pressure of his body on hers unleashed a panic inside of her that was more powerful than any she'd felt in years.

Not again.

That was all she could think, all she could feel.

Not again.

Rose shoved and kicked with all of her might, but he didn't move. The feeling of doom expanded inside her.

"You're terrified, aren't you?" Theron said in her ear. "I smell your adrenaline."

Anger and revulsion boiled inside of her. "Get off of me! Now!"

But Theron just placed his hand over her mouth. "Quiet."

A strange, dangerous feeling unfurled in her blood—something unlike anything she'd felt before.

Theron's dark gaze fell to her neck, and before she could anticipate his movement, he sank his fangs into her neck.

The pain of his fangs tearing her skin barely had time to reach her panicked mind, before it subsided, and a new, disturbing sensation began to build inside of her.

It didn't make sense.

It was euphoric and pleasant, and somehow, Rose *knew* it wasn't real. She didn't know how she knew. It wasn't like she had any clarity in the midst of her panic, but still, she *knew*.

And she fought it.

The fight to stay in control of her mind was so exhausting that she didn't have any strength left to put up a physical fight, as well.

Until he tore open her pants.

Intense, powerful waves of both terror and anger filled her, and suddenly, something snapped inside of her.

Suddenly, something felt...*different.*

"Get off of me," Rose said. Her voice sounded wrong, somehow—darker and more powerful than a human voice should have. "Now."

The room quaked, the framed paintings rattling against the wall.

Suddenly, Theron was ripped from her and flung across the room.

Rose couldn't bite back the cry of pain as his teeth tore open her neck, but before she had time to process what had caused the pain, she heard the crash of Theron's body hitting the wall.

She didn't know what had saved her, and she didn't waste time trying to figure it out. She scrambled from the bed and ran, snatching her backpack from the floor on her way out.

"I know you're in here," Kallias sighed. "I smell you."

Dark and dusty, the small house appeared to be abandoned. Boards covered the windows, and the rooms were mostly bare. A tattered mattress lay in the center of the beige, carpeted floor.

The air felt cool and stale—with no electricity running through the home—and the entire house smelled of dust, mildew, blood, and vampires.

One of those vampires being Theron himself.

Sofia emerged from a closet, a curious smile on her lips. "Are you stalking me?"

Kallias turned toward her, and he gave an annoyed sigh. "I don't know your scent well enough to stalk you. I didn't even realize it was *you* I smelled."

"Then, who *are* you stalking?" Sofia asked.

"Theron," Kallias answered, "but you already know that."

Sofia blinked those large, doe-like eyes of hers. "No, I told you. I—"

"I don't have time for your bullshit, Sofia," Kallias interrupted. "His scent is all over this place, including the bed. He's clearly been staying here."

Sofia's full lips curved into a surprised smile. "If you recognize his scent that easily," she said, "then…you've tasted his blood!"

His lip curled. "Not by choice."

Sofia laughed. "I would've never guessed that—of *you*."

Kallias grew more impatient by the moment. "Where is he?"

"Not here," Sofia said honestly.

"I can see that," Kallias said. "So, where *is* he?"

"I don't know," Sofia said with a shrug.

"You said that last night," Kallias reminded her—though he knew she hadn't been lying *then*.

Tonight, she was less convincing.

"I didn't know then, either," Sofia said. "I've only been here since sunset. I was called to—"

"To what?" Kallias said, when she didn't finish.

With a forced smile, she said, "Share information."

"*What* information?" Kallias snarled.

Sofia laughed, as if his anger was nothing to her. "You're welcome to wait with me until he returns."

Kallias sighed. He wasn't as easily manipulated as Erik, and this was clearly a concept Sofia had yet to learn. "Perhaps I will."

Sofia's smile deepened. "I can think of a few ways to pass the time."

Kallias tried to force some sort of pleasantry into his expression, but his irritation was hard to hide. "And what might those be?"

Taking the bait, Sofia sauntered toward him, her heels sinking into the old carpet. She stopped directly in front of him, and her small figure pressed against him.

She tucked her sleek, black hair behind her ears and looked up into his eyes. "That depends," she murmured, "on what you like."

"Good," Kallias said, "because what I'd like is for you to answer my question." He grasped her wrist so that she couldn't escape, and he used his abilities to take control of her mind, once again. "Tell me where Theron is."

The panic instantly left her eyes. "He's gone to kill the human woman."

Now, it was Kallias's turn to worry. "Rose," he breathed. "*Where* does he intend to kill her?"

"She stayed home tonight," Sofia said. "He'll have to go there."

He cursed under his breath. "He knows where she lives?"

"Yes, they told him everything about her," Sofia said.

"They?" Kallias frowned. "Who is *they*?"

"Other vampires," Sofia said. "They supplied the information. I relayed it."

"Shit," he groaned. "How many of you idiots are there?"

Still under his control, Sofia could do nothing but answer the rhetorical question. "I don't know how many—only that they are more."

His gaze fell on a small blood stain, and he knew without asking that it was Theron's. "Since when do vampires break into humans' apartments? That draws attention."

"Theron has decided that this is more important," Sofia told him.

Kallias glanced at her. "More important than not pissing off Aaron?"

"He no longer fears Aaron," Sofia told him, "and he says that none of us need to. Ever again."

His gaze snapped back toward her. "Why?"

"The woman," Sofia said. "She's the key to our power and freedom."

Kallias gave her a short, disbelieving laugh. "He's just making up shit now, isn't he?" He frowned curiously. "Why her?"

"I don't know," Sofia answered. She couldn't lie under his control, so Kallias, unfortunately, had to believe her. "She has something."

"Well, that's helpful," he muttered. "How long has he been gone?"

"Long enough to kill her," Sofia said.

ROSE RAN AS FAST AS HER FEET WOULD TAKE HER.

She didn't look back. She didn't pay attention to her surroundings. She just kept running, her feet pounding the concrete beneath her.

Her heartbeat thundered in her head, and her lungs felt too tight, as if they'd explode under the pressure.

She needed to stop, just for a moment, just for a breath, but she couldn't. Theron moved faster than her. Her only chance of survival was to force her feet to keep moving.

Rose gasped as she collided with a large, hard object. The force of the collision knocked her backward, nearly knocking her flat on her back.

Before she hit the ground, however, two hands grasped her shoulders to steady her. Her stomach sunk with dread, as she realized that she'd run into a *person*.

Terrified it was Theron, she twisted and attempted to run from him, but with her head spinning so violently, the first wobbly step sent her toppling forward.

His arms circled her stomach, catching her before she hit the ground. He pulled her back against him, her feet leaving the ground as he lifted her. Her back pressed against his front, and she felt his breath on her ear. She continued to fight and flail—until she heard him speak.

"Rose, it's okay. I've got you," he said in her ear. "You have to breathe, all right? Your heart's beating too fast. *Breathe.*"

Her body went slack against him. "Kallias?" she said in shock.

Suddenly, his entire body seemed to stiffen, as if he were experiencing the worst pain imaginable. "You're bleeding," he said in a strained voice. "Your neck is bleeding."

Rose lifted her eyebrows. "Nice observation skills."

Kallias dropped her on the ground and stepped back.

He'd smelled her blood before he found her, of course, but he'd been so focused on getting to her before Theron killed her that he hadn't considered how the blood would affect him.

Rose pulled herself onto her knees and rubbed her palms against her jeans to scrape off the little rocks that had embedded themselves in her hands. "You know," she complained, "it kind of defeats the purpose of catching someone if you're just going to drop them on the ground without warning."

Kallias watched blood seep slowly from that gruesome bite wound in her neck, and his mouth watered at the sight.

Rose stood, the dizziness making her stagger, and she turned toward him, slowly and unsteadily. She glanced around at her surroundings—at the trees and dark buildings—realizing for the first time how far she'd run.

The street was empty, which didn't surprise her, considering it was barely an hour before dawn, but it was definitely a lot further than she'd *thought* she could run.

Rose frowned at Kallias, wondering why he still hadn't said anything.

He stood just a few feet away from her, black jeans hugging his hips and a leather jacket hanging open over his thin black T-shirt.

His golden skin seemed much paler than usual, and she nearly gasped when she saw his eyes.

They looked much darker than usual and...*feral.*

"Kallias," Rose said nervously. "Are you okay?"

Sucking in a ragged breath, Kallias tore his gaze from the blood on her neck and forced himself to meet her gaze.

The blood loss had left Rose's skin papery white, but a deep flush darkened her cheeks as she panted for air. Blood covered the top half of her blue T-shirt, turning the fabric a dark, blackish burgundy.

Rose took a step back. "On second thought, stay away from me."

He blinked out of his daze. "What?"

Her wide, blue eyes narrowed at him. "You heard me."

Kallias noticed the spike in her pulse. "You're afraid of me," he realized. He smelled the adrenaline in her blood. "Why are you afraid?"

"Isn't that what you wanted?" Rose said sharply.

"Excuse me?" Kallias said.

"You *wanted* to make me afraid of you," she said. "You *tried* to scare me."

He scowled. "Yes—because I wanted you to run, to save yourself."

"You know," Rose said breathlessly, "I don't think it's a good idea for me to listen to you anymore." She stepped back. "After all, whatever you'd say would probably just be another lie."

Kallias scoffed at the accusation. "Wow. Could you explain to me where all of this is coming from?" he snarled. "Because I can't keep up with your irrational mood swings."

Mood swings?

He'd lied to her, and now, he wanted her to question her own judgement, too?

"I am not irrational!" she said.

He crossed his arms. "Let's agree to disagree on that."

Rose glared at him. "You're saying you've *never* lied to me?"

His smug look faltered. "Well, I mean, I..." he trailed off.

"I knew it," she said. "You told him where to find me, didn't you?"

Kallias stared blankly at her. "You think I'm helping Theron?"

"Maybe," Rose said with a shrug. "You're the one who told me to stay home."

"Because I didn't realize that he would kick down your damn door just to get to you," Kallias said. "I thought he was smart enough not to risk being seen by any human in your apartment building. A bad judgement on my part, I'll admit." Kallias stepped toward her. "But why the hell would you think that I would help Theron?"

"You warned me not to trust you. I should've listened," Rose said.

"Well, yes," Kallias agreed, "but still, you're being ridiculous." He lifted his eyebrows. "Think about what you're saying, Rose. Why would I save you from Theron if I were *helping* him?"

"To earn my trust," Rose said easily.

"I don't *want* your trust," Kallias told her. He took another step toward her. "Why would I want your trust? So I could kill you? Is that what you're thinking? If I wanted to kill you, Rose, I could do it right now. You'd never see it coming."

"You seem awfully sure of that," Rose noted. "Tell me something. How many people did you have to kill before you felt *that* sure of it?"

He froze, and hesitation flickered in his light brown eyes.

Rose took a step back. "I knew it," she whispered.

"Rose," he said hoarsely. "You're panicking. You need to stay calm."

She threw her hands up. "Sure, I'll stay calm while you kill me," she said, her voice cracking with nervousness. "No reason to panic!"

"Damn it, woman. For the last time, I'm not going to kill you!" Kallias snarled. He leaned closer to her. "Listen to me closely. I hate Theron. My hate for him runs so deep that someone as kind and pure as you could never even *comprehend* that kind of darkness. So, believe me when I tell you that Hell will freeze over before I will ever *help* him."

Her resolve faltered. "Why do you hate him so much?"

"It's none of your business," he said. "All you need to know is that I'd never help him. You're an intelligent woman. Use your damn brain."

Rose narrowed her eyes at that. "I *am* using it," she assured him, "and something isn't right about you."

Kallias hesitated at that. "You're right," he admitted, "but that doesn't mean I'm trying to kill you. You saw how badly I injured Theron? Do you honestly think he would've let someone split him open just to gain a human's trust?"

Rose shrugged. "He seems psychotic enough to me."

Kallias chuckled. "Yes, but not smart enough."

Rose's shoulders relaxed slightly. "Okay, you have a point there," she relented, "but how did he know where to find me? Last night, *you* made me promise to stay home."

"He's had vampires watching your every move, Rose," he said with a sympathetic frown. "Probably humans, too. They've been stalking you."

Rose shuddered, suddenly feeling sick. "Talk about creepy."

"Vampires are creatures of darkness. Creepiness comes with the territory," Kallias sighed. He kept his gaze on a closed, Italian restaurant across the street. He could barely look at her without wanting to attack her and feed from her—to drink the blood that called to his predatory nature and threatened to overtake his self-control. "I told you to stay home because vampires don't usually attack humans in their homes."

"Well, Theron did," Rose said, "and I didn't even invite him inside."

Caught off guard by the last part, a short laugh escaped his lips. "Why would it matter whether you invited him inside or not?"

Rose sighed irritably, as she recalled her hours of fruitless research. "In the stories, vampires have to be invited inside."

Kallias burst into a fit of laughter. "Right. Vampires are terrifying monsters that enjoy brutally murdering humans, but don't worry. They're actually really polite. They'll wait until you invite them inside before they kill you," he snorted. "You actually believed that shit? That's hilarious!"

And suddenly, his laughter, paired with her own resurfaced trauma, was too much. "No, it's not! There's nothing hilarious about it!"

Kallias froze, stunned by her reaction. He sputtered as he saw the tears threatening to spill out of her bright blue eyes. "Oh, shit."

"You told me I'd be safe at home, but I wasn't!" Rose reminded him. "Theron attacked me! He tried to kill me! And worse, he tried to—to—" Her unfinished sentences gave way to sobbing.

"He tried to *what?*" Kallias asked, his voice a quiet, dangerous growl, but he heard the answer in her thoughts. "Shit," he said again.

Rose shoved him with both hands, which accomplished nothing, really, because he didn't even budge. "It's your fault! You lied!"

She didn't believe that. He could hear it in her thoughts.

She was just…drowning.

Overtaken by some sort of strange, human instinct, Kallias pulled her against him and wrapped his arms around her. She stiffened, shocked by the embrace, but then, she relaxed—and wrapped her arms around him, too.

"I'm sorry," he whispered. His voice became a low growl as he added, "He will *never* touch you like that again. I'll make sure of it."

Rose didn't know how to react. The kindness he showed her now was so drastically different from his usual callousness.

It was as if she were seeing a part of him that was normally buried deep inside, beneath all of that bitterness and anger.

"It's not your fault. I know that," she admitted, her voice muffled by his chest. Her shoulders shook with emotion. "It's just that there's so much pain and anger inside me right now. I feel like it's going to rip me apart."

"It's all right," Kallias said. His hand seemed to move of its own accord, much like his body had done moments ago, and soon, his fingers began to stroke her long, red hair.

Her pulse, which had been racing since he'd run into her, slowed to a normal pace, and her blood flow slowed, as well. Again, his gaze fell to the wound, and despite everything, the hunger flared inside of him. Her blood smelled so sweet and powerful, and he was *so* close.

Even though Rose sensed that there was something very wrong about him—that he was dangerous, somehow—for reasons she didn't understand, she felt safer with his arms around her.

Just a typical hormonal reaction, perhaps?

Or was it deeper?

She felt him his head lean against her shoulder, and she shivered as his lips brushed her neck. It felt nice.

That is…until he sniffed her neck.

Rose extracted herself from his arms. "Did you just *sniff* me?"

Kallias took a step back, and to her surprise, rather than arrogance or annoyance, she found nervousness in his eyes.

Maybe even…embarrassment?

Kallias rubbed the back of his neck. "No. I mean, yes, technically, but," he stammered, "it was an accident."

She raised both eyebrows. "You accidentally sniffed me?"

"It's just an instinct," he said without thinking.

"An instinct?" Rose repeated.

Kallias cursed his own dumb reactions. "Look, do we have to make a deal of this?"

"I don't stink, do I?" Rose mumbled. "I just showered like—"

"No, you smell delicious," he assured her.

Rose blinked. "Delicious?"

"Damn it," he groaned in frustration. "What is wrong with me tonight?"

"I mean, I was trying not to say anything," Rose said with a frown, "but you are acting a little creepy."

"Yeah," Kallias agreed. He raked a hand through his long, brown hair, feeling humiliated for the first time in ages. His gaze shifted back toward her neck, and he frowned. "Why are you still bleeding?"

Rose scowled at the strange question. "Well, you see, blood flows through the veins," she said slowly, "and when there's a wound…"

"I know how blood works," he interrupted. "I'm asking why *your* wound hasn't healed. The healing enzymes in Theron's saliva should've healed you."

Rose shrugged. "Now, that, I don't know."

"And how did you get away from Theron?" Kallias asked.

"I ran," Rose reminded him. "Don't you remember me running into you?"

"Yes, I remember," Kallias said irritably, "but there's something you're not telling me. There must be. Humans can't outrun vampires."

She shrugged. "I just know I ran."

"It doesn't make sense," he muttered. "And where is he now?"

"Now, *that* is a good question," Rose admitted, glancing behind her.

"Come on," Kallias said. He grabbed her arm and began to pull her along. "I have to get you out of here before he finds you."

Rose scowled, as she allowed him to lead her who-knows-where. "What do you mean by that? Where exactly are you taking me?"

"Somewhere safe," Kallias said vaguely.

"You're wasting your time," Rose muttered. "Nowhere is safe for me."

Kallias turned toward her. "I won't sugarcoat this. Theron is stronger than I am, and I have no idea how many vampires are helping him," he said. "But I *will* protect you. I have friends. We can help you."

"Friends?" Rose repeated worriedly. "Kallias, I don't know."

"It's the only way. You're not safe here," he insisted. "Theron knows where you live, where you work, where you attend classes…" He sighed, "He even knows about your friends. He won't stop until he has you. There's nowhere left in this town for you to hide. Let me take you somewhere safe."

She gave him a suspicious look. "Last night, you said the safest place for me was my apartment, and now, you're saying there's somewhere safer?"

"Last night," he told her, "I didn't consider what I'm going to do an option."

"Why not?" Rose asked. "What changed?"

He looked away, suddenly uncomfortable. "I realized my choice is to either let you die or risk everything. For some reason, I'm choosing the risk."

She frowned at that. "How will this risk everything?"

Kallias shoved his hands in his pockets. He stared at his boots, avoiding her gaze. "I have secrets—secrets that are best left in the dark—but I'm sure you already realize that." At her nod, he sighed, "I don't need anyone uncovering those secrets, and no matter what you *think* you want to know, you don't want to know this. You won't like what you find." He looked at her. "But if I do this, I'm afraid you'll uncover everything."

"Then, tell me now," Rose suggested.

"There's no time," Kallias insisted. "Theron could find you at any moment. He's tasted your blood. He can track you easily." He frowned. "I honestly don't understand how he hasn't *already* found you. But… there will be time for questions later. Right now, I need to get you out of here," Kallias said. "If you want to survive, you'll come with me."

Rose watched him curiously. "Fine. I'll trust you for now, but I'm warning you: If you try to kill me or hurt me, I'll kick your butt."

He chuckled, "I'll keep that in mind."

Rose followed, as he led the way down several streets. They'd just turned down a back alley that cut between an apartment building and a clothing store when Kallias suddenly grasped her arm and jerked her to a stop. Before she could even open her mouth to ask why they'd stopped, Kallias clasped his hand over her mouth.

Rose glared at him, but he seemed too preoccupied to notice.

"He's close," Kallias said, dropping his hand. "Run. I'll deal with him."

Rose frowned. "How do you know where he is?"

He glared at her. "The questions can wait. Right now, you need to run."

Rose returned the glare, ready to tell him exactly how she felt about being told when she can and cannot ask questions, but he nudged her in the other direction. And she sighed.

Maybe this *was* a bad time.

She'd barely taken three steps before a flash of movement whirled past her. She gasped, as she found Theron suddenly standing in front of her. She stared up at him, noticing the dark blood that coated his mouth and face.

Her blood, she realized.

"Where did you even come from?" she complained.

Theron offered her a condescending smile. "You can't escape me."

"Really?" Kallias asked from somewhere behind her. "Then, how does she keep doing it?"

Theron looked past her. His eyes narrowed at Kallias. "Why are you *always* here?" he whined. "I just want to kill her. That's all."

"Yeah, that's all," Rose repeated with a scoff.

Theron glared at her, as if she were a fly that needed swatting, but then, his brown eyes darkened with a hint of something else—something that turned her stomach, something she'd seen in his eyes earlier.

Lust.

"You're more attractive with your clothes torn like that," Theron sneered. "Perhaps you should be attacked more often."

Rose felt sick at the reminder of what he'd tried to do.

Kallias chose that moment to punch Theron in the face.

Hard.

So hard, in fact, that the blow sent Theron across the alley, where he slammed into the wall and crumpled to the ground.

As Theron climbed onto his hands and knees, he spat out a mouthful of blood and what looked like crushed teeth.

"I'll kill you for that," he snarled.

Kallias shrugged. "It was worth it."

Rose glanced back and forth between Kallias and Theron, her mouth ajar and her eyes wide with shock. "How did you… You punched him, and he just flew…" she trailed off, apparently too confused to finish the sentence. "What?"

Theron jumped to his feet and raced toward Kallias, shoving him into the opposite wall.

The force of the collision created such a thunderous crash that for a moment, Rose wondered if something had exploded. She blinked, fearing the worst, as the bricks and dust fell to the ground.

When some of the dust cleared, Rose saw Theron holding Kallias by the throat, against the damaged wall.

Rose stepped toward them. "Kallias, are you okay?"

Kallias groaned in pain. "I'm fine," he said. "Just stay back."

Theron scoffed, "If by fine, you mean dead, then yes, you'll be *very* fine soon enough."

"He'll be very *dead*?" Rose said dryly. "Are there degrees of deadness?"

Theron growled in frustration and spun to glare at her, his hand still clasped around Kallias's throat. "Are you always this irritating?"

"It depends on who you ask," Rose said, trying to keep Theron's attention on her, while Kallias recovered. "To stupid people, yes, I can be very irritating."

Theron released Kallias and raced toward her. He grasped her wrist and snatched her to him, moving his face closer to hers. She cringed.

The blade of a dagger slid in front of Theron's throat, as Kallias came up behind him.

"Let her go, or I'll slice off your head," Kallias warned.

Theron visibly paled. He dropped Rose and held up both hands.

Rose staggered, barely catching herself before she fell. She frowned curiously, as she noticed the fear in Theron's eyes—realizing that, apparently, decapitation was one thing that a vampire *couldn't* survive.

Finally, she'd separated a fact from the fiction.

"Are you out of your mind?" Kallias demanded to know. "You must be—to continuously insult a vampire who wants to murder you!"

"Well, it worked, didn't it?" Rose pointed out. "He let you go."

Kallias rolled his eyes. "Fine. It was clever—but also insane."

"I released the human," Theron reminded him. "Now, you'll let me go, right?"

Kallias glanced at him. "I think you're overestimated my honor," he scoffed. "I'm not the man I used to be."

Theron paled a little at that. "If you kill me, other vampires will come for her," he warned. "I'm not the only one who knows what she is."

"*What* I am?" Rose repeated. "What do you mean by that?"

"You said you wanted answers," Theron said, his voice a little shaky. "If you let me go, I'll tell you whatever you want to know."

Kallias rolled his eyes. "Oh, of course. Now, you want to talk."

"Think about it," Theron said. "How did she escape me? Don't you want to know?"

Of course he did. "You have my attention," Kallias said.

"I already told you," Rose reminded him. "I ran."

"Humans can't overpower vampires," Theron said.

"He's right," Kallias told her. "Humans are too weak."

"I'll tell you the truth about her," Theron offered, "if you let me go."

Kallias rolled his eyes. "I don't have time for this," he grumbled, but his curiosity won. He kicked Theron to the ground. "You have three minutes. What is she, and how did she escape you?"

Theron climbed onto his knees. "She threw me across the room."

Rose frowned. She remembered him flying across the room and crashing into the wall, but she hadn't done it. Had she? "I didn't touch you."

Kallias glanced at her and then back at Theron. "What you're suggesting is impossible," he told Theron. "She's human. She can't throw a vampire."

"Is she?" Theron said. "And...I never said she used *physical* force."

Kallias turned to look at Rose, as he finally understood why she smelled so powerful. In all the years he'd been alive, he'd never met anyone with that ability—human *or* vampire.

"She isn't an ordinary human," Theron said, "and I'm not the only one who knows it. Others will come for her, whether you kill me or not."

Rose frowned. "What is he talking about?" she asked Kallias. Her apprehension grew. "And why are you looking at me like that?"

Kallias's brows furrowed, as he realized that she didn't even *know*. "You really don't remember how you got him off of you?"

Rose's blue eyes darkened with frustration. "No, and quite frankly, I don't want to think about it." Her chest tightened, and anger burned through her. "The memory still makes me..." she trailed off for a moment, giving Theron a thoughtful look. Then, without warning, she kicked him in the groin and finished, "...upset."

Theron curled into the fetal position, whining.

Kallias raised an eyebrow at Rose.

She ducked her head sheepishly. "Sorry."

He laughed, "No, I understood that, actually."

Theron launched himself at Rose, but Kallias quickly stepped between them. He caught Theron and shoved him backward.

"I assume this means you're done answering questions?" Kallias said.

Theron snarled like a rabid dog, "Humans do *not* attack vampires!"

Kallias rolled his eyes. "Oh, stop. After what you did to her, if she'd the chance to kick you in the balls and *didn't*, I'd be disappointed."

Theron glared at Kallias. "Even now, you sympathize with them."

"You thought I'd sympathize with *you*?" Kallias asked in disbelief.

Theron's eyes were dark with hatred and bloodlust. "I'll kill you soon enough, bitch!" he snarled at Rose. "I will cause you more pain than you can imagine!"

Rose rolled her eyes. "You know, the misogyny behind that word grates on my nerves. Women are not canines, and the only reason you try to compare us to them is—"

"Rose," Kallias interrupted, "this really isn't the time."

"I know, I know," Rose said, as if her tangent were only interrupting something as simple as lunch, "but it's something to think about."

A blur of movement flashed before her eyes, and Rose gasped as Theron snatched her backward. She felt his fangs brush her throat, before Kallias pulled him off of her.

She collapsed the moment he released her, falling face-first onto the pavement.

"Are you okay?" Kallias yelled.

Rose climbed to her feet and dusted the dirt off of her jeans. "Yeah."

As Rose tried to pull her tattered clothing together, out of the corner of her eye, she noticed her backpack sitting, unnoticed, among a pile of rubble. She realized that she must have dropped it, at some point.

"This would be a good time for you to run," Kallias called.

Rose glanced at him. He faced Theron, and she saw only his back. If, for whatever reason, the strange man in Greece had been right about keeping the Stone away from dangerous hands, she knew she'd need to hide the backpack before Theron noticed it.

"Okay!"

"That was *way* too easy," Kallias muttered under his breath.

"Why even bother telling her to run?" Theron asked him. "You know I'll still catch her."

"I'll tear you apart if you try," Kallias told him.

Theron's laugh was as arrogant as ever. "You're starved and weak. You don't stand a chance against me," he sneered. "You'll be dead before sunrise. I guarantee it."

Kallias shrugged a shoulder. "I was starved and weak last night and the night before, and I kicked your ass easily enough *then*."

Theron growled at that. He charged toward Kallias, and Kallias spun to dodge him.

He kicked Theron's feet out from under him, but Theron didn't stay down. He jumped to his feet and shoved Kallias into the wall.

As Kallias recovered from the painful impact, he noticed Rose's scent again. He glanced toward the end of the alley, his brows furrowing, as he realized that she was still there.

But that moment of distraction costed him.

Before he could block the attack, Theron grasped his arm and slung him across the alley—into the opposite wall.

Pain exploded throughout his body, the powerful collision knocking a few bricks loose. Kallias felt warm, sticky liquid flowing down his head, and he slumped to the ground as Theron approached him.

Theron made a lazy attempt to kick Kallias while he was on the ground, but Kallias caught his foot and twisted. Theron growled in pain, as he hit the ground face-first.

Kallias climbed back to his feet, and before Theron could attack him again, Kallias kicked him hard enough to send him across the alley. Theron groaned, and Kallias staggered toward him, clearly injured.

After hiding her backpack, Rose found herself entranced by the fight, baffled by what she was seeing. Occasionally, she'd see one of them hit the wall or fall to the ground, but most of the time, she saw only a blur of movement that seemed to bounce back and forth from one side of the alley to the other.

It was unreal, and the sounds were just as strange.

Sometimes, the fighting seemed eerily fluid and soundless, and other times, when one of them would collide with the wall, it sounded more like a car crash or an explosion.

Rose was relieved, at least, that all of the shops around were closed. She could only imagine the type of disturbance this would cause, if anyone were around to hear it. She returned her attention to the fight, studying the blurred flashes of movement. She couldn't even discern which blur was Theron and which blur was Kallias.

The fighting seemed to come to an abrupt stop, when Theron finally gained the upper hand. He shoved Kallias against the wall and kicked him with so much force that a loud crack echoed through the alley.

Kallias groaned and clutched his side, wincing when his palm pressed against the broken rib. Theron took advantage of the injury and cornered Kallias. He wrapped his hand around Kallias's throat, and Kallias reluctantly stilled.

"I think I should kill you this time," Theron said. "Don't you?"

"If you were smart, you would," Kallias muttered.

Theron looked conflicted. "I can't have you screwing this up."

"And what *is* this?" Kallias asked.

"Why would *you* need to know?" Theron said. "You'll be dead."

Rose realized that she needed to act now if she wanted to help Kallias. As always, Theron was talking too much, and that gave her time to act. She inched quietly toward them, kneeling to pick up a stray brick. When she reached them, she lifted the brick above her head to bash it against the back of Theron's head, but before she could, he released Kallias and spun around to catch her wrist.

He jerked her wrist forward, causing her to drop the heavy brick as she collided with him. "I told you before, human. You're too slow."

She gasped as he squeezed her wrist almost hard enough to break it.

"But I'm not," Kallias said, and he pressed the blade of a long, steel dagger against Theron's throat. "If you want to keep your head, let her go."

"Fine," Theron said.

In one fluid motion, he released Rose and grasped Kallias's arm.

Theron squeezed, and another crack echoed through the street, as the bones in his arm shattered. The steel dagger fell to the ground, clanging as it hit the pavement, and Kallias staggered, losing his balance, as pain exploded through his arm.

"Oh my goodness!" Rose gasped, stepping toward him. "Are you okay?"

"I'm fine!" Kallias yelled. "Stay back! For fuck's sake, just stay back!"

She froze, startled by his reaction—and conflicted about what to do.

"As if those few steps would save her," Theron scoffed.

Kallias held his broken arm with his other arm. His face twisted with pain, but he still stood his ground, as if he were preparing for another attack.

Theron knelt and picked up the dagger Kallias had dropped. "You lost your weapon," he said. "Now, what will you do?"

"I don't need weapons," Kallias said. "I just enjoy them."

"Oh?" Theron asked. "And what about your arm? Do you need that?"

Kallias kneed Theron in the stomach, but before he could attempt another blow, Theron—moving at a much faster speed—grabbed Kallias's injured arm and twisted, forcing Kallias to his knees.

Theron grabbed his head and slammed his face into the pavement.

Kallias's head spun, as he lifted himself onto his arms.

For what felt like an eternity, he watched blood drip from his forehead and nose, the crimson liquid seeping into the pavement. The scent of his own blood filled the air.

Rose's quiet whimper interrupted the incessant ringing in his head, and the haze that had momentarily separated his consciousness from reality cleared.

He wiped the blood from his brow with the back of his hand and turned toward the sound. He blinked, trying to make out the images through his swirling vision. He saw Theron standing a few feet away, clutching Rose's tattered T-shirt with one hand, as he roughly searched her pockets with the other hand.

Rose fought against him, shoving her hands against his chest and pressing her feet against his knees in an attempt to make him let her go.

"Where is it?" Theron growled in her face. "It wasn't in your apartment."

"Get your hands off of me!" Rose snarled at him.

She collapsed on the ground, when Kallias snatched Theron away of her and slung him across the alley.

Kallias turned, staggering, to check on her, but before he could even look at her, Theron raced toward him and shoved him into the wall.

Still disoriented and injured, Kallias slumped to the ground, and his head fell back.

Theron began to kick him repeatedly in the ribs, shattering his other ribs along with the one that was already broken.

Kallias groaned at the pain.

"Stop!" Rose screamed. She scrambled to her feet and ran toward them. She could barely breathe, as she saw what Theron was doing to Kallias. "Stop hurting him! Please! I'm the one you want to kill, right?"

Theron froze for a moment and cast an amused glance her way.

Kallias coughed, and a blood filled his mouth. He turned to the side and spat out a mouthful of the blood. He clearly wasn't healing quickly enough.

He leaned back against the wall. "Damn it, Rose, just run," he panted. His voice was so hoarse she could barely hear it. "Just save yourself."

Theron turned and stomped on his leg. The crack of bones shattering echoed through the streets, and Kallias's head fell back again, as he yelled at the pain.

Rose's stomach turned at the sound of his agony. "Stop! Please! Please!"

Theron smiled, obviously pleased by her reaction. "You really care that much about a man you know nothing about? Why?"

"Because he's a person, you sick, psychotic monster!" Rose snarled. "How can you hurt someone like that? How can you *enjoy* seeing him in pain?"

"A person," Theron repeated, and his lips curved into a smug smirk.

"Yeah, a person. What else would he be?" she scoffed. "Look, you wanted me, right? Leave him alone, and you can have me, instead."

"Well, now, you're making it too easy," Theron complained.

Rose could barely breathe anymore, too overwhelmed by her own empathy. "What is that supposed to mean?"

She glanced worriedly at Kallias, as he coughed up more blood. He needed medical attention sooner rather than later, and she couldn't get that for him. Still, she tried to reach him.

But before she could step past Theron, his hand shot out and grasped her arm. Before she even realized what was happening, Theron threw her against the wall.

Kallias wiped his hand across his mouth and looked at her, anxiously watching her crumpled body. She'd curled into the fetal position after she hit the wall, and she'd yet to move or even make a sound.

The scent of her blood filled the air, enticing his ravenous hunger.

Fortunately, her heartbeat remained steady.

"Leave her alone," Kallias said. "You've tormented her enough."

Theron studied him. "Why do you care? She's just a human."

"I don't care about her," Kallias insisted, but then, too quietly for her to hear, he added, "But none of them are *just* humans. They're living beings. They think. They feel. They dream. They change things. They're not just food."

Theron rolled his eyes. "I turned you into a monster, and you're still spouting philosophical bullshit," he complained. "You should *want* to kill her."

Kallias glanced uneasily at Rose. By this point, she'd managed to pull herself into a sitting position. She held her head in her hands, and watery blood flowed between her fingers, most likely pouring from her nose. The scent of that blood plagued his hunger.

He'd struggled to resist it before, but now that he was injured so severely, he didn't know if he'd be able to fight it much longer.

"You and I are the same. You just refuse to see it," Theron said.

"No," Kallias argued. "We crave the same things, but *I* resist."

Theron shrugged. "I embrace what I am. It's better than being in denial."

"I'm not in denial," Kallias said sadly. "I know that I'm a monster."

Theron knelt in front of him. "Then, feed."

"No," Kallias said sternly.

He shifted to make a weak attempt at climbing onto his uninjured leg, but before he could, Theron rose and stepped on that leg as well.

The bone cracked loudly from the pressure, and then Theron pressed down harder to ensure that both legs were shattered.

Kallias fell back against the wall, growling.

"You'll die tonight. Surely you've realized that," Theron said. "Your legs are crushed, and the sun's rising soon. You will burn."

"Then, just go ahead and kill me," Kallias rasped.

Theron knelt in front of him again, watching with a sadistic smile. "That's too easy. I'd rather let the sun kill you. It'll be *much* more painful."

"Fine," Kallias said, feeling weak and defeated.

"Of course, there is one way that you could still survive," Theron reminded him. "You know those injuries would heal with just a tiny bit of blood. All you have to do is feed. If only there were a human nearby that you could eat. Oh, wait," he taunted, turning his gaze toward Rose for emphasis, "there is!"

"No," Kallias said. "Leave her alone. I don't want her blood."

"Liar!" Theron snarled. "You want her blood as much, if not more, than I do. I see the hunger in your eyes. Just accept what you are, and kill her!"

"No," Kallias said again. "I'm nothing like you."

Theron laughed, "I suppose I'll just have to *prove* my point, then."

Kallias cursed under his breath, as Theron went to grab her. "Rose, you have to run!" he yelled, even though he knew it was too late.

Rose glanced up at the sound of his voice. Her head continued to spin from the impact of the wall, and her body felt too bruised and too weak to move. She tried to process what he'd said, but her mind was just too fuzzy.

Theron snatched her up by her already bruised arm and dragged her over to Kallias. Before she could understand what was happening, Theron tossed her on top of Kallias.

Kallias caught her arms before she could slam into him, lessening the impact of her fall. Her legs fell on either side of him, causing her to straddle his hips. Blood flowed from her nose and her neck, and their faces were too close.

Rose reached out to hold his arms, her head spinning violently. "Kallias?"

The physical contact with her caused a wave of desire to course through his body, and that desire intensified his already intense hunger.

He stared at the blood on her face and neck.

He needed to taste it. He needed to feed.

Rose watched, as his brown eyes darkened. "Are you okay?"

His breath fell from his lips in an uneven rhythm, quick and shallow, like the pant of a dog, and painful hunger twisted at his stomach.

"Run," he breathed. He licked his lips. "You have to run."

"Kallias, what's wrong?" Rose said worriedly. "Are you hurting?"

"Please. I don't want to hurt you," he pleaded. "Get away from me."

"Why would you hurt me?" she asked softly.

He leaned closer, staring at the dark, sticky blood that coated her neck. His mouth watered at the sweet, powerful scent of her blood.

He felt his own lips part, as if of their own accord, desperate for her blood. Kallias felt his self-control slipping, but there was nothing he could do about it. He suddenly grasped the back of her neck and jerked her toward him.

His mouth had nearly reached her neck before he managed to stop himself. Even so, he barely retained control of his hunger. He couldn't bring himself to push her away.

His breath fell harshly against her neck, and she shivered at the sensation.

"What are you doing?" Rose said, paralyzed with shock.

"Rose, you have to get away from me," he said in her ear.

Rose pulled back and frowned, but she gasped when she saw how dark and feral his eyes looked. Though she didn't understand it, she decided to do as he asked, just this once.

Rose tried to stand, but before she could climb onto her bruised knees, Theron pressed his foot against her back.

She gasped at the pain, as Theron pushed her back into Kallias's lap.

Kallias caught her again, as her body fell flush against his, and the shift had caused their bodies to meet in all the wrong places.

He glanced down as her body pressed against his groin. "Well, that's not going to help anything," he muttered.

"Why is he doing this?" Rose hissed.

Kallias looked up at her, and with just one look at her worried, blue eyes, he began to regain control of his hunger. "He's trying to prove something."

"Okay," Rose said, "and what is that?"

His gaze shifted back toward her neck. "It's none of your business."

Her bright blue eyes narrowed. "It clearly involves me, somehow, so I think that it's *definitely* my business. Tell me what's going on."

Kallias groaned, when Rose tried to shift into a more comfortable position and somehow made it worse. He reached out and grasped her hips to stop her. "Can you, *please*, be still?"

She froze, as she began to understand why he was acting like that. She looked down, and her cheeks flushed.

"I think I've proven my point," Theron announced.

Kallias scowled at him. "You've proven nothing, except that I want it, which I already admitted. But I'd die before I ever acted on the urge."

Rose frowned at them, finding herself confused all over again.

"Pity," Theron said. "I'm sure she would prefer you do it, instead of me."

Rose gasped, as Theron grabbed her arm and snatched her off of Kallias. He moved his mouth to her neck and traced a finger through the blood that oozed from her shoulder.

Rose tried to push away from him—and froze when she felt his fangs press against her neck again.

Then, suddenly, Theron laughed.

He dropped her on the ground. "Tomorrow," he promised. "Right *now*, I need to take shelter before the sun rises."

Theron returned to Kallias and knelt in front of him. He swiftly shoved the dagger into his stomach and twisted it.

"Just returning your dagger," Theron sneered.

8

ANSWERS

*T*heron moved so quickly that he seemed to disappear into the
night.

Rose pushed herself up onto her hands and knees, and she blinked in
shock when she saw the hilt of the dagger protruding from Kallias's
abdomen.

With a grunt, Kallias winced and jerked the dagger out of his stomach. He clutched the wound, but still, blood poured through his fingers.

Rose covered her mouth in horror.

She scrambled to her feet and ran to him. When she reached him, she
fell to her knees, gasping at the sheer amount of blood. Instinctually, she
reached toward him, her fingers nearly brushing his blood-soaked T-
shirt, but he caught her wrist with his blood-coated hand.

"Don't touch it," he said, his eyes dark.

"Right. Of course," Rose said. She shook her head. "I'm sorry."

He let go of her wrist and pressed his palm against the wound, as if
that light touch were enough to stop the bleeding.

His hand left a thick handprint of blood around her wrist, and Rose's
heart raced with worry.

"It's so much blood," she whispered.

His dark, feral gaze swept over her. "You're one to talk."

Rose glanced down at her own tattered, blood-stained clothes. Blood stained the blue T-shirt, and the tear down the middle of her shirt revealed blood-stained skin, as well, trailing from her neck to her breasts. Nervously, she pulled her shirt closed.

Kallias continued to stare at her, overwhelmed by the urge to feed. His injuries intensified the hunger he usually felt. He needed blood in order to heal, and his body knew that.

His body *also* knew that a source of very powerful blood knelt in front of him now, easily within his grasp.

His mouth watered at the sight of her blood.

"You need a hospital," Rose said. "Give me your phone. I'll call 911."

"I don't need a hospital," Kallias said, his voice strangely calm.

"Look, I get it," she sighed. "I hate hospitals, too, but this isn't just a scratch. You need medical attention. You could die."

"I don't," he insisted.

She squinted bewilderedly. "Kallias, maybe you haven't noticed, but there's a hole in your stomach," she said. "Do you expect me to sit here while you *die*?"

"No," Kallias said. He shifted, wincing with every movement, and he pulled out a cell phone. His hand left a coating of blood on the plastic, as he typed something into the screen. "I expect you to leave."

"What?" she said with frown. "Why would I leave?"

He shifted again. Rose winced sympathetically at the pain that showed in his face each time he moved.

Kallias pulled a leather wallet from his pocket and tossed it onto the pavement in front of her. "There's several hundred dollars of cash in there. Take it, and get out of town. Find a hotel, but don't give them your real name. Then, call Erik, and tell him to come get you."

She blinked, confused. "Erik? Your friend? Why would I call him?"

"Erik is the only person I've *ever* come close to trusting. He'll help you," he said. His voice sounded so strained now. "You'll need his help, if you want to survive."

"Are you planning on going somewhere?" she sputtered.

"Rose, I'll be dead by sunrise," he sighed. "You need to be gone before then."

Rose paled. She didn't want to believe it. "Why are you saying that? Why would you be dead by sunrise?"

Kallias stared at her for a moment, debating whether to tell her or not. In any other circumstance, he would've lied, but he figured she'd know soon enough anyway. He reached out and took her hand.

Rose frowned nervously, when he led her hand to his mouth.

Without breaking eye contact with her, Kallias took her index finger and pressed it against one of his canine teeth.

Well...she'd *assumed* it was a canine tooth anyway.

Rose gasped, as she felt the abnormally long and incredibly sharp tooth—so sharp, in fact, that its point pricked her fingertip the minute she touched it.

Rose jerked her hand away, watching in horror as blood surfaced on her fingertip. She glanced back at Kallias, her eyes wide.

He closed his eyes, as if savoring the small drop of blood he'd tasted from her finger, and Rose felt dread coil deeper within her.

Rose leaned forward, and his eyes snapped open, watching warily, as she reached out toward him.

She pried his lips open, needing to *see* the teeth, and with a sigh, he reluctantly opened his mouth for her.

Rose's eyes widened when she saw his fangs.

Kallias pulled back and closed his mouth, watching as she grew pale.

"You're a—a..." she trailed off, shaking her head in disbelief.

"Vampire," he provided. "Yes, I'm a vampire. Just like Theron."

Rose continued to shake her head, almost as if it were a subconscious action. "No, no. You can't be. You saved my life. It doesn't make sense."

"But it *does* make sense," he argued. "And deep down, you already knew."

Rose frowned, confused by the accusation. "No, I didn't."

"You suspected," Kallias said. "You asked all the right questions. How did I know about vampires? How did I know Theron? How could I fight Theron, if human police couldn't? Why did I behave so strangely whenever you were bleeding? Why did I do other strange things?"

"Like sniffing me?" Rose said.

He winced, obviously still embarrassed about that. "An animalistic urge. Vampires are more animal than human. Sometimes that fact is difficult to hide."

Rose sighed. "You lied to me."

"And you believed me," Kallias said, "because you *wanted* to believe me."

"When Theron threw me onto you," Rose said with a frown, "you grabbed me and—"

"Yes," Kallias said. He answered her question as if she'd finished it already. "I nearly bit you. I was injured and hungry, and you were bleeding. And you smelled amazing." As he spoke, his voice dropped lower, growing more breathless with each word. He leaned closer to her and growled, "I still want to bite you."

"You do?" she asked worriedly.

Kallias tilted his head to the side, as he studied her, and she realized, not for the first time, that he moved like a predator, that he watched her as if she were his prey. "It wasn't the first time, either. When Theron attacked you that first night, you passed out in my arms, and you were bleeding, and I...wasn't prepared."

"But you didn't bite me," she assumed. "Right?"

"Of course not," Kallias muttered. "I told you. I don't want to hurt you."

Rose nodded, relieved to know that, at least. She sighed and glanced up at the sky. The previously black sky looked navy blue now. She looked back at him and bit her lip nervously. "So, sunlight *does* kill vampires? I mean...it kills you?"

"We're creatures of darkness," he said. "We're not meant to walk in light."

"Okay," she said, trying to stay calm. "Do you dissolve or burn or..."

"We burn," he told her. "It's not pretty. It's slow and painful. Trust me when I say that you won't want to be here when it happens."

Rose just nodded, as if she were lost in thought. "How long until sunrise?"

"Thirteen minutes," Kallias said.

Her brows furrowed. "How did you know that? You didn't even look at your phone." But then, she sighed, "Never mind. It doesn't matter. Just tell me what I need to do in order to save you."

Kallias blinked. "What?"

"I thought vampires had sensitive hearing or something," she muttered.

"Rose," he said. He leaned toward her. "I just told you that I'm a vampire—a *monster*—who has almost bitten you on multiple occasions, and you want to *save* me? Are you completely insane?"

Rose shrugged. "I'm a human, and you saved *me*."

"It's different," Kallias scoffed. "Monsters are evil. Humans are not."

"I can think of plenty of humans that would prove you wrong," Rose said. "What you are doesn't make you good or evil. Your choices do."

"My kind has always been considered evil," he argued.

"Considered?" Rose scoffed. "I have never let *anyone* tell me what to think, and I'm not starting now. I'll decide for myself what to think of you."

He frowned in surprise. "It doesn't matter anyway. There's no way to save me. I don't have time to find shelter before sunrise."

"Shelter?" she repeated. "So, you'd be safe, if you were *inside*? There are stores all along this street. You could stay in one of those during the day."

Kallias laughed bitterly. "You honestly think I could just hang out in a store all day? I'm pretty sure any sane worker would call the cops the moment they saw a large man sleeping in the floor and bleeding all over the place."

"Right," Rose said with a sigh. "Well, where do you usually stay during the day?"

"I've been staying in a hotel room," Kallias said, "but I don't have enough time left to make it back to the hotel before sunrise."

She frowned. "Hotel rooms have windows."

"One or two, usually," Kallias agreed, "but I cover them."

"So, windows are okay if they're covered," Rose realized.

"As long as they're covered well enough," he admitted.

"What about my apartment? Is it close enough?" she asked hopefully.

"No," Kallias said, "nor is it a safe option. Theron could be there now."

"But you're a vampire. You can move really fast, right?" Rose assumed.

"If I weren't injured, yes," he sighed, "but in my current state, no."

"Okay," she said. "Then, how far *do* you think you can get?"

Kallias shrugged. "A few blocks, at most."

Rose cast a thoughtful glance down the alley, toward a more well-lit street. "There's an abandoned warehouse about a block from here," she said. "It's been boarded up since before I moved here—at least four years ago. But I don't know if I can get us inside. The doors are locked up with chains."

He laughed at her concern. "Chains won't be a problem."

Rose glanced at him, lifting her eyebrows. She climbed to her feet and held out a hand. "Come on, then. Let's get you inside before you get all crispy."

He grimaced at the thought. "Not funny."

Kallias braced his hands against the wall and pushed himself up onto his injured legs. He wobbled and fell back against the wall, groaning in pain.

Rose frowned at her outstretched hand—that was apparently invisible to him. "I was going to help," she muttered, as he made another attempt to stand.

"It's adorable that you think you can," he scoffed.

She dropped her hand. "Never mind, then. Enjoy your pain."

He chuckled at her acidic tone. "I'm fine. Just lead me to that building."

She didn't look convinced. "If you say so," she sighed. "Come on."

But before Rose could take a step, Kallias grasped her hand and jerked her back toward him.

Rose gasped, as her body collided with his.

Kallias swallowed, too, when her soft curves pressed against him. He hadn't meant to pull her against him. He'd only intended to pull her to a stop. She smelled of vanilla, honey, and blood, and the lust and hunger that swept through him were a dangerous mix. It threatened to override his self-control.

He moved his hand along her arm, toward her neck.

"Your neck is bleeding," he murmured. "It'll draw attention."

For a moment, Rose didn't respond. She just stared up at him, her azure-blue eyes wide and curious.

Her mouth felt too dry, her throat too tight. His nearness affected her in ways she didn't want to admit.

Rose shuddered, as his fingers trailed along her skin—until they reached her neck. Her heart raced.

She cleared her throat. "Well, what do you want me to do? Stitch it up?"

His lips twitched at her snarky remark, but he didn't meet her gaze. He couldn't tear his own gaze from the blood that coated her neck.

His mouth watered at the sight of the blood—at its sweet, delicious scent. He needed to heal her wound, and he knew of only one way to do so—without creating a blood bond, that is.

Rose froze in shock when the injured vampire pressed his lips against her neck. Just as she was about to ask him what the heck he was doing, his mouth parted against her skin, and his tongue traced the bleeding wound on her neck.

Rose's hands seemed to act of their own accord, clutching at his jacket as if her life depended on it.

As Kallias licked the wound, a strange, euphoric sensation surged through her body. Her head fell against his chest, and she couldn't hold back the soft moan that escaped her lips.

With a soft chuckle, Kallias said, "You can let go of me now."

Rose blinked, only just then realizing what she was doing.

Her cheeks burned, as she took a wobbly step backward, purposely avoiding eye contact.

He laughed at the pink flush that darkened her face.

Rose narrowed her eyes at him. "Did you just drink my blood?"

Amusement danced in his brown eyes. "Baby, you insult me," he said in a gratingly arrogant tone. "You would've enjoyed it *far* more than that, if I'd fed from you."

Rose glared harder.

"But I did taste you," he admitted, "and you taste amazing."

Rose shook her head in disbelief. "See, there's this line between normal and creepy," she said slowly, "and you blew right through the creepy line and just...*kept* going."

Kallias laughed at that. "I healed your neck," he explained. "I told you, remember? Vampires have healing enzymes in their saliva."

She frowned and reached up to touch her neck.

Rose's eyes widened as her fingers met smooth skin.

It felt as if there'd never been a wound there.

"So, you licked me," Rose muttered.

"Yes," Kallias said, "and as you can see, it worked."

Rose shook her head. "Yeah, well, next time you decide to act like a dog and lick me, at least give me some kind of warning first."

His smile faded. "I'm not a dog."

"Yes, that's what *like* means." Rose glanced anxiously at the blue-streaked horizon. "We should hurry."

His dark gaze swept over her again. "Your shirt's covered in blood, too," he said, his tone somehow low and taunting, despite his own impending crispiness. "Maybe you should take it off."

Rose rolled her eyes. "Right. Because walking around in just jeans and a black bra would totally be less conspicuous."

Kallias glanced down at her breasts. "I knew it looked black."

Rose crossed her arms over the torn shirt and glared at him. "I can still leave you here to burn in the sun, you know."

He laughed and staggered away from the wall. "I'll keep that in mind."

Rose watched the uneasiness of his steps worriedly. "Do you need help?"

He snorted, "I'm six and a half feet tall. What could you do? Carry me?"

"Forgive me for being concerned," she muttered.

He glanced at her. "I'm fine. My legs are a little broken. That's all."

"Broken?" Rose sputtered. "You're walking on broken legs?"

Kallias shrugged, as he walked unsteadily down the alley. "They're already healing. Besides, I've endured worse than this. I can handle it."

She fell into step beside him. "What about your stomach? Will it heal?"

Kallias braced one hand against the wall as he walked, and he held the other over his stomach. Thick, dark blood oozed through his fingers. "Eventually," he muttered. "Healing usually requires blood, and I haven't fed in...*a while*. I'll still heal without feeding, but the process will be much slower."

Rose wanted to ask how long he meant by *a while*, but she wasn't sure if she'd like the answer. "Hang on a second," she said, as they turned the corner. She snatched up her backpack from where she'd hidden it and slung it over her shoulder.

She ignored the curious look that Kallias gave her—*and* the way he continued to watch her suspiciously afterward.

Eventually, Kallias interrupted the tense silence. "I'm almost out of time."

"We're almost there," she assured him, as they turned onto a dark street.

Kallias noticed that the buildings that lined this street looked significantly older than the other buildings in the city. Some of them looked as if they were still in use—like the computer repair shop and the used goods store—but others appeared to have closed long ago.

Kallias breathed a sigh of relief because he knew that rundown buildings like these were less likely to have cameras outside.

As they continued down the street, his steps grew more unsteady. They'd nearly reached an old restaurant when he staggered.

"Careful," Rose warned, as she noticed him losing balance.

She reached out to grab his arm, intending to help him regain his balance, but instead, she only wound up trapping herself between his body and the wall as he caught himself against it.

She swallowed uneasily at their closeness.

Kallias braced his hands on the wall on each side of her. "Are you okay?"

"Yeah," she said breathlessly. "Are you?"

He removed his hand from the wall and tucked her hair behind her ear. "Yeah." He stepped back. "We should keep moving. I'll be dead soon."

She sighed at his pessimism and brushed past him, leading the way toward the warehouse.

Between a mechanic's shop and an old flea market set a rectangular building that spanned across a large portion of the street. Built of blocks that looked as if they'd once been beige or yellow, the building seemed long forgotten. A sign hung crookedly over the entrance with illegible, faded blue letters.

The old warehouse had very few windows—just four or five small, rectangular windows around the top of the building—and those windows were covered with boards.

Thick, heavy chains looped through the door handles, and a sign with shiny red letters that read, "No Trespassing," hung from the chains.

"Like I said," Rose said, gesturing toward it. "Chains."

Kallias stepped forward, and with a smirk, he grasped the chains and tore them from the door with one easy pull.

The locks and broken chains fell to the ground, clanging against the concrete, and he shoved open the doors.

Rose blinked. As he stepped inside the dark, dusty building, she knelt to look at the chains. She picked them up, examining where they'd broken.

The chains felt heavy in her hands, too heavy to have broken so easily.

Kallias hissed as his skin began to burn. "Rose, hurry!"

Rose jumped to her feet, gasping at the sight of the faint, pink line along the horizon.

She rushed inside, and the doors slammed shut behind her.

Kallias finished locking the doors and turned around. Just one, large room stretched before him, full of boxes and dust.

Boxes covered most of the floor, but the back corners of the building were empty, offering plenty of space to sleep. Planks of wood covered the windows, leaving the building in total darkness and, fortunately, shielded from sunlight.

He frowned when he noticed Rose's racing pulse. He stepped behind her and placed his hand on her shoulder, intending to ask her if she were all right, but the moment his fingers brushed her shoulder, she screamed.

Kallias spun her to face him. His rough hands cradled each side of her face. "Shhh," he soothed, his breath falling against her forehead. His thumbs rubbed gently under her ears, calming her. "It's okay. It's just me."

"I'm sorry. I'm sorry," she whispered, her blue eyes wide and frantic. "I didn't mean to scream. I just can't see, and... Do you think anyone heard me?"

"Relax," he said in a surprisingly gentle tone. "No one heard you."

She blinked at the darkness, hoping her eyes would adjust enough for her to see something—*anything*—but it was as if her eyes were covered by a black blanket, a blanket too thick to see the slightest light or outline.

It was unnerving to be stripped so suddenly of sight, but at the same time, she felt intensely aware of certain things—like how close Kallias stood to her, how he touched her with such surprising gentleness, how he smelled of leather and blood and *mint*...

"Can you see?" she said breathlessly.

"Of course," he said. "I'm a nocturnal creature."

"I can't see anything," she admitted, "at all."

"Relax," he repeated. "I'm here. I'll take care of you."

She frowned at the way he worded that.

Kallias must have thought twice about it, as well, because he suddenly dropped his hands. "Uh. I just meant I'd make sure you don't fall," he muttered. He winced as he saw the prints of blood on her face. He glanced down at his blood-covered hands. "Oh, sorry. I got blood on your face."

Rose laughed. "Well, my skin isn't exactly clean anymore, anyway."

His eyes darkened, as he looked over the blood stains on her skin—lines that trailed from her throat to her exposed chest. "Yeah," he said in a sort of husky tone. "I noticed."

Rose frowned worriedly at the dark hunger she heard in his voice, suddenly realizing how foolish it was for a human who's currently covered in blood to get herself trapped in a deserted building all day with a hungry vampire.

She shivered at the sudden coolness of the air—and realized that she couldn't feel his closeness anymore. She heard his footsteps moving away from her and then the shuffling of cardboard and paper.

"Are you okay?" she called out. "I mean, did the sun—"

"I'm fine," he said before she finished the question.

She'd noticed that he did that often, almost as if he could hear what she was going to ask before she asked it.

"The light never really touched me," he assured her. "It just feels like a mild sunburn."

Rose tried to follow the sound of his deep, slightly accented voice, but she lost her balance and fell forward, when her foot hit the corner of a crate.

Before she hit the ground, Kallias caught her, his arm sweeping roughly around her stomach.

He pulled her back onto her feet, and the wooden crate scraped across the floor as he kicked it out of the way. "If you would've just waited, I was *trying* to clear a path for you," he grumbled.

"I was following your voice," she said.

He had yet to let go of her. "There are boxes and crates everywhere. Are you *trying* to hurt yourself?" he growled. "Forget it. I'll just carry you."

"Look, I don't appreciate you using that tone with me, Mister Vampire," Rose grumbled, "so I'd suggest you..." she trailed off, as she realized what he'd just said. "Wait. You'll *what*?"

Rose gasped, as he suddenly hoisted her into his arms. "What do you think you're doing? Put me down right now!"

"I told you," Kallias complained. "I'm carrying you. Obviously."

"No. Absolutely not," she said, kicking her legs. "Put me down."

"Be still," Kallias grunted, as he carried her across the room.

"You'll drop me!" she shrieked.

He rolled his eyes, even though she couldn't see them. "No, I won't."

Rose sighed in defeat, accepting her fate. "That's it. I'm going to die."

He stepped around a stack of boxes. "I'm a vampire, remember? I have supernatural strength. I could carry a car if I wanted, and I'd never get tired. I'm not going to drop a *human*," he scoffed. "So, stop insulting my strength, and just be still."

Rose rolled her eyes. "Have I mentioned lately that you're an arrogant jerk?"

He laughed, "A few times."

When he reached the back corner of the room, Kallias lowered her onto the cold, concrete floor. The movement stirred up the dust into the air, and she coughed as she breathed in the thick air.

Kallias stared at her for a moment, noticing the blood that stained her face and the blood stains along her throat and chest. The top of her torn shirt looked nearly black from blood, instead of the blue color of the rest of the shirt. Her red hair fell around her shoulders—disheveled and tangled. Purpling red marks covered her arms.

"How badly did he hurt you?" he heard himself ask.

"I'm fine," she said. She coughed when she inhaled another lungful of dust. "I mean, yeah, I'm a little sore, but at least I don't have a hole in my stomach."

He flashed a sarcastic smile that she couldn't see. "Cute."

She heard shuffling near her, as he found a place on the floor to sit. It drove her nuts to not be able to see him.

"Where are you?" she asked impatiently.

"A foot or so to your left," he answered. He sounded distracted.

Rose reached out toward him to feel the distance, and her breath caught in her throat as her hand collided with bare skin.

She knew she should've pulled away as soon as her fingertips brushed his feverish skin, but her fingers had a mind of their own, curiously tracing the lines of his muscles.

Rose blushed. "You…took off your shirt," she realized.

Kallias watched her, amused. "If you keep touching me like that, I might take off more."

She pulled her hand back and looked away, her face hot.

He chuckled at her reaction, and then, he returned to pressing his crumpled T-shirt against the wound in his stomach, soaking up as much blood as he could.

After a brief period of unnerving silence, Rose said, "I have a question."

"Of course you do," he muttered.

"Your friend, Erik," she said. "Is he a vampire, too?"

He glanced at her. "Yes."

"Oh," she said, nodding. "And the ones that are trying to kill me? The *others* Theron kept mentioning? They're vampires, too, right?"

"Yes," he said again. "Where are you going with this, Rose?"

She shrugged. "I just find it interesting that you think my best chance for survival is to rely on the same kind of creatures that are trying to kill me."

"Only a vampire can take down a vampire," Kallias told her.

"And you really think that your vampire-friend would've come when I called him?" Rose asked skeptically. "To protect a human?"

Kallias watched her for a moment. "Yes," he said. "Erik has questionable morals, to say the least, but when it matters, he's...*good*, in a sense."

"So, he's like you, then?" Rose asked.

He scowled. "You misunderstand. I never claimed to be good."

"No," she agreed, "but you *proved* you are. Several times."

"You're speaking too soon," Kallias said with a dangerous edge to his voice. "I chose to save your life, but I may not get such a choice, if I lose control and act on the instinctual urge inside me—the urge to kill you."

She blinked at the warning. "I don't think you will."

"You shouldn't be so sure," he said. "I know I'm not."

A tense silence settled between them after that.

Rose heard only the soft rustling of fabric, as Kallias continued to press his shirt against his wound. She stared at the blackness around her, desperately wishing her eyes would adjust.

After a while, Kallias announced, "I don't understand you."

She jumped, startled by his deep voice. "Uhh, what?"

"Most humans are terrified of me," he said, "but you aren't."

"Well, in their defense," Rose said, "you're not exactly trying to be *less* intimidating. You walk around all decked out in leather and tattoos with weapons strapped to every part of your body." She shrugged.

"Even without the fangs, you'd be intimidating. *Theron*, on the other hand, dresses like a retired schoolteacher."

"That's because Theron wants humans to trust him," Kallias said. "I don't."

She nodded slowly. "So you intimidate people because you think it protects them."

"Something like that," Kallias muttered.

"Because you don't trust yourself not to hurt them," Rose added.

He fell silent for a moment. Finally, Kallias said, "I've never met a human who wasn't intimidated by me, and yet, here you are, sitting next to me, all alone in the dark, and you're calm. And the most ridiculous part is that you *know* what I am now! So, why aren't you afraid of me?"

"Maybe I just see through the façade," Rose suggested. "I see you."

"Dangerous is not a façade for a vampire," he told her. "It's reality."

She shrugged. "Sometimes, you just have to have faith in people."

"Bullshit," Kallias said, shocking her with his sudden change in tone.

Rose heard movement, and she realized that he must've stood up. She heard his footsteps moving back and forth in front of her, as if he were pacing.

"Don't you get it? Don't you know what people see when they look at you?" Kallias snarled. "They see a weakness they can exploit! You might as well be asking someone to hurt you!"

Rose raised an eyebrow. "I can see this is a sensitive topic for you."

The sound of his footsteps stopped. She heard him growl in frustration, and then, she heard a wooden crate scrape across the floor and crash against the wall.

Rose realized that he must've kicked it.

She blinked in shock, waiting for him to say something to her, to yell at her or insult her, but his voice never came. Instead, she heard only his harsh pants of breath.

"Bad tempers seem to be a common issue for vampires," Rose said.

"Animalistic emotions and urges," Kallias said quietly.

The tired sadness that she heard in his voice surprised her. "Oh."

"They're...hard to control," he muttered.

Rose couldn't imagine what it felt like to be so out of control of her own emotions—so instinctually-driven. If anything like the panic attacks or nightmares she'd often experienced, she thought it'd be horrible.

Rose suddenly remembered her backpack.

"What's wrong?" Kallias said, when he saw the worry in her expression.

She patted the floor around her, feeling for her bag. "My backpack."

He didn't respond. Rose assumed that meant he didn't know where it was, but then, something suddenly dropped into her lap, startling her.

"You dropped it by the door," Kallias said, "when you fell."

"Oh," she said, running her hand across the bag. "Thanks."

He watched her with a suspicious scowl. "What's in it?"

"Uh," she said nervously, "just my books and stuff."

"Then, why did you hide it from Theron?" he asked.

"I didn't want anything to happen to them," Rose said. It was sort of the truth, after all. "I love my books, and I like carrying my favorites with me. Even if I can't read them at the moment, I feel a little better having them around, you know. Because the stories are already here." She pointed to her heart. "And looking at them reminds me."

And *that* was definitely the truth.

Kallias just stared at her for a few moments.

"It's okay," she said, blushing. "You can call me a geek. Everyone else does."

He laughed, "I have to be honest. It's hard sometimes to keep up with human jargon, but it's my understanding that humans use the term *geek* to describe someone who's passionate about something." He offered her a rare smile. "There's nothing wrong with passion."

Rose smiled shyly, surprised by his response.

She heard shuffling, as Kallias sat down next to her again. She considered reaching her hand out to find out how far away he was, but the earlier incident of accidentally touching him had been embarrassing enough. He grunted in pain, as he moved.

"How is your wound?" she asked. "Is it healing yet?"

"Not yet," he sighed. "It'll heal before tomorrow night, I'm sure."

"Theron was split open," she remembered, "and he was still walking."

"Theron feeds," Kallias explained, "*often*. If I consumed as much blood as Theron does, I would've healed as quickly as he does. But I don't."

"So, just out of curiosity," she said, biting her lip nervously, "if you *were* to drink someone's blood right now, would it kill the person?"

He laughed. "Why? Did you have someone in mind?"

"No," she said quickly. "I was just wondering."

"Not necessarily," he said.

His voice sounded closer now, nearly at her ear, meaning he must've leaned toward her. She felt his breath on her cheek, and she had the distinct feeling that he was staring at her neck.

Rose swallowed. "What do you mean?"

"Well, most vampires *do* kill their victims, and Theron would've killed *you*, obviously," Kallias said. "But it *is* possible to feed from a human without killing them. It's the blood loss that kills you, ultimately. So, hypothetically speaking, if I fed from you and only took a *little* of your blood, you'd survive."

Rose shivered as she felt his breath on her neck. "Hypothetically."

He laughed, "Yes. Hypothetically."

He moved again, and she no longer felt him near her.

Rose remembered how to breathe again—once she no longer felt his breath on her neck. "Then...why don't all vampires just feed without killing?"

"You'd get a different reason from every vampire you ask," Kallias said. "Some vampires, like Theron, simply enjoy the kill. We're violent creatures. It's in our nature to hunt and kill." He sighed, "And there are other who kill by accident. The hunger's all-consuming. It's difficult to stop feeding once you've had a taste of human blood." A note of disgust colored his voice. "And then, there are the majority who kill out of convenience. It's the easiest way to ensure our *food* doesn't warn the rest of the food that we're out there."

"Even if they did warn people," Rose told him, "people would just assume they're crazy, wouldn't they?"

"Until there's too many of them saying the same thing," Kallias said.

She frowned, considering that. "So, they just kill them?"

"You sound shocked," he said bitterly. "We are monsters, after all."

His use of the term *we* stunned her. "You think you're a monster?"

"I know I am," Kallias said, as if it were just a simple fact. He sighed, "Honestly, I think most vampires just don't see a way around it. The hunger drives them to take too much blood, which forces them to choose between letting the human die or healing them with vampire blood."

"Healing?" Rose repeated. "You mean, like what you did to me?"

"No," Kallias said. "I healed a minor wound on your neck. Your artery wasn't severed, and he hadn't taken too much blood. If I'd needed to heal you from something as serious as blood loss, I would've had to feed you my blood."

"Umm, eww," Rose said.

He laughed. "Not to me."

Rose squinted. "So, vampires can heal people, and yet, they...don't?"

"Feeding someone vampire blood creates a blood bond," he said, as if that explained it.

She frowned, as she tried to make sense of that. "Can you, umm, pretend I don't know what a blood bond is? Because I don't."

"It's an eternal link between the two people," Kallias said. He sounded distracted again, or perhaps just bored. "It's intensely intimate and invasive—and also very sexual. Most vampires prefer to avoid them."

"Sexual?" she sputtered.

He looked at her and snorted, "Yes, Rose. Sexual."

"I don't want a sexual bond with you," she blurted out.

Kallias laughed. "Good," he said, "because I don't want an *intimate* bond with you. Or anyone else, for that matter."

She blinked at that last part. It was clear to her that someone had hurt him, violated his trust somehow, because why else would he have such a negative view of intimacy and trust?

She wanted to ask, but she doubted he'd ever answer a question like that. "If vampires can heal from anything, how do you kill one?"

He smiled. "Should I be concerned?"

"Only if you make me very angry," she teased.

He laughed. "Well, you already know that sunlight kills us," he began.

"And beheading," Rose added.

Kallias glanced at her in surprise. "How did you know that?"

"It was the only thing that seemed to scare Theron," she explained.

Kallias nodded. "Our regenerative abilities only go so far. We can't just regrow our heads. So, yes, beheading is the most practical way to kill a vampire."

"Well, that's the first time I've heard *beheading* and *practical* in the same sentence," Rose muttered. "So, what about wooden stakes?"

Kallias rolled his eyes. "You watch too much television."

"I barely watch *any* television, actually," she said. "TV's bad for the brain."

He snorted. "Is that so?"

She winced and mumbled, "I also kind of…don't have room for one."

Kallias laughed, "I figured that's what it really was."

"I'm not getting rid of my wonderful bookshelves for a stupid TV," Rose said, as if she'd argued about it a billion times, and Kallias figured she probably had.

"So, your books are what gave you these ridiculous ideas?" he asked.

She glared at him—or in his direction, at least. "Maybe."

"Do you really think fiction and superstitions are the best things to consult for information on how to kill *real* monsters?" he asked.

She narrowed her eyes at his condescending tone. "Well, I tried to find a non-fiction, non-superstitious book, but *shockingly*, it didn't exist." She leaned toward him. "Because, get this! Vampires are *mythological* creatures! Well, you're supposed to be, anyway."

A smile curved at the edges of his lips. "You really should calm down. Your cheeks are all flushed. A vampire might find that…enticing."

Rose gave him a withering look. "We've been over this," she warned. "Fangs to yourself, Mister Vampire."

Kallias grinned at that. "And what about my hands?"

She blushed. "Those, too."

He laughed. "To answer your question," he said, returning to the issue at hand, "it doesn't matter if it's made of wood. Vampires don't have a *magical* allergy to wood."

"What about silver?" Rose asked curiously.

Kallias frowned. "I thought that was werewolves."

Her eyes widened. "Werewolves exist, too?"

He scowled at her, even though he knew she couldn't see him. "You think I'm some all-knowing source on supernatural creatures?"

"Is that your arrogant way of telling me you don't know?" Rose countered.

Kallias sighed. "If werewolves exist, I've never met one."

"So, would *any* kind of stake kill a vampire?" Rose asked.

He shrugged. "Have you ever seen a stake?" he scoffed. "If you shove that thing into *anything's* chest, and it gets up and walks away afterward, well...that'd be some scary shit."

"Then, I *could* kill a vampire by staking him?" she asked hopefully.

Kallias rolled his eyes. "You'd never even get close enough to do it. Humans aren't fast enough or strong enough to shove a stake into a vampire's heart."

She pursed her lips. "Then, how *does* a human kill a vampire?"

"A *human* doesn't," he said. "We're too powerful to be killed by humans."

Rose sighed, "But surely, there is some way..."

"Oh, how human of you," Kallias said—in a tone that made it clear he didn't mean it as a compliment. "You all want to believe there's some way to fight back, some way to defeat the monsters. Your scariest horror tales don't even scratch the surface of how scary vampires *really* are." He leaned toward her. "Humans wouldn't be able to sleep at night if they knew the truth. We're the ultimate predators, and we're immortal. Humans don't stand a chance."

She listened to him quietly. There was an edge to his voice—a cynicism. He hated what he was, and that hatred seeped into every word he said. "So, you're saying I have to depend on you?"

He glanced at her. "That bothers you, doesn't it?"

"It's not who I am," Rose told him. "I don't depend on anyone for anything. I won't."

Kallias sighed, "I'm afraid you don't have a choice, sweetheart."

"I do have a choice," she argued. "I, unlike you, can leave right now."

"And go where?" he challenged. "Theron likely took shelter at your apartment today, assuming you'd come home after I was dead." He leaned forward. "He's probably lying in wait for you right now, and nowhere else in this town is safe for you, either. Not even during the day —because Theron has no problem coercing humans into doing his bidding. The moment you set foot outside this building alone, he'll have someone there to kidnap you and take you to him. I understand this is an unfortunate situation for you, but *you* need to understand that you're in danger."

Her eyes narrowed. "You can't keep me here against my will."

"I can, actually," Kallias snarled.

"I am not your prisoner!" she told him.

"I didn't say you were, did I?" he said bitterly. "I was just correcting you. Technically, I *am* capable of keeping you here against your will."

Rose gave him a challenging glare. "So I can leave right now, if I want?"

He blew out an annoyed sigh. "It'd be extremely foolish."

That wasn't the question.

"But I can. Right?" she prompted again.

"I told you I'd keep you safe," Kallias said. "If you leave, I can't do that. Your only chance of survival is to stay with me until we kill Theron. If you value your life, you *will* stay with me."

"For how long, exactly?" Rose said.

"It doesn't matter," he said dismissively.

"Yes, it does!" she argued. "I don't know what life is like for vampires, but humans have responsibilities. We can't just leave all of that behind!"

"Your responsibilities will mean nothing, if you're dead," Kallias said.

"But if I live, I still have bills to pay," she insisted.

"Damn it, Rose, I can take care of all of that! You have no idea what kind of power I have!" Kallias growled. "But I'm not leaving you here to die."

"What are you going to do?" she snarled. "Kidnap me?"

"Maybe," he said in an equally acidic tone. "If that's what it takes."

Rose's eyes widened. "Do you have any idea how wrong that is?"

"I'm a vampire, sweetheart," he said in that patronizing tone. His voice dripped with bitterness and cynicism. "It shouldn't surprise you that I'd do something that's wrong."

She shook her head. "I never asked for your protection. I didn't want you to die, and I'm glad we got you here in time," she said, "but I'm not going to sit here and let you tell me what I can and can't do."

Rose jumped to her feet.

Kallias frowned as he watched her attempt to leave. She picked the right direction, at least, but she walked directly into a stack of crates and fell backward.

The stack of crates collapsed on top of her, and then, another stack of boxes wobbled and fell on top of her, as well.

Rose whimpered beneath the pile of crates and boxes.

Kallias sighed. He stood and walked over to her, kicking boxes out of his way.

Rose couldn't see anything in the dark building, so she had no idea how many boxes and crates were on top of her at this point.

She knew they felt too heavy, covering her chest, arms, and legs. She could barely breathe, much less move, but she shoved at the crates anyway, wincing at the pain it caused her.

Rose froze, as she heard shuffling noises all around her. Then, slowly, she felt the weight being lifted off of her.

She inhaled deeply, relieved that she could breathe again, and then tried to sit up. She gasped when Kallias slid his arms beneath her legs and back. He lifted her and cradled her against his bare chest, and then, he carried her several steps forward before he set her on her feet.

"I should've just left you there," Kallias grumbled.

Rose couldn't help but notice that despite the anger in his voice, his touch had been surprisingly gentle. "Why didn't you?"

"I don't know," he muttered. "The door is behind you, if you want to leave."

She heard his footsteps moving in the opposite direction. She frowned in surprise, as she realized he'd left her at the door.

She reached out in the direction she'd heard his footsteps. Then, she tentatively stepped forward.

His footsteps stopped. "The door is the other way, sweetheart."

"I don't want the door," Rose said, slowly following his voice. "I want you."

His brows furrowed at that. He rolled his eyes when he saw her nearing another stack of crates. "Wait," he muttered. "I'll come to you. Please, for the love of god. Don't move."

She froze.

The warmth of his body closed around her before he spoke.

He took her hands into his and led them to his chest. "I'm here."

"You're a jerk," Rose said, absently tracing the lines of his chest.

He inhaled sharply at her touch. "You called me over here to say that?"

"No," she said. Her fingertip brushed over a raised portion of skin—a scar, she thought—but he quickly grasped her hands and pulled them away. She frowned curiously at that. "I called you over here because I want to apologize."

His brows furrowed. "For what?"

"For giving you a hard time," Rose said. "You're a total jerk, and you apparently don't know how to talk to someone without ordering them around. But...I can see you're trying to help and that you care—even if you do have a screwed up way of showing it. So, I'm sorry if I overreacted."

"If?" Kallias said.

She narrowed her eyes. "Don't push it, mister."

Kallias snorted. "It's fine," he muttered. "Don't apologize."

She reached out and touched him again. Her fingers traced the lines of his tattoo, even though she couldn't see it.

Kallias kept his hands on her wrists, but he didn't stop her this time. Instead, he closed his eyes and leaned into her, his breath coming harsher and quicker.

"Will you forgive me?" she asked softly.

"Stop apologizing," he breathed again.

Her brows furrowed. "Why?"

"I don't know how to respond," he said.

With a baffled laugh, she said, "To an apology?"

"No," Kallias said. "To kindness."

She froze. Empathy wrenched her heart raw. It hurt her to think that something as ordinary as kindness would confuse him.

Kallias pulled her hands away from him again and cleared his throat. "I will, umm… Well, if you want, I can take you back to where you were sitting."

Rose nodded. "Okay."

Her stomach flipped, as he scooped her up into his arms again. He didn't speak as he carried her across the building, to the back corner, and set her on the ground.

Rose frowned as he placed something soft into her arms. She ran her fingers across the smooth leather, realizing that he'd given her his jacket.

"You can sleep on that," he said. His voice sounded different now—so nervous and unsure. "I assume you aren't used to sleeping on concrete."

"What about you?" she asked.

"I've slept in worse places," Kallias said dismissively.

Rose heard movement behind her, and she realized he was settling down on the floor, behind her, to sleep.

She wanted to see him—to see whether he was sitting or lying, whether he looked angry or sad, whether he was close enough to touch. "What's it like?" she heard herself ask. "Being what you are, I mean."

Kallias was quiet for such a long time that Rose assumed he'd already gone to sleep. Then, she heard him answer, softly, "Maddening."

"How so?" she asked gently.

"Have you ever been hungry?" he asked. "I don't mean a craving for food or wanting to eat out of boredom. But…really, truly hungry. *Starving.*"

That wasn't a question Rose wanted to answer, but she knew that she couldn't expect him to answer, if she wouldn't. "When I was a child."

Kallias glanced at her, surprised. "It feels like that, except so much worse, and it never stops," he said breathlessly. "The hunger is always there, always burning, always consuming you. Blood becomes the center of everything. Your senses are attuned to it. You hear it. You smell it. You see it. And you *want* it—no matter the cost."

Rose swallowed uneasily at that. "How do you stay sane?"

"I didn't, at first," he admitted. "In the beginning, I went mad. I couldn't reconcile the part of myself that was a monster and the part of myself that hated it. I couldn't be within a hundred miles of another person without wanting to rip their throat open. So, I isolated myself. Between the pain of starvation and the solitude, I lost whatever sanity I had left."

Her throat felt tight with sympathy. "That sounds terrible."

He shrugged. "I cheated death. It comes with a price."

Rose blinked. "You cheated death? Are you saying you actually *died*?"

He scowled at her. "How did you think I became this?"

"You died?" she said in disbelief. "As in...your heart stopped beating? You didn't just fall unconscious or something? You actually...*died*?"

"Of course I died," he muttered.

She stared in his direction, stunned. "And...are you still dead?"

Kallias rolled his eyes. "Do I seem dead?"

Rose frowned. "Well, no, but—"

"My heart beats just like yours. I breathe. I think. I feel. I am just as alive as a human, only I'm not human," he explained. "I awoke from death as a vampire."

She nodded, trying to process the information. "How did you die?"

"I'm finished being interrogated," he said, suddenly. "I need sleep."

Rose lifted her eyebrows. "Believe it or not, there *is* a nicer way to say that," she said with a sassy smile. "It's this complicated English word you might've heard before? *Goodnight*?"

She could almost hear the smile in his voice as he recited, "Goodnight."

9

A KISS OF DARKNESS

W hen Rose opened her eyes, she saw nothing.

Darkness surrounded her—not the darkness of her apartment, where the dim streetlight outside still shone through the curtains and the alarm clock on the nightstand cast that slight, green glow.

No, this was total, blinding darkness. She blinked several times, expecting whatever blocked her eyesight to clear, but it didn't.

She shifted on the cold, concrete floor—and winced when her muscles protested its hardness.

Her heart raced, as she realized she wasn't in her own bed.

She traced her hand over the soft, leather jacket beneath her, and the events of the previous night flooded her mind.

She breathed a sigh of relief, as she remembered where she was.

Her relief was short-lived, however, because she then noticed the sound of someone shuffling restlessly. When she heard a pained groan, she jumped up. He sounded hurt.

"Kallias?" she called. "Are you okay?"

Rose listened for an answer, but she heard only the sound of shifting and pained groans. "Are you hurt?" she said louder.

Rose waited for a few more moments, but the groaning and shuffling continued. She worried that something had gone wrong. Maybe his wound hadn't healed like he thought it would.

She climbed onto her hands and knees and crawled toward the noise. As she reached out her hand, her fingers brushed his arm. She felt it tremble and jerk convulsively beneath her fingers.

At first, she wondered if vampires could have seizures, but as she listened to his groans, she thought, instead, that it was a nightmare.

A pretty terrible one, too, if the sounds were any indication.

She shook his arm gently, but he didn't wake.

Rose shook him harder, but he didn't budge. His arm was just too heavy for her to move. "Kallias!" she yelled. "Wake up!"

In desperation, she shoved his arm as hard as she could, and lo and behold, it moved.

And *he*...went totally still.

For just a fraction of a second, his muscles went rigid, and then, before Rose even realized what was happening, she felt her back hit the concrete.

Kallias lay on top of her, his weight pinning her to the floor. His hands gripped her wrists so tightly that it hurt, pinning them to the floor beside her head.

She couldn't move.

Rose realized a little late that shaking a vampire while he was having a nightmare *might* not have been the wisest course of action.

Her entire body ached from the impact of the floor. She opened her mouth to speak, but no sound came out. The breath had left her lungs and had yet to return.

Kallias blinked a few times, slowly coming awake. He tried to remember what had happened.

He remembered Theron torturing him, and then...

No, he realized, that was a dream—a memory from long, *long* ago.

Which meant...

His eyes widened, as he noticed her beneath him. "Rose?"

"Yep," Rose choked out. She offered a pained smile, as she finally managed to make a coherent sound. "You were having a nightmare. I tried to wake you, and you just kind of...*attacked*."

"Shit," Kallias breathed. "*Shit.* Rose, I'm sorry."

The panic in his voice surprised her. "It's all right."

He looked her over. "Did I hurt you?"

"Nah," Rose said, but her smile was pained.

Kallias sighed, "I should've warned you not to touch me when I'm asleep."

Rose laughed in surprise. "Why? Does this happen often?"

He didn't answer. Instead, he loosened his grip on her wrists and turned them in his hands, examining the red marks he'd left. "I hurt you."

"I'm used to it," Rose assured him. "Audrey throws pillows at me when I wake *her* up. Vampire tackle? Basically the same."

Kallias didn't laugh. "I should've warned you," he repeated.

"No, no. Look," Rose said, suddenly serious, "I get it, okay? I, uh... I have it, too."

"It?" Kallias repeated. "What is it?"

"Uhh, PTSD?" Rose said—because he had to know, right? "Nightmares, flashbacks, Prozac? You know, the whole nine yards." She flashed what she hoped was a reassuring smile. "Been there, done that."

Kallias shook his head. "What is a Prozac?"

"Well," Rose said, frowning, "they probably don't make a vampire version yet."

He massaged her wrists with his thumbs, and the pain dulled.

But as his fingers alleviated the pain, they also created new sensations —a flutter in her stomach, chills across her wrist.

Kallias studied her disheveled appearance, as he looked for any other marks he might've left on her. He watched those wide, blue eyes of hers, and as he noticed the way she gazed slightly to the left of his face, he remembered she couldn't see.

A pink flush darkened her cheeks from the spike of blood pressure, and her messy, red hair fanned around her head like a fiery halo.

She breathed rapidly, her soft, pink lips parted.

The scent of adrenaline in her blood made it smell all the more enticing, and even covered in blood and dust, she still smelled of honey and vanilla.

There was a certain wildness to the way she looked after waking, and Kallias couldn't help but find it a little sexy.

Her pulse pounded in his ears, igniting his hunger. He wanted her, and his instincts were driving him to take what he wanted.

Rose hated not being able to see. She wanted to know if he was all right. She wanted to know why he'd gotten so quiet, all of the sudden.

Was it because she'd mentioned her own trauma? She'd only been trying to make him feel better, but maybe he was judging her now.

Some people did.

But no matter how hard she tried to see him, she could only feel him.

His legs rested between her own, and his bare chest and stomach pressed against her. Rose didn't know how to react to the sensation of his body on hers or the way her *body* reacted to that sensation.

Her physical experiences with men—and women, for that matter—had always been so limited. Attraction wasn't something she responded well to.

And, as if the situation she'd found herself in weren't awkward enough, she suddenly realized that she could feel his erection pressing against her stomach.

She blushed profusely. "Uh! So, are you going to get off of me, or…"

His lips pressed against hers, suddenly—effectively ending her stammering.

Rose blinked in surprise, but then, as if it had a mind of its own, her mouth molded to his. His lips felt feverish and surprisingly soft against hers, and all of the awkwardness that she'd felt moments ago melted away under his kiss.

Her stomach clenched, and her skin felt overheated. His tongue moved against hers, drawing a moan from her lips.

She squirmed and pulled at her wrists, and she felt him smile against her lips before he released her hands.

Kallias groaned, as Rose intertwined her fingers in his hair, pulling him closer. One of his hands cupped her face, tilting her head back, as he deepened the kiss.

He ran his other hand along her body until it reached her thigh. Then, he lifted her thigh to curve around his hip.

Rose gasped, as his body pressed harder against hers.

Her lips felt even softer than Kallias had imagined, and she kissed with a passion that left him hungry for more.

She became the focus of all of his senses—her body, her scent, her blood. He felt an overwhelming urge to tear open her shirt and sink his fangs into her neck.

He pulled away the moment he realized he was losing control. His face remained inches from hers, as he panted, breathless from the intensity of the kiss.

For a few moments, Kallias didn't move. He just stared at her in shock.

Finally, he rolled off of her, but he still didn't speak. He sat next to her, wondering what had possessed him to kiss her in the first place—and why it had affected him so intensely.

He could see her out of the corner of his eye. She hadn't moved. She just lay there on the concrete floor, trying to catch her breath.

Eventually, Rose sat up, wincing at the soreness in her muscles. She knew Theron must've left some nasty-looking bruises on her skin—if the pain were any indication, anyway.

But really, the pain was the last thing on her mind, at the moment—because her mind was more fixated on the other sensations she felt.

Rose traced her lips with her fingertips, noticing how they seemed swollen and tender from the kiss.

Her mind raced with hundreds of questions: Why had he kissed her? What had he stopped? Why was he so quiet now? Did he not enjoy the kiss? It seemed like he enjoyed the kiss, but what would she know?

But Rose asked none of those.

Instead, she asked, "Do you always kiss women after you attack them?"

He snorted, "No, you're unique in that aspect."

"Oh. Good," Rose said. She grimaced at her awkward response. "I have no idea what I'm saying," she muttered under her breath.

Kallias glanced at her, raising an eyebrow in amusement.

"So," she said, her voice still a little breathless. "Can we leave yet?"

He shook his head. "The sun won't set for another hour, at least."

Rose sighed, "What are we supposed to do in the dark for an *hour*?"

He chuckled. She could almost hear the smirk in his voice as he said, "Oh, I can think of a few things, but with my stamina, we'd need more than an hour."

She rolled her eyes at him. "Does that usually work for you?"

"Flirting?" Kallias said with a laugh. "I don't know. You tell me."

"Uh, no," she scoffed. "It doesn't work on me."

"No?" he said, smiling. His voice dropped lower, becoming breathy. "Well, you could've fooled *me*—with the way you kissed me just now."

"I didn't..." Rose stammered. "You kissed *me*!"

"And you kissed me back," Kallias informed her. "Very passionately, might I add."

Rose blushed. "I didn't want to be rude."

"You expect me to believe that you kissed me like *that* out of politeness?" Kallias laughed. "Sorry, sweetheart, but you're a terrible liar."

Her eyes narrowed. "*You* kissed *me*."

"You already said that," he reminded her. "I'm aware of what happened. Are you?"

Rose rolled her eyes. "Well," she sputtered, "why?"

"Why did I kiss you?" Kallias said with a puzzled frown. He looked away. "I don't see why that would matter."

Rose scowled. "It matters because you've made it clear on plenty of occasions that you don't like me very much. So, why would you kiss me?"

"How I feel about you has nothing to do with it," Kallias muttered.

"It has everything to do with it!" she argued.

Kallias rolled his eyes. "Rose, it was a kiss, not a proposal," he said, quite hurtfully. "It was just a physical action between two people. You're making something out of nothing."

"Nothing," Rose said coolly. "Right. Of course."

Kallias looked at her, suddenly feeling a hint of regret. "Rose..."

"No, I get it," she interrupted. It looked, at first, as if she were done with the conversation, but then, her blue eyes narrowed. "You know, many cultures throughout history considered kissing to be *something*.

Ancient Rome, for instance, considered kissing so meaningful that it signified a binding contract."

He rolled his eyes. "And some ancient Norse villages didn't consider two people married until the Viking fucked his bride in front of an audience. Do you suggest we base all of our interpretations of things on ancient cultures?"

She pursed her lips at his crudeness. "No."

"Face it. Kissing is just light foreplay," he muttered. "It arouses you. That's all."

"What? It does not..." Rose blushed. "You're so arrogant. You think that...*aroused* me?"

She didn't realize that he'd closed the space between them—until she felt his breath against her face. Her breath caught in her throat, and she blinked, wishing that she could see him.

"I know it did," Kallias said, his breath against her lips. "You can't hide much from a vampire, Rose. We have incredibly attuned senses." He moved his mouth to her ear, and she shivered when his breath fell against her ear. "We hear when your heart races, when your breath hitches. We can feel the slightest spike in temperature on your skin. We can smell your—"

"Okay, I get it!" Rose squeaked. She shuffled backward to put some space between them. She breathed slowly, trying to calm herself. When she heard him laugh at her, she narrowed her eyes at him. "Well, it's not like you weren't! I know you were! Because...I felt your..." she trailed off, blushing.

He lifted his eyebrows. "Well, *I* never denied it."

Rose frowned. "So...that's why you kissed me, then," she realized, "so I'd have sex with you."

The humor faded from his voice. "No."

When she heard the harsh thud of his boots, she realized that he'd stood. His voice came from above her when he spoke again.

"I know I'm a monster, Rose," he muttered, "but I didn't realize you thought that lowly of me."

Now, Rose was *really* confused. "I—I don't," she sputtered. "I'm just trying to understand. You said it meant nothing, so..."

"So, you assume I'm manipulating you for sex?" Kallias interrupted.

Rose shrugged. "No, I just… That's what men usually do, isn't it?"

He glanced down at her. "Someone hurt you," he realized.

She shrugged. "Someone…hurts everyone. Right?"

"Yeah," Kallias said, after a moment. "Yeah, I suppose so."

Neither of them spoke for a while, and the heat of their conversation dissolved into a cold, sterile silence.

It was obvious that neither of them were eager to share the details of the pain they'd experienced.

Kallias leaned against a support beam in the middle of the warehouse, watching her. After noticing her rub her eyes for the eighth time, as if that would help her see, he shoved his hand in his pocket and pulled out his phone. He wiped the dried blood on his jeans—or tried to, at least—and pressed the power button.

Rose blinked, as a faint light suddenly illuminated his face. His light brown eyes shifted to meet hers, as he stopped in front of her and held out his phone.

"The battery's low," he said, "but it'll give you some light for a few minutes."

She reached out and took the phone, a surprised smile curving at her lips.

He took a step back and crossed his arms, still watching her.

Rose stared at him, finally able to see him for the first time since the night before. He'd apparently slept in most of his clothing, just as she had, with the exception of the leather jacket and the blood-soaked T-shirt. His black jeans hung low around his hips, and her eyes widened as she saw his bare chest.

His brown hair fell almost to his shoulders, and those intricately colored flames that colored the skin of his neck traveled down his shoulders, disappearing behind his back.

The flames seemed to glow in the faint light of the phone, reminding her of real fire.

His chest and abdomen were muscular. She didn't know if that were a trait of all vampires—or something relating to his lifestyle before his death.

But she was struck—again—by the strange perfection of his features.

That, she figured, was definitely a trait of vampires.

But the scars?

Those were unexpected.

Everything about his skin looked perfect—his golden complexion, his muscles, everything…except for the scars.

Her throat constricted, as she stared at the gruesome scars across his chest and stomach.

Some of the scars were tiny, while others were clearly caused by fatal wounds. Some of the scars looked like burns, while others looked like jagged cuts and gashes.

"What happened to you?" she blurted out—before she could stop herself.

When Rose had asked that, Kallias had been examining his stomach wound that, surprisingly, was nearly healed. Now, he glanced at her, frowning. "What?"

"The scars," Rose said breathlessly. "How did you get them?"

His eyes narrowed. "That's none of your business."

She bit her lip, and her brows creased with sympathy. "Right," she said quickly. "Of course. I'm sorry."

His glare melted away, and he watched her with a frown.

"And I'm also sorry," Rose added, "about whatever happened to you."

He looked away. "I told you to stop doing that."

She laughed softly. "I can't just…*not* be kind to you, Kallias."

"Why not?" he said, frowning. "I'm unkind to you."

"No, you're not. You're rude *sometimes*—maybe even most of the time —but you're also kind sometimes, like when you saved my life or when you comforted me after Theron tried to…" Rose trailed off, stifling a gasp. It was still hard for her to say the word—even so many years later, even after so much therapy. "After he tried to rape me."

Kallias was quiet for a moment, and then, he growled, "He'll suffer for that. I swear."

Rose looked up, blinking. "Uh…" she sputtered. "Why?"

He seemed taken aback by her reaction. "Don't you want him to?"

She shrugged. "Revenge isn't really my thing."

Kallias rolled his eyes. "Well, that just makes me want to hurt him more."

Rose's brows furrowed. "Why would it do that?"

"Because you're too...*good*," Kallias said with a frustrated scoff. "You don't deserve any of this."

Rose blinked. As much as he'd insulted her in the past, she wouldn't have thought he considered very 'good.' "No one deserves it," she said easily. "That's the whole thing."

Kallias nodded slowly.

"Whatever happened to you," Rose said, her gaze shifting toward his scars, "you didn't deserve that either."

Kallias gave a bitter scoff at that. "If you believe that," he muttered, "you don't know me very well."

Rose didn't know how to respond to that, not that he gave her much of a window to respond, anyway. Instead, he turned away from her, glancing around the warehouse, as if he'd rather look anywhere else.

She sighed and, deciding that the concrete floor wasn't being too kind to her tailbone, tried to stand. Unfortunately, her numb and tingling legs didn't cooperate, and she fell.

Kallias's hand wrapped around her elbow and pulled her back to her feet so swiftly and easily that it seemed as if he'd been beside her the entire time—even though she'd *just* seen him standing several feet away.

"Well, that was embarrassing," she muttered.

"Are you okay?" he asked worriedly. "Are your legs injured?"

"No, *you* were the one with broken legs," Rose reminded him. "Is your *memory* injured?"

He snorted at her sassy remark. "And yet, you're the one who fell."

"My legs are asleep," Rose said, thumping her thigh. She glanced at him, and her gaze flicked briefly toward his hand, which felt warm against her elbow. "I bet vampires don't have that problem. You guys are probably *always* graceful."

Kallias grinned. "Compared to *you*, yes, we're all graceful."

She huffed at him and grumpily jerked her elbow out of his grasp.

He laughed again. "Not that I mind, but you're losing your pants."

Rose froze, as she suddenly realized that her jeans *did* feel awfully loose around her hips. She shifted the phone in her hand to shine it down at her pants, and she paled, as she saw that they'd slidden lower around her hips—low enough to reveal the band of her black, cotton panties.

She jerked her jeans up to her stomach, grumbling under her breath about the missing button. Her face felt like it might melt, when she finally glanced at Kallias, who stood there with his arms crossed.

"I need another pair of pants," she told him, "and another shirt."

That cocky smirk that he'd been wearing faded from his face. "We have to get out of town first," he said with a regretful sigh, "but then, I'll buy you whatever you need."

"Buy?" she sputtered. "No. I have plenty of clothes in my apartment."

He let his arms fall to his sides, and he gave her his most exasperated scowl. "We've been over this, Rose," he said irritably. "Theron will expect you to show up at your apartment. You can't go back there. Once we get out of town, we'll stop somewhere and pick up whatever you need."

"I don't even have my wallet," Rose complained.

"I have more than enough to get you whatever you need," he assured her, "and even if I didn't, I could handle that, too."

Rose shook her head. "No. Absolutely not. I'm not letting you pay for it."

Kallias rolled his eyes. "Not this again," he groaned.

"I don't need a man to pay for things for me," she complained.

"So, my penis is the problem?" he asked incredulously.

"No, I just—" Rose sighed in frustration. "I'm an independent person. I've spent my entire life taking care of myself, and I don't need that to change."

"Except you *do*," Kallias argued. He stepped closer to her. "Right now, by no fault of your own, you're in a situation in which you *do* need help. It doesn't change who you are to accept help when you need it." His gaze softened slightly. "Look, I get that this is a big thing for you—

doing everything for yourself and all—but right now, there are some things I can do that will help. So, just let me, all right?"

She sighed, her frustration deflated by his tone. "Fine," she relented, "but only because I don't want to walk around naked."

His eyebrows lifted. "That was an option?"

"Not *actually* naked," she said, rolling her eyes. "Naked, as in *this*."

He scowled at her torn clothing. "That's not naked. At all."

She ignored him. "But if we do this, we're considering it a loan. I'll pay you back. Eventually." She pursed her lips and admitted, "It might take a while, though. I don't make much at the café."

"I figured," Kallias said. "You're kind of a terrible waitress."

Rose lifted her eyebrows. "I thought you said you liked my service."

"It was amusing," he admitted, "but I doubt everyone feels that way."

Rose couldn't argue with that. She'd once had a customer demand that Eleanor fire her, just because she'd corrected the customer's spelling of *twelve*. But come on, how hard was it to spell *twelve* correctly? It was a one syllable word, for goodness sakes!

And she was only trying to help.

Rose frowned when she noticed Kallias grinning at her, almost as if he could see the entire memory playing out in her head.

"I have questions," she said suddenly.

"You always have questions," Kallias reminded her.

"I have questions about you," she added, "and vampires."

"Very well," he sighed. "I *might* answer some of them."

Rose nodded. "Well, first, I need to know if you eat people."

"I'm a vampire, not a zombie," he grumbled.

She sighed, "You know what I mean. Do you drink human blood?"

Kallias stared at her for a moment, as if she'd asked him a complicated question that required a lot of thought, but then, he said, "No."

She sighed in relief. "Okay. So, what kind of blood do you drink, then?"

His brows furrowed. "What *kind*?" he repeated.

"Animal blood?" she guessed.

He grimaced. "Where did you get a disgusting idea like that?"

"Uh," Rose said, shrugging. "Well, blood is blood, right?"

"No," Kallias said, his lip curling. "Not right."

She didn't understand how she'd disgusted him so thoroughly with one, harmless question. "Umm…okay. Then, what's the difference?"

He sighed tiredly, as if *she* were the one acting weird. "Feeding is sexual."

Rose blinked, not sure she'd heard him right. "What?"

"Drinking blood," he rephrased, "is an intensely sexual interaction."

She wrinkled her nose. "You're kidding."

"No. Not at all," he said. "In all of that *reading* you did, you never noticed the link between vampires and sex?"

"Well, yeah. Of course," Rose admitted. "Vampires were often depicted as having some sort of seductive power over their victims, and yeah, a lot of the paintings and stories depicted them drinking the victim's blood during sex."

Kallias nodded. "Every culture had their own stories about us— usually influenced by that culture's beliefs or fears. For example, the Ancient Greeks believed in the Pantheon, but of course, our gods were different from your culture's God in that our gods were imperfect. Greek gods could be vengeful and selfish."

Rose was nodding alarmingly quickly now, apparently excited by this particular topic. He briefly remembered her saying she liked history.

"So, they were feared as well as worshipped," Kallias added. "Greek gods were said to be beautiful and powerful. So, it only made sense that when the people of Ancient Greece encountered vampires, they often assumed we were gods or demigods."

"I need to write this down," Rose whispered.

Kallias just frowned, before continuing, "On the other hand, a severely puritanistic *Christian* culture was more likely to fear sex, murder, or demons. So, when people of *that* culture encountered seductive, murderous creatures like vampires, they assumed we were demons who needed to be hunted and killed—which was what happened during the 1700s."

"I wrote a paper on that once," Rose told him. "It was so much fun."

Again, Kallias's frown deepened. "The only thing every culture agreed on was that vampires were sexual creatures who drank blood."

Rose bounced a little on her feet, as if she were about to burst with excitement. "Keep going, keep going," she pleaded. "Why did they all think vampires were sexual creatures?"

He blinked in bewilderment. When he'd been a philosopher, as a human, he'd had a couple of eager students—but none quite as strange as Rose. "Well," he said slowly, "what did you feel when Theron bit you?"

Rose's smile faded with an alarming abruptness. "Revulsion."

His brows furrowed. "You must have felt something else."

Rose looked away, remembering that terrible, almost *bewitching* pleasant sensation. "No," she lied.

"Don't lie to me, Rose," Kallias said. He stepped closer and placed his hand under her chin, tilting her head back so that he could meet her gaze. "Let me rephrase the question," he said, trailing a finger toward her neck. "What did you feel when I put my mouth on the bite wound?"

She shivered at the memory. "It was," she paused, blushing, "pleasant."

He felt her rapid pulse beneath his fingers. "Do you know why?"

"A brief lapse in judgement?" she guessed.

He laughed. "No, it's physical, not mental. You would've felt it with Theron, too," he explained. "Like the healing enzymes in our blood and saliva, our bodies *also* release sexual endorphins. It creates pleasant sensations in the victim when a vampire feeds from them. It usually ensures you don't fight us."

She blinked. "So, it causes humans to enjoy...being murdered?"

He dropped his hand. "Ultimately, yes."

She stared, aghast at the realization. "That's horrific."

"Yes," he agreed. "Nature's cruel. And the worst part is...we don't *need* that advantage over you. We're already hundreds of times stronger and faster. Even if you did fight, you wouldn't stand a chance against us."

Rose stepped back. "I did—" she paused to suck in a deep breath. "I did feel a pleasant sensation when Theron bit me," she admitted, "but I also felt revulsion."

He frowned curiously at that. "Interesting."

"How is it interesting?" Rose said.

His dark eyes seemed intensely focused and blank, at the same time, as if they weren't seeing her, but instead, seeing *through* her. "You have an extraordinarily strong will." Then, he blinked, and his expression seemed normal again. He chuckled and cocked his head to the side. "I guess that explains why you don't throw yourself at me like most women do."

Rose frowned. "What is that supposed to mean?"

"Well," Kallias said, crossing his arms, "you must've noticed that I'm incredibly attractive."

"I've noticed that you're incredibly arrogant," she muttered.

He laughed at her snarky remark. "It's, umm...another example of nature's cruelty," he explained. "We have these predatory senses that make it plenty easy for us to hunt down our prey, but we don't even need to because *they* come to us." He sighed sadly, "We're designed to attract you. We appear physically perfect. And as if that weren't enough, that seductive power you mentioned? It's real, too. I don't know what it is, exactly. I just know humans can't resist it."

Rose nodded, remembering the way Audrey and Owen had acted.

"Except," Kallias added, "*you* do."

She frowned at that. "Why am I able to resist it, if no one else can?"

Rose thought she saw something flash in his eyes. Hesitance or nervousness, maybe? But he quickly looked away.

"I don't know," Kallias said.

She narrowed her eyes, as she realized he was hiding something...*again.*

"Anyway," he said, flinching at the glare she gave him, "feeding is sexual for the vampire, too. Our...*cravings* are linked. When we *want* someone, we crave their blood, as well, and when we feed from them, we usually want to..." He smiled. "Well, I think you understand."

The light drained from her eyes, and she suddenly looked sick. "Is that why Theron tried to..." she trailed off. She didn't have the strength to say it again. Not just yet.

Then, the strangest thing happened.

Kallias growled.

Like an animal.

Exactly...like an animal.

Rose bit her lip to suppress a laugh. "Uhh? Are you all right?"

Kallias blinked, as if he were coming out of a trance. She shook his head slowly. "Theron is just," he paused, gritting his teeth in anger. "He's the kind of evil that makes me...*sick*." Hatred dripped from every word. "He's not losing control. He just enjoys it."

Rose paled a little at that. "Oh. Right."

"He wanted you to suffer," Kallias said simply. "That's why he did it."

Rose nodded uneasily. "I take it vampires don't usually do that? To... unwilling victims, I mean?"

"Why would they?" Kallias scoffed. "Most humans are more than willing."

Rose swallowed. "But isn't taking advantage of that a little—"

"Immoral?" he interrupted. His voice grew more and more bitter, by the moment. "Isn't that what we are? What we *have* to be? To kill just to sate the hunger?"

Her heart clenched at the self-hatred in his tone. "But you don't do that."

His gaze drifted down to her neck. "I still want to. I still crave it."

Rose reached up and touched his jaw, and he shuddered at her touch. She tilted his face downward, until his gaze met hers.

"But you don't," she reminded him. "That counts for something."

His face contorted, as if the thought caused him pain. "Not enough."

She sighed, wishing she knew how to change his mind. She dropped her hand, and with a grimace, said, "Okay, so, I think I understand why animal blood isn't an option now."

He shuddered in disgust. "You think?"

"So, then, how do you survive?" Rose asked. "If you don't feed?"

Kallias frowned, as if he found her question ridiculous. "I'm immortal," he reminded her. "I can't die from starvation. My body heals itself."

She froze, and her stomach twisted in horror. "Wait, are you—" She gasped at the realization. "Are you saying you starve? Over and over? Without dying?"

He shrugged. "You sound appalled," he said bitterly. "Would you have preferred I killed multiple women a night?"

"Of course not," Rose said, "but that doesn't mean I think you being in agony is just...*fine*."

Kallias shrugged again.

"You said the hunger is all-consuming," she said. "How do you resist it?"

"You can resist anything with enough conviction," Kallias said.

Rose nodded. "And what is it? The conviction that allows you to resist?"

He sighed, "I don't like to watch people die."

"Ah," Rose said softly.

"And," he added, "I've always hated people who prey on weak." He looked away. "I can't be one."

A gentle smile pulled at the corners of Rose's mouth. "How can you not see the goodness that's inside of you?"

Kallias glanced at her. He seemed shocked, at first—his eyes wide, his chest rising and falling with shallow pants—but his shock quickly morphed into anger.

He stepped toward her so suddenly that she nearly fell back. He caught her arm, gripping it tightly to keep her from falling, and he leaned toward her, his face inches from hers. "You don't know what's going through my head. Your blood smells sweet and powerful, and I don't *want* to resist it, Rose," he growled. "I want to drain every drop of blood from your body." He enunciated each word, as if he were in pain. "Does that sound *good* to you?"

She glared at him. "Let go of my arm."

He glanced down at her elbow, as if he were only just realizing how tightly he'd gripped it. He took his hand off of her arm, and his brows creased with regret. He opened his mouth to ask her if she were okay, if he'd hurt her or scared her, but then, thinking better of it, he shook his head and walked away.

Rose watched him. The flames on his neck and shoulders traveled a third of the way down his back, and along his spine, she could see more scars. Scars, she realized, from injuries that had gone all the way through him. From the looks of it, he'd been stabbed—not just once, but *many* times.

"You never told me how you died," she said softly.

"And I don't plan to," he said without looking at her.

"Fine," she sighed. "Will you at least tell me how old you are?"

He was quiet for a moment. "Do you want to know how old I was when I died, or do you want to know how many years I've been alive altogether?"

She shrugged. "Both, I guess."

Finally, he turned back toward her. "I was twenty-six when I died."

Rose nodded. She *had* noticed that he looked close to her age, definitely in his twenties. "Your body never changed?"

"I don't age, if that's what you're asking," Kallias said. "Our bodies don't deteriorate, like a human's does."

"Because of the regenerative enzymes," Rose assumed.

"There were *some* changes during the transformation, though," Kallias admitted. "For the most part, we remain the same as we were when we died, but during the transformation, our bodies do *perfect* themselves, in a sense. We become more appealing to humans."

"And the fangs!" Rose threw in. "Don't forget the fangs!"

He snorted at her enthusiasm. "Yes, the canine teeth elongate and sharpen," he said, sliding his tongue across the sharp teeth, "becoming fangs."

She nodded in approval. "And how long has it been since you died?"

"Approximately 2,485 years," Kallias said—without missing a beat.

Her jaw dropped. "Did you, uhh... Did you just say two thousand?"

"I guess that means, technically, I'm 2,511 years old," he added.

She stared, her eyes wide and her mouth ajar. "You're kidding."

He frowned. "That'd be a pretty dull joke, don't you think?"

"Holy crap," she breathed. She waved a hand. "I mean, I won't lie. If you'd said even one hundred, I would've had a hard time wrapping my mind around it, but twenty-five hundred?" She laughed, a note of hysteria in her voice. "That's insane!"

Kallias shrugged. "Theron's older than I am."

Rose blinked at that. "Is *he* the oldest?"

"No," he said. "Aaron's the oldest."

He'd said it as if the first name were enough.

"And," Rose said with a frown, "who is Aaron?"

"Pray you never find out," Kallias said darkly.

Rose frowned, but her mind quickly shifted back to the issue at hand, which was the historical artifact in front of her. "You're from the Ancient Greek Empire."

"Yes," he confirmed. "I lived in Athens."

She gave a happy, little squeak at that and bounced on the balls of her feet.

"Uh," Kallias said worriedly, "are you okay?"

"Better than okay!" Rose exclaimed. "You can tell me *everything*!"

He glanced down, raising an eyebrow at those large breasts of hers, which weren't exactly holding steady—you know, with all of that erratic jumping and all.

When Rose noticed the direction of his gaze, she immediately went still. Blushing, she jerked her torn shirt closed.

Kallias just grinned at her.

"Anyway," she grumbled. "I study history! And you are...history!"

He frowned. "You want to...*study* me?"

"Yes!" Rose said. "You have to tell me everything you've ever seen!"

"That would take a while," he muttered.

That didn't seem to deter her at all. "This is the coolest thing that has ever happened to me!"

Kallias stared blankly at her.

"I'm going to need notebooks! So many notebooks!" Rose said, glancing toward her backpack. "I hope I have enough notebooks."

Kallias shook his head in bewilderment. He'd never seen someone so excited in all of his two and a half thousand years—and this was, apparently, her reaction to...*history*.

Not fame or riches or sex. Just history.

"So, this is what it takes to impress you, then?" Kallias teased. "Living twenty-five hundred years and then teaching you *history*?"

She scowled at his teasing. "It's not *that* hard to impress me."

He snorted, "Name one other thing that has impressed you."

She glared at him. "Just because *you* can't impress me, doesn't mean—"

He cut her off. "Oh, I assure you," he said with a deep, lascivious smile. "Given the right circumstances, I *can* impress you."

She crossed her arms. "I hope you're not expecting me to kiss you again," she said, "because I don't plan on kissing you ever again."

He gave her an amused smile. "Who said anything about kissing?"

"You implied kissing," Rose said.

He laughed. "I said circumstances. I never said anything about kissing."

"Okay, I'm not *that* naïve!" Rose said, pointing a finger at him. "I know what you meant!"

With a smirk, he said, "I think you let your imagination get a little too wild there."

Rose glared at him. "You... You..." she trailed off, unable to think of an insult strong enough to voice her anger. "So, we agree? The kiss was a mistake?"

If she didn't know any better, she would've thought she saw his smile falter. But, before she could question it, he fixed the cocky smirk back in place.

"Of course," Kallias said. He leaned closer and said, "I don't even *want* to kiss you again."

Rose opened her mouth to reply to that, but she frowned, when she noticed him suddenly straighten.

His eyes fluttered a little, and he lifted his chin slightly, almost as if it were some kind of instinctual reaction. A convulsive shudder seemed to travel down his spine and through each limb of his body.

She blinked in shock. "Are you okay?"

He opened his eyes. "The sun's setting."

She looked around, confused. "And...*how* would you know that?"

"I'm a creature of the night," Kallias said. "The night calls to me."

"I don't know if that's a real thing or if you're just trying to sound cool," Rose muttered.

He turned and walked back toward the back corner of the building. He knelt and snatched up his shirt and jacket. "Get your things. We'll leave soon."

She sighed at his tone. "You're a very rude person. You know that, right?"

"Yes," he said simply.

He then pulled on his black T-shirt. The fabric looked permanently wrinkled and still wet with blood, and a large, jagged hole rested over his stomach. He picked up the leather jacket and slid his arms into it.

Rose glanced down at her own clothes. "I can't walk around in these."

"We'll stick to secluded streets," he said. "No one will see you."

Rose ran a hand through her hair in a useless attempt to tame the long, tangled mess of red hair. "I need a brush and clothes and...a shower, preferably."

She jumped, startled, when she felt Kallias suddenly behind her— even though she'd never seen him move. He moved her arm so that he could slide the strap of her worn, black backpack over her arm.

He turned her to face him. "Relax," he said. "We need to get to my car and get away from here as fast as possible so Theron can't track your scent. Then, I promise you we'll get whatever you need."

The phone dinged, a *low battery* alert flashing on the screen.

Rose glanced down at it, and when she looked back up, Kallias had disappeared. She blinked and held up the light, shining it around the room until she finally found him. He stood in front of two large metal doors, his hands on the door handles.

"Wait!" she called, running over to him. "What if someone's out there?"

He glanced at her. Then, he leaned toward the door and sniffed twice.

Rose lifted both eyebrow. "Umm... What are you doing?"

"If there were anyone out there, I'd smell them," he said. "It's clear."

"Oh," she said, blinking. "And you're *sure* the sun is down?"

"I'm about eighty percent sure," Kallias said.

She glared at him. "You're going to stake your life on eighty percent?"

He shrugged. "I normally wait an extra hour, but we don't have time."

She rolled her eyes. "I'll check. Just get out of the way."

He looked amused by the demand, but he didn't challenge her. Instead, he just took several steps back—until he seemed to disappear into the darkness. "You can open the door now," he said from somewhere behind her.

Rose exhaled slowly, and then, shoving the phone in her back pocket, she placed her hand on the handle of one of the double doors and pulled it open. She squinted as the light burned her eyes.

In comparison to the total darkness her eyes had grown used to, the dim glow of the streetlights was blinding, but slowly, her eyes adjusted to the light. She frowned at the horizon, looking for any pink light tracing the palm trees in the distance, but the sky, instead, looked blackish blue, lit only by the moon and stars.

"It's safe," she announced loudly, not sure where he was.

"Good," he said, his voice inches from her ear. "Let's go."

Startled by his sudden closeness, Rose squeaked and spun around. She knew for a fact that he hadn't been there a moment ago.

Before she could stop herself, she reflexively kicked his leg.

He looked only mildly irritated. "What was that for?"

"You scared me!" she snapped. "How did you move so quietly?"

He shrugged. "Creature of darkness, remember?"

"I'm going to put a bell around your neck," she muttered.

Kallias chuckled and brushed past her. "Come on. Stay close."

———

ROSE STEPPED OUTSIDE AND SIGHED HAPPILY, AS THE AUTUMN BREEZE encircled her, brushing off the dust and stuffiness of the warehouse.

Kallias walked with long strides that Rose had to sprint to catch up with him. They turned the corner onto a dark, narrow alley and continued down it, until they turned onto another secluded street.

The moon shone brightly in the black sky, lighting even the darkest alleys. Rose crossed her arms as they walked, attempting to hold her shirt closed, just in case they ran into anyone *before* they reached his car.

Occasionally, she'd find herself watching Kallias, noticing how he moved so quietly and gracefully through the night, how his skin practically glowed in the moonlight, and how, even after everything that had happened, he looked perfect. She could only imagine how terrible *she* looked—with her bloody and tattered clothes, her disheveled hair, and the blood stains that discolored her skin. She blinked, as she noticed his light brown eyes staring back at her.

"Uh," she said awkwardly, "why are you looking at me?"

His lips twitched. "You were looking at me first."

"I was not," she lied. "I was looking at...something else."

"Of course you were," he snorted.

Rose narrowed her eyes. "You're so arrogant."

"You've already said that. You're not very good at insults, are you?" he taunted. "Sarcasm, sure, but not insults."

Rose opened her mouth and then closed it. She decided to ignore him.

Eventually, she noticed that the buildings were growing taller and newer, and the sounds of the cars grew closer. She realized they were headed toward the busier part of the city.

"Where exactly *is* your car?"

"The hotel parking lot, where I was staying," he answered, and then, somehow predicting her next question, he added, "The Hampton."

She frowned, wondering if he'd *really* predicted her question or if she were just reading too much into it. "The one by the Interstate?"

"Is there another one?" he asked.

"Well, no, but..." she sputtered. "That's on the other side of town."

"We're cutting across the city," he told her. "It won't take long."

She didn't know how he intended to do that—when there weren't any roads that cut across the city—but she didn't have time to ask. It was all she could do just to keep up with his long strides.

He led the way onto a quiet, residential street, and they slowed, as they approached an alley that connected two of the busiest streets in town.

Chains blocked off the alley, and a yellow *No Trespassing* sign hung from the chains.

He leaned forward and grabbed the chains, preparing to tear them off.

"Wait. What are you doing?" she said. "Don't you see the sign?"

He glanced at her. Shrugging, he snatched the metal sign off of the chains. He closed his hand around it, easily crushing it into a yellow ball, as if it were only a piece of paper. He tossed it aside.

"There. Now, there's no sign."

Rose stared at the rolled up metal sign in disbelief.

Kallias tore the chains from the hinges with the same nonchalance. He stepped into the narrow alley and turned toward her expectantly.

She followed him reluctantly. "You're turning me into a criminal."

He laughed. "Relax. We're taking a shortcut, not committing murder."

This alley ran behind an expensive apartment complex. Because of this, it was much cleaner than the other alleys they'd been down, and porch lights behind each apartment lit the way for them to walk.

"What if we get caught?" Rose asked—a little louder than she'd intended.

Kallias shot an irritated glare in her direction, before his eyes suddenly shifted toward the apartment a few feet to their left. He cursed under his breath and froze, pulling her to a stop.

The door opened, and a short, stout man stepped out, clutching a garbage bag.

A small wave of relief washed through Rose, as she realized the man wasn't looking at them. Instead, he was looking over his shoulder at his wife who stood just inside the door, cleaning out their fridge.

"Babe, I don't know what you're talking about. I didn't hear anything," he called over his shoulder, but then, he turned to throw the garbage bag in the dumpster and noticed them. His grey eyes widened, as he glanced over Rose's tattered, bloody clothes. "What the—"

Kallias released her arm, and moving so quickly that the movement blurred before her eyes, he suddenly stood in front of the man. The man paled and backed into the wall. He began to hyperventilate.

"Stop panicking," Kallias said. He took control of the man's mind and, using his telepathic abilities, commanded, "Go inside. You didn't see anyone."

The man calmed instantly. "Okay."

Rose watched in complete bewilderment, as the man threw the garbage bag in the dumpster and returned to his apartment without another word.

As the man stepped back inside the bright apartment, he yelled to his wife, "I *told* you there was no one out there."

Kallias glared at her. "Next time, could you keep your voice down?"

Usually, Rose would've shot back with some sassy remark, but she was too shocked by what had just happened. "What did you just do?"

He shrugged, as if it were obvious. "I controlled his mind."

Rose gaped at him, but he didn't notice because he was already walking again. She jogged to catch up before he reached the end of the alley. "I'm sorry," she squeaked, "but it sounded like you just said you controlled his mind?!"

"I did," Kallias said without looking at her.

"Vampires can control minds?" she said.

He scowled. "That is *not* keeping your voice down."

She felt breathless from the ridiculously brisk pace they were keeping. "I just found out that vampires control minds! Forgive me for freaking out a little!"

"I never said *vampires* do," he sighed, as if she were overreacting. "I said *I* do. Telepathy is a rare ability, even amongst vampires. I happen to have it."

"Oh," she said, a little calmer. "Wait. You mean you have full-blown telepathic abilities? Like Professor X?"

"Who?" Kallias said.

"From *X-Men*," Rose said slowly. "The comic?"

"I don't know what that is," Kallias muttered.

Rose frowned. "Well, we have to fix that."

Kallias turned onto a darker alley that ran behind a diner that had closed down a couple of years before. "After a lifetime of believing vampires were fictional creatures, you discovered we're real. Why would it surprise you to find that psychic abilities exist, too?"

"Touché," Rose admitted. "So, you can hear *my* thoughts?"

"Yes," he said with an amused smile, "when I pay attention."

"And you didn't think that was something I should know?" she said, alarmed at what all he might've heard.

"No," he said, shrugging. "Why would you need to know that?"

Her eyes narrowed. "Oh, I don't know. Maybe because I—"

She never finished her sentence because Kallias suddenly grabbed her and pulled her back against him.

He clasped his hand over her mouth before she could ask him what the heck he was doing. His muscles were rigid and alert behind her. She felt his chest expand as he inhaled slowly, as if he were trying to inhale a specific scent—or identify it, maybe?

Kallias cursed under his breath, as he recognized the scents of two vampires. He pulled Rose behind a nearby shoe store and opened the door to a small storage room that looked as if it hadn't been touched in years. He grabbed Rose's arm and pushed her toward the room.

Rose pulled her arm from his grasp and twisted away from him. "What the heck do you think you're doing?" she snarled.

"Shhh!" Kallias hissed, his eyes wide. "Get inside that room. Hurry."

"Why would I do that?" she asked with an alarmed frown.

He sighed and leaned in so he could whisper, "Vampires. I don't know if they're working with Theron, but if they are, I can't let them find you. I need you to stay in there—until I find out who they are."

Rose cast a worried look at the storage room that wasn't much larger than a closet. "I'd rather stay with you."

"No," he said. "If you get too close, they might recognize your scent. Just stay in the storage room for a few minutes. I'll come back for you."

Rose's heart raced at the thought. "You don't understand. I can't—"

"You can't what?" Kallias said, exasperated.

Rose might've told him of her PTSD earlier to make him feel better, but giving him the details was a little much for her. "Do you realize the likelihood of a poisonous spider being inside that room?"

He rolled his eyes. "Which do you think is more deadly? Spiders or vampires?"

She shrugged. "I don't know the statistics on *vampires*, but one out of—"

"Rose, get inside," Kallias interrupted. "We don't have time to waste."

Rose sighed in defeat and stepped inside the small, dusty room. It *was* a little bigger than a normal closet. Perhaps she could handle the small space, just this once.

But her pulse still skyrocketed when he closed the door. She turned on the flashlight on Kallias's phone and glanced around the room, focusing on the spider webs that hung from the corners, rather than on the smallness of the space.

"It's okay, spiders," Rose whispered, after he left. "I'm more scared of the walls than I am of you. I'm a weirdo that way."

VAMPIRE ROADKILL

"*I* don't know why Theron sent you," a young vampire complained. "I could've done this by myself."

He leaned against the wall of an alley, behind a closed café. His baggy blue jeans and oversized hoodie hung loosely over his slender form. His dirty-blonde hair was gathered at the nape of his neck in a low ponytail. He held a cigarette to his mouth and lit it with a small, blue lighter.

The other man who stood in that dark alley shot a look of disgust at the one who'd spoken. This second man's clothing was totally unlike the loose, unkempt clothing of the younger vampire.

While the first man looked almost natural, hanging around in a dark, secluded alley, *this* man stuck out like a sore thumb.

He wore black dress pants and a pressed, white, button-down shirt, buttoned all the way to the collar. His hair fell close to his head in short, black ringlets. He looked more like someone who'd gotten lost on his way to an office job than someone hiding in the shadows of a dirty alleyway.

"He obviously thinks you're incompetent," the man sneered.

"Don't know why," the first man said, blowing out a mouthful of smoke.

"You're a baby vampire," the older one said. "Babies need a babysitter."

The *baby* vampire scowled at the other vampire. "I've been a vampire for fifty-seven years already. They'd call me old if I was human."

"But you're *not* human," the second vampire stated.

"What's so important about this human girl anyway?" the younger vampire said, white smoke falling out of his mouth with each word.

The older vampire wrinkled his nose, his senses overwhelmed by the scent of cigarette smoke. "Why are you smoking that?"

The younger vampire shrugged. "Human habit."

"But you're *not* human," the other vampire said again.

The younger vampire blew out a ring of thick smoke. "Sure. But now, I can smoke all I want, and it can't kill me. So, why bother quitting?"

"Because the smell is nauseating," the second vampire complained.

The first vampire ignored him and inhaled again.

"Well, are you going to put it out or not?" the older vampire asked.

The younger vampire glanced down at the cigarette. "I still have half the cigarette left," he complained. "I'll put it out when I'm done."

The older vampire shook his head slowly, his jaw tight, as if he were barely holding back his anger. "Let me rephrase the question," he said slowly. "If you don't put it out, I'll use it to burn off your face."

The first vampire paled at the threat. He quickly tossed the cigarette on the ground and crushed it under his shoe. "Happy?"

"Mildly," the other vampire muttered.

The first vampire sighed, "Has anyone ever told you you're a snob?"

"Most are smart enough not to," the second one said. Now that the overpowering scent of smoke had faded, he sniffed the air and frowned. "Do you smell that?"

The younger vampire crossed his arms, clearly pouting. "I get it. The cigarette stinks. I put it out already," he grumbled. "Give it a rest."

"Not the cigarette, idiot," the second vampire hissed. "The blood."

The younger vampire froze, his eyes widening as he, too, noticed the scent of dried blood. Sweet, *powerful* blood. "Do you think it's hers?"

"How would I know?" the older vampire said, rolling his eyes. "Go find the human and bring her here. I'll call Theron."

"Why do I always have to do the dirty work?" the younger one groaned.

WHAT LITTLE LIGHT ROSE HAD *LEFT* DISSOLVED INTO TOTAL DARKNESS, AS THE phone gave its last, dying beep. She sighed at the phone's betrayal and slid it into her back pocket.

The longer she waited, the more she wondered why she'd agreed to this ridiculous plan in the first place. She wasn't the type of person to hide and wait.

Not to mention the fact that small spaces and Rose just...*didn't* mix.

Rose jumped, as she felt someone touch her shoulder. She squealed and spun around, wrapping her hands around the person's arm.

Except it didn't feel like an arm.

It felt like wood—old, cracked wood that left splinters in her skin. She ran her fingers along the wooden handle, and she rolled her eyes at her own overreaction, as she realized that it was a broom.

She propped it against the wall.

Just as her pulse began to slow to its usual pace, the door swung open. Rose spun around, paling as she found herself face-to-face with a stranger.

His green eyes assessed her, lingering on her tattered, bloodied clothing. "What are you doing in there, human?"

"Debating philosophy with the spiders," Rose said.

He frowned at that. "Uhh, and why are you covered in blood?"

Rose shrugged. "The spiders got violent?"

His frown deepened. "You don't lie very good."

"Well," Rose said.

"Well, *what*?" the vampire asked.

"It's *well*, not *good*. *Good* is an adjective. *Well* is an adverb," Rose explained. "You should have said, 'You don't lie *well*,' instead of 'You don't lie *good*.'"

The vampire shook his head in disbelief. "Whatever," he muttered, as he grabbed her arm and jerked her out of the closet. "Come on."

She tried to pull her arm free, even though it hurt to do so. "Let me go."

"You know," the vampire mused, "if I pull too hard on your arm, it'll tear right off. Learned that the hard way a couple of times." He grimaced at the memory. "Messy situations. Anyway, I think you should stop fighting before that happens. He wants you in one piece."

Rose stopped pulling. "What a coincidence," she muttered. "I want me in one piece, too."

"Let her go," came a familiar voice.

Rose rolled her eyes. "*Now*, he comes back."

The vampire turned to look at Kallias, and his brows furrowed. "Who are you?"

"Your locking-me-in-a-closet plan worked brilliantly, by the way!" Rose called out.

Kallias sighed at her sarcasm.

He stepped forward, keeping his attention on the vampire. "I'm Kallias," he told the vampire. "I'm twenty-five hundred years old, and I'm from Ancient Greece. And you, Robert Hickerson, are a seventy-seven-year-old vampire from New Jersey."

The vampire's grip loosened on her arm. "How did you know that?"

Kallias took another step forward, and when the faint, orange glow of the streetlight danced across the blood-stains on his face, he looked even more dangerous than usual.

"I know a lot about you, Robbie," Kallias said, using the vampire's old, human nickname—to prove Theron hadn't given him the information. "I know you're the same coward today as you were when you were human. You spent your human life afraid of other humans, and now, you spend your vampire life afraid of older vampires." He offered a tight smile. "Well, Robbie, I'm a *twenty-five-hundred*-year-old vampire. Do the math. You don't want to face me."

"I'm not a coward!" Robert spat. "And I'm not falling for your mind games."

Kallias shrugged. "The information's coming from *your* mind, so whose games are they, really?"

Rose felt the vampire's fingers tremble against her arm.

"You're—you're a telepath?" Robert realized. He paled. "No, you can't be. I thought the psychic ability thing was just a myth. I've never met anyone with one."

"You still have a lot to learn, Robbie," Kallias said.

Rose wasn't sure what this conversation was meant to accomplish, exactly, but she did notice the vampire's grip loosening. Slowly.

Robert swallowed. "What do you want with the human?"

"What does Theron want with her?" Kallias countered. "He's going to kill her, Robbie, and you know it. You don't enjoy killing. You're just afraid of him." He cast a concerned glance Rose's way. "Let her go, and you'll walk away from this."

"I'm a vampire," Robert said. "I've killed hundreds of humans."

"That doesn't mean you enjoy it," Kallias said.

Robert sighed, "If I let her go, Theron will kill me."

"And if you don't, I'll kill you," Kallias warned. "Pick your poison."

The abrupt change in tone caused Robert to drop Rose's arm instinctually. He took a step back. "Marius, we have a problem!" he yelled, hoping for the older vampire's help. He grabbed a small gun from his belt and pointed it at Kallias, his finger trembling. "Come any closer, and I'll shoot you."

Kallias laughed, "I'm not afraid of a gun," he scoffed. "Just leave her and run. It's your best chance of survival."

Robert seemed to consider that for a moment, but ultimately, his expression hardened. He pressed his shaky finger against the trigger. "If you really can read my mind, you already know what I'm going to do."

Kallias turned his attention toward Rose. "Run," he told her.

Rose glanced at the gun, noticing the way Robert's finger pressed against the trigger, and she panicked. She ducked back into the closet and grabbed the broom. Before Robert could pull the trigger, Rose swung the broomstick at his head, and the handle hit him with a loud thud.

Robert dropped the gun, and he staggered and grasped his head, blood trickling from a cut along his brow. He spun toward her, and with a feral, blood-curdling growl, he snatched the broom from her hand. The handle splintered under his harsh grip, and then, he grabbed her torn shirt and jerked her against him.

Rose leaned away from him, as he bared his fangs at her. She gasped as his hand wrapped around her throat.

Just as she thought the vampire would kill her, she suddenly felt warm blood spray across her face.

She stood there, frozen in shock, as the vampire's head slid from his shoulders and hit the ground with a thud. His headless body followed.

Behind the dismembered vampire, stood Kallias, still clutching the blood-soaked dagger that had decapitated the vampire. Hundreds of tiny drops of wet blood covered his face and neck—evidence of the kill that had happened too rapidly for Rose to see.

"I didn't have a choice," Kallias said. "He would have killed you."

"Yep," Rose managed to choke out, her blue eyes wide.

"I heard *you* were dead," said a sharp voice.

Kallias turned in the direction of the voice. "You know who I am?"

Rose leaned to the side so that she could see around Kallias's tower of a body. Behind Kallias, a man stood under the streetlight, apparently unconcerned with drawing attention.

Inky, black curls set neatly on top of his head, and his dark complexion and dark eyes seemed at odds with the bright light behind him. He looked strange, she thought, standing near that dirty alleyway in his perfectly pressed pants and button-down shirt.

"I know you're Greek," the vampire said. His lip curled into an unflattering grimace, as he snarled, "I'd recognize Greek filth anywhere."

"Oh, perfect," Kallias muttered to Rose. "We've run into a Roman."

Rose's eyes lit up with excitement. "He's from the Roman Empire?"

Kallias glared at her, and she immediately suppressed her smile.

"Right. Romans are bad," Rose said with an exaggerated frown, "apparently."

Kallias rolled his eyes.

She leaned toward him. "Do you think he could tell me about the hallucinogenic fish?" At his peeved silence, she said, "No? Well, the coliseum, surely?"

"Rose," Kallias said irritably.

"To my knowledge, there's one other Greek still alive," the vampire continued, "besides Theron, of course. Which means you must be Kallias of Athens, the traitorous vampire who's been protecting a human. Except…Theron said you died."

Kallias shrugged. "A misunderstanding."

"Apparently," the vampire sneered.

"I mean, he wasn't totally wrong," Rose pointed out. "You all were dead once, right?"

"Why is the human speaking?" the vampire asked Kallias.

Kallias gave another shrug. "Must be a factory defect."

"Plumbing!" Rose blurted out hopefully. "Come on! *One* historical anecdote before I'm murdered. That's all I'm asking."

"I'm trying to *stop* you from getting murdered," Kallias grumbled. "Now, can you, please, shut up?"

The vampire watched them with a look of disgust. "Your human doesn't listen very well, does she?" he said to Kallias.

"*His* human?" Rose said with a frown. "I'm my own human, thank you very much." When the vampire ignored her, she leaned toward Kallias. "Tell him I'm not your human."

Kallias rolled his eyes. "He *knows* you're not my human, Rose. He'd smell the bond, if you were."

Rose frowned at him. "Wait, what does *that* mean?"

"At least, if she *were*," the vampire said, "you'd have a halfway decent reason for protecting her." He stepped forward. "As it is, you have no claim over her. So, you should hand her over—or *at least* step aside."

"Theron has no claim over her either," Kallias pointed out.

Rose scowled at both of them. "*No one* has claim over me!"

"That's irrelevant," the vampire said, still ignoring Rose's existence. Apparently. "We're vampires. We don't need reasons to kill."

"I disagree," Kallias said.

"You're a traitor," the vampire spat. He shot a pointed look at the headless corpse on the ground. "You choose humans over your own kind."

"I chose an innocent person over a murderer," Kallias corrected.

"Say it how you want," the vampire snarled. "You're still a traitor."

Kallias shrugged. "I've been called worse."

"I hate traitors," the vampire said. "When I was human, I crucified people like you."

"Oh," Rose said with a frown, "I should've been more specific about the anecdote." She pursed her lips. "Can you do one that doesn't involve methods of torture?"

"Now, I see how you ended up with Theron," Kallias scoffed. "Trading torture stories, I suppose."

The vampire shrugged. "Theron offered me what I want. He's not a friend. Just a stepping stone, like all of you Greeks were."

"What *is* this?" Rose muttered. "It's like some kind of sports rivalry, except the sports are ancient empires—and *dead*."

"Keep talking, human," the vampire said, finally addressing her, "and I'll rip your tongue out."

Kallias stepped in front of her. "If you even *touch* her," he countered, "*I* will rip *you* apart."

Rose blinked in shock. Throughout her entire life, only one other person had ever defended her. It had been her brother.

The vampire cocked his head to the side, his dark eyes studying Kallias. "Theron told me about this—about how you seem to have a fixation on this human, some strange concern over her well-being. I see he was right about that." A sickening smile curled at the vampire's lips. "He told me a lot about you, actually. He even told me the story of how he killed your wife."

Rose's breath caught in her throat. She glanced sympathetically at Kallias, but she could only see his back and the position of his shoulders. From what she could see, he'd given no indication of the comment affecting him in any way.

"How sweet," Kallias sneered. With a bitter smile, he said, "Do you braid each other's hair while you trade these murder stories?"

The vampire's lip curled. "He also told me you haven't been feeding," he said, between clenched teeth. "You're starved, which means you're weak. I, on the other hand, *have* fed. I'm not afraid of you."

"You should be," Kallias warned.

"I was a soldier when I was human," the vampire continued, "and you were what?" He smiled, apparently already aware of the answer.

"As eager as I am to hear a historical anecdote or two," Rose whispered to Kallias, "I think we better go. I don't think he's just taunting you. I think he's trying to keep you talking."

The vampire glared at her.

Of all times for him to acknowledge her presence.

"I warned you to keep your mouth shut, human," the vampire said.

When Kallias cast a curious look at her, Rose said, "He's stalling."

A worried frown twisted at his brows.

But the vampire was already racing toward them. He snatched Rose up by the wrists, his fingernails digging into her skin. "You think you're clever, hu—"

The vampire never finished his sentence. Instead, the last word trailed into a scream, as Kallias jerked the vampire's hand off of her.

Or, at least, that's what she thought happened—until she saw the blood.

Rose stumbled back in shock as she saw the blood pouring from the vampire's shoulder, pouring from where his arm had been.

"I did warn you," Kallias said, as he tossed the severed arm aside.

Despite his injured state and what must've been *a lot* of pain, the vampire still made an attempt to attack Kallias, but Kallias moved just a bit faster. He shoved his dagger into the vampire's stomach and said, "You're right. I am weak and starved, but I'm still older than you, Marius. Even starved, that means something."

Marius froze. As his white shirt became less and *less* white—drenched in blood from both the stomach wound and the shoulder wound—his skin turned *more* white. "How do you know my name?"

"Another thing you didn't consider," Kallias said. Before Marius could make any more attempts to fight, he leaned forward and commanded, "Don't move."

It apparently worked—because Marius began to breathe faster, and his dark eyes widened.

"How?" Marius breathed. "How are you doing this?"

"You must know," Kallias said with a taunting smile. "You're not stupid, are you?"

"No," Marius said. "Theron would've told me if you were a—"

"Unless he didn't know," Kallias pointed out.

The vampire's breath came even quick, desperate gasps now. "No."

"And now for the fun part," Kallias said, as the vampire panicked, "stop breathing."

The gasping immediately stopped, and his face began to redden.

"We don't die without air," Kallias said, "but it does hurt. Doesn't it?"

Marius, of course, couldn't answer.

Rose watched in horror, as the vampire's face turned a terrible shade of purple. "Kallias," she said, tormented by the sight.

Kallias turned toward her, suddenly, as if he'd forgotten she was there, watching him.

"We should go," Rose said again.

Kallias nodded. He turned to Marius, and with no further torment, he turned the immobile vampire, pulled him back against him, and slid a dagger through his throat.

Rose looked away this time.

She looked up, when she heard his footsteps approaching her.

"I'm sorry," he said, as he stopped in front of her. "I caught his scent. He's close. Which means we don't have time to waste."

Rose frowned. "Sorry? Sorry for what?"

"This," Kallias said, and then, he picked her up and tossed her over his shoulder.

She didn't have time to protest before the world tipped before her eyes. The world around her soon became a blur, as her body lurched forward at a speed her mind couldn't comprehend. Her head whirled, and her stomach twisted.

Finally, the motion stopped, and he set her on her feet.

Rose's palms found the brick wall behind her, as she fell back against it, her head still spinning.

It reminded her of the way she'd felt as a child, after getting off of a merry-go-round.

You know, if the merry-go-round had been moving at *light-speed*!

She didn't dare move a muscle until her vision cleared, and then, finally, she saw Kallias in front of her, watching her worriedly.

"Did we just teleport?" Rose said breathlessly. She pressed a hand to her stomach and leaned forward, trying not to puke. "Because that's how I always imagined teleporting would feel."

His lips twitched. "We ran," he said. "Well, *I* ran. You kind of...*rode*."

She glared at him. "Well, next time, could you maybe *warn* me before you toss me over your shoulder like a sack of potatoes and move at freaking light-speed?!"

"I said sorry," Kallias said defensively. He watched, as she took deep breaths, trying to calm her racing pulse. "Are you okay?"

"Well, my stomach feels a bit inside-out at the moment, but I'm sure that will pass. Eventually," Rose grumbled. "*Hopefully.*"

"I didn't mean physically," he said, his voice quiet.

She looked up, stunned by the sadness she heard in his voice.

"I assume you're not...used to seeing that kind of...violence," he said.

Rose stared at him, and sympathy twisted inside her stomach, as she noticed a flicker of something in his eyes—something she'd seen before. Guilt or self-loathing, perhaps?

Or both.

She wanted to soothe that pain in his eyes, for some reason.

"I cut open Sebastian," she confessed. "It was very sad."

Kallias blinked in shock. "*What*?"

"In my freshman Biology class," Rose explained, "we dissected frogs. I named mine Sebastian—after Johann Sebastian Bach." She sighed, "They made us cut them open. It was sad."

He shook his head, confused. "Sebastian was a frog?"

"Yes," Rose confirmed.

"Oh," Kallias said.

Well...at least he didn't look like he was in pain anymore.

Now, he just looked confused.

"So," he asked again, "you're all right?"

With a nervous smile, she said, "Yes."

Kallias nodded. He turned away, glancing around the alley, as if he were looking for something.

Rose watched him with a puzzled frown.

Spotting a fire hydrant on the corner, he walked to it and knelt in front of it. Then, he ripped a long strip of fabric from the bottom of his black T-shirt.

"What on earth are you doing?" Rose asked.

Kallias didn't answer. Instead, he hit the fire hydrant with the side of his hand. Rose blinked in surprise as the force of his hand chipped it, causing water to pour out of the small hole.

He held the piece of fabric under the stream of water until the water soaked it thoroughly.

She glanced around nervously. "Are you *trying* to get us arrested?"

He returned to her. She straightened, frowning. Kallias touched her face, his fingers curling around her jaw. His touch warmed her skin, and her chest tightened, as she stared into his light brown eyes.

He tilted her head back and wiped the fabric across her face, the icy cool water at odds with his warm touch. Rose stood, frozen to the spot, as he washed the blood from her face.

Finally, he stepped back. "There was blood."

She watched as Kallias headed back over to the hydrant.

Avoiding her gaze, he shoved the sleeves of his jacket up to his elbows, revealing his blood-stained arms and hands. He knelt in front of the hydrant again and held his hands under the water.

The water ran over his hands until the dark red bloodstains lightened —becoming pink first and then, disappearing. He cupped his hands together and then splashed the water on his face.

Rose watched his actions curiously, noticing how routine his actions seemed. His hands didn't tremble. He didn't pause to think about what he was doing. He simply washed the blood from his skin, as if it were nothing but dirt.

"How many people have you killed?" she asked.

"They're not people. They're monsters," he said, "like me."

"How many vampires have you killed?" she amended.

He splashed his face again. "I don't keep count."

She watched the reddish stream of water flow along the pavement.

How could he act so callous about killing vampires when he was one himself?

She'd seen him be kind, hadn't she? How could she reconcile that side of him with the way he acted now?

"Right," she said nervously. "Of course."

Kallias stood and returned to her. Water dripped from his face and hair, his skin now clean of blood. She blinked in surprise as he took her arm and pulled her away from the wall. He shrugged off his jacket and walked around to stand behind her.

"What are you doing?" she asked.

He lifted her arm. "Theron could find us at any moment. Luckily for us, he assumed I died when the sun rose. So, he's not in much of a hurry." He slid the sleeve of the jacket over her arm. "Because he doesn't think he needs to be, but once he sees those bodies, he'll realize I'm alive, and he'll be right behind us." He moved to her other arm. "So, we need to get to my car as quickly as possible, which means crossing the highway. And your clothes are torn and covered in blood."

Rose knew she should pull away and finish putting on the jacket herself, but something about the way his fingers felt sliding along her arms and shoulders kept her frozen in place.

"So are yours," she managed to say.

As he pulled the other sleeve over her other arm, his breath fell against her ear. "Yes, but I'm also six and a half feet tall," he chuckled, "and a *man*. No one will assume you've hurt or kidnapped *me*. You, on the other hand..."

She scowled. "That's sexist."

"But true." He finished circling her.

Rose gave him a peeved look, and then, he stepped closer and pulled the leather jacket closed around her.

He zipped it all the way up to her neck.

He watched her lips—the same, soft, light-pink lips he'd felt against his own just an hour or so before. He cleared his throat and stepped back, offering her a teasing smile. "If you're going to keep getting blood all over you, you should invest in some black clothes," he said. "It'd be less noticeable."

She glanced at his all-black outfit and laughed, "I'll think about it."

Rose followed Kallias, as he led the way out of the alley and onto a sidewalk that ran alongside the highway. The jacket hung halfway down her thighs, covering her torn, bloodied T-shirt and her torn jeans.

Even so, she felt as if someone might see through the jacket somehow —that someone would know. She cast wary glances at the people who passed her on the sidewalk.

"None of them are paying attention," Kallias said, "and you look fine."

Rose looked up at him in surprise. "Were you reading my mind?"

"Yes," he said. He pointed across the street, where she could see the hotel parking lot, well-lit beneath the streetlights. "My car is parked over there."

"Don't you think that's a little invasive?" she asked.

His brows furrowed. "Parking a car in a parking lot?"

"No, idiot," Rose said sassily. "Reading people's minds."

"No," he answered. His gaze darted from one side of the street to the other, searching for any sign of vampires. He grabbed her arm and began to pull her along behind him, as he rounded a bus stop, approaching the crosswalk. "Come on. We have to hurry."

Rose scowled at his hand. "What do you think you're doing?"

Kallias stopped and followed her gaze down to his hand, which was wrapped tightly around her upper arm. "I need you close to me," he said, frowning at her, "in case someone attacks you. I need to maintain physical contact with you."

She scowled at him. "And you figure the best way to do that is to grab my arm and drag me along, like a puppy on a leash?"

He took his hand off of her arm. "Do you have a better idea?"

"Uh, yeah," Rose shot back in her most smart-aleck tone. She grabbed his hand and peeled it open, ignoring the bemused look he gave her. She placed her hand in his larger hand and curled her fingers around his. "If you don't want it to look like you're kidnapping me or something, you probably shouldn't drag me by the arm. Holding hands, on the other hand, looks more natural. There's a lot of couples on this street. We'll look like one of them."

He stared at their joined hands apprehensively. "But we're *not* a couple."

"I know that," she muttered, "but *they* don't have to."

"Fine," Kallias sighed. He reluctantly intertwined his fingers with hers.

Rose stared at him curiously. Her bright blue eyes sparkled with amusement, as she noticed how nervous he seemed. "So, let me get this straight. Kissing means nothing, but holding hands—that makes you uncomfortable?"

His jaw tightened. "It's just been a while."

As they crossed the highway, Rose found herself watching the people walking along the sidewalks, coming and going from stores and restaurants. The sounds of laughter, conversation, and cars passing blended into an unintelligible chorus of noise as they walked.

It felt strange to Rose to see people enjoying their night, as if everything were normal, after everything that had happened.

"Ignorance is bliss," Kallias remarked.

She blinked and turned to look at him. "You're reading my mind again."

"Yes," he said, as if it were the most normal thing in the world.

She sighed, "I don't envy them, actually. Ignorance isn't bliss. It's the illusion of bliss." Rose glanced both ways before continuing across the next part of the crosswalk. "I'd rather know the truth, even if it makes me miserable. At least then, I know what I feel is real."

"A nice sentiment," he said, "until the truth stabs you in the back."

Rose sighed at his cynicism. She frowned, as she noticed a woman standing at her car, watching them.

Her boyfriend or husband or whoever-he-was-to-her stood beside her, talking, but the woman seemed to be in a trance, her brown eyes focused intensely on Kallias.

Rose grunted as her Converse hit the curb, nearly causing her to trip.

Kallias's hand tightened around hers. "Watch where you're going."

"I was looking at a woman," she said defensively.

He followed her gaze. "Honestly, babe, I don't think she's your type."

"Why not?" Rose said automatically. Then, when he raised an eyebrow at her objection, she blushed and mumbled, "I meant...she's staring at *you*."

"Of course she is," Kallias said. "Humans do that."

Rose glanced up at him, confused by his answer. "What?"

"The better question is," he said with a frown, "why is that man by the grey car staring at us? If he were gay, he'd only be staring at me and not *you*." His frown deepened. "I'm worried he has a more sinister reason for watching us."

She followed his gaze—and noticed a figure leaning against a car at the far end of the parking lot. He was too far away for Rose to even make out his appearance, much less the fact that he was watching them, but she supposed vampire vision was much better than hers.

"Can't you just read his mind to find out why?"

"He's too far away," Kallias said. "I can't connect with his mind from here."

"Like Wi-Fi," Rose said.

"Wi-Fi?" Kallias repeated. He looked at her. "Not like Wi-Fi."

"*Sounds* like Wi-Fi," Rose muttered.

She heard him chuckle.

The traffic noise grew louder as they crossed the parking lot—coming from the Interstate, which was just downhill from the parking lot.

A steep, grassy, downward slope separated the other end of the parking lot from the busy Interstate. The cars raced by below them, and the lights from the highway and Interstate illuminated the parking lot.

As they neared the man who watched them, Rose stared back at him, finally able to make out his features. She wondered if Kallias's suspicion had been misplaced. The man didn't look like much of a threat to *her*. His blue, flannel shirt hung loosely over his scrawny form, and his wavy, brown hair hung over worried, brown eyes.

Those brown eyes did seem to watch them awfully closely, but he looked *afraid*—not threatening.

Kallias pulled on her hand, drawing her closer, as they cut through a line of closely parked cars. Rose swallowed uneasily when his body brushed against hers, instantly affected by his closeness.

She glanced down at their joined hands, trying not to notice how nice his hand felt, wrapped around hers.

"Your hand is sweating," Kallias said, his mouth near her ear.

She blushed. "It's a normal physiological response to anxiety."

He chuckled. "And why are you nervous?"

She could practically hear the smirk in his voice. She glared at him. "Well, in case you've forgotten," she hissed, "I'm being hunted down by vampires."

Just as she predicted, there was a smirk. "It has nothing to do with me, then?"

Rose's cheeks reddened even more. "Of course not."

"If you say so." His hold tightened around her hand, suddenly, pulling her to a stop. He tilted his head toward the car beside them—a black car with a shiny, silver Lexus symbol on the front. "This is it."

Rose scowled at the car that was obviously brand new. "*This* is your car?"

Kallias dropped her hand and pulled a small set of keys out of his pocket. He pressed a button, and the car beeped twice, its headlights flashing in unison with the sound. "No, we're stealing it. I just *happen* to have the keys."

She rolled her eyes at his sarcasm. "It's a bit excessive, don't you think?"

Kallias frowned. "The...car?" He left her on the passenger's side and rounded the car, toward the driver's side. "It's practical. It blends in."

"My 1984 Buick is practical," Rose muttered. "*This* is excessive."

He leaned forward, toward her, casually resting both arms over the roof of the car. "If you think this is excessive, I can't wait to hear your opinion of Erik's car," he said with a laugh. "Erik doesn't do *anything* practical."

Rose opened her mouth to reply, but she stopped, as she noticed Kallias straighten, his nostrils flaring. "Is something wrong?"

He turned toward the man leaning against the gray car and squinted, as if he were concentrating on something. He spun back toward her and stepped away from the car, his brown eyes widening in alarm.

That's when Rose realized that he wasn't looking at her. He was looking at someone behind her.

"Rose, get in the car," Kallias demanded. "Now."

Rose felt a delicate hand curl around her shoulder, and a thin, feminine body pressed against her back.

"I have to admit. You do smell amazing," a woman murmured in her ear, her voice laced with a heavy Spanish accent.

Rose turned to find a woman standing behind her. Her eyes widened, as she took in the woman's appearance.

The woman was easily the most attractive woman Rose had ever seen —more attractive than any model or actress. She was tall and slim, though not quite as tall as Rose. She wore a black, satin dress that clung closely to her thin figure, drawing attention to every slight curve of her body.

Her shiny black hair framed her face, hanging just past her chin, and the woman's flawless, bronze skin practically glowed under the streetlights.

"Oh," Rose said awkwardly. "You're a vampire, aren't you?"

The woman offered her a wide, dazzling smile, complete with fangs.

"Walk away, Sofia," Kallias warned. "This isn't the place or the time."

Sofia laughed sweetly, "For what? A conversation?"

Rose stepped back cautiously, her back colliding with the car behind her.

The woman stepped forward, cornering her. "What's wrong, sweetie?"

Before Rose could think of a response, the seductive vampire was suddenly thrown back, as Kallias put himself in between her and Rose.

Sofia pulled herself back to her feet, straightening her dress. "Relax, Kallias," she said, somehow still smiling. "There's no need to cause a scene."

Kallias scowled at the veiled threat. "Don't do this, Sofia."

Sofia closed the space between them. She pushed a strand of sleek, black hair out of her face and flashed an enticing smile. "Hand over your little girlfriend, and I'll do whatever you want." She pitched her voice lower. "And I *do* mean *whatever*."

"I think you're confusing me for Erik. That doesn't work on me," Kallias said.

It didn't?

Rose wasn't totally sure it wasn't working on *her*.

Kallias leaned closer to the vampire. "I'd have to actually *want* you for that to work."

Sofia's smile faded, and an inhuman snarl sounded from her throat.

Kallias straightened. "Rose, get in the car," he repeated. "Hurry."

The man who'd been watching them suddenly started to approach. "Sofia? Is everything okay?" he called out. "Should I call the police?"

All three of them turned to look at the unsuspecting human, and he froze, watching Kallias nervously.

A smile curved at Sofia's lips, and then, before anyone realized what was happening, Sofia raced toward the man, grabbed his head, and twisted. His neck gave a loud *crack*.

The human man collapsed onto the pavement, unmoving, and Sofia turned back toward Kallias and smiled.

"Oh, by the way, you were right," Sofia said. "I *am* killing humans now."

Kallias glanced back at Rose. "In the car. Now."

Rose was too shocked to hear him. She stared at the man, who lay motionless on the pavement. "Please, tell me that guy's not dead."

"Rose," Kallias said anxiously, "I need you to get in the car."

She looked at him, surprised by the urgency in his voice. She opened the passenger door and slid inside the car.

Kallias slammed the car door closed before she'd even finished sitting down. She watched through the window, as Sofia rushed toward her.

Kallias wrapped one hand around Sofia's arm and slung her, sending her halfway across the parking lot. Her body slammed into the pavement and slid back several feet.

Rose heard the driver's door open, as she watched the vampire through the windshield, and she glanced over to find Kallias sliding into the driver's seat.

He shoved the key into the ignition, staring straight ahead at the motionless vampire.

"What about the man?" Rose said. "We have to help him."

Kallias sighed, as he cranked the car. "He's dead, Rose."

Her throat felt tight. "Surely, there's something we can do."

Kallias watched, as Sofia climbed back to her feet. He knew she was injured. He could smell the blood. "There's nothing we can do. He's dead."

"But," she said, her voice soft and sad, "it's not right."

Kallias didn't look at her. His gaze remained on the vampire in front of the car. "You can't save everyone, Rose. You need to learn that sooner, rather than later."

"And if I choose not to accept it?" she asked.

As Sofia began to approach with a noticeable limp, Kallias shifted the car into reverse. "Then, the darkness inside you will eat you alive."

Rose frowned, but before she could respond, she heard the vampire's voice again. She leaned forward, watching through the windshield, as Sofia approached with a torn dress and scrapes all over her body.

"You think you're safe inside your car?" Sofia yelled. "I'll just chase you."

"You're welcome to try," Kallias said, not even bothering to yell.

Rose turned toward him. "Who is she?" she whispered.

"Sofia Pérez," he answered, "a 347-year-old vampire from León, Spain."

Rose glanced back at the approaching vampire. "She's gorgeous."

Kallias raised an eyebrow at her.

"Objectively," Rose added quickly. "I meant: *Objectively*, she's gorgeous."

"Right," he snorted. "Have you fastened your seatbelt?"

"Of course," she said. "Why?"

"You'll see," Kallias said, and then, he slammed his foot on the gas.

The car jolted back so fast it took Rose's breath.

As the car sped backward, Sofia began to run toward them, but then, just before she reached them, Kallias slammed his foot on the brakes, causing the car to jerk to a screeching stop. Unable to stop in time, Sofia slammed into the car, her body falling forward onto the hood of the car.

Before Rose could even recover from the abrupt, terrifyingly fast stop, Kallias jerked the gear shift forward, back into drive, and slammed his foot on the gas again. Sofia fell backward onto the pavement as the car shifted, and before she could even move, the car jolted forward and ran over her.

The car continued speeding forward until Kallias jerked the steering wheel, causing the car to spin around in a complete circle, and then, before Rose could say anything or even fully process what had just happened, he slammed on the gas again and ran over the vampire a second time.

This time, he turned the steering wheel and continued forward, and with a crash that Rose felt all the way into her bones, the car jumped the barrier, skidded down the hill and onto the Interstate without even slowing.

Kallias was laughing. "I'd like to see her chase us now."

11

GROCERY STORES DON'T SELL HUMANS

"*A*re you insane?" Rose screamed, as soon as she could breathe again.

Kallias continued to speed down the Interstate. He seemed totally unfazed by the ridiculous daredevil stunt he'd just pulled. He glanced at her, laughing as he saw the look of horror on her face. "Maybe."

"You just ran over someone!" she said, clutching the door handle.

He leaned back against the leather seat, his arm relaxed. He looked more like someone who'd been driving on the Interstate for several, boring hours than someone who'd just squished a vampire under his car. "Maybe you've forgotten, but she was trying to kill you."

She stared blankly at him. "So…is she dead now?"

"I doubt it." He snorted, "But she's probably not gorgeous anymore."

Her jaw dropped. "Oh my gosh. You're so…"

"So *what*?" he interrupted. His smile faded, and his hand tightened around the steering wheel. "Violent? Brutal? Animalistic? *Monstrous*?" All the humor that had been in his expression a moment ago was gone, replaced by bitterness and anger. "What's wrong, sweetheart? Do I not act human enough for you? I'm a vampire, Rose, in case you've forgotten. A monster. And if I weren't, you'd be dead by now. You don't have to like the way I do things. You don't have to agree with it. But don't expect me to act human for you. What I *am* is the reason you're alive."

Rose looked away. She wasn't going to say *any* of those things. She wanted to argue that point, but she'd clearly hit a nerve. And she didn't want to make it worse. After a long silence, she said, "I'd never ask you to pretend to be something you're not." She looked at him. "And I'd also never call you a monster."

"Why not?" he asked quietly. "It's what I am."

"I don't think so," she told him.

He glanced at her, his brows furrowed.

"I'm sorry if my reaction insulted you," Rose said, "but what reaction did you expect after squishing some lady?"

Kallias returned his attention to the road. "A vampire," he corrected.

"Still squished," Rose muttered.

"And you didn't insult me," he sighed. "I just assumed you would."

Rose glanced at him, sympathy twisting at her chest. "You hate what you are, don't you?"

He didn't look at her. "Wouldn't you?" he asked. "If you woke up as *this*? If you wanted to bite people? To drink their blood? To kill?"

"I don't know," she said softly.

Kallias flexed his fingers, forcing his grip on the steering wheel to relax. He glanced briefly at the rear view mirror and then swerved into the left lane.

"Someone must've seen you run over that vampire," Rose realized, suddenly worried. "Someone will call the police. We'll get arrested."

"*If* anyone saw that, and that is a big *if*," he said, scowling at her, as if she were crazy. "Do you honestly think anyone will believe that a woman got ran over twice and then just got up and walked away afterward?"

Her eyes widened. "You think she got up and walked away after *that*?"

He shrugged nonchalantly. "She may have crawled."

"Vampires can't be *that* resilient," she argued.

"As long as we feed, the healing's practically instantaneous," he told her. "Sofia probably feeds at least once a night. As a matter of fact, she'd

fed once already *tonight*. So, she'll feed again, and then, she'll be fine."
He gritted his teeth. "Unfortunately."

She frowned curiously. "How do you know she's already fed?"

"I smelled human blood on her breath," he answered.

"Oh," she mumbled. "What about the hotel's cameras?"

"They're faulty on that side of the parking lot," he said. "I checked."

"It's *so* comforting to know that I'm in a car with someone who prepares *ahead* of time to run over people," Rose said sarcastically.

Kallias laughed. He glanced at the rear view mirror and switched lanes again, pressing down on the gas to pass a line of fast-moving cars.

The swerving of the car jolted Rose's body sideways, making her suddenly aware of how fast they were moving. She leaned forward to look at the speedometer, and her jaw dropped. "You're speeding!"

"Yes," he said, frowning.

She glared at him. "Speeding is against the law."

"Human law," he said. "I'm a vampire."

"It has nothing to do with species!" Rose snapped. "It has to do with you driving a car on a road—and the fact that if you crash it, we'll die!"

He shrugged. "*You* might die, but I'd survive."

"Kallias! You're driving a hundred miles per hour!" she realized.

He rolled his eyes. "Ninety-something, *maybe*."

"You need to slow down before you kill us," Rose insisted.

"I don't think you're qualified to give *me* driving advice," Kallias said.

"Oh, right, because you drive so well," she said sarcastically. "In the few minutes I've been in the car with you, you've run over someone twice, jumped a barricade and entered the Interstate in the most dangerous way possible, and now, you're so far over the speed limit that reckless driving isn't even a suitable description anymore! Where did you learn to drive? The depths of Hell?"

"Backstreets of Harlem in 1917," he said.

"And did you run over the people there, too?" Rose said in her sassiest tone.

Kallias laughed, "Only a few."

She glanced back at the speedometer. "Do you plan on slowing down?"

"No," he said.

Rose crossed her arms irritably. "Well, this is just great," she said sarcastically. "I survived all of those vampire attacks just so I can die in a car wreck."

He laughed at her pessimism. "Relax. I've been driving for almost a hundred years, and I've *never* wrecked. I'm a very skilled driver."

"So skilled you run over people," Rose added.

Kallias shrugged. "I'd like to see *you* try it."

Rose watched as his gaze darted toward the rear view mirror again. She leaned over and checked the mirrors, too, but she saw only blackness behind them. They'd left the other cars behind. She looked back at him. "You're not thinking Theron's behind us, are you?"

"I doubt it," he said. "Even if he's already found Sofia, he won't be able to chase us. Not immediately, anyway. He'll need to return to his car —*if* he even has one. By the time he does that, we'll have crossed the state line."

"Couldn't he just hotwire one of the cars in the parking lot?" she asked.

He raised an eyebrow. "You think Theron knows how to hotwire a car?"

She shrugged. "It's not hard."

He stared at her, his eyes wide.

"I haven't stolen a car before, if that's what you're thinking!" she snapped, when she saw the look he was giving her. "My brother, on the other hand—"

"You have a brother?" Kallias asked suddenly. "Where is he?"

Rose frowned at his suddenly panicked tone. "He's...in prison. Why?"

"Oh," he said, nodding. "Good."

Her frown deepened. "It's good that my brother's in prison?"

He sighed, "Once a vampire knows your scent, they can sniff out family members, as well. Yours and your brother's blood would smell similar." He glanced at her. "If Theron had access to your brother, he'd use him to get to you. But since your brother's in prison, he'll be fine."

"No one knows about him," Rose said, "except Audrey and Owen."

He frowned curiously at that. "Why? Are you ashamed of him?"

"No," Rose said quickly. She sighed. "It's just...people look at me differently when they know my past. It's like they think mistakes are genetic."

He nodded in understanding. "Why is he in prison?"

"Drug possession," she answered. "He's lucky, really. Zach was involved in all sorts of stuff. Gang violence. Petty theft. Grand theft. Selling drugs. He was lucky that when he *did* get caught doing something, it was relatively minor."

"How long is his sentence?" he asked curiously.

"Seven years," she said. "He's been in there for five. So, two more."

"Do you have any other siblings?" Kallias asked.

She shook her head. "Nope. Just Zach."

"What about your parents?" he said.

"My mom's dead," Rose told him.

He froze. Hesitantly, he asked, "Was she the one you found?"

"The one I found?" she repeated.

Kallias exhaled slowly, drumming his fingers nervously on the steering wheel. "The night Theron killed your teacher," he began, not sure whether to continue, "I saw something in your mind. A memory. A corpse lying in the floor of a living room. Was it your mother?"

Rose's expression was blank. "Yeah."

He nodded slowly. "I'm sorry."

"When I found her, she'd been dead for three days," she said, still staring at the windshield. "I'd moved away for college, and Zach was in prison. She wasn't answering my calls, but that really wasn't unusual for her. After my last class that Friday, I drove home to check. I should've checked sooner."

He glanced at her. "How did she die?"

"Drug overdose," she said. "Accidental."

Kallias watched the road, his brows creased. "You were alone?"

"For a day or so," Rose said uneasily. "Audrey drove down to help me plan the funeral. She'd…had experience with that." She blew out a shaky breath. "Audrey and I—we were the only ones who attended."

"What about your father?" he asked.

She shrugged. "I don't know who he is."

"You never wanted to know?" he said curiously.

She laughed—a short, bitter laugh. "My mom slept with drug dealers when she wanted more drugs. Have you ever met a drug dealer? They're not exactly the kind of people you want to call '*Dad.*' Well…not in my experience, anyway."

His eyes narrowed at that last part. "Did one of them hurt you?"

Rose changed the subject as quickly as she could. "So," she said, flashing a fake smile, "am I allowed to know where we're going now?"

He scowled at her, but he didn't press the issue. He knew what it was like to not want to talk about the past. "My home," he answered.

"Oh," she said, nodding. "Not a cemetery, though, right? You don't live in a cemetery."

He snorted. "I live in a normal house, just like a human," he assured her. Then, he frowned and corrected himself, "Well, it's an *almost* normal house."

"It's the *almost* part that worries me," Rose muttered.

He grinned. "If it makes you feel any better, there are nowhere near as many tombstones in my house as there are in a cemetery."

"But the bones," Rose said. "Are there bones?"

Kallias just laughed. He leaned forward and glanced at the clock on the dashboard. "I think, if I drive fast enough, I'll have us there by tomorrow night."

"I don't think driving fast is a problem for you," she muttered. Her eyes widened. "Wait. Tomorrow night? Where do you live?"

"Just outside of New York City," he answered.

She blinked. "Are you kidding me? That's a long drive!"

"I know," he said. "I've driven it."

"What happens when the sun rises?" she sputtered.

"You know, humans have invented these great places, where you can sleep while you're traveling," Kallias said. "They're called hotels."

Rose glared at him. "I am not sleeping in a hotel room with you."

A small smirk tugged at his lips—one that Rose had come to recognize as a warning that he was about to say something flirty and totally inappropriate. "Well, we don't *have* to sleep, if you have something else in mind."

Yep. Just as she'd predicted.

She rolled her eyes and leaned toward him, resting her arm on the leather console. "I wouldn't have sex with you if you were the last person on earth."

His smirk didn't falter. "Who said anything about sex?" he teased, faking surprise. "Rose, I never would've guessed you had such a dirty mind."

She blanched. "I don't! I wasn't thinking about that! *You* said…" she trailed off, her cheeks flushing. "You set me up for that."

He laughed loudly, obviously having fun at her expense. "I did."

She watched him laugh, transfixed by the uncharacteristic smile on his face. He looked genuinely happy, for once.

The lights from passing cars and streetlights danced across his face, and she blinked, as she noticed his fangs flash in the darkness.

"You hid your fangs from me, when I thought you were human."

His smile faded. "If it makes you uncomfortable, I'll keep hiding them."

"It doesn't," she told him.

He frowned, surprised. "It doesn't?"

"I'd rather you *not* hide things from me," Rose said.

A strange look passed over his face—a look that seemed…*guilty*, Rose thought. But he quickly hid it behind a smile. "Sure."

"Is it difficult to hide them?" she asked curiously.

"It hasn't been for a long time," Kallias said, "but at first, it was."

She watched, as he shifted lanes to pass another car that—unlike *them* —was moving at a reasonable speed. "Can I ask you something?"

He sighed, "I assume you will anyway."

She pursed her lips. "That vampire… He said Theron killed your wife."

His entire body seemed to suddenly tighten—his jaw, his shoulders, his grip on the steering wheel. "That's not a question."

"Her name," she said, swallowing uneasily. "Was it Phoebe?"

At the mention of her name, his grip around the steering wheel tightened so much that his knuckles turned white. "I don't want to talk about this, Rose."

"It was," she realized. Her stomach sank with guilt. "That's why Theron said what he did. He wanted to hurt you. And then, *I* made that comment. No wonder you reacted the way you did." Her voice cracked, and when she turned to look at him, her blue eyes were bright and watery. "I feel horrible."

His brows furrowed. "I overreacted. It just…surprised me. That's all."

"I hurt you," she said shamefully, "by mentioning her."

He shook his head. "You didn't know."

"I'm normally more considerate," she mumbled.

"Stop it," he said, frowning at her. "Stop feeling guilty. Stop apologizing."

It wasn't something Rose *could* stop. "Were you human when you were married to her?"

He looked back at the road. "Obviously," he said. "It's not like I could marry someone as a vampire. Legally, I don't exist."

She nodded. "And Theron murdered you, too, didn't he?"

His eyes narrowed. "I said I don't want to talk about it."

"Yeah. Sorry," she mumbled, still lost in thought. "Did you have children?"

He glared at her. "What part of this are you not understanding?"

"I just want to know more about you," she explained. "We're going to be working together—or whatever you want to call it. I want to understand you."

"How could you possibly understand me?" Kallias scoffed.

"I can try," Rose said softly. "Anyone can try."

He sighed, "No. We didn't have children."

"Why not?" she asked curiously. "I assume you were married long enough to have them. You were twenty-six when you died, and during that time period, I think the average age for men to marry was around nineteen or twenty. And fourteen or fifteen for women. Right?"

Kallias lifted his eyebrows. "You're just a vault of information, aren't you?" With a sigh, he confirmed, "I was twenty when we married, and Phoebe was sixteen."

"You didn't want kids?" Rose guessed.

He shrugged. "Phoebe became pregnant twice, but she lost it both times."

Rose's brows creased. "I'm sorry."

"Don't be," he scoffed. "It was better that we didn't have children. If we had, I can only imagine what Theron would've done to them."

Her stomach turned at that. "You think he would've hurt a child?"

"I think Theron will hurt anyone he gets his hands on," he answered.

She exhaled shakily. She watched him for a moment, relieved to see his muscles relaxing. "It's hard to imagine you married."

His lips quirked up at that. "Why? Because I'm an ass?"

"Well, there is that," Rose said playfully. "But it's more that kissing-means-nothing-and-I-don't-believe-in-love-or-anything-good   attitude you have."

"Marriage was more about convenience back then," he pointed out.

"You didn't love her?" she asked.

He was quiet for a while. "Of course I loved her," he said finally.

She nodded in understanding. "So *this* attitude came later?"

Kallias sighed, "I never said I didn't believe in love."

She looked at him. "Well, do you?"

"I believe it exists," Kallias admitted. "It's just not worth the pain."

"What *is* worth it, if not love?" Rose said. "Love makes life worth living."

He rolled his eyes at that. "*Nothing* makes life worth living," he scoffed. "Every day we wake up in this godforsaken world is a curse."

She blinked. "Well, aren't you just a ray of sunshine?"

Kallias scowled. "I'm of the darkness. Sunshine kills me."

"It's...an expression," Rose said with a frown. He did know that, right? "Have you ever considered the fact that a little optimism might help you? If you're always looking at the bad in everything, you'll never see the good."

"Optimism is foolish. It sets you up for disappointment and pain," he argued. "The higher you set your expectations, the further you fall."

"At least *then,* you'd get off the ground," she chimed.

"That's easy to say when you've never been in love," he countered.

Rose narrowed her eyes at that. "Maybe I haven't experienced romantic love, but I do *love* people. I love my brother. I love Audrey. I love Owen. I even loved my mom, despite all the ways she hurt me. I know what it's like to give part of yourself to people, and I know what it's like to have that piece of your heart ripped apart." She glanced at the window, watching trees blur past. "I believe that even the darkest parts of love are worth it."

"I disagree," he said, offering no further explanation.

"You can't tell me that if you had the chance to go back and live your human life all over again, you'd choose to never love your wife at all," Rose said.

"That's exactly what I'm telling you," Kallias replied.

Rose fell silent, stunned by his response. She'd never known of anyone to feel that way. Even the people she'd known who had lost a spouse or a lover had always said they'd go back and fall in love all over again, if they could. The kind of pain she saw in his expression, that she heard in his voice—that wasn't the kind of pain that *death* caused. "She must've really hurt you," she realized.

He blinked in surprise. He didn't understand how she could read him so easily. She wasn't even a telepath. "I'm finished with this conversation."

Rose nodded, finally giving up. Uncomfortable with the sudden tense silence, she leaned forward and switched on the radio. Her eyebrows lifted, as a contemporary rock song filled the car. "You listen to modern music?"

"Just because I was born thousands of years ago, doesn't mean I've never turned on a radio," he grumbled. "I like many types of music."

"Of course you do," she said with a laugh. "It's just...this isn't the type of music I expected a *big, bad* vampire to be listening to."

He rolled his eyes. "Are you mocking me?"

"Maybe," she teased.

He couldn't help but laugh. "So, what kind of music *did* you expect a big, bad vampire to listen to?"

"Ooh!" she said excitedly, as if she'd been hoping he'd ask. "I watch horror movies at Owen's apartment sometimes, and well... Do you know that scene where the unfeeling murderer is listening to some peaceful opera song, while he kills people?"

He snorted, "You expected me to listen to opera?"

"If you were *really* as big and bad as you *think* you are," Rose teased, leaning close enough for him to smell the honey in her hair, "you'd listen to opera."

Kallias laughed, amused by her playfulness. Not willing to let her win, he grinned and countered, "It doesn't get much bigger than me, sweetheart."

She leaned back with a huff. "Ugh." Rolling her eyes, she said, "Anyway, on a *less weird* note, I have a question! Do vampires, umm, well, use the bathroom? Like humans do?"

He scrunched up his face in disbelief. "You think *that's* less weird?"

She frowned. "Right. Yeah, I didn't really think that through before I said it," she said under her breath. She looked at him. "Anyway, do you?"

He suppressed a laugh. "Why?"

"Well, I'm just worried you might be expecting to make this drive without bathroom breaks, and well," Rose said, shrugging, "we've been in a building without a bathroom all day, and I've *kind of* had to pee for hours."

Kallias snorted, "I'll take the next exit."

———

LATE INTO THE NIGHT, ROSE'S STOMACH BEGAN TO GRUMBLE IN HUNGER.

Kallias glanced at her. "What time do humans usually eat breakfast?"

"Usually?" Rose said, brows high. "*Before* midnight."

He glanced at the clock on the dashboard, seeing that it was indeed midnight, and cursed. "Shit! Why didn't you say something?" he said, as he swerved dangerously fast into the outside lane. "I didn't save your life from Theron just to let you *starve!*"

As his maniacal driving jolted her back and forth, Rose found herself extremely grateful for the seat belt that kept her from flying through the windshield. "Relax," she said, too jostled to think. "I won't die from going *one* day without eating. If I could, I would've died a long time ago." She grimaced as she let that last part slip.

"When you were a child?" Kallias remembered.

Rose avoided his gaze, her face warm. "I'm just going to blame my talkativeness on the lack of coffee," she said, embarrassed that she'd blurted out something so awkward and personal. "I've usually had a whole pot of coffee by this time of the night."

"How long?" he said, a sharp edge in his voice.

"How long?" Rose repeated. She shifted uneasily in her seat. "You mean how long did I go without eating?" She'd never even discussed this with Audrey. Only one living person knew about her childhood, and he was in prison. "Only a few days, usually."

"*Usually?*" he repeated in a low growl.

She glanced at him, startled by the sudden anger in his voice.

His grip tightened around the steering wheel. "This happened often?"

Rose frowned, confused by his reaction. "Didn't you have drugs in your culture? Don't you know what they can do to people?"

"Of course we had drugs," he muttered. "Various types of opiates. The Lotus flower."

Rose smiled at that. "Like the *Odyssey!*"

Kallias shook his head in disbelief. "You and your books."

Rose's smile faded. "The point is," she explained seriously, "addiction changes people. It takes everything someone is and leaves a hollow shell. That's what it did to my mother."

"That's not an excuse," Kallias said. "You should've been fed and protected."

Her lips curved into a small, sad smile. "My brother did that sometimes. Most of the time, he was a typical sibling, picking on me and giving me a hard time, but sometimes, he acted beyond his age." Her smile softened at the memories. "When I was really little and my stomach would start to hurt—when I'd start to cry—he'd steal food for us from the gas station down the street. It was usually candy. He was a kid, too, after all." Her voice cracked a little, but she fought back the emotions. "But he took care of me, you know? Even if he had to break the law to do it. I don't know what would've happened, if I hadn't had him."

Kallias looked at her when he stopped at a traffic light. "You're very fond of him."

"He's the only family I have," Rose said simply. "He's a bit of an idiot sometimes—especially when he gets himself locked up in prison..."

He nodded slowly. "You're still angry at him for getting arrested."

It hadn't been a question. Or an accusation, even. Just an observation.

"Angry?" Rose said with a frown. "No! Just...annoyed."

"You're angry because you miss him," Kallias added.

"I—" Rose sighed and shook her head. "He was arrested. He didn't leave me by choice."

"You can't reason with me about your emotions," Kallias told her. "Emotions aren't reasonable."

It was so unnerving—the way he saw right through her. How did someone get used to a telepath, anyway?

"I'm not saying there are good reasons to break the law," Rose sighed, "but there are better reasons. Getting food so that we didn't starve was one thing. But getting involved with gangs and drugs? That was stupid. He saw what that life did to us—to our mom. He knew better."

Kallias didn't respond to that, and the silence gave time for guilt to rise up in Rose's throat again.

"I know it's terrible to be angry at him, but..."

"It's not terrible," Kallias interrupted. "It just means you care."

She sighed, "I appreciate your attempt to make me feel better, but..."

"I had a little sister," Kallias admitted.

She blinked, stunned that he'd shared something personal. "You did?"

"I had a few brothers, too, but I hated most of *them*," he said unapologetically. "But my sister was so young and kind. I protected her from my father whenever I could." His jaw tightened as he mentioned his father.

"From your father?" she repeated.

He glanced at her but chose to ignore the question. "We cremated the dead in Athens—back when I was human. We'd place the ashes in a decorated urn. Sometimes, the family would set candles around the urn and build a kind of shrine in their home to honor the dead. But after my death, there was no body to cremate. Most of my family didn't give a shit about honoring me, but my little sister, on the other hand, did. She didn't have an urn, but she set up a small shrine in her courtyard to honor me, and every few days, she'd tear it down."

She scowled at that. "Why would she tear it down?"

He smiled. "My sister had a temper. And she was angry at me."

"For dying?" Rose asked incredulously.

He shrugged. "I had always been there for her, and then, I wasn't."

"But it wasn't your fault," she argued.

"Like I said, emotions don't listen to reason," he said.

Rose shook her head, still confused. "Why didn't you go to her, and show her you were alive?"

"It would've been too dangerous—for her and for me," he explained. "I couldn't control my hunger. I couldn't get near anyone without wanting to…" He sucked in a harsh breath, shuddering at the memory. "I might've killed her, if I'd gotten too close. Besides, I was a monster, and the moment she saw me alive, she would've known. Death would have been a happier ending."

She watched him sympathetically. The streetlights danced across his face as he drove, highlighting the sad lines in his expression. "But you watched her."

He slowed the car as he neared the next turn. "I hadn't gone totally mad yet," he muttered. "I worried about her. She had other brothers, but none of them checked on her. So, I did."

"From the shadows," Rose added.

"Yes," Kallias agreed. "Always from the shadows."

"Couldn't you have just told her that you didn't die?" she asked. "They never found your body. She couldn't have known *for sure* that you were dead."

He suddenly looked uncomfortable. "The evidence was pretty convincing. Based on what they found, I was either dead, or I…" he trailed off.

Rose nodded in understanding. "Or you'd killed your wife."

He turned to look at her, startled by her guess. "What?"

"You already admitted Theron killed your wife," she reminded him. "And my guess is…he probably killed you, too. You just came back as a vampire—however *that* happens. So, if I'm right, and he killed you both at the same time—or on the same night, at least—then, they would've found her body but not yours."

Kallias stared at her, his eyes wide. She was so perceptive for a human. She read into every little word and detail until she came to a conclusion—an *accurate* one. He'd never dealt with anyone like her before. "I'm done talking about this," he said, as he pulled the car into a parking lot of a twenty-four-hour Walmart.

"Yeah. Of course," she sighed. "I'm sorry."

Kallias cut off the car and pulled the keys from the ignition, staring straight ahead. He sighed. "I told you about my sister because I want you to know you shouldn't blame yourself for feeling angry about having to go on without your brother. It's natural. It just means you miss him and that you care."

Rose blinked at him, stunned by the kind words. "Thank you."

He shrugged and cocked his head back, motioning toward the store. "Come on. Let's get you inside so you can get some clothes and food."

Rose opened her door and stepped out of the car. As the cold, night air chilled her skin, she crossed her arms, thankful for the leather jacket. She jumped, as she felt Kallias come up behind her. He'd moved so quickly that she'd assumed he was still on the driver's side of the car.

"Did I scare you?" he asked, a hint of amusement in his voice.

Rose turned and looked up in surprise, as she realized how close he was to her. She rolled her eyes. "It'd take more than that to scare *me*."

"Uh-huh," Kallias said with an amused smirk. He pressed the button on his keys, locking the doors, and motioned toward the store. "I'm afraid this is all that's open at this time of the night that sells clothes. I hope it's okay."

Rose rolled her eyes at him. "You hope it's okay," she snorted. "Do I *look* like the type that only wears clothes from some fancy boutique?" She raised an eyebrow and patted her thighs. "These jeans? Two dollars at the thrift store."

Kallias glanced down at the blue jeans that hugged her thighs and hips. "Well, I have to admit, for a two-dollar pair of jeans, they fit you very nicely."

She narrowed her eyes at him. "Kallias."

He smiled. "What? It was just an innocent observation."

"Innocent?" Rose scoffed. She rolled her eyes and started walking toward the store, crossing the mostly empty parking lot.

Kallias fell into step beside her. He leaned in close, and with a mischievous grin, he murmured, "Now, if I'd said your ass looks nice in those jeans, that would have been a little less innocent."

She laughed, "Could you behave for a little bit?"

"Doubt it," he chuckled. He swept his gaze across the moonlit parking lot to make sure there were no vampires nearby—even though he doubted anyone would've followed them this far.

As they stepped into the bright building, Rose noticed Kallias wince, as if the lights blinded him momentarily. "The lights hurt you?"

"Yes," he agreed, blinking a little more than normal. "Electric lights haven't been the kindest to our vampire eyesight. But I've gotten used to the pain."

"That sucks," she said, as she stopped beside the shopping carts.

Kallias glanced questionably at the shopping carts and then grabbed one. He awkwardly pushed it forward ahead of them, as if he weren't used to it.

As she followed him, she barely held back laughter as she noticed how strange he looked pushing a shopping cart. "You don't do this often, do you?"

"Well," he said quietly, "more often than most vampires, I'm sure."

"What?" Rose teased. "Vampires don't go grocery shopping?"

"Not usually," he said, frowning. "Grocery stores don't sell humans."

"Yeah, I know," Rose said dryly. "What's up with that?"

Kallias snorted. He held back for a moment, allowing her to lead the way toward the clothes section. Rose heard the heavy thud of his boots and the clicking of the cart as he followed her. She didn't see many people in the store, only a few workers and the occasional customer, but she became increasingly aware that each time one of them would look up, they'd suddenly start staring.

"Should I just grab a pair of jeans and a T-shirt?" she asked.

"You'll need more than that," he said. He stopped behind her and leaned forward onto the cart's handle. "Grab enough clothes for a week or so, at least."

She spun toward him. "A *week* or so? Just how long are you expecting this arrangement to last? I have a life, you know. I can't just stay with you forever."

"You won't have a life for long if Theron gets his hands on you," Kallias reminded her. "Rose, you have my word. The moment it's safe, I'll take you home. You can go back to your normal life, and you'll never see me again."

Rose didn't understand why, but it stung a little to hear him say that. She cleared her throat, not wanting him to notice. "So, what do you expect me to do? Am I supposed to quit my job and drop my classes?" she said nervously. "And if so, then what do I do when it's all over? I have bills to pay."

"Wow," he scoffed. "You obsess over those bills, don't you?"

"That's what it's like to be human," Rose muttered.

Kallias sighed. Then, he rounded the shopping cart and stopped directly in front of her. He leaned in—so that she could see the sincerity in his eyes. "Listen to me, Rose. You won't be safe at home until Theron's dead," he reminded her. "But as soon as I can kill him, I will. I promise I'll take you home, and I'll make sure you can return to your job and your classes. My telepathic abilities go a long way in smoothing things over with people."

She bristled. "I don't need you to fight my battles for me."

"I know," he said. "But that doesn't mean I can't help."

Rose sighed, "Do you have a washing machine and a dryer?"

Kallias frowned. "Yes. Why?"

"So, I can get seven pairs of clothes," she said, shrugging, "and then, if I have to stay longer than a week, I can wash the clothes and wear them again."

"Either that, or I can take you to get more," he suggested.

She scowled. "I'll just wash them."

He rolled his eyes. "You're so stubborn." He frowned, as Rose began to sift through a stack of T-shirts. "You realize this is the men's section, right?"

She tossed an oversized, navy-blue T-shirt in the cart and continued her search. "Yeah, believe it or not, I can read," she said—without looking at him. "I know. Crazy, right? Who would've thought that a college student with a 4.0 GPA, who happens to be at the top of her class, would *actually* be able to read?"

He chuckled. "Okay, smartass. Then, why are we in the men's section?"

"The T-shirts," Rose said, spinning around to hold up a T-shirt with superheroes on the front. "They're cheap and comfortable."

He sighed, "Would you stop worrying about the cost?"

"It's not in my DNA," Rose muttered. "Besides, did you miss the comfortable part?"

She blinked in shock, as she glanced across the aisle and noticed a woman in pink sweats, standing totally still and staring at Kallias.

Rose turned toward Kallias, surprised to find him still looking at her, as if he hadn't even noticed. She glanced around, her brows furrowing, as she saw several workers staring, as well.

She didn't understand how he managed to *not* notice all of the people staring at him.

"I notice," Kallias told her. "It just doesn't affect me."

Rose frowned at him. "You were listening to my thoughts?"

"Yes," he said simply, leaning against the shopping cart.

She glanced again at the woman. "How does *that* not affect you?"

"I'm used to it," he muttered. "It's always been this way."

"People have always stared at you like that?" Rose asked.

"Since the night I awoke from the dead," Kallias said. He stepped closer to her so that he could speak in a lower tone. "It's human women, usually. Some human men. It's that allure we talked about. Humans are vulnerable to it. They find vampires attractive. They can't help it."

Rose frowned at that—and cast another glance over his body. She couldn't deny that he was objectively attractive, but it certainly didn't give *her* the urge to stare at him like a brain-dead zombie. "All humans?" she said skeptically.

He shrugged. "It doesn't overrule sexual orientation or anything. It follows along the lines of who you're *usually* attracted to."

She nodded, as she remembered the over-the-top way Owen and Audrey had reacted to his appearance. "So, a gay man would be affected by you."

He nodded. "And straight women. And bisexual men and women."

Rose quirked an eyebrow at that last part. "And a bisexual woman would also be affected by a female vampire, too, right? Like Sofia?"

He smiled curiously. "You mean a bisexual woman like...*you*?"

"Wow. Nosy," Rose said with a sassy smile. "But yes, if you must know."

He chuckled. "Yes," he confirmed, "I would assume so."

"Then," she said, "why doesn't it affect *me* like that?" She frowned. "I mean, I don't stare at you like that. And Sofia was clearly gorgeous, but..." She paused when Kallias lifted his eyebrows again. "Well, objectively attractive. You know what I mean!"

Kallias snorted, "Erik felt similarly."

Rose blew out a frustrated sigh. "The point is," she said, her cheeks hot, "despite my observation, I wasn't...*allured* by her or anything."

He shook his head, grinning. "No one says it like that."

"You're the first vampire I've ever befriended," Rose said defensively. "Give me a minute to learn the lingo."

He just laughed.

"So," she said uneasily. "Why *doesn't* it affect me?"

His smile faded, and an odd look passed over his face—one he didn't hide quickly enough—before he shrugged. "I don't know. I guess you're just too stubborn."

"You're lying," she realized.

"We can't waste too much time in here," Kallias said, quickly changing the subject. "I'll grab some snacks while you pick out your clothes."

She frowned suspiciously. "What are you not telling me?"

He ignored her question. "I'll listen for you. If anything happens, just say my name, and I'll be by your side again in less than a second. Okay?"

She sighed, and realizing she wasn't going to get an answer from him at the moment, she turned back toward the T-shirts. She wasn't done with this, though. She knew he was hiding something from her, and she was determined to find out what it was.

"I don't understand how it doesn't affect you," she said off-hand, under her breath. "I'd love for people to look at *me* like that."

Kallias stopped behind her, his body heat warm against her back. His lips brushed her ear, as he whispered, "Thanks for the permission."

Rose straightened, shivering a little at the sensation of his breath on her ear. By the time she'd recovered from her shock and turned around, planning on offering some kind of snarky comeback, he was already gone.

"Seriously?" Rose said to the empty space. "Keep doing that, and I swear I'll put a bell around your neck." He might've been out of sight, but as he'd said, he could still hear her. "Don't say I didn't warn you!"

Unfortunately, whether or not *he* could hear her, Rose had failed to realize that the woman in pink sweats could, too.

And that it would look like she was talking to herself.

"Oh, great," Rose said under her breath. "Now, everyone thinks I'm insane."

She picked up another T-shirt and tossed it into the shopping cart.

"Can you introduce me to that man?"

Rose squeaked, startled by the woman who'd just snuck up on her. She spun around, surprised to find it was that same woman in the matching, pink sweats. She had her blonde hair pulled back into a high ponytail, and she somehow managed to look more stylish in sweats than Rose had ever looked in her nicest clothes.

Her grey eyes studied Rose curiously.

"Uh, what?" Rose said awkwardly.

The woman's pushed her shopping cart up next to the one Rose was using. Her shopping cart was empty, aside from a bag of socks and a small box of diapers. She turned back toward Rose, giving her an intense, pleading look.

"He's gorgeous, don't you think?" the woman said excitedly. "I have never, ever, in my entire life, seen anyone that attractive! Is he your boyfriend?"

"Boyfriend?" Rose snorted. "No. Of course not."

The woman glared at her, as if she considered Rose some kind of freak of nature. "What is wrong with you?" she said, suddenly.

Did this allure make humans *angry*, too?

"Uh, what?" Rose sputtered in shock.

"Never mind," the woman muttered. "Can you introduce me to him?"

"Well," Rose said with a frown, "that'd be hard because I don't know you. The basic introduction routine requires I say your name, at least."

The woman bristled. "You know what, lady? Screw you."

Apparently, that was the wrong way to ask for someone's name.

Rose watched in confused shock as the woman grabbed her shopping cart and stormed off. "I have *such* great people skills," she sighed.

If only socializing were as simple as ancient history or calculus…

She sighed, shaking her head at the baffling conversation, and grabbed her cart. She headed toward the women's section to pick out some jeans. The T-shirts in the men's section might've been cool, but the jeans would never fit her thighs or hips.

As she pushed her cart onto the aisle, she heard something begin to buzz. She stopped and glanced around, searching for the source of the sound. The aisles were empty, except for her.

As whatever-it-was continued to buzz, she realized it sounded too close, as if the sound were coming from her own body. She reached into the deep pockets of the leather jacket and noticed a small bottle and Kallias's phone—which happened to be vibrating.

She pulled out the bottle and the phone, frowning as she realized it was a bottle of lighter fluid.

"Oh, for goodness sakes, who carries a bottle of lighter fluid in their pocket?" she said, as she stuffed the bottle back down into the jacket pocket. She glanced at the screen of the incessantly buzzing phone.

The name *Erik* flashed on the screen.

"Kallias, your phone is ringing," she announced to the empty aisle.

When he didn't somehow manifest himself in front of her to stop her from answering his phone, she shrugged and placed it against her ear. "Hello?"

Silence filled the line for a long time—so long that Rose thought there was no one on the other side of the line. Just as she started to hang up the phone, she heard a low, lilting voice say, "You're a woman."

Rose frowned at his unfamiliar accent. It lilted like a European accent, but it didn't sound like any accent she'd heard before.

"Thanks for telling me. I would've never known," she said dryly.

He laughed loudly, the sound echoing through the line. Unlike his voice, which sounded smooth and melodic, his laugh sounded loud and short, like a bark.

"Ooh, you are sassy," he said in a flirty tone, "I like you."

She frowned worriedly. "Uh…thanks? I think?"

Wind crackled over the phone line. "Why do you have Kallias's phone?"

"I'm wearing his jacket," she said, "and the phone was in his pocket."

"Oh?" he said in an interested tone. "Why are you wearing his jacket?"

"To cover the blood," she blurted out, "and my boobs."

He was quiet for a moment. "I'm going to need you to elaborate, babe."

Rose scowled at the pet name. "My shirt's torn and covered in blood."

"Oh," he said, disappointed. "I envisioned something *totally* different."

"What?" she mumbled. "Never mind. I don't want to know."

He chuckled. "So… Why *are* you with Kallias right now?"

"Long story," she said, as she threw some jeans in the cart and moved toward the underwear aisle.

Rose noticed the sound of sloshing water and a car buzzing past in the background. She realized that Erik must've been outside, probably on a sidewalk.

"Well, babe," Erik said into the phone line, "I'm not busy at the moment. I'd love to hear this long story of yours."

She rolled her eyes. "Stop calling me '*babe.*' You've never even met me."

He laughed, "My apologies, babe." Apparently, her irritation had only encouraged him. "But how can I call you by your name if I don't know it?"

"It's Rose," she said irritably.

"Rose," he repeated. "That's not a very sexy name, is it?"

She held out her one, free hand, a bra dangling from it. "Wow. Thanks."

"It's not sexy, but it *is* beautiful," he amended. "Simple. Elegant."

Rose frowned. She liked this less than the insult. "Umm...thanks?"

"Yep," he said. "Well, *Rose,* my name is Erik Olafsson."

"Yes, I *can* read the caller I.D., actually," she muttered.

His short, barking laugh filled the line again. "This is fun." His voice took on a more excited, boyish sound, all of the sudden. "Hey, I can make a few dirty jokes with your name. Would you like to hear them?"

Rose blinked. This conversation had gone south quickly. "No."

"Aww, come on," he whined. "Most women find it charming."

Her eyebrows lifted. "Are you sure they said charming? Maybe your big head just mistranslated the words *inappropriate* and *immature* to charming."

"Ha!" he barked. "I could have so much fun with you."

Her frown deepened, and she pulled the phone away from her ear. She glanced around the empty aisle and said, "Kallias, if you can somehow hear me with your crazy-sensitive ears, please come save me from your perverted friend!"

When she put the phone back to her ear, his voice filled the line again, but this time, all of the humor was gone from his voice. "Crazy-sensitive ears?"

Rose cringed as she realized he'd heard her. "Uh..."

"Fucking hell," Erik said. "He's told you, hasn't he?"

She winced. "It's a long story?" she offered.

"Okay, now, you *are* going to tell me this story," he growled.

Rose opened her mouth to speak, but then, a woman suddenly screamed.

"Shit. I have to go," he sighed. "Tell Kallias that I'll call back."

The phone clicked.

Rose pulled the phone away from her ear and frowned at it. Someone had definitely screamed on his end. She was sure of it.

"I found the food," Kallias announced, suddenly, from beside her.

Rose jumped, as she heard his voice suddenly close to her. She spun toward him. "Dang it! I told you to stop sneaking up on..." she trailed off, as she saw the stack of snacks piled up so high in his arms that it nearly hid his face. "Yep," she said, "you definitely found the food."

He dropped the snacks into the cart, the drinks and junk food clanging loudly as they hit the bottom. "In case you get hungry."

She stared blankly at the food. "Yeah, I think that should cover me," she told him, "for the rest of my *life*! Please, tell me you don't think I eat that much."

Kallias shrugged. "I don't remember how much humans eat."

She scowled at him. "Audrey is the only human that eats *that* much."

He glanced at the phone in her hand. "Did Erik already hang up?"

Rose blinked in surprise. "You heard me from the *grocery* section?"

"Of course. I told you I'd listen for you," he said. "But if I'd rushed over here, considering how fast I can move, I would've risked a human seeing me, and since Erik isn't *really* a threat, I figured you'd be okay for a few moments. Besides, I needed more food."

She glanced again at the obscene amount of food. "Of course you did," she said sarcastically. She frowned. "I never said his name. I only said it was your perverted friend. How did you know it was Erik?"

"I only have one perverted friend," Kallias told her.

"Well, that's a relief," Rose said, making a dramatic show of wiping her hand across her forehead. Then, remembering his question, she said, "Someone screamed, and then, he said he had to go. He said he'd call back."

Kallias nodded, as if he had expected as much. "Nice bra."

She glanced at the bra dangling from her forefinger and blushed. Black and lacy, it wasn't *at all* the kind of underwear she usually wore. She shoved it back onto the rack and looked at him. "I was never planning on getting that."

"Of course not," he said, as he picked up a freezer meal of spaghetti and started reading the back of the box. "It wasn't your size. It was too small."

"How the heck would you know my bra size?" she sputtered.

He squinted at the ingredients, as if he found them suspicious somehow. "I don't. I guessed."

She flushed. "Just how much *have* you been staring at my breasts?"

He tossed the box back into the cart. "They lied. They said it's real Italian, but I know real Italian when I see it. Those aren't the right ingredients."

She stared blankly at him. "You need to stop staring at my breasts."

He smirked. "I'm not. At the moment. Never mind. Now, I am."

"You're as bad as your perverted friend," she said, crossing her arms.

Kallias laughed. "You have *no idea* what you're saying."

"You're probably right," she admitted. "He's pretty terrible, isn't he?"

Kallias leaned on the shopping cart and flashed a playful grin at her. "Well, if he can make an ancient Greek look like a puritan, he's obviously pretty bad."

"He kept calling me *babe*," she complained.

He tilted his head at that. "Interesting."

She frowned worriedly. "Why is that interesting?"

"It means he read you as an, umm, innocent type," he said with an apologetic smile. "Erik uses different pet names on different kinds of women. 'Babe' is more of a playful name. The names he calls other women are much...dirtier."

Rose stared at him in disbelief. "And that works for him?"

"Very much so," Kallias said. "Erik takes great pride in his ability to charm his way into women's pants. He's even more proud of that than he is of his ability to make vicious vampires cry like babies with one touch."

"What?" she sputtered. "He makes them *cry*?"

"Erik is an empath," Kallias explained.

Rose frowned. "He makes them cry by understanding them?"

"Empath, in the supernatural sense of the word," he corrected. "Erik can manipulate emotions the way I can manipulate the mind. He's very powerful."

She blinked in shock. "Oh."

Still stunned by the realization that another vampire had a psychic ability she'd never even realized existed, Rose headed toward the next aisle to get some socks. She heard the clicking of the shopping cart, as Kallias followed her. "Oh, by the way," she said, glancing back at him as she walked, "you have an admirer."

He frowned. "What?"

"The woman in the pink sweats," she provided.

He shrugged. "I don't know who you're talking about."

She scowled at him. "Well, anyway, she was attracted to you, apparently. She thought you were my boyfriend, but don't worry. I set her straight."

"Good," Kallias said dryly. "I'd hate to ruin your reputation."

"She acted like I was a freak of nature or something," Rose continued. "What? Because I don't fawn over your appearance like some lovesick puppy, I must be insane?"

"Either that, or you're not human," he added in the middle of her rant.

Rose glared at him. "You're so arrogant. You think everyone wants you."

He flashed a smug smile at her. "Everyone *does* want me."

"*I* don't," she countered.

His eyebrows lifted. "Oh? Is that so?"

He seemed…entertained, rather than offended, as if she'd challenged him to a game she could never win. He rounded the shopping cart with that playful smile, and Rose swallowed uneasily and took a step back.

Unfortunately, that step sent her into the shelf behind her, and she squealed and jumped forward as the metal pieces on the shelf stabbed into her back.

The jump forward sent her colliding into him, and his hands found her arms, steadying her before she fell. Blushing at her clumsiness, she looked up, and she realized his eyes looked darker than usual.

He moved his face toward hers, his lips not even an inch away.

Rose realized she wasn't breathing anymore. She couldn't—not with his body and lips so close.

Besides, she was afraid that if she decided to breathe, she'd forget to squash that nonsensical voice in her head that was currently nagging her to close the distance between their lips and kiss him already.

His thumbs traced the chill bumps on her arms. "Are you sure you don't want me?" he murmured, his breath warming her lips.

"I need socks," Rose announced.

Kallias just stared at her, his lips twitching.

He took a step back. Then, finally, he started laughing loudly and hysterically, as if he could barely breathe.

Her face burned with embarrassment, as she quickly distanced herself from him. She headed toward the next aisle without another word. She heard the warm, melodic sound of his laughter behind her, as he followed her with the shopping cart. She was careful to keep the cart between them as she grabbed a bag of socks from the shelf and tossed it into the cart. She didn't trust herself anywhere near him—not with that nagging urge to kiss him fresh on her mind.

"Socks," Kallias snorted. "You do know how to hurt a man's ego, don't you? In twenty-five hundred years, I have never gotten *that* reaction before."

"Yes, well, it's not like your ego can't take the hit," she muttered. Flashing a sassy smile at him, she said, "You could deflate your ego to half the size it is now, and you'd still be a cocky, arrogant, smug, bigheaded jerk."

"That was all a little redundant, don't you think?" he teased.

Her eyes narrowed. "I wanted to make sure you got the point."

Kallias watched her with a smile, as she lowered her head and rushed past him—clearly avoiding getting close to him again. He chuckled and pushed the cart behind her, following her toward some clothing racks full of pajamas.

A cascade of messy auburn hair fell over her shoulder, as she read the labels of the pajamas, squinting, as if she were having trouble seeing the words without her reading glasses.

"Did the woman say anything else?" he asked curiously.

Rose glanced up at him. "Why? Are you interested in her?"

He tilted his head to the side. "Would it bother you if I was?"

"No," she scoffed. "Why would it? We're not together or anything."

He smiled as he noticed the hint of nervousness in her voice. "Right."

She tossed a pair of pajamas into the cart. "No, she didn't say anything else. She asked me to introduce you to her, and I tried to…talk or something, and she got angry and stormed off." She shrugged. "I think I made a friend!"

He laughed, "Let me guess. You overanalyzed everything she said."

Her gaze snapped up—and narrowed. "What is *that* supposed to mean?" she snapped, much louder than she'd intended.

He held his hands up in a show of surrender. "Easy, baby, it was just a guess," he said, his voice smooth and honeyed and *so* annoyingly patronizing. He grinned. "Don't kill me."

Her eyes narrowed even more. "Don't mock me."

Kallias burst into laughter again, laughing too hard to even conceal his fangs. "You actually scare me a little, sometimes. You know why? Because you are the only human in this world insane enough to threaten a monster that could rip you apart with his bare hands."

Rose bit back a smile. "Yeah, well, you *should* be scared," she said, tossing another pair of pajamas in the cart. "I'm…you know…*fierce*…or something."

"Or something," Kallias repeated with a grin.

She rolled her eyes. "I *don't* overanalyze what people say," she said defensively. "I mean, the word 'overanalyze' implies that I focus on details that are not relevant to…" she trailed off, as she noticed him watching her with a smug smile and a raised eyebrow. She sighed in defeat. "Okay. Fine. Maybe I do. But I can't help it. It's like a nervous tick. Some people twiddle their thumbs. Some people bite their fingernails. I explain and define things," she admitted.

He shrugged. "I'm not judging. I'm not good at making friends either."

Rose smiled. "Yeah, but that's because you're a jerk."

He chuckled, "True. My social etiquette errors are usually intended."

She returned to her search for pajamas, and as she ran her fingers over one of the pairs of flannel pants, she realized, for the first time, that she was actually having *fun*. She'd barely stopped laughing the entire night, which was pretty insane, considering there were vicious monsters after her, fully intent on killing her.

As much as Kallias frustrated her, she also enjoyed their banter, for some reason, and that realization scared her more than she wanted to admit. She absently tossed the pajamas in the shopping cart.

When she finally turned back toward Kallias, her chest tight, she breathed a sigh of relief to find him reading the back of another freezer meal, not paying any attention to her. "I...uh..." She cleared her throat. "I need to get shower stuff."

"Do people actually eat this stuff?" he asked absently.

"It's cheap and convenient," Rose said. "So, yeah."

He grimaced and tossed it back into the cart. "Right. So, toiletry items."

She nodded and led the way across the store until they found the aisle with shampoos and conditioners. She scanned the hair products with a frown.

"We should hurry," Kallias said with a bit of impatience. "I doubt Theron followed us this far, but the longer we stay in one place, the easier it'll be for him to find you."

"Okay, just let me find my shampoo and conditioner and..." she trailed off, as Kallias suddenly chunked two, familiar, golden bottles in the cart. He walked away again and then returned with a beige bottle of body wash.

"Shampoo. Conditioner. Body wash," Kallias listed, as he tossed the body wash into the cart, as well—as if what he'd just done was totally normal. He looked at her curiously. "What else do you need?"

Rose pointed at the bottles in the cart, which just so happened to be the exact types of shampoo, conditioner, and body wash she used. "You read my mind?"

"I didn't need to read your mind," he said. "I just sniffed them out."

"You sniffed...them out?" she repeated, enunciating each word.

Kallias looked at her, as if suddenly realizing that might've sounded strange to her. "The scents," he explained. He pointed at the golden bottles. "The scent in your hair is honey. Specifically, it's the same honey scent that is in *those* bottles of shampoo and conditioner." He pointed at the beige bottle. "And your skin smells of vanilla, just like *that* vanilla body wash."

She stared blankly at him. "You know my...scent?"

He looked away. To her surprise, he actually looked embarrassed. "We've spent a lot of time together in the past few days. Of course I know your scent."

Rose looked down at the bottles and laughed, "Sometimes, you seem completely normal, just like a human, and other times, you're so...odd."

He nodded. "Yeah. I get that."

She laughed, "Please, tell me you can't do that with the deodorant, too."

He shifted nervously. "Umm, no?"

She crossed her arms. Kallias being embarrassed was a pretty comical sight, actually. "Are you lying?"

Kallias bowed his head shamefully and grabbed the deodorant she usually used. He held it out to her. "This is what you're wearing right now."

Rose started giggling. "You're like one of those drug dogs!"

He bristled. "I'm far more advanced than a canine. It's true that I share certain characteristics with canine predators, but I also share characteristics with feline predators and other animals. As a matter of fact, I actually have more in common with humans than canines."

She laughed at his defensive rant. "That's too bad," she teased—and pushed the shopping cart past him. "I think I like dogs better than people."

His offended scowl faded—and gradually morphed into a grin.

"Toothpaste?" Rose asked curiously.

"Crest. Spearmint," Kallias said easily. "Toothpaste *and* mouthwash."

Her eyes widened a little. "You didn't even sniff that one out."

"I recognized the taste," he said with an intense stare.

She frowned. "The taste?"

His gaze darkened and shifted down, toward her lips. "When we kissed."

Rose blinked. "Oh. Right," she said nervously. She busied herself with finding her toothbrush and toothpaste. She dropped them in the cart and wiped her sweaty palms across her jeans. She glanced nervously at Kallias, swallowing, as she found his dark eyes still watching her. "I, umm, think that's everything."

He nodded, but his heated gaze remained on her. "If you're sure."

Kallias may have been the telepath, but this time, it was Rose who knew what *he* was thinking. She would've had to be blind to not know. She'd seen that flicker of lust and hunger flashing in his eyes, and she noticed the way he watched her lips.

He was thinking about that kiss, just like she was—except contrary to what he'd said, it didn't *look* like he regretted it. And at the moment, Rose was having trouble remembering why she regretted it, too.

She squirmed under his scorching gaze and quickly grabbed the cart and pushed it in the direction of the registers. She felt him following behind her, but he never spoke.

They were silent, as they waited in line at the cash registers. The cashier—a brunette woman in a white polo shirt and blue vest—openly gawked at Kallias, her big brown eyes wide with shock and awe.

They waited for several moments for the woman to begin scanning the items, but she didn't move. She just stood there, gaping at Kallias, with a pack of Oreos dangling from her hand.

"Does this happen often?" Rose asked Kallias.

"We're in a hurry," he told the woman—that rudeness back in his voice.

The woman blinked several times. "Oh. Oh!" she said, seeming to finally realize what she was doing. She glanced sheepishly at the Oreos, and her cheeks reddened with embarrassment. She fumbled with the pack until she managed to scan it, avoiding their gazes the entire time. "I guess I forgot where I was for a moment."

Rose frowned, as she considered the woman's reaction to Kallias. She was beginning to understand what Kallias meant. Every human that looked at him seemed transfixed by him.

Except for Rose.

Sure, even Rose had noticed that he was attractive, but he didn't affect her like *that*. No one affected her that strongly. Not Kallias, Theron, or Sofia. She wondered what was so different about her.

"Are you coming?" Kallias said impatiently.

His voice tore her from her thoughts, and she suddenly realized that the bags were in the cart already. She glanced at Kallias, meeting his glare with her own. "Yes, *sir*," she snarled with a sarcastic salute.

Out of the corner of her eye, she noticed that the cashier gaped at her, as if she thought Rose was out of her mind, but Kallias just chuckled at her snarky response.

Rose pushed the shopping cart out of the aisle and headed toward the exit. She felt Kallias behind her, and she heard his heavy footsteps following.

As they stepped out into the parking lot, the wind enveloped them, cooling Rose's skin. She suddenly realized how stuffy it'd felt in that store. Pale moonlight bathed the parking lot, highlighting the few cars parked there. Kallias appeared to relax—relieved by the darkness after being in such a bright building.

They were nearly to the car when Kallias suddenly placed his arm in front of her, stopping her in her tracks. She frowned at him, her brows creasing with worry, as she noticed the difference in his countenance. He seemed on edge, his body rigid and straight—which made him look even taller than usual. His stance seemed defensive and protective, more intimidating than usual.

"What's wrong?" Rose asked nervously.

His brown eyes scanned the parking lot, searching for something out of place. He sucked in a deep breath, inhaling deeply, and then, his eyes fluttered closed, as he discerned each individual scent and sound.

"Nothing," he said, finally opening his eyes. He seemed surprised by his own answer. "I thought I'd smelled a vampire, but then, there was nothing."

Kallias dropped his arm, and Rose was able to walk again. He walked next to her, in step with her, as if he were afraid that putting too much distance between them might result in her death.

He'd yet to relax even the least little bit.

"Do you think Theron followed us this far?" Rose asked.

His eyes continued to scan the parking lot around them. "I highly doubt it," he said—without looking at her. "I'm sure Theron's still in Florida."

She slowed, as they neared his car. "Then, why do you seem so worried?"

"I'm not worried," he stated. When she gave him a skeptical look, he sighed, "I'm not. But no vampire is good news, Rose—especially not for you."

He'd said that last part under his breath, but Rose had still heard him. She scowled suspiciously. "Especially not for me? What does that mean?"

"Nothing," he said—a little too quickly. They stopped next to his shiny, black car. "It means nothing."

Rose eyed him suspiciously, as he pulled the keys from his pocket and unlocked the car. She stayed near the shopping cart, as he rounded the car and lifted the trunk. "It must mean *something*," she argued.

His gaze darted toward her again, and he returned to the cart and grabbed nearly half of the shopping bags with one hand. He tossed the bags into the trunk and returned to the cart for more bags. Before he could grab the rest of them, Rose snatched up all that she could and added them to the trunk, as well.

"What is it that you don't want me to know?" she asked.

Kallias slammed the trunk of the car closed. "Nothing."

Just as she expected him to get back inside the car, he suddenly jerked his torn T-shirt over his head. She sputtered and glanced around at the empty parking lot, as she tried to figure out why her new vampire friend had suddenly decided to be half-naked.

"Uh," she stammered. "Is this really the place for that?"

He opened the car door and tossed the torn T-shirt inside. "I got a few weird looks in the store. I need to change." He sifted through a duffel bag and pulled out another black T-shirt. He pulled it on over his head.

"I thought the weird looks were about the vampire thing," she said.

"That's a different kind of look," he said, as he pulled his shirt down.

Her frown deepened as he locked the doors. The car beeped twice. "Wait, we're not getting in the car? Where are we going?"

He motioned for her to follow him. "We need to eat."

Rose froze mid-step, her skin suddenly paling. "*We?*"

Kallias turned to frown at her—and then rolled his eyes as he realized why she looked so worried. "Oh, for goodness sakes, Rose, I'm not going to bite you," he assured her, "no matter how much I want to."

"Oh," she said. She frowned again. "Wait. What was that last part?"

12

INTOXICATED VAMPIRES

"I should've grabbed a pair of clean clothes—so I could change once we're inside," Rose said. She cast a worried glance at her torn jeans and the jacket that covered her from her neck to her thighs. "I feel gross, walking around in these bloody clothes." She looked up. "And I'm sure you want your jacket back."

The parking lot of the Walmart they'd just left extended to the end of the street, connecting with the parking lot of a strip mall.

It was mostly dark, empty stores that had closed hours ago, but near the end of the strip mall, light shone through the windows of a twenty-four-hour diner.

Rose assumed they were headed there.

"I don't need it," Kallias said. With a small smile, he added, "Besides, it looks good on you."

Rose's eyes widened at the unexpected compliment. He'd said it so nonchalantly that she thought she might've imagined it. "I doubt that."

"It does," Kallias insisted. "It looks natural on you."

Rose blinked twice, as she realized he really *had* complimented her. She wondered if he'd been possessed by some kind of *nice* demon. "I guess I missed my calling, then," she muttered. "All this time, destiny was calling to me, telling me I was meant to be a biker or a dangerous, leather-clad vampire, and I was like, *'You said nerd, right?'* Close enough."

Kallias snorted. "Well, we could fix that, you know."

Rose glanced up at him, her eyes wide. "Uh," she stammered. "Fix which part, exactly? The vampire part or the—"

He scowled at her. "The motorcycle part, obviously."

"Oh, no," she said, grimacing. "You have a motorcycle?"

His brows furrowed. "Is that a bad thing?"

She gave him an unimpressed eye roll. "You're just so stereotypical."

They slowed, as they neared the entrance of the diner. It seemed small—almost as small as the café where Rose worked. A white sign with the words *"Open 24 Hours,"* printed across the center, hung inside the glass door.

Kallias pulled the door open. "Stereotypical for what? A vampire?"

He'd said it quietly enough, but Rose still cast a wary glance around them before responding.

"Oh, come on. You know," Rose said. When he shook his head, she said, "You're an adrenaline junkie. The fighting, the weapons, that *ridiculous* stunt you pulled with your car?" She spread out her hands. "And now, I find out you even have a motorcycle."

He frowned. "I'm not sure any of those things are actually related."

"You ran over someone and jumped a barricade onto the Interstate," she reminded him. "Normal people would be terrified. You were *laughing*."

"It was…innocent fun," he said defensively.

She stared blankly at him. "Ran. Over. Someone."

"You're overreacting," he said. "You didn't die."

"Right," Rose said sarcastically. "I should wait until *after* I'm dead to freak out."

He shrugged one shoulder. "Sounds good to me."

"I'm sure it does," she muttered.

She stepped inside, and he let the door close. It was surprisingly busy for this late at night, but then, it *was* close to the Interstate.

Several groups of people filled the booths and tables, and some of the tables were pushed together to accommodate slightly bigger groups.

"Just so you know," Rose added, "I will *never* ride a motorcycle with you."

He gave her a wry smile. "Why? Are you afraid?"

"No," she scoffed. "I'm just smart. Do you know how much more likely you are to die in a motorcycle crash, compared to a car crash?"

"Do you just sit around and memorize statistics all day?" he asked.

"I do a lot of things during the day," Rose said defensively.

He chuckled. As they stood near the hostess stand, waiting for someone to seat them, Rose felt him lean closer to her, until his mouth was almost at her ear, and say, "I think you're just scared."

Rose made a frustrated noise in her throat. She stepped closer to him and raised herself on her toes. She poked a finger against his chest and hissed, "Besides, if you think I would *ever* climb on the back of a motorcycle, wrap my arms around you—all close to you and clinging to you and all that—then you, sir, are severely mistaken."

He glanced down at her finger, and his lips curved tightly as he fought the urge to laugh. He leaned in, too, and whispered in her ear, "I seem to remember that you've already been that close to me—*clinging to me and all that.*"

Rose shuddered.

She told herself it was just a natural, physical reaction—to someone's breath falling against somewhere as sensitive as the shell of her ear.

But the memory of that kiss they'd shared wasn't helping matters.

She stepped back and turned toward the hostess stand, desperate to avoid his gaze. She watched as a woman, dressed in a black, polo shirt and black pants, with shoulder-length, purple hair, glanced up and saw them.

She hurried toward them.

Rose could still feel his eyes on her. "You know, for someone who *says* that kiss didn't mean anything, you sure do mention it a lot," she said breathlessly. "*I* had practically forgotten it."

"Liar," Kallias said.

The hostess stopped in front of them and flashed a bright smile. She glanced back and forth between Kallias and Rose, and her round, green eyes sparkled with excitement. "Oh, yay! A couple!" she sang. "I love couples!"

Rose frowned. "Oh, no, we're not—"

"Just two?" the hostess asked.

"Yes," Kallias answered.

The hostess gathered two menus into her arms. "Table or booth?"

Kallias cast an expectant look at Rose, apparently waiting for her to answer.

Rose scowled at him. "What? I don't care."

"Booths are more *romantic*," the hostess said sweetly.

"Table," Kallias and Rose both responded in unison.

The hostess blinked in surprise, and her smile faded. Clearly, she'd expected the opposite answer. "Oh! Umm, okay. Sure. Follow me."

Kallias and Rose followed the purple-haired hostess to a table near the center of the dining room—just a few feet in front of the kitchen.

As they walked, the hostess kept casting curious glances at Rose, but Rose never lifted her gaze long enough to notice.

The table seemed safe enough from the dreaded *romance*—certainly not as dark and secluded as the booths.

Kallias took a seat on one side of the table, and Rose took a seat on the other side. The hostess set their menus on the table, and as Rose busied herself with looking through it, the hostess cast another curious glance her way.

Kallias snorted.

"I like your jacket," the hostess told Rose.

Rose looked up, blinking. "Me?"

The hostess lifted her eyebrows. "Yes."

"Oh," Rose said, blushing. "Thank you." She tilted her head toward Kallias. "But it's his."

Kallias shook his head in disbelief and returned his attention to the menu.

The hostess glanced at Kallias, and her brows furrowed, as she tried to figure out the relationship between Kallias and Rose.

She gave Rose another flirty smile. "Your waitress is Leslie. She'll be out soon. But if you need *me* for anything, just ask for Starr."

"Well, that's really nice of you," Rose said. "Thank you, Starr."

The purple-haired hostess nodded shyly and turned to leave.

Rose leaned across the table to whisper to Kallias, "I think that was the first woman that didn't stare at you like you were a god."

Kallias glanced up, his brows high. Did she really not know? "That's because she was too busy staring at *you*," he muttered.

Rose frowned. "What?"

She glanced back toward the door, and sure enough, the sweet, purple-haired girl was still staring at her.

The hostess blushed and looked away.

Kallias shook his head again and returned his attention to the menu. "You didn't notice?"

"No," she said, shrugging. "She must think I'm weird or something."

Kallias blinked at her. "*Or...* she's attracted to you."

Rose glanced at him. "What?"

He shrugged and turned another page. "She likes women."

"Seriously?" Rose said. "Did you see that in her mind or something?"

He nodded and turned to the steak section of the menu. "She likes you."

"No, she doesn't," Rose scoffed.

He looked up—and rolled his eyes when he caught her *also* watching the hostess. "You know, instead of staring at her like an idiot, you could just go talk to her," he said with an amused snort. "Tell her you want that booth, after all."

"What?" she said, turning her gaze back toward him. "No."

He chuckled and returned to reading his menu.

A waitress appeared at their table, her gaze on the floor, as she pulled a notepad and pen from her apron. She wore the same black polo and black slacks that the hostess wore, and her brown hair was sleeked back in a high pony tail. "Hi, I'm Leslie, and I'll be your waitress tonight," she recited. "Can I— Oh, my goodness." The moment she saw Kallias, her practiced speech ended in a gasp.

Rose looked up to find the waitress's brown eyes wide and full of awe.

Okay...

So, maybe the hostess *had* been gay.

Kallias didn't even look up. "I want Coke, and she wants coffee."

"Oh. Oh! Okay!" the waitress stammered. She tried to shift the notepad in her hands, while still staring at Kallias, and wound up dropping it.

With a puzzled frown, Rose leaned forward and grabbed it for her.

The waitress took it without ever looking at Rose. "I'll be right back with that."

"I—" Rose mumbled. "I think she forgot to write it down."

"They do that sometimes," Kallias muttered.

This *allure* of his was starting to sound inconvenient.

Rose glanced at him. "You ordered for me," she complained.

He shrugged. "You wanted coffee."

"You don't know that," she said stubbornly.

"I *do* know that, actually," he said. He pointed to his head.

Rose sighed. "Oh, right. I don't think I'll ever get used to that."

Kallias cast a curious look at her. "I thought humans drank coffee in the mornings."

She bristled at that. "Coffee isn't restricted to a time of day!"

He snorted at her seriousness. "I guess I was mistaken, then."

Rose flipped through her menu—pretty aggressively, actually. "I guess you were."

He chuckled. "You're testy about your coffee, aren't you?"

She glared at him. "Coffee is awesome." When he continued to stare at her with that amused half-smirk, she added, "It's better than *blood*."

Kallias leaned forward. "Not better than your blood."

Rose nearly dropped her menu. "W-what?" she sputtered.

Rose was still staring at him in shock, when the waitress set a cup of coffee in front of her and a glass of cola in front of Kallias.

"Are you ready to order your food?" Leslie asked. She offered Kallias a sweet smile. "I can give you more time, if you need it."

"I want a steak," Kallias muttered. "The biggest one."

She jotted something in her notepad. "How do you want it cooked?"

"Rare, probably," Rose quipped. "As rare as it gets. Still full of blood."

Kallias looked up from his menu and narrowed his eyes at her.

Rose ignored him. "As a matter of fact, you should probably just bring him the cow's artery."

The waitress wrinkled her nose, obviously appalled by Rose's attempt at humor.

Kallias, on the other hand, actually had to suppress a smile. "Medium rare will be fine."

Rose flashed a cute smile at him.

Leslie looked at Rose with obvious distaste. "And you?"

Rose glanced at the menu wistfully—but then sighed, "Salad."

Kallias frowned at her. "That's not what you want," he scoffed.

Rose blinked, glancing back and forth between him and the now *very* confused waitress.

"She doesn't want salad," Kallias told the waitress. "She wants the grilled fish."

"Now, wait a minute," Rose said irritably.

But Leslie nodded, as if Rose's answer didn't matter. "I'll be right back with it."

Rose lifted her shoulders in an irritated shrug. "What the heck was that?"

Kallias looked at her as if *she* were the one acting weird. "You didn't want the salad. I heard you think it."

Rose rolled her eyes. "No one *wants* to eat healthy all the time," she informed him. "But I can't just eat whatever I want."

Kallias's frown deepened. "Why not?"

"It doesn't matter," Rose said. She didn't exactly want to explain to Kallias that the *last* guy she'd kissed had made her overwhelmingly insecure about this sort of thing. "The point is...I don't need you to order for me."

"Well, apparently, you do," Kallias scoffed.

Rose sighed heavily. "I'm on a diet."

"A what?" Kallias said. He squinted, as if he were trying to read some small print in her mind. "You think you're fat?"

Rose gave a defensive shrug. "I just...think I should lose weight."

Kallias looked more confused than ever. "Why?"

Rose's frown deepened. "To...be thin. Why else?"

Kallias waved a hand at her. "You have breasts and an ass," he said bluntly. "I'm not sure what the problem is."

Rose sighed, "It's like you've never met a modern human."

"You mean because you're all insecure," Kallias assumed. "Yeah, I've noticed." He returned his attention to the menu. "When I was human, women didn't worry about all of that."

"I'm sure they didn't," Rose said skeptically.

"They didn't," Kallias insisted. "Back in those days, women knew they were beautiful, no matter which body shape they had."

"You mean, in the good ole' days?" Rose teased. "You sound like an old man."

His lips twitched in amusement. "Shut up."

Rose reached for her coffee cup, but she gasped in surprise, as Kallias caught her wrist.

Had anyone seen him move that fast?

Rose certainly hadn't.

He leaned forward in his chair and pulled her wrist closer to himself so that he could see it.

"What are you doing?" Rose said breathlessly.

He pushed the sleeves of the black, leather jacket up to her forearm. He traced the bluish red ring around her wrist, and his brows creased with worry. "Did I do this?" he said quietly.

Rose tried to pull her hand back, but his grip was unrelenting. She glanced at him, and her gaze immediately softened, as she saw the guilt in his eyes. "I don't know," she answered honestly. "Theron grabbed my wrists many times. Much harder than you did. And that other vampire grabbed them, as well. It could've been anyone."

He looked back down at her wrist, tracing the sensitive skin with his thumb. "Which means it might've been me," he sighed. "I said I'd protect you, but I hurt you."

She rolled her eyes and jerked her wrist back. He immediately let it go, afraid he'd worsen the bruise if he didn't. "Stop beating up yourself about it. You *didn't* hurt me," she told him. "And even if you did, it was an accident. I'm not going to blame you for something you couldn't help."

He looked away. "You shouldn't trust me."

"You only say that because you don't trust yourself," Rose said—without thinking.

Kallias glanced up at her, his brown eyes wide and unreadable.

Unable to make eye contact with him after what she'd just said, Rose grabbed her coffee. She watched the thin, black liquid, as she stirred in a bit of cream and sugar, but even without looking, she could feel his gaze on her.

She hadn't meant to say what she said, but it was the truth.

She knew it was.

Rose sipped her coffee, listening to the silverware clanging against plates and the voices blending around them. The hot coffee soothed her, and she relaxed, slouching in her chair.

"How are you feeling?" Kallias asked after a few moments.

Rose looked up, suddenly noticing the way the amber glow of the lamps complimented his golden skin. She cleared her throat, as she tried to remember his question. "What? Yeah. Fine. I'm fine."

His lips curved into a knowing smile at her stammering, but he didn't comment on it. "Your back, your legs, your head—it all feels better already?"

Now that he mentioned it, Rose realized that she *did* feel pretty sore, but after being thrown around by Theron several nights in a row, she'd grown used to it. She set down the cup of coffee. "Yeah, I feel fine."

He nodded. "Good," he said, and then, he fell silent again.

Everything suddenly felt awkward, and Rose felt the need to break the silence. "I hate that I don't have my money. I *never* let people pay for my food."

He chuckled. "You must be a terrible date."

She'd intended to glare at him, but somehow she wound up laughing, instead. "Yeah, I probably am—if my track record of *second* dates is any indication. But come on! It's not like you'd be any better! I mean, you're not exactly fitting into any 'old-fashioned gentlemen' stereotypes yourself."

"Old-fashioned?" he scoffed. "You forget that chivalry is brand new in *my* timeline. I was over a thousand years old before chivalry was thought up."

"I see your point," Rose admitted, "but you *did* live during the Middle Ages."

"In the Middle Ages, I was killing vampires, not courting ladies," Kallias said.

She gave him a skeptical look. "You expect me to believe you don't date?"

"Why would I? It's a ridiculous activity," Kallias scoffed. "Modern dating is barely any different from courting in the Middle Ages. The rules are just a little more lax these days." He sipped his own drink. "And courting was just a game of seduction, or rather...a *drama*, in which each person had a part to play."

Rose sat back, listening curiously to his theories. Dating might've been uninteresting to her, but *history* wasn't.

"The man played the part of the polite, chivalrous knight who rides in on his horse to save the damsel in distress," he told her, "and the woman played the damsel in distress who *needed* him." He leaned forward. "But those were just the parts they played. It wasn't who they were. It was a game. Glorified dishonesty."

Rose nodded in understanding. "And you think dating is the same?"

"Isn't it?" he said. He waved a hand at a couple who sat at the table behind Rose. "I can hear their thoughts right now. Neither of them has told the truth about who they are or what they want since they arrived."

Rose glanced curiously at the man and woman, and then, she quickly shifted her attention back toward Kallias, when one of them noticed her. "Why are they lying to each other?" she whispered.

"Lots of reasons," Kallias said. "She has a sexual trauma—obviously doesn't want to talk about it or admit how it affects her sex life. And he's..." He shrugged. "He's just another guy who doesn't care about her."

Rose leaned back in her seat, her stomach sinking. "That's awful."

Kallias gave another shrug. "I suppose."

"It must suck for you," she commented.

He looked at her curiously. Glass clanged against the tabletop, as he set down his drink. "What? Knowing all this shit about people I don't know?"

"No," Rose said quietly. "Knowing that everyone lies."

His impassive expression faltered for a moment, and she noticed that sadness again, softening his eyes. "It's better than the alternative."

"Ignorance?" she assumed.

"No," Kallias said. "Trust." He shrugged. "It's better to know everyone lies than to trust and have your heart shredded into a billion pieces when you finally learn the truth."

"Ooh, vivid imagery there," Rose muttered.

Plates clanged against their table, as a man in a long, white apron set them in front of Kallias and Rose. When Rose looked up, he smiled and nodded toward the plate of grilled fish. "That's my favorite."

Rose returned the smile. She had to admit that it really did look delicious.

The man turned to head back to the kitchen, but before he reached the door, their purple-haired hostess pranced over to him. Pushing him playfully, she teased, "You need to get back in the kitchen before you scare away the customers."

He rolled his eyes. "Who died and made you the boss?"

She smiled sweetly. "This is my domain. Yours is in the kitchen."

"Go bother someone else, Starr," he said, but he smiled as he said it. He brushed the purple hair out of her face and planted a chaste kiss on her forehead.

Rose smiled sadly. She didn't know what relation they had to each other, but their sibling-like teasing made Rose miss her own brother.

The hostess turned and smiled at Kallias and Rose. "Need anything?"

Kallias didn't even look up at her. The steak in front of him had *his* full attention.

Rose scowled at his rudeness—and then offered Starr a friendly smile. "We're fine. Thanks."

The hostess blushed and nodded, quickly returning to her podium.

"You shouldn't smile at her like that," Kallias said, as he cut up his steak. "She thinks you're flirting." He glanced up from his food and flashed a wry grin, before adding, "I mean, that is, unless you *are* flirting with her."

Rose blushed at the mere idea. "I wasn't flirting," she muttered. "I was being polite. But then, how can I expect *you* to recognize politeness? You've probably never been polite."

He chuckled. "Probably not."

She watched, as he placed a bite of steak in his mouth. "You're eating."

Kallias swallowed and then looked up at her. "It is *so* impressive to see your genius mind in action."

Rose pursed her lips at his sarcasm. "No. I mean, you're eating *human* food," she said. She leaned forward and whispered, "I assumed vampires couldn't eat human food."

A smile tugged at his lips, as he cut another piece of steak. "I ate human food in your café the night we met. Don't you remember?"

She rolled her eyes. "Believe it or not, I wasn't staring at you all night, like some lovesick puppy," she sassed. "I didn't know whether you ate your food or not."

"Lovesick puppy?" he repeated.

"It's an expression," she said. "You know, puppy love? Infatuation?"

Kallias nodded, as he cut up another bite of steak. "It's hard to keep up with the modern idioms sometimes," he told her. "To answer your question, yes, I *can* eat food, but it does nothing for the hunger."

Rose frowned. "Then, what's the point of eating it?"

When he looked at her, his eyes were dark with hunger. "The point is that, for just a moment, I'm distracted from the urge to rip the throats out of every person in this room. I'd say that's a good enough reason, wouldn't you?"

Rose blinked. "Yeah. Great reason."

He returned to eating his food. "The metabolism of a vampire is astronomically fast," he continued, still speaking too quietly for other people to hear. "So, when we eat or drink anything other than blood, it's burned away too quickly for it to make a difference. Blood's the only thing our bodies hold on to long enough to extract nourishment."

Rose nodded at that. "Does food taste the same to a vampire?"

He frowned, considering that. "My senses are more advanced than yours, so no, I suppose it doesn't. I can taste everything—every individual flavor."

"And does that make it taste better or worse?" she asked.

"Both, I suppose," Kallias said. "It's better because I can appreciate the flavors more than a human can. It's worse because the only thing I *want* is blood."

Rose nodded. "But does it—"

"I refuse to answer any more questions until you eat," he interrupted.

Rose narrowed her eyes. "Maybe I don't want to eat."

"Of course. That explains why your stomach's growling," he said sarcastically. He gave her a bitter smile. "You need to eat."

Rose blushed. After a day in a warehouse without food and a night in a car without food, *of course* her stomach was resorting to grumbly measures. She picked up her fork and cut into her fish.

Kallias had already returned his attention to his drink, when he heard what was clearly a moan escape Rose's lips. He choked on his drink. He watched, as she closed her eyes and chewed another bite, again moaning softly.

He snorted, "I take it you like it?"

"Mmm-hmm," Rose murmured. "What is this sauce? It's so buttery and..." She opened her eyes and looked at him, suddenly realizing that he was staring at her—*grinning* at her, really—and amended, "I mean, it's *okay.*"

He smirked, clearly gloating. "More okay than the salad would've been?"

Her eyes narrowed. "Fine! Yes! It's amazing," she admitted. "Thanks for being a total jerk and changing my order without my permission."

"You're welcome," he said, ignoring her glare.

She rolled her eyes. "You got lucky this time. Don't try it again."

He chuckled at that.

They'd been eating in silence for several minutes, when Kallias suddenly dropped his fork, and the loud clang caused Rose to look over at him. He straightened in his seat, and his gaze darted toward the window. He inhaled deeply, breathing in the scents of the diner and the outside parking lot, and a worried scowl twisted at his face.

"Are you okay?" Rose asked hesitantly.

"Yeah. Fine," he grunted.

She continued to watch him with a wary frown. "Because you got all straighter and taller in your seat, and that's saying something because you were already tall," she added. "Kallias, what is it? What's wrong?"

"Do you remember how I thought I noticed the scent of a vampire earlier?" Kallias asked. "I may have dismissed that a little too soon."

Rose leaned forward. "As an animalistic creature, don't you think it'd be wise to *rely* on your instincts, instead of dismissing them?"

He glared at her. "Yes, Rose. Thank you. That's very helpful right now."

Rose flashed a sarcastic smile. "You're welcome."

His brown gaze darted toward the door again. "We need to go. Now."

"What? We haven't even paid yet," she reminded him.

Kallias pushed back his chair, preparing to stand. "Now, Rose."

Her eyes narrowed. "That's stealing, and I don't steal."

He glared at her, his eyes wide with disbelief. "You have really fucked up priorities! You know that, right?" he said in a furious whisper.

"Whoa. What's with the F-bomb all of the sudden?" Rose complained.

His eyes shifted toward the door, widening in alarm. "Shit."

Rose continued to tease, "It's been said that people who use excessive profanity are filling in the gaps of their lackluster vocabulary. Maybe you should try reading…"

"Rose!" he interrupted. "Would you shut up for a second?"

Before she could reply, the door opened, and a cool rush of air swept through the diner. Kallias looked toward the door, and his eyes narrowed at the men who entered.

Rose followed his gaze.

Near the door, two men stood—one tall and one short. The taller man looked young—younger than Rose, even. He wore a blue, ball cap over his shaggy, brown hair, and he wore faded jeans and a blue T-shirt. The shorter man looked around Rose's age. Mid-twenties, perhaps? He was dressed a little nicer, as well.

Both of them, however, looked unnaturally attractive.

Their obnoxious jokes and laughter carried across the diner, and while there were a few people in the diner who looked annoyed, the blonde woman closest to them looked absolutely enchanted by them.

The allure was the *only* explanation, Rose thought, for anyone being attracted to those two—especially after some of the things she'd heard come out of their mouth.

With an annoyed scowl, Rose said, "They seem drunk."

"Not drunk. Intoxicated," Kallias said quietly, "on *blood*."

Her brows furrowed. "Blood can intoxicate you?"

"Shhh!" he hissed. He leaned toward her—so that he could whisper in her ear, "Yes. Blood has power and endorphins. If a vampire takes too much, it intoxicates them and dulls their senses. Which is lucky for you and me, considering *you're talking so fucking loud!*"

She jerked back in shock, when he snarled that last part in her ear. "I wasn't that loud," she complained, "and don't talk to me like that."

He glared at her. "I don't think you understand how bad this is."

"It's two vampires," Rose said with a small shrug. "Isn't that the same as what we faced earlier?"

"Yes, but that was in an *alley*, not in a crowded restaurant," Kallias reminded her. He cast another wary glance at the vampires, as the hostess attempted to calm them. "I also took on each of *them* separately."

Rose nodded. "So, you're worried about people seeing?"

He turned to her. "Yes. Of course I'm worried about that," he said. "Humans *can't* find out about us. I don't know how to make that any clearer."

"I get it," she said between clenched teeth. "I'm just thinking."

Kallias sighed, "If I fought them here, the people in this restaurant could die."

"Okay, so, you obviously can't fight them here," Rose agreed. Anger rose in her stomach, as she noticed them turning their attention toward the purple-haired hostess who'd been so sweet. "If I left, would they follow me?"

Kallias scowled at that. "What do you mean 'if *you* left?'" he said. "You're not leaving without—"

"Kallias," Rose interrupted. "Just read their minds and tell me."

He narrowed his eyes at her, but then, he shifted his gaze toward them. He watched the vampires for a moment, and then, he said, "No. They're not here for you."

Rose blinked in surprise. "They're not?"

Oddly enough, that didn't seem to ease Kallias's anxiety any. He leaned back in his chair and blew out a weary sigh. "It's just a coincidence," he muttered. "They're here for blood. Not us."

Rose's eyes widened. "They're going to kill someone here?"

Kallias looked at her. "Not someone," he said in an exhausted tone. "Everyone."

Rose paled. "What?"

"It happens sometimes," Kallias muttered, "when vampires take too much blood—especially if they fed from a human who was drunk or high." He sighed, "The last thing you'd ever want is for a powerful monster with bloodlust and insatiable hunger to have lowered inhibitions." He scoffed, "They'll feed on every human they can, just because they want to. And the hunger never fades, so they never stop. Not until the sun forces them to, anyway. But by then, they've killed countless humans." He shook his head. "Intoxicated vampires are *very* bad news."

Rose watched the vampires worriedly. "So, if we'd left earlier, like you wanted to—"

"They'd all be dead," Kallias admitted. "Your weird obsession with human law may have saved their lives—*if* I can find a way to save them."

"We," Rose corrected. "*We'll* find a way to save them."

Kallias narrowed his eyes at that. "No. You're leaving."

"Leaving?" Rose scoffed. "What am I supposed to do? Just walk out the door?"

"Once you get outside, run straight to the car," Kallias said, proving that he was indeed serious, "and wait for me."

She jumped when she felt his hand on her thigh. "What are you doing?"

He paused in the middle of his instructions, and his lips twitched up as he realized what she'd assumed. "Relax, *moro mou*," he said playfully. "I wouldn't touch you *there* in the middle of a restaurant."

Rose glanced at him, surprised—and a little amused—by the Greek pet name. "Did you forget that I know Greek?"

His smile tilted wickedly. "No."

Rose blushed.

Kallias pressed something into her hand, and when she wrapped her fingers around the keys, she understood.

Which then led to her replaying the entire conversation in her head and *finally* having a proper reaction to it.

"Wait, no, no, no!" she said quickly. "The correct way to say that was: I wouldn't touch you there *at all*!"

Amusement danced in his light brown eyes. "Of course," he said. "That's what I meant to say."

Rose glared at him. "I'm not leaving you here."

Kallias rolled his eyes. "Not this again," he groaned. "You have to! If they realize what you are—"

"There it is again," Rose said. "*What* I am—you keep saying that."

He froze, his dark eyes suddenly guarded. "You know what I meant."

"No, I don't, actually," Rose said with a suspicious glare, "because you've yet to tell me."

"You're just...a human that Theron wants," Kallias lied. "That's all I meant."

But Rose knew there was more to it than that. He knew something— or *believed* something—about her that he refused to tell her.

But she didn't have time to press the issue. "How exactly do you expect me to leave?"

"Go to the bathroom, and crawl through the window," he told her.

"Oh!" Rose said. "So, you want me to do the oh-crap-I'm-not-doing-well-on-this-date-and-I'm-too-awkward-to-explain-so-I'll-just-crawl-out-the-bathroom-window move?" she asked, somehow cramming every word into one breath.

He frowned at her for a moment, as he processed the long name she'd given it. His lips twitched in amusement. "You've done that?"

She blushed. "Only a few times."

He snorted, "Right. Well, then, it shouldn't be too difficult for you."

Rose inhaled sharply, far too aware of his hand still on her thigh. His touch was warm and gentle, radiating heat through her jeans. She grasped his hand and took it off her thigh, ignoring the smirk he gave in response. "I'm *still* not leaving you."

His smile instantly faded. "Yes, you are."

She rolled her eyes, as if she weren't the least bit intimidated by a powerful, telepathic vampire. "Okay, so, you said people might die, right?"

He scowled suspiciously at that. "Yes. I doubt I'll be able to save everyone."

"Then, the first thing we need to do is evacuate the restaurant," Rose said.

His eyebrows lifted in surprise. "Well, yes. Is that possible?"

Rose glanced at the vampires again, and her eyes narrowed, as she noticed that they were harassing the hostess now. And unlike the other women, the hostess wasn't irrationally attracted to them. She was annoyed.

Starr said something to them, gesturing toward the tables and booths, and the shorter one grasped her arm. She jerked it away from him.

"They're not being very nice to Starr," Rose muttered.

Kallias raised an eyebrow. "Worried about your girlfriend, are you?"

She shot a peeved glare at him. "I'd be worried about anyone who was being treated like that—no matter who they were," she assured him, "but...it *does* give me an idea."

His brows furrowed. "What kind of idea?"

"You said," Rose began, "you saw in her mind that she's a lesbian?"

Kallias followed her gaze toward the hostess. "Yeah. That's why she's not falling for their allure like the other women," he said. "Why?"

She turned toward him. "If she's only into women, then who's the cook?"

He frowned. "What cook?"

"The one who brought us our food earlier," Rose said. "He was affectionate toward her, and she was comfortable with it. He's not her boyfriend, so who is he?"

Kallias shrugged. "We're in another room. I can't read his mind from this far away," he told her, "and he'd need to be thinking about her."

"But you said you could tell by scent," Rose reminded him, "if the person were family. So, you could *tell* if he was her brother, right?"

Kallias frowned curiously. "Possibly." He inhaled deeply, and his frown deepened. He sniffed again. "Yes, there *is* a human in this restaurant who shares similar blood with her. If I had to guess," he said, looking at Rose, "I'd say he's her brother."

Rose smiled. She pushed back her chair and stood. "I know what to do."

He spread out his hands. "What? What are you doing?"

"I'm going to look for a bathroom," Rose announced.

Kallias continued to frown because, after she said that, she turned and marched straight into...not the bathroom, but the *kitchen*.

PETER STOPPED SLICING ABOUT MIDWAY THROUGH THE TOMATO, WHEN THE steel, kitchen doors swung open. He frowned, his knife still frozen above the tomato, as he stared at the strange woman standing in his kitchen. Her dusty, dirt-stained jeans hung loosely on her hips, as if nothing really held them there, and a black, leather jacket draped over her body, hanging to the middle of her thighs. Her fiery auburn hair hung past her breasts and looked tangled and messy.

"I know you. I just brought you food," he said. "You're a customer."

She nodded awkwardly. "Yep."

His frown deepened. The woman seemed to be looking past him, studying something on the wall. "This is the kitchen. You're not supposed to be in here."

Rose finally looked at him, smiling as she noticed the obvious similarities between him and the hostess. He had the same big, green eyes and the same smile. The only noticeable difference between him and his sister was the hair. His was short and black, while hers was long and dyed bright purple.

She shrugged apologetically. "I was just looking for the bathroom."

He stared blankly at her. "In the kitchen?"

"Right. What was I thinking? They don't put toilets in the kitchen. That would be weird...and gross...and unsanitary," she rambled.

Peter continued to frown, seriously doubting her mental state, at this point. "If you were looking for the bathroom, why didn't you just ask Leslie or Stephanie?"

She frowned worriedly. "Stephanie?"

"Sorry, I mean Starr," he said. "She goes by Starr with everyone else."

Rose nodded. "Oh. Starr. The hostess that seated us?"

"Yeah. Why didn't you ask her?" Peter asked suspiciously.

Rose mentally chided her racing heart. She told herself there was no reason to be nervous. True, she was a terrible liar and had never successfully deceived anyone, but *technically*, she wouldn't be lying this time. "Uh, well, I would have. It's just that I didn't see the waitress, and I didn't want to bother Starr," she explained. "She already had her hands full with those *guys*."

He straightened. "What guys?"

"Just these jerks that came in," she said, trying to sound nonchalant.

His grip tightened around the knife. "And they're bothering her?"

"Well, I assume so, yeah," Rose said, "but I might be wrong. It's just that they're so obnoxious and...*handsy*."

"They touched her?" he said.

"Well, yeah, but...maybe she's okay with that?" she suggested.

"No, she's not," he said irritably. "My sister is *not* okay with strange men touching her."

Rose tried to hide her smile. "Oh."

"My sister wouldn't want men touching her at all," he continued.

"Well, in that case," Rose said, "I guess it *is* unwanted."

The cook stared at her for one more moment, before he tossed the knife onto the counter and stormed out of the kitchen.

For a moment after the doors swung closed behind him, Rose stood there in the middle of the empty kitchen, stunned that it had actually worked. She laughed in disbelief and then walked toward the back of the kitchen.

She stopped in front of the back wall, between two steel sinks and the back exit. She probably shouldn't have been proud of herself. On the list of achievements in her life, trickery was definitely at the bottom of the list, but she just couldn't believe it had actually worked.

She'd vacated the kitchen, and maybe, just *maybe*...she'd helped the hostess out a little, as well.

Rose studied the small, clear box that enclosed a fire alarm, scowling at the lock along the side.

Even though she already knew the kitchen was empty, she still glanced around before pulling at the box. It didn't budge.

She sighed and went to the counter to take the cook's knife. She returned to the box. She slammed the handle of the knife into the glass with all of her strength, breaking the case.

Then, Rose reached in and pulled the alarm.

She winced, as a shard of glass cut her hand.

But it was done. Shrill alarms began to screech through the diner, and icy water drenched her, as the sprinklers sprayed water from the ceiling. Rose ran toward the door, praying she wouldn't slip.

"Stop!" a woman screamed over the alarms. "I have a gun!"

Rose froze immediately. She turned in the direction of the woman's voice. Standing just outside of a wooden door in the corner—which Rose now realized was probably an office—a middle-aged woman stood, her eyes wide and grey.

Rose glanced at the ceiling, squinting through the water that pelted her face, and sighed as she saw the black lens, "Cameras. Of course."

The woman moved toward her, slowly, as if she were afraid of *Rose*—which, to Rose, seemed totally absurd, since the woman had just announced she had a gun.

Rose hesitantly wiped the water from her face, as she tried to see the woman. From what she could see, a messy bun held the woman's grey hair out of her eyes, and the woman wore normal clothing—a loose, flowery shirt with khakis.

Rose figured the woman was probably the owner or manager.

The woman found a phone on the wall and pulled it to her ear. "Now don't you move, lady! I'm calling the police, but I *will* get my gun if I need it."

"I think you're overreacting," Rose muttered. "It was just a fire alarm."

"What?" the woman said, unable to hear over the alarms.

Before the woman could press the buttons on the phone, the doors swung open, crashing against the wall, and Rose felt something fly past her. She didn't see anything. She just felt the swoosh of air.

The woman gasped, and Rose turned to find Kallias standing in front of the woman, holding her wrists.

"Drop the phone. Now," he demanded.

The woman dropped the phone immediately.

He jerked the woman closer to him. "Look at me. Look at me!"

The woman looked at him, trembling in fear. "Please," she cried.

"Kallias, you're frightening her!" Rose yelled. She moved closer to them, squinting as she tried to see Kallias through the downpour of water that obscured her vision.

She froze, as she noticed the blood pouring from his ears.

"Relax," Kallias told the woman. It was impossible for Rose to hear him over the alarms. With what little strength he had left, he took control of the woman's mind. "Everything's all right. No one will hurt you."

The woman instantly relaxed. "Okay," she said emotionlessly.

Rose watched in shock, stunned that the woman had calmed so easily.

"Cut off the alarms, Rose," Kallias demanded.

She stared at him worriedly. "Are you okay?"

"Rose. Alarms. Now," he said, still not looking at her.

"Okay, okay," she said. She ran over to the alarm box, hoping that it'd be as simple as flipping the lever. Luckily, it wasn't a complicated alarm system. The alarms and sprinklers ceased immediately when she flipped the lever.

Rose wiped her hand across her face, wiping the water from her eyes, relieved that she could finally hear and see. As she returned to the corner of the kitchen, she realized that Kallias looked even worse than she thought. His skin seemed pale, and a long, dark stream of blood poured steadily from his ears.

Kallias fought to stay in control of the woman's mind, despite his injured state. "You won't remember seeing us," he told her. "You'll only remember worrying that there was problem with the wiring. You evacuated the restaurant out of fear that a fire might start, but everything's fine now. There's no need for police or firefighters. You just wanted to be sure. You were doing what was best for your customers."

The woman's grey eyes were blank, as if every ounce of her personality had been hidden away for a moment. "Yes," she said impassively.

"Good," Kallias said. "Now, go, and don't return until tomorrow. Once you leave, you won't remember any of this. Okay?"

"Okay," the woman said.

He released the woman's wrists so she could run. As soon as the woman was gone, he fell back against the counter, nearly collapsing. His eyes fluttered closed, and his breath came in shallow pants.

Rose moved closer to him. "Kallias, what's wrong? Why are your ears bleeding?" she asked worriedly. Her eyes widened, as she watched blood —thin as water—pour from his nose as well. "And your nose, too? What's happening to you? Are you hurt?"

Kallias opened his eyes and wiped the back of his hand across his face. He scowled at the blood that coated his skin. He looked up, fighting his overwhelming hunger. "It's always a bad idea to use psychic abilities when you're injured, but I didn't have a choice."

Rose stepped closer, and she reached out instinctively. But before she could touch his bleeding face, his hand closed around her wrist.

Rose gasped at how tightly he held her wrist and opened her mouth to say something about it. But she froze, when she saw the ravenous look in his eyes.

Kallias stared at the cuts in her palm, his fangs bared like an animal.

"Kallias?"

He looked at her then, and his eyes widened. He dropped her hand and turned away, panting heavily as he tried to regain control of his hunger. He growled at her, "Are you insane?"

Rose pulled her hand back to herself and glared at him. "Me? I'm not the one who was just staring at someone's hand like it was my next meal."

Kallias looked at her again, and his eyes darkened hungrily. "*Skata. Get away, you hazo koritsi,*" he snarled, blending English and Greek together as if they were one language, instead of two. "Do you *want* me to lose control?"

Her eyes narrowed at the Greek words that she knew meant *stupid girl.* "Okay, I am *not* stupid," she said, really only concerned with that part.

He stepped toward her, rising to his full height. "You're bleeding, and I'm injured. Do you have any idea how close I was to biting you just now?"

"Injured," Rose said worriedly. "How did you get injured?"

Kallias eyed her pointedly. "Next time you decide to set off some loud-ass alarms, give me a warning first."

She froze, as she realized why he was bleeding. "Oh, no, I didn't know it'd do that. Kallias, I am so sorry! It was a stupid idea."

"Stupid?" he scoffed. He laughed. "It wasn't stupid, Rose. It was brilliant. You saved a whole restaurant full of people."

She gaped at the compliment, but he seemed to be too distracted by the blood to notice. He probably didn't even realize what he'd said. "It worked?"

Kallias nodded. "Everyone left, except for the vampires," he said. He studied her, his lips curving. "How did you get the cook to leave the kitchen?"

"I told him his sister was being manhandled by some creeps," she said.

To her surprise, he threw his head back and laughed. "Brilliant."

She smiled shyly and shrugged one shoulder. "Nah. Overprotective older brothers just happen to be a breed of human I have experience with."

He snorted at that. Then, he straightened and glanced at the doors, as if he'd heard something. "Rose, I need you to do something else for me."

She nodded. "Okay. What do you need?"

"I need you to turn off the cameras," he answered. "The last thing we want is for humans to have documented footage of what I'm about to do."

She grimaced. "You realize there's a difference between a computer nerd and a book nerd, right? I'm the latter. I don't know *everything*."

"Oh, really? I could've sworn you thought you did," Kallias teased.

"Oh, you're so funny," Rose said sarcastically.

His smile faded, and he suddenly looked serious. "Look, I just need you to try. Those vampires are recovering as we speak. One or both of them will be in here within a minute or two. I'll take care of *them*, but I need you to take care of the cameras. You have cameras at your café, right?"

"Yeah, but that doesn't mean I know how to run *these* cameras," she said.

Kallias spun toward the doors again, and his entire body stiffened. It was as if every muscle and nerve in his body was suddenly alert and prepared for danger. In less than a second, he had his hand wrapped around her arm and was dragging her toward the office, away from the doors. "Just try. Please."

Rose scowled at his hand—but allowed him to pull her toward the office, anyway. "Even if I did know how to operate the cameras, I'd need a key to the office and the password to her computer. I have neither."

He stopped and jerked the office door open, the lock breaking with a loud *click*. "No key needed. Try Thomas for the password. It's her son's name."

She threw up her hands in defeat. "Fine. I'll try."

"Thank you," he said. "Don't leave that room until I say."

She gave him a sarcastic salute. "Yes, *sir*. Any other orders for me, *sir*?"

Kallias rolled his eyes at her sarcasm. "Yeah. Shut up."

13

TEARING HEARTS OUT, LITERALLY

"*W*ell, it's not Thomas," Rose sighed. She leaned back in the office chair and stared thoughtfully at the computer screen. She glanced around the office, looking for any hints of a possible password.

The office was uncomfortably small—not small enough to trigger Rose's panic, but small enough that the wall brushed against her back any time she leaned back in the chair.

A long, wooden desk set against the wall, in front of her, cluttered with paper and pens. The computer—an old desktop—set in the far corner of the desk, and a bulky, old cash register set next to it. On the other side of the computer, a calendar hung on the wall.

Rose froze as she noticed the calendar. She tilted her head thoughtfully, as she realized it was the wrong month, and when she saw one of the dates circled in blue ink, she smiled.

Inside the circle, someone had scribbled, "Thomas's birthday."

It was worth a try.

Rose leaned forward and typed the birthdate into the password box. The screen went dark, and then, after a moment, the desktop screen appeared.

"I did it!" she announced. She glanced around and, remembering that no one was in the room to share her giddy excitement, she turned back toward the computer and muttered under her breath, "Stop talking to yourself, Rose."

THE STEEL DOORS SWUNG OPEN, AND KALLIAS FOUND HIMSELF FACE-TO-FACE with one of the intoxicated vampires—except he seemed a little more aware now. The agony of the alarms had no doubt sobered him.

Blood stained the vampire's skin—a line of blood beneath his ears, along each side of his neck, down to the collar of his shirt.

"Who the hell are you?" the vampire said with a heavy, Southern drawl. "And why'd you do that?"

Kallias straightened, careful not to let the vampire see any signs of his weakened state. Using his telepathic abilities while he was injured had been a mistake. It had severely weakened him. His head pounded, and every muscle in his body felt fatigued.

"You don't need to know who I am," Kallias said.

The vampire narrowed his eyes. "Listen here, asshole," he snarled. "Those alarms hurt like hell. I'm not in the best mood right now."

Kallias forced a smile. "Neither am I."

"And," the vampire added, hooking a thumb back toward the dining room, "you also ran off our food."

"Good," Kallias said, and the vampire glared harder. He took a slow step forward. "What were you thinking anyway? This is a public place. If you'd killed that many humans and got caught on camera doing it? Those alarms would be the *least* of your worries."

The vampire scoffed at that. "Says who? You?" He laughed. "Who died and made you king? You don't get to tell me who I can and can't eat."

"Was that what you were planning to tell Aaron?" Kallias asked.

The vampire frowned. "Who the hell's Aaron?"

Kallias sighed. There were an awful lot of vampires being made lately without being taught the basics. "You must be a baby then."

"Baby?" the vampire said. He had such a deep accent that the word sounded like it had three syllables. "I ain't no baby."

"You haven't been a vampire long, have you?" Kallias said. When the vampire tilted his head a little at that, he said, "Then, you're a baby."

"Well, how long have *you* been a vampire?" the younger vampire complained.

"Quite some time," Kallias told him. "Definitely long enough to know who Aaron is."

"You talk like he's the boogeyman or something," the vampire scoffed.

"He's worse," Kallias said. "Look, the vampire who turned you should've told you this. You *don't* want to get on Aaron's radar. He's not going to sit down and have a talk with you about responsible feeding. He'll just send that pet assassin of his to kill you."

The vampire frowned, but he seemed to be listening, at least. "Who's he going to send? You?"

"What? No. I would *never* work for Aaron," Kallias said, his lip curling in disgust. "No, his assassin is Kara Unnarsdóttir."

The vampire shook his head, clearly unfamiliar with that name. "Well, seeing as he and his assassin ain't here, I don't see any reason to be afraid."

Kallias sighed. He'd thought he'd gotten through to the guy. "Except I'm also an ancient vampire, and while Aaron and I don't see eye-to-eye on many things, we do happen to agree on this issue."

The vampire frowned worriedly. "How ancient?"

"Twenty-five hundred years old," Kallias said.

"Well," the vampire said, his eyes wide, "all of the sudden, I ain't feeling so pissed off."

Kallias snorted, "Good choice."

The vampire nodded. He turned to leave, his hand on the steel door already, but then, he sniffed curiously. He turned toward Kallias. "There's still a human here."

Kallias took a step to the side, placing himself between the vampire and the office door. "You will *not* touch her."

"Oh," he said, nodding, "is she yours?"

"Yes," Kallias lied.

To his relief, the vampire relaxed. "You're lucky. She smells delicious."

Kallias lifted his eyebrows at that. "Yeah, she does."

The younger vampire nodded. "Yeah, Brent explained that part to me —about blood bonds and respecting other vampires' property and all that."

"She's no one's property," Kallias said—without thinking.

The vampire's brows furrowed. "What?"

Kallias sighed, "Nothing. Just...go. Now."

"Yeah," the vampire said. He turned and pushed open the steel doors to head back toward the dining room, but before he could leave, the shorter vampire appeared in the doorway.

"Where do you think you're going?" he said to the younger one.

"It's fine, Brent. I talked to the guy," the younger vampire said, waving an arm toward Kallias. "Turns out he was just helping us out."

The one called Brent glared at the younger vampire. "What?" he said. "Chris, I told you to kill him, not talk to him."

The younger vampire shook his head. "No, no, look," he said, leaning toward the older vampire. "There's this vampire Baron or something and an assassin called Laura—"

Kallias frowned. "*Aaron* and *Kara*."

"Aaron isn't an issue," Brent interrupted.

Chris leaned back on his heels, and his brows furrowed. "You knew about him and didn't tell me?"

Brent gave a disgusted scoff, "Oh, don't be so sensitive." He shot an annoyed look Kallias's way. "We don't have to worry about that kind of shit anymore. We're with Theron now."

"Shit," Kallias mumbled.

Chris shook his head, his shaggy hair shaking with the movement. "Well, even if the Baron's not an issue..."

"Aaron," Kallias said under his breath.

"That guy's ancient, too," Chris said, pointing at Kallias.

"He also ran off our food," Brent said. "He needs to pay." He turned to Kallias. "There's a human in here somewhere. We'll take her as payment."

"No, no," Chris said. "She's his. We can't have her."

Brent rolled his eyes. "Damn it, Chris, why are you so stupid? Do you smell a blood bond? No, because there isn't one. She's not his."

Chris looked at Kallias, and the young vampire actually looked *betrayed*. "You lied to me?"

Kallias shrugged. "Sorry," he said insincerely.

"Give her to us, and all's forgiven," Brent offered.

Kallias scoffed at that, "I don't need your forgiveness, and your friend was right. I am ancient. You don't want to fight me."

"Come on," Chris said to his friend. "Let's just go. We'll find another human."

"Why does she smell like dried blood?" Brent said suspiciously.

"What does that matter?" Chris complained. "It ain't fun any more. Let's just go."

Brent glared at him. "Think about it, Chris. He's protecting a human that isn't bound to him. Sound familiar? She smells like dried blood. She's obviously been injured at some point. And she smells powerful. Ringing any bells yet?"

Chris shook his head. "No."

Brent rolled his eyes. "The call we got earlier! These are the ones Theron wants us to keep any eye out for!"

Chris glanced at Kallias, his eyes wide. "Oh."

"Great," Kallias said with an annoyed sigh. He pulled out his dagger. "Let's get this over with."

"DONE!"

Rose shut down the computer, eager to tell Kallias the good news— that not only had she turned off the cameras, but she'd erased all of the footage of Kallias and her for the entire night.

"You really *do* smell incredible."

Rose spun the office chair. She swallowed nervously, as she found the shorter, black-haired vampire in the doorway, watching her with dark, hungry eyes.

The vampire took a step toward her, his head cocked to the side. "They said your blood would smell powerful, but that didn't prepare me for this. What *are* you? Humans don't smell the way you do."

"Don't come any closer," Rose warned.

He laughed darkly, as if he didn't find her the least bit intimidating. "Or what?" he sneered. "Your boyfriend isn't here to save you."

She sighed at that. "He's *not* my boyfriend."

"Listen, Rose. That's your name, right? *Rose?*" he said, taking another step toward her. "I'll make a deal with you. Come willingly, and I won't make it any more painful than it has to be. Otherwise, well...I think you understand."

"To make a deal with me, you'd have to have some power over the situation," Rose said, "but you don't. Theron's going to hurt me regardless of what *you* promise. So, no, I'm not stupid enough to come willingly."

A sadistic smile pulled at the vampire's lips. "The negotiable part isn't how much *Theron* will hurt you. It's how much I will."

"A deal would also require me to trust you, and I don't," Rose said.

He scoffed in disbelief. "Then, I suppose I *will* make this painful."

She leaned forward. "I told you not to come any closer."

"Or what?" the vampire taunted. He took another step. Only a few feet separated them now. "What will you do? *Talk* me to death?"

Rose shoved her hand under the desk and snatched the gun from the clip beneath it. She turned so quickly that the chair rolled backward and hit the wall. She aimed the gun at him and clicked off the safety. "That, or I'll could just shoot."

The vampire froze, apparently so surprised by the gun that he could only stand there, glancing back and forth between her and the desk. Finally, he seemed to recover, and he smiled. "Bullets don't kill our kind, human. I guess your boyfriend forgot to tell you—"

"Oh my word. He's not my boyfriend!" Rose said, and then, before he could respond, she pulled the trigger.

The gunshot echoed so loudly in the small room that even Rose winced at the noise. For a moment, she just stared in shock, as blood poured from the vampire's shoulder, darkening the navy blue fabric of his shirt—until it turned black.

It wasn't exactly where she'd meant to hit him, but…if it wasn't going to kill him anyway, it was as good a place as any.

"You shot me!" the vampire screeched.

Rose nodded.

His eyes narrowed murderously. "You'll regret that, you psychotic bitch!"

She rolled her eyes. "Of course. You almost murdered an entire restaurant full of people, but *I'm* the psychotic one."

He moved so rapidly that his movement blurred. He was standing directly in front of her before she even realized he'd moved.

He wrenched the gun out of her hand and tossed it aside. Then, he jerked her up by her arm, her body slamming into him.

Rose cried out, as he nearly crushed her arm in his hand. "Let go."

"You're lucky Theron wants you alive because if he didn't," the vampire snarled in her face, "I'd snap your neck right now."

She turned her face away. His breath smelled strongly of metal.

No.

Blood.

She glanced toward the table, wishing she could reach a pen, a heavy stapler, *anything…*

Heck, she'd try to hit him with a computer monitor, if she could reach it.

The vampire had gone quiet, and Rose glanced at him, as she suddenly felt his face against her wrist. He inhaled deeply, and her frown deepened.

"What *are* you?" the vampire breathed. "You're irresistible."

"Why do people keep saying that?" Rose mumbled. "*'What am I.'*"

The vampire shook his head, as if he were trying to talk himself out of something. "I can't resist it. They didn't warn me! I can't."

When the vampire opened his mouth and grazed his fangs against her wrist, Rose groaned in frustration. "Haven't I been bitten enough this week?"

"I won't take too much," the vampire whispered—not to her, but to himself. "They'll never know."

Rose fought against him, but he was so much stronger than her. She winced as his fangs tore into her wrist, and she pulled away from him as hard as she could, blindly grasping at the table.

The vampire groaned at the taste of her blood and began to feed relentlessly.

Rose's fingertip brushed a pen, and she snatched it up. As her head began to spin from the endorphins, she twisted and jabbed the sharper end of pen into the side of his head.

He released her with a growl and jerked the pen out of his head.

Blood streamed down his face, matting his inky, black hair, and he tried to grab her again.

But before he could wrap his hands around her, he froze.

The emotion seemed to vanish from his eyes, and then, his body fell to the floor.

Rose scrambled out of his way, as he collapsed face-first onto the floor. Her eyes widened, when she saw the gaping hole in his back and the blackish-burgundy blood that bubbled up out of it.

Blinking slowly, she looked up, and her mouth fell open.

Kallias stood in front of her. Blood sprinkled his skin and left wet patches of blood on his dark clothing. A thick layer of blood coated one arm—from his fingers to his elbow—and in that hand, he held a fleshy object, coated in dark blood, which dripped steadily into the floor.

"Kallias," Rose said, eyeing the fleshy object warily, "there's a heart in your hand. *Literally*. A heart. In your hand."

Kallias looked at it and then back at her. "Yes."

Rose nodded. "Just making sure you knew."

His eyes darkened with hunger. "Your wrist is bleeding."

"Oh," she said, and then, she glanced down at her own wrist. Thin, watery blood streamed from her wrist and pooled in the floor.

Kallias dropped the heart on the floor and wiped his blood-soaked hands on his jeans, which...didn't help much.

He stepped closer to her. His breath came quicker, as he took her wrist into his hand. He turned her hand palm-up, his eyes darkening with hunger, as he watched the blood ooze from the cuts in her wrist.

"This isn't a clean bite," Kallias said breathlessly. "It's not healing."

Rose stared up at him, studying the feral hunger that flashed in his eyes. She knew she should've been afraid, but she wasn't. She felt stunned, perhaps, but not afraid. "Do I need to go to the hospital?"

"We don't have time," Kallias said. "I'll have to heal the wound."

Before Rose could object, Kallias lifted her wrist to his mouth. She inhaled sharply, as his tongue slid over the torn, sensitive skin. Those strange, pleasant sensations coursed through her body again—just as they had the last time he'd healed her.

She bit down on her bottom lip, fighting the urge to moan.

Kallias groaned. Even the blood already drying to her skin tasted sweeter and more powerful than anything he'd ever tasted before.

The wound on her wrist began to heal, but the hunger twisted harder in his stomach and burned hotter in this throat.

He *needed* her blood.

Rose frowned when his fangs pressed into her wrist. "Kallias?"

His eyes snapped open, and he looked at her, her wrist still against his mouth. Realization lightened his brown eyes, and he suddenly dropped her hand and stepped back. He panted, gasping for breath.

She watched him warily. "Are you okay?"

Kallias wiped the blood from his mouth with the back of his hand. "Yeah."

Rose wasn't sure he was telling the truth. He looked as if he were experiencing the worst agony she'd ever seen.

She glanced down at her wrist, stunned to see that the wound had completely disappeared.

"We need to hurry," Kallias announced.

Rose looked up at him. Despite his calmer demeanor, she could see the barely restrained hunger in his eyes. "What about the other vampire?"

"I killed him first," he said. He tilted his head toward the heartless —*literally* heartless—one. "That's what I was doing when he slipped past me."

"Right," Rose said.

He reached behind him and pulled a white cloth from his back pocket. Then, he stepped forward and knelt to grab the small, black handgun from the floor. "Where did you find the gun?"

"Underneath the desk," she said.

Kallias ran the cloth along the gun—cleaning off her fingerprints, she assumed. "How did you know it'd be there?"

"I guessed," Rose said with a shrug. When he gave her a quizzical look, she explained, "When my brother, Zach, was a kid, he nearly got shot—because he was with some older guys who robbed a convenient store. The owner of the store kept a gun clipped to the bottom of the counter, underneath the cash register. That way, if he were robbed, he could just reach under and grab the gun as he opened the cash register." She pointed at the cash register on the desk. "That's the master cash register. The woman said she had a gun. So, I just guessed and hoped for the best."

"Good guess," he muttered. Holding the gun with the cloth, Kallias knelt and returned the gun to its clip. "Stay in here, all right? I need to clean up this mess."

Rose blinked. "Mess?" she repeated, as he left. "These are body parts, not a ketchup spill. What are you going to do? Sweep up the dead vampires?"

When no answer came, Rose walked into the kitchen. She frowned, as she watched Kallias drag in a garbage can from outside.

"Oh, even better," Rose said. "You're throwing them in the trash."

He didn't respond to that either.

She watched in silence, as he gathered up the dead vampire from the floor, as if he were just picking up trash. The severed head of the second vampire lay in the kitchen floor, just a few feet from her shoes, along a blood-stained ball cap.

Rose shifted her feet away from it, and Kallias crossed the distance between them, picked up the head at her feet, and carried it back to the garbage can.

"You don't think anyone will notice a corpse in trash?" Rose said. She lifted her shoulders in disbelief. "Here I go, throwing out a normal bag of restaurant trash, and oh, look! It's a severed head! I'm sure *that's* normal."

He didn't laugh, but his lips twitched.

Rose counted that as a success.

He walked past her. "I told you to stay in the office."

Rose followed him into the office and then stepped out of the way, as he dragged out the heartless dude. "And I told *you* I don't follow orders," she reminded him.

He returned to the kitchen with the body, and she followed him. He tossed the body into the garbage and turned back toward her, finally meeting her gaze. His black T-shirt looked wet with blood, and there were a few partially-healed cuts on his forearms and neck.

"You called me good," he said bitterly.

"Uh," she stammered. "Well, yes. I have. Once or twice."

"Look around you," he said, spreading out his arms. "This is what I am, what I do. I kill. I'm *designed* to kill. What is *good* about that?"

Rose fixed her gaze on the blood-stained, tile floor and sighed. It was clear he hated these things about himself, and she wasn't totally sure how to help. It wouldn't stop her from trying, though.

He approached her, and she glanced up at him.

"Don't you get it?" Kallias asked. He gestured toward the blood-covered room behind him. "*This?* Killing? Violence? It comes naturally to me." Then, he cupped her face with his hand and said, his voice softer now, "But *this?* Gentleness? It doesn't."

Rose covered his hand with hers. "And yet, your touch is gentle, anyway."

His brows furrowed. "That's not the point."

"It is, though," Rose told him. "It's the *whole* point. It's the important part!" She stepped closer. "Your nature doesn't determine who you are. It's natural for everyone to hurt people. Even humans. But that doesn't mean we can't *choose* to be better," she explained. "The violence and killing may come naturally to vampires, but the way you're touching me right now? You *chose* to do that, and that's what matters. Nature doesn't decide whether you're good or evil. You do."

Kallias sighed, "Why are you so determined to find good in me?"

"Why are you so determined *not* to?" she countered.

He blinked at that, suddenly at a loss for words. "Believe what you want," he said, dropping his hand. "Just remember... I warned you."

Rose frowned and opened her mouth to argue, but she froze, when he suddenly leaned into her. He slid his hand into the pocket of the leather jacket she wore, and she looked down, blinking, as his hand brushed her hip. "What are you—"

He pulled out the bottle of light fluid and held it up her to see. A small smile twitched at one corner of his lips, but he turned away before Rose could really appreciate it.

She watched in stunned confusion, as he returned to the garbage can and poured lighter fluid into it.

"You're going to burn them?" she sputtered.

At her horrified tone, Kallias turned to scowl at her. "First, you're sympathizing with me. Now, you're sympathizing with the corpses? This is getting out of hand, Rose."

She sighed, "I wasn't—"

"They're dead," he reminded her. "They can't feel anything."

"I know that," Rose muttered. She crossed her arms. "What I don't know," she added, "is whether you've thought this through—because burning doesn't fully dispose of the human body. If you burn them, there will still be remains left."

"They're not human bodies, Rose," Kallias reminded her.

"But vampire bodies are human-*like*, aren't they?" she pointed out.

"Oh, sure," he said sarcastically. "Because human bodies can also run faster than the eye can see and break even the strongest metal."

Rose held out a hand, as if he'd just confirmed her point. "So, what you're saying is," she said, "vampire bodies are stronger than human bodies and should be able to survive *more*."

Kallias sighed at that. "In most ways, yes," he admitted, "but vampires do have one major weakness that humans don't."

Rose nodded. "The sun."

"And what is the sun?" Kallias prompted.

She frowned. "It's a yellow dwarf star, made of burning gases, such as—"

"Short version, Rose," he interrupted.

Her frown deepened. "That *was* the short version."

"It's fire, correct?" Kallias asked impatiently.

"Oh. You were looking for the preschool answer," Rose said, flashing a sassy smile. "Why didn't you just say so?"

He ignored that remark. "Our bodies are weak to fire."

"Why?" Rose asked curiously. "What's the science behind it?"

Kallias gave her an exasperated look. "I don't know. I doubt anyone knows," he scoffed. "But if you're that curious, you can talk to Geoff. I'm sure he has some theories."

"Who's Geoff?" she asked.

"Geoffrey Cossington," he said. "He's another friend of mine. You'll meet him soon. I'll need his and Emma's help in protecting you." Kallias closed the bottle of lighter fluid. "He was a scientist when he was human. He still meddles around with it when he gets bored."

"How many vampire friends do you have?" Rose asked worriedly.

"Just three," he assured her. "Erik, Geoff, and Emma."

Rose nodded. "And none of them are going to eat me?"

He didn't answer.

Before he could set fire to the corpses, Rose said, "You can't burn them in here, genius." She waved at the sprinklers above them. "Fire alarms, remember?"

Kallias looked up at them and blinked. "Oh."

When he glanced back at her, he found her by the supply closet, dragging out an old mop and a blue bucket. "What are you doing?"

"Well, I figured I'd mop up the blood while you're burning the dead out there," Rose muttered. When he gave her a confused look, she lifted her shoulders and said, "To save time? Right?"

"That's the opposite of saving time," Kallias told her.

She leaned against the mop and gave him a peeved look. "Are you implying that I'm slow?"

"Compared to me, yes," Kallias said.

She narrowed those bright blue eyes of hers. "Well, we can't all be vampires, can we?"

"Go to the dining room, and leave this to me," Kallias told her. "You'll just get in my way."

Rose glared at him and dropped the mop. "Fine. See if *I* offer to help again."

He just laughed.

ROSE SAT, CROSS-LEGGED, ON ONE OF THE DINING ROOM TABLES, READING A travel pamphlet she'd found near the hostess stand. It listed all sorts of semi-interesting facts about the state of Georgia.

She frowned as she noticed that the writer of the pamphlet had gotten some of the historical facts wrong. So, she grabbed a pen from the hostess stand and started making corrections to the pamphlet.

"What are you doing?" Kallias asked curiously.

Rose didn't even look up at him. She just continued crossing out entire sentences. "I'm fixing the mistakes in this pamphlet."

His eyebrows lifted. "You're correcting someone else's pamphlet?"

"I have a duty to prevent ignorance," she said defensively.

He snorted, "And to be anal retentive, apparently."

Rose scowled at him. "Did you decide you wanted my help, after all?"

"No," Kallias said.

"Because I'm more than willing to help," Rose added, "but I'll need you to admit you were wrong first."

He laughed loudly at that. "Rose, I'm finished."

Rose's smile faded. "With the dead-vampire-burning?"

"No," Kallias said, "I'm finished with it all."

She blinked in shock. "It's been two minutes!"

He grinned. "I told you. I'm much, *much* faster than you."

Rose pursed her lips. "There's no way," she muttered. She hopped off of the table and rushed past him to check. She raised herself onto her toes and peered through the small, square window in the door.

Her jaw dropped, as she saw the spotless—and bloodless—kitchen.

"Are you satisfied?" Kallias said impatiently. "Can we go now?"

Rose turned to look at him, and she spread out her hands in disbelief, as she noticed that he'd even cleaned the blood off of himself. "How?"

Kallias grabbed his partially eaten steak and stuck it in his mouth, holding it between his teeth like a dog. He pulled money from his wallet and tossed it on the table.

Oh, good. They *still* weren't stealing.

"I may be wrong," Rose said, as she followed him, "but I think most people use a fork and a knife to eat steak."

The edges of his lips quirked up. "Most people don't have fangs."

"Touché," she admitted.

As the two of them left the restaurant, the rush of cool air outside soothed Rose. It was as if the wind were cleansing the fear and shock from her mind, allowing her to think clearly.

She tilted her head back and closed her eyes, relishing the peacefulness of the night.

"Are you trying to walk into something?" Kallias asked grumpily.

She opened her eyes. "There's nothing in front of me," she said, gesturing toward the empty parking lot. "I'm just enjoying the night while I can."

"You're a human," Kallias muttered. "You're not supposed to enjoy the night."

"Oh, I'm sorry," Rose sassed. "I forgot you owned the night."

He pursed his lips at her sarcasm. "Humans are instinctually afraid of the dark. They teach themselves to overcome that fear, but in the most basic part of their minds, they know it's dangerous at night," he said, "because it's when the monsters come out."

Rose scoffed at that. She stared up at the twinkling stars in the black sky and thought about how she'd always loved the night. He was wrong. "Monsters come out during the day, too," she muttered. "Trust me."

Kallias glanced at her, struck by the thinly veiled pain in her voice. "Rose," he said, his brows creasing, "tell me who hurt you."

She looked at him, blinking. She'd been too lost in thought to even realize what she'd said. "It was nothing," she lied. She quickly changed the subject. "You know, now that I think about it, I probably should've kept that gun. With as often as we get attacked, it'd help if I had some kind of weapon."

"No," he said, scowling. "No guns for you."

Rose lifted her eyebrows. "Oh? And why not, Sir Bossy Pants?"

He frowned. "Am I a knight now?"

"A bossy one," Rose muttered.

Kallias rolled his eyes. "Because you'd end up accidentally shooting me," he said, "or yourself."

"What?" she said. "I thought I did pretty well with that gun."

His eyebrows lifted. "Oh, so you were *aiming* for the shoulder, then?"

She narrowed her eyes at that. "Maybe."

Kallias sighed, "Rose, had you ever even used a gun before tonight?"

"Of course!" Rose said.

Kallias eyed her skeptically. "Oh, really? What kind?"

"Many kinds," Rose said. "Nerf guns, paint guns, water guns…"

Kallias laughed, "Of course." He stopped and turned to face her. "But you're right. You *should* have a weapon. So, I'll let you use this one."

Rose stared at the short, steel blade. "You're giving me your dagger?"

"No," he said, his eyes flashing at the mere suggestion. "I'm *loaning* you my dagger. I don't give away my weapons. I expect this back!"

"Yeah, yeah," Rose muttered. "So, you're *loaning* me your dagger?"

He cracked a smile at her sassy tone. "If it makes you feel safer, yes."

A surprised smile spread across Rose's face. "Thanks," she said, and she wrapped her fingers around the handle of the dagger. But then, she bit her lip thoughtfully and asked, "So, uhh, where exactly am I supposed to put it?"

Kallias laughed. He knelt in front of her and rolled up his own jeans. Rose watched as he unsnapped a small, black strap from his ankle, and her frown deepened when he moved to kneel in front of her.

"Umm, what— Kallias?" she sputtered, when he began to roll the left leg of her jeans up to her knee. "What are you doing?"

He chuckled and then leaned forward to wrap the belt-like strap around her ankle.

Rose glanced around the empty parking lot, feeling incredibly awkward, all of the sudden.

Even on his knees, Kallias was so tall that his head was level with her stomach, but that still left her having to look down in order to see him.

His hands felt rough against the smooth, sensitive skin of her ankles.

"I'm suddenly glad I shaved last night," Rose said under her breath. "This would be even *more* awkward, if I hadn't."

Kallias snorted at her weird remarks, and he pulled the belt tight around her ankle. He looked up at her and held out his hand. "Dagger?"

Rose carefully placed the sharp weapon in his hand, and he slid the dagger into a black sheath, before attaching it to the strap on her ankle.

"Is this illegal?" she asked.

"Probably," Kallias said. He grinned wickedly and suggested, "If someone sees us, just start moaning."

Rose's eyes widened. "Excuse me?"

"Then, they'd think I was doing something else to you," he teased.

She stared blankly at him for a moment. Slowly, she glanced at the crotch of her pants—which he was embarrassingly close to—and then back at him.

"Of course that's probably illegal, too," he added.

"It is," she assured him.

Finally, he climbed to his feet. He snorted at her expression. "But it'd make for a more interesting story, wouldn't it?"

Rose just stared. "Kallias, this is the South," she reminded him. "We'd be *less* likely to go to jail for the illegal weapon."

He laughed at that. Then, he turned and started toward his car.

When Rose's brain finally started up again, she jogged to catch up with him. The weight of the dagger made one leg feel slightly heavier than the other.

When they reached the lone, black car in the parking lot, she looked down at her ankle. "It feels weird."

Kallias gave her an offended look. "If you're going to complain about it, just give it back."

"You have to give me time to get used to it," Rose said defensively. "Gosh, you'd think your weapons were *people* with as much as you care about them."

"That's not true," Kallias teased. "I like them much more than *people*."

Rose remembered making a similar remark earlier and laughed.

Kallias pulled the keys from his pocket and pressed the button to unlock the doors. The car beeped twice, and the headlights flashed.

He opened his door and slid into the driver's seat. "Get in," he told her, but she was already sliding into the passenger's seat when he said it. He checked the clock on the dashboard, grimaced at the time, and shoved the keys in the ignition.

"Kallias?" Rose said, once they were along inside the car.

"Yeah?" he asked.

"The vampire that attacked me mentioned Theron," she told him.

He sighed, "Yeah."

"So, even this far away, they're still hunting me?" she asked.

"Apparently," he said.

Rose's stomach turned with dread. "What does that mean?"

Kallias shifted the car into reverse, as he muttered, "Nothing good."

14

MORE LIES

"*R*ose? Rose. Rose!"

Rose squeaked in surprise, when he snatched the horror novel out of her hands. "Hey!" she complained. She spun toward the driver's seat. "You can't just go around stealing people's books!"

Kallias turned the book over, reading the summary on the back. "I called your name fourteen times. You never even heard me."

She shrugged unapologetically. "It's a good book."

Kallias glanced at her. "That's great, but we need to go."

Only then did Rose notice how dark it was inside the car. The radio and dashboard were no longer lit up. The only light inside the car, now, was the one above her seat—the one she'd been using to read.

She leaned forward, glancing out the window. Outside, she saw the empty parking lot of a hotel.

And beyond that…pink and purple streaks bordered the night sky.

"Oh," she said, suddenly understanding his urgency. "Oops."

"We still have plenty of time to take shelter," Kallias assured her. He turned the book and looked at the cover. "But only if we go now."

"Okay," Rose said, holding out her hand. When he cast a puzzled look at her outstretched hand, Rose said, "My book. I need my book."

Kallias chuckled at her impatience. "I think I'll keep it until we're inside—just to be on the safe side," he said. "We wouldn't want to lose you to another world again, now would we?"

"What?" Rose said, horrified. "You can't do that. Taking someone's book is the darkest kind of evil!"

He laughed at that. He leaned closer to her. "Aww, but baby," he said in a low, taunting tone, "I'm a vampire. Evil's just my nature."

Rose's eyes somehow managed to narrow even more. "Not funny."

She tried to snatch the book out of his hand, but he moved it to the other side before she could. Her seatbelt caught her and jerked her back, and as she struggled to unbuckle it, he climbed out of the car.

In her desperation, she chased him across the console and seat—and then out the driver's side door.

He was cackling by the time she caught him.

"I need to know what happens!" she said breathlessly.

He held it above his head, laughing hysterically as he did.

"The serial killer just captured the heroine and forced her to watch while he peeled the skin off of his previous victims. He plans to kill her next!" she gasped. "I have to know if she escaped!"

Kallias cast another puzzled look at the book's cover. "What the hell are you reading?"

"Give it back," Rose pleaded. "It's my book!"

He laughed, as she chased him all the way to the trunk. "You'll get it back when we get inside," he said, turning to face her, "unless you *want* to watch me burn to death?"

Rose sighed in defeat. "Now, that's just unfair."

Kallias just grinned. "That's a no on me burning to death, right?"

Rose scowled at his gloating tone. "I *guess*."

He chuckled, "I appreciate your sacrifice."

"You *better*," Rose said, crossing her arms. "No one comes between me and my books. I'm breaking precedent just to save you from getting barbecued."

He snorted at that. The trunk was already open, and he reached into it and grabbed a duffel bag.

Rose reached into the trunk, too, and grabbed her backpack. She slung it over her shoulder and then grabbed a few bags of her clothes. She adjusted the bags to one hand so she could carry more, but when she returned, she found the car's trunk suddenly empty.

She glanced at Kallias. He held the rest of the bags in one hand, as if they weighed nothing.

"I was going to get those," she complained.

He ignored her. "When we get inside, let me do all the talking."

Rose scoffed at that. "Seriously?"

"Yes," Kallias said. "I need you to keep your mouth shut, okay?"

Rose lifted her eyebrows in disbelief. "No. Not okay."

"But I know it's a foreign practice for you," Kallias continued, "so I'm not setting my expectations too high."

"Ha," Rose said with dangerously sharp sarcasm.

Kallias couldn't help but watch the way her bright blue eyes narrowed and the way her full, pink lips pressed together.

Even in her disheveled, unkempt state, she looked beautiful. She hadn't taken off her reading glasses yet—thin, black ones that never set straight on her face. Her cheeks were flushed, and several locks of red hair had fallen out of its ponytail, cascading around her shoulders.

She stood with most of her weight on her left foot, her soft, wide hips tilted slightly.

Kallias didn't understand why he was so attracted to this human. They were as different as night and day, and yet...

He was.

"Oh, don't worry," Rose continued, her tone as sharp as before, "I'd never *dream* of speaking for myself. Of course I'll keep my mouth shut and let a man speak for me. It's the 1950s. What else would I do?" She tilted her head. "Oh, wait. It's *not* the 1950s, is it?"

He laughed at her unending sarcasm. "It's not like that, and you know it," he said with an amused smile. "You're just the worst liar I've ever met, and right now, it's imperative that no one knows we're here." He closed the trunk. "And I—unlike you—have done this before."

"What?" Rose challenged. "Lied?"

His smile faded, suddenly. "I've hidden who I am," he said, his voice quieter than before. He spun around and started walking toward the glass doors of the hotel. "Just keep your mouth shut, all right?"

The drastic change in his countenance stunned her for a moment, but when she'd blinked out of her shock, she followed him, jogging to keep up with his long strides.

When he stopped to open the doors of the hotel, Rose reached ahead and opened them for him.

He didn't even look at her.

Was he upset because she'd mentioned him lying?

Well, he *was* lying about something.

She knew it, and she didn't intend to let it go, either.

Kallias turned when they were in the brightly lit lobby and added, "We also need to give the impression that we're a happy couple, and every time you open your mouth, you make it undeniably clear that we're not."

"Ew," Rose said with a grimace. "Why would anyone want to look like a happy couple?"

That remark *did* earn a small smile from him. "We're checking into a hotel room together," he said quietly. "That's typically something that happy couples do."

"And people on study trips!" Rose said, as she followed him through the lobby. "Though it *would* be hard to convince someone we're on a study trip when the only thing around to study is the Interstate."

Kallias passed a set of maroon sofas and a television on his way to the hotel lobby's desk. The meteorologist on the television screen spoke of a thunderstorm that would arrive the next day, and his voice carried across the empty lobby.

Kallias and Rose stopped at a counter, where a middle-aged hotel clerk stood, typing on his desktop computer.

The hotel worker's brown eyes shifted toward them, and he offered a polite smile. He stepped away from the computer and clasped his hands together. "Such a lovely couple!" he chimed, earning another grimace from Rose. "Can I get you two a room for the night?"

Kallias set the bags down at his feet and leaned casually onto the counter. "Yes. Make it two nights," he said. "We won't be able to check out until late tomorrow evening."

"Of course," the man replied cheerfully, and he began to type.

"Also, we'll be sleeping during the day, so I need you to make a note that we don't want to be disturbed," Kallias added, "at all. Regardless of the reason."

The worker nodded. "Let's see. We have a honeymoon suite available for the next two nights. It's on special pricing all month." He looked up, flashing his brightest customer service smile. "Only a few dollars more than a regular room, but much larger and more private! It comes pre-stocked with beverages! Wine, beer, and liquor, I believe."

Kallias tapped his foot impatiently. "Sure. Whatever."

Rose scowled at Kallias. "Honeymoon suite?"

"Shut up," he mouthed back.

Rose rolled her eyes—and then froze, as she noticed the hotel clerk was watching them curiously. She flashed a fake smile. "Sorry. I guess I forgot my place."

Kallias glared at her, but the hotel clerk just chuckled.

"Okay. Almost finished. So, this room is for Mr. and Mrs. —?" The hotel clerk stopped typing and looked up at them.

Rose's eyes widened. "Oh, we're not…"

She never finished the sentence, however, because Kallias clasped his hand over her mouth before she could.

The hotel clerk suppressed a laugh, apparently amused.

"Uh," Kallias stammered, "Smith?"

Rose bit his palm to make him remove his hand, but Kallias just glanced at her and smirked, as if it hadn't bothered him at all.

When he finally dropped his hand, Rose hissed at him, "Smith? *So* creative."

Kallias shot another glare at her. "Will you, *please*, shut up?"

"Since you *asked* this time," Rose told him, "I'll think about it."

He just sighed.

"Roses," the hotel clerk said, suddenly.

Both Kallias and Rose turned to stare at him.

"What?" Kallias asked.

He smiled, still typing on the computer. "Give her a dozen roses," he told Kallias. "Trust me. I've been married for fifteen years. Roses *always* work. Give her some roses."

"Oh," Kallias said, relieved that he was only referring to the flower.

Rose laughed. "That would *never* work on me."

The clerk looked up from his computer. "If you say so," he said with a skeptical smile. He turned to Kallias. "You're almost ready. I just need your license."

Rose frowned worriedly at that. She didn't think a vampire would *have* a license, and hers was back at her apartment, still.

But Kallias pulled the worn, leather wallet from his back pocket and flipped it open. He watched the hotel clerk with that strangely intense stare, as he leaned over and glanced at the wallet.

The clerk nodded and began typing, as if he were copying the information straight into his computer.

But that didn't make sense—because when Rose glanced at the wallet, she saw that the license and credit card sections were empty.

Assuming she'd been mistaken, she stepped forward to take a closer look. But, just as she'd suspected, the wallet contained nothing but cash. She glanced questionably at Kallias, but he didn't look at her.

"All right," the hotel clerk said. "That'll be $476.37."

Kallias was moving faster now, recklessly tugging cash out of the wallet and tossing it onto the counter. He cast a frantic look at the windows.

The hotel clerk collected the cash and filed it into the cash register. "Okay, Mr. and Mrs. Smith," he said, sliding the room keys toward them, "your room will be on the seventh floor."

"Yeah, just keep the change," Kallias grunted, when the clerk tried to count it out. He grabbed the room key and the bags and started off toward the elevator.

Rose flashed an apologetic smile at the stunned clerk and then hurried after Kallias.

As they waited for the elevator, he narrowed his eyes at her. "Is it really that hard for you to shut up?"

"Is it really that hard for you to not be a jerk?" she countered.

The elevator dinged, and the doors slid open.

Kallias stepped inside and turned, frowning when he saw Rose still standing out in the hallway. She looked paler than usual.

When the doors tried to close, he placed his hand on one side to stop them. "What are you waiting for?"

Rose swallowed uneasily. "I'll just take the stairs."

Kallias stared blankly at her. "It's seven floors, Rose. Get *in*."

Rose shook her head. She looked as if she were about to pass out. "It'll be fine. I'll meet you up there."

"The sun's rising soon," Kallias insisted. "Come on."

"I—I just," Rose stammered.

What was wrong with her?

"I hate elevators," she breathed.

He laughed. "You'll sass a vampire, but you won't ride an elevator?"

Rose didn't laugh. She couldn't. "It's different. It's...*much* different."

Kallias snorted. He leaned forward and grabbed her hand, pulling her into the elevator with him. "I'll protect you from the dangerous elevator."

Rose glanced down at their joined hands, as the doors closed. She was so stunned that Kallias was willingly holding her hand that she almost forgot about the elevator.

Until it began to move.

Her chest tightened, and she stepped back, mumbling an apology when her backside collided with Kallias's front.

She felt his gaze on the back of her neck, but she couldn't bring herself to look away from the doors—her only escape from this tiny space.

"Are you...*actually* upset?" Kallias said, surprised.

"No! I'm fine," she lied. She tried to suck in a breath, but her lungs wouldn't respond. "Say something. Anything. Distract me."

His voice was low, almost a growl, as he said, "You smell amazing."

Rose glanced back at him, blinking at the feral look in his eyes. "Umm, let me rephrase," she said. "Say anything that doesn't relate to you wanting to suck all the blood out of my body."

Kallias blinked twice, as if coming out of a daze. "Yeah. Sorry."

Rose frowned at him. "There was no I.D."

He looked at her. "What?"

"When the hotel worker asked to see your license," she said, "you pulled out your wallet, and there was no I.D."

"Yeah, I don't legally exist," he reminded her.

"No, I get that," Rose assured him. "What I *don't* get is why the worker acted like he saw a license that wasn't there."

Kallias pulled his wallet out of his back pocket and flipped it open. "He *did* see it," he said, as Rose, once again, frowned at the empty I.D. section. "You didn't see it because I didn't *make* you see it."

She glanced up at him. "What does that mean?"

"What part of telepathic control do you not understand?" he asked.

As the elevator came to a squealing stop, he slid the wallet back into his pocket. Rose practically leapt out of the elevator the moment the doors opened, and Kallias followed her with a puzzled frown.

"So, you're saying you can create illusions," Rose said, as they walked down the narrow hallway together.

Kallias shifted the bags to one hand. "Illusions happen in the mind, don't they?"

"Well, yeah," Rose muttered, "obviously." She stopped at the end of the hall and turned to face him. "It's just so crazy that you can do all of this. I mean, people don't even know."

He stopped, too. "That's kind of the point, isn't it?"

The door to their hotel room was red. Not a light, inconspicuous red either. An exaggerated red. The *reddest* red.

As Kallias rifled through his pockets for the room key, Rose leaned against a decorative table.

"But you've never done that to me," Rose said, "right?"

He checked the other pocket. "I've never done what to you?"

"Kallias," she said, her apprehension growing, "you've never tried to control *my* mind, have you?"

He frowned at her. "Tried? Yeah, of course I tried."

Rose's stomach sank. "How could you do that to me?"

He found the envelope in his pocket and pulled the room key out of it. He turned toward her, his frown deepening. "I'm a telepath, Rose," he said, as if that were explanation enough. "You've seen me use mind-control on other people. Why would you be surprised by me trying to use it on you, too?"

"You had good reasons to use it on them," she said nervously.

"And you think I didn't have a good reason to use it on you?" he asked.

Rose considered that. "When?"

Kallias slid the key in the door. He pushed the door open and turned back toward her, leaning casually in the doorway. "Do you remember the night we met? When I stopped you outside the café?"

"You mean when you attacked me," he stated.

His eyes rolled toward the ceiling, as he blew out an exasperated sigh. "I thought we covered this already," he grumbled. "I didn't hurt you, did I?"

"No," Rose said, crossing her arms, "but you did scare me."

That seemed to change his countenance. His shoulders dropped, and his dark eyes softened. "And for that, I apologize," he said quietly. "You needed to be scared, but...not of me."

Her eyebrows lifted. The last thing she'd expected was an apology.

"So," he continued, "you were a little angry with me, if you remember."

"A little?" she said with a laugh.

"You were fighting me," Kallias added. "You couldn't have understood this, at the time, but vampires are unbelievably strong. If I don't want to hurt someone, I have to be *very* careful. After twenty-five hundred years, I've practically mastered that skill, but I don't like to push it. By fighting me, you could've hurt yourself, and I didn't want that to happen."

"You could've just let me go," Rose pointed out.

"Yeah," Kallias said, "but Theron was waiting for you."

She shrugged, acknowledging that.

"So, I commanded you to be still," he added.

Rose frowned. "You did?"

"And then," he said with a small smile, "you stomped on my foot."

She blinked. "But you said you used—"

"You asked if I tried," Kallias interrupted, "not if I succeeded."

"It didn't work?" Rose realized.

He shrugged. "Apparently not."

With a curious frown, she asked, "Does that happen often?"

"Never," he said.

Her frown deepened. "Then, why did it happen with me?"

He shut down so quickly that she *saw* it when it happened—each subtle change suddenly obvious. "I don't know," he muttered. He grabbed the bags and stepped into the room.

Rose narrowed her eyes at his dismissive answer. "You're still lying," she said, as she followed him into the room. He didn't look at her, but she noticed his shoulders stiffen. "I'm not stupid. Do you think I don't notice the way you evade questions like that?"

"I'm not evading anything," Kallias lied.

"What is so bad that you can't tell me, now?" Rose asked. "I already know you're a vampire. What could be harder to tell me than that?"

He dropped the bags onto a king-sized bed in the center of the room. "Close the door," he muttered. "The sun's rising soon."

But Rose was already closing and locking it before he asked. "I want the truth," she continued, "and I think..."

She fell silent the moment she reached the main part of the room.

She'd never stayed in a hotel like this one before, and she'd foolishly assumed the rooms wouldn't be much different from those of the cheap motels she'd stayed in before.

So, as she took in the sheer size of the room—probably three times the size of her apartment—and the colorful paintings and lamps, she found herself at a loss for words.

Kallias turned, lifting an eyebrow at her uncharacteristic silence.

"Who needs a room *this* big?" she muttered.

"Well, the clerk called it a honeymoon suite," Kallias reminded her, "so I assume...newlyweds."

"Nope," Rose said, shaking her head in denial, "there's no way two people need a room this big."

"How would you know?" he asked.

"I've stayed in hotel rooms before," Rose scoffed.

He gave her a doubtful look, and Rose wasn't sure if he were suggesting she didn't have enough money or that she didn't have enough friends.

Either way, he was…kind of right.

"On study trips," Rose added, and to that, he nodded. "But it wasn't like I was there *alone*! There were four other women in my room, and that room was a quarter of the size of this one."

Kallias leaned against the counter, next to the stainless steel mini-fridge, and crossed his arms. "Yes, but I assume you and those four other women weren't having passionate sex on every surface of the room during your hotel stay," he said, casually—as if that kind of remark would fit in a casual conversation. Then, misinterpreting the look on her face, he tilted his head to the side and added, "Unless you were?"

Rose stared blankly at him. "Did you just ask me if I had an orgy with four other women?"

He snorted. "Not in so many words."

She blinked slowly. "Do I *seem* like the kind of person that gets involved in those kind of…extracurricular activities?"

He grinned. "I try not to make assumptions about people."

Rose rolled her eyes. "They were straight." She frowned, as if she were suddenly rethinking that. "I think." She shook her head. "And I am *very* focused on my studies."

His grin didn't waver.

"And socially awkward," Rose added.

He laughed.

She spread out her arms. "It was a study trip, and we studied. Revolutionary idea, I know."

"Sounds like *so* much fun," Kallias teased.

"It was, actually," Rose informed him. "I enjoy studying."

"Of course you do," he said with a laugh. He pushed away from the counter and walked toward her, closing the space between them in a few, long strides. "Speaking of fun in hotel rooms…"

Rose stepped back, squeaking in surprise when her back hit the wooden footboard of the bed. "Speaking of *what*?"

Kallias reached behind him and pulled something out of his pocket.

He held up the small, worn horror novel she'd been reading in the car and grinned. "I was just giving you back your book," he said playfully. "What did you *think* I was doing?"

Rose narrowed her eyes at that, and she snatched the novel out of his hand. "What?" she sassed, glaring at the nonexistent space between their bodies. "Are you suddenly incapable of reaching across more than an inch of space?"

"Well," he teased, "I *was* injured last night."

"But you're not anymore!" she argued.

Kallias laughed, and raising his hands in a show of surrender, he took a step back.

Just one step.

Not nearly enough for comfort.

Rose tried to ignore him, as she set the novel on the bed.

She blinked.

The bed.

One bed.

"Uhh, Kallias?" she said, her eyes wide with alarm. "There's only one bed."

"Yes, I can see that," Kallias said slowly. "I have perfect eyesight, remember?"

Normally, Rose would've appreciated the snark, but right now, she was too focused on the problem. "I'm not sleeping with you."

"I don't remember asking you to," Kallias muttered.

Rose scowled at him. "I *meant*," she corrected, "I'm not sleeping in that bed."

He rolled his eyes. "Don't be ridiculous," he grumbled. "If it makes you that uncomfortable, you can sleep in the bed, and I'll sleep on the sofa."

"You're like three times the length of that sofa," Rose argued.

He snorted, "I'm tall, yes, but I'm not eighteen feet tall."

"It makes more sense for me to sleep on the sofa since my body might actually fit on it," she insisted. "Besides, people have probably had sex on that bed."

Like many of Rose's strange remarks, that one earned a fit of laughter from Kallias. "What does that have to do with anything?"

"Well," Rose said pointedly, "it's kind of gross when you think about it."

He couldn't seem to stop laughing. He laughed so hard it reddened his normally golden skin. "And you think no one's had sex on the sofa?"

"Oh," Rose said, blinking. "Then…I guess I'll sleep in the floor."

He snorted, "I'm sure they've used the floor as well."

Rose glanced down at the floor and lifted one Converse shoe, as if it were contaminated. "Fine," she said with a heavy sigh, "I guess I'll take some blankets into the bathroom and sleep in the bathtub." She glanced toward the bathroom, where a large, cream-colored bathtub set in the center of the tile floor. "It looks big enough."

When she turned back toward Kallias, she found him staring at her, his lips pulled into a tight smile, as if he were trying not to laugh.

"Oh, come on!" Rose said, her voice high with disbelief. "Not the bathtub! Surely not. It's slippery! That doesn't even *sound* safe!"

He laughed. "Rose, people have been having sex in bathtubs for as long as I can remember," he scoffed. "I consummated my marriage with Phoebe in a type of bathtub, and that was in *Ancient Greece*."

"I don't think I needed to know that," Rose mumbled.

He shrugged. "You're the one who keeps talking about sex."

"No," she said slowly, "I'm pretty sure *you're* the one who usually brings it up."

"Hmm," he said with a taunting grin. "Must be a sign from destiny or God or whatever." The patronizing bite in his tone came through strongly. "You believe in that kind of bullshit, don't you?"

Cynicism was understandable, but mocking her? Rose drew the line there. She shrugged away from him. "Don't insult my beliefs, if you don't want me to insult your lack of them."

He straightened, and his brows furrowed. "I didn't mean to offend you."

"Yes, you did," Rose said, while setting down her bags.

Kallias sighed heavily. "Yeah, I suppose I did."

Rose glanced at him, and her gaze softened, as she noticed that he looked genuinely remorseful. His light brown eyes were wide and sad. The dangerous vampire was giving her puppy-dog eyes, Rose thought with amusement. "Why does it bother you so much for someone *else* to believe in something?"

He shrugged. "I think that people get hurt when they believe in things."

Rose smiled in surprise. "And...you don't want me to get hurt?"

"I—" Kallias shook his head, avoiding her gaze. "I don't care."

Rose suppressed a laugh.

She wanted to trust him. She really did. But he'd admitted to trying to tamper with her free will, and she needed some assurance that he wouldn't do it again.

"About what we were talking about earlier," Rose said, after a few moments, "how can I know you won't do that again?"

His frown deepened. "What? Fuck a woman in the bathtub?"

Rose blinked. "Umm," she stammered, too shocked to form words, apparently, "no." She stared absently at one of the white walls, her eyes still wide. "That is not what I meant," she said slowly. "That is *so far* from what I meant. So...*so* far."

He chuckled at her reaction. "It did seem like a strange question."

"I meant," Rose said, returning her gaze to him, "how can I trust you not to control my mind?"

"I don't know," Kallias said simply.

Rose frowned at the unhelpful answer. He couldn't make this one promise to her?

He stared at her for a moment, as if he weren't quite finished with his answer, but then, something behind her seemed to catch his attention. Anxiety flickered in his dark eyes, and he stepped toward the bed, unzipping his duffel bag in one quick, fluid motion.

He fished out a roll of black tape from the bag and turned back toward her.

"Uh..." Rose sputtered. "Why do you need tape?"

His lips twitched. "To tape your mouth shut, of course. You talk too much."

Her eyes widened. "What?"

"I'm joking. Obviously," Kallias told her. He waved a hand at the window, and when Rose turned to look at it, he stepped past her.

She watched, as he pulled the darkening shade over the window and then taped the edges to the wall so that no light could enter the room.

"Right. Sunrise equals crispy vampire," she reminded herself. "Has anyone ever told you that you have a strange sense of humor?"

He didn't look at her. "And you don't?"

"Oh, no, I know *I* do," Rose assured him.

He snorted at that. "Usually, they just call me an asshole."

She laughed.

When he was sure the window was secure, Kallias turned back toward her. He sighed, "I don't really know how to answer your question." He gave a tired shrug. "You *can't* trust me. I don't even trust myself. I'm animalistic, Rose. A little rage, a little blood—and I lose control. All vampires do."

Rose started to point out that she'd only meant his telepathic abilities, but he didn't give her the chance.

"When you're with me," Kallias said, "you're always one step away from death." He crossed his arms. "And so I don't *want* you to trust me."

She studied him curiously. She could *see* concern etched into his features. "If that's how you feel, why did you insist I come with you?"

"Because with me," he said, "there's still that one step. You still have a chance." He shrugged. "Without me, you're dead. You're only human. Or...well..."

"Well, *what*?" Rose asked.

But he'd closed himself off again.

It was right *there*—whatever he was hiding from her.

It was on the tip of his tongue, and she just couldn't get him to spit it out.

"The point is," Kallias said, "I may not trust myself around you, but I still know you're better off with my help than without it."

She nodded. "But," she sighed, "Kallias, why don't you just let them kill me? At least then, there'd be no risk of you doing it. Then, if I died, you wouldn't have to feel any guilt over it."

He gave a disgusted scoff at that. "How could you even *think* that?"

He stepped closer to her. "You don't think I'd feel any guilt over letting you die? Doing nothing would be as evil as committing the murder myself."

An understanding smile curved at the corners of Rose's lips. "You follow a code of ethics."

He scowled at that familiar tone of hers. "That doesn't mean I'm good."

She shrugged. "I feel safe with you."

His eyes narrowed. "Feelings lie."

She sighed in defeat. "Look, I'm not looking for anything extreme here," she told him. "I just need to know that you won't control my mind. That's all. Tell me you won't do *that*, and I'll be fine."

"How would that prove anything?" Kallias asked. "I could be lying."

"*Or* you could be telling the truth," Rose countered. "I'd trust your word."

"That's stupid," he said harshly. He shook his head in frustration. "People lie. Believe me. I would know. I've spent centuries in other people's minds. Everyone does it. They think one thing and say another. You shouldn't believe anything without proof."

"There's not always proof available," Rose told him. "Life requires a little bit of faith sometimes."

"People will take advantage of you, Rose," Kallias warned.

"And why would *you* care, if they do?" Rose asked.

"Because..." he trailed off, looking away in frustration. "I don't."

She eyed him skeptically. "I just need to know you won't try to make me do something I don't want to do. Can you not assure me of that?"

His brows creased. "Fine," he sighed. "You *can* trust me not to use telepathic control on you—not because of anything I say to you—but because, even if I did, it wouldn't work."

Rose frowned. "How could you possibly know that?"

Kallias shrugged. "Because I've already tried."

"Yes, but that could've been a fluke," she argued.

Kallias nodded slowly. "Well," he said, crossing his arms, "we could always test it."

Rose was sure, if she'd been moving at the time, she would've stumbled. "Test?" she squeaked. "No, no, I don't think so."

He grinned, and Rose soon realized that grin of his was contagious. He stepped closer. "Come on," he said playfully. "Aren't you curious?"

Rose pursed her lips and pointed a finger at him. "That's not fair," she complained. "I'm always curious. It's a personality trait. You're just preying on my weaknesses now."

He pressed his hands together. "One command?"

Rose couldn't help but laugh at the sight he made, pleading with her like that. "Fine," she said, drawing out the word. "How does this work? Like Simon Says?"

His brows furrowed. "Who's Simon?"

"Simon Says? The kid's game?" Rose offered. "Never mind."

Kallias looked away, his eyes distant and thoughtful. "Okay," he said, glancing back at her, "imagine the mind as layered, and each layer is guarded by a wall." He spread his hands. "On the surface, you'd find conscious thoughts: inner monologue, pictures, sounds, etc. That's the easiest part of the mind for a telepath to access." He shrugged. "It's as if the wall guarding it is made of paper. You can walk through it without even realizing it."

"You walk through paper walls without realizing it?" Rose interrupted.

He ignored that. "Deeper in the mind, guarded by *much* stronger walls, you'd find the will," he continued. "Breaking through those walls requires power and concentration, but once I've broken through them, I can *see* the will and bend it to my own."

She nodded. "And that's what you're going to do to me?"

"That's the idea," Kallias agreed, "but I'm right—and I'm sure I am— I'll find that your will is too strong for me to bend."

Rose frowned worriedly. "And if you're wrong?"

"It'll be a harmless command," he said, "I promise."

Rose sighed, "Fine." She closed her eyes and held out her arms, as if she were waiting for something to crash through the ceiling and crush her. "I'm ready. Mind-control me."

He snorted, "You're not ready."

She opened one eye, squinting. "I'm not?"

He laughed and shook his head. "No." He reached out and pushed her arms back down to her sides. "At any given time, a person's will is stronger or weaker, depending on how they feel."

"Right..." Rose said slowly.

"Well, one only has to spend five seconds around you before they realize that *you* are the most strong-willed when you're angry," Kallias explained.

Rose narrowed her eyes at him. "You think so?"

He smiled. "In order to really test this, I need you to be angry."

Rose crossed her arms. "Well, you're in luck—because one only has to spend five seconds around *you* in order to *get* angry," she countered.

He laughed. "That's great, but I need you angrier than *this*."

"Well, what do you want me to do?" she complained. "I can't just hulk out at will."

His brows furrowed. "Hulk out?"

"The big green guy? *'You won't like me when I'm angry'*?" Rose prompted. When he just shook his head, she gave him a disapproving scowl. "Haven't you ever even *seen* a comic book?"

His brown eyes lightened. "I have an idea."

"I agree," Rose said, nodding. "You *should* read a comic book."

"No. That...wasn't my idea," he muttered. "What I meant was: I know how to make you angry."

She lifted her eyebrows. "Yes, we've covered that."

"No," Kallias corrected, "I mean I know how to make you angry right *now*."

She shrugged. "I mean, I guess you're off to a good *start*."

He rolled his eyes at her off-hand remarks. "Look at me."

"I *am* looking at you," she said dismissively. "Also, I'm not angry yet."

"Don't worry," he assured her. "I'll take care of that part."

Rose frowned. "That's supposed to make me *not* worry?"

Kallias stepped closer and lifted his hand. He tipped her head back, his thumb lightly tracing her jaw. "Eye-contact. Please."

Rose met his gaze uneasily. "Uhh," she said breathlessly. "Is that required?"

His gaze didn't waver. "No, but it helps me concentrate."

Rose wasn't sure how *that* helped him concentrate. It did the opposite to her. Still, she gazed into his light brown eyes, and her body warmed at his closeness.

Then, she *felt* something.

Like fingers creeping over her mind.

"My head feels funny," she said, as her head began to spin. "Why does my head feel funny?"

"You can feel me in your mind," Kallias realized. His eyes widened. "That's interesting. Most people can't," he added under his breath.

"Oh," she mumbled. "Would you just hurry up and do it already?"

"If you insist," he said with a smile. "Rose? Take off your clothes."

Her jaw dropped, and without thinking, she shoved him backward.

Well, she tried, anyway.

He didn't budge.

"You said *harmless*!" she snarled at him. Since shoving did no good, she picked up a pillow from the edge of the bed and tossed it at him. "Harmless, Kallias! You said freaking harmless!"

He didn't respond because he was too busy laughing hysterically.

She tossed another pillow, and he deflected it with the last one. "You lying creep!" she continued. "What kind of person does that?"

He doubled over, laughing too hard to catch his breath. When he saw her reach for another pillow, he grabbed her arms. "Rose," he said, as she glared up at him, "look at your clothes."

She looked down, blinking at the jeans and leather jacket. "Oh."

"You resisted the command," Kallias added in explanation.

She narrowed her eyes at him. "But what if I hadn't been able to?"

His smile faded, suddenly. "Obviously, if you hadn't been able to resist, I would've released you from my control the moment I felt your will bend."

"Right, because you're *so* honorable," Rose scoffed.

His jaw tightened, and his eyes narrowed. "Whether I am or not," he snarled, "I still wouldn't do anything like *that*." He stepped back, clearly angry with her. "If I want to look at a naked woman, there are plenty of women who are more than willing to be with me. Damn it, Rose, you keep telling me you think I'm good, and then, you say shit like that?"

Rose winced a little. She'd clearly hit a nerve, but that didn't make what he'd done any less alarming for *her*. "Don't blame this on me," she complained. "You're the one who commanded me to freaking strip. Why would you even do that?"

He shrugged tiredly. "I told you," he muttered. "I needed you angry."

Her lips twitched at that. "Well, you accomplished that."

He matched her smile—warily. "It would seem so, yeah."

Rose's smile deepened. "I'm sorry if I hurt your feelings."

He grimaced at her. "You didn't hurt my *feelings*."

"Right," she teased, "because big, bad vampires don't have feelings."

Kallias rolled his eyes. "You know I can't control your mind now," he reminded her. "You're welcome."

Rose sighed. She'd given him a whole apology, and all she'd gotten in return was a *'you're welcome.'*

She glanced down at her hands. "My wrists hurt."

He laughed. "Well, sweetheart, that's because you tried to fight a *vampire*."

"It was an accident," she grumbled.

"Also, because," he added, "if you *were* expecting that shove to do anything at all...your form was terrible."

Rose glared at him. "I changed my mind. It was on purpose."

He snorted. Then, he reached out and took her wrists, turning them over in his hands. Her breath caught, as he traced her wrists with his thumbs.

"If my form is so *bad*," she said, trying not to think about his touch, "why don't you teach me the correct way?"

Kallias smiled and shrugged. "Maybe I will."

Rose lifted her eyebrows in surprise. "Really? When?"

"After all of this is over," he said, letting go of her wrists, "if you want to learn to defend yourself better, I'll teach you whatever you want to know."

Her chest warmed at the thought. "I'll hold you to that."

He laughed—and then turned away from her.

She tried to follow, intending to make him shake on it, but she suddenly staggered, as agonizing pain filled her head.

Kallias was beside her in less than a second, his hand on her arm, steadying her.

She grasped her head, as it throbbed in time with her pulse.

She felt his arms encircle her, holding her up, as her head spun violently. Despite the constant lurching of her head, she couldn't help but notice how warm his body felt against hers.

She felt his hand brushing her hair out of her face.

"Rose," he said gently, "are you okay?"

"Yeah. Just. Headache," she said, resorting mostly to monosyllables.

He led her to the bed and urged her to sit down. When she finally opened her eyes, she found Kallias kneeling in front of her, his brows creased with worry.

"Thanks," Rose breathed.

"Yeah," he said dismissively. But then, as she continued to tense in pain, he leaned forward, pressing more of his weight onto his toes. He lifted his hands. "Come here."

He began to massage each side of her head with his thumbs, and her eyes fluttered closed. His thumbs moved in slow, soothing circles, instantly easing the tension in her head.

Rose moaned at the sudden pain relief. "You're really good with those fingers," she murmured.

He snorted. "Sweetheart, you have no idea."

Her eyes popped open. "Oh. Ugh. Not funny."

Kallias laughed. "It's helping, though?"

"Mmm-hmm," she said, and her eyes fluttered closed again.

He suppressed another laugh. She kept reaching out, like she meant to stop him, but then, she'd let her hands fall and sink into it again.

"It came on so suddenly," she murmured, after a few moments. "It's strange, don't you think?"

Kallias sighed, "It's not strange—considering it wasn't a normal headache."

She opened her eyes, and her brows furrowed. "What do you mean by that?"

"Keep your eyes closed. It'll help you stay relaxed," he said.

Her eyes slid closed again, and her reddish-blonde eyelashes brushed against her cheeks.

"The pain you're feeling is a symptom of overuse," Kallias explained. "It happens to me sometimes."

Her frown deepened, but she kept her eyes closed. "Overuse?"

"Have you ever gotten a headache after studying too long?" he asked.

"Sure," she mumbled. "Like a stress headache?"

"Well, it's kind of like that," he said hesitantly. "Overusing certain parts of your mind causes pain—sort of like soreness in your muscles after you exercise." He let his hands fall. "When I overuse my telepathic power, I get the same sort of headache you have now."

Rose opened her eyes. "Yeah, but I'm a human," she reminded him. "I don't have any...power."

Kallias shifted uncomfortably. "Right," he said, purposely avoiding her gaze. "But you did resist the command of a powerful telepath."

Rose didn't fall for his evasiveness. "Kallias, what are you not telling me?"

"Nothing," he lied.

It was an obvious lie—more obvious than any other lie he'd told Rose so far. Everything about his body language screamed that he was lying to her.

He stood. "This is my fault. If I'd known that testing your will like that would cause you pain, I wouldn't have suggested it." *That*, on the other hand, had been honest. He sighed, "I'm sorry."

Rose scowled, as he walked over to his black duffel bag that set at the foot of the bed. He was so *obviously* hiding something from her, and she was fed up with it. "It's fine," she said dismissively, "but what's *not* fine is—"

A buzzing phone interrupted her, and Kallias was all eager to answer it.

He pressed the phone to his ear without even looking at it.

"What do you want, Erik?" he said into the phone.

Rose sighed in defeat. At least she *felt* better. Physically.

She stood and went to pick up a few of the store bags on the bed, fishing out the clothes she'd need.

Kallias turned away from her, obviously avoiding her gaze.

When she had everything gathered into her arms, she looked at him. "I'm going to take a shower now."

He still didn't look at her. He just waved his hand dismissively.

Rose rolled her eyes and headed to the bathroom.

She'd have to find her way past his lies some other time.

"She's *still* with you?" Erik said—on the other side of the line.

Kallias collapsed onto the bed. He sat up against the headboard and stretched out his legs. "Yeah, about that," he sighed. "We need to talk."

"I agree," Erik said. "Why the hell did you tell her that you're a vampire?"

Kallias ran his hand through his hair. "I didn't really have a choice."

"You bit her during sex, didn't you?" Erik assumed. "I knew this would happen. I should've showed you how to—" He paused. "Wait. You're a telepath. Couldn't you just erase her memory?"

"I didn't bite her, Erik," Kallias sighed, "or have sex with her."

"You haven't had sex with her?" Erik sounded horrified, as if Kallias had just confessed to an atrocious crime.

Kallias glanced toward the bathroom door, when he heard the water cut on. "I know you must find this unbelievable," he said slowly, "but it *is* possible to be within five feet of a woman without having sex with her."

"I know," Erik said with a scoff. "You can't have sex with *anyone* from five feet away."

Kallias rolled his eyes. His nostrils flared, as the scent of honey filled his senses, making its way through the entire room. He knew that scent. It was her hair—her *shampoo*. He clenched his jaw, trying to ignore the appealing scent, trying not to think about the fact that she was naked just one wall away from him, trying not to picture her in the shower, wet and naked, rinsing the shampoo from her hair.

"If you're not having sex with her, why is she with you?" Erik asked.

Kallias cleared his throat. "She needs protection."

"Right, right. Humans and their reproductive stuff," Erik said, as if he'd only just remembered. "Look, you just pick up some condoms from a gas station, and... You know how to put one on, right?"

Kallias sighed into the phone. "Not that kind of protection, Erik."

"Yeah, they're pointless for us, anyway—since we're infertile and immune to everything," Erik muttered, "but try explaining *that* to a human woman."

Kallias shook his head tiredly. "Erik," he said, before his friend's mind could wander again, "the woman with me now—she's the same woman Theron attacked that first night. He attacked her three nights in a row." He breathed out a heavy sigh. "He's not going to stop until she's dead. He even broke into her apartment. And just since we left the warehouse, we've been attacked three times by vampires that were acting on Theron's behalf. Without protection, she'll die."

Erik was silent for a while. Finally, he asked, "Why is he fixated on her?"

Kallias cast a nervous glance toward the bathroom. "I don't know."

"Bullshit," Erik accused. "You know something."

"I have a theory," Kallias admitted, "but I think there's more to it."

"Well, it's a start anyway," Erik said. "What do you know?"

Kallias eyed the bathroom door warily, before lowering his voice so that she wouldn't hear. "She's not normal," he said quietly.

"What? Like she's kinky?" Erik asked.

Kallias rolled his eyes again. "I swear," he grumbled, "carrying on a serious conversation with you is like derailing a train that's hell-bent on going the wrong direction."

"Sorry, I didn't follow that. I was stuck on the kinky bit," Erik said.

Kallias sighed. "What I meant was: she's not an ordinary human."

"What makes you think that?" Erik asked.

"The allure does nothing to her," Kallias explained. "You know most humans can't resist vampires, but she's fought back against every vampire that's attacked her." He cast another glance toward the bathroom, before adding, "And she can resist my telepathic control."

"What?" Erik said. "That's impossible. No one can resist your mind-control, just like no one could resist Alana's. Except you, of course, but that's only because—" He paused. "Wait, is she a telepath, too?"

"No," Kallias said quickly. "No, I don't think so." He sighed, "I think…she's something *much* more powerful."

"No one's more powerful than a telepath," Erik scoffed.

It *was* one of the most dangerous abilities, and considering Erik's history with his telepathic ex-lover, Alana, it was easy to understand why he feared it so much.

But there was one ability that was more powerful.

Kallias cast another paranoid glance toward the bathroom. He heard the water running, still, and he smelled her honey-scented conditioner. "Theron attacked her in her apartment last night," he said quietly. "I wasn't there to save her."

"Then," Erik said, "how is she still alive?"

"Because she threw Theron across the room," Kallias told him.

Kallias heard Erik let out a short laugh at that. Apparently, Erik had assumed Kallias was joking, and honestly, Kallias couldn't blame him.

"Impossible," Erik scoffed. "Humans aren't physically strong enough to overpower vampires."

"I never said that she used physical strength to do it," Kallias said.

Erik was silent for nearly a full minute. "Shit," he said, finally.

"She doesn't know," Kallias told him.

"How can she be that powerful and not know?" Erik asked.

The scent of vanilla filled the room next—the scent of her body wash.

Kallias shifted uncomfortably. "I think it's best if she doesn't know," he told Erik. "She's impossibly stubborn. She'd only end up hurting herself, if she knew."

"Or she could use her power to wipe out Theron for good," Erik argued.

"No," Kallias said. "We're not gambling with her life like that. She's not a weapon."

"But she *could* be," Erik said, "if she knew."

"No," Kallias said firmly.

Erik laughed. "Holy shit. You have feelings for a human."

"That's a bit of a leap, don't you think?" Kallias scoffed. "I'm not an idiot, Erik. I'd never fall for a human—or anyone else, for that matter." When Erik didn't immediately agree, Kallias continued, "She needs protection. That's it. I feel nothing for her. Nothing!"

"Nothing. Got it," Erik said, the amusement in his voice audible.

Kallias rolled his eyes irritably. "We'll be there tomorrow."

"You're bringing her here?" Erik asked.

"I don't have a choice," Kallias said defensively. "There are too many vampires looking for her. It's the only place she might be safe."

"So, let me get this straight," Erik interrupted. "You're bringing a human—or whatever the hell she is—here? Even though she's being hunted by Theron and countless other vampires. Even though that will undoubtedly lead to those vampires coming here. Even though that will lead to a battle between us and them. You're putting us in danger just so you can protect one human?"

Kallias grimaced. "Yeah."

"Good," Erik responded.

"Good?" Kallias repeated in disbelief.

"Yeah, good!" Erik laughed. "I've been itching for a good battle for centuries. It looks like we'll finally get one!" Something shifted in the background. "I'll call Geoff and Emma, and let them know."

Kallias laughed in relief. "Thanks, Erik. I knew you'd understand."

"Yeah, whatever," Erik said dismissively. "Have you kissed her yet?"

Kallias heard the water cut off. "Bye, Erik. We'll see you tomorrow."

"Fine. Don't tell me," Erik complained. "I'll figure it out myself!"

Kallias hung up the phone and climbed out of bed. He slid his phone into his pocket and walked over to his duffel bag.

As he reached into the bag to get his soap and shampoo, he noticed his leather jacket lying beside it.

Rose had left it with his things, when she went to shower.

He picked it up, meaning to toss it aside, but as he took hold of it, her scent filled his senses. Instinct took over, and before he knew what he was doing, he had the jacket against his face, inhaling her scent.

He dropped the jacket, suddenly. "What the hell am I doing?"

He picked it up again, but this time, he quickly tossed it onto the chair, afraid his instincts would take over again if he didn't get it out of his hands fast enough.

But her scent—that sweet, powerful scent that was unique to her—was already working its way through him, igniting hunger and desire.

At that moment, the bathroom door swung open, and Rose stepped into the room. The scent of vanilla and honey moved with her.

Her pale skin looked softer and cleaner, free of those pinkish blood-stains that had marred her skin before. Drenched, red hair fell on either side of her shoulders, and drops of water sparkled in her eyelashes. She wrung out her wet hair with a small, white towel.

Her bright blue eyes shifted toward him, and she froze.

Kallias stared blankly at her—mostly because he couldn't think of a proper response to seeing her in those clothes.

Her entire body—from her neck to her ankles—was covered in thick, red-and-black flannel pajamas that looked as if they were six sizes too big for her.

"What are you wearing?" Kallias managed, finally.

Rose glanced down at her pajamas, plucking absently at the fuzz on the thick material. "What does it *look* like I'm wearing?"

Kallias stepped closer and made a dramatic show of assessing her clothing. "It *looks* like you're wearing a quilt I saw on the side of the road once."

Her eyes narrowed. "They're supposed to be comfortable, not pretty."

He smiled wryly. "That's obvious."

Rose glared at him. "You're such a jerk."

Kallias arched a challenging brow. "Is that the only insult you know?"

She let out a short laugh at that. "I memorized the dictionary *and* the thesaurus when I was a kid," she told him. "I have *plenty* more."

Kallias took another step forward, and she stumbled backward, her back hitting the wall. "Prove it."

"Fine," Rose said, lifting her chin. "You're an inconsiderate, annoying, insensitive, barbarous, uncivilized, malicious, cantankerous, scurrilous, vexatious, imbecilic simpleton!"

He snorted, *"Now*, you just sound silly."

Rose laughed, but she continued to taunt, anyway, "What's wrong? Am I talking over your head now?"

Rose fell back against the wall, as he stepped forward and slid his hand into her hair, his fingers entangling in the long, wet strands.

She didn't have time to ask—or even *wonder*—what he was doing because his lips were suddenly on hers, warm and relentless.

She moaned at the first contact of his lips, and she suddenly found herself wrapping her arms around his neck and kissing him back.

Kallias tasted the spearmint toothpaste on her tongue. He smelled the honey shampoo in her wet hair and the scent of vanilla on her damp skin. And he smelled *her*—that unique scent of her blood, the scent that had been on his jacket.

Needing more contact with her, he took one last step forward, pressing her into the wall.

Rose gasped, as he pushed her up against the wall, as the front of his body pressed against hers.

One of his hands remained in her hair, gently tugging her head back so that he could kiss her more deeply. His other hand was on her face, his fingers splayed from the top of her neck to the lower curve of her ear, holding her face steady as he kissed her senseless.

His legs pressed against hers—one between her thighs and the other against the outside of her left leg.

His strong torso pressed against her over-sensitized breasts, making her far too aware of the fact that she hadn't put on a bra after her shower —since she usually didn't sleep in one.

His fingers tugged at the buttons on her shirt, unbuttoning the first, then the second, then the third.

"I thought you weren't going to kiss me again," Kallias breathed out, between kisses.

When their mouths separated long enough for them to both draw in a quick breath, Rose managed to reply, "I did, too." Her fingers clutched at his thin, black T-shirt, and when their lips separated again, she breathed, "I thought you didn't *want* to kiss me again."

"I lied," he groaned against her lips.

Her lungs constricted, and her skin felt overheated and feverish. Each kiss left her lips feeling oversensitive and sore, and the facial hair along his jaw left her skin raw.

But none of this made her want to stop kissing him. Nothing could've made her want that.

Her heart raced frantically against her chest, and she felt an ache between her legs—a feeling she'd never really felt before.

Not like this, anyway.

Kallias pulled away from her mouth and tilted her head back so that he could press his lips to her neck. He kissed the sensitive skin between her jaw and ear, and then, he trailed downward, kissing her over and over, until he reached her neck.

Rose's eyes slid closed, her wet eyelashes fluttering against her flushed cheeks, and her head fell back against the wall, as his mouth scorched her skin. Her mouth fell open, and she couldn't help but moan softly each time his lips met her neck.

The sound of her rapidly pounding heart and her soft moans fed his hunger, and he traced the pulsing artery in her neck with his tongue.

He felt the blood pumping through her veins, beneath his lips, and the sweet and powerful scent of her blood filled his senses. He grazed his fangs against her neck.

"Oh, wow," she said, surprised by how pleasant it felt.

He groaned softly against her neck. Acting on instinct, he cradled one side of her neck and pressed his fangs into her skin.

She moaned at the prick of pain.

It would've been so easy to feed, then. She would've enjoyed it. They both would have.

Until he couldn't stop—and accidentally killed her.

Kallias pulled away, suddenly. "Shower. I need a shower."

Rose stood there, leaning against the wall with her flannel shirt halfway unbuttoned, as he disappeared into the bathroom.

15

THE TRUTH, FINALLY

Kallias cast a curious glance at Rose, when he stepped out of the bathroom. She sat, cross-legged, on the bed with a book in her hand.

And she still wore those pajamas that were so hilariously unflattering that he couldn't help but find them kind of cute. Kallias shook himself out of his thoughts and turned to face the sink. He turned on the water and sifted through his bag for a razor.

The sound of running water must've interrupted Rose's reading—because she suddenly looked up and shrieked, "Ahh! What are you doing?!"

His brows furrowed. He looked up from his bag, glancing briefly at the mirror, before turning to look at her. He lifted both eyebrows, when he found her with both hands clasped over her face.

"I'm shaving," he said. He cast a wary glance at the razor in his hand. "What is it? Do you have some kind of phobia to shaving cream?"

"No," Rose squeaked. "I meant...why are you naked?"

Kallias looked down, blinking at the long, white towel that was...*still* firmly around his hips, it would seem. "I think someone taught you the wrong definition of the word *naked*."

She waved one hand blindly, the other still tightly clasped over her eyes. "Towels don't count!"

"I don't see why not," he muttered. "They cover what needs to be covered." He turned back toward the mirror and began to shave.

"Why aren't you wearing *clothes*?" she complained.

He looked at her reflection and chuckled again at the sight of her with her hands over her eyes. "I don't wear clothes in the shower. Do you?"

"No, but I put them on before I leave the bathroom!" she said.

Kallias just laughed.

Rose eventually dropped her hands. Kallias faced away from her, still, but as soon as she dropped her hands, his gaze met hers in the mirror. She watched his reflection for a moment, blushing, as he watched her, too.

She slipped a bookmark into her book and set it on the nightstand. Then, she climbed out of bed and crossed the space between them.

She joined him near the sink and leaned her shoulder against the partial wall that connected to the sink. She crossed her arms.

"Can I ask you something?" she said nervously.

Kallias held the razor under the water and looked at her. "Do you realize ninety-nine percent of the things you say begin with, '*Can I ask you something?*'"

She shrugged. "I told you. I'm a curious person."

He looked at the mirror, as he began to shave again. "Sure. Ask."

Those scars of his captured her attention again, glowing white under the lights above the mirror. They looked even worse under the light than they had when she'd seen them in that dark building.

The flame tattoos on his neck and back hid some of them, but others were obvious and unhidden. She couldn't imagine what had left them— or how painful it'd been to receive them.

Kallias cleared his throat and gave her a hard stare. "You had a question."

"Right," she said, shifting uneasily. "Umm...did I do something wrong?"

He stopped shaving and turned to frown at her. "When?"

She chewed on her bottom lip nervously. "When we were kissing," she said. "I mean, I just assume you've had a lot of experience with women, and I'm, you know, *less* experienced. As in *much* less. *Much, much* less. I think I may have kissed three people, including you, and one of those didn't count because she was my best friend—in middle school, during a game of Truth or Dare. I didn't know what I was doing, and I don't even think I knew I *liked* girls yet. So…"

Kallias turned toward her. "Rose," he said, interrupted her rambling, "why are you telling me all of this?"

Her face reddened, and she looked down at her own bare feet. "I'm just saying, you know," she stammered, "that if I did something wrong, you should tell me—so I can fix it. I'm a fast learner."

His lips tugged into a smile. He picked up a white towel and patted his face dry. "You didn't do anything wrong, *koukla*."

Rose looked up at him, her face burning. "But you left."

He rinsed off the razor and dropped it in his bag, and then, he turned to face her. "And you automatically assumed that meant you were a bad kisser?"

She shrugged sheepishly. "It seemed like a logical conclusion."

"No, Rose," Kallias said gently, "it seems like an *insecure* one."

Rose glanced down at the plush carpet beneath her feet, before giving him another uneasy shrug.

"The problem wasn't that you didn't kiss well enough," Kallias said with a laugh. "If anything, you kissed a little *too* well."

Rose squinted bewilderedly. "What does that mean?"

He flashed his fangs at her.

"Ohhhhh," she said, dragging out the syllable. "It…affected you?"

He laughed at her vagueness. "Yeah, Rose. It affected me."

Rose turned to watch, as he walked over to his duffel bag. He pulled out a pair of black sweatpants. "My blood bothers you."

He frowned, but he didn't look at her. "Obviously."

"More," she added, "than other people's blood?"

He glanced at her, his expression guarded. "I never said that."

"But it's true," Rose asked, "isn't it?"

He looked away. "It bothers me because it's blood. That's all."

"You're lying," she said sadly. "There's more to it than that."

Kallias returned to her, the sweatpants balled up in his hand.

Rose instinctually leaned back as he closed in on her—only to realize the wall was preventing her from putting any space between them.

His eyes darkened. "Yeah, there is more to it, but I already told you that. Hunger and desire are linked," he reminded her, "and I'd *think*, after what just happened between us, it'd be obvious that I want you."

"You do?" Rose said, temporarily forgetting her argument.

"Yes," Kallias said harshly. "Unfortunately for you, that also means I want your blood."

Rose tried to ignore the way her body temperature spiked at the thought. She forced her lips to form words, despite their reluctance. "I think," she said breathlessly, "there's *another* reason my blood affects you more than most—a reason you've been hiding from me."

His jaw tightened. "I need to get dressed."

He tried to step past her, but she grabbed his arm.

"Tell me the truth," Rose said. "Please."

"Unless you prefer me naked, you should let me get dressed," he said.

Rose immediately let go of his arm. She looked away, blushing, and he wordlessly continued into the bathroom, slamming the door behind him.

When he came out less than a minute later with black sweatpants hanging from his hips—instead of the towel—Rose hadn't moved.

He sighed irritably at her.

And though she wanted to wither under his glare, she didn't. "I know you haven't been celibate for twenty-five hundred years," Rose said.

He shrugged. "And your point is?"

"My point is," she explained, "you've had *sex* with people without losing control of your hunger. You've taken things much further than kissing with other people, but with me, you can't even kiss me without wanting to bite me."

Kallias stepped toward her and placed a hand on the wall, trapping her against it. He tilted his face closer and growled, "I *always* want to bite you, whether I'm kissing you or not. It's just part of what I am."

Rose swallowed nervously. As she stared into his light brown eyes, she realized that she could actually *see* it: the hunger. It was that flash of darkness she saw in his eyes—that dangerous spark. She'd seen it so many times, just as she saw it now.

"Something's different about me," Rose said softly, "and I need to know what it is."

Kallias dropped his hand and stepped back. "I'm *done* with this conversation," he snarled. He turned to walk away. "Goodnight."

In her desperation, Rose chased after him. "Well, I'm not done with it," she told him. "Friends…shouldn't lie to each other like this."

He turned, giving her a skeptical look. "Friends?"

Well, *that* stung a little.

"After all we've been through, we're…at least friends," Rose said nervously, "aren't we?"

He shrugged tiredly.

Rose swallowed. "Kallias, you're not the only vampire who's had trouble resisting my blood. Every vampire who attacks me mentions something about it," she tried to explain. "They say it smells powerful— whatever *that* means. They say it's irresistible. Don't you think I need to know why *all* vampires want to kill me?"

His shoulders drooped with defeat. "Stop. Please."

Rose's gaze softened with sympathy. She'd never seen him like this. "You hate dishonesty. I know you do. I can hear it in your voice when you talk about it, when you warn me not to trust people," she sighed. "If you hate lying so much, why are you lying to me?"

He recoiled as if she'd just slapped him. "I'm not *lying* to anyone," he said between clenched teeth. "I'm just—"

"Lying by omission?" Rose interrupted. When he didn't deny it, she said, "I think you care about me, even if you'd never admit it. Why else would you go through all of this to protect me?"

He looked away, refusing to confirm or deny it.

Rose continued, "And I know I care about you."

His dark gaze darted back toward her. "Rose—"

"Please, let me finish," she said, before he could ask her to stop again. She sighed, "I want to ask you a question, Kallias, and I need you to be honest with me—for once. If you cared about someone, and you realized they were hiding something from you—something that affected you—don't you think that would bother you?"

When his face twisted with pain, Rose suddenly regretted asking the question. She'd wanted him to understand, but she hadn't expected it to hit *that* close to home for him.

"Yeah," Kallias said, his muscles tenser than she'd ever seen them. "Yeah, it did."

"Oh, goodness," she mumbled. "I'm sorry. I didn't know it would—"

"Sorry for what?" he interrupted. "I'm the one lying to you, remember?"

Rose sighed. That cold distance was back in his voice again. "Your telepathic control works on everyone, except me. Everyone, except me, is enthralled every time they look at a vampire because of your…seductive pheromone…or magical allure…or whatever the heck it is."

Kallias looked away, clenching his jaw.

"Even *you* can't seem to go more than a few minutes without making some strange remark that hints at what you're hiding from me," Rose said. "And that day that Theron tried to—to *hurt* me…" The word *rape* refused to come out of her mouth, shackled down by the pain in her chest. "He said I wasn't an ordinary human, and the way you looked at me afterward—it was like a light bulb had just come on in your head. You looked at me as if you *knew* something, as if you were scared, and I've *never* seen you scared, Kallias. Clearly, there's something wrong with me—something you're not saying."

Kallias looked at her, and his brows creased. "There's nothing wrong with you," he told her, "not in my opinion."

"Then, tell me the truth," Rose pleaded.

He sighed in frustration. "Have you considered that I might have a good reason for keeping this from you? That I'm trying to protect you?"

"Protect me from what?" she asked. "The truth?"

He just shrugged, as if he thought that was an acceptable answer.

"I don't know what you think my life has been like," Rose said, her voice shaky, "but I have *never* been protected from the truth—from anything, really. I wasn't some sheltered princess, locked away in a castle. I was a child in a house that was falling apart—that always had drugs but never had food." She narrowed her eyes. "I faced the truth that mom didn't care about me the first time she let a boyfriend beat me until I was bleeding for sassing him. I faced the truth that I was losing the only person who ever *had* cared about me, when my brother went to prison. I faced the truth that my mother was dead when I found her lying in a puddle of vomit, after her body had been decaying for two days." She sighed, "I mean, I knew what happens to the human body when it decays, but you don't really face the truth of it until you have to *look* at it. I've *never* been sheltered from the truth—not once—and guess what? I'm still standing. So, you can keep your patronizing *I-have-to-protect-you* attitude—because I don't need it."

Kallias stared at her, his brows creased.

This time, it was Rose who looked away. She hadn't meant to say all of that, but the words had just seemed to spill out of their accord.

For a while, Kallias didn't speak. Then, finally, he murmured, his voice low and dangerous, "Is he still alive?"

Rose frowned. "Is who still alive?"

"The person who hurt you," he said.

"I don't know," she said, her frown deepening. "Why does it matter?"

Rage simmered in his light brown eyes. "You don't know because he was just one of many, right?" he assumed. "You can't even remember all of the people who hurt you."

Rose gave an uneasy shrug. "My mom didn't associate with the nicest people," she said dismissively. "Why does that upset you?"

"Because someone should've protected you," he said.

"My brother tried sometimes," Rose said softly, "and I tried to protect him, too—even though I was too young to ever do it successfully."

Kallias shook his head in frustration. "How can you live through things like that and then tell me you still believe in good?" he said. "How can you believe in light, when you've experienced nothing but darkness?"

Rose considered that. "Because the people who hurt me don't define me. I won't give them that kind of power," she said. "I don't know why people suffer, but I refuse to go through life angry about it. I choose who

I am, not the people who hurt me, and if I ever lose that," she sighed, "that would be *worse* than what they did to me."

"How?" Kallias said. "No choice you make will ever stop people from hurting you."

"But it'll stop me from ever hurting anyone else," Rose said. "Wherever the pain started, it stops with me."

"How is that good for you?" he asked.

"Because I *want* to be kind," Rose stated. "I *want* to be compassionate."

Kallias shook his head, stunned. Whether he could read her thoughts or not, he didn't understand her. Suffering had changed him, hardened him, but it hadn't done that to her. His chest tightened, and he stepped closer. He reached up to push her wet hair out of her face, tucking it behind her ear.

Her skin was *so* soft.

She blinked, her bright blue eyes wide and surprised.

"Are you sure you want to know this?" he asked. "Are you even ready to accept that you're not an ordinary human?"

Her brows furrowed. "What does that mean?"

He stepped back and exhaled slowly, as he considered how to say it. "Theron said you're not an ordinary human because…you're not, Rose."

A surprised laugh escaped her lips. "Be serious."

His frown deepened. "I am."

"What am I, then?" she said with a giggle. "Half-alien? I guess I *could* be half-alien. I don't know who my father was, after all. Maybe he was this weird, green guy from another galaxy." She laughed again. "But he must've been a weird green guy with red hair because my mother had this beautiful blonde hair, and I wound up a freaking ginger. I knew my alien father was to blame for this."

Kallias scowled. "You're not half-alien."

"Maybe I'm half-Bigfoot!" she continued. "No, I doubt that, actually. If my father was Bigfoot, I'd be much hairier, don't you think?"

He suppressed a smile. "Can you shut your mouth for a minute?"

"Well, I would," she told him, "but my allergies are acting up tonight. So, I'm kind of *breathing* through my mouth at the moment."

Kallias sighed, "Do you want me to explain this to you or not?"

"Fine," Rose said, holding out her hands. "Just don't be surprised when you have to give me CPR."

He suppressed yet *another* laugh. "Okay. So when you did all of that reading about vampires, did you ever find an explanation for *why* we crave blood?"

Rose didn't answer. She just stood there, staring at him.

He sighed, "Rose, I asked you a question."

"I thought you wanted me to shut my mouth," she said defensively.

He narrowed his eyes at her.

She laughed. "Okay, okay. Yes, of course I found one. But then, I found another. And another. And another. There was never anything conclusive. Every culture had their own theories about it."

He crossed his arms. "What were they?"

Rose looked away. She studied a painting on the wall—a beautiful creek in the mountains—as she tried to remember everything she'd read that night. "Well," she said, finally, "some cultures believed that vampires needed blood because they were soulless—and that they somehow extracted the human's soul through their blood." She shifted her gaze back toward Kallias. "But that's nonsense because even if a soul *could* be taken through blood consumption, vampires clearly aren't soulless. The soul is personality and emotion, and you have those. You're not *zombies*."

Kallias nodded. "What else?"

"Some cultures believed vampires were cursed," she added. "They thought the need to consume blood was a punishment for cheating death."

"I could see that," he muttered. "What else?"

"Some cultures believed vampires obtained immortality through blood magic," she suggested, "which would require blood, of course."

He shrugged. "I don't believe in magic."

She squinted at that. "You're a vampire."

"What does that matter?" Kallias said.

Rose shrugged bewilderedly. "Okay. Well," she said, "there was this one theory, proposed by a group of scientists. They thought vampires could have a rare anemic disease—and that they crave blood because of its high iron content."

Kallias stepped toward her. His fingers curled around her wrist, and he turned her hand so that her palm faced upward. "It's not the iron," he said, tracing a blue vein. "I smell the iron in your blood, of course, just as I smell the water, salt, sugar, plasma…but those are just *details*." His dark gaze shifted up to meet hers. "It's not what I *crave*."

Rose tried not to react to his touch. "Dang," she said breathlessly. "I kind of liked that one."

He chuckled. "Were there any others?"

Rose found it increasingly hard to think with him touching her wrist like that. "There was another," she admitted. "Many ancient religions believed that blood symbolized life. So, they figured vampires obtained the *power* of life by consuming blood, and they craved it because they were dead. Or…were supposed to be dead."

"I like that one," he said softly, not looking at her. "I doubt it's true, but I do prefer that theory over the others. It's…closer."

"Closer?" she repeated. "Closer to the truth? What *is* the truth?"

Kallias studied her cautiously. "The truth is," he sighed, "I'm not sure what it is that we crave. I can tell you it's a kind of…power, but I can't tell you much more than that." His light brown eyes grew distant. "When you awake as a vampire, there are some things you instinctually know. One is that you need blood, and the other is that blood is power."

"Power, like strength? Or…" Rose trailed off, confused.

"I don't know," he admitted. "I just know that there's some kind of power in blood, and we crave it." He lifted her wrist slightly, as if he were showing it to her. "The scent we're so drawn to—it smells different depending on the amount of power that's in the blood."

Rose frowned warily at that. "What?"

"The power in blood nourishes us and empowers us," he continued. "It heals our injuries and soothes our hunger. But not all blood is the same. Powerful blood offers more strength than other blood. That's why a few sips of vampire blood can do as much for us as a whole body's worth of human blood."

"So, vampire blood is more powerful than human blood," Rose said.

"Yes," Kallias admitted, "but human blood can have power, as well. As a matter of fact, it's only *because* humans have that latent power that it emerges when they become a vampire."

Rose looked away, her heart racing. "Latent?"

"It usually remains latent until after your death," he told her.

She swallowed uneasily. "And how does power...*smell* to vampires?"

"Sweet. Appealing," Kallias murmured. "Like you."

Rose looked at him, her eyes wide. "Like *me*?"

"I've *never* smelled blood as powerful as yours," Kallias confessed. "In twenty-five hundred years, no human or vampire has ever smelled as enticing as you."

Rose shook her head in denial. "That doesn't make sense."

"No, it doesn't," he agreed, "but it's true, nonetheless."

"It can't be," she said nervously. "I mean, you just said vampire blood is more powerful than human blood, right? And I'm human. Right?"

"It would seem," Kallias said.

"I am!" Rose said, breathless with disbelief. "I'm obviously human."

"Even if you are," he said, only confusing her more, "you're not an ordinary human. *That*, I'm certain of."

"Well, what am I, if I'm not ordinary?" she asked worriedly.

"I haven't figured that part out yet," he admitted. He sounded as if he were apologizing for that. "All I know is that there's something different about your blood. It smells human, but it also smells...*more* than human."

"So," she said, her face pale, "I'm just some sort of freak?"

His gaze softened. "Come on now," he said, and with his hand still on her wrist, he pulled her closer. "Don't think like that."

Her chest tightened, and she couldn't force out even a single word.

"There's nothing wrong with you," Kallias told her. "You're different from most humans, but that isn't necessarily a bad thing." He brushed his free hand against the softness of her cheek. "You're different. Not wrong."

His touch comforted her—but not enough to dissolve that sinking ball of dread that had begun to weigh down her chest. "No, it can't be true," she said breathlessly. "I'm just like everyone else."

"No, you're not," he sighed. "You know you're not."

She looked up at him. "How? How would I know that?"

"Think about it," he said. "People who grow up the way you did don't usually end up becoming successful adults like you."

"Successful?" she scoffed. "I'm a socially awkward college student, working a part-time job I'm no good at—just so that I can *maybe* pay half my bills and send a small allowance to my brother."

"You're successful in college, aren't you?" Kallias pointed out.

"If you'd call an academic scholarship and a perfect GPA successful, then," Rose said hesitantly, "I suppose so."

He snorted. "The point is," he explained, "most people who grew up the way you did—*if* they survive, they end up like your brother. *That's* ordinary. You're not."

"I chose to be different. That's all," she told him. "I chose to break the cycle. There's nothing supernatural about that."

"Maybe not," Kallias said, "but most people can't make that choice. Most people don't have the willpower. Their lives aren't a series of deliberate choices, like yours. Their lives are just one, long equation of cause-and-effect. They become what life makes them, but you—you don't."

"What does that have to do with my blood?" Rose asked.

"Don't you see the common factor?" Kallias asked. "I can't control your mind because your will is too strong. A vampire's allure doesn't affect you because your will is too strong. What happened to you didn't change you because your will is too strong."

Her frown deepened. "Are you trying to tell me that my blood smells more powerful than anyone else's because…I'm stubborn?"

"I'm trying to tell you," he corrected, "that your will is too powerful to be controlled. Even…by the laws of nature."

She blinked in shock. "What?"

Kallias sighed, "Rose, how did you get Theron off of you?"

"We've already been over this," she reminded him. "I didn't."

"Then, who did?" he prompted. "There was no one else in the room."

"Why would you assume it was me?" Rose asked. "You know it's not possible. You were the one who told *me* that humans aren't strong enough to fight vampires."

"They're not," he confirmed, "physically."

She nodded slowly. "Then, it's settled. I couldn't have—"

"But mentally," he interrupted, "*you* just might be."

Rose scoffed at that. "What did I do? Throw him with my brain?"

He raised an eyebrow. "Haven't you ever heard of telekinesis?"

Her smile faded. "No. That's impossible."

"Come on, Rose," Kallias muttered. "How many times does your entire worldview have to be flipped upside down, before you realize that you have no *idea* what's possible?"

"Everything that's happened was more possible than *telekinesis*," Rose insisted.

"An ancient, telepathic, immortal being is more possible?" he asked.

"Yes," Rose said stubbornly.

He lifted both eyebrows in disbelief.

"There are…*possible* explanations for how vampires could exist—even if most people doubt them," she insisted. "And regarding telepathy, well, if you believe anything can happen in the mind, then…it's not *too* far-fetched."

His expression grew more skeptical by the moment.

"But telekinesis is different," she said. "It deals with the physical world, and there are laws that govern the physical world."

"Yes," he agreed, "but *you* can't be controlled by those laws."

"That's ridiculous," Rose said.

"Fine. Then, tell me," he challenged. "Who threw Theron off of you?"

"I don't know," she answered, "but it must've been someone else."

"I *saw* the memory. There was no one else," Kallias told her.

She shook her head. "I can't have a psychic ability. I'm not a vampire."

"I never said vampires were the *only* ones with psychic abilities," he reminded her. "After all, you know a human with a psychic ability, don't you?"

Rose frowned worriedly. "How do you know about Audrey?"

"I met her," he said simply. When her frown didn't fade, he tapped his the side of his head. "Telepathic, remember?"

"Audrey wouldn't want you to know," Rose told him. "She'd assume I told you."

"I'm not planning on spending a lot of time around your human friend, Rose," he muttered.

That didn't seem to extinguish her worry, but she moved on, anyway. "Were you telepathic when you were human?"

"Technically, yes," Kallias said, "but I had no idea."

"How?" she asked.

"It was latent," he said with a shrug. "The transformation into a vampire doesn't *create* psychic abilities. It just awakens them."

"But Audrey's not a vampire," Rose told him. "I've seen her—in the sunlight. *Plenty* of times."

"Of course she's not," he said, to her relief. He sighed, "Most humans will never know if they had psychic abilities or not. They remain latent until death. I don't *know* why, but I suspect it's for your own protection."

"Protection from what?" she said.

"You can't heal yourself the way I can," he reminded her. "If *you* do any damage to *your* brain, it might be permanent. Whereas, for a vampire, all injuries are temporary. I think humans brains suppress psychic abilities to prevent them from harming you, but when you become a vampire, you have regenerative abilities. So, your power awakens."

"Is there a way to know you have them," Rose asked, "when you're human, I mean?"

"There are signs," he told her. "The abilities reside in certain parts of the brain. So, naturally, people who have special abilities often display exceptional strength in those areas of the mind. As a human, I was intelligent and influential—common traits of a telepath. I excelled in strategy and leadership."

Rose nodded slowly.

"Erik's an empath," Kallias added, "which means he can feel and manipulate emotions. When he was human, he was emotional and sensitive. He was often mocked by other men of his time—for the amount of sympathy he showed toward opponents. And despite his obsession with sex, he was and still *is* a romantic."

"You're kidding," Rose said with an amused smile.

He returned the smile. "No."

She laughed softly and nodded. "And you think there are signs in my case, too?"

"Absolutely," Kallias assured her. "Your IQ's off the charts, which already suggests your mind is capable of more than most people's. And as I said before, your strong will, resilience, and determination are traits I'd also associate with telekinesis."

"But if you're right—which I don't think you are, by the way," she added quickly, "but *if* you are, why didn't mine remain latent until death, like yours did? Why was I able to use mine against Theron?"

Kallias rolled his eyes at her continuous denial. "For the same reason a human mother can lift a car, when her child's trapped beneath it—but not any other time."

"Adrenaline?" Rose assumed. "Fight-or-flight?"

"Because it's necessary," Kallias provided. "When there's real danger, the body lets you access your full strength—even if it might hurt you."

"Right," Rose muttered, "so adrenaline."

He sighed. "When Theron attacked," he began, "you were upset, weren't you?"

She didn't meet his gaze. "I was more than upset."

"Maybe you felt it was life-or-death?" he assumed.

A soft, pained breath escaped Rose's lips. "Worse."

"So, you accessed the power to protect yourself," Kallias said.

"Without even realizing it?" Rose said skeptically.

He sighed. "Telekinesis is the manipulation of the physical world to your will—to your *choice*," he reminded her. "You *decided* you wouldn't let it happen, and it didn't. You *decided* you wanted him off of you, and he was thrown off of you."

A surprised laugh escaped her lips. "Yeah, right."

He shook his head. "I knew you weren't ready to accept it."

"Oh, come on," she said, when he walked away from her. She followed, her smile wary. "I'm trying. I really am. But...you're saying I can move things with my mind!"

He turned to scowl at her. "Yes."

Rose offered a helpless shrug. "It's insane."

"Look, you asked for the truth, and I gave it to you. If you don't want to believe it, don't," he snarled. "I don't give a shit."

She breathed out a pained sigh. "I'm trying."

"The sun's up," Kallias said. "I need sleep."

"Wait," Rose pleaded. "Will you answer one more question?"

He raised an eyebrow. "One more or one *billion* more?"

"Definitely a billion," she said honestly, "but one, for now."

"Hmm," he grunted. "Fine."

"Even if I do have a psychic ability," Rose said, though she was skeptical, "I'm clearly not the only one. So, why would my blood smell so much more powerful than anyone else's?"

He sighed tiredly.

He really *was* beginning to look pale, but Rose didn't know why.

"Telepathic power, like mine, is considered the rarest and most powerful ability," he told her, "but *only* by people who don't know about telekinesis. If telepathy is rare, telekinesis is *unheard of.*"

She frowned. "Well, what about the other people with telekinetic abilities?"

Kallias was silent for a moment. "Rose...there is no one else."

Her frown deepened. "How do you even know it exists, then?"

"There's no one else *alive* with telekinetic abilities," he amended, "but even the vampires who *did* have it in the past weren't capable of doing what you did. You threw a vampire across the room with a single thought. Your mind carried more force than your body." He shrugged. "In the past, vampires with telekinetic abilities could barely knock over a candle with their minds."

Rose was stuck on that first part. "Kallias, why aren't they alive?"

He pursed his lips, before admitting, "They were killed."

She swallowed uneasily at that. "By whom?"

"Aaron," he said, "or possibly by his second-in-command: Kara."

"You mentioned Aaron before," she noted. "The ancient vampire."

"Yes," he confirmed. "He's the most powerful vampire I know of."

"Why did he kill them?" Rose asked.

Kallias shrugged. "He considered them a threat."

Rose's brows furrowed. "That's it?"

He nodded. "An older vampire almost always overpowers a younger vampire. Age is power. But psychic abilities throw off that balance—*especially* telekinetic abilities. No one's ever actually been powerful enough to threaten Aaron, but he doesn't take any chances. He sends his second-in-command to kill them—just in case."

She gaped at him. "He has them killed *just in case*?"

"He's a ruthless, power-hungry asshole," Kallias said simply.

"Will he try to kill me, too?" Rose asked.

"He'd never consider a human a threat," he assured her. "Besides, he lives in Europe. He doesn't even know you exist."

"You don't think Theron would tell him?" she asked.

Kallias snorted, "Aaron doesn't take Theron seriously. If he did, he would've killed him back when he killed all of the other ancient vampires."

"When he did what?" she sputtered.

"Aaron's path to power was paved with blood," Kallias told her.

Rose lifted her eyebrows. "Like most tyrants."

She half-expected Kallias to defend the ancient vampire, but instead, he just nodded.

Clearly, Kallias wasn't a fan of the guy.

"Well," Rose said with a smile, "I promised I'd only ask one question. I guess you can go get in your coffin now."

He let out a loud, surprised laugh. His smile was so wide that she actually caught a glimpse of those razor-sharp fangs he usually hid so well.

Without thinking, she reached out to touch them.

His smile faded, and he grasped her wrist to stop her.

"Don't hide them from me," she said softly, "please."

His brows furrowed, and he released her hand.

He left his mouth open, his fangs still visible, and she hesitantly reached up to touch them.

"You don't mind?" she whispered.

He shook his head slowly.

It was important to Rose that she did this—not just out of curiosity, but also because Kallias needed to know that she wasn't afraid.

That he didn't need to hide them from her.

Rose traced his left fang with the tip of her finger, and his eyes darkened with hunger. Aside from its sharpness, it felt just like a canine tooth, but of course, the sharpness wasn't something she could ignore. The fang felt sharper than any blade she'd ever felt.

His eyes fluttered closed, and he leaned into her.

"Ouch," Rose said, as she accidentally cut her finger.

His fingers curled around her wrist almost instantly, and she glanced up at him. His eyes were dark with hunger, but to her surprise, he seemed in control of it, this time.

He closed his mouth around her finger, tasting the small drop of blood that had surfaced.

Rose's mouth fell open, and her breath came rapidly.

Kallias released her hand, and his lips curved into a slow, hungry smile. "Your heart is racing," he told her.

Rose placed her hand over her chest, as if she could stifle the sound of her rapid pulse with her palm. "Yeah, that's embarrassing."

He laughed. "You know I won't let him hurt you, right?"

Rose blinked at his sudden seriousness. "Who?" she said softly. "Theron or Aaron?"

"Either," he said. "I'll keep you safe. Somehow."

Her chest fluttered at the promise. "I didn't ask for that."

"You don't have to," Kallias told her.

She fidgeted nervously. "I'd prefer to protect myself."

It was the truth, after all. She appreciated the kindness he was trying to show her, but she couldn't depend on him like that.

She couldn't depend on *anyone* like that.

He opened his mouth—perhaps to argue—but he suddenly staggered.

His hand shot out to catch himself against the bedpost, and his body leaned heavily against it.

"Kallias?" Rose said worriedly. "Are you okay?"

Aside from the fact that he was still standing—or leaning, really—he didn't even look conscious, but he somehow managed to answer, anyway. "Mmm," he grunted. "The sun's weakening me. I need to be asleep."

Rose placed her hand on his chest to steady him, but as soon as her palm made contact with his overheated skin, his eyes came open. He looked down at her hand, as if he were wondering why it was there.

"Let me help," Rose said.

He raised his head and frowned at her. "Help?" he mumbled.

"Yes, it's a one-syllable word. I assumed you knew it," she quipped.

He squinted, as if *that* had confused him, as well.

Rose sidestepped him to get out from between his heavy, unsteady body and the footboard. Then, she wrapped her fingers around his arm and pulled gently.

"I don't need help," he grumbled, but then, he stumbled and nearly fell into the floor.

"Yes, you clearly have it all under control," she said, as he nearly knocked her down, too. She pulled again, trying unsuccessfully to pull the large vampire forward. "Come on, big guy," she said in a strained voice. "I can't pull you all by myself."

"*Skata, moro mou,*" he cursed. Apparently, the sleepy version of him preferred to speak in Greek. He caught her, when she nearly fell, but then, he nearly fell, too.

"Are all vampires like this in the daytime?" Rose muttered.

"Weakens the mind," he said—for the second time.

Did he *know* he'd already said it?

"Let me help you to bed," Rose said in as firm of a tone as she could.

He leaned into her, which nearly sent them both sprawling backward into the floor, and sneered, "Will you tuck me in, *manoula*? Kiss me goodnight?"

Rose scowled. "Oh, yeah, very mature," she said sarcastically. She rolled her eyes. "And did you really just call me *mommy*?"

He pushed her hand away again. "I can do it myself."

Rose put her hands on her hips. "Yet, when I say that, it's a problem."

He grumpily pushed her away again and tried to walk on his own.

Rose lifted her eyebrows, when he stumbled *again*. She sighed and went to his side, wrapping her hand around his arm. "You walk. I'll lead," she offered.

They had almost reached the bed when Kallias grunted, "No."

"Chill, Grumpy," Rose muttered. "We're almost there."

"Not the bed," he said, looking down at her. "Sofa."

Rose rolled her eyes. "You're half-asleep already. Just get in bed."

"Sofa," he repeated, like some kind of sullen toddler with fangs.

"I'm not letting you sleep on a sofa that's half your size," Rose told him, "especially not when you're like this. Just lie down."

He leaned heavily on the bed and grasped her arm before she could walk away. "Then, I'm not letting you sleep on the sofa either."

His words slurred together, and he could barely keep his eyes open.

She sighed. "Fine." She lifted her shoulders in a defeated shrug. "We'll both sleep in the bed. We're adults. I'm sure it'll be fine."

Kallias nodded vigorously—but apparently couldn't manage a vocal response.

"I sleep in the same bed with Audrey, after all," Rose muttered under her breath. "Then again, Audrey's like a sister to me, and you're...*less* like a sister."

"I'd hope so," he slurred.

"I'm sure it'll be fine," Rose said, as if she were still trying to convince herself. "We can just—"

She blinked, as Kallias suddenly fell backward. Aside from the slight twitching of his lips, he looked comatose.

"You just fell," Rose pointed out, in case he hadn't noticed.

"Shut up, and get in bed," he murmured.

Rose just lifted her eyebrows. "Is this how you always are during the day?"

"No," he slurred. "I'm usually *asleep* during the day."

"Yeah," she said, wincing guiltily, as she realized her questions were what had kept him awake. "Sorry about that."

Her jaw dropped, when he suddenly raised his lower body up off the bed and started clumsily tugging his black sweatpants down.

She quickly clasped her hands over her eyes and shrieked, "What are you doing?"

"Taking off my pants," he said, as he tossed them in the floor.

She dropped her hands to glare at him, and her eyes widened as she took in his nearly nude appearance. The only clothing that covered his body now was a pair of thin, black boxers. "Yes, I can see that. But *why?*"

"I'm not sleeping in *clothes,*" he scoffed, as if they were disgusting.

"Oh, no. You will wear clothes," Rose stated. "You're not sleeping naked!"

He shrugged, his eyes still closed. "Fine. I'll leave on the boxers."

She cast a brief glance at the boxers, and she quickly looked away, as she noticed how they clung to his... She blinked at the ceiling as she tried to clear *that* image from her mind. "Those don't help much!"

With an annoyed groan, he jerked the blanket over his body. Thankfully, *that* helped a little more. "Get in the damn bed."

She glared at him. "Sun or no sun, you're not going to order me around like that. I'll get in bed when *I* decide I'm ready."

"Fine. Whatever," Kallias mumbled, "but I'm going to sleep."

Rose had every intention of standing there for a long time afterward —just to prove a point—but she'd been awake for a little too long, too. And while the sun didn't have a *supernatural* effect on her, time had a natural one. She yawned, her eyes watering.

"Okay, I'm ready for bed now," Rose announced.

She circled the bed and frowned at how much of the bed his long body covered. She grabbed her pillows and wedged them between them —but then, she sighed, as she realized her two pillows barely reached his waist. "I need your pillows."

Kallias opened his eyes, scowling. "What the hell are you doing?"

"I'm building a wall," Rose explained. "Give me your pillows."

He closed his eyes again. "You're not getting my pillows. Just get in bed."

Rose sighed in defeat and grabbed her own pillows again. She returned them to the top of the bed. "Fine. But keep your hands and fangs to yourself, okay?"

He kept his eyes closed, but his lips twitched into a smile. "I'll try."

Rose pulled the blanket down and crawled into bed. She swallowed uneasily, as she noticed how close his body was to her own. Even without moving, her arm nearly brushed his.

She turned on her side, facing away from him.

"Turn off the damn light," Kallias grumbled. "It's giving me a headache."

Rose rolled back toward him and glared at him—even though she knew he couldn't see her with his eyes closed.

As she rolled back onto her side, toward the nightstand, she complained, "You'd think, after twenty-five hundred years, you would've learned how to say *please*, at some point."

Rose gasped as she suddenly felt Kallias move behind her. His strong arms circled her waist and pulled her back against his front.

"Please," he breathed into her ear.

The combination of his breath in her ear and the low, accented tone of his voice sent heated waves of desire down her spine.

He chuckled and rolled over onto his back, as if nothing had happened.

Rose, on the other hand, had forgotten how to move. She blinked, shocked that he'd somehow managed to turn her on with one, innocent, little word. She wondered if *that* were some kind of supernatural power vampires possessed, too, but there was no way she was going to humiliate herself by asking.

"Light, Rose," Kallias grunted.

"Okay, Grumpy," Rose muttered, as she switched off the lamp.

———

KALLIAS PAUSED ON THE TEMPLE STEPS AND GLANCED UP AT THE TEMPLE OF Aphrodite. Wide columns stretched before him, as far as he could see, with gorgeous, ornate designs carved into the white stone.

He sighed. "Do you really think this is necessary?"

Phoebe turned toward him, her pale pink peplos swirling around her figure as she did. She stood several steps above him—so far ahead that he actually had to look up at her. She had her long black hair elegantly pinned to the top of her head, leaving her neck bare.

"We're getting married!" she reminded him. "We have to offer the traditional gifts to Aphrodite, so she'll bless our marriage. You want to marry me, don't you?"

"Of course I do," he sighed. "I just don't see the point in these ridiculous traditions. I'll love you with or without an imaginary goddess's blessing."

Her brown eyes widened, and she ran down toward him, her sandals clacking against the stone steps. "You know you can't say that!" she hissed. "Here, of all places! What if the gods hear you?"

"If they existed," Kallias said, "I'd imagine they'd have more important matters to worry about than my skepticism."

Phoebe gave him a reproachful look. "Well, I, like most people, believe they do," she reminded him. "So, I'd appreciate it if, for just one day, you could pretend to care about this."

He smiled and held up his hands. "Fine. I'll behave."

Phoebe giggled at that, and she grabbed his hand, tugging him along behind her, as she climbed the steps.

When they stepped inside the temple, Kallias blinked, stunned by how dark it was. At the Temple of Athena, where he taught lessons each day, the priestesses kept the temple well-lit with candles, but for some reason—on that day, at least—Aphrodite's priestesses seemed to have neglected that task.

He followed his fiancée, as she led him toward the statue of Aphrodite in the center of the temple. Further into the temple, it grew even darker, but his eyes slowly adjusted.

Kallias froze, as he saw two, pale blue eyes in the darkness.

Phoebe tugged at his hand. "What's wrong?"

He shook his head in confusion. "Nothing."

Kallias followed Phoebe through the temple, going through motions of the tradition without truly participating, but repeatedly, he found his gaze drawn to those strange, pale blue eyes.

He squinted, trying to see the person behind them, but it was just too dark. Those pale eyes followed them, though, the entire time they were in the temple.

There was something so unnerving about those eyes.

Eyes were windows of emotion. Normally, you could know what someone felt by looking into their eyes—by seeing the spark of anger, the dance of amusement, the flash of pain, or the darkening of lust.

But *these* eyes—it was as if the person felt...nothing.

After about an hour, Phoebe said, "Are you ready to go?"

"Yeah. Of course," Kallias said distractedly.

"The sun's setting," she added. "Father expects me home by nightfall."

He glanced at her, finally, and he blinked as he realized he hadn't been paying attention. "I'll...come in and explain it to your father."

She laughed nervously, her eyes wide. "That's not necessary."

His brows furrowed. "But your father likes me."

"Y-yes," Phoebe said hesitantly, "but he's busy. You can't come in."

His frown deepened. "Uh, okay. Let's get you home, then."

She nodded uneasily and turned to leave. Kallias followed her toward the front of the temple, but he chanced one, last look at those pale blue eyes.

He froze, as he found them directly behind him.

The man had kept himself so well-hidden throughout their time in the temple that Kallias hadn't been able to tell much more than his height and the color of those strange eyes of his.

But now, he'd emerged, and he stood just a few feet behind Kallias and Phoebe. Much like his eyes, his skin was far too pale.

Was he sick?

Dead?

No, of course he wasn't dead. What a strange thought.

The man wore the white chiton and Aphrodite pendant of a priest, but most people in the service of the gods were cheerful and friendly.

This man was the opposite.

Phoebe squeezed his hand. "What's the matter?"

When Kallias didn't answer, she turned to look at what Kallias had seen, and she froze, too. "Who is that?"

"I don't know," Kallias said. "Have you seen him before?"

"No," Phoebe whispered. She stared longingly at the man, as if she were sinking into some sort of trance. "I think I'd remember if I had. He's so...*attractive*, don't you think? And...seductive."

"Uh, no?" Kallias said with a frown. "I don't find other men attractive."

Phoebe didn't respond. It was as if she'd forgotten where she was.

"Phoebe?" Kallias said, his frown deepening. "What the hell?"

"Hmm?" she murmured, but she didn't look at him.

Puzzled by her behavior, he turned toward the man who watched them. "Who are you," he demanded to know, "and why are you following us?"

The man didn't answer, but his lips tilted slightly.

Growing impatient, Kallias approached the strange man. Phoebe let out a nervous squeak—but followed him anyway.

Kallias expected the man to retreat back to wherever he'd been hiding, but instead, he waited, as Kallias approached.

Kallias felt Phoebe's trembling fingers tug at his chiton, pleading with him to go back.

"Tell me who you are," Kallias snarled at the man.

"Erastos," the man said, his voice as emotionless as his eyes.

"Well, Erastos," Kallias snapped, "why are you watching us?"

"I was watching *you*, Kallias," Erastos said.

Kallias frowned worriedly. "How do you know my name?"

"I know many things about you, Kallias of Athens," Erastos told him.

"Oh, really?" Kallias said coldly. "Do you mind telling me how?"

"I know things," Erastos said, as if that were an actual answer.

Kallias frowned. "That was even vaguer than the first statement!"

His long, blonde hair swayed slightly, as he stepped forward. "How I know what I know isn't important right now," Erastos said.

Kallias narrowed his eyes at that. "Fine. I don't have time to deal with you, anyway," he muttered. He placed his hand on Phoebe's arm, startling her out of that strange trancelike state she'd fallen into again. "Come on. Let's get you home."

"You can't leave yet," Erastos said. "There's something I must give you."

Kallias scoffed at that. "I'll leave whenever the hell I want."

"It's of utmost importance that you take it," Erastos insisted.

Kallias pulled at Phoebe's arm, but she hesitated, still.

"What is it?" Phoebe asked curiously.

Erastos opened his hand, revealing what he'd been holding. At first, it just looked like a rolled up piece of cloth, but then, Erastos unfolded the cloth with his other hand, revealing a strange, blood-red stone, unlike anything Kallias or Phoebe had ever seen before.

The stone looked large and heavy, and the jagged edges of the stone jutted out in all directions. "You need to take this, Kallias."

Kallias frowned at the strange priest. "Why?"

Erastos stepped forward and held out the stone, wordlessly insisting that Kallias take it from his hand.

Kallias reluctantly picked up the stone, and he examined it carefully, turning the weighty stone in his hand. He squinted as he noticed a tiny inscription carved into the stone. In Greek, it read: εκλεκτός, or Eklektos —which, translated into English, could've meant chosen, selected, or fated.

Kallias glanced at Erastos. "Why does it say, 'Eklektos?'"

"Maybe the stone was chosen for something," Phoebe said. She leaned over to look at it. "Although I can't imagine *what*. It's ugly."

"It says, 'Eklektos,' because it belongs to the Eklektos," Erastos stated.

Kallias scowled at him. "Am I supposed to know what that means?"

"It means it belongs to a person called the Eklektos," Erastos said.

Kallias sighed. Nothing this guy said made sense. "So, what does that have to do with me?"

"She'll one day come under your protection," Erastos explained, "and when she does, you'll want to give her the Stone."

Trying to get a straight answer out of this priest was exhausting. "I don't even know what you're talking about."

"The Eklektos will play an important role in the fate of the world," Erastos told him, "and you'll play an important role in *her* fate."

"Whose?" Kallias said irritably. "Who are you even talking about?"

"The Eklektos," Erastos said with a frown. "I explained this already."

"What the—" Kallias muttered. He sighed heavily, "I'm asking who the Eklektos is!"

"She has many names," Erastos said. "The name you'll call her is not the name I call her."

Kallias rolled his eyes. "Wow. You're clearly out of your mind. I don't know how you haven't gotten kicked out of the temple," he muttered. He held out the Stone. "Here. You can have your rock back. Phoebe and I are leaving."

Erastos shook his head firmly, but his eyes remained cold and unfeeling. "You're not listening, Kallias of Athens. *You* must take the Stone of the Eklektos and protect it—until you meet her. It's her fate to take it, and any deviation from fate is bound to be painful."

"He's really lost his mind, hasn't he?" Kallias muttered to Phoebe.

Erastos sighed—and reluctantly turned his gaze toward Phoebe. "You'll convince him to take it, won't you?" There was sinister edge in his tone now. "It's very dangerous. It will unlock limitless power."

Kallias rolled his eyes. "It's a rock."

But Phoebe was hanging onto every word. "It sounds terrifying."

"It will be," Erastos told her, "if it falls into the wrong hands."

Kallias grabbed the strange priest's hand and shoved the Stone into it. "Take your stupid rock. And see a physician—because you're insane."

"You're choosing the more painful route," Erastos warned.

Kallias turned toward Phoebe. "I don't understand anything he's saying. Let's just go, before he wastes more of our time."

"Wait," she whispered. "I think you should take the Stone, just in case."

"Just in case *what*?" Kallias asked. "In case I meet *another* crazy person, who calls herself the Eklektos? I think I'll pass. Let's go."

"He said the Stone is powerful," Phoebe hissed. "Just take it."

"The Stone can't be powerful, Phoebe. It's a *stone*," Kallias muttered.

Phoebe sighed and turned her gaze toward Erastos. "Could I take it, instead? I'll put it somewhere safe in his home. I am his fiancée."

"I know who you are, Phoebe of Corinth," Erastos said. His strange, pale blue eyes assessed her coldly. "I know more about you than Kallias does."

Kallias scowled at that. "What are you? Some kind of stalker?"

"No. I don't obtain information in that way," Erastos answered.

Phoebe shifted nervously. "Well, I can take it—if you want."

Erastos shifted that cold gaze of his toward Kallias. "I'd advise against it. It should remain in your hands alone, Kallias."

"I'm not taking your stupid rock," Kallias insisted. "I'm leaving."

Erastos shrugged and walked toward them. He placed the Stone of the Eklektos in Phoebe's hand. "Although I know it's pointless to tell you this, I must warn you that the consequences will be tragic if the Stone of the Eklektos doesn't remain in Kallias's possession."

Phoebe squirmed nervously, wondering how much he knew.

Kallias narrowed his eyes. "Are you threatening her?"

Erastos turned toward him. "I'm merely warning her. I should remind you: any deviation from fate is painful, Kallias. The route you're choosing will cause you suffering."

"And I should remind *you* that you're insane," Kallias scoffed.

"When the time has come, we'll meet again," Erastos said.

"I sure as hell hope not," Kallias said under his breath. He held his hand out to Phoebe. "Come on. Let's get out of here."

She nodded and took his hand, clutching the Stone of the Eklektos in the other.

But before they left, she spun around and called out, "What is so important about the Eklektos, anyway?"

The strange priest seemed to almost smile.

Almost.

"She'll either save the world or destroy it."

16

KINDNESS AND MURDER

*K*allias awoke with two questions on his mind: *Why was I dreaming about that stupid stone again? And why am I aroused?*

He groaned miserably and shifted—only to realize that there was someone on top of him.

Only then did he realize that the warm, enticing comfort he felt was *her*—her soft, ample curves against his skin. He glanced down to find Rose curled against his side with her arm wrapped around his stomach and her long legs entangled with his own.

Her red hair fanned over her face, hiding it from his gaze.

Still, he heard her steady breathing and slowed heart rate and knew she was asleep. Her bare feet, which brushed his ankle, felt colder than the rest of her body. He could feel her soft, full lips against his skin and her breasts squashed against his waist.

"Well, that explains it," Kallias muttered.

At some point while they slept, he'd draped his arm casually around her shoulder, and he'd rested his hand against her back.

He couldn't believe he'd actually slept like this. She was right that he hadn't been celibate all these years, but he hadn't been sleeping like *this* with women. The last woman he'd cuddled with like this had been Phoebe—twenty-five hundred years ago.

Kallias shifted, absentmindedly trailing his finger up her spine.

He'd only been acting on impulse and hadn't expected a response. But when his fingertip moved along her spine, she moaned sleepily, and her back arched ever-so-slightly, which pressed the warm, soft area between her legs against his thigh.

His eyes widened at the arousing sensation. "Damn it, woman."

He scowled at the sleeping seductress, blaming her entirely for this. She made a soft murmuring sound in response and snuggled closer to him.

Slowly, his scowl morphed into a smile, and he ran his fingers through her soft, auburn waves. Her hand rested against his bare stomach, her fair, freckled skin contrasting starkly with his darker complexion.

Kallias shook her shoulder. "Wake up."

Rose groaned softly in protest, holding him tighter.

"Rose, wake up," he murmured in her ear.

Her eyes opened, and she blinked slowly at the darkness. As the sleepy fogginess of her mind began to clear, she gradually became aware of his body against her.

She patted his lean stomach, frowning in confusion.

"Uh, Kallias?" she said nervously.

She could hear the suppressed laughter in his voice as he replied, "Yes?"

Rose remained completely frozen. "Can you turn on the lamp?"

Kallias stretched out his arm and flipped on the switch.

The light burned her eyes, at first, but when her eyes adjusted, she realized that she was lying against Kallias, literally curled up around him.

Rose jumped up so fast that her head spun, and she immediately hung her head in her hands and groaned. When the dizziness eased, she decided to stare at a painting on the wall—rather than face him.

Unfortunately, Rose then felt him sit up behind her, his bare chest brushing against her back and his hand braced on the other side of hers. She heard his low laughter in her ear.

"What was it you said last night about wanting *me* to keep my hands to myself?" he teased.

Her blush deepened. At this point, her cheeks felt so hot that Rose worried they'd spontaneously combust. She directed her deadly glare at a poor, innocent painting on the wall—because glaring at Kallias would require looking at him, and she was *far* too embarrassed to face him. "It was an accident. I clearly thought you were my pillow."

He laughed. "You curl up around your pillow like *that*?"

Rose pressed her fingers against her cheeks to make sure her face wasn't actually on fire yet. "Look, I'm sorry, okay?" She turned to look at him. "Can we, *please*, just forget this happened?"

A slow smirk spread across his face. "Not a chance."

With a frustrated growl, Rose hopped off the bed and nearly tripped over her actual pillow, which she'd apparently dropped in the floor at some point while she slept.

See? It was the pillow's fault.

She sifted through her bags, which were scattered across the table. She found a pair of blue jeans and a T-shirt.

Out of the corner of her eye, Rose saw Kallias crawl off the bed after her. She stared very pointedly at the table—in an effort to avoid looking at his half-naked body.

He leaned in close and murmured in her ear, "Has anyone ever told you that you make these really sexy sounds when you're sleeping?"

Rose blushed harder than she'd ever blushed before. She turned to him, careful to keep her gaze above his waist. "Has anyone ever told *you* that you're the most frustrating person on the planet?"

Kallias laughed. "Just you."

Rose waved her hand irritably. "You're still not wearing pants."

"I'm aware," he said, as if there were nothing unusual about that.

She lifted her eyebrows. "Don't you have any shame?"

He snorted at that. "I'm from Ancient Greece."

She laughed softly. "Touché." She gathered her clothes into her arms and stepped past him. She didn't look at him until she reached the bathroom. "I'm getting dressed. I'd appreciate it if you did the same."

He grinned. "I'll think about it."

WHEN ROSE CAME OUT OF THE BATHROOM, FULLY DRESSED AND HOLDING HER toothbrush and pajamas, she found Kallias lounging lazily on the sofa, already dressed in a pair of black jeans and a black button-down shirt. He flipped through the channels on the television, and he tilted up a beer bottle and downed half of it.

Rose sat down beside him. "Isn't it a little early to be drinking?"

"I didn't realized humans considered eight at night *early*," he said.

She lifted her eyebrows. "You just woke up. Your 8 P.M. is like our 5 or 6 *A.M.*"

"Yeah," he said. He held out the beer bottle. "Do you want some?"

She glanced at the half-empty bottle. "No, thanks. I don't drink."

Kallias looked at her, then, for the first time since she'd left the bathroom. His lips twitched into an amused smile. "You don't break the law. You don't drink. You don't use profanity. What *do* you do for fun?"

Rose shot a peeved glare at him. "There are plenty of fun things to do that don't involve criminal activity, intoxication, profanity, or sex."

He raised an eyebrow. "Rose, I, uh—I never said anything about sex."

Her eyes widened, and her cheeks flushed scarlet. She clasped her hand over her mouth. "That's—that's not what I meant!"

His lips twitched in amusement. *"What's* not what you meant?"

"That I'm a virgin! I'm not. I mean, I am, but that's not what I meant. That's the opposite of what I meant!" Rose said, her words spilling out in a rush. Her face was redder than he'd ever seen it. "Not the opposite of virgin—but the opposite of saying it."

For several moments, Kallias just sat there, staring with that tight-lipped smile, as if he were desperately trying to hold back laughter.

Rose paled in horror. "Did I just tell you I'm a virgin?"

Kallias nodded slowly, his lips twitching upward. "More than once."

Rose whimpered and buried her face in the corner of the of the sofa, underneath a pile of cheesy, heart-shaped pillows. As if the excruciating humiliation wasn't bad enough, Kallias finally lost control and burst into hysterical laughter.

She lifted her head and spun toward him. "It's not funny."

"You're right," he said, still laughing. "It's hilarious."

"No, it's not," she said, and then, she jumped to her feet.

Kallias stopped laughing, when he saw her heading toward the door. "Rose," he called worriedly. "Where are you going?"

"Away from *you*," she said—and pulled open the door.

Rose gasped, as the door suddenly slammed shut.

Rose found her back pressed against the door, her body trapped between the red door and Kallias. His hands pressed against the door, one hand braced on each side of her head.

Rose looked up at him, expecting to find anger in his eyes, but instead, he just looked confused. "Was the moving-at-the-speed-of-light-thing necessary?" she complained.

"Why were you trying to leave the room?" he asked.

"We just went over this," Rose reminded him. "To get away from you."

His brows furrowed. "There are windows in the hallway, and the sun hasn't fully set yet," he said worriedly. "I wouldn't have been able to follow you."

She rolled her eyes. "Yes. That's the point. We *just* went over this."

His eyes narrowed. "What if Theron knows where we are right now?"

"He wouldn't be able to attack me," Rose said. "Windows, remember?"

Kallias sighed. "Don't you remember the human who tried to kill you at the college—the one with the gun?" he asked. "Don't you think, if he had her do that, he could do the same thing now? Don't you think, if he knew where we were, he'd have a human attack you the moment you left the room without me?"

Rose wanted to argue, but as much as she hated to admit it, he was right.

"I'm sorry, but I can't let you leave the room until it's dark," he said.

"Don't you think you should let me decide for myself?" Rose challenged.

To her surprise, he agreed, "Of course that's what I *should* do. But I never promised to do what I should do. I only promised to keep you safe."

Rose felt so conflicted. On one hand, she felt justifiably angry about his dismissive response. She needed to make her own decisions.

On the other hand, there was something different in his voice just then—something soft and warm, like concern or worry. "All right."

He let one arm fall. "Now, can you please stop acting crazy, and tell me why you're upset."

Her irritation immediately returned. "Crazy?"

For some reason, he'd yet to step away from her, even though she'd already assured him she wouldn't leave.

He shrugged, amusement dancing in his light brown eyes. "Well, I figured *insane* was too strong of a word, but if you prefer..."

"I'm *not* acting crazy," she scoffed.

He grinned at her. "That's what crazy people say."

"You laughed at me," she told him. "I'm upset because you laughed."

His brows furrowed. "Is laughing a crime now?"

Rose looked away, her brows creased. "What's so funny about me being a virgin?" she said lowly. "I have a right to process it however I need to process it."

"Process what?" Kallias said.

She shook her head, visibly upset. "You're just like everyone else. You think it's some kind of joke, but it's not. What? Am I less of a person because I'm not ready for..." she trailed off.

"I never said that," he said. "I *wouldn't* say that."

But she didn't seem to hear him. "Of course, what did I expect from the man who thinks kissing is just physical?" she scoffed. "You're too emotionally-stunted to understand."

He stepped back. "I'm sorry. I must have missed the memo. Have we reversed roles? Are you the rude asshole now? What does that make me? The person who defines random words in order to prove I know more than you?"

She crossed her arms and narrowed her eyes.

He continued, "You see, the Kudzu plant is defined as a—"

"This is you *not* being the rude butthole?" Rose interrupted.

He stopped mid-sentence and smiled. "Sorry. Old habits."

"For the record, the words I define are not *that* random," she scoffed.

Kallias stepped closer again, and he put his hand beneath her chin, tipping her head back so that she'd meet his gaze. "Listen," he sighed. "I don't care if you're a virgin. That's your business. I *certainly* don't think it makes you less of a person. I don't know what asshole said *that* to you, but it wasn't me."

Rose winced—because it was true.

Her ex-boyfriend had thought that. Not him.

"I didn't laugh at you because you haven't had sex," he said with a small smile. "I laughed because you're so damn awkward sometimes it's hilarious. And cute."

Rose blinked in shock. "Cute?"

Kallias stepped back and leaned beside the counter that happened to have a coffee pot sitting on it. He chuckled, as he noticed her eyeing the aforementioned coffee pot hungrily.

He trailed his gaze downward, a flirty smile pulling at his lips. "I can't say I'm not a *little* surprised you've managed to not have sex, though."

With her attention now fully on her need for coffee, Rose stepped forward eagerly and picked up the packet of coffee grounds. Her hip brushed his, as she opened the complimentary coffee packet and started preparing it.

She scoffed, "You say that like I've had a lot of opportunities or something."

He stared down at her, amused by her obsession with coffee. *Were all humans like that?* "Haven't you?"

"Are you serious?" she asked incredulously. Rose looked up at him, as she opened a pack of paper coffee cups. "Do I *seem* like the type of woman men want to have sex with?"

"You like women, too," he pointed out.

"Yeah, and I'm not much of a catch for them either," Rose said.

His smile faded. "Why would you think that?"

As she filled the coffee pot with water, she shrugged. "You've seen me. I'm so awkward I can barely carry on a conversation, much less make it successfully through a date. I'm bad at the social stuff, and my idea of a wild night is finishing a six-hundred-page-book in one night." She turned off the water and carried the coffee pot back to counter. "Not to mention, the fact that I'm completely and utterly unattractive..."

"What?" he interrupted. "Why the hell are you so insecure?"

His hostility caught her off-guard. She glanced at him, blinking in shock. "Well, psychologists say that insecurities come from—"

"Rose," he interrupted again. He sighed. "Stop doing that."

"Stop doing what?" Rose said.

"Hiding behind impersonal facts and definitions," Kallias said. "I didn't ask you what the statistics say or what psychologists say. I asked what *you* think." He stepped closer. "It's not them I want to understand. It's you."

"Fine," she sighed. "I don't know. Do you like *that* answer?"

"It's better. It's personal, at least," he said.

Rose shifted uneasily. How had seen through her answer like that?

But then, she supposed it was easy when you could literally read someone's mind.

Aside from the low, crackling thunder that rumbled outside, and the ambient noise of the television in the background, only silence stretched between them for a moment.

"And you're not unattractive," Kallias added. "Whoever told you that was just trying to hurt you. And he obviously succeeded."

Rose looked up, her eyes wide. "No, no," she sputtered. "You can't read my mind. Not about him!"

His brows furrowed. "I didn't. I just assumed—"

But the memories were already flashing through Rose's mind—of the awful things he'd said to her, *done* to her.

She set down the coffee pot before she could drop it, and she gripped the counter, as her breath came faster.

Kallias frowned worriedly. "Rose, what's wrong?" he breathed. "Your heart's beating *way* too fast. What are you— You're panicking."

"No, no, no," she said, gasping for breath. "Don't read my mind. You can't read my mind. I can't stop—"

But he'd already seen it.

"Shit," Kallias said, his eyes widening at the memories. "Shit."

Rose looked up at him, and the absolute terror in her eyes was impossible to miss. "Don't say that. Why are you saying that?"

He looked away. "I'm an idiot."

"Well, I wouldn't go *that* far," Rose said, even though she could barely breathe. "You seem a *little* intelligent."

Talking more to himself than to her, he said, "No wonder your power awakened when Theron tried to rape you. It wasn't the first time. You were panicking because it was happening again. All of that trauma from before was—"

"You read my mind," she whispered. "I told you not to read my mind."

Kallias looked at her, his eyes wide with worry and regret. "Rose..."

"Stay out of my head!" she snarled at him.

He reached out for her, wanting to explain or apologize or comfort her or...*something.*

But she shrugged away from him and fled to the bathroom.

ROSE CLOSED HERSELF IN THE BATHROOM AND LOCKED THE DOOR behind her.

She crossed the bright, white-tiled room and leaned against the large bathtub. She wrapped her arms around herself, hugging her chest, as she desperately tried to slow down her breathing.

She'd never felt so humiliated.

She should've known he'd read her mind. She should've never let herself start thinking about it again.

Three short raps at the door drew her attention.

"Rose, open the door. Please," Kallias said from the other side.

"Go away," she yelled—needlessly, since he would've heard a whisper.

"Please. Just open the door," he pleaded, his voice quieter this time.

"No," she said, hugging herself tighter. "Just go away."

The doorknob turned and gave way with a loud *crack*.

The door swung open to reveal Kallias, standing uncomfortably in the doorway, with the broken doorknob in his hand.

He stared at her with a horrified expression, as if he'd found her mortally wounded, rather than just leaning against a bathtub.

Rose blinked at the broken doorknob. "I actually said *go away*, not break the door and come inside," she muttered, "but you know, close enough."

"You're crying," he said, as if that were the only explanation needed.

"What? I am *not* crying," she scoffed. But when she ran her hand under her eyes, she felt the wetness. She scowled at her tear-covered hand. "Oh."

He walked over to her, setting the doorknob on the sink. "Rose…"

"They're not tears," she lied. "I accidentally got toothpaste in my eyes."

He lifted an eyebrow at that. "Toothpaste?"

Rose winced at her error. "Soap. Soap would've been a better lie."

"Or dust," he said with a gentle smile.

She nodded.

He reached out and wiped a tear away with his thumb. "Don't cry over him," he murmured. "He doesn't deserve your tears."

Rose blinked, and another tear fell. The two sides of her warred against each other. Part of her wanted to accept the comfort he offered her, and the other wanted to push him away.

"I don't usually do this," she muttered. "It just…caught me off guard."

"Let me explain. Apologize," he pleaded. "Something."

"Well, I can't kick you out *now*," Rose said. "You broke the door."

"I'm sorry," Kallias said. He brushed a strand of red hair behind her ear, before it could get wet with her tears. "It wasn't my intention—to see *that*, I mean. It's like I told you last night: reading conscious thoughts is the simplest of my abilities. It's so easy that sometimes I do it without meaning to. I just *wonder* what someone's thinking, and suddenly, I'm in their mind."

"I just…didn't want anyone to know," she said softly. "No one knows, except for Audrey and Owen."

He frowned at that. "Did you think I'd think badly of *you* because of it?"

She shrugged. "I dated Ethan for a long time. Most people are ready for sex after a certain amount of time, and I…wasn't." She looked away, her throat tight. "Not with him. It felt wrong."

"It felt wrong because he was an abusive asshole," Kallias said.

Rose nodded. "I figured that out a little late."

"Look at me," he said. When she looked up, the look in his eyes shocked her. There was anger and concern, all at once. "You decide when and *if* you're ready. It doesn't matter how long you expected him to wait. He should've waited."

"I know. I agree," she sighed, "but—"

"No. No *buts*," he interrupted. His brows creased with frustration. "Damn it, Rose. How can you be so kind to others but so cruel to yourself?"

She chewed on her lip and shrugged, as her eyes began to burn again.

He drew her close, wrapping his arms around her. "I'm sorry I read your mind," he murmured. "But maybe it's good I did—because *someone* needs to tell you you're wrong, that you have to stop believing the things he said." He pulled back and looked down at her. "Of course he said it was your fault. Of course he said you were unattractive. That's what people like him do. He did what he did because he wanted to hurt you, just like Theron does what he does to hurt people. Rose, you don't deserve *any* of the terrible shit that's happened to you."

Rose blinked back more tears. "Thanks."

His brows furrowed. "For what?"

She shrugged. "Understanding, I guess."

He studied her for a moment, and then, he seemed to suddenly realize he was holding her. He immediately dropped his arms and stepped back. He leaned against the sink, as she returned to her place beside the bathtub.

As the awkward silence stretched between them, Rose tried to break it with her usual snark. "I can't believe you're actually being kind, for once," she teased. "It's weird."

Kallias didn't respond to her teasing with one of his usual quips. He didn't respond at all, actually. It was as if he hadn't heard her. He just stared at the wall, as if he were lost in thought.

A crack of thunder resounded outside.

"I could kill him, if you want."

Rose looked at him, her bright blue eyes wide with shock. "K-kill?"

He nodded easily, as if they were discussing something normal, like the thunderstorm or the color of the walls—not the murder of her ex-boyfriend.

"Well, so much for being kind," she said under her breath.

"Ethan. The one who tried to rape you," he said, apparently mistaking her lack of response for confusion. "Do you want me to kill him?"

Rose shook her head in disbelief. "Are you being serious right now?"

"I'll have to wait until after I deal with Theron, unfortunately," Kallias admitted, "but yes, once this is over and I'm sure you're safe, I will kill him, if you want."

She blinked at him. "If I want? You think I *want* you to murder him?"

"I wouldn't call it murder," he mused. His lip curled. "I think *slaughter* would be a more appropriate term. Like a butcher slaughtering a pig."

She frowned. "But he's not a pig. He's a human."

"I disagree," Kallias said.

Rose sighed, "Kallias, you don't kill humans. You told me that yourself."

He shrugged. "I can make an exception for this one."

She sighed in exasperation. "No, Kallias. I don't want you to murder my ex-boyfriend," she said, since he apparently expected an actual answer to that ridiculous question. "Because murder is wrong, in case you've forgotten."

"What he did to you was wrong," he reminded her.

"Yeah, and you can't fight fire with fire," she told him.

"I don't need fire. I have fangs," he assured her. "And my hands."

"That's not what I meant," she sighed. Reasoning with a vampire who apparently only understood about forty percent of the expressions humans used was a *little* exhausting. "You can't right a wrong with a wrong. Two wrongs don't make a right. Is *any* of this making sense to you?"

Thankfully, he nodded this time, apparently familiar with at least one of those. "I know," he said. Then, to her surprise, he moved closer to her, invading her space again.

Rose smelled the clean scent of soap on his skin, the unfamiliar scent of aftershave on his face, the peppermint toothpaste on his breath.

His brown eyes, dark and dangerous, bore into hers. "But as I told you before, I'm not afraid to be the bad guy. I don't *want* to make a right with two wrongs. I want to *wrong* a wrong person." He leaned closer. "You're good. You're always worried about doing what's right. I like that about you. But understand this: I don't mind being the bad guy, if it means assholes like him can't hurt you anymore."

Rose stared at him, stunned by the sincerity in his voice. Even her brother had never been *that* passionate about protecting her. But then, she guessed that was just who Kallias was.

He protected people—because he cared about them, no matter how much he liked to pretend he didn't.

Rose sighed, and quietly this time, she said, "I don't want you to kill him."

"Fine," he said, stepping back. "I won't kill him. I'll just hurt him."

Rose held out her hands, not sure where she was going wrong. "You're not beating up my ex-boyfriend, Kallias," she laughed.

He didn't understand why she was laughing. "When I was human, the punishment for attempted rape was castration," he began ominously.

Rose immediately stopped laughing, and her eyes widened.

"Since I'm not comfortable with cutting off another man's balls," he continued, "punching him in the face will have to do."

Rose shook her head slowly. She held up her hands in defeat and then stepped past him. She didn't speak until she reached the bathroom door—the *broken* bathroom door.

Then, Rose turned toward him, and with an amused smile, she said, "I'm going to overlook this *insanity*. Because that's what this is, by the way. *Insanity*." She pointed playfully at him. "*But* I'm going to ignore it, just this once, because I know it's your weird way of showing me you care."

Kallias followed her out of the bathroom and into the room. He watched as she perched herself on top of the bed and sat cross-legged. "So, is that a no?"

Rose laughed, her bright blue eyes sparkling. "Yes, that's a no."

"Okay, but just so you know, if I happen to encounter him, and my fist accidentally hits his face," he said, heading toward the fridge, "it's not my fault."

She laughed at that, too. "Well, in that case, I should warn you that Ethan's dad is the best lawyer in the state." Her smile faded, and she muttered under her breath, "One of the many reasons it would've been pointless to report him."

Kallias grabbed another beer. "I don't legally exist, remember? How's he going to file a lawsuit against *me*?"

"Ooh. Nice loophole," Rose said, her brows high. She eyed the beer bottle with concern. "Uh, should you be drinking another beer before you drive?"

His brows furrowed. "What does beer have to do with driving?"

"Uh, it's a law?" Rose said. "You can't drink and drive."

"Human law," he reminded her. "I'm not human."

"It really doesn't work that way," Rose informed him. "Did someone *tell* you it worked that way?"

"I'm a telepath," Kallias said. "They're not going to be able to arrest me."

Rose rolled her eyes. "It's not about you being arrested, Kallias," she scoffed. "It's about you putting people in danger."

He frowned. "Danger?"

"Yes, danger," Rose said. "I'm not going to let you endanger people by driving while intoxicated."

His lips parted in surprise, and then, he laughed. "Oh. I see."

Rose squinted at that. "You see what?"

He smiled. "Alcohol doesn't intoxicate vampires, Rose."

She frowned. "It doesn't?"

"Our metabolism works too fast," he said. "It doesn't even affect us."

Rose scowled suspiciously. "Are you sure?"

"Of course I'm sure," he chuckled. "Don't you think I'd know by now? The only thing that *can* intoxicate us is blood—as you saw at the diner."

"So, what's the point in drinking alcohol?" she asked curiously.

His eyes darkened, and his gaze drifted toward her neck. "It burns the throat. Only a little—but it's enough to distract me for just a moment from the constant fire in my throat. The hunger."

"Oh," Rose said.

He popped the lid off of the bottle. "Your coffee's ready."

Rose hopped off the bed and raced over to it. "Yay!"

Kallias leaned against the wall. He raised an eyebrow in amusement, as she danced happily, while stirring her coffee.

She turned with her coffee and almost ran directly into him. She cradled her coffee against her chest, glaring at him. "You almost made me spill it!"

He laughed, "I didn't do it. You're the one off in your own little world."

Rose sipped her steaming cup of coffee, humming a classical tune. After several sips of her scalding, magical, caffeine-infused liquid, she suddenly remembered he was standing there. "Do you want some?"

He let his smile tilt suggestively. "Not of the *coffee*."

Rose blushed.

Was that flirting?

Why was he flirting?

In an attempt to *not* be awkward, she hurried past him and climbed into the bed, cradling the cup of coffee in her hands.

"If you don't want coffee," she mumbled, not looking at him, "you must be hungry, at least."

He looked at her neck, and his smirk only grew. "Are you offering?"

Her eyes widened, and her hand flew to her neck, as if it alone could protect the pulsing, carotid artery. "What? No. I just meant—"

Kallias pushed away from the wall and strode toward the nightstand. He picked up the phone. "Relax. It was a joke."

"Hilarious," Rose said dryly, "especially the part that involves killing me."

Kallias held the phone between his shoulder and his ear, as he thumbed through the phonebook, searching for a number. He flashed another grin at her and teased, "Even if I *did* feed from you, I probably wouldn't kill you."

"*Probably*," she repeated. "How comforting."

He laughed, and then, he dialed the number he'd found in the phonebook.

Rose leaned over to look at the book. "What are you doing?"

"Ordering us a pizza," he said, as the phone line rang.

She leaned back against the headboard and smiled. "You mean you can eat pizza? I thought vampires were afraid of garlic or something."

His brown eyes shifted toward her, as he waited for someone to answer. "Hilarious," he said, mimicking her sarcastic tone perfectly.

Rose laughed. Then, she grabbed her novel from the nightstand and flipped it open to read.

AFTER SHE'D BEEN READING FOR A WHILE, KALLIAS SAID, "DID SHE DIE?"

Startled, Rose glanced up at him. He leaned casually against the wall with his arms crossed, watching her read.

"What? Who?" she sputtered. "Did who die?"

"The protagonist of your book," he answered. "The last I heard, you were worried because she was going to be skinned alive by some crazy serial killer."

Rose laughed. "Nah. They rarely kill the main character when the book's written in first-person. It's too awkward," she explained. "She did lose a finger, though."

"Oh. Well, that's promising," he quipped.

Rose set the book aside. "So, the garlic thing is a myth, too, huh?"

"Of course it is," he scoffed. "Like most things you humans say about us."

"I didn't realize I was answering for the entire human race," Rose muttered.

"Garlic has a strong, unpleasant scent," Kallias admitted, "and considering vampires have such sensitive olfactory senses, it's obviously not a *pleasant* scent for us. But it certainly doesn't scare us away or repel us. I do like pizza, after all."

Rose nodded. "And the myths about crosses and holy water?"

He rolled his eyes. "Those originated with the Christian church when they hunted vampires during the eighteenth century. They believed vampires were demons, and I guess if that were *true*, then maybe holy water and crosses *would* repel us."

"Vampires obviously aren't demons," Rose scoffed. "Demons were fallen angels. Before you were a vampire, you were a human, not an angel. And your human self—your soul, as they say—is still there. It's just...different."

"It's less than human," Kallias muttered under his breath.

He hadn't meant for Rose to hear that, but she did. Her chest tightened at the bitter loathing laced in his voice. He obviously hated vampires, which meant, by extension, he hated himself, too.

"You're wrong," she told him. "You're not less."

Kallias looked at her, surprise lightening his eyes for just a moment, but then that impassive mask came over his face, once again.

He continued, as if she'd never said anything, "Humans like to have their little superstitions—because it gives them a sense of power when they're helpless. Our only weakness is the sun, but that's too scary for them to accept."

Rose nodded. "I can see how it would be—powerful, attractive creatures with barely any weaknesses, hiding in the shadows, waiting to kill us?"

"Exactly," Kallias said. "We're humans' worst nightmare in the most brilliant disguise."

Rose frowned. That bitter edge was back in his voice again—the self-loathing hidden just beneath the surface of his words. How could she get him to see that regardless of what he was, he *wasn't* a monster?

She offered a wry smile. "So, you don't sleep in coffins. Your heart beats. You touch crosses. You eat garlic. And you don't even speak with that fake, Transylvanian accent." She shook her head in disappointment. "I hope you know you're ruining my childhood."

He laughed. "Your childhood consisted of corny horror stories?"

A wistful look passed over Rose's face. "Oh, I have *always* loved scary stories," she told him with an excited smile. "Bram Stoker was like my Dr. Seuss."

He raised his eyebrow at her. "No wonder you're so strange."

"I'm strange?" she countered. "You're one to talk, *vampire*."

Kallias smiled and shrugged. "Touché."

Rose sighed, "Please, tell me you *at least* have a cape."

He scowled. "Do I look like the kind of person who owns a *cape*?"

"If I were a vampire, I'd totally wear a cape," Rose said, "so I could stand on top of a building with my cape blowing in the wind, like Dracula or Batman."

He snorted, "I imagine this is why people call you a geek, Rose."

"I know," Rose said with a grimace. "I can't help it."

A smile tugged at his lips. "Good."

Her eyes widened, but before she could respond to his remark, four knocks at the door of the hotel room interrupted her.

Kallias straightened and sniffed. "It's the pizza."

"Oh," Rose sighed. She'd halfway expected it to be another vampire, wanting to kill her. She watched as Kallias pushed away from the wall and strode toward the door.

Kallias turned back toward her, his hand still on the doorknob. "Get your bags. Quickly," he urged. "We'll eat in the car."

Her worry returned with a vengeance. "Is something wrong?"

The thunder outside seemed to punctuate her question, filling her with unease.

"Not yet," Kallias assured her, "but we shouldn't stay any longer."

ROSE WATCHED THE RAIN CASCADE OVER THE WINDOWS, AS KALLIAS DROVE through the downpour. She wondered how he even saw through that opaque layer of water that constantly covered the windows.

"Can I ask you another question?"

Kallias scowled. Despite the storm that raged outside, he seemed completely at ease, one hand relaxed around the steering wheel and the other lying idly on the gearshift. "Rose, you've been asking me questions for the last six hours. How could you possibly have any more?"

"Just one more," she said, holding up one finger for emphasis.

"That's what you said two hours ago," he said under his breath.

Without waiting for an answer, she flipped open the notebook in her lap and straightened the reading glasses on her nose. With her pen poised above the paper, she asked, "So, you said you were in England during the 1500s, right?"

"Something like that," he said noncommittally.

She frowned. "What do you mean by that?"

"I *mean*…I've been alive for 2,511 years," he said, rolling his eyes. "Do you honestly think I remember where I was every year of that? After a few centuries, the years—and decades, even—blend together."

She sighed. "All right. Well, if you *were* in England during the 1500s, like you said, my question is: Did you ever meet Shakespeare?"

"No, Rose. I never met Shakespeare," Kallias said.

She dropped the notebook into her lap and glared at him. "How could you not meet Shakespeare? He was such an important historical figure!"

As he pulled the car to a stop behind the long line of slow-moving traffic, he turned to look at her. "Rose, I read minds. I don't see the *future*. How was I supposed to know some raggedy playwright would become a famous historical figure?"

"How do you know he was raggedy, if you never met him?" she challenged.

"I glimpsed him briefly," he admitted, "when I fought a vampire outside the theatre."

Her bright blue eyes lit up with excitement. "That's amazing!"

He laughed. "I didn't meet Jesus either. You didn't scold me for that."

"That's because you already told me you were in Africa during those years," she reminded him. She flipped back several pages in her note-book and held it up for him. "See? It says right here that you stayed in South Africa from 100 B.C. until 20 A.D. So, you couldn't have met him because you were nowhere near Nazareth, Jerusalem, Rome, or anywhere else he went."

He scowled at her notebook. "You're writing down everything I say?"

Rose shrugged. "I'm a nerd. We've been over this."

He chuckled. When the traffic began to move again, he returned his attention to the partially flooded road.

Rose scribbled something in the notebook and then flipped to another page. "And in the 1600s, you were in France. So, my question about that is—"

"Rose! You said *one* more!" Kallias complained.

She winced. "Well, yeah, but then I thought of another one."

"No." He snatched the notebook out of her lap and tossed it in the backseat. "You've reached your quota of questions for the next century."

"But I won't even be alive a century from now," she whined.

He shrugged. "Then, I guess you're done asking questions."

"You can't stop me from asking questions," she said stubbornly.

"Fine. Ask," he said, "but I won't answer."

Rose blew out a disappointed sigh.

They'd been driving all night, only stopping at the occasional gas stations so Rose could use the restroom and so Kallias could fill the back-seat with more snacks than she could ever eat.

He'd also stopped at multiple fast food restaurants.

If there was anything she'd learned about vampires over the last two nights, it was that they severely overestimated how much food a human could eat.

Rose glanced at the clock on the dashboard. It was after three in the morning already. She was beginning to worry that Kallias had overesti-mated how far he could drive in a thunderstorm.

The sun would rise within the next few hours.

"Where are we?" she asked.

"Rose," he grunted. "That's a question."

Rose rolled her eyes. "Fine. We're at a place, of which I don't know," she said slowly. "Therefore, I hope the grumpy guy next to me will tell me where we are." She shrugged. "There. Now, it's not a question."

He snorted. "We just crossed the New York state line."

"Oh," she said, surprised. "So, what will we do for the rest of the ride?"

He smiled. "I think I've earned the right to question *you* relentlessly for a while."

Rose frowned. "But I'm not as interesting as you are."

His gaze flickered toward her. "*I* find you interesting."

She blinked in shock. "You do?"

These compliments he kept throwing at her, all of the sudden, were completely blindsiding her. She waited for him to correct himself or say he'd been joking, but he didn't.

Rose gave an uneasy shrug. "You've...seen inside my mind," she reminded him. "You already know me better than most."

This time, it was Kallias who looked stunned. He looked at her—briefly—before returning his attention to the road.

Neither of them spoke for a long time after that.

It was Rose who eventually broke the silence. "Can I use your phone?"

He frowned curiously. "Is something wrong?"

"Umm, well, I just realized," she said, her heart racing, "tomorrow is when Audrey's supposed to go home. I need to warn her that Theron knows where we live."

He shifted to one side so he could pull his phone from his pocket. He held out the phone to her, but when she started to take it from him, he held it tightly. "First," he said with a grave expression, "promise me you won't tell her where you are."

She rolled her eyes. "There you go again. Ordering me around."

"It's not an order," he said. "It's a condition—for getting the phone."

"Condition, order, ultimatum..." Rose muttered. "Haven't you ever heard of a synonym?"

"I can't let you call her, if you don't," he said again.

"Am I your prisoner now?" Rose scoffed. "What next? Are you going to handcuff me?"

A smirk twitched at his lips. "Only if you want me to."

"Not funny," she said. "Kallias, you can't just order me around."

With a long, exasperated sigh, he said, "Must you always be like this?"

"Yeah," she sassed. "Apparently, it's my superpower."

He snorted at that. "I know it seems like I'm just being an ass—"

"Seems?" Rose interrupted.

"But I'm just trying to keep you alive," he finished.

"By not letting me call Audrey?" she asked skeptically.

Kallias sighed, "I never said you couldn't call her. I *want* you to call her."

"Good," Rose said. "So do I."

"But," he added, "I also want you to stay alive."

Rose lifted her eyebrows. "It's a phone, Kallias, not a gun."

He ignored her snarky remarks. "Theron knows everything about you. He knows where you live, where you work, where you attend classes…" He sighed, "If he knows all of that, don't you think he also knows who your friends are? And if he wants to know where you are, who do you think he'll ask first?"

"Audrey's my best friend," she said. "She'd never tell him where I am."

"You're so naïve," he scoffed. "People will say anything under the right circumstances. Even your best friend." The traffic inched forward on the wet Interstate. "You think she'll endure torture, rather than answer a simple question? Even if she does, how long do you think she can hold out? Most humans don't last long."

Her throat constricted. "Torture?"

"You still don't understand what Theron is, do you?" he muttered.

"I know he's cruel," Rose told him. "Pure evil."

"Evil?" he scoffed. "Evil doesn't even *begin* to cover it." He kept his gaze on the road, as he spoke. "Even evil people have a reason for what they do. They have a moral code of some kind—a line they won't cross. They *believe* what they're doing is right." He sighed. "Theron's different.

There are no lines he won't cross. He kills because he *enjoys* it. He tortures because he *likes* to cause pain."

She nodded. "He's sadistic."

"Yeah," Kallias agreed. "He's absolutely insane. I don't know why. I don't know when he became this way. Maybe he's always been like this."

Rose watched the way his jaw tightened and his knuckles whitened, when he discussed Theron. She heard the way his voice rung with intensity and agitation. A sinking ball of dread weighed down her stomach.

"I should've left you that night," he said quickly. "You said you didn't want my help. I should've given you your wish and walked away. Most people would have." He glanced at her, pain flashing in his eyes. "Do you know why I couldn't leave you?"

"I can't say I haven't wondered," she mumbled.

"Because all I could think about was what Theron would do to you," Kallias said, his voice strained. "If you were lucky, he'd just kill you, but if you weren't..." He shook his head, unable to finish that.

Rose's stomach turned with nausea, as she finally pieced it all together, arriving at a terrible conclusion. "Kallias, your scars—"

"Don't," he interrupted.

Her lungs constricted, not allowing her to breathe. "Don't what?"

"I know what you're going to ask," he said. "Don't."

Rose nodded hesitantly, empathy twisting in her stomach. If she'd thought he seemed intense before, it was nothing compared to how he was now. He sat rigid in his seat, his arm locked and his grip tight around the wheel. She wished she knew what to say, but all she could say was, "Do you think he'll hurt Audrey?"

"If she knows where you are," he told her, "he'll jump at the chance."

"No," Rose breathed. "Kallias, please. I have to warn her. I can't let that happen."

Kallias glanced at her, stunned by the fear in her voice. His gaze shifted toward her hands, which lay in her lap. "You're shaking."

Rose looked down at her hands to confirm that, yes, they were indeed trembling. "Am I supposed to be calm after what you just told me?" she said breathlessly. "I'd rather die than let him hurt someone I care about!"

His jaw tightened. "Don't say that."

"Why not?" she sighed. "It's the truth."

"I won't let that happen," he said, his gaze back on the road. He held out the phone. "Call your friend, but if you tell her where you are, you'll only give Theron more reason to hurt her. Do you understand?"

"Yes," Rose assured him. "I understand now."

He nodded and let her take the phone. "Tell her to stay away from your apartment until all of this is over. One moment is all he needs."

She shivered at that. "Okay."

Rose dialed the familiar number and placed the phone to her ear. She hoped Audrey was awake, but by the fifth ring, Rose assumed Audrey had already fallen asleep.

The sixth ring was cut short. "Umm, hello?"

"Audrey!" she said quickly. "It's Rose."

"Oh! Rose!" Audrey said with a laugh. "I was worried you were a telemarketer."

"At this time of the night?" Rose asked.

"I don't think they sleep," Audrey said. "Did you leave the country?"

Rose frowned. "What? No. Why?"

"The number you called from has a foreign area code," Audrey said.

Rose rolled her eyes. "It's not foreign, Audrey. It's just out-of-state."

"Yeah, yeah, same thing," Audrey said dismissively. "So, where are you?"

"Uh…" Rose paused, glancing warily at Kallias. "I'm with Kallias."

That succeeded in steering Audrey's mind away from the question. Audrey squealed into the line, "Holy bologna! You're sleeping with him?"

"There is nothing holy about bologna," Rose muttered.

Audrey continued, as if she hadn't heard Rose's off-hand remark, "I can't believe you're actually sleeping with him! I mean, I knew you sort of liked him, but I never thought you'd actually— Well, you know, I always figured you'd *die* a virgin."

"Wait, what?" Rose said, blinking. "Audrey, I'm not having sex with him."

Kallias glanced at her, raising an eyebrow in amusement.

Audrey was silent for a moment. "But it's almost four in the morning."

"What does that have to do with anything?" Rose asked.

"What else could you be doing with him at *this* hour?" she asked.

"Lots of things. Lots of *non-sexual* things," Rose said indignantly.

"Ah, crap," Audrey complained. "You really *are* going to die a virgin."

"Thanks for the vote of confidence," Rose said sarcastically.

"So, why *are* you with Mr. Tall-Hunky-Scary-Guy?" Audrey asked.

"His name is Kallias," Rose reminded her.

"Yeah, yeah," Audrey said impatiently. "It's four in the morning, Rose. Get to the point."

Rose sighed, "I'm with him because...he's taking me somewhere safe."

"Umm, Rose?" Audrey said, a note of concern in her tone. "Do you remember when I ran off to Vegas with that guy in the prison costume, and you went on and on about how you didn't think that was a wise thing to do?"

"It was a *mime* costume, not a prison costume," Rose told her.

"Whatever," Audrey said. "You said he might be an axe-murderer."

"Oh, come on," Rose objected. "I didn't jump *straight* to axe-murderer."

"You said I didn't know him well enough," Audrey continued.

"You didn't even know his name," Rose pointed out. "You still don't."

"Yeah, well," Audrey said irritably, "now you're doing it."

"I'm going to Vegas with a fake mime?" Rose asked.

Audrey huffed out an irritated sigh. "You're trusting someone you don't know. You just met him. Rose, he could be *anything*!"

Rose looked at Kallias. "I know exactly what he is."

"Fine," Audrey said. "At least tell me where you are, just in case."

Kallias shot a look of warning Rose's way, and she sighed.

"I can't tell you," Rose said.

"Excuse me?" Audrey snapped.

"It's dangerous for you to know," Rose said quietly. "If I tell you where I am, Theron might hurt you, and I can't let that happen, Audrey. Please, understand."

Clearly, she didn't. "Rose Melanie Foster, if you don't tell me where you are, I'll—"

"Use my full name again?" Rose interrupted.

"I will hunt you down, woman," Audrey warned.

Rose glanced at Kallias, who was still eyeing her as if she were a child, about to misbehave. Rose didn't appreciate that look. "I'm sorry, but I can't," she said into the phone. "It's too dangerous."

Audrey blew out a frustrated breath. "When will you be back?"

"I don't know yet," Rose admitted. "Once Theron is no longer a threat, I guess."

"You're not making me worry any less here, Rose," Audrey said.

"Sorry," Rose sighed. "But speaking of *worry*...that's why I called." She shifted uneasily in her seat. "Theron knows where I live, Audrey—which means he knows where you live. You can't go home. He broke into the apartment once already, and he might come back."

Audrey inhaled sharply at that. "It happened."

"Yeah," Rose said dismissively, "but I'm all right. He didn't hurt me." He glanced at Kallias, remembering the bite wound he'd healed. "Not permanently, anyway."

Audrey was silent for a moment. "Did he..." she trailed off.

"Did he what?" Rose prompted.

"Nothing," Audrey said—a little too quickly. "Forget I said anything."

But Rose was already piecing it together. "You knew," she breathed. "You saw him try to—to... You saw."

Audrey breathed a sigh of relief. "Try? So, he didn't succeed?"

"Why didn't you tell me?" Rose said.

"How could I?" Audrey sounded sad and breathless. "It was so terrible."

"You should've warned me," Rose insisted.

"I'm sorry!" Audrey said. "You just— You don't understand."

Rose's frustration melted at the pained sound in Audrey's voice. It wasn't her fault, after all. "It's all right," she told her friend. "Just, please, promise me you won't go home. I'm worried about you."

She could practically hear the smile in Audrey's voice. "I'm worried about you, too," Audrey said. "I'll stay with my grandparents for a bit longer. I promise. But…are you sure you can trust Mr. Tall-Hunky-Scary-Guy?"

Rose rolled her eyes at the ridiculous nickname. "Yes, I'm sure."

Audrey yawned. "Well, I should probably go. Henry's waiting for me."

"Henry?" Rose said with a frown. "High school boyfriend, Henry?"

"Ex," Audrey corrected, "but yes, he lives next door to my grand-parents."

"With his mom?" Rose said.

"You don't forget a thing, do you?" Audrey muttered. "Anyway, we've been catching up—and stuff."

Rose frowned. "And stuff?"

Audrey cackled loudly, "Why else would I be awake right now?"

Rose sighed, "Sixty years from now, you'll be an old woman, sitting in your rocking chair, reflecting on your life, and you'll think, 'What on earth did I do with my first thirty years of life?' And then, you'll remember, 'Oh. That.'"

Audrey laughed. "A girl's gotta sow her wild oats, Rose."

Rose shook her head, smiling. "Not me."

"Well, that's because you don't have any wild oats, Rose," Audrey teased. "Your oats are all organic and wholegrain."

"My oats are not organic and wholegrain!" Rose argued.

She didn't realize how strange her declaration must've sounded until *after* Kallias started laughing.

Audrey snorted. "Goodnight, Nerd."

"Goodnight, Weirdo," Rose replied automatically.

She ended the call and handed the phone back to Kallias.

"Were you listening the entire time?" Rose said, as he slipped the phone into his pocket.

"I can't help it. Sensitive hearing." He tapped his ear with one finger.

"Great," Rose said sarcastically. "That's not embarrassing at all."

Kallias grinned. "If it makes you feel better, I agree with you. You do have one or two wild *'oats,'*" he said with a laugh, "buried somewhere underneath that cautious, anal-retentive exterior of yours."

She glared at him. "Anal-retentive?!"

He just offered her an infectious, wolfish grin.

Rose wrinkled her nose, feeling somewhere between baffled and amused. "There's no wildness in me," she assured him. "Everyone knows that."

"You like to read things that excite you and scare you," he reminded her.

"That's not wild," she said with a laugh. "That's nerdy. Everyone says so."

His smile deepened. "There's also the way you kiss."

Rose's eyes widened. "What? How do I kiss?"

Kallias laughed at her panicked tone. His gaze drifted toward her lips, and he lowered his voice. "Like you're on fire."

Rose blushed. "Everyone knows I'm not wild," she said again.

"They see what you want them to see," Kallias said. "You hide that part of yourself. It's almost as if…" he trailed off.

Rose glanced at him. "As if what?"

He met her gaze briefly, before returning his attention to the road. "It's almost as if you're afraid of it."

An eerie chill traveled through Rose's veins, as if something deep inside of her agreed with that statement. She looked away, deciding to focus on the rain, instead.

As they merged lanes, Rose noticed the faint outline of a skyline in the distance, the lights blurred by the cascade of the rain. She leaned closer to the window, squinting, as she tried to see through the layer of water.

Kallias answered the question she hadn't asked yet. "New York City."

She glanced at him, her lips curving in amusement. She wondered how often he did that: answering thoughts before they were spoken.

He didn't even seem to realize he'd done it.

Rose leaned back, the leather of the seat cooling her skin. "So, when we get to your house, what should I expect?" she said with a smile. "How many vampires are we talking, exactly?"

His gaze darted briefly toward her. "Vampires?"

"Do you live with one of those creepy covens?" she asked.

He snorted, "Vampires don't have covens, Rose."

"Packs?" she guessed.

He scowled at her. "No."

"Well, that's disappointing," Rose said. "None of you live in groups or anything?"

"Groups, yes," he clarified. "Vampires often live in very *large* groups, but we call those groups *colonies*, not covens or packs."

"Oh," she said with a sigh. "It sounds so normal."

Kallias laughed at her disapproving tone. "You think so?" he said. "If you ever set foot in one, you'll change your mind. Vampires who live in human society, like I do, act more human than vampires who live in colonies."

Her eyebrows lifted in disbelief. "You think *you* act human?"

He chuckled. "Compared to them, I do."

"So, then, you're not part of one?" she asked.

"No," Kallias said, glancing at her. "I don't play well with others."

Rose laughed at that. "And your friends?"

"Erik lived in a colony once," Kallias admitted, "with Alana and Kara."

Rose quirked an eyebrow at that. "Who?"

"His ex-girlfriend," Kallias said, "and his ex-girlfriend's girlfriend."

Rose's brows furrowed. "I'm confused."

"So am I," he muttered.

Rose watched him curiously. "But he doesn't live there anymore?"

"No," Kallias said. "He lives with me now. And Geoff and Emma— our other friends—they have their own house, as well."

"How long have you and Erik known each other?" Rose asked.

Kallias frowned. "I believe it was around 800 AD, when I met him. So, I suppose that would be...about twelve hundred years?"

"Wow. Most countries can't even stay together that long," Rose said. She flashed a playful smile at him. "Are you sure you're not gay?"

Kallias rolled his eyes. "One-hundred percent."

"No one's *that* sure," Rose scoffed.

He snorted at that. He pulled into the outermost lane, preparing to take the next exit.

Rose noticed the streets becoming increasingly darker—the streetlights fewer and farther between. "So, how did you meet him?"

Kallias frowned. "Well, I...tried to kill him."

"Oh, yeah," Rose said sarcastically. "That's how I make friends, too."

Kallias laughed. He glanced at the mirror, as he shifted lanes. "Erik had earned quite the reputation in his early years," he told her. "Hell, even I had heard of the infamous Erik Olafsson, and I kept to myself back then. Well, I still do, really."

"A reputation for what?" Rose said warily. "Killing?"

"Erik has always been a man of insatiable appetites," Kallias explained, "whether that be his appetite for alcohol, sex, or, well...*blood*."

"Right. So, killing," Rose said. "He was known for killing."

"Not exactly," Kallias said after a moment of hesitation. "It's true that he killed a lot of humans in that first century or so, but that wasn't what he was known for among *vampires*."

"What was it, then?" Rose asked.

Kallias glanced at her. "His unique method of torture."

Her eyes widened. "Your *friend* tortured people?"

He sighed, "It's not what you think."

"Okay," she said, deciding to hear him out.

"I told you Erik's an empath," Kallias reminded her, "and he's an exceptionally powerful one, at that." He turned onto an even darker road than before. "Telepaths are some of the most dangerous people to exist, but an empath can be dangerous, too—in his own way."

Rose frowned. "How could empathy be dangerous?"

"We're not talking about the human understanding of empathy," Kallias told her. "Erik doesn't just sympathize with you. He *feels* what you feel, and he can manipulate what you feel, as well."

Rose nodded in understanding. "He controls emotions the way you control thoughts."

"Yes," he said.

"But what does that have to do with torture?" Rose said.

Kallias flexed his fingers, forcing them to relax around the wheel. "Physical torture—well, it's terrible, obviously. There's nothing good to say about it," he said quickly, "but at least you still have *some* control over your reaction. You can still hold on to that *small* shred of dignity. You can't do that with emotional torture."

"Emotional torture?" Rose repeated.

He glanced at her. "Erik can project pure terror. You have no control over the way your body or mind reacts to it," he told her. "It feels just as real—if not *more* real—as it'd feel, if you'd felt it on your own."

Rose swallowed uneasily. "Well, this makes me feel *great* about meeting him."

"He doesn't use it much anymore," Kallias assured her, "but back then, he used it on every vampire who pissed her off."

"Her?" Rose said with a frown.

"Alana," Kallias said.

Rose nodded. "His ex-girlfriend," she remembered, "who...*also* had a girlfriend."

"Yes," he said. "Every vampire was afraid of her, and because of what she made him do, they feared him, too."

"*Made* him?" Rose repeated.

"I'm getting ahead of myself," he muttered. He turned onto the next street and sighed, "Erik killed *a lot* of people in those early years, and Aaron didn't seem to care enough to stop him—not even when he risked the exposure of the colony."

Rose's frown deepened.

"Eventually, I decided that, if no one else was going to do it," Kallias said, "I'd have to kill him myself."

"For the sake of the humans," Rose assumed.

"Of course," Kallias scoffed. "I didn't care about the vampires he tortured. I figured they probably deserved it, anyway."

There it was again—the contempt for his own kind.

Was he even aware of it?

"When I found him, I was...ready for a fight, obviously," he muttered, "but Erik didn't fight me. He just sat there. *Weeping*."

"He was crying?" Rose said. Her stomach twisted with sympathy at the thought. "Why?"

"He hated it," Kallias said, "the things she made him do." His light brown eyes shifted toward her. "He didn't do what he did because he enjoyed it. He did it because he had no choice."

Rose's brows furrowed. "There's always a choice."

"You're making the same mistake I did," Kallias told her. "I don't mean he *thought* he had no choice. I mean he *literally* didn't."

Rose's eyes widened, as she realized, "She's a telepath, too."

"Was," he corrected. "Alana's dead now."

Rose blinked. "How many others *are* there?" she asked breathlessly. "Like you?"

"Aaron typically kills telepaths, as well," he told her. "He sees us as a threat to his power, just like he sees people with telekinetic abilities as a threat to his power." He glanced at her. "People like you."

"So, why didn't he kill you," Rose asked, "or Alana?"

"Technically, he did kill Alana," Kallias said, "eventually."

Rose swallowed at that. "But he never tried to kill you?"

He shrugged. "He must've had some selfish reason not to," he scoffed. "He's not capable of anything else."

Rose didn't think that made much sense, but she didn't argue.

"Alana was the vampire who turned Erik," Kallias explained, "and he loved her—despite all of the terrible things she made him do."

"Why?" Rose asked curiously.

Kallias shrugged. "He sympathized with her—for *some* reason," he said. "I'll never understand it, but...his power is his curse, I suppose."

Rose's frown deepened.

"Anyway, when I realized he hadn't *wanted* to kill anyone," Kallias said, "I realized I didn't need to kill him." He glanced at her. "He just needed someone to break her control over him, and I was a telepath. I could do that."

Rose nodded. "And she didn't try to stop you?"

"Oddly enough, no," he admitted. "I was older than her. Perhaps she knew there was no point in fighting me."

Something about that didn't sound totally right, either.

"Erik didn't even know it was possible to resist blood," Kallias continued, "so I taught him how. Eventually, we had him completely weaned off of it."

Rose smiled. "And then, you married him and lived happily ever after."

He grimaced at her teasing. "Stop that."

Rose tilted her head back and laughed, and Kallias couldn't help but smile at the sight. She had such a beautiful smile.

Silence settled between them, as they continued to move farther and farther away from the bright, city skyline.

After a while, Rose said, "You've saved people—me, Erik, other humans. Yet, you still don't see the good in yourself."

"Erik saved himself," Kallias said uncomfortably. "I just gave him the chance to do it. And you—well, you saved me, too, remember?"

"Not quite as gallantly," Rose muttered.

Kallias looked at her. "You helped a starved vampire, knowing it could cost you your life. It was very foolish—but also brave."

A surprised smile curved at the corners of Rose's lips. "You think so?"

He narrowed his eyes. "But *mostly* foolish," he reminded her.

Rose laughed softly.

Kallias turned onto a roughly paved road that was so dark that Rose could barely see—even *with* the headlights.

It had been growing increasingly darker for quite some time, but until now, the moon, at least, had shone brightly in the sky.

Now, trees lined each side of the road, creating a canopy of leaves that shielded them from the moonlight.

The road winded between the trees, like a serpent, leading toward a destination that Rose could no longer see.

"Well, this looks like a nice place," Rose muttered, "to be murdered."

Kallias snorted at her sarcasm. "Believe it or not, you'll be safer in these woods than you were in the city. The trees and wildlife mask your scent."

"I bet that's what you tell all the girls before you murder them," Rose teased.

Kallias laughed, amused by her strange sense of humor.

The trees veered farther and farther away from each other, as the forest gave way to an opening of grass. At first, Rose saw only the grass, but as the car slowed to a stop between a motorcycle and a red car, the car's headlights fell upon a two-story, stone house.

"That's your house?" When he nodded, she said, "It's big."

His lips twitched. "I suppose so."

The house was made up of a combination of dark grey and light grey stones—with a large, darkly-stained, wooden front door.

Rose vaguely recognized the style. It looked similar to many of the historical homes from the eighteenth and nineteenth centuries, but there was something different about this house.

Something...*strange.*

Rose laughed when she realized what it was. "No windows?"

He shrugged. "Sunlight kills us, so it's safer without them."

"No, no, I get that," she assured him, "but your house looks freaking weird without windows."

He laughed at her teasing. "Come on. Let's get you inside."

Rose nodded and turned in her seat, but she froze, when she saw the gleam of sleek, red car outside her window. "Oh, for goodness sakes," she complained. "What's with the fancy car?"

"It's called a Ferrari," Kallias told her.

"It's called impractical," Rose countered.

"It's Erik's," he added. He pulled the keys from the ignition. "I told you Erik's car makes mine look practical, didn't I?"

"Mmm-hmm," Rose grunted in disapproval.

Kallias laughed. "You don't like extravagance, do you?"

Rose feigned shock. "How did you ever figure *that* out?"

He snorted and opened the driver's side door. "Come on."

The interior lights cut off the moment he closed the door.

Rose froze, blinking at the darkness. The trunk creaked open, and plastic bags rustled.

Rose reached out, blindly grasping for the door handle, but before she could find it, the car door opened, nearly causing her to fall out.

Rose felt a hand curl around her shoulder, steadying her.

"What's wrong?" he said impatiently. "Why are you still in the car?"

"I don't know," she muttered. "I'm sure it has nothing to do with the fact that I can't see."

Kallias glanced around, noticing, for the first time, that there was no light outside. "Oh," he said. "Well, I'll help you, then." He grasped her hand and pulled her out of the car.

"Thanks," Rose said, but as soon as she was on her feet, she started walking in the direction she'd seen the house.

"There's a car there," he said—at the exact moment she ran into it.

"Dang it," she grunted. Her knees and stomach ached where she'd run into it. "Who put a car in the way?"

"No one put it in the way," Kallias laughed. "You're the one who went the wrong way." He took her shoulders and turned her entire body. "The house is that way."

"Right," Rose said, and she started walking again.

"Oh, hell," he muttered, when she tripped over a large stone. "Can you just stop walking for a minute?"

Rose's toes throbbed from the impact of the stone, and she glared into the darkness. "Great," she complained. "I can't even walk without your help."

His voice was closer now. "I could just carry you."

"Oh, yeah," she said sarcastically. "That's *very* dignifying."

Kallias's hand curled around her elbow. "Step over the rock."

With plenty of indignation, Rose let him lead her toward the house. "Why don't you have porch lights?"

"Porch?" he said, as if he'd never seen another house before. "Oh, like a veranda. Yeah, I don't have one of those."

"And no lights, either, apparently," she grumbled.

He laughed. "Don't worry. There are lights inside."

"I sure hope so," she said. "I don't want to fall into any coffins."

Kallias snorted at that. He pulled her to a stop when they reached the door, and he lifted her hand and placed it on the doorknob. "There's the door. Go on inside. Erik would've left it unlocked."

Rose wanted to ask him something else, but the chill in the air let her know that he was gone. Somewhere behind her, she heard the trunk pop open again.

Rose turned the doorknob and stepped inside, the hardwood floors slick beneath her tennis shoes. She practically melted with relief, as she saw the soft, golden glow of the torch-like lamps along the walls.

She could see again.

She swept her gaze around the foyer, first noticing the lack of pictures and personalization, and then, she noticed the stairs.

Her eyes widened, as she saw what was lying on top of those stairs…

Rose screamed and ran, slamming the door behind her.

17

THE LOST CAUSE

"hat happened?"

Unfortunately, when Rose closed the door, she'd also cut off her only source of light. So, while she could hear in the closeness of his voice that Kallias was beside her, she couldn't actually see him.

His hands curled around her shoulders. "Rose? Are you okay?"

"I think so," Rose said, blinking in the darkness.

"What happened?" Kallias said. His hands skimmed her face, turning it, as if he were looking for injuries. "Rose! What the hell happened?"

"I just saw something I didn't want to see," Rose said. "That's all."

His hands left her. "What do you mean *that's all*?" he snapped. "You screamed! You didn't even scream when Theron tried to kill you!"

"Well, that's because Theron kept his clothes *on*," Rose muttered.

"What does that even…" Kallias trailed off. He glanced at the door, blinking, and then, with no warning whatsoever, he burst into a fit of hysterical laughter.

Rose glared at him.

Well, she glared at *something*, anyway. She couldn't see well enough to know whether she was glaring at him or a tree.

"What's so funny?" Rose said.

Kallias straightened, his grin wide. "I see you met Erik."

Rose blew out a peeved sigh.

"Well, come on," he laughed, and then, Rose heard the doorknob turn.

"Wait!" she said, chasing after him. "You *really* don't want to go in there right now…" she trailed off, blinking in shock.

A blonde man stood—*alone*—at the bottom of the stairs, pulling on a pair of black pants.

The black pants contrasted starkly with his pale skin. His skin wasn't unnaturally pale, exactly, but it *was* lighter than Rose's fair, freckled skin —which was…saying something.

He looked a couple of inches shorter than Kallias, which meant he still towered over Rose—and most other people, she assumed.

A large, black, dragon tattoo stretched across his slender chest, starting near his right collarbone and curling around his left hip.

It was the standard European dragon from storybooks—winged with four legs. The ink was a blend of black and electric blue—black scales, blue eyes, and blue flames.

"There was a woman. A *naked* woman," Rose told Kallias. "She was naked."

"Oh, I'm sorry," the man said with a soft, lilting accent. "Were you hoping to see her again?" He grinned, his fangs flashing. "*Naked*?"

Rose recognized that strange accent—from the awkward phone conversation she'd had with him the night before. "No," she said slowly. "That is *not* what I was hoping. At all."

His lips curved into a deeper smirk, and amusement sparkled in his bright green eyes. "Sure, it isn't."

Rose frowned. "You just met me," she reminded him. "You don't even know enough about me to be using sarcasm there."

"You just saw a naked woman," Erik said, as if she'd somehow forgotten that. He waved a hand at his chest—that he hadn't bothered to cover with a shirt yet. "And I'm an empath."

Rose shot a worried look at Kallias. "What does he mean by that?"

"You don't want to know," Kallias muttered. "The woman's still here. She's upstairs—probably cleaning up," he added, as if it were totally normal for him to know that. He turned to the blonde vampire and sighed, "The *stairs*, Erik? You have a bedroom. With a door...that locks."

Erik shrugged. "We were headed there. We just didn't make it."

Kallias rolled his eyes, as if he'd heard that excuse before.

Erik snatched his black T-shirt from wooden rail. "Besides," he said, tugging the shirt over his head, "having sex in a bed gets boring after a while."

"It's never boring if you do it right," Kallias scoffed.

"Says the guy who hasn't brought a woman home in decades," Erik said.

Rose glanced back and forth between them. "Are you two *really* bickering over sex?"

The two vampires fell silent and looked at her. Rose nearly laughed at the sight—because they reminded her of two dejected children, who'd just been scolded for fighting over a box of cereal.

Erik flashed a charming smile at Rose—no doubt the same smile he used on every woman he met. "Anyway," he said happily, "you must Kallias's lover. Rose, isn't it?"

Rose stared blankly at him. "No, I must *not* be his lover—since, you know, there's no actual reason for you to assume I am," she sassed. "Also, I think the term people use in *this* time period is *girlfriend*."

Erik threw his head back and laughed loudly. "I like her."

Rose shot another worried look in Kallias's direction.

Kallias sighed. "Erik has a thing for spunky women. So, when you sass him, you're basically just encouraging him."

Rose grimaced. "Crap."

With a snort of amusement, Erik stepped forward and extended his hand. "I'm Erik Olafsson," he said with practiced courtesy. "It's a pleasure to meet you."

Rose looked down at his hand, her eyes widening in horror, as she realized he intended for her to shake it. "I'm not touching that hand," she informed him. "I don't know where it's been."

Erik glanced down at his hand and nodded. "Fair point."

"I think the problem is that you *do* know where it's been," Kallias reminded her.

Rose covered her ears. "Ugh! No! I'm trying to *forget* what I saw!"

Erik laughed. "What's the big deal? It was just sex," he scoffed, "and we were practically finished, anyway. Well, I was finished. She was still…" His grin widened. "Well, you saw."

Rose glared at Erik—who, unlike Kallias, actually looked taken aback by her irritation. "What do you mean *just* sex?" she said. "Sex is a big deal!"

Erik lifted his eyebrows. "You're a virgin."

Rose turned her glare on Kallias. "You told him?"

Kallias winced at her mistake. "No."

"It was just a guess," Erik said with a smirk, "but thank you for confirming."

Her face reddened. "Crap," she said again.

Erik's bright green eyes shifted downward, assessing her. "Aren't you a little old to be a virgin?"

"Old?" Rose said incredulously. She narrowed her eyes at the obnoxious, blonde vampire. "I'm twenty-three, not eighty!"

Erik shrugged. "Twenty-three's pretty old. I was two years younger that when I died, and I'd already slept with *hundreds* of women by then."

"You realize you're not the standard of *normal*, right?" Kallias said.

"My sex life is none of your business," Rose said.

Erik offered a taunting smile. "Don't you mean your *lack* of sex life?"

"Either way," Rose said between clenched teeth, "it's none of your business."

Erik just laughed. Then, he took her *totally* by surprise—by stepping forward and sniffing her, as if she were a candle.

Or some kind of scratch-and-sniff sticker.

"What the heck?" she muttered.

Erik's brows furrowed. "You've never been attacked by a vampire before?" he said, as if he found it difficult to believe. "Before Theron attacked you, I mean."

"No," she said slowly. "Why?"

His tongue traced his right fang. "Because your blood's appealing."

Rose frowned worriedly. "Kallias?" she called. "Could you, *please*, tell your friend to stop staring at me like I'm a Thanksgiving dinner?"

Erik grinned at that. "More like a Thanksgiving *feast*."

Her eyes widened. "Kallias," she whined.

"Erik," Kallias said. "Cool it."

Erik pouted at him. "Traitor."

Kallias rolled his eyes. "She's from a small town. You know, as well as I do, small towns aren't good for vampires. People notice too much."

"If you think *that* was a small town, you should see where I grew up," Rose muttered under her breath.

Erik considered that. "Still..."

"She'd probably never encountered a vampire before Theron," Kallias told him.

Erik glanced at her. "Surely, you've traveled?"

"I'm not made of money," Rose scoffed. "I've traveled twice—on scholarship—to Greece."

Erik nodded slowly. His gaze shifted toward Kallias. "She had to have encountered a vampire *then*, at least."

"She wasn't there long," Kallias assumed. "Maybe she...got lucky."

Erik lifted an eyebrow. "Back when I fed from humans," he told Kallias, "there's no way I would've been able to resist *her* scent."

"What are you saying?" Kallias asked. "You think someone's been protecting her?"

Erik shrugged. "It would explain how someone as appetizing as her has survived this long."

"Hey, I'm right here," Rose said, waving her hand. "You know, the person you're discussing like she's one of the five main food groups?"

Erik smiled. "Technically, you're the *only* food group for us, so..."

"Shut up," Kallias said, and with a tilt of his head, he gestured toward the top of the stairs.

Erik spun around to face the woman at the top of the stairs.

The human woman was small and thin and—to Rose's relief—no longer naked.

She descended the stairs, her black heels clicking against each hardwood step. Her red shirt and black skirt clung to her petite figure, and her sleek, brown hair hung around her chin.

She stopped in front of Erik, and she seemed to sink into some sort of adoring trance. "Hi."

Flashing that charming smile again, Erik said, "Hello, gorgeous."

Kallias rolled his eyes, and Rose had to suppress a laugh.

But then, the woman's hazel eyes shifted toward Kallias, and her eyes widened. Her gaze traveled the length of his body, and her lips parted. "And hi," she breathed.

Rose glanced back and forth between the woman and the two vampires, but no one else seemed to blink an eye at the woman's reaction.

"Yeah. Hey," Kallias said impatiently.

When the woman finally tore her gaze from the vampires and spared one, quick glance for Rose, her eyes narrowed.

"You're the woman who walked in on us."

Rose blushed profusely. "Yeah, I, uhh…"

"Erik," Kallias called. He gestured impatiently at the woman.

"But…" Erik whined, glancing back and forth between the angry woman and Rose. He sighed, "Come on, babe. Let me drive you home."

The woman glanced back at him, and her smile returned. "Or," she said hopefully, "I could call in to work, and we could spend the day together."

Erik didn't show the slightest bit of unease. He wrapped his hand around hers and brought it to his mouth. He kissed the back of her hand. "I'd love that, but unfortunately, I'm…busy during the day."

Kallias rolled his eyes. "Yes, and that day starts very *soon*."

Whatever the woman might've said about the rude remark was lost the moment she turned her gaze on Kallias. Her eyes widened again.

Rose sighed. How did vampires even carry on conversations like this?

Well, *Erik*, at least, seemed to enjoy it.

Erik touched the woman's arm, bringing her adoring gaze back to himself. "Let me get you home. I'm afraid we'll have to hurry."

"You're not going to introduce me to your friends?" the woman asked.

"What part of *hurry* does she not understand?" Kallias complained.

"Sure," Erik said, though he seemed to be getting a little anxious himself. He gestured toward them. "That's my best friend, Kallias, and that's Rose, his *lover*."

Rose sighed irritably, "Stop calling me that. I'm not his lover."

Erik grinned. "Could've fooled me."

The woman frowned at him. "You're not going to tell them my name?"

Erik looked at her, his eyes suddenly wide. "Er, yeah," he stammered. "Guys, this is a beautiful woman called...er..." He glanced at Kallias.

Kallias rolled his eyes. "Anne! Her name is Anne. Now, take her home."

The woman turned to Kallias. "How do *you* know my name?"

"Erik told me," Kallias lied, "while you were upstairs."

Erik mouthed, *"Thank you,"* to Kallias while the woman wasn't looking.

"Oh," the woman said. She adjusted her purse on her shoulder and smiled shyly at Erik. "For a minute, I thought you'd forgotten my name."

Erik scratched his head, mussing his wavy blonde hair. "No. No. Never," he said, wincing. He tugged her toward the door. "Come on."

When they left, closing the door behind them, Rose turned to Kallias. "He *just* had sex with her, and he's already forgotten her name?"

Kallias lifted his eyebrows. "I doubt he was even listening when she told him her name." He gathered the bags into his hands and headed toward the stairs. "Come on. I'll show you around."

Rose followed him up the stairs, glancing around as she did. The stone and hardwood of the house reminded Rose of a rental cabin—comfortable yet impersonal.

"How long have you lived here?" Rose asked curiously.

"Not long," Kallias muttered. "Maybe a century or so."

"Not long?" she said with a scoff. "That's longer than I'll even *live*—even *if* I reach my projected life expectancy." She laughed. "But with all these vampires trying to kill me, I probably won't make it past tomorrow."

He stopped and turned toward her, his tall form suddenly blocking her way. "Why do you make jokes about things like that?"

She blinked, stunned by the sudden emotion she saw in his light brown eyes. Was that...*anger*? Or fear? "I don't know," she mumbled. "I guess...because it's easier than being afraid?"

His gaze softened a little at that, but he didn't say anything. He turned and continued down the hallway—with Rose trailing closely behind.

She wished she could stop him and demand to know what was bothering him, but she knew, even if she did, he'd never answer. Letting her help or comfort him would mean tearing down the walls around his heart, and he clearly had no intention of doing that.

He slowed as he came to the end of the hallway, where there were three wooden doors—two across from each other and another at the farthest end of the hall, between the other two.

With his shoulder, he pushed open the door on the right.

He dropped the bags on the floor. "This will be your room."

Rose followed him—only to freeze in the doorway.

She didn't know what she'd expected, but it wasn't *this*. This room was two or three times the size of her entire apartment. Why would anyone even need this much space?

Despite its size, the furniture *did* fill it. A large bed, covered in a blue quilt, set in the center of the room with an oversized desk along the farthest wall and two large dressers along the other wall.

Noting her silence, he looked at her. "If you don't like it, I can—"

"No, no! It's fine! Of course it's fine," she assured him. "It's just...*big*."

"Is it?" he said obliviously. "I suppose it *is* the largest guest room. It's the same size as my room and Erik's room." He pointed toward a wooden door across from the bed. "And it has its own bathroom."

She glanced at the door, blinking. "Wow," she muttered. "I've never had my own bathroom before. I'm not sure I know what to do with it."

He snorted at that—and then leaned toward her.

She straightened, as the zipper of his leather jacket brushed against her elbow, followed by the warmth of his body.

Closer to her ear than necessary, he teased, "Well, if you take off your clothes, I'll show you how the bathtub works."

She started laughing. "Nice try."

He chuckled. "I thought it was my most charming line yet."

"Oh, yeah. So charming," she said sarcastically.

Kallias watched as Rose laughed. He watched those soft, full lips of hers curve into a beautifully bright smile, and he found himself enthralled.

When her bright bright blue eyes shifted his way—and widened with a hint of curiosity—he quickly averted his gaze.

Kallias rubbed the back of his neck. "My room is next to yours, and Erik's room is across the hall," he said slowly. "If you need anything, just come to my room."

Rose tilted her head, studying him curiously. He'd been staring at her, hadn't he? But why?

She thought about the doors they'd passed on their way to this one. "How many rooms does your house have?"

"Bedrooms?" he said with a distracted frown. "Seven, I think."

Rose blinked. "Why so many? Do you bring a lot of humans home?"

"No," Kallias said, glancing at her. "You're the first."

Rose's eyes widened. She understood the need for secrecy, but...Erik hadn't hesitated to bring a human home, had he?

"Oh!" Kallias said—so suddenly that it startled her. "There's another room I have to show you!"

Rose had never seen him so...*excited* before. It was a cuter side of him. A *cute* side of a deadly vampire? She nearly laughed at the thought. "What kind of room?" she said with a curious smile.

"You'll see," he said. His grin was so wide she thought she saw a flash of fang. "Come on."

With an agreeable shrug, she followed him into the hallway.

His excitement only seemed to grow, as he led the way down the stairs. He opened a door in the foyer, and it opened into another hallway. Fewer doors lined this hall—one at the end and one just a few feet past the foyer.

As they continued down the hall, Kallias slapped one door with his palm, as they passed, and said, "That's another bathroom."

Rose nearly tripped, while trying to look at the door they'd already passed. "Slow down," she muttered, jogging to keep up with his brisk pace. "And what about the other two rooms?"

"Kitchen and living room," he said, as if neither of those were important.

Rose would need a map, if he wasn't going to give her a better tour than *this*.

The end of the hallway seemed to descend into steps, perhaps leading to a basement, but Rose couldn't see enough to tell.

Aside from that, there was just one other door along that hallway—an oversized wooden door that apparently led into a *very* large room.

Kallias turned and leaned against the door, as if he were hiding it from her. With an enticing smile, he said, "Are you ready?"

Although an excited Kallias was certainly an amusing sight, the curiosity was killing her. "Are you trying to kill me with anticipation? Because there are easier ways," she muttered. She tried to glance around him. "What is it? A room full of coffee?"

His smile faded. "Uh, no. We keep the coffee in the kitchen."

"Dang. I had my fingers crossed for a coffee swimming pool," Rose quipped.

His lips twitched. "I'm sure you'll find this just as pleasing."

Rose waved her hand impatiently. "I *can* die of old age, you know."

She regretted the joke when his smile faltered.

But rather than comment on it, he let his weight push open the large, heavy door, and then, held it open with his forearm.

With a wary smile, Rose stepped through the doorway—and then froze, her jaw dropping in awe.

Kallias let her gape for a moment—before saying, "You can go inside."

Rose took a wary step forward, as if she thought the illusion might dissolve beneath her feet. "You have a lot of books."

The understatement of the century.

Kallias laughed. "I've been alive for a lot of years."

Another understatement.

She'd thought the guest room was huge, but the library made the guest room look like a *closet*.

It was nearly half the size of the house!

Or the first floor of it, anyway.

Much like the rest of the house, the library had hardwood floors, and somewhere beneath the bookshelves, the walls appeared to be stone.

But the bookshelves—towering, impressive bookshelves—covered every wall from floor to ceiling.

In the center of the room—the only part of it left empty—three leather sofas set catty-cornered to each other.

"How long do you have to be undead before they give you one of these?" Rose said breathlessly.

He snorted, "I think it has more to do with the telepathic control."

"Right," Rose mumbled, but she didn't look at him.

She couldn't seem to tear her gaze from the shelves upon shelves of old, dusty books.

Kallias leaned against the wall and crossed his arms, as he watched her. A vampire's allure might not affect her, but a *library* clearly did.

Her bright blue were wide and beautiful, and her arms were outstretched slightly, as if she were about to ask a question.

As if she were in a perpetual state of awe.

She was so beautiful like that.

With a laugh, Kallias said, "So, do you like it?"

She pinned him with the snarkiest stare he'd ever seen. "It's a library," she said dryly. "Of course I like it."

With a soft chuckle, he strode toward her. He stopped behind her—so close that his shirt brushed against her back. "It looks like I can impress you, after all," he teased.

Rose tilted her head back to stick her tongue out at him, but she nearly lost her balance when she did. His arms came up around her stomach—almost instinctually—and suddenly, it felt as if they were a normal couple, comfortably embracing each other.

"This is yours?" she asked.

He snorted, "Well, it's definitely not Erik's. He hates reading."

"I'm surprised," she admitted. "I didn't expect *you* to have a library."

He released her and stepped past her, heading toward a nearby book-case. "Why does that surprise you? Do I seem illiterate?"

Rose followed him, still wearing that cute smile of hers. "I just find it hard to picture *big, tough* Kallias curled up on the couch with a book."

He snorted at that. He turned toward her, smiling. "What do you think I did when I was human? As a profession, I mean."

Rose shrugged. "How would I know?"

"Ah, come on," he chided. "You know Greek history. You're intelligent. Make an educated guess. Humor me."

Her eyes narrowed at the challenge. "Fine," she sighed. "Soldier?"

His smirk widened, as if he'd just beaten her in a game. "Wrong."

"Aww," she pouted. "I was close, though, right?"

He shrugged. "My father and brothers were military."

She crossed her arms. "Okay. So, what did you do, then?"

His brows furrowed, as if he were trying to figure out how to explain it. "I, uhh… I learned and taught. I was like a modern…*professor*, I suppose."

Her eyes widened. "You were a Greek philosopher?"

"Yes," he said, "which involved vigorous reading, by the way."

"Like Socrates, Plato, and Aristotle?!" she squeaked.

He frowned. "I wasn't famous, Rose. The job description was similar, but that's like comparing an amateur songwriter to Bach or Mozart."

"Yeah, but still," she said, her brows high. "You're serious?"

"Why is this so shocking to you? Do I not seem intelligent?" he asked.

She giggled, "No, you seem plenty intelligent. You just don't seem nerdy."

Kallias laughed, "What threw you off? Was it my irresistible sexiness?"

Rose burst into hysterical laughter. She laughed so hard that it made her stomach sore. "No, I think it was the muscles, actually," she teased back.

He chuckled. "Is that what made you guess soldier?"

"Well, no. Not just that," she admitted. "You seem really skilled in combat."

He nodded, accepting the compliment as fact. "I was trained as a child," he told her, "and of course, I've had plenty of time to perfect my skills since then."

"Also," she added shyly, "you're brave. And kind. And protective. Qualities I imagine would be important in war."

He froze, obviously caught off guard by that. "You're mistaken," he stated, averting his gaze. "I'm not kind."

Kallias heard her soft footsteps and glanced curiously at her. He blinked, as she stood before him with a defiant spark in her blue eyes.

"You can say that as much as you want," Rose said, "but I'm not going to give up." She reached up and touched his jaw, causing his eyes to flutter. "I'll show you the good in yourself, if it's the last thing I do."

Kallias stared at her for a moment, stunned by her declaration. He reached up, covering her hand with his own. Then, he dragged her hand down to his chest.

Rose watched him curiously—the way his brown eyes seemed to simultaneously darken with desire and soften with affection.

His heartbeat thumped against her palm, and her own heart pounded, as well. Then, acting on a sudden impulse, she tugged lightly at his shirt and lifted herself onto her toes to kiss him.

She couldn't have surprised him, really—since he had to lean forward to kiss her—but the groan that escaped his lips *sounded* surprised, all the same.

Only a moment into the kiss, Kallias pulled away sharply.

Rose hesitated, thinking she'd made a mistake. But his eyes flashed with hunger and lust, and he took a step forward, backing her into the bookshelf.

When Kallias pressed her against the bookcase—and it didn't wobble —Rose had only a moment to marvel *again* at the library, before his lips pressed against hers. His hands pressed hers on either side of her head, and Rose closed her fingers around his.

His mouth left hers, and Rose frowned for just a moment, before he pressed his lips to the sensitive skin between her ear and neck.

Rose's eyes instantly fluttered closed, and chills rose over her skin.

Maybe it was a bad idea to let her mind sink into an aroused haze, while a vampire's fangs were this close to her neck, but she trusted Kallias not to hurt her—whether he thought she should or not.

His mouth trailed lower, finding the place where her neck met her shoulder, and he kissed there, too, setting fire to Rose's skin.

His fangs nipped lightly at her skin, and she gasped.

The soft scents of vanilla and honey and the powerful scent of her blood overwhelmed Kallias, and his sharp fangs pressed harder against her throat.

A sudden realization struck Rose.

Some part of her *wanted* him to bite her. She didn't know why, exactly —or what strange part of her mind the desire had emerged from—but somehow, the thought of being bitten felt...*right.*

But Kallias managed to pull himself away from her neck before he gave in to the hunger, and when he kissed her lips again, the strange desire that had surged inside Rose slinked back into the more...*hidden* part of her mind.

Kallias pressed his body against hers, and his breath came in harsh, heavy pants. He breathed something into the space between their lips— something he hadn't expected her to understand.

"*Se thelo.*"

But Rose *did* understand. "Me, too," she whispered—without thinking. "I want you, too."

With a surprised groan, Kallias kissed her harder, and Rose's mind whirled with unfamiliar emotions—and questions.

Why had she said that?

After all of those years of trying to be ready and *not* being ready, could she truly be ready now?

She couldn't honestly say.

Rose only knew that she *did* want him in some sort of way—and she trusted him to take things slowly.

Except...the desperate kiss they shared now didn't *feel* slow.

And Rose wasn't bothered by it either.

She fumbled clumsily with the first couple of buttons of his shirt, and she slipped her fingers beneath it, tracing the brightly-colored flames that were inked into his skin.

His hand moved, as well, tracing the wide curve of her hip, and his thumb curled into the waistband of her jeans.

"*Gamoto,*" Kallias cursed.

He pulled away so suddenly that Rose stumbled forward, nearly falling flat on her face.

Which...would *not* have been romantic.

Kallias caught her elbow, steadying her, and Rose frowned up at him, worried she'd done something wrong.

But Kallias's glare was directed toward the person in the doorway—not her. "What the hell are you doing, Erik?"

Rose blinked and followed his gaze to find Erik leaning against the doorframe and watching them with an amused smirk.

Erik shrugged one shoulder. "Just enjoying the show."

Rose's cheeks burned with embarrassment. "You're disgusting," she tried to grumble, but it came out more like a breathless gasp than a grumble.

Erik clasped a hand over his chest. "You've wounded me."

"Wounding you," Kallias mused. "That sounds like a good idea, actually."

Erik raised both hands in surrender. "Hey! It's not my fault you two decided to have sex in the library, of all places," he teased. "Seriously, though, why here? This is the *least* arousing room in the house."

"It's not the..." Rose was just about to defend the library's honor, before she fully realized what had been said. *Priorities.* "We weren't having sex," she said, instead.

Erik ignored that. "I also think it's a bit hypocritical, considering how you acted about Amy and I having a little fun on the stairs."

"Anne," Kallias corrected. "Erik, her name was Anne."

Erik waved a hand dismissively. "Close enough."

"We were not having sex," Rose insisted—louder this time.

Erik grinned at her. "Maybe not *yet,* but..."

"You act like you didn't *know* this was a bad time," Kallias interrupted. "You knew what was happening. You would've *felt* it."

"Uhh, what?" Rose said, glancing at Kallias. "What does that mean?"

Erik answered her—before Kallias could. "I feel your emotions," he reminded her with a sickeningly smug look. "Desire's an emotion, babe."

Rose's eyes widened. "I don't think this could get any more embarrassing."

Kallias rubbed the back of his neck and offered her a wary smile. "Don't say that. He'll take it as a challenge."

Erik pushed away from the doorframe and walked into the room. "So, is this what you meant by *'just'* protecting her?"

Kallias narrowed his eyes at his friend. "I *am* protecting her."

"Clearly," Erik snorted. Amusement sparkled in his green eyes. "Ah, come on. Don't look at me like that. You know I like to gloat when I'm right."

Rose frowned. "Right about what?"

"Nothing," Kallias muttered. He directed his next words at Erik. "So, did you have an actual *reason* for coming in here at such an inappropriate time?"

"Aside from you being a creepy pervert, that is," Rose added.

Erik grinned, as if that had been a compliment. With a nonchalant shrug, he said, "What you call perverted was considered normal when I was human."

"Erik, you were never considered normal," Kallias muttered.

Erik laughed. He strode over to one of the leather sofas and perched himself on the arm of the sofa. "Actually, I did need to talk to you."

Kallias nodded. He buttoned his shirt and walked over to the sofa.

Rose blushed at the reminder of how eagerly she'd unbuttoned those few buttons.

Erik glanced at her and grinned, and her blush deepened, as she realized that he must've sensed her embarrassment. He winked, confirming her fear.

Kallias turned toward her. "Are you coming?"

"I was actually thinking about standing here and dying of embarrassment," Rose told him. "I prefer to die near the books, instead of the perverted, empathic vampire."

Erik laughed. "I don't think she likes me," he said to Kallias.

Kallias sank onto the sofa across from Erik. "I don't blame her."

Erik just chuckled. "So, I talked to Geoff and Emma. They've agreed to help," he told Kallias. "Geoff, of course, expressed his…concerns. He thinks she's a lost cause."

Kallias narrowed his eyes at that. "She's not a lost cause."

Erik raised both hands. "Hey. I didn't say it. He did," he said defensively. "Don't shoot the messenger."

Kallias's glare didn't waver.

"You know how Geoff is," Erik tried again. "He has nothing against her. He's just being *rational*." He rolled his eyes, as if he thought rationality was as fictional as Santa Claus. "You have to admit, though: The odds aren't in her favor."

"I don't give a shit about the odds," Kallias snapped. "I won't let her die."

A strange look passed over Erik's face—a mixture of surprise and curiosity, perhaps? His eyebrows lifted, as if he and Kallias were having a silent conversation.

Which, of course, they *were*.

Peeved about being left out of their telepathic conversation, Rose walked over to join them. "I'm a lost cause?"

Erik looked up at her, as if he'd only just remembered she was there.

"No, you're not," Kallias said.

"I didn't ask you," she told Kallias. She turned to Erik and crossed her arms. "I asked *him*."

Erik winced a little. "No, you're not?" he repeated—though he sounded a lot less sure than Kallias. He shrugged. "Or yes, you are. I don't know. My abilities are empathic, not precognitive." He leaned forward. "Geoff was a scientist when he was human. He sees everything in black and white—facts and numbers…"

"Then, he's right," Rose said. "You can't argue with statistics."

"Sure you can," Erik argued. "Numbers treat everyone as if they're the same, but they're not the same. People *feel* differently. Emotions change things. I'd trust feelings over facts any day."

Rose frowned curiously at that. "That sounds like an irrational line of thinking."

Erik shrugged. "I'm an empath. We're not exactly known for our rationality."

"It's true," Kallias agreed. "He's the most irrational person I've ever met."

Erik chuckled at Kallias's remark. He returned his gaze to Rose and shifted his body toward her. "Think of it this way," he explained. "All the experts in the world can say that you *can't* do something, but if you feel strongly enough about it, you can prove them wrong. People do crazy, impossible things for the ones they love all of the time—because of what they *feel*."

Rose considered that. "Why does your friend think I'm a lost cause?"

Kallias shot a worried look at Erik. "Erik, don't."

"You know that thing you do?" Erik asked him. "Where you get all overprotective of people you care about?" He offered a small, amused smile. "You're doing it again. Every vampire in this country wants to kill her—including an ancient psychopath who likes to torture people. Trying to protect her from being afraid is pointless."

Rose couldn't but smile a little at that.

Kallias, on the other hand, shot glares at both of them. "Fine." He turned to Erik and sighed, "Tell her what she wants to know."

Erik gestured toward the sofa. "Sit down," he told Rose.

Rose shook her head. She was too anxious to sit down, too worried about Erik's answer. "No, thanks. I'm good."

Erik rolled his eyes. "Well, I'm not." He climbed to his feet and stepped toward her. "You see, I'm not usually an anxious person, but *you're* anxious—which means I'm anxious, too, because I feel what you feel." He grabbed her arm in the middle of his speech and dragged her toward the sofa. "And I don't like feeling anxious." He pushed her down beside Kallias.

With a yelp of surprise, Rose scoffed, "Who do you think you are?"

"Erik Olafsson," he said with a grin. "We just went over this, didn't we?"

Rose rolled her eyes at that.

Then, Erik surprised her by leaning forward and pressing his hand to her shoulder. Before she could ask him what he was doing, she felt a strange wave of serenity wash over her, slowing her heartbeat and calming her anxiety.

For a moment, she wondered if she'd been drugged with a sedative or something, but it wasn't drowsiness she felt.

She just felt...calm.

Erik sighed in relief. "That's better."

"What did you do to me?" Rose said—with even more anxiety than before.

"Holy hell. Your emotions are almost as unstable as mine," Erik complained. "I just calmed you, and you're already upset again."

"I'm not not upset," Rose said with a frown, "or unstable."

"Well, you're definitely not *calm*," Erik muttered.

"You said you calmed me," Rose said curiously. "What did you mean by that?"

Erik sat on the sofa across from theirs. "That's how my abilities work. I control emotion. I can manipulate your current state, or I can create an emotion and project it. In your case, I manipulated."

Rose nodded, her curiosity only rising. "Do you have to touch the person to do that?"

"Not necessarily," Erik said. "Physical contact just helps me control it."

"If he didn't touch you, he'd accidentally manipulate the emotions of everyone in a five-mile radius," Kallias said. He lowered his voice to a whisper. "He doesn't have the best control."

Erik scowled, his sensitive hearing clearly unhindered by a whisper. "You're one to talk," he scoffed. "At least I don't carry on conversations with people's thoughts without even realizing it."

Rose couldn't help it. She started giggling. When she noticed Kallias scowling at her, she covered her mouth with her hand in an effort to stop herself from laughing. "Sorry. It's just...he's right," she said. "You do that. A lot, actually."

"Did she just say I'm right?" Erik asked. "I need to write that down."

"Wait," Rose said, turning her attention back toward Erik. "Five-mile radius?"

"It happened once," Erik said defensively, "and my emotions were a little unstable, at the time."

"Your emotions are always a little unstable," Kallias pointed out.

"My emotions were a *lot* unstable," Erik amended.

Rose could nothing but laugh in disbelief, her eyes wide. "So, uh," she said, returning to the question he'd sort of evaded, "why am I a lost cause?"

"You're not," Kallias said again.

Erik glanced at Kallias, before answering Rose. "Because Theron is ancient and powerful. And, *apparently*, not alone."

Rose nodded uneasily at that.

"Theron isn't a problem," Kallias said stubbornly. "I'll kill him myself."

Erik lifted his eyebrows. "You keep saying that, and yet, he's still alive."

"I told you," Kallias muttered. "I've been distracted."

"And you'll continue to be distracted, as long as *she* is alive," Erik said, jabbing a finger in Rose's direction. "That's how emotions work. They can empower you, but they can also distract you."

Rose cast a puzzled look at Kallias, but he shifted away from her gaze.

"Besides, even if you weren't distracted, he's older than you, which means he's physically stronger," Erik added. "And don't forget: you're starved. Any advantage your telepathic abilities give you doesn't change the fact that he feeds, and you don't. You might as well be centuries younger than him."

Rose thought about that. "What if Kallias *wasn't* starving himself?"

Kallias narrowed his eyes at the question. "It doesn't matter. I am."

"Oh, calm down," Rose scoffed. "I'm not trying to feed somebody's puppy to you. I'm just curious."

Kallias grimaced at that thought. "It *might*...even the odds," he admitted, "but it doesn't matter because I *am* starving, and that's not going to change."

Erik lifted his eyebrows in disbelief. "It'd do *more* than even the odds."

"Erik," Kallias said in warning.

"He's a telepath," Erik told Rose. "Theron is nothing compared to a telepath—*if* the telepath isn't weakened by hunger, that is." When Kallias continued to glare at him, he added, "Theron still outnumbers us, though. We don't know how many vampires he has helping him, but it's clearly more than we have."

Rose turned to Kallias. "Why didn't you tell me this?"

Kallias kept his gaze on the floor. "I'm not afraid of numbers."

"You should be!" Rose said. She shook her head in disbelief. "Did you honestly I think I'd be okay with you risking your life for me? With *all* of you possibly dying?" Her words grew breathless. "For me?"

"Well," Erik said with a tilt of his head, "if we're all dead, it won't matter if you're okay with it." He shrugged. "Because you'll be dead, too!"

They both frowned at him.

"How is that helpful?" Kallias said.

Erik shrugged.

"It's not your choice," Kallias told Rose. "I can risk your life, whether you're *'okay'* with it or not."

Rose narrowed her eyes at the patronizing bite in his tone. "It's my choice, whether I *let* you protect me. I could leave."

Erik snorted. "And what? *Walk* back to Florida?"

Rose turned her glare on Erik.

He cringed. "She's going to kill someone with that glare one day."

"If you leave, I'll just follow you," Kallias informed her.

"Even if I tell you not to?" Rose said.

"Yes," Kallias assured her. "I won't let you die."

Rose sighed. "Well, maybe I don't want to let you die, either," she said—softly now. "Have you considered that? How is my life more valuable than yours?"

"Because my life is stolen. I should've died long ago," Kallias told her. "You haven't lived yours yet. You have infinite possibilities ahead of you."

"They're hardly infinite," Rose scoffed. "And it wouldn't matter, anyway. I don't want any of you to risk your lives for me. So, *don't*."

"I've made my decision," Kallias said, clearly not willing to budge an inch. "What they do is their choice."

Rose glanced at Erik. "Your choice is no, right?"

"What?" Erik laughed, as if that were absurd. "My choice is *hell* yes."

Confusion twisted at Rose's face. "Why?" she asked. "I don't understand why *any* of you would do this."

Erik leaned back, his grin playful. "Well, first of all, because I love a battle, and I haven't had a good one in a while..." He lifted his narrow shoulders in a careless shrug. "And second...this is what we *do*. We go out and save humans from other vampires."

A small smile tugged at the corners of Rose's lips, and she asked again, "But *why*?"

"Because Kallias did it for twelve hundred years by himself, and he was *so* overwhelmed that he actually forgot how to get women," Erik joked.

Kallias scowled at him.

And Rose didn't fall for the evasion. "You must have a real reason."

At that, Erik's smile slipped. With a soft sigh, he said, "How many lives do you think someone has to save in order to ease the guilt of taking so many?"

"I don't know," she admitted.

"Neither do I," Erik said softly. "I haven't reached that number yet."

Sympathy tightened in Rose's chest.

Should she feel sympathy for someone who murdered people? Was that wrong? She didn't know.

She couldn't help it, though. It had always been her problem. She sympathized with everyone, even when she shouldn't.

These two people were vampires—violent and dangerous—but to her, they were still people. Damaged and hurting people, just like her.

"I can feel your, er, sympathy. It's," Erik paused, shifting uncomfortably, "strange."

With a nervous smile, Rose said, "Sorry."

Erik cast another curious glance her way.

Rose turned to Kallias. "And you?" she asked gently. "Is it a redemption thing for you, too?"

Kallias didn't meet her gaze. "No."

"What would *he* need redemption for?" Erik scoffed. "He's been starving himself since day one. He's almost as boring as you are, *virgin*."

Rose chose to ignore the immature vampire. "Then, why?" she asked Kallias. "You're not killing humans. They are. Why would you risk *your* life?"

Kallias spread out his hands. "What's the alternative? Stay home and pretend it's not happening?" he pointed out. "Is it any less evil to do nothing, when I have the power to stop it?"

An understanding smile curved at the corners of her lips. "'The only thing necessary for the triumph of evil is that good men do nothing.' Edmund Burke," she quoted.

Erik squinted. "Who? What?"

Kallias, on the other hand, just nodded.

Kindness and empathy burned in Rose's bright blue eyes. "You're just trying to be good in the only way you know—as what you are."

His jaw tightened, but he didn't deny it.

Rose leaned closer to him. "You've already done your good with me," she told him. "You don't have to keep risking your life for me. You've done enough. Just...hand me over to Theron."

Kallias shifted toward her so fast it startled her. "What?" he growled. Lines of anger twisted at his strangely beautiful face, and she could practically *feel* the rage radiating off of him. "Hand you over?"

Rose leaned back against the side of the sofa, wary of his anger. "I—"

"How can you even say that?" he snarled.

Rose continued to stare at him, not sure how to respond. She'd only said the obvious truth, hadn't she?

That she wasn't worth this much trouble...

More shock and rage flickered in his light brown eyes, and Rose realized he must've heard that thought.

"You *are* worth it," Kallias said. "Don't say you're not."

Rose swallowed uneasily. She wanted to argue with such an absurd statement, but no words came readily.

Kallias didn't break eye-contact, but he *did* move—up and closer, pressing his weight onto his left arm.

He was practically hovering over her now.

The rage in Kallias's brown eyes seemed to fade, then—revealing something softer beneath it.

"Leave, Erik," he said.

Erik jumped to his feet. "Yep. Got it."

The door closed behind him with a soft click.

There was so much emotion in Kallias's eyes in that moment. Rose wanted to look away—to pretend she hadn't seen it.

She didn't want to face what she might feel for him—or what he might feel for her. She didn't want to be hurt again.

And she *definitely* didn't want to hurt him.

Or to watch him and his friends risk their lives for her.

"I'm just one person," Rose whispered. "I'm not worth—"

His jean-clad knees brushed her legs, as he leaned closer. "Yes, you are."

His breath warmed her lips, and her gaze flickered downward.

"I'm trying to argue with you, but," she paused, her face warming, "I sort of just want to kiss you."

Her clumsily-worded confession seemed to amuse him, and his anger gave way to a wide grin.

Rose's blush deepened. She'd never admitted anything like that before, and she wasn't sure what had prompted her to say it then.

"Well," Kallias said with a laugh, "you could just do it, then." He waited for a moment, before adding, "Kiss me?"

He might've been a dangerous vampire, but Rose couldn't help but think that what he'd just said was sort of...*adorable*.

Kallias must've heard that thought, too, because he leaned back, his eyes wide. "Wait a minute, now. I was only responding to—"

Rose interrupted his objection with a gentle kiss.

Kallias froze, and his eyes slid closed, as her soft mouth pressed against his. He lifted his hand, brushing his fingers along the soft curve of her jaw, and he deepened the kiss.

Without thinking, Rose lifted her hands to touch his long, brown hair —and then promptly fell back against the arm of the sofa, as she remembered that one of her arms had been holding her weight.

"Oops," she mumbled.

But Kallias just laughed.

He wrapped one hand around her soft hip and tugged her downward so that she lay beneath him—in a much less awkward position.

He pressed the other hand against the sofa to hold his weight, as he leaned over her.

Rose swallowed nervously, as his body pressed against her own.

Kallias kissed her again, groaning softly against her lips. As Rose gasped for breath, he trailed his mouth downward, kissing her neck.

Kallias hesitated when his lips brushed the warm skin over her carotid artery. He heard the blood coursing through the artery, and he felt it—pulsing, beneath his lips.

Her blood smelled so sweet and so powerful—better than anything he'd ever encountered—and he could practically taste it already.

His fangs grazed her skin, and Rose moaned at the sensation.

That sound only intensified his hunger, and he slowly began to lose control of it. He pressed his razor-sharp fangs into her neck, and the soft skin nearly gave way beneath that slight bit of pressure.

Hunger burned in his throat and stomach, and his mind whirled with the possibility of tasting her, consuming her, creating a blood bond with her…

"*Shit.*" He jerked back, suddenly.

Rose watched him warily, as she tried to catch her breath. Pressing her hand to the back of the couch, she pulled herself into a sitting position. He was still nearly on top of her, but he'd pulled back enough for her to sit up.

He kept his head turned to the side and his eyes closed. He looked paler than she'd ever seen him—sickly pale.

He panted heavily, his fangs bared, like an animal.

"Is it your hunger?" she asked gently.

His eyes snapped open, and he moved toward her so quickly that she gasped and nearly fell backward *again*. Feral hunger burned in his dark eyes, and his fangs gleamed in his mouth.

"It's *so* difficult to control it around you," Kallias growled. He pressed his face into the curve of her neck, inhaling her scent.

Rose swallowed nervously. "Would it hurt?"

His fangs pressed into her skin again.

"If you fed from me," Rose tried again, "would it hurt?"

"No," he murmured against her skin. He nipped her neck, and she couldn't help but moan. "You'd be *writhing* in pleasure."

Rose shuddered, a warm rush of longing spreading through her lower body. Instinctually, she tried to clench her thighs, but she couldn't —because he was there, kneeling between her legs.

"I should be afraid," Rose stated.

"Yes, you should," Kallias agreed. His voice came out as just a soft growl against her skin. "You have *no* idea how much I want to taste you."

"You won't," Rose said breathlessly.

His fangs pressed harder against her skin. "How can you be so sure?"

Rose closed her eyes, her breath coming faster. "Because," she gasped out, "you'd never hurt me."

Kallias froze.

Rose watched curiously, as he leaned back, resting his weight on his knees. Her chest tightened with sympathy, as she realized that she was seeing him in his most vulnerable state. His skin was pale, and his lips trembled.

"I could never hurt you," he agreed.

The foreign longing that ached in Rose's chest—the one she'd been ignoring for days—grew stronger and more insistent, then.

She *shouldn't* feel what she was feeling. She didn't *want* to feel it, but it was becoming harder and harder to deny that she was falling for him —much too quickly and much too hard.

Kallias lifted himself onto his knees and moved off of her. He moved to sit in the opposite corner of the sofa—as far away from her as he could get. He hung his face in his trembling hands and took deep breaths, as he tried to regain control of the overwhelming hunger that surged inside of him.

Rose leaned toward him. "Is there anything I can do to help?"

"Don't come any closer," he said, his voice muffled by his hands.

Rose nodded and scooted backward. "Okay."

After several moments of tense silence, Kallias lifted his head and looked at her. That dangerous spark of hunger had vanished from his light brown eyes, and now, it was pain that twisted at every part of his face. "I'm sorry."

Rose shook her head, offering him a gentle smile. "It's okay."

"No, it's not," he said between clenched teeth.

Sighing at his angry tone, she said, "Do you want to talk?"

"About what?" he said miserably.

"Anything," Rose said. She searched her ever-curious brain for a good distraction. "Okay. Can I ask you a question?"

Despite his sullen anger, that still managed to earn a laugh from him. "Yes, Rose," he sighed, "for the billionth time."

Rose suppressed a smile. "We were talking earlier about your career," she reminded him. "I'm just curious. If the rest of your family were military, what made you decide to become a philosopher?"

Kallias shook his head in disbelief. "That's what you want to talk about right now?"

Rose shrugged. "I always want to talk about history."

Kallias rolled his eyes, but his smile betrayed his amusement. He rested his elbows on his knees and lifted his shoulders in a tired shrug. "Above all else, my father believed in strength, and he believed a nation— or empire—demonstrated their strength over another nation with military force," he sighed. "And as an individual, he believed *people* demonstrated their strength over others in the same way—through brute strength."

Rose tried to read between the lines of what he was saying. *His father was cruel.* Was that what he meant?

"My brothers followed in his footsteps. They thought strength was all that mattered," Kallias told her, "but I believed differently."

Rose nodded, listening curiously.

"I didn't want to be like my father or brothers. They were basically just bullies, preying on anyone they perceived as weaker than them," Kallias said. "I *hated* it." He shrugged. "So, I chose a different career— one that didn't involve violence. I'd always had a great admiration for those who dedicated their lives to learning. So, that's what I did. I thought, by doing that, I could be different and *better* than them."

"You wanted to break the cycle," Rose said.

That was a feeling she knew well.

Kallias laughed bitterly. "I was so naïve," he scoffed. "Look at me. I'm more of a monster than my father ever was. I thought I could escape it, but I can't."

Rose leaned forward and rested one of her hands over his. She feared he'd pull away, but instead, he just stared at her hand. "That is *not* true," she told him. "You're not a monster."

Kallias rolled his eyes. "Rose—"

But she continued, "Despite being a vampire, you *still* choose not to prey on those weaker than you. You still choose not to hurt others."

He shook his head, refusing to meet her gaze.

"Every night, you choose to fight your demons," Rose added. "That makes you different—whether you realize it or not."

Kallias stared at her, stunned by her words, stunned by how they made him feel. "What are you doing to me?" he whispered.

Rose frowned at the question. "What do you mean?"

But he jerked his hand away and stood. "Nothing."

Disappointed that he was pulling away again, Rose stood and followed. She just wanted to understand—and to help.

He was in pain, and she knew all too well what that was like.

Kallias stopped by a bookcase near the door, and he pulled out a book that appeared to be written in Spanish. He thumbed through it distractedly.

Rose crossed her arms. "Do you know why I love to read?"

"Because you're curious," Kallias said without looking at her, "and you enjoy learning."

Rose nodded. "That, too," she agreed, "but also because anything can happen in books."

He stared at the book in his hand, still attempting to ignore her.

"I fell in love with reading as a child," Rose said, though her pulse raced as she said it. "My life was...not great, and things felt so hopeless that...it just wasn't worth living anymore."

Kallias glanced at her curiously.

"Things were never going to get better. No one was ever going to love me," Rose said with a shrug. "When you start thinking like that, giving up seems like a good option."

The book lay forgotten in Kallias's hands.

"But them I started reading, and I started believing," Rose said. "In books, you can overcome anything. Good can defeat evil. People can change. Life can get better. The good guys can slay the monsters and save the world. A little girl can grow up in the worst of circumstances and *not* become bitter or cruel because of it. Love can win, and hate can be extinguished." She smiled. "Books taught me to believe."

"You were reading *fiction*," Kallias told her. "You can't apply that to real life."

"Why not?" Rose argued. "You can learn so much from fiction—hope, faith, love..."

"I stopped believing in those things a long time ago," he interrupted.

Rose dropped her arms to her sides, and sympathetic pain twisted at her brows. "Everyone needs to believe in something," she said softly. "Isn't there *anything* you believe in?"

Kallias looked away, his brows furrowed in thought. "Yeah," he said, as he returned the book to the bookcase. He turned toward her. "I believe in you."

He then turned and walked out of the room, leaving Rose standing in the middle of the library, stunned.

18

THE STONE

It was midway through the day, while everyone else slept, when Rose's pen fell from her hand and clacked lightly against the desk.

She didn't move for a moment, her hand poised over the notebook— frozen the way it'd been before she'd read that last line. The words blurred before her eyes, and cold dread poured through her veins.

This was bad.

Really bad.

Rose shoved the scrolls aside, no longer taking care to be gentle with the ancient documents. Their appeal to her—as a piece of history—was overshadowed by the *other* emotions reeling through her, now.

It wasn't that she'd never considered the possibility. It was just that… it was too much of a coincidence.

Right?

Apparently not.

Rose pinched the bridge of her nose between her thumb and forefinger, but it did nothing to dull the throbbing headache that had been bothering her for hours.

If she'd been able to sleep—and not plagued with nightmares, as usual—she'd still be blissfully ignorant.

And maybe Theron would've killed her before she'd ever translated that sentence.

Wishful thinking.

As it was, she had no doubt that Kallias would kill her before Theron had the chance.

"Can't sleep?"

Startled, Rose spun the office chair so quickly she nearly tipped it over.

Kallias stood in the doorway, leaning tiredly against the frame. A pair of sweatpants hung around his waist, but his chest was bare—his scars illuminated by the lamplight.

Aside from those scars, most humans would've thought he looked physically perfect tonight, as vampires always did, but Rose noticed the subtle differences that others would've missed.

Like the ashen tint of his skin.

And the bruised circles beneath his eyes.

With a concerned frown, Rose said, "You look tired."

Kallias slumped heavily against the wall. "I'm supposed to be asleep."

Rose frowned at his posture, worried that he'd fall. "Why aren't you, then?"

"I heard you awake," he said softly. "Your heartbeat...your breathing..."

Rose reflexively placed her hand on her chest, feeling her elevated heart-rate against her own palm. "Sorry," she said softly. "I tried to stay quiet."

He rubbed his hand across his face, as if he could wipe off the tiredness. "You didn't wake me. My body *wants* to sleep during the day, whether there's noise or not. It isn't the noise. It's *you*."

Rose's brows furrowed. "Me?"

"I can't sleep," Kallias stated, "knowing you're upset."

Rose's eyes widened. It wasn't like him to say something so...transparent.

Apparently, daylight did more burn him.

It also made him more...*open*.

"I'm not upset," she said.

"Your heart-rate says otherwise," he slurred, "and I'm sure your thoughts would, as well, if I—"

"Don't," Rose interrupted.

Despite his sun-induced near-comatose state, he still managed to narrow his eyes at that. "You're hiding something."

Rose swallowed down the anxiety surging in her throat. "I'd rather tell you the truth myself," she told him. "You don't need to invade my mind for it."

That seemed to shake him out of his semi-comatose state for a moment. He placed his hand on the doorframe and pushed himself to stand in a more upright position. His heavy-lidded, brown eyes studied her for a moment, and then he shuffled toward her, clearly too weak to be walking around.

Still, he slumped onto the edge of her bed and leaned forward, his elbows resting on his knees. He rubbed his face again and then looked up, meeting her gaze with a suspicious glare.

"What is it, Rose?" he said, his voice already rough with irritation.

Rose wished she could've waited until nightfall to tell him—because the sunlight clearly didn't have him in the best of moods.

And she was about to make it a lot worse.

With an uneasy sigh, Rose began, "Before I met you, I'd—I'd just gotten back from a study trip. I'd been to Greece."

Kallias shrugged impatiently. "And?"

"While I was there," Rose continued, "someone approached me."

Kallias rubbed the side of his head. "Who was he, Rose?"

The tension in her shoulders pulled tighter with each word. "I don't know," she said honestly. "He didn't tell me his name. He just pulled me aside and gave me this old, stone box."

He squinted bewilderedly at that. "A box? Why?"

Rose shrugged. "He said it belonged to me—whatever *that* meant," she said, "and he told me not to tell anyone about it. He said people would die if it fell into the wrong hands."

"Well, what was in it?" Kallias said impatiently.

"I'm getting to that," Rose said with a peeved look. She leaned forward in the chair. "There were these ancient scrolls inside—written in a *very* ancient dialect of Greek."

His frown deepened.

"I've been trying to translate it," Rose told him, "since that first night —at the hotel—but it hasn't been easy." She shook her head. "Some of the words are unregistered, even in the best historical databases. Others are recognizable but don't make sense in the context of the sentence. It's like they're the wrong words, even if they aren't."

He leaned his face against his hand and nodded tiredly. "Ancient Greek is complicated. If one letter is written wrong, it can change the entire word," he told her. "You were probably just dealing with some misspelled words."

Rose blinked. She hadn't thought about that. "You think so?"

He gave another nod. "You should've brought it to me."

"Yeah," Rose said with a regretful sigh. "I *should've* done a lot of things I didn't do."

His scowl grew wary. "What's the matter with you?"

"I know what Theron wants from me," Rose confessed.

His eyes narrowed dangerously. "You told me you didn't know."

"I didn't!" she said. Then, she cringed. "Not for sure, anyway."

Kallias growled, "Rose—"

Rose held up her hands in a placating gesture. "Just let me explain. Please," she said cautiously. "I wasn't...*intentionally* dishonest."

His glare didn't waver. "I'm listening."

Rose gulped at his tone. "The scrolls in the box—they were written by a woman. It was some sort of journal, I think," she explained, "but, well, Theron was pretty much all she talked about."

He leaned toward her. "How long have you known this?"

"The Theron part?" she squeaked. She winced. "Umm, a while?"

A frightening, animalistic growl resounded from his throat, and within a moment, he was in front of her, gripping the arms of the office chair. His face was so close to hers that she could feel the warmth of his breath on her face, and his brown eyes were dark with a feral kind of rage—a rage that raised every hair on her body.

His fangs gleamed dangerously in the lamplight. "Why didn't you tell me this before?" he snarled.

Rose leaned back in the chair, her eyes wide. Everything about his stance reminded her of a dangerous, feral animal. She'd expected anger, but this was worse. This...was a dangerous loss of control.

A sudden, loud crack drew her attention to the arms of the chair. She frowned as she realized that they were cracking under his grip.

"I didn't know it was important," she said, careful to keep her tone even. "The scrolls are about her sex life, for goodness sakes. She goes on and *on* about her sexual encounters with Theron. *Why* she felt the need to describe her sex life in such descriptive detail, I have no idea. I mean, seriously, why would anyone want to write about Theron—"

"Get to the point," he interrupted.

Ignoring the fact that he had her trapped and clearly wasn't himself at the moment, Rose snapped back, "What is your problem? Did you catch rabies or something?"

His eyes remained cold and steely. "I'm not a dog. I'm a vampire," he snarled. He tilted his head, eyeing her with murderous hunger. "Or have you forgotten that fact? That I can kill you anytime I choose?"

"I don't care what you are," Rose told him. "You're not going to treat me like this." She lowered her voice slightly. "Back off. Please."

Her response seemed to catch him off-guard, and he *did* ease back on his heels—though he still didn't let go of the chair.

Rose crossed her arms, and because of his closeness, her arms brushed his bare chest. And she blushed—which sort of ruined her attempt to appear as tough as possible. "You heard my heart racing," she reminded him, "because I had *just* found out what was so important about those scrolls. The final half of the final scroll was where she finally said it: the thing that Theron wants."

His frown deepened. "What is it?"

Rose cast a wary look at the box on the desk and bit her lip nervously. "The other thing that was in the box?"

His eyes narrowed again. "There was something else?"

"Yes?" she said uneasily. "There was a stone."

Kallias released the chair and stepped back, his expression suddenly guarded. "What kind of stone?"

"It has a name," Rose said, "according to the scrolls. Eklektos? Stone of the Eklektos?" Her brows furrowed. "I guess the translation would be Stone of the Chosen? Or Stone of the Destined? Or…"

But Kallias wasn't listening to her anymore. He'd turned ghostly pale the moment she'd spoken that word. He took another step back, and Rose studied him with a concerned frown.

"I'm going to go out on a limb here and assume you've heard of it?" Rose said.

He glared at her—though she still didn't understand why. "What did the scrolls say about it?"

"Not much," Rose said honestly. "It's not even mentioned until the last page." She reached for the scrolls and flipped to the part that mentioned it. "Near the end, the woman begins to worry about Theron's obsession with the Stone. She regrets telling him about it."

Kallias stiffened. "What?"

Rose glanced up at him. "Uh, I said that the—"

"I know what you said," Kallias said—quite harshly, actually. "The woman who wrote the scrolls was the one who told Theron about the Stone?"

"Uh, yeah?" Rose said. "Is that bad?"

He held out his hand. "Give me the scrolls."

"All right," Rose said warily. She held out the old parchment, watching with a puzzled frown, as he took it from her.

Kallias sat down on the edge of the guest bed, scowling at the Ancient Greek words. His entire countenance had grown cold and distant.

"Do you want my notebook?" she offered. "It's where I translated it."

He didn't look at her. He just held out his hand. "I need a pen, too."

Rose turned toward the desk, searching for the pen she'd been using.

He must've heard her thoughts—because without looking up, he said, "Behind your ear."

"Ah," Rose said, snatching the pen from its temporary holding place

—between her ponytail and ear. She held it out, and he took it without looking.

Kallias wrote quickly in her notebook, crossing out words and adding others, and Rose's curiosity grew with each stroke of the pen.

Only a few minutes later, he stood. He dropped the notebook in her lap and said, "It's done." As she glanced down at his notes, he added, "I could've saved you a lot of time and effort, if you'd told me earlier."

The barely controlled rage beneath those words seemed disproportionate to the situation—unless there was something Rose had missed.

Rose scanned his corrections to her translation curiously. She couldn't believe he'd translated it so quickly, but perhaps he'd been alive during this particular dialect.

She pointed at one of the words. "How did you get this?" she said curiously. "I mean, obviously, it makes more sense this way, but I know that word. It means *'sun.'*"

"Technically, yes," he agreed, "but it's not what she meant."

Rose looked up at him, frowning. "But how could you know that?"

"She misspelled it," Kallias explained. "She always did."

Rose's frown deepened. "Always?" she repeated. Anxiety flipped inside her stomach. "You...*know* who wrote this?"

"Of course," he said. "I was married to her."

Rose's eyes widened.

"I'd recognize my own wife's handwriting," he said, bitterness seeping into every word, "don't you think?"

Rose glanced down at the notebook, her skin pale. The horror settled in waves, as she considered every word she'd translated.

Her gaze fell to one particular line: *'Sometimes, I have moments of clarity, when I understand the danger, when I regret everything, but then, I look at him, and I think I love him again.'*

The allure.

His wife had been powerless against it.

Rose's fingers tightened around the parchment. "Oh my word."

"I taught her to read and write myself," Kallias said coldly. "I tried to correct her spelling, but she didn't listen."

Rose held out the scroll, clinging to one, final ounce of disbelief. "Your wife," she said. "This was...your *wife*?"

Kallias didn't seem to hear her. "Her father didn't think women needed literacy skills," he said bitterly. "But hey, if I hadn't gone against his wishes and taught her to read and write, she never could've never written those scrolls about how amazing of a time she had, fucking someone else. What a tragedy that would've been."

Rose frowned at that assumption. "I mean, it seems that way at first, but there are times when she realizes—"

"You're defending her?" he scoffed.

"Of course not," Rose said quickly. "I just thought you'd want to know—"

"I don't," Kallias snarled.

Rose shrunk back in her chair. "Kallias, I—" she trailed off with a pained expression. "If I'd known, I..."

"What?" he interrupted. "You would've kept lying to me?"

Rose sighed at his tone. "I never meant to hurt you."

Kallias leveled her with an unfeeling glare. "Fuck you, Rose."

It took Rose a moment to stop reeling from his reaction, but then, she jumped out of the chair and chased after him.

Vampire or not, she couldn't leave him alone with this much pain.

People needed friends at times like this.

And besides, even though she truly empathized with his pain, there were a few things Rose needed to say, as well.

He'd left his bedroom door open, and Rose came to a stop in the hall, lifting her hand to knock.

His room wasn't much different from the guest room she'd stayed in. It was just darker—and bit messier. More lived-in.

Only one lamp lit the room—a small, dim lamp on his nightstand.

The nightstand and dressers were made with black-stained wood, and a few daggers scattered the surface of the dresser.

There was a weapon cabinet on the wall, where he stored the rest of his weapons. So, the daggers on the dresser must've been the ones he'd used recently.

A large, wrought-iron bed set in the center of the room, covered in sheets and blankets that were as black as the metal itself. Kallias leaned over that bed, now, facing away from her, with both hands gripping the black, wrought-iron bed-frame.

Rose hesitated, as the metal let out a frightening groan.

Being angry was understandable, but breaking a whole dang bed was a little much.

"You know what?" Rose said, instead of knocking. "You're the one who told me not to trust you, and now, you're angry at me for doing what you asked? How is that fair?"

Kallias turned to look at her, his eyes dark and murderous. "What are you doing in here?"

"The man who gave it to me said that people would die if I told anyone," Rose explained, "and even though I thought it sounded totally crazy, it still made me nervous enough to keep it to myself."

"Rose," he said again. "Why are you in my room?"

"I should've told you about the scrolls and the Stone," Rose admitted. "I wish I had now. But you don't get to treat me like this, just because I made a mistake. Especially when you're the one who told me *not* to trust you." She spread out her arms. "What do you even want from me?"

"I want to know," he growled, "why you're in my room."

Rose shrugged. "You told me to come to your room if I needed you." She spread out her arms and flashed a sassy smile. "Well, here I am."

"Let me rephrase," he snarled. "Get out."

"Fine," Rose said, and she took one step backward, placing herself firmly in the hallway and *not* in his room.

He wasn't amused. "Rose—"

"You're in pain," she said, her voice gentler now. "At least let me be close—in case you need me."

"I would *never*," he snarled, "need you."

Rose sighed sadly at that. "I'm only here because I care."

His words were more growl than voice. "I don't want you to care."

"Well, that's not really your choice," Rose said simply.

He didn't look too happy about her response, but...Rose was only stating the facts.

"We have to talk about this," Rose said. "We can't just sweep our problems under the rug. We have to face them and fix them. Everyone knows that sweeping things under the rug just causes bugs. Or... rodents. Or something..." she trailed off, frowning. "I think that analogy got away from me somewhere."

He moved so quickly that her eyes barely registered the movement.

One moment, he'd been standing near the bed, and the next, her back hit the wall behind her, as he pushed her back and pinned her there, his hands clasped around her wrists.

"I don't think you understand," he said, his fangs bared. "I'm not telling you to get out because I'm running from a problem. I'm telling you to get out so that I won't kill you."

Rose swallowed down the fear that tried to rise in her throat. "No offense, but I think murder would be a bit of an overreaction."

"You really don't get it, do you?" Kallias said. His voice sounded strangled, as if something were choking him. "I'm an animal. I feel emotions on a level that you can't possibly understand. I feel rage like an animal." He moved his face closer to hers and hissed, "And when you piss off an animal, it bites."

"Well," Rose pointed out, "some animals scratch..."

"Damn it, Rose," he snarled. "This is not the time for jokes!"

Rose chewed on her lip, resisting the urge to say what she was thinking—because what she was thinking was that it *was* the time for jokes.

Jokes hid the fear and pain she felt when he lashed out at her like this, and that was something she needed to hide.

"The sun is weakening me," he tried to explain. "I can't control myself right now, and I don't want to hurt you."

Rose's eyes softened with sympathy. "And that's why I know you won't."

"How? How could you know that?" He moved one hand to her neck, feeling her rapid pulse against his finger. "It'd be *so* easy to kill you. I could snap your neck just by closing my hand." The rest of his fingers curled around her neck, too, as if to make his point. He leaned closer. "Or better yet, I could sink my fangs into your neck and devour you—finally sate this damn hunger I've been fighting since we met."

Rose couldn't help but shudder at the thought.

Why *wasn't* she afraid of being bitten? Why *was* she so comfortable around vampires?

It was strange—as if…some part of her knew something she didn't.

"I'm not afraid of you," Rose told him.

His brows furrowed. "You should be."

"I'm not, and do you know why?" Rose said gently. When he gave her a puzzled look, she said, "Because I see through this, Kallias. You're the bravest person I've ever met, and yet, you're *terrified* of letting someone hurt you. You're also terrified of hurting someone else. So, you push people away—like you're doing to me now." Sympathy sparkled in her bright blue eyes. "You think as long as someone hates you, they're safe, and you're safe, too. It's a defense mechanism." She shrugged sadly. "I may not be an empath or a telepath, but I see through *you*."

He let go of her and stepped back, as if he'd been burned. "Just go," he said softly. He stared at the floor. "Go back to your room."

He turned to walk toward the bed, but before he reached it, he staggered and reached out to grasp something for support.

What he found there, ready to help, was Rose's hand.

She'd come to his side the moment she saw him stagger. "I'll help you to bed," she offered.

Kallias let go of her hand as if it had hurt him to touch it. "I don't need your *help*," he snarled.

Rose resisted the urge to point out that he'd almost fallen just a moment before, and instead, said, "I'll be here when you change your mind."

He narrowed his eyes at her use of *'when,'* instead of *'if.'* "I told you," he said, before stumbling again, "to get out."

"And I will," Rose said easily, "as soon as you're in bed and not stumbling all over the place."

He glared at her—and then stumbled again.

Rose spread out her hands helplessly.

When he'd almost reached the bed, he grasped the footboard to prevent himself from falling. "What do you want from me?"

"Well, for you to make it to your bed without injury, for one," Rose muttered, "but also...talking through this would be nice."

"Why?" Kallias said, looking back at her. "What's the point?"

"Of talking?" Rose said with a look of disbelief. "It's part of the process. You fight. You talk. Then, you make up. That's how relationships work."

"Relationship?" he repeated. He let out a bitter laugh. "Is that what you think this is? You think we're *together*?"

Rose nodded to herself, already understanding what was happening. "You're doing it again."

But he continued to sneer at her, "Did you think you were my lover or something? My *girlfriend*? Did you really think I'd fall in love with you? With a *human*?"

Rose sighed heavily. "I never assumed *anything* would happen."

"Of course it won't," he spat. "Because I'm a vampire, and you're a human. Our lives don't fit. Even if I *were* interested in you, it'd never work."

Rose tried to ignore his attempts to upset her, but her insecurity surged anyway. "You kiss me a lot," she muttered, "for someone who's not interested."

"I'm a monster," he stated. "I'm not capable of love."

"I don't believe that," Rose said simply. "Not even a little bit."

"And if I loved *anyone*," he added with cruel resentment, "it certainly wouldn't be a liar like you."

"Wow," Rose said dryly—though there was real pain hiding beneath her sarcasm this time.

She'd either hidden her pain well enough, or he just didn't care.

"You're just like her," Kallias snarled. He wasn't even looking at her anymore. "Lying about Theron and that damn Stone."

Rose spread out her hands in defeat. "You know? I was willing to overlook how much of a *jerk* you're being because I know you're hurting. I know you're hurting *really* badly." Her chest ached, and her eyes burned. "How could you not be? Thousands of years ago, someone broke your heart, and you never healed. You buried the pain and let the wounds fester." She sighed, "So, yeah, I get it. The pain is unbearable right now, and you don't know how to deal with it. On top of that, you're a vampire. You feel everything in extremes, and you can't control your emotions. And on top of *that*, you're also awake during the day, which apparently weakens your mind as well as your body."

He glanced at her, waiting for the *'but'* of that statement.

"I know you're angry at me for not telling you about this, but I'm not the only reason you're angry, Kallias," Rose reminded him. "A lot of this anger existed before I was even *born*." She shrugged. "But I let you take it all out on me, anyway—because I know you need someone, whether you want to admit it or not."

A strange, red glow flashed in Rose's blue eyes, like a spark of fire.

Kallias blinked. What the hell was that?

Had he hallucinated it?

It was the middle of the day, after all.

"But I have to draw the line somewhere, Kallias," Rose said, apparently oblivious to whatever he'd just seen. "I've...made the mistake of not drawing the line before—of staying with people who were cruel for the sake of being cruel. And I promised myself, then, that I wouldn't do it again."

Kallias closed his eyes and opened them again—but her eyes were just their normal hue of blue, now.

There wasn't even a hint of the red he'd seen moments before.

"I genuinely hope this pain heals for you," Rose said sadly, "but...I think *this* is when I have to leave."

Kallias blinked again. *Leave?*

What had she been saying again?

"I'm sorry. I really did want to be here for you," Rose sighed. "Goodnight, Kallias."

"Wait," Kallias said.

But Rose's chest ached too severely to look at him now.

She'd nearly reached the door, when Kallias suddenly blocked her path. Blinking at his speed, she muttered, "You can barely walk, but you can still teleport?"

"It's...not teleporting," Kallias said with a frown.

Rose suppressed a smile at that. "You told me to leave, Kallias," she reminded him. "So, why are you stopping me when I try?"

Kallias looked away, his brows furrowed. "You *should* leave..."

One corner of Rose's lips lifted encouragingly. "But?"

"But..." he said slowly. His gaze shifted upward, meeting hers. "But I don't you want you to."

Rose's smile softened at that confession. "Then, I won't."

His brows furrowed, and then, he stepped forward. He cupped her face in his hands and kissed her, and she wrapped her arms around his neck.

Between kisses, Rose said, "I thought you were angry with me."

"I am," he grunted.

They kissed again, and then, Rose asked, "So, why are you kissing me?"

"Rose, for fuck's sake," Kallias grumbled. "Stop overanalyzing everything, and shut up."

Rose laughed, as he kissed her again.

Mentally, she was aware of the fact that they needed to talk—definitely more than they needed to kiss—but her body disagreed.

Kissing him was...nice.

Kallias turned and pressed her against the wall, and his hand found her hair, his fingers sinking into the soft, red strands and tugging back, angling her head for a deeper kiss.

Though Rose had barely thought about it while they'd talked, his body being pressed against hers like this made it far more obvious that Kallias was wearing nothing but sweatpants.

She trailed her hand downward—tracing his neck, then his chest. She felt the faint outline of his tattoo, the raised, jagged lines of his scars...

Rose gasped when his sharp fangs brushed her tongue, but she only clung tighter to him—not a trace of fear left within her.

There were so many problems, so many reasons a human shouldn't be with a vampire, but when they kissed, all of that faded. Nothing mattered, except for the emotions that rose between them.

Kallias moved his hands to her thighs, and Rose gasped as he lifted her off the floor. Being on the curvier end of the spectrum, Rose wasn't exactly used to people lifting her, and she panicked a bit, wrapping her legs around his waist and clinging tightly.

Kallias chuckled and kissed her again, before carrying her to the bed.

An anxious squeak escaped Rose's lips when he dropped her onto the soft mattress. She scooted backward, watching curiously as Kallias crawled onto the bed with her.

She didn't know whether it was the daylight or his hunger, but for whatever reason, his movements seemed more…animalistic than usual.

He pressed his face against her neck, kissing the sensitive skin, and his fingers began to unbutton her flannel pajama shirt.

The air that met her skin was cool—especially compared to the thick fabric of her shirt…and especially compared to the warmth of his touch.

Rose shivered, and Kallias moved to kiss her exposed collarbone.

Her eyes fluttered closed, and she sighed softly.

His fangs grazed her skin, and his fingers tightened in the flannel shirt.

Kallias pulled back suddenly, his breath coming in quick, harsh pants. He moved to sit at the edge of the bed, gripping the edge of the mattress. "I can't do this," he breathed.

Rose sat up, blushing, as she pulled her shirt closed over her breasts. His back was turned to her, and he had his face buried in his hands.

"Is it your hunger?" she asked gently.

Kallias turned to look at her, and almost as if they had a mind of their own, his eyes trailed downward, narrowing on the opening in her shirt.

Rose's blush deepened.

He returned his gaze to her face. "I am hungry, yes," he told her, "but it's more than that."

"Okay," Rose said slowly. "What else is bothering you, then?"

He sighed, "We both know where that was leading."

"I guess," Rose said with a shrug. "I mean…I'm not *that* naïve."

"You've never…" Kallias trailed off. "It'd be your first time, and it shouldn't be like this. You deserve better."

Rose frowned. "Better than what? Angry…sex?" She lifted her eyebrows. "Or better than *you*?"

His jaw tightened. "Both."

Rose offered him a gentle smile. "Well, regarding the sex...I might not have even gone through with it."

Kallias frowned curiously.

"I might've gotten nervous," Rose admitted. "I do that sometimes."

Kallias nodded. He didn't seem bothered by that possibility, and Rose appreciated that.

"And as for whether I deserve better than you," Rose said—with the gentlest smile Kallias had ever seen, "you're who I want, Kallias."

He exhaled sharply, as if her words caused him pain. "Rose," he said, his brows twisting with pain. "Can't you see I'm not good for you?"

Rose's smile softened, and she climbed up onto her knees. She crawled to the end of the bed to sit beside him.

"That should be obvious," Kallias continued, "especially now—after I...said the things I said..."

"Oh, hush," Rose said. She wrapped her arms around his right arm and leaned her head against his shoulder.

Kallias closed his eyes, soothed by her touch.

"You know I've already forgiven you for that," Rose said.

Kallias opened his eyes. "What?" he said, looking down at her. "You can't *do* that, Rose!"

Rose squinted up at him. "I can't forgive you?"

"No!" he said—as if she'd just suggested they go for a jog in the sunlight. "I don't deserve forgiveness."

Rose laughed, "No one deserves forgiveness, silly. That's the whole point."

Kallias shook his head bewilderedly. "I don't understand you."

"I told you," she said with a playful smile. "You can't push me away. I'm too stubborn."

He couldn't help but laugh at that. "Rose," he said, after a moment, "you know that when all of this is over, you and I won't—"

Her smile faded, and pain twisted inside her chest. "Could we just... not talk about that yet?"

He stared at her for a while—and then nodded. "Okay."

Kallias then surprised her by resting his head against hers. "You're nothing like Phoebe," he said into her thick, red hair. "I shouldn't have said that."

Rose smiled. "I'm sure she wasn't all bad."

"No, she wasn't," Kallias admitted. "But still…"

"It's true, isn't it?" Rose said, looking up at him. "You have less self-control during the day?"

Kallias nodded. "Our bodies run on basic instinct during the day," he admitted. "On the need for rest and the need for, well, blood."

Rose traced a soothing pattern on the side of his arm, and he looked down at her, his eyes dark.

"My true nature shows during the day," Kallias told her, "and my true nature is that of a monster. Do you see that now? Whatever good you thought you saw in me wasn't real."

Rose rolled her eyes. "Well, that's just totally flawed logic," she scoffed. "You fought those instincts. You didn't give in to them." A smile curved at her lips. "That's proof that the good I see in you *is* real."

Kallias rolled his eyes. "You really are the most stubborn person I've ever met."

Rose laughed, "I know."

He breathed out a long sigh. "Would you…want to sleep with me today?"

Rose jerked upright, her eyes wide. "Uhh," she sputtered. "But you said—"

Kallias grinned, his smile so wide that Rose could see the razor-sharp fangs in his mouth.

Rose blinked in surprise—because that was the first time she'd seen him smile like that all day.

"Sleep, Rose," Kallias clarified. "Just sleep. No sex."

Rose's blush deepened. "Oh. I, uhh, might've misunderstood."

Kallias laughed at that. "I noticed."

Rose's cheeks refused to cool. "Umm, why?"

He shrugged. "You have to admit…we both slept a lot better at the hotel."

Rose offered a shy smile. "You are kind of…comfortable. Sometimes."

He snorted, "It's settled, then."

Kallias moved to lie back on his bed—and then tugged his sweat-pants off right in front of her.

Rose squeaked and—just like the first time—clasped her hands over her eyes. "What are you doing?!"

"We went over this yesterday," he said with an amused laugh. "I don't sleep in clothes."

"There's nothing wrong with clothes!" Rose complained. "They cover stuff. Covering stuff is…good!"

"I think most people would disagree with you on that," he teased.

Rose peeked out from behind her fingers and sighed in relief, as she found him already beneath the blanket.

He snorted, "If you'd come in earlier, you might've found that I normally sleep nude."

Rose blinked. "I don't know if that's a joke or not," she muttered, but when he opened his mouth to respond, she added, "Don't tell me."

Kallias tilted his back and laughed. He was clearly in a better mood now, and Rose was grateful for that—even if he *was* making her blush as red as a tomato because of it.

"Come on, *moro mou*," he said, lifting the blanket. "Get in bed, before I pass out."

Rose's smile deepened. It was sort of…intimate when he spoke in Greek to her.

Not intimate in a sexual way—but intimate in a *no-one-else-knows-what-this-means* way.

Rose moved to lie down on the opposite side of the bed, careful to keep plenty of space between them.

She'd accidentally cuddled up to him once. She had to be more careful this time.

But he just held out his arm and grumbled, "Get over here."

A surprised smile curved at Rose's lips, and she obliged him, curling against his side and draping an arm over his stomach.

He curled his arm around her, too, and he closed his eyes. He buried his face in her soft, honey-scented hair and murmured—so sleepily that his words were slurred and strangely accented, "Good-night, *agapi mou*."

Rose's eyes widened. He'd called a few Greek endearments recently, but he'd never called her *'my love'* before. "Kallias?" she breathed.

But only his slow breathing filled the silence between them.

He'd already fallen asleep.

Rose sighed and decided it didn't matter. Lots of people used the word *'love'* without meaning it. She was just taking things too literally—as usual.

But even as she told herself that, she doubted Kallias was the type to do that.

Strangely enough, despite the fact that she'd spent all morning trying to fall asleep in the guest room and had repeatedly failed, next to him, like this, she quickly and easily drifted into a comfortable sleep.

WHEN ROSE AWOKE, SHE FELT WARM—*REALLY* WARM—AND COMFORTABLE.

She blinked, hoping her eyes would adjust to the darkness, but they didn't. At some point in the day, someone had cut off the lamp, plunging the room into total darkness.

Rose poked the arm that encaged her curiously—and her fingertip met with hard, unyielding muscle.

Well, *this* wasn't good.

Kallias lay behind her, curled around her—with his face buried in the crook of her neck and his arm tightly imprisoning her.

Rose tried to wiggle out of his arms, reaching for where she thought the lamp would be, but his hold allowed no such movement.

Whoever had decided that vampires should be this strong *clearly* didn't have a bladder.

"Kallias?" she said warily.

He let out a soft groan of protest against her neck, and his warm breath raised chills on her skin.

"Umm, Kallias?" she tried again. "Could you wake up?"

He gave her another miserable groan.

"Yeah, see...it's comfortable and all," Rose admitted, "but I have this thing called a bladder..."

Her conversation with the comatose vampire was interrupted by a knock at the door. She jumped, startled by the sound, and peered worriedly in the direction of the door.

"Relax. It's just Erik," Kallias said in her ear.

Rose froze. "How long have you been awake?"

"Don't know," he slurred. "Long enough to find out that you have a bladder." His lips curved lazily against her ear. "Such sexy talk to wake up to."

She scowled at his sarcasm. "I wasn't kidding. I really do have to pee."

The bedroom door opened, and light from the torch lamps in the hall flooded the room. Even though the light was dim, Rose winced as it momentarily blinded her—so drastically different from the total darkness that had cloaked the room a moment ago.

Kallias groaned miserably and buried his face in her hair, which caused his warm breath to fall against her neck again.

Erik tilted his head curiously, as he noticed them in bed together. "Interesting."

"Nothing happened," Rose said—a little too quickly.

"I see that," Erik said sarcastically.

"I mean it!" Rose said, desperately trying to pry Kallias's arm from her stomach. He grunted and reluctantly released her. It was so sudden, she nearly rolled off the bed. "Nothing at all."

She scrambled to her feet, and Erik glanced down at her pajamas.

"What the hell is that supposed to be?" Erik said.

"Go away, Erik," Kallias groaned.

Erik looked at him. "Hey, I came to tell you your breakfast is ready, you asshole."

"Yeah, yeah," Kallias grumbled. "I'm sure that's the only reason you're here."

"Breakfast?" Rose repeated with a frown. "What time is it?"

"It's breakfast for us *nocturnal* creatures," Erik clarified. "It's about 8:30."

Rose blinked. "Wow. That late?"

Erik returned his attention to her flannel pajamas. "Seriously…what the hell are you wearing?"

Rose glanced at her pajamas and then looked up, narrowing her eyes at him. "They're not that bad!"

Erik wrinkled his nose. "Are they a form of birth control?"

She gave him a peeved look. "Really?"

"You know you don't need that with vampires, right?" Erik added. "We're sterile."

Rose's glare turned murderous.

"Erik, shut up before she throws the lamp at you," Kallias grumbled.

"They're comfortable, okay?" Rose informed the blonde vampire. "Comfortable and warm!"

Erik shrugged one shoulder. "So are naked bodies."

"Go *away*!" Kallias said again.

Erik just laughed, "All right. I'll see you two lovebirds downstairs."

When he left, Rose turned to glance back at Kallias—and blushed, as she found him staring at her with dark, hungry eyes.

"Stop that," Rose muttered.

He smiled lazily. "Stop what?"

Rose shook her head nervously and turned to leave. "I need to shower," she said, as she hurried toward the door, "and pee. Not in that order."

Kallias laughed at her nervous rambling. "The towels are in the closet."

"Yep. Thanks!" Rose said, fleeing the room as if her life depended on it.

19

TRAINING

*R*ose froze at the bottom of the stairs. She cast a puzzled glance around the foyer—at multiple identical doors.

The library was awesome, but…she really *had* needed a tour.

"Note to self," Rose muttered. "Next time you stay in a mansion with vampires, while other vampires are trying to kill you, ask for a map—so you'll at least know the dang kitchen is."

From somewhere behind her left shoulder, a voice came, suddenly, "Or you could just follow the scent of bacon."

Rose jumped at the sound and then nearly tripped over her feet, as she turned to find Erik standing on the other side of the stairwell.

"Stop…*sneaking*!" Rose complained.

Erik bit into the slice of bacon in his hand, chewed, and then, muttered, "Creature of darkness, babe. Sneaking's kind of our thing."

"I'm not your babe," Rose reminded him. "Stop calling me that."

Erik didn't spare a glance for her complaints. He had eyes only for the bacon. "Do you want me to call you a dirtier name?"

Rose stared blankly at him. "I want you to call me *Rose*."

"Well, that's not very creative," Erik said, stuffing the rest of the bacon in his mouth.

"Neither is calling everyone with female genitalia the same pet name," she countered, "but you don't seem to have a problem with that."

Erik grimaced at her. "Female genitalia?" He glanced at his empty hand, grateful he'd already finished his bacon. "Who calls it *that*?"

"Umm, lots of people?" Rose mumbled. "Science books, for one."

Erik pointed a greasy finger at her. "I'm starting to understand why you're a virgin."

Rose cast her eyes upward and breathed out a long sigh. "Kitchen? Please?"

"Of course," Erik said with a taunting smirk. "Wouldn't want you to get lost in this *mansion*."

Rose followed him, muttering under her breath as she did, "It feels like a mansion to *me*."

Erik chuckled and opened a door, motioning toward it with a tilt of his head.

Rose stepped into a kitchen that was *easily* larger than her entire apartment.

Like the rest of the home, the floors were hardwood, and the walls were some kind of grey stone.

Though most of the house looked normal enough, the kitchen struck her as strange—because some of the appliances were stainless steel and possibly brand-new, while other parts of the kitchen, such as the chimney-stove that probably hadn't been used in decades, looked almost a century old.

"Wow," Rose mumbled. She dragged a fingertip across a long, wooden table. "Is every room in this house massive?"

"Massive," Erik scoffed, as he made his way over to the long counter in the center of the room. He snatched another slice of bacon from the wooden platter. "It's a kitchen. Kitchens are supposed to be big."

Rose lifted an eyebrow at that. "The kitchen in my apartment is like *this* big," she said, holding her hands *maybe* a foot apart.

Erik leaned back on his heels, his eyes wide. "That's horrific."

Rose laughed at his melodramatic response. "No, it's not."

Erik leaned against the counter. "You should've seen the kitchens in the Norse mead halls," he told her. "*This* is nothing, compared to those."

"Norse?" Rose said with a curious smile. "You lived during the Viking Age?"

He scoffed, "Lived during? I *am* a Viking."

Excitement brightened Rose's eyes. "Really?" she said, stepping closer. "Tell me *everything!*"

Erik gave her a puzzled frown. "Usually, when women are hanging to my every word, they're feeling a different emotion from," he paused, waving a piece of bacon at her, "this."

Rose rolled her eyes. "I'm sorry to break it to you, but I'm immune to your allure."

Erik leaned forward and rested his elbows on the countertop. He lowered his voice and squinted knowingly. "Is that because you're...*gay?*"

Rose narrowed her eyes at him. "My sexual orientation is none of your business."

Erik shrugged, as if to say, *'Worth a try.'*

"For the record, though," Rose added, "I wouldn't be affected by a female vampire's allure either."

He gave her a skeptical look. "Have you *tested* it, though?"

"Yes," Rose said. Then, she frowned. "Kind of."

Sofia had been gorgeous, obviously, but Rose had resisted the vampire easily.

"Erik Olafsson," Rose repeated to herself. "I should've known. That's a Norse name."

Erik poked her shoulder with a slice of bacon. "I like it when you say my name."

"Ugh," Rose said, rolling her eyes again. "Do you ever stop?"

He took another bite. "Not really. No."

Rose circled the room, searching the counters, only to turn ghostly pale when she found them all empty.

Erik glanced back at her, as he sensed her panic. "What's wrong?"

Rose gestured wildly at the empty counter. "You have no coffee pot," she gasped. "I can't live without coffee."

Erik held up a finger and a slice of bacon, leaving Rose unsure of what that gesture was supposed to mean. He moved a pan to a different eye of the stove and then joined her at the counter.

He flipped open a cabinet above her head and waved a hand toward the old coffee pot inside. "Your life is saved."

Rose nearly collapsed in relief. "You're my best friend now," she said, as she snatched out the old coffee pot. But as she leaned forward to plug it up, she added, "Well, not really. I already have a best friend—and I kind of can't stand you. No offense."

Erik snorted at her teasing. "None taken."

Rose removed the plastic lid from the can of coffee grounds. "Where's Kallias?" she asked curiously. "Has he come down yet?"

Erik glanced up toward the ceiling, listening to the sounds coming from upstairs. "Unless he left the water running," he said, returning his attention to the food, "I think he's still in the shower."

"You can hear the water?" Rose said. "From all the way down here?"

"Yep," Erik said, as he grabbed yet *another* slice of bacon.

Rose frowned, as a somewhat disturbing thought occurred to her. "You..." she hesitated. "You don't have sex while Kallias is in the house, do you? Because it seems like that would be awkward."

Erik laughed loudly. "You make a big deal about the strangest things."

Rose scooped out another spoon of coffee grounds.

"Kallias isn't a prude," Erik informed her. "He's an Ancient Greek, for Odin's sake." He moved another pan onto the stove. "His people were perverts. They had sex in the middle of the street, *and* they had sex twenty-four hours a day!"

Rose frowned. "That...isn't even remotely accurate."

Erik continued, as if he hadn't heard her. "I heard that their women would have sex in public where any onlooker could watch. I would've loved to be alive for that."

Rose sighed heavily. "Can you hand me two knives, please?"

"Sure," Erik said. He pulled open a drawer beside him and picked up two knives. He held them out. "Why do you need them?"

Without missing a beat, Rose said, "Because I need to shove both of them into my ears so I never have to hear you say anything like that ever again."

Erik turned to stare at her for several moments, his eyes wide. He tossed the knives back in the drawer. "You know what your problem is?" he said, leaning toward her. "You're a prude."

"I'm not a prude," Rose complained. She scooped out another spoonful of coffee, her long, red hair falling over one shoulder. "It only seems that way to *you* because you're a pigheaded pervert."

Erik grinned, as if she'd just handed him an award. "Thank you!"

Rose just rolled her eyes.

"For a vampire, you're moving awfully slow tonight," Erik said.

Realizing that Erik must've been talking to Kallias, Rose turned to glance toward the door.

Kallias stood in the doorway, dressed in a black T-shirt and a pair of black jeans. His drenched hair hung around his face, dripping water onto his clothes. Even his skin was still wet, as if he'd only just stepped out of the shower.

Kallias crossed the room and slumped tiredly onto a bar stool. "I was up until three in the afternoon. You're lucky I even got out of bed."

"Damn, Kallias. It doesn't take *that* long to have sex," Erik said with a grin. "Foreplay and all, I'd say maybe an hour, at the longest."

Rose spun around with a full pot of water in her hand. "We didn't have sex!"

"He knows that," Kallias said. "He's just trying to get a reaction from you."

Erik grinned at her. "Trying *and* succeeding."

Rose rolled her eyes and then poured the water in the coffeemaker.

"Hypothetically speaking, though," Kallias said to Erik, "as vampires, we have limitless stamina. If we didn't *want* to stop after an hour..."

Rose blinked. She turned back toward them. "Don't you two ever have *normal* conversations?" she asked. "You don't ever talk about the weather or new discoveries in science and archeology? Or the possibility of extraterrestrial life?"

Kallias glanced at her. "Sometimes, we discuss efficient ways to behead an enemy. Does that count?"

"No," Rose said slowly. "No, that doesn't count."

"How is it *normal* to discuss aliens," Erik said, waving a hand, "and whatever else you said?"

"Science and archeology?" Rose asked. "Those are interesting topics."

"Maybe for a virgin," Erik scoffed.

Kallias gave Erik a tired look. "Behave."

"I'm not a child," Erik whined.

"Are you sure?" Rose said. "Because you could've fooled me."

Erik laughed loudly, before leaning toward Kallias. "Can we keep her?"

Rose scowled at the back of his head. "I'm a human, not a puppy."

Kallias took a bite of scrambled eggs and then looked down at his plate, his lips drawn into a pouty frown. "It needs more salt."

"Well, wake up earlier next time, and make them yourself," Erik said, but even as he said it, he stood up and grabbed the saltshaker.

Erik placed the saltshaker on the counter, but when Kallias reached for it, Erik covered it with his hand. "Wait." He turned to Rose, offering a scheming smile. "I want *you* to give it to him."

Rose glanced up from the coffeemaker, which was doing its best in its elderly age, and frowned at him. "Okay," she said with a puzzled frown. She stepped forward and reached out to grab the saltshaker, but Erik grasped her wrist before she could.

Rose froze, glancing down at the fingers around her wrist. "What the heck?"

"Don't use your hand," Erik told her. "Use your mind."

Rose glanced up at him. "What?"

Kallias leaned across the counter and grabbed the saltshaker forcefully enough to draw their attention back toward him. "Stop being an ass, Erik," he grumbled. "She's a person, not a weapon."

Erik flashed a very *un*-apologetic smile and released her wrist. He leaned toward Kallias, resting his arms on the counter. "Think about it, though," he said softly. "If she *can* move things with her mind, she could be useful. She could be the advantage we need."

Kallias looked up at Erik, and Erik straightened nervously, when he sensed the anger radiating from Kallias. "She's here so we can protect her," he snarled. "You *agreed* to protect her."

"I know," Erik said, holding up his hands. "I won't break my word. I swear. I just think we should explore this opportunity."

"Opportunity?" Kallias repeated. "She is a *person*, Erik."

"I know," Erik said warily.

"And a human, at that!" Kallias added. "We have no idea what would happen if she used her abilities—how much she could even handle."

Erik nodded. "Right, but—"

"Hey," Rose interrupted. "Would you two quit talking about me like I'm not here?"

They both turned to look at her, faces blank.

"Sorry," Kallias said, before returning his attention to his food.

Rose turned to Erik, who looked as unrepentant as ever. She crossed her arms. "What was that with the saltshaker?"

"I wanted to see you do it," Erik said with a shrug. "Telekinesis."

"Two problems with that," Rose said. "First, I'm not a circus monkey. And second," she sighed, losing a little of her resolve, "I can't."

Erik frowned. "Why not?"

Rose shrugged. "I don't know how," she told him, "and I'm not even sure if I believe it in the first place. I mean...me? Telekinesis? It sounds crazy."

"You wouldn't smell the way you do, if you weren't powerful," Erik said simply.

"I just—" Rose sighed. "I can't accept that I have some kind of superpower."

"Well, maybe if you tried," Erik said, "you'd see—"

"Drop it, Erik," Kallias snapped.

Erik's bright green gaze shifted back toward Kallias, and his brows furrowed. He tilted his head slightly, and his lips curved, as if he'd just noticed something interesting.

"Ah," he said with an amused laugh, "now, I get it."

Kallias's glare turned murderous.

Erik leaned toward Rose and whispered, "Let me know if you change your mind."

Then, he strolled out of the room, whistling an unfamiliar, happy tune.

Rose frowned in the direction he'd gone. "What was that about?"

"Nothing," Kallias grunted—and immediately returned his attention to his food.

Rose watched as Kallias stabbed his fork into his food so forcefully that Rose feared for the plate.

When Kallias looked up and noticed that Rose was still stubbornly waiting for an answer, he sighed, "Erik reads too much into things."

"Okay," Rose said warily, "and what does that mean?"

"It doesn't matter," Kallias said dismissively. "He's wrong. That's all you need to know."

Rose sighed. She wanted to argue, but then, she thought about Erik's last remark and realized that she'd probably have more luck asking *him*, instead.

Rose finished pouring her coffee and then hopped onto the barstool across from Kallias.

Kallias gestured toward the food. "Do you like bacon and eggs?"

Rose usually skipped breakfast. Normally, she was too anxious in the mornings to eat, but the sudden flip of sleeping schedule had left her hungrier than usual. So, she nodded.

Rose reached for a plate, but instead of giving it to her, Kallias started scooping food into the plate for her.

Too *much* food, she quickly realized.

"Okay, okay! That's enough!" Rose squeaked, snatching the plate from his hand. "What are you trying to do? Fatten me up before you eat me?"

His brows furrowed. "That's...not how it works."

She giggled at his seriousness, as she picked up a fork and began to eat.

He watched her for a moment. "Rose, I have to go out tonight."

She looked at him, her fork still in her mouth. "Out?"

"It's what I always do," Kallias explained. "I go out and try to stop a few vampires from making meals out of humans." He shrugged. "There are a lot of vampires in big cities like this one. But…I have a more immediate reason to go out tonight."

"Theron?" Rose guessed, as she took a sip of her coffee.

"Yeah," Kallias sighed. "I'm the only one who knows his scent. I don't know if he followed us, but if he did, I need to find him before he finds you."

Rose set her coffee cup down. "Okay. I'll get that dagger you loaned me."

He reached across the counter and grabbed her hand before she could stand up. "Rose, you misunderstood. *I'm* leaving. You're staying here."

Rose narrowed her eyes. "Oh, I am, am I?"

Either he didn't recognize the snark in her tone, or he chose to ignore it. "I can't take you out there with vampires trying to kill you," he told her. "This is where you're safest."

"And what about *you*?" Rose countered. "Where are *you* the safest?"

His brows furrowed. "That doesn't matter."

"Yes, it does," Rose said with a look of disbelief. "It matters to me."

Rose didn't realize she'd said anything wrong, until he released her wrist and leaned back.

His jaw tightened. "It shouldn't."

Rose didn't understand why being honest about her feelings was such a problem, but clearly, it was.

Speaking in a foreign language was easier than speaking in her own sometimes. People were…complicated.

"But it does."

Anger darkened his eyes, and he snarled, "You want to know when I'm safest? When *you're* not around to distract me."

Rose leaned back, too, and she pulled her hand back toward herself. She suddenly didn't want to be touched at all. "Oh," she said. She stood and flashed a sarcastic smile at him. "In that case, let's just hope Theron finds me here and kills me. Then, I won't distract you anymore. Problem solved."

Rose turned to leave with every intention of locking herself in the library for the rest of the night, but before she could take even the first step, Kallias appeared in front of her.

Rose gasped in surprise—before pinning him with another glare. He'd said something to hurt her, and he'd succeeded.

What more could he possibly want?

"Don't say shit like that," Kallias said softly.

Surprised by the sudden pain in his voice, Rose frowned. "What other response could you have expected?"

"It's not…a lie," he admitted. "You do distract me—because…I don't want anything to happen to you. I want to know you're safe."

Rose sighed, the prick of anger quickly softening into sympathy. "You don't even know I'd be safe here," she tried to explain. "If there's anything I've learned from reading hundreds of horror novels, it's that being alone usually ends badly."

"I never said you would be alone," Kallias corrected.

Rose frowned. "What?"

"Erik will stay here with you," he told her.

"Umm, no." Rose shook her head quickly. "Absolutely not."

"Erik will do what?" asked the aforementioned person.

Kallias and Rose both glanced toward the door.

Erik stood there with what Rose was *pretty* sure was a mixing bowl—and a regular-sized spoon.

Kallias stepped away from Rose. "I'm the only one who can track Theron by scent," he told Erik. "So, it'll have to be me who searches for him."

Erik shoved a spoonful of something pink into his mouth. "Right."

"So," Kallias added, "I need you to stay here with Rose."

He pulled the spoon out of his mouth. "Yeah, okay."

"I don't need a babysitter," Rose complained.

Erik scooped out another bite of pink stuff and pointed the spoon at her, nearly spilling it. "Well, that's a relief because I would *not* be a good babysitter," he muttered. He shoved the pink stuff into his mouth before continuing, "Once, when I was human, my mother asked me to babysit my sister, and I nearly killed her. But come on. How was I supposed to know newborn babies couldn't eat wild boar?"

Rose stared at the blonde vampire, her eyes wide with horror.

Kallias sighed, "He's not a babysitter. Think of him as a bodyguard."

"Now, *that*, I can do," Erik said. "Much less hazardous job."

Rose shook her head, as if that would shake Erik's horrifying babysitting story from her head. "I'm not staying here with him."

"Ah, come on. I'm the fun one!" Erik whined.

Kallias shrugged. "I guess, if you're that uncomfortable with it," he said, "I could call Emma."

Rose cast a glance at Erik as an idea occurred to her. "Actually, no," she amended. "I think I'll be fine with Erik."

Kallias just smiled. "Good."

Erik slumped into a wooden chair at the dining room table and set the bowl of mushy, pink desert in front of him.

Rose blinked. "Is that ice cream?"

"Yeah," Erik said, holding out the spoon. "You want some?"

Rose scowled at the spoon that had literally *just* been in his mouth. "No, thanks," she said with a grimace. "How much ice cream is that?"

Erik shrugged and took another bite. "About…a gallon and a half."

Her eyes widened. "That's a bit too much sugar for the human body to process at one time," she said warily. "You'll put yourself in a diabetic coma."

"Vampire, remember?" Erik said, flashing his fangs at her.

"Oh, right," she said, though she still worried.

"Where did you even get all of that?" Kallias muttered. "There hasn't been any ice cream in the freezer in months—not since those five gallons disappeared."

"Oh, those didn't disappear," Erik said.

They both stared at him, waiting for him to explain.

Erik glanced up at them. "I put them in the deep freezer in my room," he said, as if it were obvious, "where I keep all of my sex-related desserts."

Rose turned to Kallias. "On second thought, don't leave me with him."

"Erik, do you see what you've done?" Kallias complained.

"What? I don't know what she's worried about," Erik said defensively. "I didn't say I was going to use them on *her*."

Rose didn't even know what he meant—nor did she want to. "Can this conversation get any more inappropriate?"

"Yes," Erik assured her.

Kallias ran his hand through his hair, exasperation clear on his face. "If you make her uncomfortable," he warned Erik, "I'll kick your ass."

Erik waved a hand dismissively. "Yeah, yeah, I know."

———

ROSE SIGHED AND CLOSED THE BOOK, LETTING IT FALL TO HER STOMACH. SHE gazed up at the ceiling, trying to decide whether to find another book to read or to find Erik, instead, and ask him about what happened earlier.

Her curiosity won.

She returned the book to its shelf and left the library.

She found Erik in the living room, watching television.

Rose sat on the leather sofa next to him, frowning curiously at the romantic comedy he was watching. The crunch of popcorn interrupted the quiet, romantic scene, and Rose turned to look at the massive bowl of popcorn in Erik's lap.

"I was afraid you'd never leave that library," Erik complained.

"Oh, yeah," Rose said sarcastically, "because watching television is *so* much more productive."

"It's more fun," Erik corrected, and then, she could argue, he held out the bowl. "Popcorn?"

Rose laughed, "You have no concept of germs, do you?"

"Nope," Erik said.

Rose leaned back against the back of the sofa, surprised by just how comfortable it was. "I have a question."

Erik shoved a handful of popcorn in his mouth. "Questions are boring."

Rose sighed and climbed to her feet. "Fine."

"Whoa, whoa. Wait a minute," Erik said, before she could leave. "You have my attention. What is it?"

Rose turned to face him. "You gave Kallias this…strange look earlier," she reminded him. "He said you read too much into things, that you were wrong."

Erik laughed at that. "Of course he did."

"Wrong about what?" Rose asked.

Erik set the bowl of popcorn beside him and leaned forward. "Kallias heard my thoughts," he told her. "If he were comfortable with you knowing my…*observation*, he would have told you." He scratched his clean-shaven chin. "He's my best friend, Rose."

Rose's curiosity immediately turned to guilt. "You're right. I shouldn't have asked."

"What I *will* tell you," he said, before she could finish her apology, "is that Kallias protects the people he cares about. He may act like an asshole, but…he doesn't like to see people hurt. Protecting you is how Kallias shows he cares."

Rose frowned. "Are you saying you think he cares about me?"

He lifted his eyebrows. "If that were *all* I was saying, I'd only be stating the obvious."

Rose shook her head in bewilderment. "Am I supposed to *understand* this gibberish you're speaking?"

Erik laughed at her teasing. "Sorry, babe. You'll have to figure out the rest on your own," he said, winking. He patted the spot next to him. "Now, sit down, and watch something with me. Watching television by myself is boring."

"Is *everything* boring to you?" she laughed.

"No, not everything," Erik said, his gaze on the TV. "Sex is fun."

Rose rolled her eyes. "I *really* should've expected that answer."

"We can watch something different, if you want," Erik offered, waving the remote. "It's already past my favorite scene, anyway."

Rose started to ask what a *Viking's* favorite scene in romantic movie might be, but then, she realized…it was probably the sex scene.

Of course it was the sex scene.

"I'd rather read," Rose told him.

"Ah, come on," Erik whined. He might've been over a thousand years old, but he *sounded* like a twelve-year-old. "We don't have to watch

TV! We can do whatever you want. It's insulting that you prefer that boring library over me."

"There is nothing boring about a library," Rose informed him.

"Yeah, yeah, whatever," Erik muttered. "Surely there's something else you want to do. We can do whatever you want! I'm the fun one, remember?"

Rose laughed. "Fine. I have another question."

"Questions," Erik scoffed, throwing up his hands. "Questions are your idea of fun."

Rose ignored that. "Hypothetically," she began, "if I *do* have telekinetic abilities...you really think I could use them to fight Theron?"

Erik shrugged. "At the very least, you could hurt him a little."

"Because," Rose added in explanation, "I *hate* feeling helpless." She stared at the floor, unsettled by her own confessions. "Depending on people is just...*not* something I can do. I need to fight my own battles." She looked up. "If there's a way for me to fight Theron, I'd like to know how."

Erik studied her curiously. "What are you asking me, Rose?"

"I'm not saying I believe you," Rose added for clarification, "about me having a psychic ability, but if I *do*, will you show me how to use it?"

Erik moved the bowl of popcorn from the sofa to the table and rested his elbows on his thighs. "I'm an empath," he explained. "My power deals with the emotions—the heart or...*soul*, really. Telekinesis deals with the physical plane of existence—the *body*. My power is drastically different from yours."

Rose nodded. "Yeah, sorry," she sighed. "I didn't realize." She turned to walk back to the library, only to gasp as she walked into someone. She clasped her hand over her chest, her pulse racing beneath her palm. "I didn't even see you move!"

Erik just grinned. "I'm good at what I do."

Rose lifted her eyebrows. "Oh. In that case, why don't you show me how good you are at moving out of my way?"

He snorted, clearly amused. "You misunderstood me," he told her. "I never said I wouldn't *try* to help you."

"Oh." Rose chewed her on lip nervously. "I mean, this is all hypothetical, still. I doubt I even have telekinetic power, so—"

"Move that glass," Erik interrupted.

Rose turned and frowned at the glass he'd gestured at. It was a small, square glass on the coffee table, full of whiskey. "I must be insane to even be considering this."

"You'll never know if you don't try," Erik said—so close to her ear that she could practically smell the popcorn on his breath.

For a vampire, he sure loved his snack foods.

With a defeated sigh, Rose stepped toward the coffee table. Feeling very silly, she muttered, "Now, what?" She waved a hand, mimicking a storybook witch. "Move, glass! Abracadabra and other silly words!"

Erik laughed at her sarcasm. He stepped closer. "If you want it to work you have to take it seriously," he said. "Look at the glass, and will it to move."

"You make it sound so simple," Rose said sarcastically. She inhaled deeply and concentrated on the glass. She stared, imagined it moving, everything...but nothing worked.

Finally, she threw her hands up in defeat. "See? Nothing is happening. I told you. I don't have any psychic—"

She never finished that sentence—because at that moment, Erik grabbed her shoulder.

Before she could ask what he was doing, an intense, spine-chilling wave of terror worked its way through her body, setting her nerves on edge and sending her pulse skyrocketing.

Her body began to tremble, as if she were freezing to death—or convulsing. Her lungs felt constricted. Her stomach lurched.

She felt as if she were dying.

A scream like nothing she'd ever heard burst from her own lips, and the sound of glass shattering echoed through the room.

Finally, Erik released her.

Rose doubled over. She took slow breaths, knowing from experience that she'd pass out if she didn't slow her breathing.

Her body ached with each rapid beat of her heart.

Rose spun toward him, spots still dancing before her eyes. "What the heck was that?" she snarled at him.

Erik rubbed his wrist, as if his own pulse ached in the same way hers did. "Terror."

Rose clenched her hand into a fist, trying to stop her fingers from trembling. "Why would you do that to me?" she whispered.

"I wanted to know if it'd work," he said quietly.

Rose's eyes widened. "You made me feel *that* as a freaking experiment?"

"I'm sorry," he said. He held out his hands. "Let me calm you."

Rose backed away from him. "Are you insane? Like actually insane?" she said, her voice high with panic. "You're not touching me again. Not after *that*! I'm not stupid!"

Erik dropped his hands. "Sorry," he said again, "but at least now, you know it's real."

Rose frowned. "What do you mean? No, I don't."

Erik raised an eyebrow, and the remorse she'd seen briefly cross his face turned to amusement. "Then, how do you explain what you did to the glass?"

"I...didn't do anything," Rose said, but she turned to look, anyway. Her eyes widened, when she found the glass gone. The only sign that it'd ever been on the table was the thin ring of water where it'd been sitting. "That's not possible," she mumbled. "Where is it?"

Erik gestured toward the wall. "Keep looking."

She lifted her gaze to the wall, and her face paled.

She glanced down at the floor to find what was left of the glass: hundreds of tiny, broken fragments. "That's not possible. I didn't do that," she said quickly. "I couldn't have done that."

"It was you," Erik assured her. "You must've been terrified when you threw Theron across the room. So, I recreated the emotion. I know it was torture, but...you needed to see yourself do this, Rose."

Rose turned toward him, her eyes still wide. "Is it possible to control it?"

Erik shrugged. "Power's always difficult to control."

"You can control yours," Rose pointed out.

"It took me decades to learn how, and the woman who taught me was...a good teacher," Erik sighed.

There'd been a hint of pain in his voice when he said that. Was he referring to his ex-lover?

"It took Kallias much longer to control his," Erik explained. "Centuries." He leaned toward her. "And Rose, you have more power than either of us."

Rose scoffed at that. "No, I don't."

Erik shrugged. "Believe what you will, but *I* know what power smells like."

Rose frowned thoughtfully. "Do it again! The terror thing."

His jaw dropped. "I just tortured you, and you're asking me to do it again?"

"I *need* to be able to fight Theron," Rose reminded him.

Erik sighed, "Your pulse hasn't even slowed yet."

"I feel fine," Rose told him. "I feel *strong*, actually."

"That's the adrenaline," Erik said. "I smell it in your blood."

"Will you help me or not?" Rose asked.

Erik pursed his lips, clearly considering what Kallias might think of this, but ultimately, he sympathized too much with her fear of helplessness to refuse. "Fine." He stepped past her and motioned for her to follow. "But your power's a bit too destructive to have you near something as important as my TV. So, let's do this in the gym."

Rose followed him into the hallway. "You have a gym?"

When they reached the end of the downstairs hallway, Rose found another set of stairs—a basement, just as she'd suspected.

She followed him down the steps, until they reached a metal door that looked out of place in the old house. Erik opened a plastic box beside the steel door to reveal a set of number buttons.

He typed four numbers into the keyless entry lock, and the door slid open. "The passcode is 2-5-1-1, if you come down here by yourself."

"Kallias's age?" Rose said with a frown.

Erik shrugged. "He changes it every year, but you have to admit: no random human is going to guess *that* correctly." He led the way into the room, flicking on the dim lanterns that lined the walls of the room. "Watch your step."

"What's with the spike in security?" Rose quipped. "Is this where you hide your victims or something?"

He snorted, "If we had victims, we wouldn't leave them in our basement to decompose and stink up the house. We'd properly dispose of them."

"It's always *so* comforting when someone assures you that they can properly dispose of corpses," Rose said sarcastically, "as they take you into their creepy basement."

As they stepped into the basement, the air in the cold, dark gym chilled her skin, raising chills along her arms.

The walls and floors of the gym were painted black and made of rough concrete. Aside from the dim lanterns along each wall, the room was empty, which left it feeling cold and ominous.

"This is the safest room in the house, if you're a vampire," Erik told her. "If, for instance, the house is destroyed in the middle of the day by some kind of natural disaster, we'd likely survive the natural disaster, but we wouldn't survive the sunlight. Down here, though, we'd be safe."

Rose frowned. "This is New York, not Alabama. It's not like you have a ton of tornadoes ripping through here."

"Just an example," Erik said. "More importantly, if, for some reason, vampires ever come under attack by humans, we'll be vulnerable during the day. If they were blast holes in the side of the house in the middle of the day, we'd be dead." He turned to her. "That's why we had this built into the house. If that ever happened, we'd be vulnerable upstairs, but we'd be safe underground."

Rose's frown deepened.

"Not *only* do they need to know the code to open those doors," Erik continued. He stepped back into the hallway and ascended the steps again. Rose followed him, watching curiously. He reached up and pulled the handle attached to the wall at the top of the steps. The handle pulled a solid piece of flooring over them, closing off the stairs and the basement from the rest of the house. He smiled, knocked on the hardwood flooring above them, and finished, "They'll never know to check for a basement. With that closed, it looks like this house has no basement."

Rose lifted her eyebrows at the surprising amount of thought they'd put into this. "Is that something you actually think could happen?" she said worriedly. "You think humans would attack vampires? I mean, it wouldn't be wise, would it? For them?"

"Generally, humans aren't wise," Erik said. "Generally, they're scared."

"Umm, human...standing right here," Rose said, pointing to herself.

"I did say *generally*," Erik said with a grin. He sighed, "The thing about humans is that when they scared, they try to kill what scares them. Humans love war. History's proven that. So, yes, if they knew we existed, their first move would be to declare war and hunt us down. They've already tried it, after all—in the 1700s."

Rose nodded. "That's true."

"Besides, underground is *always* safest from sunlight," Erik added.

She followed him, as he returned to the gym. "Is that why there are so many myths about you guys sleeping in coffins and graves and cemeteries?"

He laughed, "I actually know the vampire that started those myths."

Rose frowned. "Really? Who?"

"Aaron," Erik answered.

Her frown deepened. "Kallias mentioned him."

He nodded. "He's the oldest vampire alive—as far as we know, anyway."

"How was Aaron responsible for the myths?" Rose asked curiously.

"He intentionally built an underground shelter for vampires beneath a cemetery," Erik explained. "Humans would see vampires going in and out of tombs at night and assume they were rising from the dead. Then, the humans would dig up corpses and stake them, rather than looking for actual creatures of darkness. It kept them off of our trails." Erik smiled. "And then, of course, that shelter became the most powerful vampire colony in the world: the Tomb of Blood."

Rose grimaced. "That's...not the most appealing name, is it?"

Erik nodded. "It sounded more intimidating in Latin," he admitted.

"It's the colony Aaron leads, though. I used to live there with Alana and Kara."

"Kallias told me about those. Vampire colonies," Rose told him. "He said the vampires who live in them are less…human…than you are."

Erik chuckled at that. "Yeah, it'd definitely be culture shock for someone like *you*."

Rose crossed her arms. "And what is that supposed to mean?"

He just laughed, refusing to elaborate. "Maybe you can convince Kallias to take you one day. I doubt it. He's not much of a fan of Aaron. But it would be *so* funny to see your face."

"Okay," Rose said slowly. "I don't think I like the sound of *that*."

"And even better, I could introduce you to Kara!" Erik added. "She'd *love* you. You're exactly her type. Trust me. I *know* her type."

Rose's frown deepened. "What? Who?"

"Kara Unnarsdóttir," he said quickly, as if he could barely stop his nostalgic rambling long enough to clarify. "She'd eat *you* alive! Figuratively, of course. Well…I suppose literally, as well." His smile widened. "That shy but sassy personality of yours—she loves that kind of thing. And the red hair! Kara loves redheads. Personally, I don't get it. I prefer blondes. No offense. But she liked them." He was talking so fast she could barely understand him. "I remember when she learned the *entire* Celtic tongue just so she could visit the Celtic villages at night and seduce their women. She always said there were plenty of pretty redheads among the Celts."

Rose blinked, totally unable to keep up. "Umm, okay," she managed to stammer out. "But who's Kara?"

"Oh," Erik said, finally noticing her confusion. "An old friend of mine. She was a Viking warrior, like me, and she's also Aaron's second-in-command."

As always, the mention of history made Rose smile. "Sounds interesting."

"So, you *are* interested in her," Erik said, delighted at the realization.

"Wait. That's not what I said," Rose mumbled, "at all."

But of course, Erik ignored her. Again. "Back when Kara was Alana's lover, dating Kara would've gotten you killed—because Alana's jealousy was a little, you know, psychotic—but now that Alana's dead, you'd *probably* survive!"

"Alana's lover?" Rose repeated. "But I thought *you*...were Alana's lover."

"Kallias told you about Alana," Erik realized. He nodded, as if that were a relief, rather than something that upset him. "Yeah. Alana had many lovers."

"At the same time?" Rose asked.

"Most vampires aren't monogamous," he said. "We *are* animals, after all."

"Sea otters are monogamous," Rose stated.

Erik frowned. "We're not...sea otters."

"I'm sure you could be monogamous, if you wanted to be," she said.

"Of course. Geoff and Emma are," Erik agreed. "But Alana wasn't."

"And you became friends with her other lovers?" Rose asked.

"Just Kara," Erik said. "I haven't seen her in twelve hundred years, though. Not since I left Alana. It's too bad, really, because she would *love* you."

"Yeah, you already said that," she said, "in like fifteen different ways."

He smiled conspiringly. "You *are* into women, aren't you?"

Rose laughed in disbelief. "Are you *seriously* trying to set your best friend's girlfriend up with your ex-girlfriend's ex-girlfriend? Because that is *really* weird."

He grinned. "You just called yourself Kallias's girlfriend."

Rose blushed. "No, I didn't. I'm pretty sure I didn't."

"Yeah, you did," he laughed, his green eyes gleaming with amusement.

"No, I—I know better," she stammered, her cheeks growing hot. "He's a vampire, and I'm a human. It's impossible. I know that. I'm realistic."

"It's not impossible. Love knows no bounds," Erik argued.

She grimaced at him. "*You* sound like a Hallmark card."

"I'm a romantic," he said with a shrug. "Curse of being an empath."

Rose laughed at that. She cast a nervous glance around the empty gym, rocking back and forth on her feet, as she tried to calm herself.

The squeak of tennis shoes against concrete was louder than she expected.

Erik studied her, as if he could see straight into her soul.

Which was kind of true, Rose realized. He couldn't see her innermost thoughts like Kallias, but he could feel her emotions.

She wasn't sure which was more unnerving: to have her mind laid bare or her soul laid bare.

"We don't have to do this, if you're having second thoughts," Erik said.

"I'm good," Rose assured him. "I want this. I need to know how to fight him."

Erik scratched his head, mussing his already messy, blonde hair. "Yeah, I feel that," he admitted. "Kallias is going to kill us for this."

She bristled at that. "Kallias isn't my boss."

"No," Erik agreed, "but he does care for you." The humor in his expression was gone. "And what we're about to do will jeopardize your safety."

"I don't care," Rose said. And perhaps that was her self-destructiveness talking, but she didn't. This feeling of helplessness was so much worse. "Just blame it all on me."

Erik snorted, "Oh, don't worry. I will."

"So, how does this work?" Rose asked. "How do I control the power? Is there a magic word? A secret formula? Do I need to join a cult? Sell my soul?"

He chuckled, "Not that simple."

"I agree," Rose said sarcastically. "Selling my soul sounds *way* too simple."

With a frown, Erik began, "These abilities work like...eh...like a gun? I guess?"

"Awesome," Rose said. "I've always wanted to shoot bullets out of my eyes."

"It's like...there's gunpowder and a trigger," he tried to explain. "For me, emotions empower me—*fuel* me. When I feel angry or afraid, I become stronger and more dangerous—because I pull my power from my emotions. So, my gunpowder is...emotion." He waved a hand. "I control my power, or *shoot*, with emotions, as well. So, emotions are also my trigger. I *feel* the emotion, and I project it."

"You're trying *so* hard to make this analogy work," Rose commented.

Erik laughed at that. "Shut up. Teaching's not my thing," he said defensively. "Anyway, Kallias is similar. He's empowered by his mind or his *concentration*—his ability to read someone, predict, and strategize. His mind is his power, but it's also his trigger. He reads and controls the mind at will. He chooses to do it, and then, he does it. So, the mind is also the trigger for him. The mind is his domain. The soul is my domain. Eh...does any of that make sense?"

Rose resisted the urge to say, *'Not at all,'* and instead, said, "But based on that pattern, my power wouldn't make sense. You manipulate the soul. Kallias manipulates the mind. Telekinesis would be...the body. And using the body to manipulate the body in the way you use emotions to manipulate emotions would just be...basic physics. There's no psychic ability there."

"I have no idea what you just said," Erik informed her.

Rose sighed and begrudgingly fell back on his weird analogy. "What is my gunpowder and trigger? It's clearly not like yours."

"Right," Erik said. "Well, you violate the laws of gravity or...whatever."

"Physics," Rose provided.

Erik waved a hand in annoyance. "Just keep making up words, why don't you?"

Rose stared at him in disbelief.

"I don't know exactly how you do it," Erik told her, "but after tonight, I'm almost certain I know what fuels you."

"My gunpowder," Rose said with a sassy smile.

Erik pointed at her, as if she were suddenly making sense. "You're like me when it comes to that. Your emotion empowers you."

Rose frowned. "But that doesn't fit the pattern."

Erik rolled his eyes. "What is it with you and patterns?"

Rose just spread out her hands in bewilderment.

"Emotions fluctuate. They don't follow patterns," Erik told her. "Sometimes they're barely there. Sometimes they're overwhelming. You couldn't move the glass until I made you feel something, and you obviously felt something when you threw Theron across the room. You need emotion to use your ability, just like I do. Which means...emotion is your fuel."

"Right," Rose said. "So, what's my trigger?"

"That's the part I don't know," he admitted. "You would know better than I would. It'd be whatever makes it happen, whatever directs your power, whatever determines what the telekinesis does..."

"Then, it's decision," Rose said simply. "Telekinesis is manipulating things to your *will*. I decide something will move, and it does. I decided I needed Theron off of me, and it happened. I decided to move the glass, and it moved."

"Your trigger is your will," Erik realized. "That's the *mind*, like Kallias."

Rose frowned. "So, I'm like...both of you?"

Erik nodded slowly. "Your power combines the two—the mind and the soul—to manipulate the physical world. It makes sense, actually."

Rose gave him a skeptical look. "How so?"

"The parts of us that control our abilities are usually exceptionally strong," Erik told her. "Kallias has a strong mind. He's intelligent. And me? I've always been sensitive, emotional, and empathetic." He gestured toward her. "And *you*—well, you're annoyingly intelligent."

Rose frowned. "Is—is that a compliment or an insult?"

"Definitely an insult," Erik said without missing a beat. "And as an empath, it's clear to me that the emotional side of you is strong, as well."

Rose suddenly remembered what Kallias said at the hotel. "Wait. Kallias mentioned that my will is stronger than most. He said that was the reason he couldn't control my mind—that my will was too strong to bend," she said thoughtfully. She tilted her head to the side. "As a matter of fact, he purposely made me angry because he said I'm the most strong-willed when I'm angry."

Erik laughed and nodded. "So, he already knew all of this. It's not surprising. He's been inside your mind. He probably knows you better than you know yourself."

"That's a disconcerting thought," Rose muttered.

Erik stepped closer. "Well, there's only one way to test the theory."

Rose swallowed uneasily. "Let me guess. You're going to zap me with an unpleasant emotion again?"

He scowled. "I don't zap."

Rose pulled her thick, red hair into a messy ponytail and quickly wrapped the hair tie on her wrist around it. "Okay! I'm ready."

Erik gave her a puzzled frown. "Why…did you need your hair up?"

"Mental thing," she said quickly. She grabbed his hand and placed it awkwardly on top of her head. "Just hurry up and zap me before I chicken out."

He removed his hand from her head. "There's no zapping involved," he argued. "It's emotion, not electricity."

Rose opened her mouth to argue that, technically, emotions do involve *electrical* impulses in the brain, but before she could speak, Erik curled his hand around her shoulder.

A deep, blood-boiling wave of anger poured through her. It caused her heart to race and her skin to burn. It set every nerve in her body on edge. Her hands tightened into fists, and her teeth clenched together.

Something in her mind seemed to snap.

Erik yelped as his back collided with the concrete wall.

He sunk to the floor, wincing in pain.

The moment his hand left her shoulder, the anger faded, leaving Rose feeling kind of…dazed.

"Well, that was fun," Erik laughed. He winced, as he pulled himself to his feet. "It hurt like hell, though."

Rose stared, her eyes wide. "I— You—" she stammered, glancing from him to the wall and then back again. "I did that? But how— I—I actually did that?"

Erik laughed at her stammering. "Normally, when I render women speechless, I'm actually *doing* something to them."

Rose wrinkled her nose. "Great. I'm in shock, and you're being dirty."

"I'm always being dirty," he said. "I just keep some of it to myself."

"It doesn't seem like you keep *anything* to yourself," she muttered.

Erik approached her. "Your fear was powerful, but I think your anger might be even stronger."

"*My* anger?" Rose said. "You're the one who made me feel it."

"It was your emotion," Erik explained. "I just manipulated it." He frowned thoughtfully. "I need to test another emotion."

"Wait," she began, but he grasped her shoulder before she could finish.

A flood of happiness washed over her—warm, light, and pleasant. Rose had never felt anything like it.

She felt her lips curve into a wide, open-mouthed smile, and she felt the urge to laugh for no reason whatsoever. She knew she was smiling like an idiot, but she couldn't stop.

When she lifted her chin to meet his gaze, he smiled back at her.

"This is amazing," she told him.

"I know," he chuckled. "Move me. Throw me. Do something."

Rose nodded, as she suddenly remembered that there was actually a purpose for the intense—but honestly, pretty freaking awesome—emotion she was feeling.

She tried to focus—to let that happiness fuel her—but she couldn't.

"It's…harder," Rose said. "I don't know if I can."

It was supposed to be a complaint, but she was too happy. Instead, it sounded more like she'd just announced that she'd won a million dollars.

Erik dropped his hand. "That's strange."

"Forget Prozac," Rose scoffed. "*You*'re the cure for depression!"

"It should've worked," Erik said under his breath. "Happiness is a powerful emotion."

"Can I just carry you around in case I start feeling crappy?" Rose asked.

Erik laughed, "You'd have to deal with all of my dirty jokes."

Rose sighed, "Never mind."

He frowned. "You are…unusual."

"Well, yes," Rose agreed, "but I don't think *you* have room to talk."

"Happiness works for me. Any emotion works for me," he continued. "But for you, the dark emotions are the strongest. Anger and fear—those are *dark*."

"Dark?" Rose sputtered.

"It's odd—because you're so full of hope and kindness," Erik added. "You seem to be all light, and yet, your power is derived from darkness."

Rose liked the sound of this less and less with each word.

"Unless," Erik paused, glancing at her, "unless you *do* have a dark side—hidden underneath all of that light."

She swallowed uneasily. "I don't...have a dark side."

Erik blinked and cleared his throat. "Do you want to try again?"

Rose frowned, surprised by how quickly he'd changed the subject. He'd seemed so concerned about it. "Sure," she said. "Why not?"

"Are you sure?" he said with a grin. He took a step backward and raised an eyebrow. "Because I won't go easy on you. I'm not Kallias. He cares for you. *I* don't." He spread out his hands. "Don't get me wrong. I don't *want* you to die. That would hurt my best friend, and I don't want that. But I don't care about your *feelings* or anything."

Rose frowned, too caught up on the *that-would-hurt-my-best-friend* part. Was it true? Kallias had been alive for twenty-five hundred years. Would it really hurt him to see one human die?

It didn't seem likely.

Rose looked at Erik, as she considered his warning. "I know you don't," she assured him. "Why do you think I asked *you* to teach me, instead of Kallias?"

Erik smiled. "Don't say I didn't warn you."

Before Rose had a chance to wonder what he had planned, Erik seemed to vanish. She glanced around, trying to follow his inhumanly fast movement, but she saw no one.

Suddenly, she felt her body jerked backward. Her back collided with the tall, slender person behind her, and his hand clasped around her neck, tilting her head. His sharp fangs then pressed into her skin.

An unseen force tore him away from her and flung him toward the wall.

Rose glared at him. "What the heck was that?!"

528

"Owwww," Erik whined.

"You attacked me!" Rose complained. "You tried to *bite* me!"

He groaned in pain again. "I'm a vampire. What did you expect?"

"Uh, not that," Rose muttered.

"Relax," Erik said, wincing. "I wasn't actually going to kill you."

"Oh, yes. Very comforting," she said caustically.

He leaned back against the wall, before pushing himself to his feet. "I just needed to scare you."

"You don't need your fangs for that!" she reminded him. "You're an empath!"

"And piss you off," he added with a lazy grin.

"Too bad you're not an *empath*," she said again. "Oh, yeah! You are!"

"I am," Erik said, "but Theron is *not*."

Rose nodded slowly. "Another experiment."

"Now, you know you can use your telekinetic abilities when you're *actually* being attacked," Erik said. He spread out his arms. "You're welcome."

Rose rolled her eyes. "Fine. I *guess* I can forgive you."

"You *guess*?" he whined. "You hurt me!"

"You tried to bite me," Rose said. "Try it again, and I'll hurt you worse."

Erik burst into a fit of hysterical laughter, his grin wide enough to reveal his fangs.

Rose crossed her arms. "What's so funny?"

He snorted, "I'm a dangerous vampire, and *you* threatened *me*."

Rose narrowed her eyes. "Are you mocking me?"

"No, but it's hilarious," he said, clearly mocking her. "And...kind of hot."

Rose rolled her eyes again. "Do you flirt with all the women your best friend brings home? Because that doesn't seem very best-friend-like to me."

"There's a difference in flirting and fucking," Erik stated.

Rose stared at him blankly. "I can't believe you actually said that."

He just laughed harder. "And what do you mean *all* the women he brings home? I think you're overestimating your boyfriend's sex life."

Rose looked away nervously. "He's not my boyfriend."

"It looked like he was earlier," Erik argued.

"Says the man who has sex with women he doesn't even know," she countered.

Erik laughed. "Having sex with a woman does not make her my girlfriend," he said with a smirk. "Cuddling with her, on the other hand, does."

"That's a *terrible* philosophy," Rose said. "And we weren't...cuddling."

"Of course not. You were just lying all curled up around each other," he said sarcastically. He snapped his fingers. "Oh! That *is* called cuddling, isn't it?"

Rose suppressed a smile. She could appreciate the sarcasm, even if he *was* being ridiculous. "Why are you trying so hard to convince me that Kallias is my boyfriend?"

He stopped laughing, and his gaze softened so suddenly that it caught Rose by surprise. "Because your life is too short for you to be embarrassed about what you feel," he said honestly. "Even if you survive all of this, you'll eventually die of old age. You have to make the most of the moments you have."

Rose blinked at his sudden change of attitude. "Aren't you supposed to be the optimistic one?"

"I can feel what you feel," Erik explained, "and you're obviously falling—"

"I think we should get back to practicing!" she squeaked, interrupting him before he could finish that sentence. She wasn't ready to hear the end. "I need to be prepared."

Erik nodded. "If that's what you want."

20

DAMAGED

The weight of the sofa shifted, as someone sat down.

Erik didn't look away from the television. "Find anything?"

As he often did, Kallias removed his weapons from their sheaths and tossed them on the table, the blades clanging against its wooden surface. "Not a thing," he muttered. He turned to Erik. "As a matter of fact, I didn't even see any vampires in the bad parts of the city—the hotspots for vampire activity. What's going on out there?"

Erik glanced at his friend, who now occupied the other side of the sofa. "That's how it's been the last few nights. I have a bad feeling about it."

Kallias leaned back, resting his head against the back of the sofa and watching the ceiling curiously. "How's Rose?"

"Don't know," Erik said, drinking his whiskey. "She went to bed."

Kallias frowned. "She's not asleep. Her breathing's uneven," he realized. He leaned forward. "I should check on her. Something might be wrong."

Erik snorted. "You don't have to make up reasons to go see her. Just admit you missed her while you were gone. I won't make fun of you. Much."

Kallias stood and shot a peeved glare at him. "Shut up."

"Love you, too," Erik teased, grinning.

Kallias grabbed his weapons from the table and headed upstairs.

The upstairs lights had been turned off, which was odd—since Rose, unlike Kallias and Erik, actually needed those lights to see.

Rose had left the guest room door cracked open, but even that light was off. Kallias pushed open her door and stepped into the room.

"Kallias?" Rose said nervously. "Is that you?"

Kallias hesitated in the doorway. "Do you need me to turn on the light?"

Rose lay on her side in the bed, her red hair bright against the pillow and curling around her face. Her skin looked paler than usual, and pain creased her brows. She clung to the blanket as if she were freezing to death. "Please, don't. The light makes it worse."

Rose heard only the clanging of his weapons against the dresser and then his footsteps on the hardwood floor.

The bed dipped beneath his weight, as he sat next to her.

"Are you sick?"

"I guess," Rose said, "but I felt fine until an hour ago."

He trailed his fingers through her long, red hair, each strand soft against his skin. Rose moaned softly and moved closer, resting her head against his thigh.

"I don't remember anything about human sickness," he said worriedly. "What do you need? Water? Soup?"

"Mmm," Rose murmured, "what you're doing now feels amazing."

He smiled, but as he continued to play with her hair, he noticed a thin layer of cold sweat along her forehead. "What is this sickness?"

"I don't know," she mumbled. "Lots of things cause headaches and nausea."

A worried frown pulled at his lips. "How severe is the headache?"

"Pretty bad. Definitely a migraine." She snuggled closer to him. "You're so warm."

Kallias placed the back of his hand against her forehead. "And *you're* cold."

"Hence the blankets, genius," she said with a weak smile.

He didn't laugh. "And you're experiencing light sensitivity as well?"

"Yeah." She giggled tiredly, "Maybe I'm turning into a vampire."

"Doesn't work that way," Kallias said, apparently missing the joke. Again. "Are you vomiting? Was there blood?" When less than a millisecond had passed between his question and her response, he repeated himself anxiously, "Rose, are you vomiting blood?"

Rose frowned at the sudden interrogation. "Umm, I don't want to discuss my puke with the person I, uh, kiss and stuff." Her cheeks warmed, despite their clamminess. "How could I ever hope to seem sexy to you after that?"

"You'll still be sexy," he said under his breath.

Rose's eyes popped open.

"Rose, please. This is something I need to know," he said. "Are you vomiting blood?"

"Is this a fever-induced hallucination? Because it sounded like you said *still*. *Still* implies you think I am sexy *now*. But that can't be right. Because I'm me: Unsexy Rose," she rambled. "I bet you're not even really here right now."

"Rose. Blood," he said impatiently. "Was there blood?"

"Maybe a little," she said with a weak shrug.

Kallias stiffened, and his hand stilled. "Erik, get your ass up here. Now." He didn't yell it. He barely even raised his voice.

"Why are you calling *him*?" Rose said. "And how is he supposed to hear—"

"What's wrong?" Erik asked, before she could finish the question.

"What the hell were you thinking?" Kallias said. There was a sudden rise in his tone—a hint of nervousness or fear. "You knew this could happen!"

Rose glanced in the direction of his voice, suddenly confused. It didn't help that she was *literally* in the dark. She attempted to pull herself up into a sitting position, as if that would help her see.

But Kallias pushed her back down. "Don't waste your energy."

She couldn't actually see him, so she settled for directing her glare at the hand that pressed gently but firmly on her shoulder.

Erik looked at Rose and then at Kallias. "I knew *what* could happen?"

"She's throwing up blood," Kallias said.

"Oh," Erik said, drawing out the word. "Sorry."

"I said it was a *little* blood. Sheesh, it's not that big of a deal," Rose complained. She pushed his hand off of her and attempted to sit up again. "And why is Erik apologizing? Will someone, *please*, tell me what's going on?"

"How could you do something so stupid?" Kallias snarled at Erik.

Erik shrugged. "I do stupid shit. You've known me for twelve hundred years. It's not like this is news to you. Remember the incident in London?"

"Rose is human," Kallias reminded him. "She doesn't heal like we do."

Rose blew out a tired sigh, as they continued to ignore her. "Hello," she said, waving a hand. "Can anyone tell me what's going on?"

"It's actually her fault," Erik said defensively. "She asked me to do it."

Rose groaned in frustration. "*What* are we talking about?"

"She didn't know what would happen," Kallias said. "You did."

Maybe she'd fallen into another dimension, and they couldn't hear her anymore. If the supernatural was real, why not sci-fi, as well?

Rose touched her forehead, as if that would still the throbbing pain for a moment. "If someone doesn't answer me right now, I will..." she trailed off. "Well, I don't know what I'll do because you're both vampires, and I'm sick. But..." She pointed a finger at...most likely, no one. "It'll be bad!"

"Wow. You are just terrifying," Erik said sarcastically.

With a sigh, Kallias turned to face her. "Do you remember when I told you I get headaches when I overuse my telepathy? That overuse debilitates me?"

Rose leaned tiredly against the wooden headboard, blinking at the darkness. "Yeah. At the hotel," she said quietly. "After you tried to control my mind."

"Yes," Kallias said. "Your power is what allowed to resist my tele-pathic control. That headache that you felt afterward was a side effect of overuse. It was your body warning you to stop using your power."

Rose frowned worriedly. "Warning? Why?"

"There's a reason Erik and I try not to depend on our psychic abilities too often," Kallias said hesitantly. "The mind and body have limits. It wasn't made to do all of this. Overusing your power causes damage."

"What kind of damage?" Rose asked.

"It usually starts with a headache," Kallias told her. "Then, there's bleeding—nose, stomach, mouth, ears, eyes…" he trailed off.

"Hemorrhaging," Rose murmured thoughtfully.

"For a vampire, it's unpleasant," Kallias said, as if that much weren't obvious. "It can weaken us and severely debilitate us—but *we* heal."

Rose looked in the direction of his voice. "I'm human," she said cautiously. "What does it mean for me?"

Kallias clenched his jaw, as if he couldn't bring himself to say it.

So, Erik answered, instead. "It means you could die."

Rose nodded slowly.

"This is why I didn't want to tell you about your power," Kallias said irritably. "I knew you'd push yourself past your limits."

Rose scowled at that. "I just want to be able to defend myself."

"At what cost?" Kallias countered.

Rose closed her eyes and sighed, "You don't know how it feels."

"Well, it's a good thing one of us doesn't," Kallias scoffed, "because the person who *does* feel what you feel put you in danger because of it!"

Erik offered no words in his own defense—or hers.

Rose froze, as she felt a warm liquid on her face. She reached up and touched the wetness above her lips. A warm, sticky liquid dripped steadily from her nose, coating the skin and pooling into her hand.

"Whoa. That smells…*incredible*," Erik muttered. "If I still fed from humans—"

"Please, don't finish that," Rose interrupted.

Someone suddenly brushed her hand aside and pressed a warm, wet washcloth against her face.

Rose recognized Kallias's touch—warm and a little rough—as he tilted her head back and wiped the blood from her face.

"Kallias, stop," Rose said, wrapping her fingers around his wrist. "I can do it. You shouldn't be so close to it."

Kallias froze. She couldn't see him, but she had the distinct impression that, if she could, she might see a hint of pain in his eyes. "I won't hurt you," he told her. "I promise."

Rose's chest tightened with sympathy, as she realized why he'd reacted so strangely. "Kallias, I'm not worried about myself. I'm worried about *you*," she explained. "I know it hurts you to be close to blood. You shouldn't torture yourself."

"Er, speaking of…" Erik interjected, "I think I should leave."

"Go," Kallias said without hesitation.

"Goodnight, Rose," Erik called out. "See you when you smell less appetizing!"

Rose blinked. "Uhh…"

Kallias continued to wipe the blood from her face.

Rose realized that he must've acted instantaneously when she started bleeding—because she'd barely even realized her nose was bleeding before he'd returned with the washcloth.

"I need to stay with you," Kallias told her. "I need to know if—" He sighed, "I need to know you're okay."

Rose could easily guess what he'd almost said, instead. "*Am* I?" she asked softly. "Do you think I'll die?"

"You won't," Kallias told her. "I'll make sure of it."

"How?" Rose asked. "If I'm dying, what can be done about it?"

"If you *are* dying," Kallias said slowly, "I'll give you my blood."

Rose grabbed his wrist again and pulled the rag away from her face. "What?"

Kallias frowned. "My blood will heal you—no matter how severe the damage."

Her eyes widened. "No. No, no, no," she said quickly. "I'm not…like you. I can't drink blood. It would be gross."

"Vampire blood tastes different from human blood," he said—as if that changed *anything*.

Rose shuddered, horrified at the thought. "Besides," she said after a moment, "you said you'd never give anyone your blood!"

"Believe me," Kallias sighed, "I don't want to. It'll create a blood bond between us—one that links us together for the rest of your life. Neither of us needs that right now." He shrugged. "But if it's the only way to save you, I'll do it."

Her brows furrowed. "Couldn't I just go to the hospital?"

"What could *they* do for you?" Kallias asked. "They won't even understand what's happening to you—much less know how to fix it."

She pinched the bridge of her nose between her thumb and forefinger to dull the throbbing pain in her head. "Okay," she said slowly. "When will we know if I'm dying or not?"

"I'm not taking any chances," Kallias told her. "If it gets any worse, I'll give you my blood." He pulled the cloth away. "I think your nose has stopped bleeding."

Rose nodded tiredly. "I think I need to splash some water on my face."

Before she could climb to her feet, Kallias leaned past her and switched on the light. She squeezed her eyes shut, the pain suddenly excruciating, but after a moment, she managed to stumble out of bed and shuffle toward the bathroom.

She braced her hands against the sink to stop herself from falling, and then, she glanced up at her reflection.

Kallias had wiped the blood from her face, but faint, red blood-stains marked the places the blood had been.

Not to mention, the bright red bloodstain on the front of her shirt.

Rose glanced down at the stained, blue-and-black flannel. "Great."

"You could be *dying*, and you're worried about your shirt?" Kallias asked.

Rose glanced up at the mirror, seeing his reflection behind her own. "It's a coping mechanism," she mumbled, glancing down at the stain. "When people are scared, they worry about the insignificant things they *can* control, rather than the uncontrollable situation that really scares them."

His gaze softened at the impersonal answer. "You're scared?"

Rose couldn't bring herself to answer the question in that way. "It would be a normal reaction to the information provided."

Kallias stepped forward and tossed the blood-stained washcloth in the sink. He placed his hand on her arm and turned her to face him.

Rose fixed her gaze on his shoulder, too anxious to look him in the eye.

"I won't let you die," he assured her. "If it worsens, I'll give you my blood. I promise you, Rose: I'll do whatever it takes to save you."

Rose cast a puzzled glance toward his face. "Why?"

He looked away. "I wish you wouldn't ask that question."

Her lips twitched. "Why?" she asked again, half-joking but...also kind of serious.

"Because it's best if neither of us answers that question," he said.

Rose watched him curiously for a moment, noting the flicker of anxiety in his brown eyes, the hint of some other feeling she couldn't quite identify...

She turned back toward the sink. The sight of her sickly pale complexion brought a wave of insecurity into her throat.

She cupped her hands beneath the stream of water, filling her palms, and then splashed the cold water on her face.

"I'd like to stay with you tonight," Kallias said, as he watched the water drip from her eyelashes, "if you don't mind."

Rose smiled shyly at his reflection.

"I need to be as close as I can," he said, "in case this gets any worse."

"Okay," Rose said nervously. "I mean...yesterday and the day before were...nice."

He smiled, too, at that.

Kallias stepped forward and wrapped his arms around Rose's waist, before saying, near her ear, "You must know by now: you're welcome in my bed anytime you want."

Rose watched her own cheeks turn scarlet in the mirror.

At her blushing, he added with a grin, "To sleep, I mean."

"Right," Rose said, laughing nervously. "To sleep."

Kallias chuckled. "Come on. Let's get you to bed."

Rose didn't resist, as he took her hand and led her back to the room. He switched off the light and helped her find the bed in the now dark guest room.

His touch left her, once she was in bed, and Rose wondered if he'd changed his mind about staying close.

But after a brief shuffling of clothing, she felt him crawl into bed behind her. He wrapped his arms around her and pulled her against him the way he had the day before, and she closed her eyes, soothed by the warmth of the embrace.

"You need to sleep, *moro mou*," he said, sliding into Greek the way he often did when they were alone. "I'll wake you, if it gets worse."

"I *am* sleepy," she admitted, her words beginning to slur. But even as she began to drift into a half-asleep state, Erik's words from earlier replayed in her mind. "Kallias? I have a question."

"Of course you do," he laughed.

Waves of drowsiness swept over her. "Would it hurt you, if I died?"

Kallias was quiet for so long that by the time he finally answered, she'd already drifted off to sleep. He nuzzled his face in the curve of her neck, and knowing she wouldn't hear, he said, "Yeah. It'd fucking kill me."

A SLEEPY MOAN ESCAPED ROSE'S MOUTH, WHEN SOMEONE'S WARM LIPS lightly touched her neck. Those lips parted, and his tongue traced the pulsing, carotid artery. She squirmed in his hold, but he curled an arm around her stomach, holding her still—his front against her back.

Rose opened her eyes. "Umm, Kallias? What are you doing?"

He nipped her ear with his fangs, and Rose couldn't help but moan.

"Waking you."

"Yeah, well," Rose said breathlessly, "most people just go with: *'Hey, you. Wake up.'*"

He laughed, his breath warm against her skin. "How are you feeling?"

Before she could answer, Kallias kissed her neck, and her train of thought instantly vanished. She shuddered when his sharp fangs grazed her skin.

What kind of silliness was it to ask a question and then effectively ruin her ability to answer it?

"You seem to be feeling better," he noted.

"Yeah. Better," she mumbled. "Better works."

He chuckled, lazily tracing the seam of her pajama pants with his finger.

When she gasped softly, Kallias rolled her onto her back and climbed on top of her. He braced his hands on each side of the pillow, holding his weight above her, and his lips descended upon hers.

Rose moaned and kissed him back with the same passion.

His fingers entangled in Rose's thick, red hair, as he deepened the kiss.

"Wait...mmm. Stop," she said, her voice muffled by the kiss.

He immediately pulled back. "What's wrong?"

"I need to brush my teeth," Rose said simply, as if this were a totally normal time to think about her routine.

"Right now?" Kallias said with a stunned frown.

"Well, preferably before you kissed me," Rose said, "but yes, right now."

His frown deepened. "I don't understand."

Rose squinted at him. "Haven't you ever heard of morning breath?"

"No," he said. Both confusion and frustration twisted at his lips. "You're seriously thinking about your teeth right now?"

"I mean, they're in my mouth," Rose pointed out.

Kallias didn't understand this human at all.

Rose added in explanation, "I'd prefer to have minty breath when you're kissing me."

Kallias shook his head in disbelief—and then climbed off of her.

He switched on the light, and Rose hopped off the bed and hurried to the bathroom.

Admittedly, it'd been a while since he'd been with a human, but he couldn't remember *this* happening before.

In the bathroom, Rose held her toothbrush under the water and watched as Kallias's reflection appeared in the corner of the mirror.

He leaned against the door. "Do you actually think I care about this?" He sounded offended by the mere suggestion. "Are you going to start insisting you have a shower and brush your hair every time I kiss you, as well?"

Rose subconsciously touched her frizzy, puffed-out mess of red hair. "Oh. The pillow wasn't too gentle with it, was it?"

Kallias rolled his eyes. "Do you think I'm that shallow?"

"What?" she sputtered, glancing back at him. "No. Of course not."

"Then, why are you worrying like this?" he asked.

"Because I...*worry*," Rose stammered. "My fear over all of this isn't because of you. I'm just nervous. I...can't help it."

His brown eyes softened a little at that. "I'd never pressure you into something you're not ready for. You know that, right?"

"Of course," Rose told him. "This nervousness is just—it's always here for me."

Kallias crossed his arms and nodded. With a glance toward her wet toothbrush, he added, "Well, you should know that nothing as ridiculous as that could make me stop wanting you."

Rose froze with the tube of toothpaste still in her hand and glanced at him, her eyes wide.

She needed to respond, but she was stuck on the *wanting* part.

He'd said that before.

He'd said it in Greek.

Se thelo. I want you.

Rose's mind whirled with all of the different things the word *'want'* could mean.

It could mean sexual desire, passing fixation, or aching longing.

You could want someone the way you want sex, or you could want someone the way you want a new object—a toy.

Or...you could want them in the way you want food and water, as if you can't live without them.

You could want them on a whole other level—the way you long for the other half of your broken soul.

She wondered which one he meant.

Rose offered him a shy smile. "I know that—I think. Sort of," she said, her tone growing more unsure by the moment. "It's just... Well, you're so perfect, and I'm so...*not* perfect."

Kallias stared at her in disbelief. "I'm not perfect."

"Well...right. No one is," Rose admitted, "but compared to me..."

"Rose," Kallias interrupted. His confusion turned to bitterness. "I'm as far from perfect as it gets. I just come in misleading packaging."

Rose looked as if she wanted to argue.

But Kallias continued, "I'm damaged. Can't you see that?" He waved a hand at himself. "I'm wrapped well. That's all. Inside, it's all messed up beyond repair. I'm not what anyone needs."

"We're all damaged," Rose told him, "and no one's beyond repair."

"If you actually think I can change after all these centuries, you're more naïve than I thought," Kallias said. "And who says I want to change?"

Rose tried not to react to his tone. "Everyone can heal—when they want to. I have to believe that," she argued, "and I think you want to."

Kallias scoffed at that.

"You don't like yourself the way you are. It's obvious you don't," Rose stated. "If it's what you want, yes, I believe you can change."

He looked away, bitterness twisting at his mouth.

"But for the record," Rose added, "I never said you needed to change. *You* said that."

Kallias glanced back at her, frowning in surprise.

Rose stepped closer to him and placed her hand against his chest, feeling his deep scars beneath her palm. "Damaged doesn't mean unlovable."

He stared at her, unblinking—too stunned to respond.

She tilted her head thoughtfully. "I remember, once, on a study trip," she said, "we saw this piece of pottery, recovered from a recent dig. It was beautiful—but ancient and damaged. There were probably hundreds of cracks in the vase." She smiled. "But it was also beautiful *because* it was damaged, you know? Despite everything, it held itself together. And the cracks seemed to make their own design—a beautiful, unintentional design. I remember thinking, at the time," Rose said, "that there really is a such thing as beautifully broken."

For the longest time, Kallias just stared at her, his gaze dark and intense, piercing right through her.

Rose wished, as she often did, that she could know his thoughts the way he knew hers.

Kallias glanced down at her hand, which was still against his chest, and he wrapped his own hand around it, interlacing his fingers with hers.

It was strange to remember how hesitant he'd been to hold her hand a few nights ago, compared to how natural the action felt now.

"I think...you're wrong," he said quietly. "You're closer to perfect than I've ever been."

Rose frowned, positive she'd heard that wrong. "*What*?"

Kallias dropped her hand and took a step backward. "I said...come downstairs with me," he lied. "I need to introduce you to Geoff and Emma."

Rose's frown deepened. "Your other vampire friends? They're here? Now?"

Kallias nodded slowly. "Don't you hear them?"

Rose lifted her eyebrows, when she heard only the creaking of air vents in the ceiling. "Well, maybe you haven't noticed, but your walls are made of stone."

He turned to leave. "Are you coming?"

She cast a sideways glance at her reflection. "I need to shower first."

"You'll have plenty of time to shower later," he called back, from the guest room. "This will only take a moment. I just need to know you're comfortable with them before I leave for the night."

"I'm still in my pajamas. You know? The ones you said looked like an old quilt?" she reminded him. She frowned worriedly. "Wait. Why would you need to know if I'm comfortable with them?"

He shrugged on his shirt. "Because Geoff is staying with you tonight."

Rose sighed. "What is this? A game of Musical Chairs? Do you really think it's smart to leave me with every single vampire you know?"

He sat on the bed and propped his leg over the other as he laced up his boots. "I *know* many vampires, actually," he laughed, "but I only *like* three."

Rose squeezed some toothpaste onto her forgotten toothbrush. "You're such a sourpuss. Out of the billions of people in the world, you only like three?"

"Four," he said quietly. "I like four people."

Rose's lips curved into a surprised smile. "I like you, too, Grumpy."

He stood. "Oh? What happened to you *kind of hating* me?"

Rose nearly choked on her toothpaste, as she laughed at what she'd said to him several nights ago. She turned on the water and leaned forward to spit out the toothpaste before it led to an early death. "I guess it's all kind of linked. I mean, *apparently*, hate is a passionate emotion."

As they headed downstairs together, they continued to tease and laugh at each other—not really noticing the vampires at the bottom of the stairs.

Rose gasped, as someone suddenly latched onto her. She could barely breathe as a small vampire squeezed her dangerously tight.

A slender man stood in front of the door. He smiled apologetically at Rose and stepped forward. He placed his hand on his wife's shoulder and gently pulled her backward. "Emma, she's human. Humans are fragile, remember?" His voice lilted with an unmistakably British accent.

Rose rubbed her sore ribs and glanced at the thin vampire who'd nearly crushed her.

Rose couldn't deny that the woman he'd called *Emma* was beautiful. Her brown hair fell around her neck, framing her small face. A short, lavender-colored dress clung to her thin figure, and her small, hazel eyes sparkled with excitement.

Her glossy, red lips were curved into the brightest and friendliest smile Rose had ever seen.

Sofia had been gorgeous, but Emma was...*stunning*.

Emma pouted at her husband. "I just wanted to make her feel comfortable."

Erik snorted, "It's hard to feel comfortable when your ribs are broken."

Erik leaned against the wall, next to Geoffrey.

Geoffrey had a slender frame—much like Erik's—but he was a lot shorter than him or Kallias. He had short, neatly cut, black hair, and rather than the casual, all-black clothing she'd become accustomed to seeing on Kallias and Erik, this vampire wore a suit—black pants, a white button-down shirt, even a tie.

He stepped forward and extended his hand. "I apologize. My wife and I aren't around humans often," he said with a polite smile. "My name is Geoffrey Cossington, but you can call me Geoff. And this is my wife, Emma."

Rose shook his hand, relieved that his grip was gentler than his wife's. "It's nice to meet you both," she said honestly. "I'm... Well, I guess you know who I am."

Emma smiled. "You are Rose. The unusual human."

Rose blinked at that. "Yes. The Unusual Human," she muttered. "That's what it says on my birth certificate."

Erik watched Rose shake Geoff's hand with an offended look. "So, you'll shake his hand, but not mine?"

Rose flashed a sassy smile at him. "His hands are probably cleaner than yours."

Erik gave a small nod to that, as if he couldn't argue.

"Yes, Geoff is very clean," Emma chimed in helpfully. "He bathes after killing *and* after sex. And he doesn't like it when I leave lingerie in the floor."

Geoffrey suddenly looked uncomfortable. "Inappropriate, Emma."

Rose stared at Emma. "You leave...underwear in the floor?"

"It's not my fault," Emma told her. "*He* takes them off of me."

"Bloody hell," Geoffrey muttered under his breath.

Rose's eyes widened at the woman's enthusiastic honesty.

"He doesn't like it when I leave lingerie *outside*, either," Emma added.

Rose shot a questioning look at Kallias, but he just shrugged.

A bright red blush had begun to creep up Geoffrey's neck.

Erik, on the other hand, was far too amused by this conversation. "When did you two have sex outside, Geoff?" he teased. "I thought you were too civilized for that."

Geoffrey narrowed his eyes at his obnoxious friend.

But Emma quickly answered, "Oh, he's never civilized when we..."

Geoffrey clasped his hand over Emma's mouth before she could finish that sentence. The blush that had crept up his neck, starting beneath the collar of his button-down shirt, had already reached his ears, turning them bright pink.

"Emma is...very honest," Kallias said in Rose's ear.

"Really?" Rose said, her voice sharp with sarcasm. "I hadn't noticed."

"Emma, do you remember that conversation we had," Geoffrey sighed, "about the things people don't like to talk about in public?"

"Which one?" Emma asked. "The one we had yesterday? Or the night before? Or the night before that? Or the night before that? Or the—"

"All of them," Geoffrey interrupted. "Do remember the list?"

Emma listed them on her fingers, "Murder, vampires, blood, sex..."

"Yes, that one," Geoffrey said. "And what were you just talking about?"

"Oh," she said. She smiled sweetly. "Sorry."

At the sight of her smile, Geoffrey's lips curved into an adoring response.

"They're kind of adorable, aren't they?" Rose mumbled to Kallias.

Kallias laughed. "Yeah, I suppose so." He glanced at the clock on the wall. "I need to shower and get dressed. Do you think you'll be all right with them?"

"They seem harmless enough," she muttered.

Kallias snorted at that, as if she didn't know what she was saying.

After Kallias excused himself to get ready, Geoffrey and Emma made their way into the living room. As Rose stood in the foyer, trying to decide whether to follow the couple she barely knew or flee to the social-safety of the library, Erik pushed away from the wall and walked over to her.

He scratched at his messy blonde hair. "Do you want something to eat?"

Rose shrugged and followed him to the kitchen, more concerned with the coffee than the food.

She made coffee, as Erik rummaged through the fridge for ridiculous amounts of food. "Do you always cook?"

He pulled out a stick of butter. "Sure. It's relaxing."

"What about Kallias?" she said, as she filled the coffee pot with water.

"Sometimes," Erik said distractedly. "Whoever wakes up first."

Rose turned on the coffee maker and turned toward him, frowning, as she watched him toss a carton of eggs on the counter. Shockingly, none of them broke from his careless treatment.

"Audrey says *my* cooking is cruel and unusual punishment, which is totally unfair, because her cooking sucks, too."

Erik turned toward her. "Who's Audrey?"

"She's my best friend," she answered, "and my roommate."

He leaned closer. "Is that all?"

Rose frowned. "Yes, that's all."

Erik cracked the eggs. "Have you ever been with a woman?"

"Would you stop asking about that?" Rose complained. "You're not setting me up with your ex-girlfriend's ex-girlfriend."

Erik laughed. "You'll change your mind, if you meet her."

Rose shook her head at his persistence. "Besides, I would've thought my lack of experience with women was covered under *'virgin.'*"

"Fair point," Erik said. "You're *such* a disappointment."

Rose cast an incredulous look at him. "I'm sorry I'm not as slutty as you."

Erik snorted, "Did you just call me a slut?"

"You called *me* a prude," Rose said with a shrug. "Fair is fair."

He laughed loudly at that. "I've never been called a slut before."

"I find that hard to believe," Rose muttered.

He flipped the eggs in the skillet, still grinning to himself, as if someone had just handed him an award. He didn't speak again until Rose sat down at the bar with a cup of coffee.

Erik glanced up at her. "There's blood on your shirt."

"Oh, sorry!" Rose said. She glanced down at her flannel pajama shirt, examining the blood-stain. "I'll go change."

He waved a hand dismissively. "It's fine. I can handle dried blood." Then, he leaned forward, bracing his hands against the counter. "Listen, I didn't just ask you in here for the food. I need to apologize."

Rose blinked in shock. "No, you don't." When he continued to look remorseful, she added, "I asked you to do it. It was my fault."

Erik sighed, "Kallias was right. I *did* know what would happen."

"Why didn't you tell me?" Rose asked curiously.

"I *did* warn you that it was dangerous," Erik reminded her, but then, he sighed, "but I should have told you everything. I'm careless. Kallias knows that, but...you didn't."

"I'm not angry at you," Rose assured him. "You did what I asked."

Erik nodded slowly. "I assumed you'd tell me when the headache started. Why didn't you?"

"I didn't realize it was related," she began.

"Still..." he prompted.

"I thought I could ignore the pain," she said. "It's...what I always do."

"Don't," Erik told her. "Pain *always* means something."

Rose blinked, stunned by his sudden seriousness. But then, she saw Erik's gaze shift past her, and she turned to find Kallias in the doorway.

He was fully dressed now—in black jeans and a black, button-down shirt. His long hair hung around his face, still wet from the shower, and he offered Rose a small smile when she looked his way.

Kallias then strode past them to grab the plates from the cupboard.

"You seem to be in a better mood today," Erik noted.

Kallias scowled at him—though it was a decidedly *less* grumpy scowl than usual. "For now."

Erik laughed and then raked the eggs into Kallias's plate. "Bacon?"

Kallias glanced around the counter. "Where is it?"

Again, Erik laughed at his impatience. "I'll have to make it."

Kallias waved him back. "I'll make it."

Erik took his own plate of eggs to the counter and sat across from Rose. "Toss me a beer," he told Kallias.

"Yes, toss a glass bottle," Rose said sarcastically. "That's such a great idea."

But then, Kallias *did* toss the glass bottle across the room, and Erik caught it—without even looking up from his food.

Rose blew out an annoyed sigh.

"Rose called me a slut," Erik bragged.

Kallias snorted, "I doubt she meant for you to take it as a compliment."

Rose rolled her eyes in exasperation. "I didn't."

Erik grinned, as he grabbed the salt and pepper. "It made my night."

Rose sipped her coffee, glaring over the top of the cup at Erik. When she shifted her gaze away from him, she nearly spat out her coffee when she saw Emma suddenly sitting across from her.

"I'm seriously going to tie bells around all of your necks," Rose grumbled.

Emma flashed an excited smile. "What size dress do you wear?"

Rose paled in horror. "Dress?"

"I'm going to grab you one while I'm out," Emma said, and then, apparently misunderstanding the horror on Rose's face, she added, "I'm promise I won't get any blood on it."

"Yes, and, umm, I appreciate that," Rose mumbled. She set down her cup. "But I...don't wear dresses. I just don't feel right in them."

"But," Emma pouted, "dresses are pretty. And they make sex easier."

"That's true," Erik said—without looking up from his food.

"I'm just...not really the *pretty* type," Rose tried to explain. She glanced down at her blood-stained flannel pajamas. "I have other clothes. I promise. This isn't my only outfit."

Emma propped her face in her hand. "I'd think you'd look sexy in a dress," she said, before sharing a sly smile with Erik. "Don't you, Kallias?" she called out.

Erik winked, and Rose realized that Erik must've shared his theories about Kallias's *feelings* with Emma.

Kallias didn't even look up from the skillet. "She looks beautiful in everything she wears," he replied automatically.

Everyone in the room—but *especially* Rose—turned to gape at Kallias.

Kallias seemed to realize what he'd said a little too late. He looked up and winced at their surprised expressions.

He quickly turned off the stove eye. "I just realized that I forgot my weapons."

As Kallias disappeared from the room, Erik scoffed, "He didn't forget his weapons. Kallias doesn't go anywhere without his weapons."

"Oh my God!" Emma whispered to Erik. "You were right! He's never called anyone beautiful before, has he?"

Erik laughed, "Not that I remember."

Rose remained silent, still shocked by the compliment. No one had ever called her beautiful before, and she certainly hadn't expected Kallias to be the first to do it.

When she finally tore her gaze from the empty doorway, she realized that Erik was watching her with an amused smirk.

He mouthed, *"Told you so,"* so that only she would notice.

A HIGH-PITCHED GRATING SOUND ECHOED THROUGH THE HALLWAY, originating from Kallias's room.

Rose cracked the door and peeked inside.

Kallias sat on the edge of his bed, sharpening his dagger on a grey whetstone. A smile curved at his lips. "You really think you can spy on vampire?"

Rose pulled the door the rest of the way open. "No," she muttered. "I just had to make sure you weren't naked or anything."

He glanced down at his clothes. "Disappointed?"

"No," she scoffed. She crossed the room and sat down next to him. Insecurity drew up her shoulders, tensing her muscles. "Kallias, why did you call me beautiful?"

He sighed, "Why do you have to overcomplicate everything?"

Rose frowned. "I'm not. I was just asking a simple question."

He set the dagger aside, clearly agitated now. "There's nothing simple about it."

Rose wanted to say that it *could* be simple—if he'd just speak the truth—but she thought maybe she was missing some social cue again. So, she kept quiet.

Kallias stood and walked over to his closet. He pulled open the door and grabbed a black leather jacket from the sea of black clothing inside.

"You have such a colorful wardrobe," Rose teased.

Kallias shrugged on his leather jacket, and one corner of his mouth tilted into a half-smile. He returned to her and surprised her by leaning over her and resting his knee on the empty space of bed between her legs. He rested his palms on each side of her hips.

Was *this* flirting? Rose had no idea.

"Well," he said with a smirk, "it'd be difficult to sneak around at night in bright-colored clothing, wouldn't it?"

She swallowed and leaned back—so that their bodies didn't touch. "Oh, I know," she said playfully. "It's like that time I wore neon yellow to rob a bank."

Kallias chuckled and rocked back onto his feet, towering over her, once again. "Hey," he asked, "what ever happened to that dagger I loaned you?"

Her smile tilted impishly. "See, here's the thing. I found out the hard way that when you throw a dagger over the edge of a cliff, it's impossible to retrieve it."

He snorted, "I'd be worried, if we'd been around any cliffs recently."

Rose shrugged. "Hey, you never know. Maybe Erik dangled me off the edge of a cliff last night. He's not the best babysitter, you know."

Kallias sighed, "He wasn't *babysitting* you. I just need to know someone's here to protect you." He looked away. "I'd be a nervous wreck, if I didn't."

Rose blinked, surprised by that confession. "Well," she said uneasily, "has it ever occurred to you that I might feel the same way? Don't you think I worry about you, too—out there all alone?"

His lips curved downward into a deep scowl. "You shouldn't."

Rose rolled her eyes. "Let me guess. Because you're a vampire?"

"Because I'm long past my expiration date," he corrected.

Rose narrowed her eyes at that. The way he viewed his own death terrified her. She stood, her heart racing. "Do you think that makes the possibility of you dying *any* easier for me to handle?" she asked, her voice cracking a little. "If something happened to you, I—I—"

Fear gripped her chest.

Kallias stepped closer, and though he looked sympathetic toward her feelings for a moment, his concern quickly turned to frustration. "It shouldn't matter to you," he said angrily. "A week ago, I wasn't even in your life."

"But now, you are," Rose said quietly, "and you always will be."

For a moment, Kallias just stared at her, his expression blank, but then, the shock in his eyes darkened, morphing into anger. "Where exactly do you think this is headed, Rose?" he snarled. "Do you really think we'll be together after all of this is over? After Theron is dead, I'm taking you back to your home, and you'll never see me again. You'll move on with your life, and I won't be part of it."

Her eyes burned. "That's not what you want."

"It doesn't matter what I want," Kallias growled.

"Yes, it does!" Rose argued. "It does to me! Kallias, stop doing this!"

"Stop doing what?" he asked.

"Trying to protect me from *everything*!" Rose said. "I never asked to be saved, okay? I don't need you to save me from heartbreak. I can handle it. I don't know if it's because you were born in a different time or if the other women you've been with were different, but I'm not like that. I don't want you to be my knight in shining armor. I just want someone who cares about me and accepts me—because that's *real*."

"I'm not the person who *should* be with you, Rose," Kallias said.

"See? That's what I'm talking about," Rose said. "You're trying to protect me from yourself—from getting hurt—but I didn't ask for that. You don't get to decide who should or shouldn't be with me. That's my decision. Not yours."

"Don't you get it, Rose?" he said. "I can never give you what you want."

"I just told you what I want," Rose reminded him, "and it's definitely something you can give me."

"You want more than that," Kallias argued.

Rose rolled her eyes. "Fine. Enlighten me, *Oh-Great-Wise-One*. What do I want?"

"What everyone wants," he said. "Someone to grow old with you, to marry you, to have a normal life with you. Someone who can give you children."

"What makes you think everyone wants that?" Rose said incredulously. "People want all kinds of things. Maybe I don't want any of that."

"Bullshit," he muttered.

Rose crossed her arms. "Or maybe I don't want any of that with anyone else," she amended. "If you knew what I want as well as you think you do, you'd know that what I want…is you."

Kallias shook his head. "Rose," he said heavily, "there are people out there who are better for you. Humans. *Normal* people. People who aren't damaged, like I am."

"Everyone's damaged! Everyone has baggage!" Rose argued. "You think I'm not damaged after all the crap that happened to me? *Normal* people—as you call them—wouldn't want to deal with baggage. And maybe you don't either! But if that's the case, then say it—instead of acting like you know what I want better than I do."

"It's not that," he assured her.

"Then, stop," Rose pleaded. "You accept my damage, and I accept yours. That's what love is. It's not about shopping for the best deal. It's about finding someone who accepts your baggage and wants to help you carry it. I accept you, Kallias. Nothing else matters."

"It does matter," Kallias insisted. "Years from now, it will matter."

She rolled her eyes. "And you call *me* stubborn."

Kallias stepped closer to her, leaning down so that his flashing, brown eyes were level with her gaze. "This isn't some fantasy story where the princess falls in love with the monster, and the monster magically becomes human again and lives happily ever after. That doesn't happen in real life."

Rose frowned. "Okay, if you're talking about *Beauty and the Beast*, Beauty was actually the merchant's daughter, not a princess," she corrected. "Well, according to the book that was written in 1756 by Jeanne-Marie Leprince de Beaumont, anyway."

Kallias stared at her, his eyes wide. Then, he shook his head and headed toward the bed. He snatched up his dagger and started toward the door.

"Kallias?" Rose called.

He paused at the door and turned back toward her. "Yes?"

"You're a vampire," Rose said. "If this isn't a fantasy story, what is it?"

Kallias watched her for a moment, his expression cold and indifferent. "It's a horror story," he said, "and in horror stories, the monsters eat the humans."

Rose collapsed on the sofa, next to Erik. Geoff and Emma sat on the sofa across from them—Emma leaning her head on Geoff's shoulder, as they watched television.

"Do antidepressants work on vampires?" Rose asked Erik. "Because I think your friend, Mr. Doom-and-Gloom, needs some. I haven't refilled my prescription recently, or I'd offer him some Prozac."

"Human medication doesn't affect vampires," Geoffrey said distractedly. "Our metabolisms work too quickly. Blood is the only thing a vampire's body can hold onto."

"You can always count on Geoff to give you a serious answer when you're trying to make a joke," Erik muttered. He turned toward Rose. "Are you all right?"

"Yeah, I'm fine," Rose sighed. "Do you know where he went?"

"Mr. Doom-and-Gloom?" Erik said with a grin. "He's in the kitchen."

Rose stood up and dusted off her pants. "Wish me luck."

Erik laughed, "Good luck."

When Rose reached the kitchen, she found Kallias in front of the sink with his back turned to her. He didn't move or flinch, but she knew he knew that she was behind him.

He always knew.

"I came to return your dagger," she said, holding the sheathed dagger out in front of her, "since I'm just going to get eaten anyway."

Kallias still didn't turn to look at her, but an amused smile curved at his lips. He managed to hide the smile before he turned to face her.

He wiped the dishwater from his hands with a small, white hand towel. "I'd hoped you would."

She lifted her eyebrows in disbelief. With an annoyed scoff, she crossed the space between them and shoved the sheathed dagger into his hands. "Here," she muttered. "Take your precious dagger."

He suppressed a laugh at her reaction. "It's not very precious," he told him. "It's actually my most inexpensive one."

"Fine," Rose said, her voice sharp. "Your cheap dagger that's *so* important to you."

When she turned to leave, he finally let himself laugh. "Rose," he called. "Wait a minute."

Rose turned back toward him, her expression wary. "What is it?"

Kallias reached behind him and grabbed something from the counter. He walked toward her, allowing himself to smile now. He held out a long, thin object, wrapped sloppily in brown packaging paper. "I wanted to give you this."

Rose glanced down at the horrendously wrapped package. "What is it?"

Kallias looked down at it. "We didn't have wrapping paper when I was human. I don't know how it works yet. I think it turned out okay, though."

"Not the paper," she laughed. "What's *inside* the paper?"

"Uh," he said. He raked his fingers through his hair. "Just open it."

Rose hesitantly took the package from him and gently pulled at its paper. Beneath, silver gleamed in the low light of the kitchen.

Before she had time to react, Kallias mumbled, "Flowers would've made more sense, I guess. Or jewelry? Do humans still give each other jewelry? I know it's a ridiculous gift, but—"

"Ridiculous?" she interrupted. She traced the design with her finger. "I love it."

Kallias smiled. "I never use it, and I—I thought of you when I saw it."

Rose stared at the beautifully engraved dagger. "Is that an owl?"

He reached out, tracing the design engraved into the handle. "Yes. It's Athena's owl, actually," he said. "The goddess of—"

"Wisdom and war," she finished with a smile. "I know my mythology."

He laughed, "Of course you do."

"I love it so much," she whispered.

Kallias's smile deepened. "Athena's owl was a symbol of wisdom and strength, and that's what you are, Rose. You're wise and strong."

Rose looked up at him, her eyes wide. "You're...confusing me with these compliments today," she said nervously, "especially after what you said in your room..."

"I'm sorry," he interrupted, but he left it at that.

Rose understood. He was sorry for lashing out at her, but he still felt the same.

"It's a silver dagger. So, it won't rust like iron daggers do," he advised, "but it might tarnish."

Rose smiled and carefully pulled the dagger from the silver sheath. Her own bright blue eyes reflected clearly in the blade. "I never realized a dagger could be this beautiful," she breathed.

"The blacksmith who made it wanted to be an artist," he said.

"He *was* an artist," Rose murmured.

Kallias smiled. "So, does that mean you like it?"

"Depends," she said with a cute smile. "Do I get to keep it?"

He snorted, "Of course you do. Why do you think I wrapped it?"

"I'm not sure that qualifies as wrapping, Kallias," she teased.

"I tried my best," he complained. "I have big fingers."

Rose laughed at that. "I thought you *never* gave away your weapons."

He shrugged uneasily. "I don't," he said, "usually."

Rose's smile deepened. "Thank you. So much. It's perfect."

"You don't have to say that," Kallias muttered. "A human would've gotten you flowers or something. I should've just gotten you flowers."

"No. Kallias," she said, stepping closer. "I like *this*. This is *you*. Your dagger. It's personal to you." She held it closer. "It means more to me than flowers ever could."

He smiled back—hesitantly. "You're sure?"

"Absolutely," she promised.

Kallias looked away and sighed, "I need to leave now."

A deep, sinking feeling settled in Rose's gut. "Can't you just...stay?"

"No," he answered. "Theron might be in the city by now."

"Yeah. That's what worries me," she muttered.

Kallias leaned forward and kissed her on the forehead—a strange, affectionate action that seemed completely uncharacteristic for him. He placed his hands on her face. "Please, don't practice your abilities tonight."

"Yeah, I know," she sighed. "I learned my lesson last night."

He gave her a small, tight smile and then turned to leave.

Rose followed him into the foyer. "Please, don't get hurt."

He froze in the doorway, and that cold distance returned to his voice. "Stop caring so much. For both of our sakes."

Rose watched as Kallias closed the front door behind him. She stared at that heavy, wooden door for a moment, trying to ignore the dread that knotted itself in her stomach, warning her that something terrible was going to happen.

Finally, she sighed and stalked into the living room.

"Are you okay? You seem unhappy," Emma said with a peppy smile.

Rose slumped onto the sofa and flashed a fake smile. "I'm fine," she lied.

"Allow me to translate," Erik offered. "She's pissed."

Rose cast a puzzled look at him. "I'm mildly irritated, at most."

Erik grinned. "This is mildly irritated for you?" he teased. "This feels like Geoff's *enraged*. Damn, you have intense emotions."

Rose sighed and pretended to be interested in the television show.

Erik moved closer to her and threw his arm around her shoulders. She stiffened and frowned at the intrusive arm.

Before she could ask what he was doing, Rose's entire body relaxed.

He was projecting calming emotions to her, and with her anxiety as high as it had been, Rose appreciated the gesture.

"He only acts like that because he's afraid of hurting you," Erik whispered in her ear.

Rose felt her lips curve into a grateful smile. "I know."

Emma raised her head from Geoffrey's shoulder and stood up. "Well," she sighed, "I should probably leave."

"No, take your time," Erik said sarcastically. "It's not like there are humans out there that might be dying while you sit here."

Rose shot a baffled look at him. "You realize you're still sitting here, too?"

"No one asked for your opinion, nun," Erik countered.

"Nun?" Rose exclaimed. "How am I a nun?"

Erik listed on his fingers, "You're a virgin, a prude, and you dress weird."

Her eyes narrowed. "They're pajamas! *Comfortable* pajamas!"

"You're a virgin?" Emma asked.

Rose sighed, "This really isn't anyone's business."

Emma offered a reassuring smile. "It's okay. Kallias can fix that," she told Rose. "Sex with a vampire is very pleasant. I enjoyed sex with Geoff *before* we were vampires, of course, but blood definitely makes it better."

Erik whimpered like a puppy—*exactly* like a puppy. "Don't remind me."

"Blood *and* sex were on the list, Emma," Geoffrey sighed.

Emma giggled. "Sorry, Erik. Sex *without* blood is good, too, though."

"The list," Geoffrey complained.

"Yes, it is," Erik agreed. "That's what I keep telling myself."

Rose just sat there, blinking at the unusual, excessively honest vampire.

Emma patted Rose's shoulder. "Just tell Kallias, and he'll fix it."

"I don't think *fix* is the correct word to use there," Rose mumbled.

"No, but she got the first letter right," Erik quipped.

Rose shoved him away. "Ugh. Go kill vampires or whatever it is you do."

Erik laughed loudly at her. He climbed to his feet and checked his weapons. Then, he grabbed his keys and turned to leave.

"Do you have your weapons?" Geoffrey asked Emma.

Emma pulled a dagger from beneath her dress to show him.

Erik froze, tilting his head. "Where did you have that?"

Without hesitating, Emma pulled the skirt of her dress up around her hips to reveal the black belts around each thigh, designed to conceal her daggers.

Rose's eyes widened as she realized that the beautiful, peculiar vampire had also inadvertently revealed her lacy, pink lingerie. She looked away, blushing.

"Nice," Erik said. "That's kind of hot."

Geoffrey scowled at him. "Seriously, Erik? I'm right here."

Erik raised his eyebrow. "You'd rather me say it when you're not?"

Rose stared at a random place on the wall, as she waited for Emma to put her dress back down and cover those *extremely* sheer panties. "Vampires are weird."

Erik grinned. "Then, you should fit right in."

"Ha. Ha," Rose muttered sarcastically.

"Are you missing anything else?" Geoffrey asked his wife.

Emma patted down her dress, frowning. "No. Wait. Keys?"

Geoffrey smiled and tossed her the keys. Emma caught them easily, but when she spun toward him, her thigh brushed a small decorative table against the wall.

The table tipped, and the glass vase slid off of it.

But the vase never hit the floor.

It stopped, suspended in the air.

Emma, Geoffrey, and Erik all stared at the floating vase.

"What..." Emma turned toward Erik with a questioning look.

But Erik wasn't looking at the vase anymore. He was staring at Rose.

Emma followed his gaze. "Did you do this, Rose? That was so neat!"

"And dangerous," Erik said harshly. He grabbed the vase from where it was suspended in the air and set it on the table. His eyes narrowed at Rose.

Rose just stared at the vase in shock. "I didn't even realize what I was doing. It just happened. I just saw it falling, and..." she stammered. She swallowed, unnerved by her own power.

Emma and Geoffrey just frowned at her, not sure what to say, but Erik's gaze was suddenly intense. His brow creased with concern, and his jaw clenched.

"I didn't mean to do it," Rose said defensively.

"Yeah. That's what worries me," Erik said.

"Well, *I* think it was neat," Emma said, elbowing Erik a little too harshly.

Erik winced and rubbed at his ribs. "Ouch," he complained.

Emma turned and started toward the door. She stopped in the

doorway to the foyer and blew a kiss at Geoffrey. "See you later, handsome."

Geoffrey smiled. "Be careful out there."

Erik gave Rose another concerned look before he turned to head toward the front door. "See you later, *handsome*," he said mockingly to Geoffrey.

Geoffrey rolled his eyes, choosing not to respond.

"You, too, Rose," Erik said seriously. "Be careful."

Rose nodded nervously. "Yeah. Sure."

21

STRANGE BLOOD AND BAD NEWS

"Can I ask you an awkward question?" Geoffrey asked.

"My life is a long list of awkward questions," Rose said with a playful smile. When he gave her a puzzled look, she said, "I mean, yes? What is it?"

The television flashed in the dark living room, as the two Roman soldiers on the show fought with swords that—as Rose had pointed out—looked more like the ones used in the late Middle Ages, rather than the time of Roman Empire.

Geoffrey loosened his tie. "Could I look at your blood?"

Rose blinked. "You're right. That *is* a pretty awkward question."

"I don't want to taste it," he assured her. "I've fed from Emma already."

Rose noticed the redness in his face and was amazed that she'd finally met someone who blushed more than she did. "Why does it embarrass you to talk about feeding?" she asked curiously. "I don't blush when I talk about what I ate for breakfast."

"Well, it's, er, different," he stammered. "We—well, *most* vampires feed during sex."

"Oh," Rose said, as she finally understood the blush. "Oh!"

He offered a nervous smile and explained, "I don't want to feed. I just want to look at your blood—to examine it."

Rose's frown deepened. "Like…scientifically?"

"Yes!" he said, apparently relieved that she'd understood. "I was a scientist when I was human. Specifically, I studied blood."

"A hematologist," Rose assumed.

He frowned. "What?"

"A person who studies blood," Rose explained. "We have a name for it now."

"Ah. Well, we were just called scientists back then," Geoffrey said. "Anyway, your blood smells different from most human blood. I'd like to see if it looks different—under a microscope."

"Last time I checked, it was red," Rose said.

"Yes." Geoffrey apparently didn't catch the dry humor in that remark. "I'm referring to less obvious differences. Vampire blood is also red, but there are peculiarities that distinguish it from human blood."

She leaned forward, intrigued. "Really?"

"Yes," he said, encouraged by her enthusiasm. "It took me many tries to identify what those differences were, but now, I believe I can identify the restorative enzymes that allow us to heal so quickly."

"That is very cool," Rose informed him.

He smiled, and with another slight blush, he added, "I've also identified the endorphins that create the…erm…*pleasant* reactions? During blood-sharing."

"This is literally the most interesting thing I have ever heard," Rose said.

Geoffrey looked a bit skeptical, but he admitted, "Erik implied that you might be…intellectually inclined, like me."

Rose laughed in disbelief. "He said those words?"

"Well, actually, he said we were both boring," Geoffrey said with a smile, "but I translated in my head."

Rose laughed again.

"Your telekinesis explains the scent of power in your blood, but I remain," Geoffrey paused, "unconvinced that it *fully* explains your unique scent."

Rose frowned worriedly.

No one else had thought that, had they? Kallias had never mentioned it.

Then again, there were lots of things that Kallias had chosen *not* to mention.

"What else could it be?" Rose asked.

"I don't know," Geoffrey said, "but maybe a look at your blood could tell us."

Rose nodded nervously. "My blood's been drawn before."

"But perhaps they didn't know what they looking for," Geoffrey pointed out, "or…perhaps they did, and they deliberately hid it."

Rose's eyes widened. "You—you think someone tampered with my blood tests? At a hospital?"

"I don't think anything," Geoffrey corrected, "but I am an overly cautious person. I've considered the possibility."

But it *wasn't* a possibility.

Was it?

"Fine," Rose agreed. "You can look at my blood—as long as you don't bite me."

Geoffrey laughed. "No biting. I promise."

He leaned forward and grabbed what appeared to be an oversized briefcase from the floor. He placed it on the coffee table, and it thudded much too loudly against the wood—as if it were heavier than it looked.

Geoffrey flicked open the clasps and let it fall open, revealing lots of lab items—including every size syringe, a microscope broken down into its smallest parts, and many flasks of strange-colored liquids.

The black velvet lining of the case held each item perfectly still.

"Who knew you could fit a biology lab in a briefcase?" Rose muttered.

"I don't know what you mean," Geoffrey said. "It's not a *room*."

"It was a joke," Rose said with a frown. "I have a weird habit of making them."

Geoffrey nodded, agreeing with the weird part, at least. "See?" he said, holding up a syringe. "No biting."

"New needles?" Rose asked.

"Of course," he assured her.

Rose nodded and rolled up the sleeve of her pajama shirt. At least if she got blood on it, it'd match the other blood-stain. "Are you sure it won't bother you?" she asked, as he moved to sit next to her. "Fresh blood seems to be a big deal for Erik and Kallias."

Geoffrey took her wrist and turned it, searching for a place to stick the needle. He traced the vein in the bend of her elbow with his thumb. "Erik and Kallias are starved. Their hunger's unbearable," he explained. "Vampires that feed regularly have more control over the hunger."

"Oh," Rose said, and then, she immediately added an, "*Ouch*," when he shoved the needle into her arm.

Geoffrey glanced up at her. "Oh. Did that hurt?"

"Little bit," she squeaked, as he pushed the needle deeper.

"I apologize," Geoffrey said. "My experience was with the comatose."

Rose nodded stiffly. "Explains a lot."

He attached a vial to the syringe to collect the blood, and dark red liquid poured into it. He placed the vial on the table and pulled the needle out of her arm.

Then, to her surprise, instead of using a Band-Aid like a normal person, he licked his finger and placed it against the small, bleeding hole on her skin, as if it never occurred to him to do otherwise.

"Wow," Rose muttered, "that wasn't gross at all."

"It works better than a bandage," was the only explanation Geoffrey gave her.

Rose glanced down at her arm and realized that he was right. There was no bruising or evidence of the needle whatsoever, which was impressive, considering how easily her fair skin bruised. "Still weird."

The clang of metal against wood drew her attention back to Geoffrey.

He connected several small pieces of equipment, putting together a microscope—one piece at a time. "Gosh, Owen would fall in love with you over this equipment," Rose scoffed. "Not literally." She frowned. "Possibly literally."

He set a small piece of glass on the table. "Owen's a scientist?"

"No, he's a waiter. For now," Rose said. "But he's also a biology major."

Geoffrey squeezed a droplet of blood onto the glass. "A what?"

"It just means he studies biology," she explained, "in college."

"Ah," he said, sliding the drop of blood under the microscope.

After meeting several vampires, Rose had decided that Geoffrey was the most normal one she'd met so far. Aside from the using-his-saliva-as-a-bandage incident, he seemed as human as anyone.

Then, Geoffrey proceeded to prove her wrong.

He neatly rolled up the left sleeve of his white, button-down shirt, and as soon as he had it up to his elbow, he grabbed another empty vial.

And then...he sank his fangs into his own wrist. A few drops of blood splattered onto the hardwood floor, before he covered one of the holes with the empty vial.

"We never did *that* in Biology," Rose muttered.

He glanced at her briefly, as he pulled the vial away from his wrist. Then, he made it all just a *tiny* bit weirder by lifting his wrist to his mouth and licking the wound.

Befriending vampires was a lot weirder than it sounded.

Geoffrey rolled his shirt sleeve back into place and buttoned the cuff.

He seemed normal again...if you ignored the blood on his face.

"It's easier," he explained.

"Mm-hmm," Rose mumbled.

Geoffrey pulled a handkerchief from the pocket of his shirt.

Not a paper napkin.

An actual, cloth handkerchief.

Rose had assumed it was one of those fake ones that were sewn into the shirt, like what she'd seen at the occasional thrift store, but nope.

The vampire had a real handkerchief.

He wiped the blood from his face and returned the handkerchief to his pocket. Then, he pulled out a second piece of glass.

Geoffrey placed a drop of his own blood on the glass, and then peered into the microscope, examining her blood in comparison to his own.

"How old are you?" Rose asked curiously.

"Er, 226 years old? I think," he said. "It was around 1818 when I became a vampire, and I was twenty-eight."

"1818," she repeated, "and you're from England? You sound...English."

"Yes. London," he confirmed. He frowned and switched the slides again.

"And Emma? How old is she?" Rose asked.

"She was four years younger than me," he mumbled. "222?"

Rose smiled. "She's outspoken for a woman from the Victorian era."

He laughed. "Yes, I always liked that about her. She was interesting."

Rose smiled at the adoration in his voice. "Did everyone appreciate it?"

"No," he admitted. "Her honesty was often considered improper and unladylike."

"Ugh, I hate that word," Rose scoffed. "Women have all kinds of personalities. We don't all fit our assigned gender role." She grimaced at the thought. "We're not all *ladylike*."

Geoff glanced at her. "Emma would like your feelings on that. She was treated badly for her inability to...fall in line."

"That's terrible," Rose said sympathetically. "I'm glad she didn't let them change her."

Geoffrey smiled. "Well, Emma was already an outcast," he explained. "She never really cared to learn perfect etiquette because...what would be the point? Even if she did, she'd never be accepted."

"Why not?" Rose asked.

Emma certainly seemed feminine—so it couldn't have been that.

Geoff checked the blood, frowned, and then checked it again. He didn't tell her what he'd noticed. He simply pulled out two more pieces of glass and prepared more blood samples.

"Emma's mother was an, erm—what is the modern term?" he mumbled. "An *escort*?"

"A prostitute?" Rose guessed. "Sex worker?"

Geoff nodded. "Yes, thank you," he said, relief in his tone. "I didn't want to call her a whore. It feels crass."

"And they weren't too kind to people of that career back then," Rose said.

It was a statement, not a question.

She was a history major, after all.

He nodded. "Emma was the product of that…career choice," he added. "Illegitimate children, especially the children of prostitutes, weren't accepted in general society. They were viewed as the lowest of classes—not only poor, but immoral, as well." He sighed, "These aren't my opinions, I assure you. They were theirs."

Rose offered a reassuring smile. "I understand."

Geoffrey continued, "Emma never knew who her father was, but apparently, he was wealthy, and most likely, a prominent member of society. When Emma's mother realized that she had tuberculosis— which, at the time, was a death sentence—she blackmailed Emma's father, so that her daughter wouldn't wind up in an orphanage, because the orphanages were…"

"Inhumane," Rose finished for him.

Geoffrey frowned. "You know a lot about Victorian society."

"I study history," she explained.

"That's a strange subject to study," he said. "What could you possibly do that with education?"

Rose laughed at his disapproving tone. "This is the twenty-first century. We have jobs in the history field now."

His frown deepened.

"History is important," Rose told him. "We can learn a lot from the past. We can learn to not repeat our mistakes—and how to move forward."

Geoff nodded, but Rose was pretty sure she'd failed to recruit him into her own area of nerdiness.

"Well, rather than have his dark secret revealed," Geoffrey explained, "Emma's father paid a boarding school to house Emma and put her to work. Girls didn't attend school back then, and even though it *was* better than living in an orphanage, it was still unpleasant for her."

"Because of the work?" Rose asked.

"Not just that," Geoffrey sighed. "She was also ridiculed for her… inappropriate behavior toward…people."

Rose nodded. "Because she didn't lie to make men feel better?"

"Exactly," Geoff said. "We met at the school." He glanced at her. "I stayed up late, and I'd sneak into the lab to study. I loved science, and I had this dream, at the time, of saving lives with some scientific discovery."

Rose smiled at that.

"One night, Emma came in to clean the lab and found me." An adoring smile curved at the corners of Geoffrey's lips. "She promised not to get me into any trouble, and I...asked her if she'd like to study with me."

"Aww," Rose couldn't help but say.

His face reddened. "I married her after I finished my education."

"So, you two were married *before* you became vampires," Rose realized.

He leaned over, peering again into the microscope. "Yes. Why?"

Rose shrugged. "How did you become vampires, then?"

Geoffrey leaned back, and anxiety flashed in his dark eyes.

Rose noticed his nervousness. "Oh, no. Have I said something insensitive?" she said worriedly. "I don't mean to. I'm just so curious, and I ask a lot of questions. And I—"

"It's fine," he interrupted. "It's just...a difficult story to tell."

"Then, don't tell it," Rose said. "I'm sorry for asking."

Geoff smiled at her concern. "It's all right. Really. It happened a long time ago."

Rose shook her head. "Yeah, but if you don't want—"

"I do," he assured her. "I told you that I worked as a scientist, right? Specifically, that I worked with blood?" When she nodded, Geoffrey continued, "Baby vampires, and by that, I mean newly changed vampires, have very little control over their hunger. In beginning, they're starving—like Kallias and Erik—except *they* don't know what they're feeling or how to control it. They're drawn to the scent of blood, and they hunt it down. But they don't understand what they're doing until it's too late."

Rose nodded in understanding. "And you worked with blood."

"Yes," Geoffrey said. "I was working late at the lab one night, and a newly-made vampire broke in, crazed by the scent of blood." He glanced at her. "While blood outside the veins—like what I worked with

—has a stronger scent, it's the blood *inside* the veins that we actually crave."

"So, the vampire came for the blood and found a whole, living human," Rose realized.

Geoff nodded. "There was no time to react. When he smelled my blood, the blood of a *living* being, he attacked me. It didn't hurt—not for long. It actually felt...pleasant, which was a bit disturbing."

"So, you died?" Rose asked.

"Yes," Geoff told her, "but baby vampires are still very human. Most of them aren't desensitized to killing yet. They still feel remorse when they realize what they've done. The vampire who killed me ran—but not before trying to heal me."

"With his blood," Rose assumed.

"Yes," Geoff said again. "Unfortunately, while vampire blood will heal a *living* human, it can't heal a dead human—not without changing them into a vampire." Then, he tilted his head and added, "Or maybe it can. Perhaps it's not the blood that changes us but death, instead. Either way, what he did brought me back...as a vampire."

"And Emma chose to join you?" Rose guessed.

He sighed, "I wish it were that simple." He turned slightly to face Rose. "When you first awake as a vampire, everything is a blur until you feed. Your body has to heal itself from death. You can't think. Nothing is functioning right. All you know for the first couple of nights is hunger."

Rose frowned sympathetically at the thought.

"For those first couple of nights, you sleep and feed. You just repeat that cycle—over and over—while your body heals and transforms."

Geoffrey seemed to have forgotten the microscope. Now, he stared at the wall, his narrow shoulders rigid. "I walked the steps to my home. They were familiar. But...I didn't know what I was craving. I didn't understand what was happening to me."

Rose inhaled sharply, as she realized where this story was going.

His jaw clenched. "I was so *painfully* hungry, but I didn't realize that it wasn't food I wanted. It was blood." He tugged again at his tie. "Emma, who *was* thinking clearly, wanted to know why I was late and why I had blood on my clothes, but I didn't want to answer. I didn't want to think. I just wanted to eat and sleep, and she was...an obstacle to that. Her questions made me...desperate. And angry."

Rose's stomach lurched with dread. "Oh, no," she whispered.

Geoffrey looked at her. "In the end, it was the hunger that caused me to bite her," he sighed. "I couldn't control it. I—I killed her."

Rose's throat felt so tight with sympathy that she could barely breathe.

"It was the worst moment of my life," Geoffrey admitted. "She was the one person I couldn't handle losing—and it was *my* fault. I had killed her." His voice cracked a little, but somehow, he kept his face clear of emotion. "You know Erik feels the emotions of others when he's in close proximity to them, but what you may *not* know is that a particularly powerful emotion can reach out to him across greater distances. They draw him in like a beacon." He looked down at his long, pale hands. "Erik and Kallias lived in London at the time. So, when I held her lifeless body, completely broken over what I'd done, Erik felt it, and he led Kallias to me."

"Did they think you'd killed her purposefully?" Rose asked worriedly.

"No," he assured her. "Erik felt my pain. He knew already. And Kallias—regardless of what he may have thought at first—saw my thoughts. He knew exactly what had happened." Geoff glanced at her. "They tried to tell me it wasn't my fault, but that didn't matter. I just wanted my wife back. I begged them to save her."

"So, they turned her?" Rose asked.

"Kallias didn't," Geoffrey said. "He was trying to explain that it might not work, and that even if it did, she might hate me for it, but I wasn't thinking rationally—and Erik...was feeling what I felt."

"Erik turned her," Rose realized.

Geoffrey nodded. "Erik isn't a rational person, anyway. If one were to place Erik near enough grieving people, we'd have hundreds of vampires being made every single night." He rolled his eyes. "Empathy makes him unreasonable. Erik will *always* act on the behalf of a hurting person—with no regard for the consequences."

"Yeah, but that wasn't such a bad thing in *your* case, was it?" Rose argued.

Geoffrey sighed, "I suppose not."

"And...Emma forgave you for killing her?" Rose assumed.

"Of course," Geoffrey said easily. "She understood—especially since she felt the same uncontrollable hunger when she awoke. I only sustained a few bruises and broken bones during the apology."

Rose blinked. "Is—is that a joke? Did you just make a joke?"

He still *looked* serious.

"It was nothing," he said with a wave. "I healed quickly."

Rose squinted bewilderedly.

Was it a joke or not?

Geoffrey leaned forward and peered into the microscope again.

"But she's so small," Rose mumbled.

Geoffrey didn't pull away from the microscope, but he did laugh. "And feisty."

Rose cast a baffled look at him.

Geoffrey's expression grew...wary. He leaned back, shook his head, and peered into the microscope again.

Rose frowned. "Is something wrong?"

"Yeah," he said, but he didn't elaborate. He leaned over and reached into his briefcase. He pulled out a small bag of thick, crimson liquid. The blood swished from one side to the other, staining the bag.

Rose recognized the blood donor bag. "Where did you get that?"

He ripped the bag open with his fangs and grabbed another empty vial. "I didn't kill anyone for it, if that's what you are thinking. I just... borrowed it."

"So, you stole it?" she asked.

Geoff filled the new vial with the donated blood. He glanced at her and smiled. "I am using it to learn. Learning is never wrong, right?"

"Oh. Uh, wow. I'm really torn here," she muttered.

He studied one drop of blood, then the next, and then the last, quickly switching between the three slides. His frown deepened. "This is so strange."

Rose continued to ponder the question he'd asked. "I mean, really, entire philosophies could be founded on that question. Law versus Learning."

Geoffrey looked at her, his eyes wide. "You're human?"

"I think I'm a dragon, actually," she told him, "or a space dinosaur."

His brows furrowed. "A *what*?"

"Sarcasm. Again," Rose said. "Sorry."

"Oh," he said, still frowning.

Geoffrey returned his attention to the blood. His lips turned downward, and he set two more pieces of glass on the table.

He applied a drop of his own blood to each slide. Then, he added a drop of human blood to one slide and a drop of Rose's blood to the other, allowing each type of blood to mix with his own.

He placed each slide under the microscope.

"What are you doing?" she asked.

"Checking something," Geoff said. He leaned back, his brows furrowed. "What the hell?"

Rose raised an eyebrow—because even the mild profanity sounded strange coming from someone so polite. "Is something wrong with my blood?"

"I'd say so," he scoffed. When he turned to her, he narrowed his eyes suspiciously. "You might think you're human, but your blood doesn't *act* like human blood."

Rose frowned. "But...I am human."

Right?

Geoffrey pushed the microscope toward her. He adjusted the scope for her, and then, he placed a slide of crimson liquid under the lens. "This is what human blood looks like when it's mixed with vampire blood. Take a look."

Rose leaned forward to check, her long, red hair falling over one shoulder. At first, she thought it looked similar to what she'd seen before, but when she adjusted the scope, she gasped, "What is this?"

"It's reacting. The enzymes in our blood react to human blood—they attempt to heal anything amiss, form a bond, and...create pleasant reactions," he explained. He removed the slide and replaced it with another. "And this is how your blood reacts. Look, now."

Rose hesitantly leaned forward and peered into the microscope. Her eyes widened. "Why is it doing that?"

"I don't know," Geoffrey said. "I've never seen anything like it."

Rose's blood didn't just *react* with the vampire blood, like normal blood did. It *changed* with the vampire blood. Strange sparks of light and hazes of darkness swirled around in the crimson liquid.

"I don't even understand what I'm seeing," she said.

"Me, either," he admitted, "but whatever it is—it's not natural."

Rose looked up at him. "Not natural?"

"Not human," he added.

"But," Rose said, her heart racing, "I am human. I mean, if I wasn't, what could I even...*be*?"

"I don't know," Geoffrey admitted.

WHEN ROSE SHUT OFF THE WATER IN THE SHOWER, SHE NOTICED A LOUD buzzing noise coming from nearby. She stepped out of the shower and grabbed the long, white towel she'd draped over the towel bar. She wrapped it around her body, before searching for the source of the incessant buzzing.

It led her to the bathroom door and then back into the guest room. Water dripped in the floor, her hair still too wet.

She found the cell phone in the middle of the floor, repeatedly lighting up and buzzing. She hadn't replaced her own phone yet, so this one must've belonged to Kallias.

She remembered him undressing for bed the night before and realized it must've fallen from his pocket.

Rose knelt to pick it up.

And her stomach lurched with dread.

She knew that number. It was Audrey's number.

Her anxious mind jumped to the worst possible conclusion: that Theron had found Audrey and that when she answered, it wouldn't be Audrey's voice on the line. It would be Theron's.

Her hands shook, as she lifted the phone to her ear.

"Hello?" Rose said hesitantly.

"Rose? Thank God it's you!" Audrey breathed. "I need to talk to you."

Rose almost sank to the floor with relief. "You're okay."

"I'm not okay! I'm an emotional wreck!" Audrey shrieked into the phone.

Rose winced. "Sorry," she mumbled. "What I should've said was: I'm relieved that you're *physically* well enough to make this phone call."

"Yeah, well, you might want to wait until you hear why I called before feeling relieved," Audrey said hesitantly. "I had another dream."

Rose returned to the bathroom to find a towel for her hair. "I thought that might be it."

"I *promise* I would've called sooner, if I'd known how to get in touch with you, but you'd lost your phone," Audrey explained in a rush. "Then, I remembered you calling me from Mr. Tall-Hunky-Scary-Guy's phone, so…"

Rose squeezed the ends of her drenched hair with the second towel. "Kallias," she corrected absently.

Audrey hesitated for a moment. "I still don't know if I should even tell you…"

Rose stopped drying her hair. "Why do you say that?"

"Just…promise me," Audrey insisted. "Promise me you won't do anything dangerous."

"You know I can't promise something like that without knowing why," Rose said honestly.

Audrey sighed in defeat. "It's Kallias. I think something's happened to him."

Rose nearly dropped her towel. Clutching the phone closer, she said, "What do you mean?"

"In my dream," Audrey said shakily, "there was…blood. So much blood."

Rose tried keep a clear head—despite her quickly skyrocketing pulse and trembling fingers. "I need more information. Please, Audrey."

"No, you don't," Audrey breathed, "because I know what you're doing, Rose. You're planning on doing something stupid."

"No," Rose lied, "I am t-totally calm." Her attempt to lie caused a slight stammer, though—which gave her away. "I just need to know where he is."

"Rose, no," Audrey cried. "You'll get yourself killed."

"More information," Rose said, a strange note in her voice, "please."

Audrey was quiet for a moment. "You...sound different."

Rose lifted her face, glancing at her reflection in the bathroom mirror. For a moment, she thought...

But that was impossible, right?

She'd thought she'd seen a red glow in her eyes.

Like the Stone of the Eklektos had glowed, when she touched *it*.

She leaned closer, but it was only her bright blue eyes blinking back at her now.

She must've imagined it.

"I have to save him, Audrey," Rose said honestly. "Please. Tell me everything you remember about his surroundings."

"You can't save him!" Audrey pleaded. "You'll die."

"I *will* save him," Rose stated, "even if I have to wander the streets blindly."

"I shouldn't have called," Audrey said. "I just needed to know *you* were okay, but now..."

"Where was he?" Rose repeated.

"He's probably dead already!" Audrey said. "There was so much blood. No one could survive that."

More panic surged inside Rose's chest, and she gripped the counter, her head spinning. "Just tell me something, Audrey. Please."

"Don't you understand? If you go after him, whatever happened to him will happen to you!" Audrey said. She sounded as if she were on the verge of tears. "Listen, I know you like him or something, but that's not a good enough reason to get yourself killed. Just...come home."

"I have to try," Rose tried to explain. Her heart raced faster and faster with each passing moment. "I love him too much to lose him."

Silence filled the line.

Rose pressed a hand against her chest, feeling her own rapid pulse against her palm. She hadn't meant to say that, but she couldn't take it back either. It was true. She loved him.

Finally, Audrey managed to utter an eloquent response. "Shit."

"Yeah," Rose agreed. She hurried to the guest room, sifting through the dressers to find the warmest clothes she could. If she had to wander the streets in the rain, it'd be cold.

She found her thin, black hoodie and considered herself victorious.

"Rose," Audrey said, but there was a note of defeat in her voice now, "whoever do that to him will kill you, too."

"Maybe," Rose said lowly, "or maybe I'll kill him first."

"What?" Audrey sputtered. "Rose, that doesn't even sound like you!"

Rose held the phone with her shoulder, as she tried to pull on her jeans. Her wet skin made the denim cling to her, but she didn't have time to wait. She hopped a little, jerking the pants up to her hips.

"Describe what you saw," Rose reiterated, "please."

Audrey sighed, "I couldn't see *much*. There were no windows. It was dirty."

"That narrows it down," Rose said, as she wrestled with her bra.

"Oh, God, the blood," Audrey said weakly. "It makes me sick to think about it."

"Deep breath, Audrey," Rose said, even though *she* was the one who was actually panicking. "The walls. Tell me about the walls."

If there was anything good at all about being an anxious person, it was that strange ability to *handle* the anxiety during a real crisis.

"Block, I think?" Audrey said, and it was almost as if Rose could hear her squinting in confusion. "No paint. Just block." She stopped talking for a moment, giving herself time to recreate the memory. "There was dirt. Through the cracks in the wall, I saw…dirt."

"He's underground!" Rose realized. "Do you remember anything else?"

"No," Audrey answered. "No, wait, I… Yes, I do! There was graffiti! I remember it! I can draw it!"

Rose nearly sobbed with relief. "Perfect! Text it to this number."

Audrey went quiet, and Rose could hear the scratch of one of Audrey's charcoal pencils through the line.

She must've placed the phone on the counter.

Rose pulled the black hoodie over her head. She didn't know if the speaker-phone was on, but she said her goodbyes, anyway. "I love you, Audrey. *Please*, be careful."

The scratch of pencil stopped. "*You're* the one who needs to be careful," she told Rose, "and...I love you, too, nerd."

It was her usual, playful remark, but there was no humor in her voice now. Only fear.

Rose ended the call and snatched her silver dagger from the bed.

She ran down the stairs, nearly tripping over a few as she did. By the time she reached Geoffrey, the phone dinged with Audrey's text.

She pulled the hood of her hoodie over her drenched hair and opened the message, studying the picture.

Geoffrey glanced up from the microscope, and his brows furrowed, as he noticed the dagger in her hand.

Noticing his frown, Rose explained, "We need to go. Now."

"What?" Geoffrey sputtered, tearing his gaze from the dagger.

"We need to go. Kallias is hurt," Rose insisted. "Possibly even dying."

His frown deepened. "He hasn't given you his blood, has he?"

"What?" Rose said. "No, of course not."

"Then you aren't bound to him," Geoffrey said.

She shifted impatiently, her sneakers squeaking against the floor. "What? Why does that matter? Didn't you hear me? Kallias is in trouble!"

"A blood bond, like the one between Emma and me, would allow you to sense that he's in danger," he explained. "But you're not bound to him. So, how could you know?"

Rose sighed, "I have a friend who has dreams that predict the future. She called me. She saw Kallias in her dream, and he was hurt. He needs our help."

His eyes widened. "You know someone with precognitive abilities?"

"How is that important right now?" Rose complained. "Kallias needs us!"

His brows furrowed with concern, and he drummed his fingers

against his legs. "That can't be right. The odds of that happening are astronomical."

Rose impatiently jerked at the strings of her hoodie, tightening the hood around her face, as she tried to calm herself. Remaining idle in this sort of panic was unbearable. "What are you talking about?"

"Your friend," Geoffrey explained with a worried frown. "Psychic abilities are rare, and most humans that have them never tap into them. How is it possible that both you and your friend have psychic abilities? It just seems unlikely. Are you sure this person is your friend?"

"Yeah," Rose said harshly. "She is my best friend *and* my roommate."

"I'm just saying that it seems awfully convenient," Geoffrey tried to explain, "almost as if someone placed you two together for some reason. And if that's the case, then I doubt they did it for a *good* reason."

"That's the craziest thing I've ever heard," Rose scoffed.

"No, the craziest thing is *you*. Everything about you is insane: your blood, your ability, your power, even the people around you," Geoffrey argued. He stood and walked toward her, his black eyes flashing with suspicion. "I'm only saying: I think you should be wary—because it sounds like something bigger is at work here. Theron may not be your biggest enemy. It might be someone close to you."

"Wonderful," Rose muttered. "Can we go now?"

"Are you not listening to me?" he asked. "I'm telling you that someone might be manipulating you right now. Like your friend, for instance."

"Audrey is my best friend," Rose said. "She'd never do that."

"Whatever she told you…it could be a trap," Geoffrey insisted.

"It's not," she snapped. "Kallias is hurt. We need to save him."

Geoffrey shook his head. "I'm supposed to protect you…*here*."

Her eyes narrowed. "Your friend is hurt. He needs you."

"Rose, I think you're forgetting that you're just a human," he said. "You can't save him. And neither can I, for that matter. If someone's strong enough to take down Kallias, they're strong enough to take down all of us. It makes no sense to leave here and possibly walk into a trap—just so we can die, too."

"He is your friend," she snarled, "and you think we should let him die?"

"*If* he's dying," he corrected. "We don't know he is. And I'm only saying that it makes no sense to put ourselves in danger, when it'll do no good, anyway. All we'll accomplish is dying with him. Surely you realize that."

"I don't care," she stated, defiance flashing in her eyes. "I can't just stay here while he's dying. I'm going to save him, regardless of the cost."

"I'm sorry, but I promised to keep you safe," Geoffrey said, as if it were final.

"Fine. I'll go without you, then," Rose said, spinning on her heels.

Geoffrey blinked in shock. "What?!" he sputtered. He chased her into the foyer, balking as she started to turn the doorknob. "How will you even get there? Are you going to *walk*? Do you even know where he is?"

Rose opened the door, shivering as the cold wind rushed in. Rain pelted the ground outside, and thunder rumbled in the distance, but without light, she couldn't see anything.

"I can't let you leave, Rose," Geoffrey said. "I promised to protect you."

Rose noticed a flicker of light through the trees. She squinted, trying to see through the rainy darkness. Her lips lifted into a relieved smile when she saw the light again. *Headlights*, she realized.

The headlights winded between the trees, heading toward the house.

"Erik," she whispered, actually relieved to see him, for once.

Geoffrey sighed, "Bloody hell. He's even more irrational than you are."

The car hadn't even reached a complete stop yet before Rose darted out the door, scrambling down the wet steps in the darkness. She reached the car, just as it stopped, and opened the passenger door.

Erik switched on the interior light for her, as she slid into the passenger seat. "What are you doing? And what the hell is up with your emotions?"

"We need to go," Rose said breathlessly. "Kallias is in trouble."

He cringed, as if in pain. "Seriously, babe. Your emotions are torture."

"Listen to me! Kallias is hurt! Your best friend is hurt!" Rose snapped.

Erik looked at her again, frowning. "How do you know?"

"My friend has precognitive dreams," she said quickly. "She called me."

Erik glanced at the dashboard. "You have a friend with psychic abilities?"

"Yes," she said impatiently. "We have to find him before it's too late."

He nodded. "Have you tried calling him?"

Rose held up the phone. "He left his phone."

"Shit," he said. "Did your friend know where he was?"

"Underground. Block walls. Ring any bells?" she asked, as she opened the text.

"Sure. Too *many* bells. I need something more specific," Erik said.

Rose handed him the phone and tapped the screen. "What about this? She saw this graffiti on the wall. Have you ever seen this?"

His eyes widened, and he took the phone. "Yeah. Yeah. It's an old warehouse," he mumbled. "That entire street is a hotspot for vampires."

"So, you can take me there?" Rose asked.

Erik scowled at her. "I can take *me* there. You go inside."

"Absolutely not," Rose said. "I'm going with you."

"That area's usually crawling with vampires, and you want me to take you?" Erik scoffed in disbelief. "Even if Theron hadn't basically issued a nationwide Vampires'-Most-Wanted alert on you, any vampire would *still* jump at the chance to taste your blood."

"I don't care," Rose stated. "I'm going with you."

"Are you crazy?" Erik said incredulously. "This is basically suicide."

"Maybe," Ross said, "but I can't just stay here, knowing he might die."

Erik studied her, and then, his gaze darted toward her trembling fingers, which were wrapped tightly around the silver dagger. "Kallias would kill me if I put you in danger like that."

"Kallias might be dying!" Rose said, every word vibrating with fear. "That's the *only* thing that matters right now."

He reached out toward her. "Here. Let me calm you."

"No!" she snapped. "You don't understand! I have to go!"

Erik dropped his hand, and his green eyes softened with sympathy. "Explain it to me."

"Explain *what*?" Rose said desperately. "That I care about him? That I love him?"

Erik leaned back. "Buckle up."

Rose blinked. The hood of her hoodie blocked her peripheral view of him, so she had to turn in the seat to look at him. "What?"

"I'm not the safest driver," Erik admitted shamelessly. "Due to your...human-ness, you should probably buckle up."

"That's not what I meant," Rose said. "You're taking me?"

Erik shrugged. "I asked you to explain it, and you did."

Rose frowned suspiciously. "You're not going to tell me that I can't love him because he's a vampire or that I haven't known him long enough to love him or...*anything*?"

Erik laughed weakly at that. "Listen," he said, one hand on the steering wheel. "No one can tell you who you should or shouldn't love. Not even you. And as for time—time has nothing to do with it. Sometimes, you meet someone, and after days or weeks, you know them—because they're real with you. And sometimes, you know someone for a hundred years and still don't know what they're capable of. Love isn't bound by time—or anything else."

Despite the emotions surging through her, Rose still felt the twist of sympathy in her chest. "A hundred years? Is that how long you loved her?"

"I loved Alana longer than that, I think," Erik admitted, his jaw tight. "It just took me a century to realize I'd never really known her."

"I'm sorry," Rose said softly.

He just offered a pained smile in response. "Geoff's coming," he warned her. "He's going to lecture me about enabling your irrationality or some gibberish like that."

Rather than admit that Geoffrey had *already* said that 'gibberish,' Rose turned her attention to the seatbelt.

Geoffrey jerked open the driver's door and crouched down to look at Erik, his white shirt and black hair drenched with rain. "Have you lost your mind?" he snarled at Erik.

"*Losing* my mind would imply that I had one at some point," Erik said.

"This could be a trap," Geoffrey reminded him, "and even if it's not, it's still a suicide mission, and you know it."

Erik sighed, "I can't drive with my door open, Geoff."

"If—*if*—he's even injured," Geoffrey said, "you'll both die with him."

Erik turned toward Rose. "Are you prepared to die for him?"

"Yes," she said without hesitating.

Erik shrugged at Geoffrey. "There you go."

Geoffrey wiped the rain from his brow. "Neither one of you is thinking clearly."

"Gibberish," Erik muttered to Rose.

"Erik!" Geoffrey yelled, when Erik put the car in reverse.

Erik sighed and turned toward him. "What if it were Emma?"

Geoffrey straightened. "What?"

Erik lifted an eyebrow. "What if it were Emma? Would you stay here while one of us went to save her, or would you insist you go, too, so that, in the end, you'd know you did everything you could to save her?"

Geoffrey frowned, pain flashing in his dark eyes. "That's different."

"Not to *her*," Erik argued, jerking his thumb toward Rose.

Geoffrey's resolve faltered, and he glanced at Rose. "Fine."

Erik fastened his seatbelt. "You stay here and wait for Emma."

"And if Kallias shows up?" Geoffrey asked. "What, then?"

"Then, explain what happened, and have him call me," Erik said.

Geoffrey gave him a blank stare. "Before or after he kills me?"

Erik shrugged. "Just blame it all on me."

"Oh, believe me. I will," Geoffrey assured him.

Erik glanced at Rose. "Ready?"

"Yes," she said, staring straight ahead.

As soon as Geoffrey closed the door, Erik shifted the car into reverse and stomped on the gas pedal, spinning the car around so fast that gravel flew up around the car.

Then, he shifted gears and pushed the gas pedal again, sending the car flying down the winding driveway.

Rose grasped the dashboard to steady herself, since the seatbelt apparently wasn't made to withstand such maniacal driving. "Don't hit that tree!"

"Which one?" Erik asked with a playful grin.

"Not. Funny," she said, her eyes wide.

The ride felt significantly smoother, once they reached the paved road at the end of the driveway—even though Erik continued to drive the car faster than *any* car was meant to go. "You have to calm down. I can't think with your emotions like this."

Rose glanced at him. It was strange to think a statement like that would've made no sense to her a few days ago, but after everything that had happened in the past week, it now sounded completely normal. "As an empath, you should know the words *'calm down'* never help anything."

Erik snorted, "True."

Then, he took his hand off of the gearshift and placed it on her forearm. Rose sighed and relaxed in her seat, as waves of calmness swept through her, slowing her rapid pulse and lightening her mood.

Erik sighed in relief, as his emotions calmed, as well. "Better."

Rose narrowed her eyes at him, when he removed his hand, just in time to shift gears. "I don't need to be calm right now. I need to—"

"Freak out?" Erik scoffed. "What good will that do? Save your emotions for when you can actually use them. For now, stay calm. Distract yourself. Distract *me*. Talk."

Rose made the mistake of glancing at the speedometer. Her eyes widened in horror. "We're going to die before we even get there."

Erik frowned. "Maybe I should've specified that you talk about something other than my driving."

"Is reckless driving a vampire thing?" she complained.

Erik considered that. "Well, I suppose the immortality does give us a little more boldness. I've crashed many times in the last century, and it's never killed me."

Rose glared at him. "Reassuring."

"Geoff drives slow, though," Erik continued. "He likes to read those signs on the road."

"Yes, those are kind of important!" she squeaked.

He swerved onto an exit so quickly that it slung them sideways. "Besides, what's the point in having a car like this, if you're not going to drive fast?"

"There *is* no point in having a car like this," Rose informed him. "It's excessive."

"And fast," Erik added. "*And* it helps me pick up women."

Rose rolled her eyes. "Like you need help," she scoffed.

He grinned. "Was that a compliment, babe?"

"For *what*?" Rose sassed. "Your attractiveness isn't an accomplishment. It's just a benefit of being a vampire. And women only flock to you the way they do because of that pheromone...or whatever it is that vampires have."

"Pheromone?" he laughed. "I have no idea what you're saying half the time."

"If you picked up a book every now and then, you'd know," Rose said.

"Yeah?" Erik countered. "Well, I guess I don't have time to read because I'm too busy having sex. You know...that thing you know nothing about?"

Rose rolled her eyes. "I don't know why you feel the need to brag about objectifying women and treating them like conquests."

"You think I objectify women?" he said with a look of disbelief.

"You only want them for sex, right?" she pointed out.

"They only want *me* for sex!" Erik said defensively.

"Oh, come on," Rose scoffed. "You're a womanizer, and you know it."

"That's not fair," Erik whined. "I appreciate women. I appreciate women a lot. And often! I just happen to enjoy *expressing* my appreciation."

"Of course—because giving someone an orgasm is the only way to show them you appreciate them as a person," Rose said sarcastically.

"If you'd ever had one, you'd feel differently," Erik countered.

She rolled her eyes. "You're such a jerk."

"Sure," he said, smiling. "But I'm growing on you, aren't I?"

"Sometimes," Rose admitted. She stared out the window, watching the downpour of rain mold to it, like a second layer of glass. "Thank you for...understanding."

"I don't really have a choice," Erik said. "I feel what you feel."

"I'm so stupid," Rose muttered. "I knew better than to fall in love with someone who would never love me back. He's a vampire, for goodness sakes."

Erik's grip seemed to tighten around the steering wheel. "You don't know *anything* about loving someone who will never love you back."

Rose glanced at him curiously. "What do you mean?"

"*I* loved someone who could never love me back. I know unrequited love when I see it, and it doesn't apply in your case," Erik told her.

"Are you saying you think he loves me?" Rose asked. "I know for a fact that he doesn't. He gets angry when he thinks that's even being *suggested*."

"Of course he does," Erik said. "If he were to ever admit that he felt something for you, there would be no going back—no stopping what he started."

Her brows furrowed. "No stopping *what*?"

"The relationship. Love," Erik provided. "And ultimately...pain."

Rose seemed hurt. "He thinks I'll cheat on him...like Phoebe?"

"He told you about her?" Erik asked in shock. "He *never* talks about her."

"It wasn't exactly intentional," she said uncomfortably.

"He has strong feelings about lying," Erik admitted, "and a bit of blindness when it comes to admitting that he does it, too. But cheating isn't what I was referring to." He glanced her way. "It's something more definite that he fears."

"Death," Rose realized.

Erik nodded. "He watched the only person he ever loved die. She died in front of him, and there was nothing he could do to stop it. That's the only thing in the world that has ever broken him."

She swallowed uneasily. "He thinks I'm going to die?"

"You *will* die," Erik said. "Eventually. Because you're human, and humans die. Even if you survive tonight, even if you survive Theron and whatever other enemies you have out there...you will *still* die of something eventually."

"I'm twenty-three," she told him. "I won't die of old age for a long time."

"It's long to *you*," he scoffed. "To us, a few decades are nothing."

Rose sighed. "So, you think he's afraid? That doesn't sound like him."

"It's true. Nothing scares Kallias," he admitted, *"except* this."

Rose stared at him. "What makes you think he feels anything for me?"

"I don't think. I know," Erik corrected. "And I know for the same reason that I wasn't surprised when you told me you loved him. I feel what you feel, and I know how love feels." His jaw tightened. "I'm not saying you two have a happy life ahead of you. I'm just saying it's not unrequited."

A small part of Rose wanted to believe him, but she couldn't.

Kallias had made it clear that he felt nothing for her, and *that* made sense.

No one had a reason to feel something for *her*.

Rose peered out the passenger's side window, trying to make sense of their surroundings through the blurry downpour. "How much longer?"

"We're almost there," he assured her. "There's no traffic through here."

"Why not?" she asked curiously.

"No reason for it. Most of these buildings are condemned or abandoned," he explained. "That's why so many vampires congregate here. There are plenty of places to hide during the day." He sighed, "One of us always checks this street. We have to clean out entire groups of vampires every few days."

"Was Kallias here tonight?" Rose asked.

"Yeah," Erik said. "He should've been fine. No one can hurt Kallias."

"Except for Theron," Rose corrected.

"Yeah. Except for Theron," he agreed. He looked at her and tilted his head toward the silver dagger. "Do you know how to use that?"

Rose followed his gaze toward the dagger. "I mean, it's not exactly a complicated weapon, is it? Just stick it in them when I get the chance, right?"

He broke into a wolfish grin. "That's usually the man's job," he said immaturely. He lifted an eyebrow and added, "Unless you like to use toys."

Rose rolled her eyes. "Do you really think this is a good time for dirty jokes?"

"It's the perfect time," he told her. "Laughter eases tension."

"Maybe," she admitted. She wrinkled her nose. "But still."

"But yes, if you're put in a position where you need to use it—which will probably happen tonight—just stab. Don't aim for the heart or head or anything because none of that's enough to kill a vampire, anyway," Erik advised. "Just stab. Don't think. Just stab."

"Don't think. Just stab," Rose repeated. "Got it."

"Your only goal is to slow them down long enough for me to kill them," Erik added. "Take any more time than *that*, and they've killed you already. Understand?"

She nodded. "Totally."

Erik parked the car. "Good. Because we're here."

THE SUICIDE MISSION

*D*ingy streams of rain-water flowed down the sidewalk, the drains unable to keep up with the steady downpour.

As Rose stepped out of the car, the icy water filled the holes of her Converse, soaking her socks. She shivered and pulled her hood higher over her head—even as the cold rain thoroughly drenched her thin, black hoodie and the clothes underneath.

Erik rounded the car and joined her on the sidewalk. Water dripped from his blonde hair, and the wet strands stuck to his forehead. But the cold rain didn't seem to bother him.

He'd even left his jacket in the car.

Along the street, large, abandoned buildings stretched before them, as far as Rose could see. Beneath a flickering, orange streetlight and behind a blurry downpour of rain, those dark buildings looked even more foreboding than usual.

Erik pointed toward the end of the street. "It's that old warehouse."

The flickering light didn't reach that far. So, no matter how hard Rose squinted through the rain, she saw only darkness.

"I'll take your word for it," she said with a shrug.

Erik led the way toward the building, water sloshing around their shoes with each step. After a few steps, he glanced back at her. "Are you all right?"

"I don't know," Rose said honestly. She could barely hear her own voice over the roar of water in the storm drains. "Ask me again when we find him."

Erik nodded sympathetically. "Stay close, all right?"

Rose shoved her hands into the front pocket of her hoodie and fell into step beside him. She wrapped her fingers around the sheathed silver dagger that she'd slipped into that pocket.

"So..." she began, as she tried to think of anything, *other* than the fact that someone she loved was possibly dying. "Emma fights vampires in dresses?" she said curiously. "And high heels?"

Erik laughed, "Yeah. She's quite good at it, too."

The sole of Rose's shoe hit a slick manhole cover, and she slipped.

Before she could hit the pavement, however, Erik grasped her elbow and jerked her upright.

"Well, you're off to a great start," Erik muttered.

"Funny," Rose said sarcastically. "There's too much water."

He glanced at her drenched Converse. "You should've worn boots."

"I have one pair of shoes, Erik," Rose informed him, "and as you can see, they're not boots."

Erik looked back down at them. "Not very sexy either, are they?"

Rose scowled at him for that remark.

He just laughed. "Just try to stay on the concrete."

"That'd be easier if I could *see* the concrete," Rose muttered.

After several steps, they turned the corner and walked through a narrow alley, which cut between two concrete buildings.

Plain, unpainted block, just as Audrey had said.

A dim light glowed at the end of the alley, and they walked toward it.

Suddenly, Erik's fingers closed around Rose's elbow, jerking her to a stop. His nostrils flared, as he seemed to inhale deeply.

Then, he growled a long string of words that Rose didn't even *remotely* recognize.

"What did *that* mean?" she asked. "Also, you're hurting my arm."

Erik glanced down at her elbow. "Oops," he said, before opening his hand and releasing her arm from his painfully tight grip.

"What language was that?" she asked curiously. "Old Norse?"

"Yeah," Erik said. With a small smile, he added, "I'd translate it for you, but it's too vulgar."

She frowned. "Vulgarity never stopped you before."

"Oh, no, I don't mean it's too vulgar for me to say. *Nothing's* too vulgar for me to say," he laughed. "I just meant that there are no words in the English language that are vulgar enough."

Her frown deepened. "There are plenty of vulgar words in the English language."

He grinned. "Not vulgar enough for a Viking."

Rose rolled her eyes. "You give your people a bad name."

"Thank you," Erik said, as if that had been a compliment.

Rose suppressed a laugh. "So, was there a reason for these vulgar words, or did you just reach your limit on how long you can go without saying something R-rated?"

His smile faded, and he glanced at her, wariness in his eyes. "Do you smell anything unusual?"

"I smell rain," she said with a shrug, "and wet concrete."

"Is that all?" he asked. "You don't smell anything…*terrible*?"

With a concerned frown, Rose inhaled carefully. It was hard to smell anything in a downpour like this one, but then, she *did* notice something beneath the scent of rain and wet concrete.

Something foreboding and unpleasant.

"What is that?" she asked.

"Rotting flesh," Erik told her. "Somewhere nearby, there are…*many* corpses."

The blood drained from Rose's face. "How many is *many*?"

"I don't know," Erik admitted, "but I *do* know what it means." He glanced at her, fear flashing in his bright green eyes. "This much death means…*a lot* of vampires. Geoff was right. This is suicide."

"I have to try," Rose insisted. "No matter the cost."

"I know," Erik assured her. Sympathy softened his gaze. "Don't worry. Kallias is all I have left. I'm right there with you."

A grateful smile curved at Rose's lips.

It was strange to hear a dangerous vampire admit something so vulnerable, but then, Erik was probably more comfortable with vulnerability than anyone she'd ever met.

A side effect of his empathic abilities, she assumed.

Erik pulled a handgun from his belt. "Are you ready?"

"I'm *always* ready for a suicide mission," she assured him. Under her breath, she added, "Or so says my therapist."

If Erik had heard that last remark, he apparently didn't understand it well enough to give it any thought.

As Rose followed him through the dark alley, she said, "A gun is your choice of weapon?"

He shrugged. "I'm all about speed."

"Yes, I remember your speedometer," Rose muttered.

He laughed at that. "What did you expect? Sword? Battle-axe?"

"Battle-axe would be appropriately Viking," Rose teased.

Erik snorted at the stereotype. "It also wouldn't be very subtle in present-day New York City."

Rose gave a disappointed sigh. "True."

He laughed again. "Kara had a battle axe. I think she stole it *after* becoming a vampire, though."

"Who?" Rose said.

Oh, right.

The ex-girlfriend's ex-girlfriend he wanted her to meet.

"I never used one," Erik said. "They're heavy, you know—not very practical for someone as small as I was."

"Yes," Rose said sarcastically, "I, too, categorize six-foot-whatever as small."

"Six feet, four inches," he provided. His lips curved into a flirty smile. "Would you like a part-by-part measurement, as well? I can tell you that, too."

"I'd rather gouge out my own eyeballs," Rose assured him.

Erik laughed. "I really *was* small—in a sense. I was tall, yeah, but too skinny."

"I wish I had that problem," Rose muttered under her breath.

Erik glanced at her. "You realize people *like* your boobs, right?"

She rolled her eyes. "I thought bullets couldn't kill vampires."

"They won't," Erik agreed, "but they will slow them down. All I need is time."

Rose nodded thoughtfully. Her dagger would serve the same purpose.

Before Rose had time to understand what was happening, Erik pushed her against the wall, beside a dumpster that hid her from the end of the alley. He slowly placed his forefinger against his lips, motioning for her to stay quiet.

He then took a step back and tilted his head, like an animal that had just heard an interesting noise.

He mouthed, *"Stay here,"* and then moved so quickly that he seemed to disappear. He stopped at the end of the alley and pressed his back to the wall.

"It was *one* human," complained a gruff voice. "I'll get you another."

"It's not even about her," the other vampire complained. "It's the principle of the matter. I earned her fair and square."

"What the hell are you talking about?" the first man scoffed. "She followed you because of your allure, and she came to me because of my allure. No one *earned* anything." He laughed. "We're vampires. We take what we want."

"It was disrespectful," the second vampire grumbled.

"Ugh. So whiney," the first one sneered. "You sound like a human."

The second guy was quiet for a moment. "Speaking of humans," he said warily, "do you...smell one?"

"A powerful one," the other vampire whispered.

It was now or never.

Erik turned and fired a few shots into the alley. At least two of the bullets hit their mark.

One of the vampires collapsed on the pavement, blood pouring from his wounds, and the other braced a hand against the wall—likely injured, as well.

Erik moved quickly, standing before them before they could realize he wasn't part of their group.

The standing vampire turned toward Erik, his brows knitted in confusion. "What—"

Erik slashed at him with a dagger, but the vampire caught his wrist. His eyes narrowed, and he stepped closer.

Erik kicked him backward, and the vampire landed flat on his back. With his dagger free for use again, Erik knelt, pressing his knee against the man to hold him down.

He then shoved the blade of his dagger through the vampire's neck, slicing off his head.

When Erik finished killing that vampire, he turned his attention to the one who was on the ground, but he was no longer there.

Erik cursed and rushed back to where he'd left Rose.

ROSE FELL BACK AGAINST THE BUILDING, STARTLED, WHEN THE DARK-HAIRED vampire seemed to appear out of thin air.

Supernatural speed and blurry, rain-obscured vision were *not* a good combination for a human.

"You," the vampire gasped, "smell *so* good."

Rose noticed the sticky, blood-soaked hair near the man's temple and wondered if he'd been shot in the head.

Maybe that was why he seemed so...*out of it.*

"Hungry," the vampire slurred. He snatched up the front of Rose's hoodie, jerking her closer. "Need to...feed."

Rose wrapped her fingers around the handle of the dagger in the front pocket of her hoodie, and when the vampire bared his fangs and went for her throat, she shoved the silver dagger into the other side of his head.

Two head wounds would definitely slow him down, right?

The vampire's eyes rolled back, and he stumbled backward.

But he never hit the ground.

Erik caught the vampire and beheaded him with one quick swipe of his dagger.

Rose turned her head, as sticky blood sprayed across her face.

The vampire's body fell to the ground in two pieces, the severed head hitting the concrete first. Erik pressed his boot against the side of the head to hold it still—and pulled the silver dagger free.

He held out the blood-soaked dagger, offering it to her.

Rose took it cautiously, and then, with a grimace, she attempted to shake a few of the fleshy bits off of it.

"You did good," Erik told her.

In a hollow tone, Rose muttered, "Thanks."

Erik frowned. "Are you all right?"

"Of course," Rose said. She wiped her hand across her face, attempting to wipe away the blood and water that had left her skin feeling sticky and dirty. "Totally fine."

Erik raised an eyebrow skeptically. "If you need to puke, hurry. They would've heard the gunshots."

"I said I'm fine," Rose repeated. "Wait. Who's *they*?"

"The vampires inside that building," Erik told her.

Rose glanced at the block wall behind her, as if she could see through the block. She couldn't, unfortunately. "How many?"

"A lot," Erik said with a sigh. "There are too many scents to discern, but I'd guess somewhere between ten and a hundred."

"That's a narrow window," Rose muttered.

Erik didn't react to her sarcasm. Instead, he lifted his own dagger to his mouth and licked the blood from the blade—as if that were a normal thing to do.

He groaned at the taste.

With a wide-eyed look, Rose pointed a finger at him. "Okay, I can handle the beheading, but *that's* just weird."

Erik's gaze shifted toward her neck, and he tilted his head to the side.

Rose instinctually covered her neck with her hand. "Erik?"

He blinked. "Oh," he said, looking up. "Don't worry. I'm just…hungry."

"Oh, yeah," Rose said sarcastically. As Erik began to drag the corpse to the end of the alley, she lowered her voice and adopted a fake accent to mimic his. "Don't worry. I'm just imagining killing you right now. No big deal."

He snorted in amusement, "My voice isn't that low."

Rose stepped in front of him and opened the lid to the dumpster—so Erik could throw the corpses inside.

"And you screwed up my accent," Erik added. "I'm Norse, not British."

"And I'm from Florida," Rose said playfully. "I can barely tell the difference."

He laughed freely at that.

In a more serious tone, Rose added, "Besides, no one alive—well, no *human*, anyway—knows exactly how Vikings sounded. So, you can't expect me to get that part right."

Erik wiped his bloodied hands on his pants and turned toward her. He said something in his own language—something that Rose didn't understand.

A melodic lilt lifted his voice—his accent much thicker than it had been when he spoke English.

Rose shrugged bewilderedly. "Was I supposed to understand that?"

"I said, '*This* is what we sounded like.'" Erik grinned and added, "I also said, 'Nice breasts.'"

She rolled her eyes. "I regret even asking."

"Well, they *would* be nice," he amended, opening the door to the building, "if you wore clothes that actually let us *see* them."

Rose narrowed her eyes at him. "There are no words for how much of a jerk you are."

"*Bacraut*," Erik said—speaking another word she didn't understand.

Rose followed, as he stepped closer to the building. "Don't we need to burn the bodies or something?"

"No time," Erik told her. "They're hidden well enough—for now."

When Erik started to step inside, Rose placed a hand on the door. "Why haven't they attacked us yet?" she whispered. "You said they would've heard the gunshots. So, where are they?"

"I don't know," Erik admitted, "but it's probably a bad sign."

Rose nodded. "Do you smell..." she trailed off. "Is Kallias inside?"

His face grew tight—painfully impassive. "Yes."

Rose glanced down, noticing the fist clenched at his side. "What are you not telling me?"

Erik blew out an uneasy sigh. "I don't want to scare—"

"Tell me," Rose interrupted.

"I smell his blood," Erik said reluctantly. "A *lot* of his blood."

Rose's pulse immediately spiked. Her hand fell to her side, and her stomach lurched with dread. "Oh."

Erik immediately released the door and placed his hands on her shoulders. Before Rose had time to react, a strange sense of calm was washing over her. "We *will* save him," he told her, "I promise."

Rose nodded quickly. "We have to."

Erik watched her for a moment, reluctant to let her go, but then, he nodded and stepped back. He motioned toward the door with a tilt of his head, and Rose led the way the inside.

Her stomach instantly turned, as the scent of death filled her lungs. Outside, in the downpour, the scent had been almost unnoticeable, but inside, it was nauseating.

The room was too dark. She could barely see inches in front of her face, much less what waited ahead. So, she slid her hand into her pocket and pulled out Kallias's phone.

"Rose," Erik warned, his voice behind her. "Don't look."

But Rose had already turned on the flashlight. She gasped and stepped back, nearly bumping into Erik.

Erik immediately curled a hand around her shoulder to calm her. "Look away."

She *did* try to look away, but the eyes were cruel when it came to truly horrific things. Rather than sparing her from the trauma of the situation, they zeroed in on it.

But, then again, Rose thought, maybe it was best to *see* the bad things —because you only felt empathy when you knew of them.

Erik stepped past her, his footsteps loud against the concrete. He made his way over to the pile of corpses, which were discarded like trash.

Rose watched as he moved them—her throat too tight to speak.

"They tied their hands," he realized. "There was no point in that."

Rose tried to force her feet to move forward, but she couldn't.

"This was—" Erik's voice lowered to a growl. "This was just to scare them, wasn't it?"

"Horrible," was the only word Rose managed to get out.

Erik turned to look at her, but he didn't seem to *see* her. Some of her emotions were mirrored on his face, but his eyes held anger, too—a quickly flashing, unstable anger. "They like to make their victims to feel fear?" he snarled under his breath. "I'll show them fear."

Rose watched him with a concerned frown. She didn't know where he'd gone emotionally, but he didn't to be in the present moment anymore. "Are you—are you all right?"

It was a ridiculous question. No one would be all right after seeing that. *Rose* certainly wasn't.

But she worried about him.

Something felt…wrong.

Erik didn't seem to hear her. He knelt and started to pull the rope from their tied hands—even though it did no good now.

A door creaked open, and Rose was the only one present enough to notice. She fumbled with the phone, nearly dropping it, before turning the flashlight in the direction of the sound.

A large, dark shadow stood in the dimly lit doorway.

The silhouette cringed and lifted an arm to shield his face. "Get that damn light out of my face, bitch."

"Oops," Rose said reflexively, but then, she added, "Why does everyone resort to that word?"

Erik spun around to look at the vampire. "Who are you?"

"Darius," he said easily, "and *you're* Erik Olafsson."

The vampire stepped forward, and a few of his features started to come into view. He wasn't as tall as Erik, but he was far more muscular.

"How do you know who I am?" Erik asked.

"Oh," the vampire said, a sneer in his voice, "everyone knows Erik Olafsson—the fearsome *lapdog* of Alana."

Erik's jaw tightened, but he didn't argue.

"You're always hiding behind someone, aren't you?" Darius taunted.

"First, Alana. Then, Kallias. And now, what?" He waved a hand toward Rose and laughed, "A human?"

Erik just shrugged. "I'm more afraid of her than I am of you."

But Rose only caught one part of that. "Kallias! You said Kallias!"

Darius let out a derisive laugh. "And they said you were smart."

Rose ignored the taunt. "Where is he?" she said in a panicked tone. "Where is Kallias?"

Darius tilted his head slightly. "Dead," he said with a sharp smile, "just like you."

Even if there had been enough light in the building for Rose to see, she still couldn't have seen such inhumanly fast movement.

Before she could process what he'd said, he was already behind her, jerking her back against him. He held her immobile, one arm wrapped around her arms and chest.

Rose cringed as she felt the prick of two razor-sharp fangs against her neck.

"Why do you smell so powerful?" the vampire asked.

Clearly, he'd recognized Erik, but he didn't know her.

Rose winced in anticipation of the bite, but she also bent her knee and tried to kick backward. He held her easily.

"Are you *her*?" Darius said worriedly. "The one Theron wants?"

Rose didn't answer, and Erik chose that moment to jerk the vampire away from her with so force that it caused her to fall face-first onto the concrete.

Erik shoved Darius to the ground and jumped on top of him to hold him still.

He tried to shove the dagger through the vampire's neck, but Darius overpowered him. He tossed Erik across the room, and with a pained grunt, Erik hit the wall.

Having dropped the phone—her only source of light—Rose grasped blindly across the floor, hoping her hand would connect with the silver dagger she'd dropped.

Before she could find it, Darius shoved her back down.

Rose gasped in pain, as her shoulders dug into the concrete. The vampire straddled her hips, and he wrapped his large hands around her throat.

Her head spun, and her lungs ached for oxygen.

Waves of tiredness swept over her.

"What scares you more?" the vampire mocked. "The possibility of me bearing down just a *little* harder and snapping your pretty little neck? Or the possibility of never breathing again?"

She could barely hear him anymore. Her muscles grew weightless, and her eyelids grew heavy.

Erik, moving slower now, pulled the vampire off of her and threw him in the opposite direction. He pointed his gun at the vampire, but before he could shoot it, the vampire was on his feet again.

Darius attacked Erik, shoving him backward. The gun hit the floor with a clang. Darius kicked Erik several times—once in the head, causing a thin, watery cascade of blood to pour from the side of his head.

Erik folded forward, grasping his blood-soaked head.

The vampire returned to Rose.

He jumped on top of Rose again, but she had her dagger this time. She shoved the silver blade into his chest.

He yelled in pain and grasped her throat again.

She knew her strength would fade without air.

So, as quickly as she could, she gripped the dagger's hilt and ripped it out of his chest. Moving beneath his large arms, she shoved it into his chest again—closer to the center, this time.

He nearly fell forward, his blood soaking her clothes, as well as her own.

Before she could attempt to retrieve her dagger, he released her wrists and pinned her hands to the concrete.

"You'll pay for that," the vampire growled.

Darius bared his fangs and went for her throat.

When he released one of her hands briefly—to grab her hair—Rose clasped it over her neck in a desperate attempt to protect the artery.

It worked.

Kind of.

His fangs sank deeply into the back of her hand, and a strange cracking noise preceded the immense pain that spread through her.

His teeth left her as suddenly as they'd impaled her, and the pain drew a scream from her lips.

She blinked at the still figure above her, as she realized why his fangs had left her hand.

Erik held the vampire by the hair, the blade of his dagger against the vampire's throat.

"Get off of her," Erik snarled.

The vampire climbed to his feet slowly, holding his hands out on either side of him.

Erik reached around and jerked the silver dagger out of the vampire's chest, tossing it onto the floor, beside Rose.

The vampire stumbled, as blood began to pour from the second wound.

"Kneel," Erik demanded.

"What?" Darius said weakly. "If you're going to kill me, just do it."

"How and when I kill you is my decision, not yours," Erik snarled. He sliced into the vampire's neck—deeply enough to draw blood but not enough to sever his head from his body. "On the ground. Now."

Darius crumbled to his knees, whimpering in pain.

The scent of blood only seemed to intensify the emotions raging in Erik's eyes. He circled the vampire, careful to keep the blade against his neck, as he moved to stand in front of him.

Rose clutched her bleeding hand to her chest and pulled herself to her knees. She watched Erik warily, unsure of what he meant to do.

They needed to get to Kallias, but Erik seemed to have forgotten that.

"You like scaring people?" Erik asked.

Darius looked up, his eyes wide, as if he *knew* what Erik meant to do. "Please, don't."

Rage darkened Erik's green eyes. "I'm sure those humans begged, too, but you didn't listen."

"It's not like I killed them by myself," Darius gasped. "Please!"

Erik's stare turned cold. "I suppose I shouldn't listen, either."

With no further warning, Erik placed his hand on the vampire's shoulder and projected terror. He didn't hold back at all, and the force of the emotion caused Erik to fall to his knees, as well.

Erik then dropped the dagger and braced both hands on the vampire's face, as he continued to project fear.

Rose watched in horror. She'd never seen this side of Erik.

Darius didn't fight—because he could no longer even *think* about fighting. His eyes widened, and his skin seemed to take on a grey tint—ashen, deathly. He trembled violently.

He opened his mouth and screamed the most blood-curdling scream Rose had ever heard—so full of fear and desperation that it made her chest ache.

The vampire fell forward and clutched his chest, as if he were in pain.

"Didn't you know?" Erik said. "Vampires can have heart attacks, too."

For the first time, Rose found herself scared of *Erik*.

She'd accepted the violence and killing because there hadn't been any way around it, but this was too much—too painful.

She pulled herself to her feet and forced her feet to move forward, taking hesitant steps toward Erik.

"Erik?" she called out, trying to speak over the vampire's screams.

Erik didn't even notice. He just continued to torture Darius.

"Erik," she said nervously, "I think you've made your point."

He still didn't hear her.

He was too absorbed in the emotions.

Something touched Rose's shoe, and she looked down at the concrete floor. She noticed the black handgun at her feet.

Erik's gun.

Rose knelt to pick it up.

She was right-handed, but Rose's right hand wouldn't respond with anything but pain, at the moment. So, she closed her left hand around it, instead.

She moved closer to the murderous vampire, who now lay in the floor, sobbing, as Erik tortured him mercilessly.

Darius looked up at her, and she thought she saw a hint of relief flash in his eyes, as pressed the gun to the side of his head.

She looked away before she pulled the trigger.

When she looked back at the vampire, he lay on the floor, unconscious, with blood pooling beneath his head.

Rose turned toward Erik hesitantly, not sure what to expect. She'd expected to see that dark, deadly fury still in those green eyes of his.

But instead, his eyes looked blank.

Erik stared at her for a few moments, blinking slowly, as if he were in shock.

"I'm sorry," Rose said softly, "but I had to put an end to that." She offered the gun to him. "I couldn't watch it."

Erik took the gun, sadness pulling at the corners of his eyes. "I scared you," he realized.

"A little, yeah," Rose confessed.

Erik leaned forward and flipped the vampire over.

"What are you doing?" she said, worried that he wasn't finished.

"You didn't kill him," Erik said. "He's only unconscious."

"Pieces of his *brain* are on the floor," she said skeptically.

"He can still heal, if I don't do this," Erik explained. He plunged his hand into the vampire's chest, ripping out his heart.

Blood and bits of flesh coated his arm as he clutched the heart, blood pouring from both it and the vampire's body. He dropped the heart on the floor beside the body and lowered his head.

"You can say it," he said without looking at her, "that I'm a monster."

Rose's gaze softened with sympathy. "Erik," she said with a sad laugh, "I don't think you're a monster."

He looked up, his brows furrowed.

"Do I think you might've gone too far?" Rose said honestly. "Yes."

He closed his eyes, as if he felt like crying.

"*But,*" Rose continued, "I also think your anger came from a good place. You felt compassion for those people, and there's nothing monstrous about compassion. My honest answer is that, yes, I do think that got out of hand. I think you forgot who you were for a moment. But that doesn't make you a monster."

He opened his eyes, staring up at her. "Why are you so kind?"

Rose shrugged bewilderedly. "It wasn't kindness. It was just…honesty."

Erik climbed to his feet and tilted his head slightly. Blood still soaked his blonde hair and stuck to the side of his face, but his gaze was light and alert. "Thank you," he said with a surprising amount of emotion. "I consider you a friend, Rose."

Rose sputtered in shock. "Uh, what?"

"I hope you know I take friendship very seriously," he added.

Rose had *no* idea how to respond to that. "Umm, okay?" she said, her frown deepening. "Or…thank you?"

Erik glanced down at the bleeding hand she held to her chest. "Let me look at it."

Rose could barely move it on its own, so she cradled the wounded hand in her left hand, before extending it to him.

"Lot of blood," Erik muttered.

"Yeah," Rose said, as she tried not to wince at the pain.

The phone lay on the floor a few feet away, offering enough light for Rose to see the dark red blood on her skin but not much else.

Erik took the injured hand in his own and turned her wrist. "I have to heal this," he told her. "I can't focus with the scent of your blood in the air."

Rose frowned worriedly at that. "Heal it…how?"

Erik lifted her hand closer to his face, watching the blood slide along her skin. "His fangs went in deep, Rose. I think I see the bone."

"Okay, just keep that to yourself, please," Rose said, her eyes wide.

"Can you squeeze it?" Erik asked curiously.

"No," Rose said, "and stop looking at my hand like you want to eat it."

Erik snorted at that. "It does look very appetizing."

"Okay, that's it," Rose said. "Give me my hand back." But when she tried to pull it back, she nearly collapsed in pain.

Erik closed his hand around hers, making the pain only that much worse. "Does this hurt?"

"Oww. Freaking oww," Rose complained. She squeezed her eyes shut, holding back actual tears. "Yes, it freaking hurts."

"It's broken," Erik informed her.

"Huh," Rose said weakly. "I'm shocked, really."

Erik smiled at her sarcasm. "You'll need vampire blood to heal that."

Rose's eyes widened. "Uhh, that's not happening."

"Relax," Erik laughed. "I don't want to feed you my blood either."

"Good," Rose said, her brows high. "Don't."

"So, we'll let the bone heal later—when we've found Kallias," Erik told her.

Rose hoped he meant an ER visit, though she doubted it.

"But for now," Erik told her, "I need to stop the bleeding, at least."

Rose shook her head quickly. "Please, tell me you're not going to—Oh, for goodness sakes."

Erik lifted her hand to his mouth before she even finished the question, and to her horror, he, indeed, licked the wound.

Erik groaned involuntarily at the taste of power, coursing through her bloodstream. It tasted sweeter and better than any blood he'd ever tasted.

He tasted her power, felt it strengthening him after only one drop, and he wanted more.

He *needed* more.

The hunger that had plagued him for hundreds of years burned stronger than ever before. It took all of his strength to drop her hand and step back.

"Are you all right?" Rose said worriedly.

Erik licked his fangs. "You taste *so* good."

"Thank you," Rose muttered. "That makes this so much less awkward."

"I'm serious," he said, stepping toward her. "If I still killed humans, you'd be dead right now."

Rose lifted both eyebrows at his earnestness. "In your head, did that like...sound like a compliment?"

"Of course," Erik said easily.

Rose shook her head in disbelief.

Erik grabbed the silver dagger—which now looked more crimson than silver—from the floor. Then, he picked up the phone, as well, and took both to Rose.

"Thanks," Rose said softly.

She tried to take the phone in her injured hand—to keep her left hand free for the dagger—but she still could barely move it.

So, she had no choice but to try to hold both in her left hand.

Erik watched curiously. "Do you need help?"

"No," Rose said stubbornly. She looked up at him. "We should find Kallias quickly. I didn't like the way that vampire talked."

"Yeah," Erik agreed. "We're close. He's further into the building."

Rose cast one last glance at the pile of corpses in the corner of the room, and her heart broke all over again. "You can't save everyone," she mumbled to herself, repeating the words Kallias had said to her several days before. "This is what he meant. Sometimes you're too late."

Erik watched her with a sympathetic frown. "We feel too much—people like you and me," he told Rose. "It's a curse."

"You and me?" Rose repeated. "You'd group us together?"

"We're a lot alike," Erik said. "We both care too much."

Rose frowned. "I wouldn't have thought I had anything in common with you."

They were different in so many ways.

"But you do," Erik argued. "We feel too much, and we're always the ones who get hurt."

Rose's chest ached at the truthfulness of that statement.

He placed his hand on her shoulder and turned her away from the horrific sight. He gestured toward the door that opened into another room, further into the building. "Let's find Kallias."

She nodded and followed, as he led the way into the next room.

The next room seemed darker and colder than the previous room. Rose tried to hold the phone out in front of her, even though it was hard with so much in one hand.

Their own footsteps echoed loudly in the empty room.

"Where is everyone?" Rose whispered.

"I'm not sure," Erik said with a worried frown. "I think they're in the basement. But…it's strange." He paused, his frown deepening. "Kallias smells…closer than the other vampires."

When they reached the other side of the room, Erik nudged the door open. It seemed to open into a narrow hallway, but once they stepped into it, Rose realized that they were actually in a stairwell.

Erik led the way down the stairs, which led into a basement. He grew more nervous and fidgety, as they descended the stairs.

By the time they reached the last step, stopping in front of a large, steel door, he looked as if he were going to be sick.

Rose grabbed his arm to stop him. "What's wrong?"

He turned toward her, his brows knitted with worry. "You'll see."

She frowned, puzzled by his reluctance to answer.

He opened the door into a warmer room, and Rose turned off the flashlight when she realized the room was illuminated by a fireplace in the corner.

This room seemed *far* more lived-in than the other rooms—with stray chairs, clothes, and bags lying around, and weapons tossed in the floor. She followed Erik into the basement.

Rose knew something was wrong the moment she saw the puddle of blood on the floor. Her gaze followed the trail of blood, which led from the door of the basement to the other end of the room.

She gasped.

Without thinking, she ran toward him. "Kallias!" she cried, falling to her knees in front of his injured body. "Kallias! Wake up! Please!"

Dark red blood coated nearly every inch of his skin.

His black shirt was torn in hundreds of places, where he'd been stabbed or cut, and several of those tears were directly over his heart.

Two chains held him against the wall, each one linked around his arms. His brown hair fell over his face, and his normally golden skin looked ashen with a frighteningly bluish tint.

Rose tried to pull the chains free. "We're here! Everything will be okay."

"Rose," Erik said softly.

Rose continued to jerk at the chains. "Erik, help me with these."

"Rose," he said again.

"Please," Rose said, gasping when the chains didn't budge.

"Rose," Erik said—a final time. When she looked at him, he said, "Kallias could've broken those chains, if he were conscious."

"But," Rose said breathlessly, "he's not conscious."

Erik ran his hand through his blonde hair. "But at some point, he was."

Rose felt dread sinking in her stomach. "What are you saying?"

"I'm saying," Erik sighed, "someone was here to stop him from breaking free." He gestured toward the empty room. "So, where are they now?"

"You're saying someone's still here," she realized.

Erik glanced around the room, as if he expected to see someone suddenly appear. "I'm saying," he said slowly, "we're surrounded."

With her pulse spiking, Rose turned back toward Kallias. She placed her uninjured hand on his face. "Wake up, Kallias," she pleaded. "We need to go. Please, wake up."

Erik scowled, as she touched his face. "You know, you *really* shouldn't hold your wrists that close to an—" He winced, when Kallias turned his face and sank his fangs into her wrist. "—an unconscious vampire."

Rose watched, frozen in shock, as Kallias mercilessly sucked blood from the arteries in her wrist—even though he still looked…unconscious.

The endorphins began to take effect, and Rose's breath grew shallow.

A strange heat burned through her entire body, and euphoric sensations washed over her in hot, pleasant waves.

With these emotions overwhelming her, it never even crossed her mind to pull her wrist away from his mouth.

"Whoa," she mumbled, pleasantly disoriented.

Erik grabbed her uninjured arm and roughly pulled her from Kallias. He held her several steps away from the unconscious vampire.

Rose stared at the blood on Kallias's lips and face, as he fell forward again. She glanced down at her bleeding wrist and then back at his mouth, too disoriented to stitch her thoughts back together.

Erik glared pointedly at the powerful blood pouring from her wrist. "You're killing me tonight."

Rose didn't fully snap out of the strange, euphoric daze—until Erik licked her wrist to heal it. Again.

When he swallowed a mouthful of her blood, groaning at the taste, Rose turned to grimace at him.

"Accident," Erik said, but he didn't look sorry.

A harsh, gurgling cough drew her attention back to Kallias. He leaned his head back against the wall and coughed again. Blood trickled from his mouth. He opened his eyes.

His brows furrowed, when he saw Rose. "Rose?!"

"He's awake!" Rose said to Erik. She tried to run toward Kallias, gasping to him now, "You're awake."

Rose didn't even make it two steps before Erik tightened his grip on her arm, jerking her backward.

"Didn't you learn your lesson?" Erik complained at her.

Kallias stared at Rose as if she were a hallucination, but when he licked the blood from his lips, his eyes widened. "Did I bite you?"

"A little," Rose admitted.

He looked at Erik, his eyes narrowing. "What the hell were you thinking?"

"It's not like I fed her to you," Erik grumbled. "*She's* the one who put her hands in your face. I don't know what she expected to happen."

Rose scowled at Erik. "Right. Because I totally knew—without anyone telling me—that vampires can bite people while they're asleep."

"Not asleep," Erik corrected. "Unconscious. Specifically because of injuries. Our bodies run on instincts when we're unconscious—to keep us alive."

"Well, I didn't know that," Rose informed him.

"No, Erik," Kallias growled. "I mean, why the hell is she here?"

"To save *you*," Rose told him, "obviously."

He coughed. "You have no idea...what you've walked into." He gasped for breath. "You have to get out of here. Now."

Erik glanced toward the door. "Yeah, I think it's too late for that."

"Oh, it is *definitely* too late," Theron agreed.

THE AWAKENING

Cold dread unfurled throughout Rose's body, when she heard that familiar voice—the one that dripped with cruel, sadistic amusement and instantly turned her stomach.

She turned, and even though she knew who she'd find, she still paled at the sight of him.

Theron approached slowly, while rolling up the sleeves of his white, button-down shirt.

Rose looked him up and down warily, her eyes widening at the dark red blotches of blood, splattered over his white shirt. She turned her attention back toward Kallias, noticing his many bleeding wounds, and she realized *exactly* what had happened to him.

A wave of scorching anger washed over her.

When she turned her glare on Theron, she found him standing directly in front of her.

Several vampires stood along the wall, behind Theron, confirming Erik's suspicion.

They were indeed…surrounded.

The deep sense of dread in Rose's stomach sunk lower.

"Rose," Theron sneered. He leaned toward her to sniff her neck, and she recoiled at his closeness. "It's so nice to see you again."

She tried to suppress the disgust that took hold of her entire body—because she knew he'd interpret every cringe and flinch as victory.

And she refused to give him the satisfaction.

Feigning a calm she didn't feel, Rose said, "Highly unpleasant would be the accurate descriptor, but hey, you were close." She patted his blood-stained sleeve. "A for effort."

Theron narrowed his eyes at her sarcasm. His gaze flicked toward her hand, and before she could pull back, he snatched up her wrist and twisted it.

The cry of pain spilled from her lips before she could stop it, and she nearly collapsed.

The satisfied smile that curled at Theron's lips hurt worse than the physical pain.

Kallias pulled weakly at the chains around his arms. "Stop!"

Theron leaned forward to hiss in Rose's ear, "I look forward to picking up where we left off." His dark gaze raked her body with cold interest that felt like slime on her skin. "I'll be sure to make it *highly unpleasant.*"

That night replayed in her mind, and her stomach whirled with nausea.

Not much could've cut through Rose's panic in that moment—but the sudden gunshot that echoed through the room did.

Her wrist came free from Theron's grasp—just a moment before she heard the loud thud of his body against the floor.

Rose cast a stunned look at Theron's body, noting the bleeding hole in the center of his forehead. She looked up, lifting an eyebrow at the gun in Erik's hand.

Before she could react, she felt her arms snatched backward. One of the vampires restrained her, while two more restrained Erik.

Erik dropped his gun, but his smug smile didn't fade—even when the vampires yanked his arms backward. He seemed more entertained than concerned.

"You had to have known that wouldn't work," Kallias muttered.

Erik laughed, "Of course I did. Still felt good to shoot him in the head, though." He offered a playful smile to Kallias. "You're welcome for that, by the way."

Kallias rolled his eyes, but the action was slow and weak.

Rose heard the clink of metal, before she felt the handcuffs close around her wrists. She winced, as the vampire tightened them.

"You're not supposed to tighten them that much," Rose informed the vampire behind her. "Didn't you read the instructions?"

"Shut up," the vampire growled in her ear.

"Oh, sorry," Rose said with a wince. "I shouldn't have assumed you could read."

Erik laughed loudly, but the vampire behind her was *much* less amused—if the way he jerked roughly at her arms was any indication.

Rose noticed that no one had bothered to handcuff Erik, but then, she figured he would've just broken the handcuffs, if they had.

For a vampire, breaking metal was as easy as ripping paper.

Which begged the question: Why hadn't Kallias broken his chains?

She cast a worried glance at Kallias, her frown deepening, as she noticed the bluish tint of his skin.

Once the handcuffs were locked around her wrists, the vampire that had seized her joined the two who were restraining Erik.

He was the smallest of the three—a short, lanky man with sandy-brown hair—but size meant nothing for vampires. Their strength was supernatural, not physical.

Rose heard the click of heels behind her and turned to look at the approaching vampire. Her arms and wrists burned from the painfully awkward position they were held in, but her feet were still free to move.

She blinked in shock, as she caught sight of that impossibly beautiful woman again. The light of the fire was yellow and orange against her perfect, bronze complexion, and her raven hair shone in firelight.

Kallias had told her Sofia would survive, but it was still strange to see the woman in perfect condition again, as if Kallias *hadn't* run her over with a car.

Sofia knelt beside Theron's body.

"You shouldn't have done that, Erik," Sofia said with that seductive smile of hers. She lifted her hand to her mouth and sank her fangs into her own wrist. She then placed her wrist against Theron's open lips, letting her blood fill the unconscious vampire's mouth. "Theron will be angry when he wakes up now." She looked up, and her smile deepened. "You should ask your dying friend over there what Theron does when he's angry."

Rose's eyes widened, and panic surged in her veins. "Dying?"

But Erik's only response was, "How does this one know my name?"

Sofia chose to answer Rose's question, instead of Erik's. "Yes, sweetie. Dying," she said in a condescending tone. "Even vampires can't survive *everything*."

"Says the person who survived being run over by a car," Rose muttered.

Erik cocked his head to the side. "Do I know you?" he asked Sofia.

Sofia glanced his way. "You *have* known me," she said with a seductive smile. "Several times."

Erik nodded, as if he'd expected as much. "We've had sex."

Sofia's smile faded. "You really don't remember me?"

"Don't feel bad," Rose muttered. "Not remembering names seems to be his thing."

Erik tilted his head in acknowledgment. "She's not wrong."

Kallias told Erik, his voice weak and raspy, "León, Spain. 1669."

Erik shrugged. "That doesn't narrow it down much."

Rose lifted her eyebrows in disbelief.

Sofia, on the other hand, just rolled her eyes. "We were in a brothel."

Erik nodded. "You were a whore?"

Sofia sighed irritably. "No." She crossed her arms. "I was there to find food for my *boyfriend*. He was the one who liked whores."

Erik stared blatantly at her breasts. "Clearly."

Her brown eyes narrowed dangerously. "Excuse me?"

"Erik, can you be *less* of a pig for five seconds?" Rose complained.

Erik offered Sofia a proud grin. "She thinks I'm a slut, too."

Rose scowled at him, but his grin didn't waver.

"We also had sex in the carriage," Sofia reminded him, "and in my dead boyfriend's home. You don't remember *any* of that?"

Erik frowned. "Dead boyfriend?"

"Yes. You killed him to stop him from killing those humans," Sofia explained. "You spared me because...I was a victim, too."

Erik glanced at Theron's body and then back at her. "Clearly."

"He would've killed me, too, if I hadn't helped him." Sofia smiled and waved a hand at Kallias. "He never really believed me, but you did."

Erik's eyes widened. "Oh, I remember you!" he said, finally. He offered an approving smile. "You were...*skilled*."

Sofia smiled, too. "I still am."

"Which makes this *such* a tragedy," Erik added.

Sofia frowned. "What?"

"I hate killing women who are good in bed," Erik said with a shake of his head. "It just seems wrong."

"Even your *morals* are immoral," Rose complained.

Sofia offered him a puzzled smile—that was still, somehow, impossibly beautiful. "You think you'll have a chance to kill me?" She glanced at the vampires who restrained his arms. "How?"

Erik's lips curved into a slow smile. "Like this."

He shifted to grasp the arms of the vampires behind him.

They immediately fell to the floor, screaming in terror.

Sofia froze, staring at the other vampires in shock.

Erik ran toward her, and before she could react, he shoved his hand into her chest. She let out a strangled gasp—just before Erik ripped out her heart.

Her body fell to the the concrete floor, blood pooling around her.

Erik dropped the mangled heart onto her lifeless body, and the other vampires scrambled forward to restrain him again, jerking roughly at his arms.

This time, a vampire placed the tip of their knife against his throat—to ensure that he couldn't pull a stunt like that again.

Erik just smiled. "Two down. Only about...a hundred to go."

Rose stared down at the gory mess, stunned.

"Thank you, Erik Olafsson," Theron said, suddenly.

Rose turned to find Theron fully conscious and standing again.

He dusted himself off, the hole in his head healing as they watched.

"I hate blood bonds, but you took care of that for me."

Erik grimaced and amended, "A hundred and *one* to go."

Theron stepped over Sofia's blood-soaked corpse. "Keep the knife against his throat, idiots," he told the vampire who restrained Erik. "He's an empath. You can't expect to restrain him with brute strength alone."

"You must be really stupid, if Theron thinks you're an idiot," Rose said.

Theron moved too swiftly for Rose to see. She didn't even realize he'd moved until his hand closed around her throat. She tried to cringe away from his closeness, but he only squeezed harder when she did.

His breath smelled of something sweet and unfamiliar. "You must *really* want to die."

"It's on my bucket list," Rose said hoarsely.

Theron further tightened his grip around her throat. Her feet left the floor, and her lungs screamed for air. Her chest burned, as if her lungs were full of fire, instead of air, and her veins pulsed as if they'd explode at any moment.

The metal around her wrists grew heavier the longer she hung there, the position awkward and painful. She thought she heard someone yelling, but the longer she went without breathing, the duller the sounds grew. Her surroundings drifted farther and farther away.

"This is apparently the only way to shut you up," Theron growled.

"Let her go, or I swear you'll regret it," Kallias snarled.

Theron laughed, "I don't think I will."

Kallias jerked desperately at his chains, but he didn't have enough strength left to break them. "You can kill me, but I'll come back for you," he warned. "I'll come back as many times as it takes."

Theron smiled at the poor excuse for a threat. "Do you...*love* her?"

Kallias froze, a hint of fear flashing in his eyes. Even as his skin had paled from blood loss, even as he'd suffered fatal injuries, he'd never let the fear show, but it showed now.

"This has nothing to do with her," he said warily.

Erik glanced at Theron. He sensed Theron's pleased reaction to Kallias's response, and he knew Theron didn't believe Kallias.

Erik shifted in the vampires' hold, wincing, as the movement caused the knife to press harder against his skin. "You…wouldn't want to kill her *yet*, would you?" he said to Theron. "Her blood won't taste good once she's dead, and *someone* should at least get to taste her, before it all goes to waste."

Kallias looked up at Erik, but he'd clearly read Erik's thoughts—because he didn't question him.

Several vampires around them looked at each other—as if they wanted to be the *'someone'* who tasted it. Kallias's jaw tightened, but Erik hoped he'd suppress the anger and save his strength.

He'd need whatever he had left.

Theron hesitated, before glancing at Erik. "Why would you say that?" He loosened his grip slightly, but he didn't totally release Rose. Not yet. "You're here with Kallias."

Erik tried to shrug. "I was with Alana before him," he said. "Do you remember Alana?"

Theron gave him a strange look. "Everyone knows Alana."

'Knows?'

Perhaps he'd meant *'knows of.'* Theron hadn't spent as much time in America as Erik and Kallias had. Maybe he still spoke differently.

"I'm clearly not the most loyal companion," Erik added.

Theron frowned suspiciously at that, but he released Rose's neck, anyway. "You have a point," he sighed. "Can't waste the blood."

Rose folded forward slightly—though her body didn't allow her much mobility. She choked and gasped, her lungs sore and desperate.

Theron watched her unsympathetically. Then, he crouched in front of her and grasped her chin tightly. "Besides," he said with a cruel smile, "it's not my style to kill painlessly."

Rose squinted at his blurry form. "You call that…painlessly?"

Theron straightened. He turned to Erik. "I like you, Erik Olafsson."

Erik sighed at that. "All psychos do, apparently."

Theron scowled. "I *meant*…because you and I are alike."

Every trace of humor in Erik's face faded. "We're really not."

"We both have a taste for torture, do we not?" Theron pointed out.

Erik paled at the accusation. "I don't *enjoy* torturing people."

"I heard Darius's screams," Theron said. "It was…*impressive*."

Erik's jaw tightened, and pain burned in his bright green eyes. He'd managed to not let Theron or anyone else affect him until now, but it was clear that he was losing control of his emotions.

Rose could feel the emotions changing the environment around him, like a heat wave. Another wave of protectiveness rose inside her. "What is wrong with you?" she snapped at Theron. "Why do you enjoy making other people miserable?"

Theron returned to her. "There's nothing wrong with me," he laughed. He touched the bruise he'd left on her neck, and she recoiled. "As a matter of fact, I'm quite pleased with the way tonight turned out. I like patterns. History always repeats itself."

Rose's knees wobbled weakly, but she didn't let herself fall. She was afraid she'd never get back up, if she did. She took slow breaths, trying to recover the oxygen she'd lost.

Kallias grunted, as if he were in pain, and then, the metal chains broke. He hit the floor with a loud thump, and he coughed up a splash of blood onto the concrete floor.

His skin looked ashen with a bluish tint, like the skin of a corpse.

Theron turned and slowly approached Kallias.

Rose pulled desperately at her hands, trying to twist them out of the handcuffs, even as they cut into her skin.

Kallias tried to lift himself onto his arms, but Theron placed the bottom of his shoe on Kallias's back, pushing him back down.

Kallias choked again on his own blood.

And then, Theron pressed harder, bones cracking beneath his foot.

"No!" Rose cried. She instantly forgot her own helplessness and stumbled forward to help, but another vampire grabbed her shoulder and jerked her backward. "Stop hurting him!" she pleaded.

"You wanted to know if I *enjoy* making people miserable," Theron reminded Rose, "but it's not that—not just that, anyway."

As Kallias groaned in pain, Rose continued to beg, "Please, stop hurting him. Just...stop."

But Theron ignored her. "It's the control that's so exhilarating." He removed his shoe from Kallias's back and turned to face Rose. "Immortality can be so boring and meticulous. I have to pass the time somehow."

Rose stared at him, horror and disgust coursing through her.

"No one's unbreakable," Theron told her, "and when I break someone, it's...intoxicating." His lips curved into a sickening smile. "It's the only time I *feel* anything."

Rose swallowed against the nausea rising in her stomach. "You're a textbook psychopath," she said. "There isn't a shred of sanity inside of you."

Theron narrowed his eyes. "I *hate* being interrupted."

Rather than point out that he'd stopped talking already, Rose said, "Makes sense—considering your obsession with control."

Theron walked back toward her. With a handful of red hair, he snatched her head backward. "It's people like you who really get to me," he growled. "You're so willful. You act like you can't be broken, but you can."

Rose glared at him, which only made him hurt her worse, but that was okay—because as long as he was here, hurting her, he *wasn't* hurting Kallias.

"I have to show you you're wrong." His eyes were wild and manic. "I have to prove that you can be broken." He leaned closer, and Rose wished she had the mobility to recoil. "Kallias thought he couldn't be broken either, but I showed him that he could."

Kallias tried to push himself up, coughing up more blood as he did.

"Kallias, you have to stop," Erik warned. "You'll die faster."

"Leave her alone," Kallias tried to say to Theron, but the words came out as gasps.

Theron didn't even hear him—not that he would've cared, if he had. "I thought it'd be fun to do a little recreation of what happened all those centuries ago—repeat each part of the torture—but it wasn't enough. I was missing the key ingredient—the one thing that actually *did* break him."

Rose tried to look at Kallias, but she couldn't move her head.

"Do you want to know what it was?" Theron asked. When Rose didn't immediately answer, he jerked her head back so far she feared her neck would snap. He knelt down, pressing his forehead to hers, as he snarled, "Ask me what it was."

With her entire body shaking from the pain, Rose couldn't do anything *but* gasp out, "What was it?"

"Killing the person he loved," Theron answered.

Theron let go of her hair so suddenly that she didn't have the time to regain her balance and fell to the floor.

Theron walked toward Kallias, who still lay in the floor. "I thought we wouldn't get to repeat that part," he laughed, "but then, you actually came here of your own volition. What are the chances?"

With her wrists handcuffed, the most Rose could manage to do was roll onto her shoulder. "The chances are high. He needed me. So, I'm here."

Kallias lifted his head a little to look at her.

"I thought he'd die before I got to repeat that crucial part," Theron said, glancing back at her, "and then, you showed up."

He grasped Kallias's shoulder and shoved him against the wall, pulling him into an upright position.

Blood stained the floor where Kallias had been.

"And I think he has just enough life left in him to see it," Theron said.

"You're replacing his wife with me?" Rose scoffed, as she finally managed to roll into a sitting position. "You actually think he loves me like he loved her?"

"She's right," Kallias said weakly. He avoided Rose's gaze. "I don't love her."

Rose looked away. She'd thought as much herself, but it still stung to hear it.

"She means nothing to me," Kallias continued. "There's no reason to kill her."

"You think I'm that stupid?" Theron scoffed.

Theron started to take a step toward Rose, but Kallias suddenly lurched toward him, throwing his body forward the best he could, and latched onto Theron's leg.

He twisted and rolled, just barely managing to knock Theron onto the floor.

Theron froze in surprise for only a moment. Then, he snatched his dagger from his belt and plunged the blade into Kallias's chest.

"No!" Rose screamed. Anger coursed through her, setting every nerve in her body aflame, boiling her blood. "Stop hurting him. Now."

Erik glanced at her, as he sensed her emotions. She didn't *feel* as much like Rose anymore. She felt more like a bundle of emotions, volatile and exposed.

Theron stood, glaring at her. "Or what?"

A flicker of red seemed to flash in Rose's eyes, and the dark energy around her seemed to pulsate. "Or I'll kill you."

Theron laughed at the warning. "You think you—a *human*—can kill me?"

Rose didn't react to his mocking tone, but that strange red light that had flashed in her eyes returned.

Erik had never seen anything like it—nor had he *felt* anything like it. "Rose?" he said warily.

Almost as if to call Rose's bluff, Theron jerked Kallias up by the shoulder and shoved the blade into his stomach again.

Nothing could've prepared them for what happened next.

Erik gasped—because the first thing he noticed was a shockwave of emotion that burst through the room like a bomb.

The energy unleashed a thunderous roar through the building, like a whirlwind, and as Erik closed his eyes and shielded his face, he realized that it *felt* like a whirlwind, as well.

He lowered his arm slowly, as he realized: the vampires weren't restraining him anymore.

Erik reluctantly opened his eyes to look at Rose.

Metal lay in tiny shards at her feet. The handcuffs had shattered as ifs they were nothing more than glass.

Her long, red hair whipped around her shoulders, as if blown by a strong wind. Power rippled around her body in a strange shape that was somehow…almost…*visible*?

Erik didn't even know how to interpret what he was seeing.

Nothing about Rose seemed human anymore.

By far, though, the most terrifying change in her appearance was her eyes.

Her eyes, which had been a bright, azure-blue, had transformed completely. A swirling red haze covered her eyes now, glowing and flickering, like fire.

Those inhuman, blood-red eyes sent a chill of terror down Erik's spine—an instinctual warning that Rose was dangerous, that…whatever she was, it was *worse* than a vampire.

"I told you not to hurt him."

The room shook with her words.

Erik glanced around the room, realizing that Rose had left no one but him standing. The other vampires were sprawled across the floor, as if held down by some invisible force.

She'd also cleared his path to Kallias.

Erik rushed to his side and fell to his knees beside him. "Kallias?" he said, grasping his friend's shoulder. "Are you conscious?"

Kallias tried to lift his head and then cringed in pain and dropped it. "Barely."

"Stop wasting your strength," Erik told him. "You'll die!"

"If I can't do it, you have to," Kallias said. "You have to stop her. She's using too much power."

Erik cast a wary glance at the person he'd originally thought was human, and he nearly gasped again at the sight of that terrifying, majestic haze in her eyes. "What is she?" he breathed. "I've never seen anything like that."

"She's Rose," Kallias said without hesitating. "That's all that matters."

Erik glanced at him and sighed, "I'll do what I can."

Kallias let his shoulders slump against the wall that Erik had propped him up against. "Thank you, Erik."

Erik nodded and climbed to his feet. He glanced from Rose to Theron, warily watching the scene before him.

Rose had flung Theron against the wall and pinned him there. He couldn't even move. His arms, legs, and body were all paralyzed.

Rose held him there with nothing more than her mind.

Theron's dark eyes were wide with shock. "What *are* you?"

Rose tilted her head, as if she were trying to make sense of that question, but there was something stopping her.

Some sort of barrier between her and the answer.

Erik took a hesitant step toward Rose. The intense emotions spiraling through her were unlike anything he'd ever felt—too dark, too powerful, too unfathomable.

"Rose?" he called. "I need to calm you."

Rose turned her strange, inhuman gaze toward him, and Erik nearly stumbled backward at the sight. The full intensity of her blood-red eyes was more than he'd anticipated.

"Stay back, Erik," she warned. "I don't want to be calmed."

"What happened to your *eyes*?" Theron asked.

Rose frowned again, as if she didn't understand the question. "My eyes?"

She didn't seem to know.

"Rose," Erik said, approaching her, "you're using too much power."

Her unnerving gaze shifted toward him again, and his feet left the ground in an instant. His back crashed into the wall behind him.

"I told you to stay away," Rose said.

"I'm not afraid of a human," Theron sneered, drawing her attention back to him, "or those weird eyes of yours. What are you going to do? Hold me here until you die?" There was a hint of anxiety in his eyes that contradicted his words.

"*Actually*," Rose began ominously. A dagger flew through the air, stopping just before it would've pierced straight through his face. It moved, hovering in the air, until the blade pressed against his throat. "I was thinking you'd die first."

Theron visibly paled. "You can't do this."

The red fire burned brighter in Rose's eyes. "Apparently, I can."

"Rose, don't," Kallias called out.

Her glowing, red gaze instantly shifted toward him.

"You have to stop, all right?" Kallias said. "You can't do this."

"He hurt you," Rose said, and the walls shook again.

"This will," Kallias stopped to gasp for breath, "kill you."

"But it'll save you," Rose stated, as if that were all that mattered.

Kallias narrowed his eyes at that, but when he tried to respond, he coughed up another mouthful of blood.

Erik tried to stand, but the invisible force pushed at him, still. "Rose, you'll have blood on your hands," he tried to warn her. "It won't matter if it's good blood or evil blood. It's still blood. It's still guilt. You'll have taken a life, and there's no going back after that."

The red fire in Rose's eyes slowed slightly at that. "If I don't do it, he'll have the chance to hurt someone else."

"Let us kill him," Erik pleaded. "We crossed that line a long time ago."

"You're killing yourself, Rose!" Kallias called again.

Rose turned her gaze back on Theron. "I don't care."

Erik glanced at Kallias, and seeing the desperation in his friend's face, he said the one thing he knew would stop her, "Kallias will die, if we don't go now."

Rose turned to Erik, and her eyes flickered back and forth between the human blue color and the inhuman red. "Now?"

"He doesn't have enough blood left to heal himself," Erik said honestly. "If you want to save him, we have to go now."

Rose's eyes faded back to blue, her decision made. "Get him out first."

"No!" Kallias snarled.

"Only if you're right behind us," Erik added—for Kallias's sake.

"I am," Rose promised. The dagger left Theron's throat and spiraled through the air, before landing in her hand. "I'll hold them long enough for you to get him out. Then, I'm coming, too."

Erik nodded. He moved swiftly and picked Kallias up, ignoring his protests.

He disappeared in a flash of movement.

Tiredness and pain pulled at Rose's mind, nearly rendering her unconscious, but she held them for as long as she could.

She took several steps backward—and then, as her power waned, she turned and began to run.

Her stomach lurched, and her head spun. But she ran up the stairs, still, stumbling as she did. She didn't hear anyone behind her yet, but she kept moving anyway.

As she caught sight of the hint of purple light beyond the door, she realized that they might've been afraid of the sunrise.

Or…more likely, they were afraid of *her*.

Rose collapsed on the pavement outside, rain pelting against her skin. She vomited a thick, red liquid that she realized was blood.

And more blood poured from her nose and ears.

"Shit," Erik gasped, stopping in front of her. "You're both dying on me!"

Rose wiped her mouth with the back of her hand, refusing to think about what he meant. She glanced up at him, squinting to make out his outline through the rain that stung like razor blades. "Where is Kallias?"

"Safe. For the moment," Erik assured her.

She folded forward, nearly passing out from the sheer relief.

Then, without warning, Erik lifted her into his arms, one arm beneath her legs and the other beneath her back, and he began to move.

He moved so fast that Rose saw nothing but a disorienting blur. So, Rose closed her eyes before the rapid movement could induce another bout of vomiting.

Rose then felt herself leave his arms, and as air rushed up around her body, she realized she was falling.

She hit the floor hard, her body sprawling on the floor. She groaned, the pain rattling through her bones.

Erik jumped down, landing on his feet beside her. "Sorry. I was in a hurry."

She blinked at the darkness. "So, you dropped me down a hole?"

"The sun was rising," Erik said defensively. "It could've been worse."

Rose pushed herself up onto her hands and knees. She fished the phone out of the pocket of her hoodie and glanced at the screen, noticing that, fortunately, a small amount of battery life remained.

She turned on the flashlight and shined it around the room, trying to figure out where they were. She noticed a long hallway in front of them —a corridor of white walls and white, dust-covered flooring.

She glanced up at Erik. "Where are we?"

"Another abandoned building," Erik told her. "Same street."

He offered a hand, and Rose took it reluctantly.

"Is that safe?" she asked.

Erik held her shoulders and lifted his eyebrows, when she nearly collapsed again. "Not for long," he said honestly. "We're safe today—because of the sun—but once it sets, we're as good as dead."

"Very encouraging," Rose said sarcastically.

He shrugged. "At least it's a comfortable place to sleep."

Rose frowned at the bare walls and floors—considering the dark, dusty basement that lacked furniture, food, electricity, and water. "I think you and I have different definitions of the word *comfortable*."

Erik nodded. "It does need a TV."

Rose blinked at him. A television was the *last* thing on her mind.

The low-battery warning flashed on the phone. "Where's Kallias?"

Erik raked his hand through his hair, ruffling the damp, blonde waves. "Yeah, about that..." he sighed. "We need to talk."

She narrowed her eyes. "Then, talk."

"He's alive," Erik said, before she could panic, "but...*barely*. He'll be dead before nightfall."

Rose's gaze hardened with determination. "Then, tell me how to save him."

Erik scratched nervously at his clean-shaven jaw. "He's not going to want you to."

"Just tell me," Rose insisted.

Erik nodded slowly. "We can heal from *almost* anything—with the exception of the obviously fatal injuries, like a missing head or heart," he explained. "The problem is...our ability to heal relies on our blood."

"And Kallias doesn't have enough blood left," Rose realized.

He watched her warily. "There *is* still one way to save him."

Rose nodded. "Tell me. Whatever it is, I'll do it."

Erik reached out and pushed the hood of her jacket aside. He pulled her hair to one side, exposing her neck. "Blood," he said. He drummed a finger against the pulsing artery. "He needs to feed."

She exhaled slowly. "Right," she said. "Then, take me to him."

He pulled back, his eyes wide. "That's it? You're fine with it?"

Rose lifted her eyebrows. "What part of *'I'd die for him'* did you not understand?"

Erik tilted his head. "Fair point," he admitted, "but good luck convincing *him*."

"What do you mean?" she asked. "You think he'll refuse?"

"He already did, when I suggested it," Erik admitted. "He doesn't want to hurt you."

"He's dying," Rose said, a dangerous edge in her voice. "He *will* feed from me, and that's all there is to it."

His lips twitched. "You scare the hell out of me sometimes. I like it."

Rose rolled her eyes at that. "Just take me to him."

Erik nodded and motioned for her to follow.

Rose tried to follow, but she staggered and nearly collapsed. She braced her hand against the wall to regain her balance.

Her head spun, and every muscle in her body grew heavy with fatigue. To make matters worse, the phone's battery chose that moment to die, plunging her into total darkness.

"You're going to need *his* blood, too," Erik realized. He moved to her side and grasped her arm, tugging her away from the wall. "Come on. I got you."

Erik led her the rest of the way, and she stumbled along beside him. She had no choice but to lean on him—in order to avoid collapsing.

Erik pushed open a door and then led her into another dark room.

Erik positioned her against a cold wall, and then, his hands left her, and his footsteps moved away.

"I told you not to bring her in here," Kallias said. His voice sounded weak—so raspy and quiet that it was barely audible in the silent room.

"Hey, I went back for her, even with the threat of the impending sunrise, because *you* insisted," Erik muttered. His voice seemed to move back and forth across the room, as he picked something up and then dropped it somewhere else. "I don't want to hear any complaints from you."

"Yes, thank you for that," Kallias grunted. "Now, get her out of here."

"No," Erik said, and then, he struck a match and tossed it into a dusty fireplace.

The spark of fire burned out as quickly as it started.

Rose heard shuffling, as Erik made a second attempt at starting a fire in the long-abandoned fireplace.

Kallias groaned in pain. "I mean it, Erik. I don't want her in here."

"Wow. Thanks," Rose muttered.

He was quiet for a moment, and even though she couldn't see him, she knew he was staring at her. "Rose, you need to stay away from me."

This time, the spark caught and quickly grew into a large, blazing fire.

Rose gasped the moment Kallias became visible in the flickering light of the fire. Blood stuck to his torn shirt, stained his jeans, and pooled around him. His skin, usually so tawny, looked papery white, and the pinkness of his lips faded, nearly matching the pale shade of his skin.

Just by looking at him, she could see that he was dying. His body couldn't reproduce the blood as quickly as he was losing it.

Despite her dizziness, she crossed the room and sank to her knees in front of him. "Kallias," she whispered and reached toward the wounds in his chest.

Kallias caught her wrist and held it tightly. His brown eyes darkened, as he stared at the veins in her wrist—blue beneath her fair skin.

His fingers dug into her skin, and his entire body—from his fingertips to his shoulders—seemed to tremble and convulse. "I can't...resist it."

Her brows twisted with sympathy. "Then, don't."

He glared at her. "Have you lost your mind?"

"You need it," Rose reminded him.

She tried to scoot closer, but Kallias stiffened and squeezed his eyes shut.

"Please, don't come any closer," he pleaded. "I can't control myself."

Rose hesitated, conflicted. She could see the pain in his features, and she didn't want to make it worse.

But...he *needed* her blood, and she refused to let him die.

Erik spun toward them. "She's right, Kallias. You need blood, and she's offering it to you. You should take her up on the offer."

Kallias finally managed to let go of her wrist. He glared at Erik. "We discussed this. I won't feed from her. I'd rather die than hurt her."

"Apparently," Erik muttered.

"You *will* hurt me," Rose offered, "if you die."

Kallias shook his head. "Rose, you *shouldn't* care. I'm just—"

"The person I love?" Rose finished for him.

He froze. "What?"

"Weren't you listening?" Rose said grumpily. "I *said* I love you."

"Rose," he said, his brown eyes wide. "You can't love me. I am a—"

"Vampire," Rose interjected, "and I'm a human. Yes, I'm aware. I know it's impossible. I know we'd never make it. And I know you don't love me back. But what I know doesn't change how I feel. So…I love you. Get over it."

"There were *way* more romantic ways to say that," Erik complained.

"Shut up, Erik," she muttered.

Erik laughed. He crouched down beside her—in front of Kallias. "Look, we've been friends for twelve hundred years, and neither one of us is easy to like. But somehow we've managed to stick together century after century. You're all I've got. So, if you think I'm just going to stand by and watch you die, you're an idiot." He shook his head and sighed, "Hell, I'd even give you *my* blood, if there were no way around it."

Kallias grimaced. "That's not happening."

"Right," Erik agreed. "It'd be weird for both of us. Luckily for us, there's another option." He looked pointedly at Rose.

Rose tilted her head slightly. "You're right," she told Erik. "Your declaration of love was way more romantic than mine."

Erik snorted and shoved her playfully—except his *playful* shove felt more like a real shove, and it knocked her flat on her face. "Shit. Sorry, Rose!"

"I've starved myself for twenty-five hundred years, and you want me to break that starvation with her?" Kallias snarled at Erik. "I could kill her."

"We both know you won't," Erik said. "I know hunger is supposed to be the strongest thing vampires feel, but we both know there are things stronger than that." When Kallias still tried to argue, Erik added, "Besides, she'll die without your blood, anyway."

Kallias glanced worriedly at Rose. "You used too much power?"

Rose offered an apologetic smile. "Oops?"

Erik stood. "I'm assuming the prude will want privacy…"

Rose glared at him.

"So, I'll find a place to sleep in the next room," Erik finished.

But on his way out of the room, he stopped in the doorway. "Oh, and one more thing," he said, spinning back toward them. "For Odin's sake, would you two quit fighting what you feel for each other? Who cares if the relationship is practical or if it'll last her entire lifetime? There's a good chance we'll all die tomorrow, and none of it will matter. What *does* matter is what you feel right now. I know I act without thinking ninety-nine percent of the time and that I occasionally make shitty choices. But if you ask me, it's better than what you two are doing. At least I *act*. So, for once, stop thinking, and just fucking act." He turned and left without another word, slamming the door behind him.

Kallias and Rose stared at the empty doorway, stunned by Erik's sudden, strangely emotional outburst.

Rose glanced at Kallias. "Was that his idea of a pep talk?"

Kallias shrugged. "He *did* get pretty emotional about it."

The door jerked open again, and Erik ducked his head through. "And Kallias, I swear…if you don't feed from her, I'll force-feed you *my* blood."

Kallias wrinkled his nose. "But—"

The door slammed shut again before he could finish his argument.

"Well, then," Rose said with an encouraging smile, "I guess it's settled."

Kallias scowled at her. "Don't ask me to hurt you."

"You're not hurting me," she argued. "You're letting me help you in the only way I can." She rested her hands on her thighs. "Didn't you once ask me to let *you* do the same?"

"I need too much blood," he explained. "I'll take too much."

Rose shrugged. "Well, it's a good thing you can heal me, then."

"That would bind you to me," Kallias reminded her.

Rose glanced down at the blood on his shirt and then leaned forward to unbutton it.

He winced, as her fingers brushed his skin. "What are you doing?"

"Sorry," Rose muttered, biting her lip, as she concentrated on not touching him. She gently pulled the shirt down his shoulders. "The shirt touches your wounds when you move. It must be painful."

He leaned forward so that she could finish removing his shirt.

Rose set the shirt aside and then looked at him, gasping as she saw how terrible his wounds really were. "What did he do to you?"

Kallias leaned back against the wall. "What he always does. Torture."

Her throat constricted with sympathy. "I wish I'd known sooner. I could've—oh, gosh."

"Hey," he said, wiping a thumb under her eye. "Don't cry."

She wiped her hands over her face, surprised to find wetness under her eyes. "It's bad enough that you went through this, and I couldn't prevent it. At least let me help *now*. You need my blood to survive."

Kallias sighed, emotions warring on his face. "But the blood bond—"

"I don't care about the blood bond!" Rose told him.

"You should!" he insisted. "It'll connect us for the rest of your life."

She shrugged. "What's wrong with that?"

"How can you ask that?" he said irritably. "It's intense and intimate. You'd feel what I feel, and I'd feel what you feel. You'd never be able to move on after me because we'd still be connected."

Rose rolled her eyes. "With *or* without the blood bond, I'll never be able to just *move on*. What part of *'I'm in love with you'* do you not understand?"

"Rose…" he sighed.

"I'm already connected to you—maybe not as literally as a blood bond, but still," she argued. "No matter what happens between us after this, you'll always be someone I've loved."

"I'm not good for you," Kallias insisted.

"Let me decide that," she demanded. She leaned forward onto her knees, closing the distance between them. "You don't see what I see. You just see your flaws, but *I* see more than that. I see the good you refuse to see. And isn't that what love is, really? Knowing and accepting someone's flaws and brokenness, choosing to love the good in them, and then, helping them love the good in them, too. You are far from perfect, as am I, but you're more than the monster you think you are."

Despite how weak and drained he felt, he reached out and placed his hand on her face because, at that moment, he *needed* to touch her. Her cheek felt warm against his clammy skin, even despite the cold rain water that still clung to her skin.

Her eyes fluttered closed, and she leaned into his touch.

He could hear her heart racing. "I just want what's best for you," he tried to explain.

She opened her eyes. "Then, don't ask me to watch you die."

He dropped his hand, suddenly seeing the connection between this and what had happened to him. She'd watch him die, just like he'd watched Phoebe die.

The only difference was *his* death could be prevented.

"I..." he trailed off.

"It'd hurt me," Rose said. "I can't watch you die."

Kallias stared at her. He knew he shouldn't do this. It'd change their lives forever. But at the same time, he couldn't ask her to endure the thing that had broken him.

He could feel himself dying, and if he didn't feed, he'd die right here, in front of her. His gaze darted down to her neck, and his mouth watered in anticipation.

"I kind of like the idea of being connected to you," she confessed. "I understand you don't love me, so you probably don't want to be connected to *me*. But..."

He placed his finger against her lips. "No. No, you *don't* understand."

"What?" she sputtered.

Kallias laughed, "For someone so brilliant, you can be so clueless sometimes."

"Well, aren't you sweet?" Rose said, frowning as his fingers moved downward. "I declare my love for you, and you... Hey, what are you doing?"

He finished unzipping her hoodie. "Taking off your jacket."

"Okay..." she said, drawing out the word.

He tossed the hoodie aside, and his hands returned to her, tugging up the hem of her blue T-shirt.

Rose stilled his hands, her eyes wide. "Okay, *now*, what are you doing?"

His lips twitched. "Taking off your shirt."

"Uhh, yeah, but...why?" she asked. "If this is your way of bargaining—"

"It's nothing like that," he said. Kallias gestured toward his chest, drawing her attention to all of the gashes and wounds. "I don't want to ruin your clothes."

Her eyes widened. "Kallias, what are you saying?"

Kallias wrapped his hand around her wrist and pulled her toward him. "I'm saying you're wrong. I *do* want to be connected to you." His light brown eyes burned with intensity. "And I do love you."

"You...love...me?" she stammered. "But...you said you didn't."

"I lied," Kallias said. "*Obviously*, I lied. Even *Theron* could see I was lying."

"But..." Rose trailed off. A slow smile tugged at the corners of her lips. "Could you like...say it again? Just so I know it really happened."

He laughed at that. "Come closer, and I will."

Rose crawled toward him, and he raked his hungry gaze down her body. She gasped as his fingers curled around her hips and pulled her closer—until she was practically on top of him.

He leaned forward and pressed his lips to her jaw, as he rolled her T-shirt upward.

Rose couldn't help but moan softly, as his fingers brushed her bare stomach and then her breasts.

He tugged the shirt over her head and tossed it aside. He pulled back to stare at her. She blushed—because not only was she not used to being looked at like this, but she'd also worn one of her simple, white cotton bras, which was probably unflattering against her pale skin.

He didn't seem to notice, though, as his gaze darkened with lust.

His fingers trailed along her stomach and hips, and he leaned forward to kiss her collarbone. Then, her shoulder. Then, her neck...

He sought out the pulsing artery with his mouth, and Rose gasped as he sucked gently at her skin.

His fingers entangled in her drenched hair, tugging her closer.

Kallias moved his lips to her ear and said, "*S'agapo, psychi mou.*"

Her breath caught at those words: *I love you, my soul.*

He'd said it again, and this time, it couldn't have been a mistake.

He tugged gently on her hair, tilting her head—to expose her neck.

Then, with no further warning, he sank his fangs into her skin.

She tensed at the brief pain as his fangs tore through the skin, but that pain soon subsided, replaced by intense waves of pleasure.

Kallias groaned, as her blood poured into his mouth.

The hunger took control, drawing out the animalistic side of him. He licked the blood, intoxicated by its sweet, powerful taste.

It tasted better than he'd ever imagined, and after two and a half millennia of hunger, he couldn't get enough.

He clutched her hair tightly with one hand, and the other hand tugged at her hip, holding her close, as he continued to feed.

Rose grasped his shoulders—one of the few uninjured parts of his body—as an intense euphoria wreaked havoc on her body.

The sensations caused by the blood sharing only seemed to intensify the longer he fed, overwhelming her with pleasure and desire.

Kallias pulled away. Blood dripped from his fangs and mouth. He stared at Rose for a moment, his gaze dark and intense. Then, he grasped her thighs and pushed her onto the dusty floor.

He climbed on top of her, nuzzling his face against her neck, inhaling her alluring scent.

"I love the way you *smell*," he told her. He licked the blood on her neck. "The way you *taste*." He lifted her legs and wrapped them around his hips.

Rose gasped as their bodies pressed together.

"The way you *feel*," he said.

The floor—not yet warmed by the fire—felt cold against Rose's back. She could feel his body pressing against hers, his weight pinning her to the floor. Every curve of her soft body molded against his.

And it was all too much and not enough, at the same time.

She tugged at his hair, urging him back to her neck, and he smiled against her skin, before sinking his fangs into her again.

Their bodies moved almost involuntarily, and the friction of his body against hers intensified the sensations caused by the blood sharing.

Soon, Rose was lost in those euphoric sensations again, blissfully unaware of her decreasing blood count.

Kallias reluctantly tore himself away from her neck, as he tried to regain control of his hunger. Blood dripped from his lips, and dark red drops landed on her skin. "You're letting me take too much."

She offered him this strange, goofy smile. "I feel fine. No, *awesome*! I feel awesome."

He snorted, "Yes, well, you're also high from the blood sharing. So, I don't think your judgement is the best right now." He licked the blood from his lips and tilted his head, listening to the slow pound of her heart. He sighed, as he realized it was already too weak. He lifted his wrist to his mouth and sank his fangs into his own wrist. Then, he held his hand out to her, his palm up with blood pooling on his wrist. "You have to drink this, Rose. You need it."

Her goofy smile faded, and she wrinkled her nose.

He laughed, "It's not that bad. It doesn't even taste like human blood."

"That's not necessarily encouraging," she slurred.

"You need it," he insisted. "It's too late to back out now."

Despite her disoriented state, Rose gave a somewhat steady nod and wrapped her hand around his wrist. She grimaced at the sight of the blood pouring from the holes, but she placed her mouth over them, anyway, gently licking and suckling the blood.

She realized he was right. Vampire blood tasted nothing like human blood. It didn't taste *good*, exactly, but it didn't taste metallic and salty, like human blood, either. She closed her eyes and forced herself to swallow the first mouthful of blood.

Kallias rolled off of her, curling against her side, as he fought the urge to bite her again. His hunger continued to gnaw at him, burning and clawing at his stomach and throat, but he'd taken too much already.

He watched her, mesmerized by the way her fair, freckled skin looked in the flickering light of the fire, aroused by the way her tongue caressed his wrist. He ran his hand through the wet strands of her hair, which shined bright orange each time the light fell upon it.

Her eyes opened, and her breath came in quick, sharp gasps. "Kallias?"

"It's the blood bond," he murmured, as he kissed her freckled shoulder. With a wicked smirk, he traced his finger along her pale stomach, chuckling as she squirmed and clenched her thighs together. "I did tell you it'd be intense."

"Yeah. Intense," she squeaked, unable to handle even the slightest touch.

He barely brushed his fingertip across the tops of her breasts, and she moaned. Smiling, he pushed her bra aside to reveal her soft, round breast. Her fingers dug into his arm as he took her breast into his hand, massaging it. She moaned and pressed herself into him, her breast overfilling his hand.

He trailed his hand downward and wrapped his fingers around her hip. She rolled toward him, and her fingers dug into his jeans, pulling him as close as possible.

Kallias froze when he noticed her eyes.

No longer blue, her eyes glowed red again. That swirling red haze that covered her eyes was unnerving and terrifying.

She frowned, as she noticed his sudden discomfort. "What's wrong?"

"Nothing," he lied, not wanting to worry her. He smiled and ran his hand through her hair, leaning forward to kiss her on the forehead. "It's nothing."

She grinned in that slightly intoxicated way again. "You have blood all over your face."

"Sorry," he laughed. "Not very romantic, is it?"

She wrinkled her nose, still smiling. "It's a little weird."

Kallias wrapped his arms around her waist and pulled her closer. "We should get some rest, anyway. We need to be ready for tomorrow."

Rose nodded, staring up at him with those glowing, red eyes. "Okay."

Kallias studied those inhuman eyes, wondering what the hell she was.

2 4

BLOOD BONDS

*R*ose awoke with a flushed face and a racing pulse. Her breath caught in her throat, and her stomach fluttered.

It wasn't fear that caused these reactions. Not this time.

It was Kallias.

His lips brushed her neck, parting to allow his tongue to trace the artery.

He was all around her, his front against her back, his arms around her stomach. It was the most intense sensation of her life because she could *feel* him.

Not in the physical sense.

That would've been normal.

Comprehendible.

This was not.

It was as if her nerves and her mind were all wrapped up in his. She couldn't tell the difference between what he felt and what she felt.

Everything—their bodies and emotions—were connected, and it made every sensation a thousand times more intense.

Rose opened her eyes and watched the light from the fire dance across the wall, flickering around the shadows of their intertwined bodies. The floor felt unforgivably hard and cold against her side.

Yet, her skin felt warm—overheated, even—as teased her with his lips and teeth. Had last night made her *like* the stab of fangs somehow?

Why did she crave it now?

"Kallias, *please*," she whispered.

He chuckled. "Please *what*?" he said in her ear. He sucked on the lobe of her ear, drawing a strangled gasp from her lips. His fingers traced her stomach. "Please stop? Please *don't* stop? What do you want?"

Rose groaned in frustration, "You *can* read my freaking mind, can't you?"

Kallias laughed loudly, apparently amused by her...*subtlety*.

Rose gasped, as he rolled her over in one swift movement, his body suddenly on top of hers. With his skin still stained with both his blood and hers, and his fangs gleaming in the glow of the fire, he looked less human than ever before, but Rose didn't care anymore.

She didn't fear him. She loved him.

All of him.

His hand curled around her neck, his thumb tracing her artery. He leaned down to kiss the sensitive skin between her ear and her neck.

It was clear that he was gravitating toward her neck—certainly more so than *before* the blood-sharing—but Rose found that she *wanted* that. Something in her longed for it to happen again.

When his fangs grazed her neck, she squirmed, her fingers curling into the waistband of his black jeans.

Kallias laughed again. "Patience, *agapi mou*."

Rose kept her eyes closed to avoid the embarrassment she'd feel, if she opened them, but she growled out, "It's... too... intense."

With a smug chuckle, he said, "I warned you it would be."

"Yes, yes. Great time for an *I-told-you-so*," she grumbled.

"Well, what is it time for, then?" Kallias teased. His sharp teeth nipped at her neck. "This?" He moved to kiss her bare collarbone. "Or this?"

As Rose struggled not to moan, Kallias tugged one cup of her bra downward, further exposing large curve of her of right breast.

He moved downward, as if he were going to kiss her there.

"Hey, you two," called a voice from the other side of the room.

Rose managed to separate herself from Kallias so quickly that even the two vampires in the room were impressed. She wrapped her arms around herself.

Kallias glared at his friend. "You're such an asshole."

Erik leaned against the doorframe, one eyebrow raised. "Usually."

Rose kept her arms tightly closed around herself. "Why are you in here?"

Erik cast a baffled look at her. "The better question is: Why are you wearing that bra?"

Rose looked down at her perfectly normal, white, cotton bra, and her face turned crimson at the realization that he could still see it. "My shirt, Kallias," she said in a panicked tone. "Where is my shirt?"

"You can't expect *me* to remember," Kallias complained. "I was dying."

"That's not an excuse," Rose hissed.

Erik pushed away from the door and walked into the room, the concrete loud beneath his boots. He knelt and snatched something off of the floor, before tossing it to Rose.

She caught it, frowning at the blue T-shirt in her hand.

"And another important question," Erik continued. "Why do you wear clothes like *that* when you have breasts like *those*?"

Rose turned toward Kallias. "Can I kill him?"

"No," Kallias said.

"I'm just saying that it wouldn't hurt to show them off a little," Erik said.

"Shut up, Erik." Kallias raked his fingers through his hair, exasperated. "Why are you even in here? You *knew* this was a bad time."

"Yes, and I'm sorry to interrupt," Erik said. At Kallias's skeptical look, he added, "Really, I am. It's one of my rules. *Never stand in the way of good sex.*"

"We didn't have sex!" Rose squeaked. "Why would you think we had sex?"

"But," Erik said, ignoring her objection, "the sun is setting, and if we're not gone by nightfall, Theron will kill us. So, I figured this *might* be more important."

Kallias nodded. "Right." He climbed to his feet and grabbed his own shirt from the floor—where it set next to a puddle of his own blood. He turned back toward Erik, as he slid his arms into the shredded button-down shirt. "Now, could you, *please*, leave the room before you give Rose a heart attack?"

Erik cast one last, amused look at Rose, before performing a melodramatic, sarcastic bow and heading into the hallway.

Kallias sighed—and then offered her a small smile. "I guess we'll have to continue that later."

Rose blushed profusely. "So, you're," she stammered, "feeling better?"

He laughed at the quick change of subject. He stepped into the light of the fire and opened his arms, allowing his still unbuttoned shirt to fall open over his bare chest. "You tell *me*. What do you think?"

Rose's eyes widened, as she realized that his wounds were...*gone*.

Blood stained his skin, still, but the wounds had fully healed, as if they'd never existed.

Only scars remained where the gruesome, fatal wounds had been.

"Wow," Rose breathed.

"That's what your blood did," he said with a smile. "You saved my life, Rose. I don't know how to thank you."

"It was," she said, blushing, "not so bad."

At that, he smirked. "I bet it wasn't."

Her cheeks grew hotter. "Shut up."

Kallias laughed and began to button his shirt. Rose wasn't sure why he even bothered. His skin and hair were still sticky with blood, and the shirt was so shredded that it barely covered anything anyway.

Kallias knelt to pick up the black hoodie, and he tossed it into Rose's lap. "Get dressed."

Rose blinked out of her daze and nodded quickly. "Right."

She quickly pulled the T-shirt over her head. When she pulled her arms through the sleeves of the hoodie, too, she glanced up and froze, as she met his intense, unblinking gaze. His dark, dilated eyes were focused on her.

"Uh, Kallias?" she said warily. "Are you all right?"

He ran his hand through his hair. "Sorry. It's the bond—it... Sorry."

She frowned, confused by his nervousness. "It's fine."

Kallias held out his hand to her. When she placed her hand in his, he jerked her to her feet. Her body collided with his, and he placed his hand on the curve of her back to steady her.

Her hands went to his arms, and her breath caught in her throat at their closeness.

Almost as if he couldn't help it, Kallias lowered his face to her neck and inhaled, his breath warm against her skin. He groaned when her scent sparked an intense wave of hunger.

And Rose...*felt* it. "Oh."

"Sorry," he murmured, but he didn't pull away. "You think the blood bond is intense for you, but it's worse for a vampire." He nuzzled closer into her neck. "And you smell *so* good."

Rose patted a hand awkwardly against his arm. "It's okay. I've accepted your weirdness."

At that, Kallias pulled back and scowled at her. "*My* weirdness?"

Rose zipped up her hoodie, smiling at his objection.

When they started toward the hall together, Kallias grumbled, "Have you met *you*?"

"Kallias, you drank my blood last night," Rose reminded him. "I think you win, just this once."

He snorted at that, and then, coming up behind her, he wrapped his arms around her stomach.

She gasped, as he pulled her back toward him.

"You don't have to remind me what I did," he teased. "I remember it *very* well."

Rose giggled at his playfulness. "You're in a good mood tonight."

Kallias kissed her neck again. "Hmmm, yes. Very good mood."

Erik stepped into Rose's line of sight. "Hurry, lovebirds. We have about thirty seconds to get to the car."

"Thirty seconds?!" Rose repeated.

"Yes," Erik said. "So, the sex can wait until we get home."

"Why does he always assume we're having sex?" Rose complained.

Rose's complaint ended in a squeak of surprise, as Kallias released her, only long enough to scoop her up into his arms.

He held her this time with his arm beneath her back and the other beneath her knees, cradling her bridal-style.

He laughed at her shocked expression. "We have to move quickly."

Rose poked his chest threateningly. "Then, you better not drop me."

He snorted, and then, so quietly she almost didn't hear him, he said, "Never."

EMMA LATCHED ONTO KALLIAS, AS SOON AS HE OPENED THE DOOR. "YOU'RE alive!" she cried, wrapping her small arms around his neck. "I'm so glad you're alive!"

Kallias patted her awkwardly on the back. "Thanks, Emma."

Emma extracted herself from Kallias and immediately latched onto Rose, nearly breaking Rose's ribs.

Again.

Then, she hurled herself at Erik who, more prepared for the attack, hugged her easily. "We were worried when you didn't come home last night!"

"We didn't have time to make it back before sunrise," Erik explained.

Geoffrey stood behind Emma, already fully dressed in his black pants, white button-down shirt, and tie. His dark eyes assessed the blood on Kallias's skin. "I assume this means Rose was right?"

Kallias glanced curiously at Rose. "About?"

Erik answered for him, "Rose knew you were injured, and she knew where to find you. We couldn't have saved you, if she hadn't."

"I tried to stop her," Geoffrey said, "but Erik let her go."

Erik scowled at him. "Thanks, Geoff."

Geoffrey held up his hands. "I told you…I'm *not* taking the blame for this."

"Thank you, Geoff," Kallias said. He shot an irritated glare toward Erik as he muttered, "I appreciate you not being a reckless idiot, unlike *some* people."

Erik shrugged. "Hey, you know what? I'm not even sorry for taking her because in case you've forgotten, the two of us would be dead, if it weren't for her."

Rose shifted uneasily at the reminder of what she'd done.

Geoffrey's dark eyes widened in alarm. "What?"

"Rose used her power to save our lives," Kallias explained.

"And she's a hell of a lot more powerful than we thought," Erik added.

Geoffrey seemed bothered by that. He cast a worried frown at Rose.

Kallias glanced at Rose. "So, how *did* you know I was hurt?"

Rose shoved her hand in her pocket, until her fingers found the phone. She pulled it out and handed it to him. "You left your phone, and Audrey called."

Kallias nodded. "Audrey. Of course. I should've known."

Geoffrey turned his scowl toward Kallias. "Wait, you knew about her friend? Didn't you think it was strange that her friend has a psychic ability, too?"

"Of course I did," Kallias agreed, "but I also saw inside Audrey's mind. She genuinely cares for Rose. I don't see any reason to be suspicious of her. Yet."

Rose smiled. "Exactly."

"She is a bit strange," Kallias added, "but so is Rose."

Her smile faded. "Less exactly."

They ignored that.

Geoffrey scratched his head nervously and then leaned toward Kallias. "I need to know exactly what happened last night," he said, too quietly for Rose to hear, "and you need to know something, too."

Rose squinted curiously at them.

"I could use a shower first," Kallias said, gesturing toward his torn, bloodied clothing. He nearly stepped past Geoffrey, but then, he froze. He turned to stare at Geoffrey, concentrating that intense stare on him. "On second thought, we'll talk now. Privately."

He'd clearly read Geoff's mind, and Rose's suspicion only grew stronger, when the two of them headed into the living room alone.

There was something Kallias wasn't telling her.

Again.

If Emma noticed that she'd been left out, as well, she didn't give any indication. Maybe because of her...*extreme* version of honesty, she was left out a lot.

Rose offered her a kind smile—one that Emma immediately returned.

She nearly jumped when she felt a hand grasp her arm. She glared at the hand that had startled her and then at the owner of it.

Erik cringed at the look. "Damn," he muttered, immediately dropping his hand. "I was just going to offer you some coffee."

Rose's irritation instantly faded, and she smiled brightly. "Well, you should've just said so."

Rose hurried to the kitchen, and whatever Kallias was hiding slipped to the back of her mind, far behind her need for caffeine.

Erik laughed and followed her. He grabbed a skillet from the cabinet. "I'll make something quick since it's late. You like grilled cheese?"

"Sure," Rose said, as she prepared the coffee. "I actually know how to make grilled cheese. It turns out a little black when I cook it, but I can make it."

Erik shot a puzzled look at her. "Black? As in...*burnt*?"

"I like to think of it as *well-done*," Rose said.

Erik laughed loudly. "You really *can't* cook, can you?"

"I have plenty of skills," she said defensively. "Cooking just isn't one of them."

Erik only laughed louder.

As Rose leaned forward to pour coffee grounds into the filter, she nearly jumped *again* when a slender shoulder brushed her upper arm. The sound of someone sniffing only increased her wariness.

Rose turned to find Emma squinting at her. "Emma?" she said slowly. "Did you just sniff me?"

Emma leaned in again, and the satin of her blue dress brushed Rose's hand. She clutched the arm of Rose's hoodie and leaned in to sniff the fabric. Then, she frowned and raised herself on her tippy-toes to sniff Rose's neck. *Then,* she grabbed a handful of Rose's hair and sniffed it, as well!

Rose lifted her hands in an effort to not touch the ridiculously pretty vampire as she continued her peculiar examination.

Erik watched from the counter, a spatula poised in his hand and a fascinated smile at his lips.

Rose shot him a questioning look, and he shrugged.

As a woman who was attracted to women, Rose had to draw the line when Emma leaned forward to sniff her breasts. "Emma?" she squeaked. When Emma didn't answer, Rose shot Erik a pleading look and mouthed, "Help."

He snorted and tossed the spatula aside. He crossed the room and wrapped his hand around Emma's arm, gently pulling her away from Rose. He looked far too amused by the strange situation. "Emma, you got to stop sniffing Rose."

Emma pulled her arm out of his grasp. "But she smells different."

Erik grabbed her and held her back, as she tried, once again, to sniff Rose. "Emma, most people wouldn't consider sniffing another woman's breasts, er, *appropriate*?" He grinned and added, "*Kissing* them, on the other hand—"

"Shut up, Erik," Rose grumbled.

"She smells different!" Emma insisted.

"Yes," Erik agreed. "Didn't you notice that Kallias does, too?"

Emma's hazel eyes lightened with recognition. "A blood bond?"

Erik finally let go of her arm. "Kallias wouldn't be alive otherwise."

Emma danced around in a circle. "Yay!" she squealed. Rose winced, as Emma patted her harshly on the shoulder. "I knew you two would have sex."

Erik raised an eyebrow at Emma's strange dance. "Do that again."

Rose rubbed her shoulder, wincing at the soreness. "Why does everyone assume we had sex? And even if we did, it wouldn't be anyone's business."

But no one was paying attention to her.

"I can't," Emma told Erik. "I have to get out of this room before you start cooking that disgusting human food."

Erik pouted at her. "But it smells fine when I cook it."

Emma grimaced. "Eww. No," she said and left the kitchen.

When Emma was gone, Rose asked Erik, "I smell different?"

Erik flipped the grilled cheese and glanced at her. "Sure. A little."

She frowned worriedly. "Is it a good different or a bad different?"

He grinned. "Don't worry, babe. Everyone still wants to eat you."

Rose rolled her eyes. "How the heck is that supposed to make me *not* worry?"

He tossed two more sandwiches into the skillet. "It's barely noticeable. It basically just warns other vampires that you're bound to someone."

Rose leaned against the counter. "And that...*protects* me?" she guessed.

"Ideally, yes," Erik said, waving his hand as he explained. "It's kind of a common courtesy among vampires not to...eh...*take* what belongs to another."

She narrowed her eyes at him. "I don't *belong* to anyone."

He winced. "Right. *I* know. I was explaining it the way *they* see it. Don't shoot the messenger. Look, most vampires view humans the way most humans view animals. To us, or...eh...*them*, humans are food. So, when a vampire decides to feed a human their blood, it's usually because that vampire became fond of that particular human, which kind of makes you a...pet."

Rose glared at him. "Did you just call me a *pet*?"

Erik stepped away from the skillet. He held both hands up in the air, including the spatula-wielding hand, as if she were pointing a gun at him. "Hey, it's what *they* think, not what *I* think. I swear to Loki."

She frowned. "You can't swear to Loki. He's the *trickster* god!"

He winced. "I was counting on you not knowing that."

Erik yelped as a saltshaker suddenly flew through the air and hit him in the head. He rubbed his head, scowling at the saltshaker as it shattered on the floor. "Oww," he whined. "That's not fair. You can't use your abilities on me."

"I don't know what you're talking about," Rose said with a playful smile. "I didn't even touch the saltshaker."

Erik laughed and then reached out toward her. "Turn-about is fair play."

Her eyes widened, and she quickly sidestepped him. "Truce! Truce!"

As Rose darted toward the other side of the room, placing the bar counter between them for safety, Erik burst into hysterical laughter. He laughed so loudly and so obnoxiously that he nearly fell over in the floor before he finally sobered and returned to the stove to try to save the food before it burned.

Rose cautiously eyed the coffee pot from the other side of the kitchen, not willing to risk the venture back to that side of the counter until the coffee was completely finished brewing. "So, they would spare me out of...*politeness*?"

"Not just that, no," he said, as he set the fourth pair of sandwiches on the plate. "Most vampires aren't willing to take that kind of risk."

She glanced longingly at her coffee, when it finished brewing. "What risk?"

Erik frowned, as if he were surprised she'd asked. "The risk that the vampire who's bound to that human will *kill* them, of course." He sighed at her puzzled expression. "The blood bond does more than just intensify the sexual feelings and hunger between you. It also intensifies the vampire's protective instincts and urges. A vampire who's bound to you will rip someone to shreds without a second thought, if that person even appears to threaten your safety or wellbeing."

Rose swallowed. "You think Kallias would do *that*?"

"Kallias would've probably done that for *you* before the blood bond," Erik scoffed. He placed two more sandwiches in the skillet, and Rose wondered how many people he was planning on feeding with this '*quick*' meal. He looked at her. "But yeah! I ripped a guy in half one time for calling Alana a whore. She was a hell of a lot more powerful than I was. She didn't need me. But it just happened. I'd only been a vampire for two days, and it was an instinct I couldn't control."

Rose blinked. "Well, I mean...I'm not a big fan of the way men use that word—what they typically mean by it—but...ripping someone in half is, umm..."

"Gross?" Erik assumed.

"Extreme," Rose corrected.

He snorted, "The point is: they'll hesitate before provoking Kallias."

"Will Theron?" Rose asked. "Hesitate?"

His smile faded. "No. This will just give him *another* reason to kill you."

"HER BLOOD GLOWED," KALLIAS REPEATED, AS IF HE EXPECTED GEOFF TO come to his senses as soon as he heard those ridiculous words together.

"In a sense, yes," Geoffrey confirmed. "I've never seen blood react like that. Kallias, I don't know what she is, but she is *not* human."

"Don't be ridiculous," Kallias said. "Her blood is human. *She* is human."

"You said her eyes glowed, too," Geoffrey reminded him. "There's nothing human about it."

"I tasted her blood," Kallias argued. "It tasted human."

"Except it tasted *much* more powerful than human blood, right?" Geoffrey pointed out. He leaned forward on the edge of the sofa, across from Kallias. "Think about it. How could she be human when her blood is more powerful than *vampire* blood? She has to be something more!"

"Keep your voice down," Kallias snarled at him. "I don't even think she knows what happened to her eyes!"

"Yeah," Geoffrey said quietly, "and if you really thought she was human, don't you think you would've told her about it?" His eyes darkened with suspicion. "You're keeping it from her for a reason—because you know it's bad!"

"She's human, and you're not to say otherwise," Kallias growled.

Geoffrey swallowed at his tone. "I understand that you care about her, but don't you think you're being—"

"No, Geoff, you don't understand," Kallias snarled. "Less than two weeks ago, she was living a normal, human life with no clue we existed, and now, she's *hanging out* with dangerous vampires, as if it's the most normal thing in the world. She has a blood bond with me—a twenty-five-hundred-year-old telepath, which is screwed up enough, as it is. She has telekinetic abilities, and after last night, who the hell knows what she can do?" His voice grew more unsteady with each word. "And on top of all of that, Theron and a bunch of other vampires want her dead. She has enough to deal with without you making her feel like some freak of nature!"

Geoffrey sighed, "But Kallias, what if she's something...*worse* than us?"

"I don't care what she is," Kallias said. "I love her. That's all that matters."

Geoffrey blinked in shock, as he processed that declaration. He'd suspected, of course, but until Kallias confirmed it, he hadn't been completely sure. "That explains your sudden irrationality, I suppose."

Kallias narrowed his eyes at that.

"If she can do what you said she did...she's dangerous, Kallias," Geoffrey told him. "We can't just let her—"

"We're dangerous!" Kallias argued. "We are vampires. She is human."

"You don't even believe that yourself," Geoffrey accused. "She nearly killed a vampire that's older than *you* are! We have no idea what she's capable of."

Kallias stood. "Rose is here with us every day. Hell, she sleeps next to me," he pointed out. "She knows we're dangerous, and she trusts us. And now, *you* think it's too hard to trust *her*?"

Geoffrey held up his hands. "You need calm down," he urged, but Kallias didn't listen. "I'm just saying that we have no idea what she is, or if she can control whatever that is inside of her." He shrugged. "You don't see humans letting wild animals roam free the streets. It doesn't matter if they trust the animal or if the animal trusts them. If there's a chance it might hurt or kill someone, you have to take precautions. They still take care of the animal! They just put it in a—"

"A cage?" Kallias interrupted, his voice a low, blood-curdling growl.

Geoffrey winced. "Okay, so, that was a bad analogy, but—"

He didn't manage to get the correction out before Kallias closed his hand around Geoffrey's neck.

Geoff paled in fear as he realized how much weaker he actually was in comparison to Kallias.

647

Kallias looked absolutely feral, his fangs bared. "Do not threaten her."

Erik was already in the room before Geoffrey could react, pulling Kallias off of him. He placed himself between them. "Hey. Hey! Kallias! Look at me."

Kallias blinked at Erik, his body still shaking with anger. "What?"

"You attacked Geoffrey," Erik informed him. "What happened?"

"I did?" Kallias said breathlessly. He glanced toward the door, as Rose stepped into the room. "I... I don't know. I didn't realize I was doing it."

Erik nodded. "It's the blood bond. Let me calm you down, okay?"

Kallias nodded his assent, still trembling, as he tried to control the anger.

Erik placed his hands on Kallias's face and used his abilities to soothe the volatile rage that surged through Kallias. He watched as Kallias relaxed, his shoulders falling and his eyes softening.

"Thanks," Kallias mumbled, when Erik dropped his hands and stepped back.

Erik nodded and turned back toward Geoffrey. "Are you all right?"

Geoffrey swallowed, still a little shaken up. "Yeah. I guess."

Kallias stared at Rose, saddened by the worry he saw in her eyes.

Emma appeared in the other doorway. She leaned elegantly against the doorframe, her normally wide, innocent eyes now narrowed with concern.

"I don't understand," Geoffrey said. "Kallias has never acted like that."

Kallias glanced at him, but he remained silent.

"Kallias has never had a full-blown blood bond with anyone before," Erik explained. "You'd do the same thing if someone had threatened Emma."

Geoffrey quickly shook his head. "I wasn't threatening Rose. I swear!"

Rose frowned at Kallias, as she realized he was staring at her again.

Erik shrugged. "It must've felt like a threat to cause that reaction."

Geoffrey's mouth fell open. "W-what? You're on *his* side?"

"I'm not on anyone's side, asshole. We're friends here, not enemies," Erik scoffed. He scowled at Geoffrey. "I just want to know what happened."

"Not here, Erik," Kallias said quietly, still watching Rose.

"I wasn't threatening her," Geoffrey insisted to Erik. "I was just suggesting that we act rationally about this. She's obviously dangerous, and I—"

"Dangerous?" Rose repeated, her eyes widening. "Me?"

"*Gamoto*," Kallias muttered, cursing in Greek.

Geoffrey glanced at her. "Well, I'd think so, after last night..."

Rose paled at the thought, but there wasn't much she could remember about last night.

Erik rolled his eyes. "Are you kidding me?"

Geoffrey flinched at his tone.

"Don't be such a baby," Erik scoffed. His voice was as strangely boyish as it always was, but there was an instability in it now. "We're literal *monsters*, and she looks at us like we're no different from her—like we're just people. A *human* is braver than you!"

"Oh, come on," Geoffrey said. "None of us are convinced on the human part, are we?"

"What?" Rose breathed. "What does that mean?"

Kallias clenched his fists at his sides, and Erik seemed to almost...*mimic* him.

"I'm just being rational," Geoffrey tried to tell Erik, "which isn't something I'd expect *you* to understand."

Erik lifted an eyebrow, but he didn't respond to that insult.

"Yes, we're monsters," Geoffrey admitted, "but she might be an even worse monster."

Erik was clearly *very* aware of Kallias's emotions—because his hand shot out to stop Kallias, before Kallias could even react. "Instinct," he reminded Kallias. "Try to control it."

Kallias took a step back, but he continued to glare.

"Monster?" Rose breathed. "You—you think I'm a monster?"

A strange growl resonated in Kallias's throat, and Erik kept his arm in front of him—just in case.

"Geoff," Emma said softly. She stepped forward, frowning at her husband. "Rose is nice to me. I don't…want you to call her that."

Geoffrey actually shrank back at that. He hadn't really listened to Erik, but Emma was clearly the one person he *did* listen to.

"You don't even know *what* I've done," Erik said darkly. "There is no worse monster in this room than me. I can assure you of that."

Geoff looked down, his resolve faltering. "We don't even know what she is."

"She's a very annoying smart-ass," Erik informed him.

Rose frowned.

"And…she's our friend," Erik added. "We promised to protect her. If you've changed your mind, that's your choice. Leave whenever you want. We'll continue to protect her without you."

"No, I still want to help," Geoffrey said. "I just think we should—"

"Well, I think *you* should shut the hell up," Erik interrupted.

Geoffrey sighed in frustration. He stood up and shoved his hands into his pockets. "I need some air."

Before he reached the door, however, he turned to Rose. "I'm sorry," he said at her wary look. "I didn't mean to offend you."

Rose tried to smile. "It's…fine," she said, but her voice cracked a little, as she said it.

Geoffrey sighed and left, closing the door behind him.

"I should go with him," Emma said, crossing the room as gracefully as ever. She stopped and lifted herself on her toes to pat Rose's red hair, like the fur of a puppy. "You're not a monster, Rose. You're our very nice human."

Rose managed a weak smile. "Thank you, Emma."

Emma curtsied to them. "I shall fix Geoffrey with sex! Wish me luck."

Rose's eyes widened.

Erik chuckled, "Good luck. I'll try not to listen. Maybe."

Rose grimaced at Erik. "Eww!"

After she left, Kallias turned to Erik. "I think you may have been a little too harsh."

Erik spun toward him. "*I* was harsh? You nearly ripped out his windpipe!"

"It was an accident," Kallias said defensively.

Erik shook his head in disbelief.

"So…" Rose said softly, biting her lip, "I'm a monster?"

They both looked at her with startled expressions.

"No," Kallias insisted. "You're not."

"He's right," Erik agreed. "You're not a monster, Rose."

"Then, why does he think I am?" she asked softly.

Kallias looked away. "Geoff is…a cautious person."

"Allow me to translate," Erik said suddenly. "He's a cowardly asshole."

Kallias cast a wide-eyed look at Erik. "Damn."

Erik groaned in frustration, dragging a hand through his wavy, blonde hair. "Don't look at me like that," he snapped at Kallias. "It's *your* emotions that are doing this!"

"Right," Kallias said, wincing. "Sorry."

"Is it because of my blood?" Rose asked.

"Your blood?" Erik repeated. "I figured it was about last night."

Kallias cast an alarmed look at Erik, but Erik didn't notice.

"Last night?" Rose said with a frown. "When I used telekinesis?"

"That's an understatement," Erik laughed. "You didn't just shatter a glass this time. You immobilized a hundred vampires with your mind, nearly collapsed a building, and almost killed an ancient vampire! And your eyes—"

"Erik!" Kallias interrupted.

Erik frowned at him.

"What about my eyes?" Rose asked curiously.

Erik twirled his finger, thinking of the swirling red haze that had consumed them, but at Kallias's glare, he simply said, "Angry."

Rose's frown deepened. "I guess I *do* remember being angry."

Erik hesitated at the confusion he'd heard in her voice. "Is that…*all* you remember?"

"It's kind of a…blur of emotion," Rose admitted, "like a blindspot in my memory."

Erik nodded. "Yeah, I sensed that."

Kallias, on the other hand, looked relieved. "It was helpful. Last night," he told her, "but there's no reason to relive it. Or to *ever* do it again."

Rose squinted suspiciously at that. "What...exactly happened last night?"

"I just *said*...there's no reason to relive it," Kallias said—a bit too forcefully.

"And I'd like to know why," Rose said with a worried frown.

Erik glanced back and forth between them, clearly torn.

"Were you afraid of me?" Rose asked.

"Of course not!" Kallias said—at the same time that Erik said, "A little bit."

Kallias glared at him.

"What?" Erik muttered. "Even without the telekinesis, she's a little scary."

"You say that about all women," Kallias reminded him.

Erik shrugged. "All women are scary." Under his breath, he added, "And sexy."

Kallias rolled his eyes. He turned to Rose. "I'd never be afraid of you, Rose, because I trust you," he said, and *that* was enough to catch her off guard. "I know I said I'd never trust anyone—that it was stupid to trust people—but I trust *you*. Whatever happened last night doesn't change that."

Whatever fears Rose had dissolved at that admission. "You do?"

"Besides," Kallias said, looking away, "we have more immediate matters to worry about."

"Like the fact that I'm almost out of alcohol," Erik agreed.

"Or the fact that a hundred vampires are trying to kill us," Kallias said pointedly.

Erik nodded. "Yeah. That's bad, too."

"Too?" Kallias repeated.

Erik sniffed the air. "Oh, shit. I'm burning the food."

Rose's eyes widened, but Erik just casually walked past her, like the house burning down was only *slightly* dangerous.

As Erik left, Kallias stepped closer to Rose. "I need a shower," he said with a small smile, "and *you* need to eat."

"Shower," Rose repeated. "A shower sounds nice, actually."

He chuckled, "Eat first, okay? I can feel your hunger."

"Oh, great," Rose muttered. "As if reading my mind wasn't weird enough."

He laughed softly at that. "I'll be back soon."

"Sure, and I'll try not to die while you're in the shower," Rose said playfully.

He frowned worriedly. "Try?"

Rose gave a cute shrug. "I can't make any promises."

Kallias glared at her. "I'll make the shower quick."

AFTER HIS SHOWER, KALLIAS FOUND ERIK IN THE KITCHEN. HE SAT AT THE counter, across from Erik, raising an eyebrow at the empty whiskey bottle between them.

Erik swirled the amber-colored liquid in his glass, his eyes blank. His mind was clearly elsewhere.

"Rose went upstairs to take a shower," Erik said, not looking up.

"Yeah. I can...tell," Kallias said, frowning, as he tried to explain it.

Erik chuckled, "Blood bonds are fun, aren't they?"

Kallias frowned, as Erik continued to stare at the glass. "Are you okay?"

"I'm having those dreams again," Erik said quietly.

Kallias nodded in understanding. "About Alana?"

Erik sighed, "The dreams are pleasant, but then, when I wake up..."

"You miss her?" Kallias asked. "Erik, she used you! She ruined you."

"I know. I know," Erik said, dragging his hand through his hair.

"Sorry. I'm just...concerned," Kallias said. "Are they memories?"

Erik grimaced. "Sometimes."

Before Kallias could ask what he meant, the door opened. Erik and Kallias glanced toward the doorway, as the scent of blood flooded their senses. Emma came through the door, her mouth, neck, and dress coated in blood.

Kallias blinked at the amount of blood, his eyes wide. "Uh...Emma?"

Emma giggled at their shocked expressions. "Sorry, I'm a messy eater."

Erik choked on his drink, as he burst into a fit of laughter that was equal-parts laugh and equal-parts cough. His head fell face-first on the counter.

Kallias and Emma both gave Erik quizzical looks.

"Do either of you mind if I bathe in your facilities?" Emma asked.

Kallias scowled at the blood dripping onto the floor. "Please, do."

Emma left the room, leaving a relatively clean Geoffrey standing by the door, scratching his neck, as a blush crept up his neck.

Kallias scowled, as Erik continued to laugh obnoxiously. "Are you done?"

"Nope," Erik snorted. "Not at all."

Geoffrey sat on the barstool next to Kallias. He drummed his fingertips against the countertop nervously and stared straight ahead, obviously still embarrassed.

"Sorry about earlier," Kallias said awkwardly.

Geoffrey glanced at him. "No, it's fine," he said dismissively. "If it had been Emma, I might've had the same reaction."

As they talked, Erik stood and walked to the sink. He grabbed a washrag and held it under a stream of hot water. Then, he tossed it to Geoffrey.

"I just..." Geoffrey stopped, as he caught the washrag. He frowned at it.

Erik tapped a finger against the side of his neck. "You missed some."

Geoffrey's eyes widened, and he quickly began wiping the blood from his neck with the rag. "I didn't get any on my shirt, did I?"

Erik and Kallias both scowled at him.

"What *are* you?" Kallias asked bewilderedly.

Geoffrey glanced at the blood on the rag. "I just got it dry-cleaned."

"What kind of self-respecting vampire dry-cleans his clothes?" Erik said.

"The kind that dresses better than the two of you," Geoffrey countered.

Erik snorted, "Hey, it's not my fault I look better in leather than you."

Kallias rolled his eyes at both of them.

Geoffrey had just opened his mouth to say something else when a knock sounded at the door. All three of them straightened, their senses on high alert.

"Were you expecting someone?" Geoffrey asked them.

Kallias scowled worriedly. "No."

Erik sniffed the air. "It's a vampire."

"A powerful one," Kallias added.

"Is it Theron or one of the vampires working for him?" Geoffrey asked.

"I don't know. I was a little too distracted by the mass amounts of Kallias's blood everywhere to memorize their scents," Erik scoffed.

"No," Kallias said suddenly. "It's not any of them."

Erik frowned at that. "Are you sure? Because you were kind of...*dying*."

"I'm sure," Kallias said. "I made a point to remember their scents, just in case I *did* survive. This is one I've never encountered before."

"It could still be a vampire working for Theron," Geoffrey advised.

Two knocks sounded again—just as calm as the first ones.

Almost begrudgingly, Kallias stood and started walking toward the foyer.

"Is it really a good idea to answer it?" Geoffrey asked cautiously.

"I might as well," he said. "It's a vampire. If he wants in, he'll come in."

"Do you have a weapon?" Erik asked.

"Of course," Kallias answered, as if the question were absurd.

As Kallias left the room, heading into the foyer, Erik glanced at Geoffrey. "I should go with him just in case this gets bad. You go get Emma."

"Okay," Geoffrey agreed, before disappearing into the hallway.

Erik joined Kallias in the foyer, as Kallias answered the door.

Kallias froze, as he saw the last person he'd *ever* expected to see at his door.

The strangely pale, blonde man looked barely any different than he had two and half millennia ago. He was...*perhaps* a little paler, the circles beneath his pale blue eyes a bit darker...

But his long, blonde hair was as pale and straight as it had been then, and those pale blue eyes that stared back at Kallias were the same lifeless, emotionless eyes that had set Kallias on edge all of those years ago.

Only his clothing had changed. Instead of a white chiton, he wore a black, button-down shirt and black slacks that contrasted starkly with his ghostly paleness.

"Hello, Kallias," he said, his voice as impassive as his eyes.

"Erastos," Kallias said coldly.

"You remember me," Erastos said.

"How could I forget the person responsible for my death?" Kallias snarled.

Erastos didn't respond to that. "Are you going to invite me inside?"

"No," Kallias said. "I'm going to ask you what the hell you're doing on my doorstep?"

"If you had listened to me, you would remember that I warned you that you'd see me again when the time has come," Erastos said.

"I can see you're still annoyingly vague," Kallias grumbled. "What *time*?"

"Her time," Erastos said simply.

Kallias rolled his eyes. "*Whose* time?"

"The Eklektos," Erastos said.

Kallias frowned. "The Eklektos."

"Yes," Erastos said. "You should have listened to me, Kallias."

"Uh, Kallias?" Erik said. "How do you know the pale guy?"

Kallias turned toward Erik. "Do you remember me telling you about the priest who gave me the Stone that caused Theron to kill Phoebe *and* me?"

"Yeah," Erik said with a frown.

Kallias jerked his head back toward Erastos. "This is the priest."

"The priest was a vampire?" Erik asked.

"Apparently," Kallias muttered.

"I am not a priest," Erastos admitted. "I only impersonated a priest because I knew Phoebe would trust one. She was very devout."

Kallias's jaw tightened. "I know what she was."

Erastos shrugged. "Anyway, it was my understanding that the Stone of the Eklektos, which you so carelessly lost, has come back into your possession."

"Wait. What?" Erik said, gaping at Kallias. "When?"

"It's *not* in my possession," Kallias said harshly.

Erastos nodded. "But she *is*."

Kallias paled in shock. "She?"

"The one who holds the Stone," Erastos said.

At the mention of Rose, Kallias lost his patience. He didn't trust this vampire at all—especially not now. "I think you should leave."

"No. The time has come," Erastos stated, disregarding Kallias's frustration. He placed his hand on the door before Kallias could close it.

Kallias growled, "What the hell does that even…"

"Kallias!" Rose yelled. She ran down the stairs, stumbling as she tried to take them two at a time. Her long hair, still drenched from her shower, hung around her shoulders, soaking her green T-shirt. "That Stone is glowing! And not the way it glows when I touch it, but *really* brightly now! Is that bad?"

She stopped abruptly, when she saw the man at the door.

Before Kallias could even react to all of the new information, Erastos answered, "It means that the Stone of the Eklektos has been activated."

Kallias gave him an incredulous look. "Activated?"

Rose's mouth fell open. "You. It's you," she whispered.

Kallias looked at her, his eyes widening in surprise. "You know him?"

Rose nodded. "He's the one who gave me the Stone."

"You didn't tell me it was a *vampire* who gave it to you!" Kallias complained.

"I didn't know," Rose said with a frown. "Kallias, why is he *here*?"

Erastos studied her intensely, as if she were a chemistry experiment he expected to react. His lips lifted into a slight, almost unnoticeable smile. "I am here for you," he said, bowing, as if she were royalty, "my Eklektos."

THE EKLEKTOS

"*Y*our *what?*"

Erastos sat on the sofa across from them, now—after insisting they let him come inside before even attempting to answer the simple two-word question that Rose had already asked several times now.

Rose sat between Kallias and Erik on the other sofa, watching Erastos with a scowl.

"Eklektos," Erastos said, as if that word were enough.

"Yeah, I heard you," Rose said. "I want you to *explain.*"

Erastos frowned. "Eklektos. It's Greek for—"

"Chosen, elected, fated, etcetera, etcetera. Yes, I know Greek," Rose interrupted. "What I want to know is: Why are you *calling* me that?"

Erik shot a disbelieving look at her. "Why do *you* know Greek?"

Rose was just about to remind him of her obsession with history, when Erastos interjected, "She feels drawn to the ancient."

Rose glanced at him, frowning.

This strange, inhuman-looking man didn't know her. So, why did that statement feel so...accurate?

Erik also eyed him warily. "He's creepy, right?" he mumbled to Rose. "It's not just me?"

Rose didn't answer, since...creepy or not, the guy was definitely within earshot.

"I called you the Eklektos because that is what you are," he told Rose.

The way he spoke was almost as strange as his habit of appearing in strange places at strange times. He didn't use contractions where most people used contractions, and his intonation sounded more like a computer than a human.

"So, I take it you're...Greek?" Rose tried to guess.

He was a lot paler than you'd expect from an Ancient Greek, but the word he kept using was Greek.

And he knew Kallias, apparently.

"No," Erastos said simply. "The awakening of the Eklektos has been awaited since long before the Ancient Greek Empire."

Rose's frown deepened. "Right. You're insane. You could've just led with that."

Erastos frowned. "My emotional state is stable."

Rose raised an eyebrow at the robotic answer. "Come on, now," she scoffed. "You can't expect me to believe that thousands of years ago, someone knew *I* would exist."

"Not just someone," Erastos corrected. "*Many* people."

Rose rolled her eyes. "Oh, yeah. *That* makes it more believable."

Kallias drummed his fingers against the arm of the sofa. "If that were true," he questioned Erastos, "wouldn't *I* have heard of this?"

Erastos shrugged. "It was long before your time."

Erik laughed in disbelief. "Just how old *are* you?"

"Older than you would believe," Erastos said vaguely.

"Older than Aaron?" Erik asked skeptically.

"Much older," Erastos assured him.

Rose sighed, "What makes you think that I'm this...*Eklektos*?"

"I do not *think* you are the Eklektos. I know you are," Erastos corrected.

"Okay..." she said, drawing out the word in confusion. "But, umm, how?"

"I know things," Erastos answered.

Rose squinted in confusion. "That's...not really an answer."

"Don't waste your time trying to get real answers from him," Kallias muttered. "All he does is make vague statements and expect you to understand."

Erastos glanced at him. "I understand that you don't trust me—"

"That's an understatement," Kallias interrupted.

"But I do have reasons for everything I choose to say or not say," Erastos continued in that strange tone. "My intentions are pure."

Kallias rolled his eyes. "Any evil person would say something similar. It's easy to justify your own actions to yourself."

"Kallias," Rose said, nudging him gently. "You're being rude."

Kallias scoffed at that. "And?"

"*And*...we should give him a chance," Rose said.

Kallias turned to look at her. "The last time I gave him a chance, I was tortured and turned into a vampire," he informed her. "Forgive me if I'm hesitant to do it again."

Rose nodded sympathetically. It wasn't in her nature to be unforgiving. To be cautious, on the hand, was.

"You didn't trust me then, either," Erastos pointed out.

Kallias leaned forward and narrowed his eyes at the pale vampire. "Let me reiterate," he said between clenched teeth, "that *you got me killed*."

"I told you that you had a choice," Erastos said. "I warned you that the path you were choosing was the most painful one."

"If you knew what would happen, why didn't you stop it?" Kallias asked.

"I cannot stop what is meant to happen," Erastos stated.

"Like hell you can't," Kallias snarled. "You could've warned me."

Erastos seemed completely unaffected by Kallias's frustration. "It's not my place to interfere with fate."

"Fate?" Kallias scoffed. "I was tortured, killed, and turned into a monster! You're calling *that* fate?"

"Yes," Erastos said simply.

Kallias glared at him. "You're lucky I don't kill you now."

"Or perhaps you are lucky you haven't tried," Erastos countered.

Kallias leaned forward. "Are you threatening me?"

"No," Erastos said—as calmly as ever.

Rose realized she could *feel* Kallias's anger. It was a calm, controlled rage, but it felt so intense—almost as intense as it might've felt, if it were her own emotion.

Physical touch was rarely Rose's first instinct, but it felt as if Kallias needed that. So, Rose reached out and touched his jean-clad knee.

His dark gaze immediately shifted toward her, and the rage faded.

"I'm not saying we should trust him," Rose assured him, "but we should give him a chance. Maybe he can tell us how to defeat Theron. We need all the help we can get."

"I don't want his help," Kallias told her. "Considering his track record, his help probably involves you *dying*."

Rose frowned suspiciously when she noticed Erastos look away. "Hypothetically," she said to the strange vampire, "if you *did* know of these things before they happened, why would you think it was okay to let what happened to Kallias *happen*?"

Erastos gave her a baffled look. "It isn't a matter of right and wrong, my Eklektos. It is simply what is."

Rose shook her head. "Everything is a matter of right and wrong."

"It is not my purpose to interfere with fate," Erastos told her.

Rose grew more frustrated with everything he said. An ounce of humanity was *not* too much to ask for. "I don't even know if I believe in fate," she said honestly, "but if I did, I still wouldn't care—not when it comes to letting someone suffer like that."

There was a slight, uncharacteristic twitch of smile at the corner of Erastos's pale lips. "Yes, you have...*acted* on that emotion before, my Eklektos."

"Emotion?" Rose said with a frown.

"Have you been stalking her?" Kallias asked.

"No," Erastos said.

Rose wasn't sure if the quickness of his answer put her mind at ease or not.

Erastos turned his emotionless gaze back toward Rose. "Each moment of the past played a role in leading to present and future events.

If I had interfered with even one thing that happened to him, this moment might've never happened."

Rose nodded. "Like the butterfly effect."

"What are you talking about *now*?" Erik complained.

Rose sighed, "It's chaos theory. Changing a minor detail can result in major differences at a later time—like the flapping of a butterfly's wings changing the path of a hurricane."

Erik rolled his eyes. "*This* is why no one has sex with you."

Rose scowled at him. "You know what? Just because you're too shallow to appreciate intelligence in a woman, doesn't mean everyone else is."

Kallias—who, until that moment, had been as tense as physically possible—suddenly started laughing.

Erik held up both hands. "I don't even have a comeback for that one."

"It only took thirteen hundred years for you to find someone who can out-sass you," Kallias told him.

Erik snorted. "This isn't over," he warned Rose.

Rose laughed—and then immediately stopped, as she noticed Erastos watching her.

He didn't laugh. He didn't react. It was unnerving.

She *wanted* to give Erastos the benefit of the doubt, but there was something so eerie about the cold intensity of his gaze. He stared at her as if he were assessing her every feature.

It reminded her of the way someone might appraise an expensive car before committing money to it.

She shivered.

"If I'd interfered in what happened to Kallias," Erastos explained, "he wouldn't have had the weak blood bond with Theron that led him to you the same night Theron tried to kill you."

Kallias frowned. "She'd be dead?"

Erastos nodded. "And the world would be doomed."

"Wait, *what*?" Rose sputtered. "What do you mean '*doomed*?'"

"You are the Eklektos," Erastos said, as if that made *any* sense.

"You're fated to either save or destroy the world. You must live in order to fulfill that purpose. If you die, no one stands a chance."

Rose actually laughed at that. "That...has to be a joke."

Erik scoffed, "Does this guy *look* like he has a sense of humor to you?"

Rose considered the impassive, stone-like expression on Erastos's face and thought...maybe not. "And you know all of this," Rose said slowly, "because you...*know things*?"

"That is what I said," Erastos told her.

Rose lifted her eyebrows at that. "You can't actually think *I* could save the world," she argued. "I'm just a human."

"You are mistaken," Erastos said. "You are not just a human."

Rose squinted at that. "What else could I be?"

"Physically," Erastos said, "Rose Foster is human, but the Eklektos is not."

Rose spread out her hands in confusion. "But you keep saying *I'm* the Eklektos!"

"You are," Erastos said. "The Eklektos is...both parts of you."

Rose's eyebrows arched higher. "As in...the left and the right?"

"No," Erastos said.

Rose sighed in frustration. "Nothing you say makes *any* sense."

"Told you so," Kallias muttered.

"All right," Rose said, deciding to try something else. "Tell me this: What *is* the Eklektos?"

"Power," Erastos said.

Well, that *still* didn't make any sense.

"And," Rose sighed, "what species is it?"

"It's older than any species," Erastos told her.

Rose threw up her hands in defeat. "I'm getting nowhere."

Erik patted her shoulder. "Good effort, though."

Kallias leaned forward. "Why are you doing this now?" he asked Erastos. "And don't give me that 'the-time-has-come' shit—because, in case you haven't noticed, this is a *bad* time. If you know as much as you say you do, you know that Theron and about a hundred vampires are looking for us and that Stone of yours."

"It is not *my* Stone," Erastos said. "It belongs to the Eklektos."

"The point is," Kallias said irritably, "while you're wasting our time with this nonsense, those vampires are getting closer and closer to killing us."

"I'm here because I am needed," Erastos answered. He held up his hand, when Kallias opened his mouth to snap at him about the vague answer. "And, more specifically, I am needed because the Eklektos has awakened."

"Umm...actually," Rose said, "I woke up a couple of hours ago."

"Not you. The Eklektos," Erastos corrected.

She sighed in frustration, "You *just* said the Eklektos is—"

"Both parts of you," Erastos interrupted, "and until last night, at least one of those parts were latent, buried in the deepest and darkest part of your mind."

"Last night," Kallias repeated. "What changed last night?"

Erastos glanced at him. "You almost died."

"What does that have to do with anything?" Kallias asked.

"This kind of power wouldn't have come forth for just any reason," Erastos explained. "It is a dark and unstoppable power. Only equally dark and powerful emotions could've awakened it."

"Like fear?" Rose assumed. "Or anger?"

"Or love," Erik said quietly.

Erastos nodded. "It could only be love."

She frowned at both of them. "Love isn't dark."

"It *can* be," Erik said, turning toward her. "Love is the most powerful emotion because it evokes *so many* emotions. It's the one emotion that is both light and dark. Love creates kindness, happiness, joy, selflessness, and hundreds of other small emotions, but it can *also* evoke fear, sadness, anger, jealousy, and pain. It is potent and all-encompassing."

Rose frowned worriedly. "And last night..."

"You saw someone hurt the person you love. You saw Kallias almost *die*. Last night, your love for him evoked some very dark emotions," Erik told her. "I've never felt *anything* as dark as the emotions that I felt radiating from you."

Rose shifted uneasily. "I...don't remember much about last night."

"That's because a different part of you took control," Erastos said. "A part that you don't understand yet."

Rose paled. "Control? What? Like...*possession?*"

Erastos didn't even react to her panic. "No, it was still you."

"I tried to kill someone," Rose argued. "That doesn't *sound* like me."

"My Eklektos..." Erastos bowed his head slightly, as if he were speaking to some kind of authority. It was *so* weird. "Light doesn't exist without darkness. The same thing that makes you kind and compassionate is what made you merciless last night. *Love.* You love more deeply and freely than most, and because of that, you are the most dangerous person in the world."

The blood drained from her face. "I don't want to be dangerous."

An odd smile tugged at his lips. "Ah, but you *are.*"

Rose froze, as an eerie chill traveled down her spine, like some kind of inner warning that something was off about that smile of his.

"Is that why her eyes turned red?" Erik asked. "The Eklektos thing?"

She spun toward him. "My eyes did *what?!*"

Kallias rolled his eyes. "Damn, Erik. Just blurt it out, why don't you?"

"Yes," Erastos said in answer to Erik's question.

"Because those eyes scared the hell out of me," Erik added.

"Erik," Kallias said again.

"What? They did," Erik said defensively. "You can't tell they didn't freak you out a little."

Rose turned to Kallias, her eyes—her normal, *blue* eyes, that is—wide. "My eyes changed, and you didn't tell me?"

"I...didn't know it was important," Kallias said.

"Really?" Rose said dryly, not believing that for a moment. She shook her head in frustration. "And they freaked you out?"

Kallias shrugged. "It was a little unnerving. That's all."

"As it should be," Erastos interjected. "The eyes of the Eklektos should be seen as a warning to her enemies that their time is up."

Rose turned her disbelieving stare toward Erastos. "What? No, no, I don't hurt people! That's not *me.* You're wrong. I'd never..."

Erastos tilted his head to the side, his long, pale hair shifting with the movement. "You'd do whatever it took to save someone you love."

Rose frowned. "Well, yeah, but—"

"*Whatever it takes* includes hurting people," Erastos stated.

Rose shook her head in denial. "No. I—I can't even process this. It's insane," she sputtered. Then, she turned to Erik. "And I still want to know why *no one* thought it was important to tell me that my eyes changed colors!"

"I think Kallias was afraid it would freak you out," Erik told her.

"It wouldn't have!" Rose snapped.

Erik lifted both eyebrows. "But you *are* freaking out."

"Yes, because I just found out my eyes change colors!" Rose said.

Erik laughed and held out his hands.

With a defeated sigh, Rose turned back toward Erastos. "I don't want this power," she told him, "not if it's going to make me hurt people."

"You cannot change who you are," Erastos said. "You are the Eklektos."

"Why?" Rose asked irritably. "What is the purpose of this *dangerous* power?"

"To save or destroy the world," Erastos repeated.

"How?" Rose asked again. "By defeating Theron?"

To her surprise, Erastos smiled at that. Really, it wasn't so much a smile as it was a smirk—a suspiciously smug *smirk*. "Theron is only one of your enemies, and he's certainly not the most powerful."

Rose's eyes widened at that. "Well, that's not reassuring."

"Theron is one of the oldest vampires alive," Erik reminded him. "Who is more powerful than that?"

"Many people, actually," Erastos told him

Erik ran his hand through his wavy, blonde hair, obviously growing frustrated. "And do you mind—oh, I don't know—maybe giving us a heads-up on these threats?"

"I will warn you when the time is right," Erastos assured him.

Erik blinked in disbelief. "Is he serious?" he asked Kallias and Rose.

"Then, what the hell are you doing here right *now*?" Kallias snarled.

Erastos turned to Kallias, his expression impassive. "Because in order for her to face these more powerful enemies, she must first defeat

Theron," he explained. "If she doesn't, well, as I said before, the world is doomed without her."

"And you're going to...*help* us defeat him?" Erik assumed.

"That is not my role," Erastos told him. "I came only to help her understand her power and the Stone of the Eklektos."

Rose raised her hand. "Uhh, for the record, you haven't helped me understand *anything*. You're actually the most confusing person I've ever met."

Erastos simply stared at her.

So unhelpful.

"What does the Stone of the Eklektos have to do with this?" Kallias asked.

"It unlocks her power," Erastos said. "It allows her to tap into a part of it that...might be unaccessible otherwise."

"Again with the vagueness," Rose grumbled.

"It's important that she has it in her possession when she faces Theron again," Erastos added.

"Do you mind telling us when that might be?" Kallias sighed.

"It's better if I don't," Erastos said.

Kallias rolled his eyes. "Okay, that's it. Get out."

Erastos didn't move.

"How does a Stone have power, anyway?" Rose asked.

"That's what I asked him," Kallias agreed.

"It doesn't have power. *You* do," Erastos corrected. "The Stone of the Eklektos is simply a tool that will help you use your power."

"Theron seems to think the Stone itself has power," Kallias told him.

Erastos nodded. "Phoebe misunderstood and miscommunicated the information," he explained. "The truth is that the Stone of the Eklektos is useless without the Eklektos. Only she can use it."

"Great," Kallias muttered. "So, when he finds that out, he'll want Rose."

"He already wants to kill me," Rose reminded him.

"Yes, but then, he'll want you *alive*," Kallias said, "so he can use you."

She grimaced. "Yeah, that *does* sound worse."

Erastos nodded in agreement. "Yes, it's important that the Eklektos never falls under Theron's control—or anyone else's, for that matter."

"Oh, I will never be under *anyone's* control," Rose assured him.

Erastos seemed amused by that. "Of course you won't, my Eklektos."

Rose frowned suspiciously at that.

"Well," Erastos said, climbing to his feet, "our time together is over."

"What?" Rose sputtered. "You've told us nothing!"

"I've told you to keep the Stone of the Eklektos close," Erastos told her. "That is all you need to know."

"Somehow, I doubt that," Rose muttered.

"The Stone of the Eklektos draws out your power," Erastos added. "It manipulates it. It will allow you to use your power without limits."

"Without limits would kill her!" Kallias said.

Erik leaned forward. "Are you saying it would save her from the physical consequences?"

"No," Erastos said. "Her body is still human." His pale, blue gaze shifted toward Rose. "When she uses too much power, she will die."

Rose straightened as she realized he'd said *'when'* and not *'if.'* She glanced at Erik and Kallias, but neither of them seemed to have noticed. She tried to calm herself. The last thing she needed was for them to notice her fear.

"I must admit that a vampire body would be more ideal for the Eklektos," Erastos continued. That eerie smile returned at his lips. "What a dangerous monster she would be then."

The unease grew heavier in Rose's stomach.

Kallias scowled at him. "What is *wrong* with you?"

Erastos bowed. "I look forward to speaking again, my Eklektos."

Erik stood, too. "You're not going to help us fight them?"

"I've helped all I can," Erastos told him. "It is not my fate to participate in this fight. My purpose is elsewhere."

"Convenient," Kallias muttered under his breath.

Erastos ignored them. "You know what you have to do," he told Rose.

Rose's frown deepened. "I do?"

Geoffrey and Emma chose that moment to join them in the living room. Emma's brown hair dripped water onto her yellow dress, and her skin didn't appear to have been dried well either.

Geoffrey pointed at Erastos and asked Kallias, "Friend or enemy?"

"Your guess is as good as mine," Kallias muttered.

"You're really pale," Emma told Erastos, "like an angelic bunny."

Rose turned to frown at the peculiar vampire. "Bunny?"

Erastos stared back at Emma, obviously confused.

"A white one," Emma said, nodding, "from Heaven."

Erik glanced at Geoffrey. "Umm, Geoff, is Emma okay?"

Geoffrey raked his fingers through his short hair and sighed, "She drank *a lot* of my blood." A familiar blush crept up his neck. "She appears to still be a bit…"

"High?" Erik assumed.

Emma poked Erastos in the chest. "You don't *feel* like a bunny."

Rose lifted both eyebrows.

Erastos stepped around the intoxicated vampire and headed toward the door. He turned and bowed to Rose yet again. "Until next time."

Rose was so confused by his strange habit of bowing that she let him leave without saying anything. When she heard the door close, however, she jumped to her feet. "Hey! Wait!"

Kallias caught her hand, when she tried to run after Erastos. He stood and pulled her back toward him. "Where are you going?"

"I just need to talk to him for a second," Rose told him.

"No. Absolutely not," he said. "You can't go out there alone."

Her eyes narrowed. "You can't stop me."

Kallias was just about to argue that technically, he could, but he sighed, instead. "I don't trust him."

"You don't trust anyone, Kallias," Rose reminded him.

"I don't trust him either," Erik interjected. "There's something off about that guy."

Rose cast a curious look at him. "Since when are *you* cautious?"

Erik shrugged. "Since I met someone who feels no emotion."

"No emotion?" Rose repeated.

"I've never encountered anyone like that before," Erik informed her.

"Not even psychopaths?" Rose asked.

"Even Theron feels more emotion than *this* guy does," Erik said. "It was like sitting across from a statue. I felt *nothing*."

She'd never seen Erik look so visibly disturbed.

"His mind is unusual, too," Kallias said. "Reading his mind is like reading a list of command prompts on a computer. There's no personalization to his thoughts. It's as if his mind is always blank, aside from the task at hand."

"Maybe he's an android," Rose muttered.

"What?" Erik said irritably.

"A robot," she elaborated.

Erik rolled his eyes. "Well, that's just silly."

Rose lifted her eyebrows at that. "You're a vampire, and you think *robots* are ridiculous?"

Erik looked at Kallias. "Why is she so weird?"

Kallias shrugged. "I think she reads science fiction."

Rose rolled her eyes. "I read *everything*."

"Well, maybe you should stop," Erik suggested.

Rose just shook her head in disbelief. "Anyway," she said loudly, "strange or not, I need to talk to him."

Kallias sighed in defeat. "Then…I'll go with you."

"Alone," she amended. "I think I need to talk to him alone."

"No," Kallias said quickly. "He could kill you before I even—"

"Do you trust me?" Rose interrupted. "You said you did."

With a reluctant nod, Kallias said, "Yes. *Only* you."

She offered him a gentle smile. "I promise I'll be fine."

He scowled. "You can't promise that."

"I just did," she said with a shrug.

Kallias breathed out a long sigh, "Fine, but if I feel you're in danger—"

"You'll come out there. Got it," she finished for him. She ran to catch Erastos before he could leave. "Thank you!"

Kallias shook his head in defeat.

"You *definitely* should not have let her do that," Erik grumbled.

"I can't tell her what to do," Kallias said quietly. "It's overbearing and…controlling."

Erik frowned. "You *are* overbearing and controlling!" When Kallias glared at him for that, Erik added, "And me telling you that has never stopped you before."

Kallias sighed in frustration. "I'll be upstairs."

ROSE STOPPED BESIDE THE LONG, BLACK CAR IN KALLIAS'S DRIVEWAY. "I WAS worried you'd already left," she said, when someone opened the back door.

"I knew you were coming," Erastos replied.

"Right," Rose said with a puzzled frown. She peered into the car, glancing curiously at the man in the driver's seat.

"Give us some privacy," Erastos told the man.

She could only see the back of the man's head and his short, black hair. He nodded and hit a button on the dashboard. Rose's eyebrows lifted, as a divider slid down between the front seat and the spacious backseat. "Huh," she muttered, "I thought that only happened in movies."

Erastos gestured toward the empty seat beside him. "Sit."

Rose crawled into the long car that might've reminded her of a limousine, if she'd ever been in one. She glanced at the strange vampire.

He stared straight ahead, his pale blue eyes fixed on the divider. His pale blonde hair fell around his shoulders, contrasting starkly with his black shirt. He sat rigidly, his posture impeccable.

She sighed and pointed at the divider. "Who's the guy?"

Erastos glanced at her. "He's unimportant. He is only a human."

Rose scowled at him. "*I* am a human."

"No, you are the Eklektos," Erastos corrected. "It's different."

She rolled her eyes. "Doesn't he ask questions?"

"No," Erastos said. "It's my understanding that he is paid well."

She raised an eyebrow. "Your understanding? You don't know?"

His lips thinned. "Ask your question."

"Who's paying him," Rose asked, "if you're not?"

"That wasn't your question," Erastos said simply.

"Well, it is now," Rose grumbled, but she knew he wouldn't answer. She sighed, "Why didn't you tell me all of this when you gave me the box? Why did you just disappear like that?"

"I've found that if I leave quickly, there are no questions," Erastos said, "and it wasn't time for you to know yet."

Rose's frown deepened. "So, you were...running away?"

Erastos turned his pale gaze on her. "With all due respect, my Eklektos, you've yet to ask me the question you were supposed to ask."

"Supposed to ask?" Rose repeated.

"There was a specific question you needed to ask," Erastos said, "without Kallias present. Ask *that* question."

As frustrated as she was with the strange vampire, Rose knew that she couldn't waste any more time. "I'm going to die, aren't I?"

Not a shred of emotion passed over Erastos's face. "Yes."

Rose nodded slowly. She'd expected that. "When?"

"It's best if you don't know," he stated.

Rose blew out a shaky breath. "And...there's no avoiding it?"

"Your death is necessary, my Eklektos," Erastos told her. "It's an important step in your journey."

"Well, it's not much of a journey if it's ending already," Rose muttered under her breath.

"You should prepare yourself for your death," Erastos told her.

"What does that even *mean*?" Rose complained.

"It's important that Kallias doesn't know," Erastos added.

Rose sighed at that. "You realize he's a telepath, right?"

"Kallias has no reason to look past your conscious thoughts. If you don't think about it, he won't know," Erastos told her.

"I'm supposed to know that I'm dying but not think about it?" Rose said with a look of disbelief.

"As long as he continues to trust you," Erastos said, "you can hide it from him."

Rose shook her head, growing more stressed by the moment. "You want me to lie to him?"

"Think of it more as an intentional omission," Erastos corrected.

Rose scowled at him. "That's still lying."

"Oh," Erastos said with a frown. "Then, yes. Lie."

"I can't do that," Rose tried to tell him.

"Do you want him to die?" Erastos asked.

"No," Rose said desperately. "I'll do anything to prevent that."

"Then, you'll do this," he told her. "It's the only way."

Rose stared at the tinted window, as she processed the imminence of her own death. "How will it happen? Will Theron kill me?" she asked, but then, she sighed, "No, that's not what you said. You said I'd die from using too much power."

"Yes," Erastos said.

Rose nodded in acceptance. "Will it hurt?"

"You will experience unbearable pain before your death," he said.

Rose raised an eyebrow. "Well, thanks for sugar-coating it."

"I'm afraid your future involves much suffering," he added.

"Again with the sugar-coating," Rose said sarcastically. She glanced at him, her brows knitted in worry. "But my friends? If I die, they'll survive?"

Erastos looked away, a sudden reluctance pulling at his features. "You...will lose *many* loved ones before this is over."

"Many?" she sputtered. Her heart pounded harshly against her chest. "How? The four vampires inside are the only ones involved, right?"

"At this time," he said, "but there will be more in the future."

Rose shook her head too quickly, her panic making her dizzy. "No, no, no. I—I can't lose anyone. I can't! I will do anything to prevent that. *Please.* Tell me how to prevent it."

"Loss is necessary for strength," Erastos said.

Rose stared at him for a moment, thinking she *must* have heard that wrong. "You...heartless *jerk*!" she snarled. "You're fine with innocent people dying because it might make me *stronger*?"

"Life is suffering," Erastos said. "Death is mercy."

"What?" Rose breathed. A strange feeling twisted at her stomach—a surge of adrenaline that rose within her, boiling her blood with fierce, fiery anger. "You're going to tell me how to save the people I love."

Erastos turned to look at her, and that unnerving smile curved at his lips again. "I'd hoped I would get to witness it. I have waited so long."

Rose frowned, momentarily stunned. "What?"

"The eyes of the Eklektos," Erastos said. "So wonderfully terrifying."

She froze. "What? Right now?" she squeaked. She covered her eyes with her hands, as if that would somehow change them back to blue.

"Yes, you should push it back for now," Erastos said. "As honored as I am to see it, we don't want to attract Kallias's attention."

"I'm a circus freak," Rose said miserably.

"No. There is no one like you anywhere," Erastos assured her, "much less at a circus."

Rose dropped her hands. "You *really* don't get metaphors, do you?"

He sighed in disappointment. "Ah, the eyes are blue again."

"Good," Rose muttered, still disturbed that they'd changed without her knowledge. "Erastos, I need you to tell me how to save everyone."

"You cannot save everyone," he said. "You must accept that."

"I *don't* accept that," Rose told him. "I *refuse* to accept that."

He smiled. "So much of you is...*her*."

"What?" Rose said breathlessly. "Who?!"

"Sacrificing yourself will save them," Erastos said. "*This* time."

"What do you mean by that?" Rose said worriedly. "If I'm dead, how will there be a next time?"

He straightened. "I must go now."

"I have more questions," Rose told him.

"None I can answer," Erastos stated. "Leave now."

She narrowed her eyes at the abrupt demand. "You can't just tell me people are going to die, and then—"

"I will see you again," he interrupted, "when you need me."

"I need you *now*," she pleaded. "I have questions!"

"None that can be answered at this time," he told her.

She sighed in frustration, raking her fingers through her long, red hair.

Even though they were in a car now, he bowed his head to her. "Until next time, my Eklektos," he said, and then, he opened the car door.

With a defeated sigh, she climbed out of the car.

As she trudged through the muddy yard, toward the door, Rose did her best to clear her mind of the conversation—so that Kallias and the rest of her new friends would remain safe.

———

"KALLIAS, STOP!" ROSE SAID. "YOU DON'T NEED TO READ THAT."

He lounged on the guest bed, one arm folded beneath his head, as he scanned one of the scrolls—as if it were a newspaper, instead of an ancient document written by his dead wife.

She crossed the room and pulled the scroll from his hand, earning his attention. "Are you trying to torture yourself?"

He seemed bored. "It doesn't bother me anymore."

"Yeah, right," Rose said sarcastically.

Kallias pulled the scroll from her hand and tossed it onto the night-stand, next to an empty coffee mug. Then, he grasped her hand and pulled her onto the bed.

Rose laughed nervously, as she fell onto him. "What are you doing?"

"I always believed that my wounds wouldn't heal," Kallias told her.

Rose shifted to get into a more comfortable position, which resulted in her straddling his hips. She immediately blushed at the realization of *where* their bodies met now. "Umm, yeah," she stammered. "I remember you saying that. Once."

"I was wrong," he told her, "because I'm healing now."

A surprised smile curved at her lips. "Oh. Well...I'm glad."

He curled a hand around her hip, his fingers brushing the bare skin between the waistband of her jeans and the hem of her shirt. "I love you."

Rose's smile couldn't have been brighter. "I love you, too."

Kallias slipped a hand into her long, red hair and pulled her closer. He kissed her, groaning as her soft, full lips pressed against his own.

His hunger immediately reacted to her closeness, burning and twisting in his stomach, and Rose clearly felt it—because she suddenly gasped and pulled back.

"Kallias?" she said, swallowing back a cry of pain.

"Sorry," he said softly. "That's one of the downsides to being bound to me. You're feeling my hunger."

"It hurts like this?" Rose whispered. "Every time?"

"Worse," Kallias told her. "You're feeling a milder version."

Rose's brows twisted with sympathy. "I don't want you to be in pain."

Kallias smiled at her empathetic response. She was more like Erik than she realized.

He grasped the collar of his shirt and pulled it down to reveal the detailed, orange and red flames that colored his skin. "Do you know why I chose this tattoo?"

"To cover the scars on your neck," Rose assumed.

He nodded. "Yes, but do you know why I chose the flames, specifically?"

"Because…they mean something to you?" she guessed.

Kallias nodded. "Fire is painful and powerful," he explained. "It changes everything it touches. It destroys weaker things, like paper and wood…"

"And human flesh," Rose offered with a cute smile.

Kallias snorted at the unexpected dark humor. "Yes, but the stronger things, like stone and metal, can withstand fire. It makes them stronger or purer. They're changed by the fire—but not destroyed by it."

Rose nodded. "I get it," she said gently. "The pain in your life made you stronger."

"No," he said, to her surprise. "I let what happened to me destroy me."

Rose's frown deepened. "Kallias…"

"You, on the other hand," Kallias paused. "You're what I wish I could be. What happened to you made you stronger. And more compassionate."

"*You're* strong," Rose tried to tell him.

"I was destroyed," he argued, "afraid to feel *anything*."

"Everyone has negative responses to trauma," Rose tried to reassure him. "I have…*a lot* of negative responses. It's called PTSD, and it makes me—"

"Rose," he interrupted. "I was destroyed *until* you put me back together again."

Rose blinked, rendered speechless by the uncharacteristically affectionate statement.

He winced immediately afterward. "Was that too corny?"

Rose laughed softly. "Never."

She leaned forward, then, and kissed him. She tried to keep herself upright—by pressing her hand against the pillow under him—but when he responded by pulling her closer, she fell clumsily.

He laughed at her but didn't give her time to feel embarrassed. He kissed her intensely, his lips pressing harshly against her. With a low, hungry growl, he rolled and pinned her to the bed beneath him.

His hunger surged, and he couldn't resist the urge to nip her lips with his fangs, tasting a drop of her blood in the kiss.

A jolt of pleasure shot through Rose, and she quickly and clumsily pulled his T-shirt over his head. The blood bond was causing strange reactions in her, and it overpowered some of her usual anxieties.

His head fell to her shoulder, his fangs nearing her neck, before he finally found the strength to pull back. He panted, unable to catch his breath.

"It's fine. You can," Rose told him. "You can bite me again."

Kallias gave her a pained look. "I have no intention of treating you like food, Rose."

"You don't," Rose assured him. "You never have."

"Rose," Kallias said, but the hunger was visible in his dark eyes.

"I don't want you to hurt like this," Rose told him. "Not if you don't have to. Let me help. Feed from me."

His fangs flashed in the lamplight. "Are you sure?"

Rose pulled her long, red hair to one side, exposing her neck. "Of course."

Kallias looked at her neck and licked his lips. "Don't let me take too much."

Rose wasn't sure how he expected her to stop him, but when he leaned down and slid his tongue along the curve of her neck, she completely forgot her question.

Kallias inhaled her scent and cradled the other side of her neck in his hand, and then, when he could no longer hold back, he sank his fangs into her neck.

THE NEXT NIGHT, ERIK HAD NEARLY HYPERVENTILATED BY THE TIME HE found Rose on the stairs. He placed a hand on her shoulder and projected serene emotions, sighing in relief when her anxiety began to ease.

She looked up at him, both eyebrows high.

"You're killing me," he told her.

"Sorry," Rose said with a wince. "I'm just worried."

"Believe me. I know," Erik grumbled, and then, he released her shoulder and sat next to her. When he noticed her anxiety already rising again, he grabbed her arm and calmed her again.

"Sorry," she said—for the second time.

Theron hadn't shown up the night before, which, according to Kallias, meant he still didn't know where to find her.

So, the four vampires, along with Rose, had spent the night hanging out and watching movies—almost like normal people. It had been fun, but like all good things do, it had come to an end.

And tonight, things would end badly. Rose was certain of it.

"He'll be fine," Erik said. "I won't leave his side."

Rose glanced at him. "And don't get me wrong. That does make me feel better," she assured him, "but you're outnumbered thirty-to-one."

Erik grimaced. "Please, tell me you didn't actually count them and do the math and everything. Who does that? You have a problem, Rose."

She rolled her eyes. "And let me guess. Sex is the solution?"

He grinned proudly. "You know me well."

She wrinkled her nose. "You're not really hard to figure out."

Erik rolled back his shoulders. "I'm going to take that as a compliment."

"But..it wasn't a compliment," Rose muttered.

He laughed. "Listen." He stretched out his legs in front of him, his own leather-clad legs stretching much further than her shorter ones. He put an arm around her shoulders to maintain contact with her, as he continued to manipulate her emotions. "Kallias has fed now. He's more powerful than he was when Theron ambushed him, and he won't be alone this time."

"Theron is still stronger," Rose said, "*and* you're outnumbered."

"But we have the element of surprise this time," Erik argued.

Rose turned toward him. "Not if it's a trap."

Erik tilted his head, acknowledging that. Then, he returned to rubbing her arm, his hand wrinkling her white sleeve, as he kept her calm. "Just have a little faith. We'll be fine."

Rose leaned her head on his shoulder and closed her eyes. It wasn't really a conscious decision. It was just a natural reaction to the emotions he was projecting into her. "I hope you're right."

"Babe, I'm *always* right," Erik said with a wide grin.

Rose opened her eyes and shoved him with her shoulder. "I think you mean *never*."

He laughed and shoved her back, nearly knocking into the floor.

A vampire push was very different from a human push.

Footsteps thudded heavily behind them, as Kallias came down the stairs. He stepped around them.

As he buttoned the last few buttons of his black, button-down shirt, he turned to frown at Rose. "I don't know why you're so worried. I've already told you I'll be fine."

"Well, maybe you've forgotten, but you said you'd be fine a couple of nights ago, too," Rose said. "You know…when you almost died?"

Kallias scowled. "It won't be like that this time."

"Just let me go with you," Rose pleaded. "I can protect you."

"You're human, Rose," Kallias sighed. "You're the one who needs protection."

"Kallias…" Rose tried again.

"No," he said, before she could finish.

Rose glared at him, but Erik cut in before she could respond.

"You can't come with us," Erik told her, "because if you did, how would you show up and save our asses when we need you to?"

Rose turned to him. "Don't patronize me."

Erik held up both hands. "I'm not. I swear."

"Don't listen to him," Kallias told Rose. "If we end up in trouble, I want you to stay as far away as possible. No more heroics, all right?"

Rose turned her narrowed gaze on Kallias. "Just so you know, I'm liking Erik more than you, at the moment, and that's bad. Because we both know how much his dirty jokes annoy me."

Erik pouted dramatically. "But I thought we were best friends now."

Geoff and Emma joined them in the foyer. Looking as incredible as always, Emma wore a sheer, white dress that clung to her petite figure. It looked more like what someone would wear to a wedding than to a board game night with Rose.

Geoff smiled and turned his gaze toward Kallias. "Are we ready?"

Kallias nodded. He stepped closer to Rose and held out his hand. She placed her hand in his, and he pulled her to her feet.

He then pulled her close and kissed her.

When Rose finally broke the kiss, she felt breathless, and her face felt warm. "Kallias, if anything happens tonight, I want you to know…"

"Nothing is going to happen," Kallias interrupted.

She sighed. "You don't know that."

Kallias reached into his pocket and pulled out a phone. "I asked Geoff and Emma to pick this up for you when they left here last night. I know yours is gone."

Rose's eyes widened, as he placed the phone in her hand. "You just…*bought* a new phone?"

"I'll call you often, if that'll ease your anxiety," Kallias offered.

She smiled at the offer. "That *would* be…helpful, I think."

He returned the smile. "Good."

Kallias followed Geoffrey outside, leaving Rose in the foyer with Erik and Emma. She slipped the phone into the back pocket of her jeans.

Erik climbed to his feet and wrapped his lanky arms around her, using the hug to project one last wave of peace toward her.

"Kallias will be fine," he said in her ear. "I promise."

Rose hugged him back. "I need you to stay safe, too, all right?"

Erik stepped back, his grin wider than ever. "You do care!"

Rose rolled her eyes. "I care about all of my friends."

"Friend?" Erik said. He placed his hand over his heart in the most melodramatic show of emotion she'd ever seen. "Stop it. You'll make me cry!"

"Please, don't," Rose muttered. "This is awkward enough as it is."

He laughed loudly at that. Turning to Emma, he said, "Have fun, you two."

Emma smiled and waved eagerly.

Rose sank back down onto the bottom step and sighed, "Why does it feel like I just told them goodbye for good?"

Emma grabbed her hand and pulled her back to her feet. "Because the angelic-bunny vampire freaked you out."

Rose frowned. Emma couldn't *still* be intoxicated.

"Come on. No more panicking," Emma said, dragging Rose by the hand. She dragged her into the living room. "I brought board games. You'll feel better after you play with me."

"Sure," Rose said—since Emma's grip on her hand was too strong to resist anyway.

IT WAS THREE HOURS LATER, WHEN EMMA SUDDENLY FROZE. HER NOSTRILS flared, and she straightened, her eyes wide. Emma jumped to her feet so quickly that it knocked the dice, board, and tea off the table.

"Rose, get to the basement," Emma hissed. "Now!"

Rose frowned worriedly. "What?"

But it was already too late.

A thunderous crash sounded in the foyer, as the door was thrown open, and seven vampires flooded into the living room.

Three of them grabbed Emma and restrained her, and one of them snatched Rose up by the arm and then bent that arm behind her back.

Emma fought against the vampires holding her, but there were too many. "No! Rose!" she cried.

Her fighting only made matters worse. A bald, male vampire hit

Emma over the head hard enough to knock her to her knees. She whimpered at the pain as the other vampires held her on the floor.

"No! Don't hurt her!" Rose said worriedly. "Just leave her out of this!"

A click behind her let her know that they'd handcuffed her. Again.

Hadn't they learned their lesson last time?

Rose tried to focus on breaking the handcuffs, but she suddenly felt a sharp pain in her arm. She tried to turn—to see what had caused the pain—but the vampire held her too tightly.

"What did you—"

Rose couldn't finish the thought—because, at that moment, her head began to spin. Her vision blurred, and she staggered backward, before involuntarily surrendering her weight to the vampire behind her.

Then, she heard a familiar laugh—the one that never ceased to turn her stomach.

"You didn't think I'd make the same mistake twice, did you?"

Rose squinted, trying to make sense of Theron's blurred shape.

"You can't use psychic abilities, if you can't concentrate," Theron told her. "You're defenseless now."

Her eyes fluttered closed, and she lost consciousness.

Theron looked at the vampire who held her. "Take the unconscious human to the car," he demanded. He then turned to the other vampires. "As for the rest of you, stay here and look for the Stone of the Eklektos. Don't return until you find it."

"What about this one?" one vampire asked. He jerked Emma up by her hair, showing her face to Theron. "What do you want us to do with her?"

Theron scoffed, as if that were a ridiculous question. "Kill her."

26

BATTLE WOUNDS

*R*ose awoke with the most excruciating headache of her life. Her heart pounded thunderously in her head, along with a low, incessant ringing.

She opened her eyes, squinting, when the flickering light of a fire in the corner of the room burned her eyes. She tried to focus on the shadowy figure in front of her, but it was too blurry to make out.

Theron leaned forward in his chair. "Ah, you're awake."

Rose gradually became aware of how uncomfortable she felt. Her arms felt as if they'd been twisted too tightly, stretched in the wrong direction. The back of a cold, metal chair dug into her back.

Her ankles burned. She tried to shift positions, only to realize she couldn't move.

She tried to move her feet, but that only caused the ropes to dig into her ankles. She winced and pulled at her hands, but that just caused the metal handcuffs to bite into her wrists.

"I wouldn't do that if I were you," Theron said. He sounded much too close for comfort, and she could *hear* the cruel smile in his voice. "You'll make yourself bleed, which wouldn't be wise, considering your present company."

"You tied me up," she said lethargically.

Her voice sounded strange to her ears. It was too low and too raspy, and her words slurred together.

She squinted again, trying to make sense of the blurry figures.

"I admit that tying you up was a little unnecessary. You're clearly in no shape to escape. But what can I say?" he chuckled, and the chair squeaked as he leaned forward. "Seeing you helpless, like this, brings me immense pleasure."

"Seeing you dead would bring *me* immense pleasure," she muttered.

"Ah, and you used to be so innocent," Theron taunted.

She narrowed her eyes at the shadowy figure in front of her and decided to ask the most pressing question first. "What did you give me?"

"I don't know what you mean," Theron said.

"You drugged me," she stated.

The longer she stared at the blurry figure, the easier it became to make out his features. She slowly became aware of the fact that Theron was sitting in the chair directly in front of her—so close that his knees nearly touched hers.

Theron smiled. "You don't miss much, do you?" He pulled a syringe from his pocket and held it up for her to see. "Honestly, I don't know what it is. One of the vampires working for me used to work as an apothecary when he was human. Wait, no, that's not what you call them anymore, is it? He was one of those people who sold medicine...or maybe it was poison..."

"Close enough," Rose muttered.

"What do you call those people now?" Theron asked.

"Pharmacist or drug dealer. Depends on the context," she said.

Theron waved his hand dismissively. "Yeah, yeah, one of those. The point is that he knows about medicines, and he helped me pick the perfect one for what I have planned. You see, this little drug impairs your mind, but it doesn't dull the pain. It was very important to me that you felt every bit of the pain."

"Of course it was," she mumbled.

"It's a great plan, don't you think?" Theron bragged. "You can't use your telekinetic abilities if you can't concentrate, but you can still *feel* everything."

"You know, it says a lot about your mental state that you need approval from your victims," Rose said. The metal handcuffs clanged together, as she tugged at her hands. She cringed as the metal cut into the side of her wrist.

Theron stood and walked over to her. He reached behind her and drew his finger across her wrist, causing her to wince in pain again. She grimaced at him, as he stepped back and licked a drop of her blood from his finger.

"It tastes funny," he sighed sadly, "because of the medicine."

"Well, that's your own fault, isn't it?" she sassed.

He knelt down, bracing his hands on her legs. His fingernails dug into her thighs, as he moved his face close to hers.

She cringed at his touch, but the ropes and lethargy trapped her.

She smelled the metallic scent of blood on his breath, as he snarled, "That attitude will get you nowhere tonight."

"It *never* gets me anywhere," she said with a weak shrug. "That's never stopped me before. It's still my default response to stupidity."

She screamed in agony, as Theron suddenly shoved a knife into her leg. Before she could even catch her breath, he smiled and twisted the blade.

"I did warn you," he snarled in her ear.

Her head fell back against the back of the chair, and her entire body convulsed from the pain.

She stilled herself for the next wave of pain as he ripped the dagger out of her leg, but a scream escaped her lips yet again.

Warm blood poured from the wound, drenching her jeans. Her stomach lurched, and her head spun violently.

Theron smiled. "Not so tough now, are you?"

"I never said I was," she rasped.

Theron stepped back. He walked back to his chair and sat down in front of her. He leaned toward her. "As I said earlier, I would rein in that attitude of yours, if I were you. You're completely at my mercy right now. I can make this as painful as possible, if I want. I have all the power right now."

"You'll never have all of the power," Rose said. "You might be able to do whatever you want to my body, but my *mind* is and always will be mine."

He narrowed his eyes at that. "I don't think you understand—"

"Oh, I understand," she said. The pain made her voice hoarse and sharp, all at once—giving it a feral edge. "I understand people like you perfectly." Adrenaline surged through her, fueled by childhood memories. "You use fear to control people. You can't *handle* not having that power over them. That's why you hate me so much. That's why you hate Kallias. You can't control us. You think you're the first person to hate me for this reason? The first monster I met almost broke me. But you? You don't stand a chance."

Rage flashed in Theron's eyes. "You better stop while you're ahead, little girl, or I'll—"

"You'll what? Kill me? Hurt me?" Rose interrupted. "But you're already planning to do that, aren't you? Do I look afraid?"

He growled dangerously, his fingers tightening around the dagger. "I'll kill you! I'll cause you more pain than you can imagine."

"Yes," Rose snarled, "but you'll *never* get the satisfaction of my fear."

Theron jumped to his feet, growling. "You're an idiot, then."

"No," Rose said. "I'm just someone who's well-acquainted with monsters—someone who knows exactly how people like you work."

"You've never met anyone like me," Theron snarled.

Rose laughed, but the sound was sharp with pain—vicious and disoriented. "You think you're unique?" she sneered. "I've been dealing with people like you my whole life. Using fear to control others? Hurting people because it gives it pleasure to see others suffer? You're no different from every other glorified bully."

Theron's lip curled. "Are you comparing me to a human?"

"Lots of them," Rose assured him. "You're nothing special, Theron. You're just another evil man in a world full of evil men." She leaned forward, too disoriented from the pain of her leg to notice the bite of metal around her wrists. "You want to know what *is* special? People like Kallias, Erik, Emma, Geoff... It takes strength to be good. It takes *nothing* to be evil. Evil doesn't scare me. The good guys are much scarier."

He moved too fast for her to see. Before she could even brace herself, he was in front of her, shoving a dagger into her stomach.

Rose screamed out. The pain pounded through her veins, blurring her thoughts. She couldn't have held back the scream, even if she'd been prepared. It was just…too much.

He waited for a moment, watching her face contort in pain, before he jerked the dagger out, leaving a gaping wound in her stomach.

Blood poured out, soaking her white T-shirt.

"You'll die from that wound," Theron told her.

She coughed, blood in her throat.

He leaned in close and hissed, "But not fast enough."

Rose watched the room spin, barely conscious through it all.

"I know you love Kallias," he whispered.

Rose looked up at him.

"You think I can't do anything worse than kill you, but you're wrong," Theron warned. "Don't think I didn't notice Kallias's scent in your blood. You share a blood bond with him. That means he will feel your pain, and he'll come to save you." He tilted his face closer. "And then, I'll kill you both."

"Kallias is," she gasped, barely able to speak, "too smart to walk into a trap."

"But he loves you," Theron sneered. "That's his weakness."

More blood gurgled in her throat, and she coughed again.

Theron walked over to the fire and held the dagger over the flame. "Tell me. How much do you know about what I did to your lover?"

As the drug in her system faded, Rose noticed a few shadowy figures along the edge of her vision. With a wave of cold dread, she realized there were other vampires in the room—*many* of them—waiting for Kallias to arrive.

She turned her blurry gaze back toward Theron. "I've seen the scars."

"Ah, but that's not really the same, is it?" Theron asked. "Don't you think you would understand him so much better, if you shared the experience?"

Rose swallowed, as she realized what was about to happen.

Theron returned to her and leaned in close, grazing the tip of the dagger across her neck. "With that wound, you'll die, but until then, you'll *wish* you were dead. Do you want to guess how we're going to pass the time until you die?"

"You're going to torture me," she answered.

"Yes," Theron said with a sickening smile. "I am."

"I'M TELLING YOU," ERIK GRUMBLED, "THIS IS WHERE THEY WERE."

Geoffrey cast another glance around the empty building. "I believe you, but that doesn't change the fact that there's no one here now."

Erik knelt in front of the fireplace and ran his finger across a thick layer of fresh ash. "There were so many of them," he muttered. "It seems unlikely that every one of them packed up and left in one night."

"The more barbaric of our kind aren't really known for carrying a lot of luggage around. Don't they just take what they want when they want it?" Geoffrey muttered.

Erik glanced back at him, his eyebrows lifting. "Is there a reason you're asking *me*?"

Geoffrey shrugged. "Well, you have more in common with them than you do me, right?"

Erik scoffed, "Asshole."

Geoffrey sighed regretfully. "I didn't mean anything by it. I just mean, realistically..."

Erik climbed to his feet and stepped past him, ignoring his friend's 'apology.'

"You've lived like them before," Geoffrey continued. "That's all I'm saying."

Erik froze, shifting his gaze around the room. "Where is Kallias?"

"He's right..." Geoffrey trailed off, as looked at the place Kallias was standing before and found no one. "He was there just a minute ago."

"Shit," Erik hissed under his breath. "The one time I'm not focused on his emotions! Shit!" He turned and placed his hands on Geoffrey's shoulders. "Show me what you feel."

"What?" Geoffrey said breathlessly. "I don't feel anything."

"Focus," Erik said. "No matter how unthreatening it feels to you, we need to...find it."

"I don't understand," Geoffrey said with a frown.

"Kallias and Rose have a blood bond. If Kallias disappeared without saying anything, he must've sensed something," Erik explained. "Rose must be in danger, and Rose was with Emma. So, what do you feel?"

"I haven't felt anything," Geoffrey assured him. "Just the usual..." he trailed off, his eyes widening. "Oh, no."

"*Fy faen,*" Erik cursed.

Not danger—but...anger.

And worry.

Erik pulled his phone from his pocket and dialed Kallias's number, even though he knew Kallias wouldn't answer.

As he listened to one ring after another, waiting for an answer that wouldn't come, he ran up the stairs, taking two at a time. When he reached the top, he gave up and shoved the phone into his pocket.

As soon as Geoffrey joined him, he said, "We have to figure out where they took Rose. That's where we'll find Kallias."

"What? No," Geoffrey said worriedly. "I have to find Emma."

"But she's not even in danger!" Erik argued. He stopped, though, when he sensed Geoffrey's fear. He closed his eyes, sighing, "No. Sorry. You're right. You find Emma. I'll find Kallias and Rose."

Geoffrey nodded nervously, his dark eyes still wide with fear.

Before either of them could step outside, though, the door creaked open.

Geoffrey sighed in relief, as Emma stepped into the building. Blood thoroughly soaked her dress, turning the material blackish-red.

Geoffrey ignored that, just relieved to know she was all right. He ran to her and scooped her into his arms, embracing her tightly.

Erik walked toward them slowly, his gaze on the blood stains. "Please, tell me there's a funny story behind all the blood."

She pulled away from Geoffrey. "They took Rose."

"That would be a *not*-funny story," Erik sighed.

Geoffrey pulled the white handkerchief from his suit pocket and offered it to Emma, as if that one handkerchief could wipe off the bloodbath.

"They left five vampires to guard me," Emma said. "Kill me, really."

"Why did I never feel your fear?" Geoffrey asked.

Emma scoffed, "I wasn't scared of *them*. I was just worried for Rose."

Erik lifted his eyebrows at that. "And what happened to the five vampires?"

Emma spread out her arms and offered a coy smile. "Isn't it obvious?"

Erik looked down at the blood. "Oh. That's...theirs."

Geoffrey took Emma's hand. "We should get you home."

Emma jerked her hand away from him. "Not until we find Rose."

Geoffrey gave her a pained look. "I've already had one scare."

"Do you know where they took her?" Erik asked.

Emma shrugged helplessly. "I wish I did."

Erik nodded and glanced around the room, desperately looking for a clue about where they could have gone, but every scrap of evidence had disappeared. They'd disposed of the bodies, cleaned up the blood, and taken everything else with them.

If they'd left even one vampire behind, maybe...

Erik froze, as he heard a soft giggle outside. Two sets of footsteps grew closer—one shuffling and clumsy and the other sure and aggressive.

He inhaled their scents.

A drunk human and...yes, a vampire.

Erik stepped back, waiting for the vampire to reveal himself.

The door opened, and the two stumbled inside, kissing and clinging to each other. The drunk woman giggled every time she tripped over absolutely nothing, but the man pursued her, holding her against the wall, as he kissed her.

Erik cleared his throat, and the two people separated and turned to look at the three vampires. The drunk woman screamed at the sight of Emma's blood-stained dress.

Erik smiled. "I hate to interrupt, but we need information."

The vampire immediately shoved the girl aside and raced toward Erik, but Erik caught him easily and threw him against the wall.

As the vampire, who looked surprisingly familiar, groaned in pain and tried to pull himself to his feet, Erik turned toward the woman.

"Go home, darling," he told her. "You're drunk, and this guy's *very* bad news."

The woman didn't need any convincing.

She fled as quickly as she could.

The vampire stepped toward Erik. "*That* was dinner."

Erik shrugged. "Well, like I said, I need information."

The vampire tried to attack Erik again, but Erik shoved him back and wrapped his hand around the vampire's throat.

"You attacked me," Erik told him, "which means you remember me."

The vampire tried to shake his head, but Erik gripped him tighter. "I don't. I don't know you."

"You saw me last night," Erik stated. "Tell me where to find Theron."

"I," the vampire gasped for breath, "I don't know a Theron."

"I don't believe you," Erik said. "You knew this building would be empty when you brought the human back—because you were here when everyone left. Tell me where they went."

The vampire's gaze hardened. "Kill me. Do whatever you like. *Anything* is better than what Theron will do to me if I help you."

Erik laughed bitterly. "It's almost as if you think Theron's the only person with experience in torture."

With that, Erik began to use his empathic abilities to project terror.

The vampire let out a shrill, blood-curdling scream, but Erik didn't stop. Erik continued to torture the vampire, even as the vampire sobbed and screamed for him to stop.

Geoffrey and Emma exchanged a horrified look.

"Erik!" Geoffrey yelled over the screams. "Stop!"

Emma, who'd never seen him do this, cringed. "Please, Erik. Stop."

Erik ignored them.

"Okay!" the vampire cried. "I'll tell you whatever you want."

Erik immediately stopped. "I'm listening."

"Just...promise me you'll kill me afterward," the vampire said, his voice hoarse from screaming. "He'll torture me, too, if he finds out I told you. I—I don't want..."

Erik nodded slowly. "That can be arranged."

Geoff's eyes widened. "What?"

"Okay," the vampire said. His shoulders continued to rise and fall—in time with his quick, shallow breaths. "There's an old morgue a few blocks here. That's where they are."

"A morgue," Erik said darkly. "How poetic."

"Just turn left at the end of the street," the vampire panted.

"Erik, don't kill him," Emma pleaded. "We can protect him."

The vampire glanced at her, his brows furrowed.

But Erik didn't hesitate. He shoved his hand into the vampire's chest and ripped out his heart. He stepped back as the vampire's body collapsed on the concrete floor—and then dropped the heart.

"That was unnecessary," Geoffrey told him. "You're as bad as the vampires we kill."

Erik shrugged easily, as if he were completely oblivious to the blood and flesh that coated his arm. "Alana was a bitch," he said with a bitter smile, "but her way *did* get results." The strange smile faded. "And my friends are in danger."

Geoffrey watched him in disbelief, as Erik headed toward the door. "You're as foolish as you are insane," he warned. "Kallias walked straight into a trap when he went after Rose, and you know it. That's what Theron wanted! And now, you want us to do the same?"

"Do you even understand what friendship is?" Erik asked, his emotions clearly running high. "It means you care about the person. It means you love them, even—and you'd do anything to not lose them, *including* walking into a trap. Kallias has been my best friend for twelve hundred years, and Rose is my friend now. I'm going after them, even if it means dying, because they're my friends."

Geoffrey frowned worriedly. "Do you know how crazy that sounds?"

Erik shrugged. "As crazy as everything else I say."

"I'm going with you," Emma told Erik.

"Good," Erik said, turning to leave. "Come on."

Fear twisted at Geoffrey's face. "Emma, no."

Emma turned to him, her smile gentle and apologetic. "I know you're worried, but Kallias is our friend. And Rose—she's *always* kind to me, and kindness is rare. I really like her, and I think, if she survives, we could be friends, and I'd really like that. So, I'm sorry, but I can't just stay here while they die."

"If you go, *you* could die," Geoffrey said.

"I have to do what I can," Emma told him.

"Emma, please," Geoffrey pleaded, his face pale.

She touched his chest lightly and murmured, "I'm sorry."

Emma followed Erik outside, and they both started in the direction of the abandoned morgue. They stopped, however, when they heard the quick pounding of footsteps behind them.

Emma turned, her eyes widening in surprise, as she saw Geoffrey. She smiled when he reached her. "I thought you said our plan was too foolish."

"It is," he said honestly, but then, he took her hands into his own, "but I can't let you go alone. Emma, you're the only person in this world I'll be foolish for."

She smiled brightly. "I'm glad you changed your mind."

"Yeah, yeah, you're both adorable," Erik said. "Can we go, now?"

Geoffrey nodded. "Do we have a plan at all?"

"Yeah," Erik said easily. "Don't die."

THERON CHUCKLED, WHEN HE WAS SLAMMED FACE-FIRST INTO AN OLD, BRICK wall. He turned his head, his cheek pressing hard against the wall, to look at Kallias. "It took you long enough," he said, as if the pain hadn't affected him at all. "I was beginning to wonder if you cared enough to try to save her."

Kallias growled, as several vampires pulled him off of Theron. They restrained him as well as they could, but with him no longer starved, it took quite a few of them. "I'll kill you," he snarled. "I will rip you apart."

Theron turned around and straightened his clothes. "I don't think you're in any position to be threatening me," he said, looking pointedly at Kallias's arms, which were being held in place by six vampires. Theron stepped closer and whispered, "I bet you were frightened when you felt her pain."

Kallias barely looked like himself. His muscles shook with rage, and his dark eyes looked wild and feral. "Where is she?"

Theron's lips curved into a sadistic smile. "Take him to her."

The vampires led him downstairs. When they reached the basement and Kallias finally saw Rose's crumpled, bleeding form, the color faded from his face. "Rose?"

Rose didn't even lift her head. Her limbs were limp and motionless, her body curled forward in the chair.

Kallias called her name again, desperate to wake her.

"I doubt she'll wake up," Theron laughed. "She's lost *a lot* of blood."

"How could you do this to her?" Kallias breathed.

Theron snorted at the question—and the despair he heard in Kallias's voice. "*How could I do this?* What a pathetic question," he sneered. "I did it for the same reason I did it to you. Because I enjoy it."

Kallias looked at Theron. "You'll pay for this."

Theron glanced at Kallias's restrained arms and scoffed, "I doubt it."

Kallias turned to look at Rose, listening for her pulse. Another jolt of fear traveled through his veins, as he realized how slow and weak it sounded. "Let me heal her."

Theron lifted an eyebrow. "Why would I do that?"

"She's dying," Kallias said. "Let her go, and you can kill me."

Theron laughed. "Why would I do that, when I can kill you both?"

Kallias twisted and swept his leg under the feet of the nearest vampire, managing to knock one of the vampires that held him off of his feet.

After he'd allowed them to drag him down the stairs so easily, the sudden fight took the vampires by surprise, and he managed to get the upper hand fairly quickly, kicking one of them in the stomach and slinging another across the room.

He used the brief break to remove his dagger from its sheath.

He heard a flurry of movement behind him and spun just in time to swing his blade, beheading the approaching vampire in one, clean sweep.

A shorter man tried to grab Kallias from behind, but Kallias elbowed him and twisted to shove his dagger into the vampire's chest.

With no time to dislodge the blade, he turned and shoved his hand into the next vampire's chest, ripping out their heart.

By now, other vampires had joined the attack—more than Kallias could count. He stopped seeing the vampires when they attacked.

He began to rely on instinct, on training he'd been given long ago, killing everything that came at him.

He didn't notice the spray of blood that seemed suspended in the air, or the shallow wounds he obtained as he fought. He simply fought and killed everyone who attacked.

The battle only lasted a matter of minutes, but in pure rage, Kallias managed to kill more than half of the vampires who engaged him.

It all came to an end when Theron decided that Kallias had killed too many of his followers.

Kallias swung a sword he'd acquired after disarming another vampire and beheaded the next one approaching him. Before he could take on another any more, however, he felt himself pulled backward, as someone placed a cold blade against his neck.

He froze, as he realized that fighting now could result in losing his head.

Literally.

Theron chuckled in his ear. "You may be stronger than every other vampire in the room, but you will *never* be stronger than me."

"That's easy to say when you have a blade against my throat," Kallias said. "Put it down, and we'll see which of us is *actually* stronger."

"I don't need to prove anything to you," Theron scoffed.

Kallias wanted to respond with the retort Theron's cowardice deserved, but he couldn't—because as the surviving vampires gathered their composure and returned to their places around the room, his gaze returned to Rose.

Despair crept up his throat, as he realized that she'd be dead soon.

He stared at the crimson stains that covered her T-shirt, the holes that opened around gruesome stab wounds.

He listened the slow, weak beat of her heart.

Theron was right. She'd never wake up in this state—not without being healed by vampire blood first. She'd remain unconscious until her heart stopped, and it would stop soon.

She'd been almost fully bled out.

"Give up, Kallias," Theron told him. "There are too many of us for you to fight. She won't make it much longer anyway. You might as well accept it."

"I will *never* accept that," Kallias said.

Theron laughed. "You'll have no choice, soon enough."

Kallias closed his eyes and concentrated. It was difficult because all he could think about was Rose. He wanted to focus on every aspect of her—her slow, labored breaths, her weakened heartbeat.

He needed the reassurance that she was still alive.

But he narrowed his focus anyway, clearing his mind of everything else.

Theron suddenly collapsed, the blade sliding across the floor, as he dropped it. His hands immediately went to his head, and he began to scream in agony.

As soon as the dagger left his throat, Kallias ran toward Rose.

While the rest of the vampires were frozen in shock or shifting nervously, while trying to understand what was happening to Theron, one vampire—a short-haired blonde man—raced toward Kallias.

He'd nearly reached Rose before the vampire caught up with him. He shoved a sword through the center of Kallias's back.

The tip of the blade protruded from Kallias's chest, the rest of the sword buried in his heart.

The vampire jerked the sword out of his chest, and Kallias fell to his knees, gasping, as blood poured from his chest.

The pain of the injury was too much. He lost his concentration.

The agonizing pain in Theron's head stopped suddenly, as if it had never been there, and Theron stopped screaming.

Still breathless, Theron glanced at Kallias in shock and then at the vampire who'd stabbed him. "What...happened?"

The blonde vampire glared at Kallias. "*He* did that to you," he told Theron. "I know because I've seen it done before. Alana does it."

Kallias glanced up at the vampire. He didn't know whether the pain was affecting his hearing or if he'd really just heard someone refer to Erik's dead lover in present tense, rather than past tense.

"Alana?" Theron repeated, still gasping. "The...telepath?"

"Yes." The vampire spoke with an obvious Norwegian accent.

Long ago, both Erik and Alana had lived in what was now Norway, but still, Kallias thought he might've heard him wrong.

When the vampire noticed Theron glaring at him, he quickly amended, "Yes, sir. She's a telepath." He winced a little, when Theron's glare didn't soften. "Telepaths can make you feel pain—or the illusion of pain. They make you think you feel it."

"Are you suggesting what I just felt wasn't real pain?" Theron growled.

The vampire stepped back warily. "Of course not. I was just..." he trailed off. "I was explaining how it works. That's all."

"And what makes you such an expert on telepathy?" Theron said.

The vampire shrugged. "I was with Alana. Once. I'm an ex-lover."

Kallias held a hand near his chest, his shirt bunched between his fingers. His pulse had already begun to slow from the blood loss, and his half-hearted effort to slow the bleeding wasn't working.

"She had a lot of those," Kallias said weakly, "apparently."

The vampire shot a disdainful look at Kallias. "What was that?"

Theron apparently didn't appreciate the guy's divided attention— because he suddenly yelled at him, "York!"

The vampire looked at him, blinking. "My name is *Bjorn*. Not *York*."

"Don't change the subject," Theron snapped. "You agreed to follow *my* commands. I am in charge. Not you. Do you understand?"

"Er," Bjorn stammered. "Yes...sir."

"I will be the one to kill him, not you," Theron added.

Bjorn gestured toward Kallias with his sword. "But I had to disrupt his concentration. He was—"

"No excuses!" Theron snapped.

"Okay," Bjorn said, drawing out the word in confusion, but then, he sighed and said, "I mean…yes, sir."

"Pathetic," Kallias muttered, and Bjorn took a step toward him again.

"Bjorn!" Theron snapped.

Bjorn stepped back again, fixing his hazel eyes on the concrete floor.

Theron frowned at Bjorn. "So, you think Kallias did something that your telepathic ex-lover did. But how could someone do that without being telepath? Did you think about that?"

Bjorn shot wide-eyed look at Theron, as if he were only just now realizing that Theron was *not* a genius. "Well," he said with a frown, "hypothetically, that would mean he's…*also* a telepath."

Theron scoffed, "I'd know if Kallias were a telepath."

Kallias might've laughed, if he weren't so injured and weak.

Theron stepped closer to Kallias, studying him curiously.

"I wouldn't get that close to him if I were you," Bjorn warned. "Proximity will make it easier for him to…use his power."

Theron narrowed his eyes at Bjorn. "Didn't I *just* tell you that he's not a telepath? Are you trying to say I'm wrong?"

Bjorn sighed, "I'm just…trying to help."

Theron stepped closer. "Are you saying… I'm… wrong?"

"No," Bjorn said quickly, "sir."

"Good," Theron said, but when he turned back toward Kallias, Bjorn tried again.

"But he didn't even touch you, and yet, you were in pain," Bjorn pointed out. "You must realize—"

Theron didn't even let him finish. He turned and plunged a dagger into Bjorn's stomach. The sword fell from the vampire's hand, and his body folded forward. "Next time," Theron snarled, "keep your mouth shut."

When Theron removed the blade, Bjorn fell to his knees—not far from Kallias.

Kallias gave a pained laugh, and Bjorn glared at him.

When Theron turned back toward him, Kallias immediately glanced down at his chest wound, hiding any amusement that had been in his expression.

He could feel himself growing tired and weak, but if he could manage just a little concentration before falling unconscious...

Theron knelt in front of him. "See? You're harmless, aren't you?"

Kallias looked up, making eye contact with Theron. "Let me heal Rose."

Theron's dark eyes grew suddenly blank. "Okay."

Kallias sighed, relieved that his abilities had still worked, despite his injuries. He couldn't stand. So, he had no choice but to crawl toward Rose.

The other vampires began to shift and mutter under their breath.

One woman stepped forward. "Um, Theron? I thought... It's just... you *said* you wanted them both dead."

Theron blinked, before glancing her way. "Are you questioning me?"

Her eyes widened. "Uh, no. It's just..."

A man spoke up, next. "You *did* say you would kill them tonight."

Theron scowled at him. "Excuse me?"

Still holding his hand over his own wound, Bjorn looked back and forth between Theron and Kallias. At this rate, Kallias would reach Rose long before Theron realized what was happening.

Bjorn lunged at Kallias, suddenly, knocking him to the ground.

Bjorn crawled on top of him and shoved his sword into Kallias's chest, twisting upward to ensure he was too injured to move this time. Already too weak and injured to fight, Kallias yelled out as the sword ripped through his chest.

His skin grew pale, and the blood drained out of him.

Theron glanced back and forth, his eyes wide. "What happened?"

"He was controlling your mind," Bjorn said in a pained voice. "I had to stop him before he healed her. His concentration should be broken now."

Theron ran a hand through his short, black, hair, and glanced around at the other vampires, furious and humiliated that Kallias had fooled him.

Bjorn fell over to the side, still holding the wound Theron had given him.

Theron noticed that Kallias was losing consciousness and turned to the two vampires who had questioned him. "You two, take him to the opposite wall and restrain him. It shouldn't take much. He'll be dead soon." He glanced at Bjorn. "And I've decided to forgive your faults. Go feed and…heal yourself."

Bjorn nodded. He climbed to his feet and staggered toward the stairs.

Once Kallias was restrained, Theron walked over to him, careful to keep a safe distance this time. "Your girlfriend seemed to think you knew better than to walk into a trap," he taunted. "Too bad she'll never wake up to find out how wrong she was."

Kallias's eyes fluttered opened. His breathing came in sharp, unsteady pants, as he struggled to stay conscious, despite the fatal injuries. "I did know better," he said hoarsely, "but I couldn't just let her die. I had to try."

"Well, you definitely *tried*," Theron laughed, "but you failed."

Kallias glanced at Rose one last time, desperately wishing he could save her.

ERIK, GEOFFREY, AND EMMA STOPPED JUST SHORT OF THE ABANDONED morgue, as they noticed the scent of fresh blood.

Erik peered into the dark alley beside the building—finding a man and woman pressed against the wall.

"Hey," Erik said under his breath, "I recognize that scent."

Geoffrey stepped into the alley, preparing to help the human, but when the man stepped back to look at them, the woman collapsed.

She had no heartbeat.

They'd arrived too late.

The vampire wiped the blood from his mouth and walked toward them. Blood soaked his blue shirt, and the ripped hole in the middle of his shirt indicated the reason for the blood.

He'd been injured recently.

The man tilted his head, his blonde hair falling to the side. "Erik Olafsson."

"You're...Bjorn," Erik realized. "Wow. It's been a *while*."

"I'd say so," Bjorn said. "You left the woman who gave you all of that power quite a long time ago. A thousand years ago, right?"

"I would say Alana *took* more power than she gave," Erik corrected, "but yeah, I've been free of her for twelve hundred years."

"Free?" Bjorn laughed. "If she only knew the way you talked about her..."

Erik frowned at that. "Well...she never will, so..."

Bjorn veered off toward the left, beginning to circle the three vampires. His bloodstained lips curved upward. "I know why you're here."

"Well, I have no idea why *you're* here," Erik muttered.

"Your friend is inside, isn't he?" Bjorn said with an amused smile.

"Both of my friends are inside," Erik corrected.

Bjorn laughed loudly. "The *human*? You're siding with humans now?" he scoffed. "What would Alana think of her favorite lover now?"

Erik frowned. "You were with her once, too."

Bjorn narrowed his eyes. "Yes, but I was never her *favorite*," he sneered. "I did everything she asked, while you and that lesbian whore betrayed her. Yet, she only loved you two."

"Wow," Erik said, his eyes wide. "You're calling *Kara* that? Do you *want* her to kick your ass?"

Bjorn scoffed at that. "I'm not afraid of her."

Erik laughed. "Are you sure? Because I don't remember you calling her anything like that to her face. You wait until you're on the other side of the world."

Bjorn sighed irritably. "Only because Alana is so protective of her...girlfriend."

Erik snorted. "Kara didn't need Alana to protect her. She would've kicked your ass herself." When Bjorn's glare grew more sullen, Erik added, "Hey, it's nothing to be ashamed of. Kara's a badass by anyone's standards. She's kicked my ass a few times, too."

Geoffrey and Emma waited awkwardly, not sure why they were talking, instead of fighting.

"What are we *doing*?" Geoffrey asked Erik.

Erik leaned toward Geoff. "This is the part where we talk before we fight because we're both waiting for the other to let his guard down."

Bjorn chose that moment to attack.

He lunged at Erik, shoving him into the brick wall behind him.

Erik winced, as pain spread across his back, but he didn't hesitate to counterattack.

He turned and slammed Bjorn against the wall, but Bjorn managed to reverse their position with surprising ease.

Bjorn pulled a sword from the sheath on his belt and placed the tip of the blade against Erik's neck. "You're weaker than you used to be."

Erik grimaced and leaned his head against the wall, putting space between the blade and his neck. "I wish I could say the same about you."

Bjorn laughed, "How long has it been since you fed?"

Erik suddenly grasped Bjorn's hand, ready to use his empathic abilities, but Bjorn quickly shifted away from him and held his sword out at arms-length.

"I remember how your abilities work," Bjorn reminded him.

Erik smiled. "What's wrong? Afraid I'll make you cry again?"

Bjorn stood his ground, his feet squared off with his shoulders, prepared to withstand Erik's next attack. Erik, on the other hand, leaned against the wall, smiling, as if he were waiting for something.

Just as Bjorn stepped forward with his sword, Erik leapt to the side, dodging the attack. Erik moved to stand where Bjorn had stood moments ago.

Bjorn growled and ran toward him again, but Erik dodged him, just as he'd done before.

Erik laughed at him. "Can't keep up?"

Bjorn stopped short before he ran into the wall. He turned around again, growling at Erik. "I could, if you'd stop running and face me already."

Erik raised an eyebrow. "Fine, but remember…you asked for it."

Bjorn attacked again.

Erik stood still for so long that Bjorn thought the ancient Viking was going to let him run him through with the sword, but just as the sword pressed against Erik's stomach, he grasped the blade, wincing as the blade sliced into his hand, and spun away from him, taking the sword from Bjorn's hand.

When Erik flipped the sword and held it out, pressing the tip of the blade against Bjorn's throat, Bjorn stepped back. He held his hands up in a show of surrender and tried to take another step back.

But Erik followed.

"It must suck to always lose to me," Erik taunted.

Bjorn grimaced, as his back collided with the wall. "You can still leave," he said quietly. "We can pretend this never happened."

Erik laughed. "After I won? Why would I want to do that?"

"They'll have heard you by now," Bjorn told him. "There's at least fifty vampires left alive—guarding different parts of the morgue, possibly headed here now. You're outnumbered. If you don't leave now, you *will* die."

Geoffrey shifted uneasily at that. "Maybe we *should* go."

"We've been over this, Geoff," Erik said impatiently. "Leave, if you want, but I'm going to do what I can for our friends."

"All you can do in there is die," Bjorn tried to tell him.

Erik shrugged. "Then, at least they won't die alone."

Bjorn tilted his head thoughtfully. "I do kind of like the idea of you being dead."

Erik laughed. "Same."

He shoved the blade through Bjorn's neck, slicing off his head. Then, celebrating perhaps a little too soon, he tossed the blood-covered sword on the ground and turned to face Geoff and Emma.

But Geoff and Emma were both looking around with wide eyes.

Erik followed their gazes, and then, his eyes widened, too. "Oh."

"We're surrounded," Geoffrey said.

Erik stared at the twenty or so vampires that surrounded them. Some gathered by the closest door, and the others were spread out around them, apparently having come from other exits.

He glanced down at the Bjorn's decapitated body. "Well, at least I killed *him* before I died."

27

DEATH AND ORCHIDS

"*K*allias, don't die on me. Not yet."

The familiar voice roused Kallias into a more conscious state—though he was still fading quickly. He glanced toward the voice, frowning, as he found Erik sitting next to him.

Was he hallucinating?

In a weak voice, Kallias said, "What are you doing here?"

Erik lifted his tied hands and flashed a guilty smile. "Same as you."

It was only then that Kallias noticed the blood on Erik's shirt and skin. Like Kallias, Erik had suffered too many injuries.

His injuries looked less fatal than Kallias's, but they were still severe enough to weaken him. The stab wound in Erik's stomach was oozing blood, still, and since he hadn't fed in hundreds of years, his body couldn't heal it fast enough.

"You *idiot*," Kallias said with a hoarse growl.

Erik offered a tired smile. "Yep."

"Now, all three of us will die," Kallias said.

Erik winced. "All...*five*, actually."

Kallias followed Erik's gaze, horrified to find Emma and Geoff also tied up. "What the hell?"

"Erik's an idiot," Geoffrey agreed.

704

"Oh, come on," Erik complained. "I'll be dead soon. You're supposed to be showering me with compliments and declarations of love."

"We're *all* dying soon, thanks to you," Geoffrey grumbled.

"I think you're a good friend, Erik," Emma said.

"See?" Erik said proudly. "I *am* a good friend." He turned to Kallias. "Your turn."

Kallias stared blankly at him.

"Tell me you love me," Erik said.

If Kallias were any less injured, he would've rolled his eyes. As it was, he simply muttered, "No."

"Ah, come on. I'll say it," Erik whined. "I love you, Kallias."

Kallias closed his eyes. "Can you just let me die in peace?"

Erik sighed, "You don't happen to have any last-minute plans, do you?"

Kallias opened his eyes and looked at Rose again, his chest tightening at the sight of all of her gruesome injuries. She'd been right.

If he'd stayed home, like she asked…

But it was too late now.

They'd both die.

"Begging?" Kallias said in a soft, broken tone.

Erik gave a weak laugh at that. "Kallias of Athens doesn't beg."

"I would for her," he said—so quietly that only Erik heard him.

Erik's bright green eyes softened with sympathy. "I know."

"I can't—I can't watch her die," Kallias confessed.

Erik's brows creased. "You've done all you can."

Unconsciousness pulled at Kallias again, and his eyes fluttered closed. "It wasn't enough."

"Kallias, you have to hold on," Erik told him. "You just need a little bit of blood to heal from this. If we can find a way—"

"It's too late," Kallias mumbled.

Erik breathed out a nervous sigh. "You tried your best. You did everything you could."

Kallias opened his eyes, when he heard footsteps moving toward them. His eyes narrowed at the sight of Rose's blood on Theron's shirt. "Not everything," he said suddenly.

"You're awake," Theron said with a smile. "I waited to kill your friends—in hopes that you'd wake up to watch—and here you are."

Kallias glanced worriedly at Rose. How long had it been since her last heartbeat?

Finally, he heard another beat, but it was too quiet.

"I have a question," Erik announced. "How did you manage to find so many vampires who can tolerate you for even a millisecond?"

Theron narrowed his eyes at Erik. "I think I'll kill you first."

"Oh, I like going first," Erik said. "It makes me feel special."

With a frustrated shake of his head, Theron turned back toward Kallias. "I assumed you've noticed how weak her pulse is," he said with that sick smile of his. "Now, you'll watch the woman you love die *and* watch your friends die, as well. I couldn't have planned this any better."

"But you *didn't* plan it," Geoffrey said with a frown. "We came to *you*," he added, turning to glare at Erik, "like imbeciles."

"I love you, Geoff, too," Erik said.

Geoffrey rolled his eyes.

"I know what you wanted from her," Kallias said.

Theron frowned. "Do you?"

"The Stone," Kallias said weakly. "The Stone of the Eklektos—you wanted it then. You want it now."

"I already checked her pockets," Theron said. "She doesn't have it." He cast an annoyed glance at Emma. "I left several vampires to look for it, but…they don't seem to be coming back."

"They were unkind," Emma said defensively. "Unkind people should die."

Theron blinked at the small, soft-spoken vampire.

"I'll give it to you," Kallias offered, ignoring the worried look Geoffrey shot his way, "but only if you let them all live."

"Do you have it?" Theron asked.

Kallias sighed, "I know where it is."

Theron laughed in disbelief. "You expect me to let you leave?"

"It's not like you don't *know* I'd come back," Kallias said. "I wouldn't leave them to die. You know that."

Theron shrugged. "Even so, you're dying. You obviously can't leave."

"Then, let them go, and I'll *tell* you where it is," Kallias offered.

"Kallias, think about this for a minute," Geoffrey said. "If what Erastos told you was true, this could endanger the whole world…"

"My whole *world* is in this room," Kallias said. "Do you think I care about anything he said right now? No. I just don't want to lose all of you."

"I love you, too, Kallias," Erik said with a victorious grin.

"I'm not letting them go until the Stone of the Eklektos is in my hand," Theron said. "So, I suppose you should tell me quickly."

"No, I have to *see* you let them go," Kallias argued. "I'll be dead soon."

Theron shrugged. "Unless you have it on you, that's impossible."

"Rose will die soon," Kallias pleaded. "You have to let me heal her."

"Not until I have the Stone of the Eklektos," Theron said.

"She won't survive that long!" Kallias tried to tell him.

"Untie me," Emma demanded.

All four vampires turned to look at her.

"Kallias, I have it," Emma told him. "The vampires he left at your house—they'd already found it when I killed them. I have it."

Kallias sighed in relief, "Thank you, Emma."

Emma looked at Theron. "So, you can let him heal Rose now."

Theron walked toward her. "When I have it in my hand."

"There's a pocket on the inside of my dress," Emma explained. "You'll have to untie me."

Instead, Theron knelt in front of Emma and shoved his hand into the dress, roughly searching for the pocket.

Despite his injuries, Geoffrey jerked at his own restraints, but Theron had found it before anything could be said. He pulled out the dark red Stone and climbed to his feet. "I finally have it."

"Now, heal her!" Emma said. "You promised."

"And let them all go," Kallias added.

"How do you use it?" Theron asked.

Kallias tried to shake his head, but he was too weak. "I don't know."

"Then, it sounds like you have no more help to offer," Theron said. He turned toward the other vampires. "Someone give me a sword!"

The vampires scrambled to follow the order, obviously wary of his psychotic temper, but few of them carried weapons at all—much less large, conspicuous swords. Finally, a tall, muscular woman with long black hair stepped forward and unsheathed a long, engraved sword from a strap slung across her back.

Theron took the sword and frowned. "Why does it feel different?"

"You're probably used to a longsword," she explained. "That's a katana."

Theron's frown deepened. "A what?"

Her eyebrows lifted. "A…katana."

Theron scowled at her. "Is it sharp?"

"Very," she assured him.

He shrugged. "Then, it'll do."

Theron turned and pressed the tip of the curved blade to Erik's throat.

"Should've seen that coming," Erik muttered.

"No!" Kallias used every ounce of strength left to try to free himself, but it was pointless. He had nothing left. His skin already felt cold from blood loss, and his heart had slowed to the point that he wondered, each time, if it would beat again. "You have the Stone of the Eklektos. You promised you'd let them go."

Theron shrugged. "And I lied. Does that really surprise you?"

"Please," Kallias said, lifting his head as much as he could. "You'll still get to kill me. I'm the one you hate, not them. Let them go."

"It's *because* I hate you that I have to kill them," Theron said. "Watching people you love die is what really hurts you."

Kallias took quick, sharp breaths, as he tried to stay conscious. "Please."

With a smile, Theron dragged the tip of the blade along Erik's neck. "This reminds me of my days as a human prince. Executing prisoners. It was my favorite part of the job. Well, that and torture."

"Seriously, what vampire looked at *you* and said, 'Hey, look, that guy's psychotic. Let's add immortality and see what happens?'" Erik grumbled.

Theron's eyes narrowed. "Say goodbye to your friend, Kallias."

"No," Kallias said hoarsely. "No. Theron, stop. Please, just—"

But Theron didn't listen. He lifted the sword and began to swing it.

Erik cringed in anticipation of the blade's contact with his neck, but then, seconds passed, and nothing happened. He looked back at Theron.

Theron pulled at the suspended blade, but it was stuck, as if being held by some invisible force. "What the—"

He didn't even finish the sentence before his body flew through the air, hitting the wall of the morgue with so much force that the entire structure shook.

Kallias opened his eyes. "Rose," he breathed.

For a moment, Theron only groaned and whimpered—in too much pain to understand what had happened.

The rest of them, however, stared at the blood-covered form in the center of the room.

Rose dragged one leg, as she walked—her jeans still blood-soaked from the stab wound in her thigh—but she didn't act as if the pain and blood loss debilitated her the way it should have.

She looked inhuman, like something from a horror film, her skin as white as a corpse, her injuries too severe for any living being, and yet, somehow, she stood there in her blood-drenched clothing.

Her eyes glowed red, that strange red haze swirling and flickering like fire.

She tilted her head to the side, watching Theron with those frighteningly inhuman eyes.

It was clear she wasn't herself.

When he came to his senses, Theron paled in horror. "What the hell?"

"Oh. I forgot to warn you," Rose said in a cold, eerily calm voice. She continued to shuffle toward him, her steps slow and clumsy. She lifted her hands to show him her unbound wrists. "I got free."

"You—you shouldn't be conscious," Theron said in a quiet, disbelieving tone. "You should be dead already."

"I think I almost was," Rose said with a frown.

"You should be in too much pain to move," Theron added.

A strange tone came into her voice, then, almost as if someone were speaking through her. "Pain has never stopped me."

"Rose!" Kallias called. "Rose, please, stop! You'll kill yourself."

Rose's strange, red gaze shifted toward the wall, where they waited, injured and restrained. "I'm dying, anyway."

"We can save you!" Kallias told her. "You just need vampire blood."

"What are you all waiting for?" Theron yelled at the rest of the vampires in the room. "Get her! Now!"

The other vampires actually looked terrified of the human—or *whatever* she was—who stood there calmly, despite fatal injuries that should've killed her already.

They'd never seen anything like her.

Two of the bravest vampires in the room—the woman who'd given Theron her sword and a small, male vampire—suddenly raced toward her. Rose didn't even turn to look at them.

Her eyes flashed a darker shade of red, and a discarded dagger, lying on the floor, flew through the air, slicing through the neck of the approaching woman, before clanging across the concrete floor.

Rose turned slowly, clumsily, toward the others, as the severed head fell to the floor, followed by the thud of the body. Her glowing, red eyes narrowed at the approaching vampire, and she stopped him with her mind before he reached her.

He froze, his eyes widening, as an invisible force prevented him from moving. He began to cry out in pain, veins bulging in his forehead.

His agonized scream stopped short, when his heart ripped out of his chest. The organ floated, suspended in midair, as his lifeless body fell, only a few feet from the other.

As soon as Rose looked away, the heart fell to the floor, as well.

Her glowing, red eyes scanned the crowd of vampires.

"Anyone else?" she said in that same, eerie tone.

Surprisingly, the rest of the vampires took several steps backward, many of them holding up their hands in a show of surrender.

"Yeah, I think I'd surrender, too," Erik muttered under his breath.

Rose turned back toward Theron. The flickering, red haze in her eyes grew darker, like shadows, when she looked at him. "You're alone."

Theron stared in shock. "What *are* you?"

A thin stream of blood began to pour from her nose. "I'm human." She touched the blood and frowned. "I think."

"You're dying," Theron warned her.

"You're right. I am dying. But the question is," Rose said, as her frightening gaze shifted toward him, "Will I die first, or will you?"

Theron swallowed. "If you stop this…now, I'll let you live."

Rose smiled. It was a weak, barely noticeable smile, but it was the first emotion she'd shown since she awoke. "That was almost funny."

"If you don't let me go, you'll definitely die," Theron told her.

She shrugged. "That might be best."

"What the hell, Rose?" Kallias snarled.

Rose didn't respond to Kallias. She didn't even look at him. Instead, she held out her hand and watched, as the Stone of the Eklektos slid from Theron's pocket, flew through the air, and landed in her hand.

The moment it touched her skin, the Stone began to glow the exact same luminous shade of red as her eyes.

"What?" Theron stammered. "Why is it glowing?"

"Because it's mine," Rose murmured, "apparently."

Theron's brows furrowed. "Yours?"

She held out the necklace, the chain looped around her fingers. The heavy, red Stone dropped and swung from the gold chain. "Can't you tell? It matches my eyes. That's like a fashion thing, right?"

Erik turned toward Geoffrey. "Is she joking, while *dying*?"

Geoffrey ignored him, his dark gaze never leaving Rose.

"No," Theron said. "You can't be. Because if you are—"

Rose finished for him, "Because if I am, then the Stone will be useless to you soon because I'll be dead, and you need me to use it."

"You…" Theron trailed off, his eyes widening. "Let me go. I'll heal you!"

"I'll be dead because of *you*," Rose said. "Isn't that ironic?"

He struggled to move, but he couldn't. "Please," he begged. "I can fix this. Just let me heal you."

She traced her thumb over the glowing Stone. "I have some conditions."

Kallias frowned. "Rose, what are you doing?"

Theron nodded. "Anything."

"My friends live," Rose said.

"Of course," Theron said. "I can heal them, too."

"And," Rose said, watching the glow of the Stone, "you'll make the other vampires leave the room. I don't trust them."

"But," Theron stammered, "then, I'll have no one to protect me."

"They're not protecting you, anyway," Erik said with a tired laugh. "They're more afraid of *her* than you."

Theron's eyes narrowed. "At least let me kill *that* one."

"No," Rose said, looking up. "You touch *any* of them, and the deal's off. I die."

"You can't expect me to send everyone away," Theron said.

"You'll send them upstairs," Rose told them. A warm liquid streamed from her ears, too, now, and she lifted her hand to touch it. She drew her hand back and stared at the blood that coated her fingers. "I'll make no deals until my friends' safety is guaranteed."

"Rose, stop," Kallias pleaded. "You're killing yourself."

"Okay!" Theron said quickly. He looked at the other vampires, who already seemed eager to leave the room. "Go upstairs, but don't leave."

Rose waited until the last one left the room, and then, finally, she released Theron. He fell forward, collapsing onto the concrete, but he quickly regained his composure and stood.

Rose staggered, her eyes fluttering, as she began to lose consciousness.

Theron stepped toward her. "I need to heal you. Now."

"No," she said. "Untie them first."

"No, Rose," Kallias said. "You don't have time for this."

"For once, I have to agree with your boyfriend," Theron said.

"You want to use me? My power?" Rose snarled, and the ground itself shook with the force of her words. "You'll untie them. Now."

Theron held his hands up in surrender.

Rose folded forward, as if she were going to collapse, but she kept herself upright. She closed her eyes, the red glow disappearing behind her eyelids.

Theron knelt in front of them, untying Kallias first. Then, Erik.

But Rose didn't have any more time to wait.

The screams started before he reached Geoffrey.

Theron looked up, stunned by the sounds of desperate screams from somewhere up above them.

Rose fell to her knees.

"Something's burning," Geoffrey said worriedly.

"That would be flesh," Erik said. "That scent is burning flesh."

"Rose! No!" Kallias yelled, as he crawled toward her.

Theron's eyes widened at the realization, and he spun toward Rose. "What are you doing?"

Rose didn't answer. She *couldn't* answer—because she was choking on her own blood. She fell forward onto her hands and knees. Blood poured from her nose and ears, and now, it had begun to trickle from her mouth, as well. When she looked up at him, he realized that the blood streamed from her eyes, too—dark red streams that matched her glowing, red eyes.

She was dying.

Theron bit into his own wrist. "I have to heal you! Now!"

"You should've listened earlier," Rose mumbled. "I already told you that you'd never control me."

Theron froze. He vaguely noticed that the screams on the upper level of the building had ceased. He opened his mouth to ask her what she meant by that, but a strangled scream escaped his mouth, instead.

He met her terrifying, inhuman gaze, as she ripped his heart from his chest with nothing but her mind.

She waited until Theron's lifeless body hit the floor, before letting the darkness overtake her.

Rose collapsed face-first on the floor, dying in a pool of blood.

HER EYES FLUTTERED OPEN, BUT AS SOON AS THEY DID, BLINDING LIGHT burned them. Pain shot like daggers through her eyes to the back of her head.

She cried out and flung her arm over her eyes. Instinctually, she curled into the fetal position, as she tried to protect her eyes from the excruciating light.

Even with her eyes covered, she couldn't stop the thundering noise that pounded at her ears, like a perfectly timed bass drum buried inside her head, intensifying the pain that already throbbed relentlessly in her head.

And if the headache weren't enough to make her feel nauseated, the scents certainly were. She smelled so many different scents at once: wood, detergent, leather, after-shave, cologne, soap, bleach, grass, trees, water, and hundreds of other scents that she couldn't identify.

She smelled everything so strongly.

It was as if someone had placed the scents right under her nose—or no, it was stronger than that, actually.

She'd never smelled anything so overpowering. The scents made her stomach swirl and lurch. She whimpered in pain.

Aside from pain, she only felt one other thing.

Hunger.

Violent, unbearable hunger.

"You can uncover your eyes now," Kallias said. "I turned off the lamp."

Rose cringed. "Stop yelling at me."

She heard him sigh, "Sweetheart, I'm barely speaking over a whisper."

Rose uncovered her eyes and rolled toward him. She didn't even have to think about where she'd heard his voice. She just knew where he was somehow. She *knew*, without looking or listening, that he was sitting next to her, on the edge of the bed.

The blinding light was gone, and she could see him now. She could see him sitting there in just a pair of jeans, one of his hands braced on the mattress and the other on the nightstand, as if sitting were a difficult task for him at the moment.

His unshaven face looked reddened, stained by blood. Her eyes trailed down his abdomen, noticing the bandaged wounds, a large chest wound and a stomach wound.

Her stomach burned, as she noticed the wet, red stains on the bandages. An intoxicating scent filled the air, calling out to her.

"What's that sound? And the smell?" she breathed. "Make it stop."

Kallias looked away, and Rose realized that she could feel his hesitation, his *fear*. "I'm afraid that would require me dying."

She winced at the pain in her ears. "I don't... I don't understand."

When he looked at her again, she saw two very different emotions warring in his eyes: happiness and pain. He seemed both relieved and fearful, at once.

A sharp pain shot through her stomach, a pang of hunger, and she curled forward, this time with her arm over her stomach.

Kallias sighed and shifted to put more weight on the nightstand. It was obvious from the slow, labored way he moved that he was still injured. He held out his other arm toward her and waited.

The drum grew louder—unbearable and thunderous—quaking her entire body, and the scent called to a part of her that she couldn't control. Before she even realized what she was doing, she'd unfurled her body and flung herself toward his arm.

She wrapped his arm up with her own and sank her teeth into his wrist, moaning as the warm, sweet blood poured into her mouth.

She sucked at the bite wound mercilessly, the taste of blood soothing the pain of her hunger.

Rose must've been feeding for a minute or so before she realized what she'd done. Her eyes shot open, suddenly, and she shoved his wrist away from her.

Her swirling, red gaze darted back and forth between him and the blood trickling from his wrist. "What..."

"It's okay," Kallias said. He looked even paler than before. "You can take more. You *need* more. I can feel that you do. I can feel your hunger."

Rose's head spun, as she tried to make sense of his words. He sounded so weak, still. "My...*hunger*?"

His brows drew together with concern and pity.

Rose looked down at the blood on his wrist, and her stomach clenched with hunger again. She quickly scurried to the other corner of the bed, drawing her knees up to her chest, as she fought against the urge to bite him.

It was so overpowering, so instinctual.

Her entire body convulsed from the pain.

He turned toward her, holding his hands up. "It's okay. Just breathe."

Her eyes widened. "What's happening to me?"

He watched her warily, as if she were a bomb that might explode at any moment. "Why don't you take a little more blood before we talk? You'll need it."

"No!" she said, scooting backward.

"Okay," Kallias said, holding up his hands again, "if you're sure."

"I bit you," Rose mumbled under her breath. "I—I bit you."

Again, he nodded. "It's fine. I knew you would…"

"I don't understand," she stammered. "Why—why would I do that?"

He winced. "Let's talk slower. For now. You're cutting your lips."

Rose frowned, but as soon as she thought about it, she realized her lips *did* feel raw.

She pressed her fingers to her lips, wincing in pain, and then, she pulled them away, surprised by the droplets of blood she saw on her fingertips.

Then, without a single thought, she licked the blood from her fingers. For a moment, the taste of blood gave her relief, but then, she realized what she'd done.

Her heart raced, and her breath came in quick, harsh pants.

"Rose, calm down," Kallias said uneasily. "This is all…normal."

"Normal?" she snarled.

Why did her voice sound like that?

Like an animal—a panicked, snarling animal.

Her eyes flashed such a dark shade of red that they looked almost black. "What about this is *normal*? I bit you! I want to bite you again! I—I—"

Her stammering devolved into sobs.

Kallias looked as if he were in pain. "Rose… Baby…please, don't cry."

Her entire body shook. "What's happening to me?"

He inhaled sharply and moved closer.

Her eyes grew wide, as another wave of hunger threatened to take over. She quickly leapt out of the bed and backed toward the wall.

He froze, his brows drawing together.

"I—I can't..." she stammered. "I can't control it."

He crawled out of bed, as well, his movement still slow and labored.

"Don't come any closer," she pleaded.

Kallias approached her slowly—with his hands outstretched, as if he were afraid of spooking her. "It's fine. You can have as much blood as you want. Erik's just across the hall. He can—"

"What's going on?" she asked, her voice cracking.

Kallias exhaled nervously. "How much do you remember?"

Rose flinched, as flashbacks assaulted her mind, more vivid than any memory had ever been. "I remember...Theron t-torturing me."

Kallias's face contorted with pain, as if the memories hurt him, too. "I'm sorry. You were right. If we'd stuck together, maybe..." he trailed off, as he noticed that she was shaking. "He can't hurt you anymore. He's dead."

Rose nodded, her eyes dark and haunted now. "I killed him, didn't I?"

He stopped in front of her, his brown eyes full of empathy. "We don't have to do this now. You don't have to process it all at once."

"Did I kill him?" Rose repeated slowly.

Kallias sighed and nodded.

"And the other vampires?" Rose asked. "What happened to them?"

He watched her apprehensively, worried that this would be too much for her, especially *now* that she was... "They're dead, too."

"Because I killed them?" Rose prompted.

With a slow sigh, Kallias admitted, "It was the last thing you did before you killed Theron."

Rose nodded woodenly. "Fifty. I killed fifty of them at once."

"You burned them. With your mind," Kallias admitted. "You saved our lives. If you hadn't killed them and Theron, we couldn't have survived the night."

Rose nodded, as the memories began to stitch themselves together in her head. Her eyes grew haunted, as she stammered, "I remember... Kallias, I remember being *dead*." She shook her head, unable to fit this memory into the others. "It was dark. I remember it. I—I died."

"You have to understand," Kallias tried to explain, "I couldn't lose you." He stepped closer. "In the end, it wasn't even me who made the decision. It was Erik. I was too upset. Rose, you were *dead*."

She stared at him, hating the agony and grief she saw in his eyes.

"You'll hate me for this," he said sadly, "and you have every right to hate me. It was selfish."

"You turned me," Rose realized.

"I couldn't lose you," he whispered. "Erik—he knew I—"

Rose nodded slowly. "Then, I'm a..." she trailed off, running her tongue across her teeth. Even though she'd expected it, she still gasped when her tongue scraped the sharp fangs, where her canine teeth should've been.

"Yes, Rose," Kallias sighed. "You're a vampire."

ERIK STEPPED OUT OF THE BATHROOM, TOWELING HIS WAVY, BLONDE HAIR dry, as he headed to bed.

He froze, when he found her standing in front of him.

"You look like you've seen a ghost," she murmured. Her voice was as soft and seductive as it always had been. She stepped closer, her long lashes fluttering. She trailed her dark blue gaze downward, a smile curving at her lips. "It seems I'm overdressed."

"You're dead," Erik said.

She didn't argue. Instead, she took the ends of her blue dress into her hands and curtsied, giving him a seductive smile as she did. "What do you think of the dress?"

"It matches your eyes," he responded—automatically.

Her plump, pink lips curved in amusement. "I knew you'd say that."

"This is a dream," Erik realized. "I'm dreaming about you again."

"Well, if I'm dead, I suppose it must be," Alana said.

He pinched himself and winced. "I need to wake up."

She tilted her head back, her pale blonde hair falling to the side, as she looked up at him through long, fluttering eyelashes. "Why would you want to wake up? Didn't you miss me? I know I missed *you*."

"It's hard to miss someone who treated me like shit," Erik said.

"That's not fair," she said with an exaggerated pout. She trailed her long fingernails along his bare stomach until they reached the towel. She cupped the other hand behind his neck and pulled his face toward hers. "I treated you very well," she said, her lips curving as they brushed his, "*in bed.*"

Erik knew he should pull away, that he shouldn't kiss her—not even the dream version of her—but he couldn't help it. His body and soul responded to her—the only woman he had ever loved.

He pressed his lips to hers, groaning at how *real* her lips felt against his, at how real she tasted.

Never breaking the kiss, Alana stepped backward, her heels clicking against the hardwood floor, the sound as real as it would've been in real life. She pulled him with her, tugging him toward the bed, as they kissed.

When the backs of her legs collided with the oak footboard, she turned and, with one easy push, shoved him onto the bed.

His eyes darkened, as she crawled onto him, her blonde hair falling over her shoulders. She straddled his stomach, and he groaned, as he felt the silk of her panties against his bare skin.

He trailed his fingers along her thighs, her skin pale beneath his hands, as white as alabaster.

"My subconscious remembers you well," he commented.

Alana moved her face closer to his. Her soft, pale blonde hair fell around them. "What is that supposed to mean?"

"You always *did* use sex to get your way," he said harshly.

Her blue eyes narrowed, and for a moment, he expected her to pull back and slap him. It was the kind of thing she would have done in real life, after all.

But instead, she just offered an innocent smile. "Only because it works."

Erik sighed, "Why do you haunt my dreams?"

"Because you still love me," Alana whispered, and then, she kissed him.

He pulled back, suddenly, and pushed her backward, until she was sitting upright, her lips far away from his. "I *don't* love you. That's not true at all."

Alana licked her lips. "Oh, really?"

He pushed her off of him, completely, so that he could sit up. He glared at her, trying to ignore the way her dress rode up her legs, revealing every inch of her thighs to his gaze. "You're a manipulative, psychotic bitch," he snarled. "You ruined me."

She lay back against his pillow, shifting her body so that her thighs would draw his gaze. She flashed another seductive smile. "You enjoyed every minute of it. Stop pretending you didn't."

"I loved you," Erik said sadly, "and you used me."

She shrugged. "People use each other. I know that better than most."

"You became just as much of a monster as the ones who enslaved you," Erik told her. "No, you became a *worse* monster."

"Worse?" she growled. She sat up, suddenly. She gripped his arm and pulled him to face her. She ignored the pained look he gave her when her fingernails dug into his skin, drawing blood. "You know *nothing*! You have *no* idea what it's like to be raped and beaten every day. You know nothing of *worse*!"

Erik glanced down, watching the blood flow down his arm. "You're right. I don't," he agreed. "And *you* know nothing of loving someone who will never love you back—someone who will never see you as anything more than a toy, a *weapon*."

She rolled her eyes. "You were always so sensitive."

"Once upon a time, you liked that about me," Erik reminded her.

"Only because it made you so easy to manipulate," Alana said.

Erik didn't react to that. He crawled out of bed and began searching his dresser drawers for a pair of sweatpants—*anything* to put between him and the evil seductress on his bed. "I hate seeing you here."

"In your bed?" Alana said with a skeptical smile.

"In my dreams," he corrected. "I should call them nightmares, really."

She giggled, "Stop being so melodramatic."

He picked up one of the daggers on his dresser and sliced his arm.

Alana sat up, suddenly. "What are you doing?"

Erik winced at the pain. "Trying to wake myself up."

Alana rolled her eyes and hopped out of bed, striding over to him.

She took the dagger out of his hand and wrapped one of her small hands around his arm.

He watched apprehensively, as she leaned down and covered the cut with her mouth. She licked from the start of the cut to the end, closing her eyes, as she swallowed the blood.

His eyes darkened with hunger, as he watched her.

By the time she leaned back and licked the blood from her lips, the cut had already healed. "You taste just like I remember."

"You're dead," Erik reminded her—or maybe he was reminding himself.

She smiled. "So you keep saying."

"I just want to wake up and not see you here," he said quietly.

Her eyes narrowed. "You'll wake up when I want you to wake up."

He frowned. "You're just a figment of my imagination—a memory. You have no control here. You can't stop me from waking up."

Alana fiddled with the dagger. "Are you sure about that?"

"Uh, yeah," Erik stated, "because you're dead."

Alana looked up at him, her lips curving into her most seductive smile. "Telepaths can control dreams, you know. Dreams are just illusions. They happen in the mind." She tapped her forehead for emphasis.

His brows furrowed. "Of course I know. You used to get into my head all the time when I was dreaming. You'd do it to Kara, too."

"Kara," she repeated with a reminiscent smile. "Kara and I had *so* much fun together."

"Yeah, when you weren't being a bitch to her, too," Erik muttered.

Her dark blue eyes narrowed. "You're being mean tonight."

He shrugged. "It's my dream. I can say whatever I want here."

She raised a challenging brow. "Are you sure about that?"

He frowned, not sure what she meant.

"Speaking of Kara," Alana said suddenly, "have you seen her lately?"

"Not since I left the Tomb of Blood," Erik said slowly.

"You should go see her," she suggested. "You might need her help."

His frown deepened. "For what? What are you even talking about?"

Alana shrugged. "I suppose I've just grown tired of waiting."

"This dream is making no sense," Erik muttered under his breath.

She stepped away from him, still carrying the dagger, and began to circle the room. "Your bed stinks of other women."

"Jealous?" Erik said with a grin.

She looked back at him. "A little," she admitted.

His smile faded, as he realized how honest she sounded. For a moment, he almost forgot it was a dream. "You had tons of lovers."

"As did you," Alana murmured. "Maybe that's why it didn't work out."

He glared at her. "It didn't work out because you controlled me!"

She shrugged. "I'm a telepath. It's what we do."

"*Kallias* doesn't do that to me," Erik told her.

"Awww. Does *Kallias* make love to you, too?" she sneered.

He rolled his eyes. "It's not like that, and you know it."

She shrugged. "I don't know anything. I'm dead, remember?"

Erik frowned at her—and that mocking tone in her voice.

Alana continued to circle the room, trailing her hand across the red, satin sheets and the oak dresser. "I've always thought this was such a sensual room."

"You've never seen it. You're dead," he reminded her.

She returned to him. She trailed the tip of the dagger along the dragon that stretched across his torso. "Why did you do this to your beautiful skin?"

He scowled at his tattoo. "I like it."

"Yeah, well, *I* don't," Alana snarled. "I liked your skin before."

Erik glanced apprehensively at the dagger. "Good thing you're dead."

Alana's eyes narrowed, and then, she leaned in close to him. She entangled her fingers in his wavy, blonde hair and pulled his face closer, until she could press her lips to his ear and hiss, "If I were still alive, I'd make you claw your own skin until there was nothing left of that ugly mess."

Erik jerked back. Icy fear flooded his veins, and his heart pounded rapidly in his chest. "My subconscious remembers you a little *too* well."

She flashed a taunting smile at him. *"Because*...you still love me."

"I think you're mistaking hate for love, sweetheart," Erik snarled.

Alana glared at him and shoved the dagger into his stomach. He fell forward and braced his hands on her shoulders to stop himself from collapsing, feeling the pain as intensely as he would've in real life.

"You hurt my feelings," Alana told him.

"So you stabbed me?!" he croaked.

Alana pulled the dagger from his stomach and looked down at the wound that wasn't healing.

Erik fell back against the wall, covering the wound with his hand, as he tried to slow the bleeding somehow.

"You're starving yourself. It's ridiculous," Alana said. "If you were still with me, I'd *make* you feed."

"I don't want to feed," he said hoarsely.

She rolled her eyes. "You can't lie to *me*. I see your thoughts."

"Fine. Of course I want to," Erik admitted. "But that's not who I am anymore."

Alana sighed, "I don't like seeing you in pain like this."

He narrowed his eyes at her. "You just stabbed me!"

"You deserved *that*," Alana muttered. "You were being mean to me."

He glared at her. "Forgive me, princess. Should I bow? Kiss your feet?"

She rolled her eyes. "Now you're just being snarky."

"This is *my* dream," Erik whined.

"Is it?" Alana said. She placed her hand over his stab wound, letting the blood ooze through her fingers.

Erik's eyes widened, as he realized that the wound was healing.

"Because it seems to me," she said, "that I'm the one in control."

He stared at the closed wound in shock. Aside from the blood left on his skin, it looked as if the wound had never been there. He had to remind himself, of course, it *had* never been there.

This was only a dream.

"I brought you a gift," Alana announced.

"A gift," he repeated dully.

Alana held out her hand, which was still coated with his blood, and an orchid suddenly materialized in her hand.

"What?" he muttered. "Are you a magician now?"

"It's pretty neat, isn't it?" she said, smiling. "This is why I like dreams."

As he saw that innocent smile on her face, he almost smiled back, but then, he caught himself. He couldn't keep doing this to himself.

She held out the orchid. "Do you remember?"

Erik glanced at the orchid. The blood on her hands stained the petals, turning some of them black in places, but he could see that it was a blue orchid.

It wasn't a common color, but he knew one place where he could always find them. He'd gone often—back when he loved her.

"Of course I remember," he murmured.

"You used to give them to me," she said. "You'd say..."

"It matches your eyes," Erik finished, returning the smile.

Alana twirled the orchid's stem between her fingers. "You loved me so much back then."

"And you didn't love me at all," Erik said bitterly.

She looked up at him, her blue eyes soft and sad. "Maybe I tried."

"Maybe," he agreed.

She strolled over to the nightstand and deposited the orchid beside an empty liquor bottle. She seemed so innocent now, so sweet, but that was the way Alana always was.

She seemed good until she wasn't.

She returned to him and pulled him in for another kiss, and he didn't resist. He was hurting too much to resist right now—not from the stab wound, but from the memory of her.

They kissed for the longest time—a slow, affectionate kiss that Erik had never shared with anyone else. Finally, he pulled away, breathless and wanting.

"I want you back, Erik," Alana whispered. She stepped backward, flashing a seductive smile at him. "And I *always* get what I want."

ERIK CAME AWAKE WITH A START, HIS HEART POUNDING RAPIDLY AGAINST HIS chest. He glanced around the dark bedroom and breathed a sigh of relief, when he realized he was alone.

He ran his hand over his stomach, paranoid that there would be blood, but of course, there was none.

He was fine, and he was alone.

"*Alana is dead,*" he told himself over and over. "*It was just a dream.*"

He briefly considered finding Kallias and Rose and telling them about the unsettling dream, but he decided against it. They had bigger problems to deal with—life-or-death problems, problems far more immediate than his weird dream about a dead ex-girlfriend.

Certain that he wouldn't fall asleep again anytime soon, he crawled out of bed and began sifting through drawers, searching for clean clothes. He froze, as he noticed something on the nightstand.

Erik forced his feet to move back over to it, his heart now thundering in his chest again. Lying on the nightstand was a blue orchid with blood-soaked petals—the same orchid Alana had given him in the dream.

To Be Continued...

Rose's story is continued in The Tomb of Blood,
Book Two of the Creatures of Darkness Series.

In the second book of the *Creatures of Darkness* series, Rose Foster is just starting to adjust to her new life as a vampire, when a series of murders throws her life into chaos yet again.

When Rose and her friends find out that the seductive and telepathic vampire, Alana, is alive—*and* forming an army—they turn to Alana's ex-girlfriend for help.

Alana's ex-lover, Kara Unnarsdóttir, is a skilled and cunning warrior, and she's the second-in-command of the largest vampire colony in the world. Rose's attraction to Kara is as intense as it is complicated, but whether or not she can trust Kara remains to be seen.

Find out more at:
www.britneyjackson.com

ALSO BY BRITNEY JACKSON

Lesbians, Pirates, and Dragons:

Pirates of Aletharia

Goddess of the Sea
(Coming Soon)

The Dragon Child
(Coming Soon)

Creatures of Darkness Series:

The Stone of the Eklektos

The Tomb of Blood

The Assassins of Light

The Reign of Darkness

ABOUT THE AUTHOR

Britney Jackson is an award-winning author of LGBTQ speculative fiction. She's adored books for as long as she can remember and has loved writing for almost as long.

She has a passion for creating the kind of heroes she needed when she was younger: heroines with mental illness, flaws, and traumatic pasts. She centers her books around strong, lesbian and bisexual women who find courage, love, and happy endings.

She resides in Alabama with her two kids and the snuggliest cat you'll ever meet. She has a Bachelor of Science in Fine Arts and Religion and did her graduate work in English.

Learn more at britneyjackson.com.

www.ingramcontent.com/pod-product-compliance
Lightning Source LLC
Chambersburg PA
CBHW030837030726
47495CB00005B/1256